African Adventures: 2

African Adventures: 2

The People of the Mist
★
Black Heart and White Heart
★
The Wizard

H. Rider Haggard

LEONAUR

African Adventures: 2—The People of the Mist,
Black Heart and White Heart & The Wizard
by H. Rider Haggard

Leonaur is an imprint of Oakpast Ltd

ISBN: 978-1-84677-796-7 (hardcover)
ISBN: 978-1-84677-795-0 (softcover)

http://www.leonaur.com

Publisher's Notes

Contents

The People
of the Mist

Dedication

I dedicate this effort of "primeval and troglodyte imagination"
This record of barefaced and flagrant adventure
To my godsons
In the hope that therein they may find
Some store of healthy amusement.

Ditchingham, 1894

Author's Note

On several previous occasions it has happened to this writer of romance to be justified of his romances by facts of startling similarity, subsequently brought to light and to his knowledge. In this tale occurs an instance of the sort, a "double-barrelled" instance indeed, that to him seems sufficiently curious to be worthy of telling. The People of the Mist of his adventure story worship a sacred crocodile to which they make sacrifice, but in the original draft of the book this crocodile was a snake—*monstrum horrendum, informe, ingens*. A friend of the writer, an African explorer of great experience who read that draft, suggested that the snake was altogether too unprecedented and impossible. Accordingly, also at his suggestion, a crocodile was substituted. Scarcely was this change effected, however, when Mr. R. T. Coryndon, the slayer of almost the last white rhinoceros, published in the *African Review* of February 17, 1894, an account of a huge and terrific serpent said to exist in the Dichwi district of Mashonaland, that in many particulars resembled the snake of the story, whose prototype, by the way, really lives and is adored as a divinity by certain natives in the remote province of Chiapas in Mexico. Still, the tale being in type, the alteration was suffered to stand. But now, if the *Zoutpansberg Review* may be believed, the author can take credit for his crocodile also, since that paper states that in the course of the recent campaign against Malaboch, a chief living in the north of the Transvaal, his fetish or god was captured, and that god, a crocodile fashioned in wood, to which offerings were made. Further, this journal says that among these people (as with the ancient Egyptians), the worship of the crocodile is a recognised cult. Also it congratulates the present writer on his intimate acquaintance with the more secret manifestations of African folklore and beast worship. He must disclaim the compliment in this instance as, when engaged in inventing the 'People of the Mist,' he was totally ignorant that any of the Bantu tribes reverenced either snake or crocodile divinities. But the coincidence is strange, and once more shows, if further examples of the fact are needed, how impotent are the efforts of imagination to vie with hidden truths—even with the hidden truths of this small and trodden world.

September 20, 1894

CHAPTER 1

The Sins of the Father are Visited on the Children

The January afternoon was passing into night, the air was cold and still, so still that not a single twig of the naked beech-trees stirred; on the grass of the meadows lay a thin white rime, half frost, half snow; the firs stood out blackly against a steel-hued sky, and over the tallest of them hung a single star. Past these bordering firs there ran a road, on which, in this evening of the opening of our story, a young man stood irresolute, glancing now to the right and now to the left.

To his right were two stately gates of iron fantastically wrought, supported by stone pillars on whose summits stood griffins of black marble embracing coats of arms, and banners inscribed with the device *Per ardua ad astra*. Beyond these gates ran a broad carriage drive, lined on either side by a double row of such oaks as England alone can produce under the most favourable circumstances of soil, aided by the nurturing hand of man and three or four centuries of time.

At the head of this avenue, perhaps half a mile from the roadway, although it looked nearer because of the eminence upon which it was placed, stood a mansion of the class that in auctioneers' advertisements is usually described as "noble." Its general appearance was Elizabethan, for in those days some forgotten Outram had practically rebuilt it; but a large part of its fabric was far more ancient than the Tudors, dating back, so said tradition, to the time of King John. As we are not auctioneers, however, it will be unnecessary to specify its many beauties; indeed, at this date, some of the tribe had recently employed their gift of language on these attractions with copious fullness and accuracy of detail, since Outram Hall, for the first time during six centuries, was, or had been, for sale.

Suffice it to say that, like the oaks of its avenue, Outram was such a house as can only be found in England; no mere mass of bricks and mortar, but a thing that seemed to have acquired a life and individuality of its own. Or, if this saying be too far-fetched and poetical, at the least this venerable home bore some stamp and trace of the lives and individualities of many generations of mankind, linked together in thought and feeling by the common bond of blood.

The young man who stood in the roadway looked long and earnestly towards the mass of buildings that frowned upon him from the crest of the hill, and as he looked an expression came into his face which fell little, if at all, short of that of agony, the agony which the young can feel at the shock of an utter and irredeemable loss. The face that wore such evidence of trouble was a handsome one enough, though just now all the charm of youth seemed to have faded from it. It was dark and strong, nor was it difficult to guess that in after-life it might become stern. The form also was shapely and athletic, though not very tall, giving promise of more than common strength, and the bearing that of a gentleman who had not brought himself up to the belief that ancient blood can cover modern deficiencies of mind and manner. Such was the outward appearance of Leonard Outram as he was then, in his twenty-third year.

****

While Leonard watched and hesitated on the roadway, unable, apparently, to make up his mind to pass those iron gates, and yet desirous of doing so, carts and carriages began to appear hurrying down the avenue towards him.

"I suppose that the sale is over," he muttered to himself. "Well, like death, it is a good thing to have done with."

Then he turned to go; but hearing the crunch of wheels close at hand, stepped back into the shadow of the gateway pillar, fearing lest he should be recognised on the open road. A carriage came up, and, just as it reached the gates, something being amiss with the harness, a footman descended from the box to set it right. From where he stood Leonard could see its occupants, the wife and daughter of a neighbouring squire, and overhear their conversation. He knew them well; indeed, the younger lady had been one of his favourite partners at the county balls.

"How cheap the things went, Ida! Fancy buying that old oak sideboard for ten pounds, and with all those Outram quarterings on it too! It is as good as an historical document, and I am sure that it must be worth at least fifty. I shall sell ours and put it into the dining-room. I have coveted that sideboard for years."

The daughter sighed and answered with some asperity.

"I am so sorry for the Outrams that I should not care about the sideboard if you had got it for twopence. What an awful smash! Just think of the old place being bought by a Jew! Tom and Leonard are utterly ruined, they say, not a sixpence left. I declare I nearly cried when I saw that man selling Leonard's guns."

"Very sad indeed," answered the mother absently; "but if he is a Jew, what does it matter? He has a title, and they say that he is enormously rich. I expect there will be plenty going on at Outram soon. By the way, my dear Ida, I do wish you would cure yourself of the habit of calling young men by their Christian names—not that it matters about these two, for we shall never see any more of them."

"I am sure I hope that we shall," said Ida defiantly, "and when we do I shall call them by their Christian names as much as ever. You never objected to it before the smash, and I *love* both of them, so there! Why did you bring me to that horrid sale? You know I did not want to go. I shall be wretched for a week, I——" and the carriage swept on out of hearing.

Leonard emerged from the shadow of the gateway and crossed the road swiftly. On the further side of it he paused, and looking after the retreating carriage said aloud, "God bless you for your kind heart, Ida Hatherley. Good luck go with you! And now for the other business."

A hundred yards or so down the road, was a second gate of much less imposing appearance than those which led to the Outram Hall. Leonard passed through it and presently found himself at the door of a square red brick house, built with no other pretensions than to those of comfort. This was the Rectory, now tenanted by the Reverend and Honourable James Beach, to whom the living had been presented many years before by Leonard's father, Mr. Beach's old college friend.

Leonard rang the bell, and as its distant clamour fell upon his ears a new fear struck him. What sort of reception would he meet with in this house? he wondered. Hitherto his welcome had always been so cordial that until this moment he had never doubted of it, but now circumstances were changed. He was no longer in the position of second son to Sir Thomas Outram of Outram Hall. He was a beggar, an outcast, a wanderer, the son of a fraudulent bankrupt and suicide. The careless words of the woman in the carriage had let a flood of light into his mind, and by it he saw many things which he had never seen before. Now he remembered a little motto that he had often heard, but the full force of which he did not appreciate until today. "Friends follow fortune," was the wording of this motto. He remembered also another saying that had frequently been read to him in church and elsewhere, and the origin of which precluded all doubt as to its truth:—

"Unto every one that hath shall be given, but from him that hath not shall be taken away even that which he hath."

Now, as it chanced, Leonard, beggared as he was, had still something left which could be taken away from him, and that something the richest fortune which Providence can give to any man in his youth, the love of a woman whom he also loved. The Reverend and Honourable James Beach was blessed with a daughter, Jane by name, who had the reputation, not undeserved, of being the most beautiful and sweetest-natured girl that the country-side could show. Now, being dark and fair respectively and having lived in close association since childhood, Leonard and Jane, as might be expected from the working of the laws of natural economy, had gravitated towards each other with increasing speed ever since they had come to understand the possibilities of the institution of marriage. In the end thus mutual gravitation led to a shock and confusion of individualities which was not without its charm; or, to put the matter more plainly, Leonard proposed to Jane and had been accepted with many blushes and some tears and kisses.

It was a common little romance enough, but, like everything else with which youth and love are concerned, it had its elements of beauty. Such affairs gain much from being the first in the series. Who is there among us that does not adore his first love and his first poem? And yet when we see them twenty years after!

Presently the Rectory door was opened and Leonard entered. At this moment it occurred to him that he did not quite know why he had come. To be altogether accurate, he knew why he had come well enough. It was to see Jane, and arrive at an understanding with her father. Perhaps it may be well to explain that his engagement to that young lady was of the suppressed order. Her parents had no wish to suppress it, indeed; for though Leonard was a younger son, it was well known that he was destined to inherit his mother's fortune of fifty thousand pounds more or less. Besides, Providence had decreed a delicate constitution to his elder and only brother Thomas. But Sir Thomas Outram, their father, was reputed to be an ambitious man who looked to see his sons marry well, and this marriage would scarcely have been to Leonard's advantage from the family lawyer point of view.

Therefore, when the matter came to the ears of Jane's parents, they determined to forego the outward expression of their pride and delight in the captive whom they owed to the bow and spear of their daughter's loveliness, at any rate for a while, say until Leonard had taken his degree. Often and often in the after-years did they have occasion to bless themselves for their caution. But not the less on this account was Leonard's position as the affianced lover of their daughter recognised among them; indeed, the matter was no secret from anybody, except perhaps from Sir Thomas himself. For his part, Leonard took no pains to conceal it even from him; but the father and son met rarely, and the estrangement between them was so complete, that the younger man saw no advantage in speaking of a matter thus near to his heart until there appeared to be a practical object in so doing.

The Rev. James Beach was a stout person of bland and prepossessing appearance. Never had he looked stouter, more prepossessing, or blander than on this particular evening when Leonard was ushered into his presence. He was standing before the fire in his drawing-room holding a huge and ancient silver loving-cup in both hands, and in such a position as to give the observer the idea that he had just drained its entire contents. In reality, it may be explained, he was employed in searching for a hall-mark on the bottom of the goblet, discoursing the while to his wife and children—for Jane had a brother—upon its value and beauty. The gleam of the silver caught Leonard's eye as he entered the room, and he recognised the cup as one of the heirlooms of his own family.

Leonard's sudden and unlooked-for advent brought various emotions into active play. There were four people gathered round that comfortable fire—the rector, his wife, his son, and last, but not least, Jane herself. Mr. Beach dropped the cup sufficiently to allow himself to stare at his visitor along its length, for all the world as though he were covering him with a silver blunderbuss. His wife, an active little woman, turned round as if she moved upon wires, exclaiming, "Good gracious, who'd have thought it?" while the son, a robust young man of about Leonard's own age and his college companion, said "Hullo! old fellow, well, I never expected to see *you* here today!"—a remark which, however natural it may have been, scarcely tended to set his friend at ease.

Jane herself, a tall and beautiful girl with bright auburn hair, who was seated on a footstool nursing her knees before the fire, and paying very little heed to her father's lecture upon ancient plate, did none of these things. On the contrary, she sprang up with the utmost animation, her lips apart and her lovely face red with blushes, or the heat of the fire, and came towards him exclaiming, "Oh, Leonard, dear Leonard!"

Mr. Beach turned the silver blunderbuss upon his daughter and fired a single, but most effective shot.

"Jane!" he said in a voice in which fatherly admonition and friendly warning were happily blended.

Jane stopped in full career was though in obedience to some lesson which momentarily she had forgotten. Then Mr. Beach, setting down the flagon, advanced upon Leonard with an ample pitying smile and outstretched hand.

"How are you, my dear boy, how are you?" he said. "We did not expect—"

"To see me here under the circumstances," put in Leonard bitterly. "Nor would you have done so, but Tom and I understood that it was only to be a three days' sale."

"Quite right, Leonard. As first advertised the sale was for three days, but the auctioneer found that he could not get through in the time. The accumulations of such an ancient house as Outram Hall are necessarily *vast*," and he waved his hand with a large gesture.

"Yes," said Leonard.

"Hum!" went on Mr. Beach, after a pause which was beginning to grow awkward. "Doubtless you will find it a matter for congratulation that on the whole things sold well. It is not always the case, not by any means, for such collections as those of Outram, however interesting and valuable they may have been to the family itself, do not often fetch their worth at a country auction. Yes, they sold decidedly well, thanks chiefly to the large purchases of the new owner of the estate. This tankard, for instance, which I have bought—hem—as a slight memento of your family, cost me ten shillings an ounce."

"Indeed!" answered Leonard coldly; "I always understood that it was worth fifty."

Then came another pause, during which all who were present, except Mr. Beach and himself, rose one by one and quitted the room. Jane was the last to go, and Leonard noticed, as she passed him, that there were tears in her eyes.

"Jane," said her father in a meaning voice when her hand was already on the door, "you will be careful to be dressed in time for dinner, will you not, love? You remember that young Mr. Cohen is coming, and I should like somebody to be down to receive him."

Jane's only answer to this remark was to pass through the door and slam it behind her. Clearly the prospect of the advent of this guest was not agreeable to her.

"Well, Leonard," went on Mr. Beach when they were alone, in a tone that was meant to be sympathetic but which jarred horribly on his listener's ears, "this is a sad business, very sad. But why are you not sitting down?"

"Because no one asked me to," said Leonard as he took a chair.

"Hem!" continued Mr. Beach; "by the way I believe that Mr. Cohen is a friend of yours, is he not?"

"An acquaintance, not a friend," said Leonard.

"Indeed, I thought that you were at the same college."

"Yes, but I do not like him."

"Prejudice, my dear boy, prejudice. A minor sin indeed, but one against which you must struggle. But there, there, it is natural that you should not feel warmly about the man who will one day own Outram. Ah! as I said, this is all very sad, but it must be a great consolation to you to remember that when everything is settled there will be enough, so I am told, to pay your unhappy father's debts. And now, is there anything that I can do for you or your brother?"

Leonard reflected that whatever may have been his father's misdeeds, and they were many and black, it should scarcely have lain in the mouth of the Rev. James Beach, who owed nearly everything he had in the world to his kindness, to allude to them. But he could not defend his father's memory, it was beyond defence, and just now he must fight for his own hand.

"Yes, Mr. Beach," he said earnestly, "you can help me very much. You know the cruel position in which my brother and I are placed through no fault of our own: our old home is sold, our fortunes have gone utterly, and our honourable name is tarnished. At the present moment I have nothing left in the world except the sum of two hundred pounds which I had saved for a purpose of my own out of my allowance. I have no profession and cannot even take my degree, because I am unable to afford the expense of remaining at college."

"Black, I must say, very black," murmured Mr. Beach, rubbing his chin. "But under these circumstances what can I do to help you? You must trust in Providence, my boy; it never fails the deserving."

"This," answered Leonard, nervously; "you can show your confidence in me by allowing my engagement to Jane to be proclaimed." Here Mr. Beach waved his hand once more as though to repel some invisible force.

"One moment," continued Leonard. "I know that it seems a great deal to ask, but listen. Although everything looks so dark, I have reliance on myself. With the stimulus which my affection for your daughter will give me, and knowing that in order to win her I must first put myself in a position to support her as she should be supported, I am quite convinced that I shall be able to surmount all difficulties by my own efforts."

"Really, I cannot listen to such nonsense any longer," broke in Mr. Beach angrily. "Leonard, this is nothing less than an impertinence. Of course any understanding that may have existed between you and Jane is quite at an end. Engagement! I heard of no engagement. I knew that there was some boy and girl folly between you indeed, but for my part I never gave the matter another thought."

"You seem to forget, sir," said Leonard, keeping his temper with difficulty, "that not six months ago you and I had a long conversation on this very subject, and decided that nothing should be said to my father of the matter until I had taken my degree."

"I repeat that it is an impertinence," answered Mr. Beach, but with a careful avoidance of the direct issue. "What! You, who have nothing in the world except a name which you father has—well—tarnished— to use your own word, you ask me for my dear daughter's hand? You are so selfish that you wish not only to ruin her chances in life, but also to drag her into the depths of your poverty. Leonard, I should never have thought it of you!"

Then at last Leonard broke out.

"You do not speak the truth. I did not ask you for your daughter's hand. I asked you for the promise of it when I should have shown myself worthy of her. But now there is an end of that. I will go as you bid me but before I go I will tell you the truth. You wish to use Jane's beauty to catch this Jew with. Of her happiness you think nothing, provided only you can secure his money. She is not a strong character, and it is quite possible that you will succeed in your plot, but I tell you it will not prosper. You, who owe everything to our family, now when trouble has overtaken us, turn upon me and rob me of the only good that was left to me. By putting an end to a connection of which everybody knew, you stamp me still deeper into the mire. So be it, but of this I am sure, that such conduct will meet with a due reward, and that a time will come when you will bitterly regret the way in which you have dealt with your daughter and treated me in my misfortunes. Goodbye."

And Leonard turned and left the room and the Rectory.

CHAPTER 2

The Swearing of the Oath

Arthur Beach, Jane's brother, was standing in the hall waiting to speak to Leonard, but he passed without a word, closing the hall door behind him. Outside snow was falling, though not fast enough to obscure the light of the moon which shone through the belt of firs.

Leonard walked on down the drive till he neared the gate, when suddenly he heard the muffled sound of feet pursuing him through the snow. He turned with an exclamation, believing that the footsteps were those of Arthur Beach, for at the moment he was in no mood for further conversation with any male member of that family. As it chanced, however, he found himself face to face not with Arthur, but with Jane herself, who perhaps had never looked more beautiful than she did at this moment in the snow and the moonlight. Indeed, whenever Leonard thought of her in after-years, and that was often, there arose in his mind a vision of a tall and lovely girl, her auburn hair slightly powdered over with the falling flakes, her breast heaving with emotion, and her wide grey eyes gazing piteously upon him.

"Oh! Leonard," she said nervously, "why do you go without saying goodbye to me?"

He looked at her awhile before he answered, for something in his heart told him that this was the last sight which he should win of his love for many a year, and therefore his eyes dwelt upon her as we gaze upon one whom the grave is about to hide from us for ever.

At last he spoke, and his words were practical enough.

"You should not have come out in those thin shoes through the snow, Jane. You will catch cold."

"I wish I could," she answered defiantly, "I wish that I could catch such a cold as would kill me; then I should be out of my troubles. Let us go into the summer-house; they will never think of looking for me there."

"How will you get there?" asked Leonard; "it is a hundred yards away, and the snow always drifts in that path."

"Oh! never mind the snow," she said.

But Leonard did mind it, and presently he hit upon a solution of the difficulty. Having first glanced up the drive to see that nobody was coming, he bent forward and without explanation or excuse put his arms around Jane, and lifting her as though she were a child, he bore her down the path which led to the summer-house. She was heavy, but, sooth to say, he could have wished the journey longer. Presently they were there, and very gently he laid her on her feet again, kissing her upon the lips as he did so. Then he took off his overcoat and wrapped it round her shoulders.

All this while Jane had not spoken. Indeed, the poor girl felt so happy and so safe in her lover's arms that it seemed to her as though she never wished to speak, or to do anything for herself again. It was Leonard who broke the silence.

"You ask me why I left without saying goodbye to you, Jane. It was because your father has dismissed me from the house and forbidden me to have any more to do with you."

"Oh, why?" asked the girl, lifting her hands despairingly.

"Can't you guess?" he answered with a bitter laugh.

"Yes, Leonard," she whispered, taking his hand in sympathy.

"Perhaps I had better put it plainly," said Leonard again; "it may prevent misunderstandings. Your father has dismissed me because *my* father embezzled all my money. The sins of the father are visited upon the children, you see. Also he has done this with more than usual distinctness and alacrity, because he wishes you to marry young Mr. Cohen, the bullion-broker and the future owner of Outram."

Jane shivered.

"I know, I know," she said, "and oh! Leonard, I hate him!"

"Then perhaps it will be as well not to marry him," he answered.

"I would rather die first," she said with conviction.

"Unfortunately one can't always die when it happens to be convenient, Jane."

"Oh! Leonard, don't be horrid," she said, beginning to cry. "Where are you going, and what shall I do?"

"To the bad probably," he answered. "At least it all depends upon you. Look here, Jane, if you will stick to me I will stick to you. The luck is against me now, but I have it in me to see that through. I love you and I would work myself to death for you; but at the best it must be a question of time, probably of years."

"Oh! Leonard, indeed I will if I can. I am sure that you do not love me more than I love you, but I can never make you understand how odious they all are to me about you, especially Papa."

"Confound him!" said Leonard beneath his breath; and if Jane heard, at that moment her filial affections were not sufficiently strong to induce her to remonstrate.

"Well, Jane," he went on, "the matter lies thus: either you must put up with their treatment or you must give me the go-by. Listen: in six months you will be twenty-one, and in this country all her relations put together can't force a woman to marry a man if she does not wish to, or prevent her from marrying one whom she does wish to marry. Now you know my address at my club in town; letters sent there will always reach me, and it is scarcely possible for your father or anybody else to prevent you from writing and posting a letter. If you want my help or to communicate in any way, I shall expect to hear from you, and if need be, I will take you away and marry you the moment you come of age. If, on the other hand, I do not hear from you, I shall know that it is because you do not choose to write, or because that which you have to write would be too painful for me to read. Do you understand, Jane?"

"Oh! yes, Leonard, but you put things so hardly."

"Things have been put hardly enough to me, love, and I must be plain—this is my last chance of speaking to you."

At this moment an ominous sound echoed through the night; it was none other than the distant voice of Mr. Beach, calling from his front-door step, "Jane! Are you out there, Jane?"

"Oh! heavens!" she said, "there is my father calling me. I came out by the back door, but mother must have been up to my room and found me gone. She watches me all day now. What *shall* I do?"

"Go back and tell them that you have been saying goodbye to me. It is not a crime; they cannot kill you for it."

"Indeed they can, or just as bad," replied Jane. Then suddenly she threw her arms about her lover's neck and burying her beautiful face upon his breast, she began to sob bitterly, murmuring, "Oh my darling, my darling, what shall I do without you?"

Over the brief and distressing scene which followed it may be well to drop a veil. Leonard's bitterness of mind forsook him now, and he kissed her and comforted her as he might best, even going so far as to mingle his tears with hers, tears of which he had no cause to be ashamed. At length she tore herself loose, for the shouts were growing louder and more insistent.

"I forgot," she sobbed, "here is a farewell present for you; keep it in memory of me, Leonard," and thrusting her hand into the bosom of her dress she drew from it a little packet which she gave to him.

Then once more they kissed and clung together, and in another moment she had vanished back into the snow and darkness, passing out of Leonard's sight and out of his life, though from his mind she could never pass.

"A farewell present. Keep it in memory of me." The words yet echoed in his ears, and to Leonard they seemed fateful—a prophecy of utter loss. Sighing heavily, he opened the packet and examined its contents by the feeble moonlight. They were not large: a prayer-book bound in morocco, her own, with her name on the fly-leaf and a short inscription beneath, and in the pocket of its cover a lock of auburn hair tied round with silk.

"An unlucky gift," said Leonard to himself; then putting on his coat, which was yet warm from Jane's shoulders, he also turned and vanished into the snow and the night, shaping his path towards the village inn.

He reached it in due course, and passed into the little parlour that adjoined the bar. It was a comfortable room enough, notwithstanding its adornments of badly stuffed birds and fishes, and chiefly remarkable for its wide old-fashioned fireplace with wrought-iron dogs. There was no lamp in the room when Leonard entered, but the light of the burning wood was bright, and by it he could see his brother seated in a high-backed chair gazing into the fire, his hand resting on his knee.

Thomas Outram was Leonard's elder by two years and cast in a more fragile mould. His face was the face of a dreamer, the brown eyes were large and reflective, and the mouth sensitive as a child's. He was a scholar and a philosopher, a man of much desultory reading, with refined tastes and a really intimate knowledge of Greek gems.

"Is that you, Leonard?" he said, looking up absently; "where have you been?"

"To the Rectory," answered his brother.

"What have you been doing there?"

"Do you want to know?"

"Yes, of course. Did you see Jane?"

Then Leonard told him all the story.

"What do you think she will do?" asked Tom when his brother had finished. "Given the situation and the woman, it is rather a curious problem."

"It may be," answered Leonard; "but as I am not an equation in

24

algebra yearning to be worked out, I don't quite see the fun of it. But if you ask me what I think she will do, I should say that she will follow the example of everybody else and desert me."

"You seem to have a poor idea of women, old fellow. I know little of them myself and don't want to know more. But I have always understood that it is the peculiar glory of their sex to come out strong on these exceptional occasions. 'Woman in our hours of ease,' etc."

"Well, we shall see. But it is my opinion that women think a great deal more of their own hours of ease than of those of anybody else. Thank heaven, here comes our dinner!"

Thus spoke Leonard, somewhat cynically and perhaps not in the best of taste. But, his rejoicing over its appearance notwithstanding, he did not do much justice to the dinner when it arrived. Indeed, it would be charitable to make allowances for this young man at that period of his life. He had sustained a most terrible reverse, and do what he might he could never quite escape from the shadow of his father's disgrace, or put out of his mind the stain with which his father had dimmed the honour of his family. And now a new misfortune hung over him. He had just been driven with contumely from a house where hitherto he was the most welcome of guests; he had parted, moreover, from the woman whom he loved dearly, and under circumstances which made it doubtful if their separation would not be final.

Leonard possessed the gift of insight into character, and more common sense than can often be expected from a young man in love. He knew well that the chief characteristic of Jane's nature was a tendency to yield to the circumstances of the hour, and though he hoped against hope, he could find no reason to suppose that she would exhibit greater determination in the matter of their engagement than her general lack of strength might lead him to anticipate. Besides, and here his common sense came in, would it be wise that she should do so? After all, what had he to offer her, and were not his hopes of future advancement nothing better than a dream? Roughly as he had put it, perhaps Mr. Beach was right when he told him that he, Leonard, was both selfish and impertinent, since was it not a selfish impertinence in him to ask any woman to link her fortune with his in the present state of his affairs?

Let us therefore make excuses for his words and outward behaviour, for at heart Leonard had much to trouble him.

When the cloth had been cleared away and they were alone again, Tom spoke to his brother, who was moodily filling his pipe.

"What shall we do tonight, Leonard?" he said.

"Go to bed, I suppose," he answered.

"See here, Leonard," said his brother again, "what do you say to having a last look at the old place?"

"If you wish, Tom, but it will be painful."

"A little pain more or less can scarcely hurt us, old fellow," said Tom, laying his thin hand on his brother's shoulder.

Then they started. A quarter of an hour's walking brought them to the Hall. The snow had ceased falling now and the night was beautifully clear, but before it ceased it had done a welcome office in hiding from view all the litter and wreckage of the auction, which make the scene of a recent sale one of the most desolate sights in the world. Never had the old house looked grander or more eloquent of the past than it did on that night to the two brothers who were dispossessed of their heritage. They wandered round it in silence, gazing affectionately at each well-known tree and window, till at length they came to the gun-room entrance. More from habit than for any other reason Leonard turned the handle of the door. To his surprise it was open; after the confusion of the sale no one had remembered to lock it.

"Let us go in," he said.

They entered and wandered from room to room till they reached the greater hall, a vast and oak-roofed chamber built after the fashion of the nave of a church, and lighted by a large window of ecclesiastical design. This window was filled with the armorial bearings of many generations of the Outram family, wrought in stained glass and placed in couples, for next to each coat of arms were the arms of its bearer's dame. It was not quite full, however, for in it remained two blank shields, which had been destined to receive the escutcheons of Thomas Outram and his wife.

"They will never be filled now, Leonard," said Tom, pointing to these; "curious, isn't it, not to say sad?"

"Oh! I don't know," answered his brother; "I suppose that the Co-hens boast some sort of arms, or if not they can buy them."

"I should think that they would have the good taste to begin a new window for themselves," said Tom.

Then he was silent for a while, and they watched the moonlight streaming through the painted window, the memorial of so much forgotten grandeur, and illumining the portraits of many a dead Outram that gazed upon them from the panelled walls.

"*Per ardua ad astra*," said Tom, absently reading the family motto which alternated pretty regularly with a second device that some members of it had adopted—"For Heart, Home, and Honour."

"'*Per ardua ad astra*'—through struggle to the stars—and 'For Heart, Home, and Honour,'" repeated Tom; "well, I think that our family never needed such consolations more, if indeed there are any to be found in mottoes. Our Heart is broken, our hearth is desolate, and our honour is a byword, but there remain the 'struggle and the stars.'"

As he spoke his face took the fire of a new enthusiasm: "Leonard," he went on, "why should not we retrieve the past? Let us take that motto—the more ancient one—for an omen, and let us fulfil it. I believe it is a good omen, I believe that one of us will fulfil it."

"We can try," answered Leonard. "If we fail in the struggle, at least the stars remain for us as for all human kind."

"Leonard," said his brother almost in a whisper, "will you swear an oath with me? It seems childish, but I think that under some circumstances there is wisdom even in childishness."

"What oath?" asked Leonard.

"This; that we will leave England and seek fortune in some foreign land—sufficient fortune to enable us to repurchase our lost home; that we will never return here until we have won this fortune; and that death alone shall put a stop to our quest."

Leonard hesitated a moment, then answered:

"If Jane fails me, I will swear it."

Tom glanced round as though in search of some familiar object, and presently his eye fell upon what he sought. A great proportion of the furniture of the old house, including the family portraits, had been purchased by the in-coming owner. Among the articles which remained was a very valuable and ancient bible, one of the first ever printed indeed, that stood upon an oaken stand in the centre of the hall, to which it was securely chained. Tom led the way to this bible, followed by his brother. Then they placed their hands upon it, and standing there in the shadow, the elder of them spoke aloud in a voice that left no doubt of the earnestness of his purpose, or of his belief in their mission.

"We swear," he said, "upon this book and before the God who made us that we will leave this home that was ours, and never look upon it again till we can call it ours once more. We swear that we will follow this, the purpose of our lives, till death destroys us and it; and may shame and utter ruin overtake us if, while we have strength and reason, we turn our backs upon this oath! So help us God!"

"So help us God!" repeated Leonard.

Thus in the home of their ancestors, in the presence of their Maker, and of the pictured dead who had gone before them, did Thomas and Leonard Outram devote their lives to this great purpose. Perhaps, as one of them had said, the thing was childish, but if so, at the least it was solemn and touching. Their cause seemed hopeless indeed; but if faith can move mountains, much more can honest endeavour attain its ends. In that hour they felt this. Yes, they believed that the end would be attained by one of them, though they guessed little what struggles lay between them and the Star they hoped to gain, or how strangely they should be borne thither.

On the morrow they went to London and waited there a while, but no word came from Jane Beach, and for good or ill the chains of the oath that he had taken riveted themselves around Leonard Outram's neck.

Within three months of this night the brothers were nearing the shores of Africa, the land of the Children of the Mist.

CHAPTER 3

After Seven Years

"What is the time, Leonard?"

"Eleven o'clock, Tom."

"Eleven—already? I shall go at dawn, Leonard. You remember Johnston died at dawn, and so did Askew."

"For heaven's sake don't speak like that, Tom! If you think you are going to die, you will die."

The sick man laughed a ghost of a laugh—it was half a death-rattle.

"It is no use talking, Leonard; I feel my life flaring and sinking like a dying fire. My mind is quite clear now, but I shall die at dawn for all that. The fever has burnt me up! Have I been raving, Leonard?"

"A little, old fellow," answered Leonard.

"What about?"

"Home mostly, Tom."

"Home! We have none, Leonard; it is sold. How long have we been away now?"

"Seven years."

"Seven years! Yes. Do you remember how we said goodbye to the old place on that winter night after the auction? And do you remember what we resolved?"

"Yes."

"Repeat it."

"We swore that we would seek wealth enough to buy Outram back till we won it or died, and that we would never return to England till it was won. Then we sailed for Africa. For seven years we have sought and done no more than earn a livelihood, much less a couple of hundred thousand pounds or so."

"Leonard."

"Yes, Tom?"

"You are sole heir to our oath now, and to the old name with it, or

29

you will be in a few hours. I have fulfilled my vow. I have sought till I died. You will take up the quest till you succeed or die. The struggle has been mine, may you live to win the Star. You will persevere, will you not, Leonard?"

"Yes, Tom, I will."

"Give me your hand on it, old fellow."

Leonard Outram knelt down beside his dying brother, and they clasped each other's hands.

"Now let me sleep awhile. I am tired. Do not be afraid, I shall wake before the—end."

Hardly had the words passed his lips when his eyes closed and he sank into stupor or sleep.

His brother Leonard sat down upon a rude seat, improvised out of an empty gin-case. Without the tempest shrieked and howled, the great wind shook the Kaffir hut of grass and wattle, piercing it in a hundred places till the light of the lantern wavered within its glass, and the sick man's hair was lifted from his clammy brow. From time to time fierce squalls of rain fell like sheets of spray, and the water, penetrating the roof of grass, streamed to the earthen floor. Leonard crept on his hands and knees to the doorway of the hut, or rather to the low arched opening which served as a doorway, and, removing the board that secured it, looked out at the night. Their hut stood upon the ridge of a great mountain; below was a sea of bush, and around it rose the fantastic shapes of other mountains. Black clouds drove across the dying moon, but occasionally she peeped out and showed the scene in all its vast solemnity and appalling solitude.

Presently Leonard closed the opening of the doorway, and going back to his brother's side he gazed upon him earnestly. Many years of toil and privation had not robbed Thomas Outram's face of its singular beauty, or found power to mar its refinement. But death was written on it.

Leonard sighed, then, struck by a sudden thought, sought for and found a scrap of looking-glass. Holding it close to the light of the lantern, he examined the reflection of his own features. The glass mirrored a handsome bearded man, dark, keen-eyed like one who is always on the watch for danger, curly-haired and broad-shouldered; not very tall, but having massive limbs and a form which showed strength in every movement. Though he was still young, there was little of youth left about the man; clearly toil and struggle had done an evil work with him, ageing his mind and hardening it as they had hardened the strength and vigour of his body. The face was a good one, but most men would have preferred to see friendship shining in those piercing black eyes rather than the light of enmity. Leonard was a bad enemy, and his long striving with the world sometimes led him to expect foes where they did not exist.

Even now this thought was in his mind: "He is dying," he said to himself, as he laid down the glass with the care of a man who cannot afford to hazard a belonging however trivial, "and yet his face is not so changed as mine is. My God! he is dying! My brother—the only man—the only living creature I love in the world, except one perhaps, if indeed I love her still. Everything is against us—I should say against me now, for I cannot count him. Our father was our first enemy; he brought us into the world, neglected us, squandered our patrimony, dishonoured our name, and shot himself. And since then what has it been but one continual fight against men and nature? Even the rocks in which I dig for gold are foes—victorious foes—" and he glanced at his hands, scarred and made unshapely by labour. "And the fever, that is a foe. Death is the only friend, but he won't shake hands with me. He takes my brother whom I love as he has taken the others, but me he leaves."

Thus mused Leonard sitting sullenly on the red box, his elbow on his knee, his rough hands held beneath his chin pushing forward the thick black beard till it threw a huge shadow, angular and unnatural, on to the wall of the hut, while without the tempest now raved, now lulled, and now raved again. An hour—two—passed and still he sat not moving, watching the face of the fever-stricken man that from time to time flushed and was troubled, then grew pale and still. It seemed to him as though by some strange harmony of nature the death-smitten blood was striving to keep pace with the beat of the storm, know-ing that presently life and storm would pass together into the same domain of silence.

At length Tom Outram opened his eyes and looked at him, but Leonard knew that he did not see him as he was. The dying eyes stud-ied him indeed and were intelligent, but he could feel that they read something on his face that was not known to himself, nor could be visible to any other man—read it as though it were a writing.

So strange was this scrutiny, so meaningless and yet so full of a meaning which he could not grasp, that Leonard shrank beneath it. He spoke to his brother, but no answer came,—only the great hollow eyes read on in that book which was printed upon his face; that book, sealed to him, but to the dying man an open writing.

The sight of the act of death is always terrible; it is terrible to watch the latest wax and ebb of life, and with the intelligence to comprehend that these flickerings, this coming and this going, these sinkings and these last recoveries are the trial flights of the animating and eternal principle—call it soul or what you will—before it trusts itself afar. Still more terrible is it under circumstances of physical and mental desolation such as those present to Leonard Outram in that hour.

But he had looked on death before, on death in many dreadful shapes, and yet he had never been so much afraid. What was it that his brother, or the spirit of his brother, read in his face? What learning had he gathered in that sleep of his, the last before the last? He could not tell—now he longed to know, now he was glad not to know, and now he strove to overcome his fears.

"My nerves are shattered," he said to himself. "He is dying. How shall I bear to see him die?"

A gust of wind shook the hut, rending the thatch apart, and through the rent a little jet of rain fell upon his brother's forehead and ran down his pallid cheeks like tears. Then the strange understanding look passed from the wide eyes, and once more they became human, and the lips were opened.

"Water," they murmured.

Leonard gave him to drink, with one hand holding the pannikin to his brother's mouth and with the other supporting the dying head. Twice he gulped at it, then with a brusque motion of his wasted arm he knocked the cup aside, spilling the water on the earthen floor.

"Leonard," he said, "you will succeed."

"Succeed in what, Tom?"

"You will get the money and Outram—and found the family afresh—but you will not do it alone. *A woman will help you.*"

Then his mind wandered a little and he muttered, "How is Jane? Have you heard from Jane?" or some such words.

At the mention of this name Leonard's face softened, then once more grew hard and anxious.

"I have not heard of Jane for years, old fellow," he said; "probably she is dead or married. But I do not understand."

"Don't waste time, Leonard," Tom answered, rousing himself from his lethargy. "Listen to me. I am going fast. You know dying men see far—sometimes. I dreamed it, or I read it in your face. I tell you—*you* will die at Outram. Stay here a while after I am dead. Stay a while, Leonard!"

He sank back exhausted, and at that moment a gust of wind, fiercer than any which had gone before, leapt down the mountain gorges, howling with all the voices of the storm. It caught the frail hut and shook it. A cobra hidden in the thick thatch awoke from its lethargy and fell with a soft thud to the floor not a foot from the face of the dying man—then erected itself and hissed aloud with flickering tongue and head swollen by rage. Leonard started back and seized a crowbar which stood near, but before he could strike, the reptile sank down and, drawing its shining shape across his brother's forehead, once more vanished into the thatch.

His eyes did not so much as close, though Leonard saw a momentary reflection of the bright scales in the dilated pupils and shivered at this added terror, shivered as though his own flesh had shrunk beneath the touch of those deadly coils. It was horrible that the snake should creep across his brother's face, it was still more horrible that his brother, yet living, should not understand the horror. It caused him to remember our invisible companion, that ancient enemy of mankind of whom the reptile is an accepted type; it made him think of that long sleep which the touch of such as this has no power to stir.

Ah! now he was going—it was impossible to mistake that change, the last quick quiver of the blood, followed by an ashen pallor, and the sob of the breath slowly lessening into silence. So the day had died last night, with a little purpling of the sky—a little sobbing of the wind—then ashen nothingness and silence. But the silence was broken, the night had grown alive indeed—and with a fearful life. Hark! how the storm yelled! those blasts told of torment, that rain beat like tears. What if his brother——He did not dare to follow the thought home.

Hark! how the storm yelled!—the very hut wrenched at its strong supports as though the hands of a hundred savage foes were dragging it. It lifted—by heaven it was gone!—gone, crashing down the rocks on the last hurricane blast of the tempest, and there above them lowered the sullen blue of the passing night flecked with scudding clouds, and there in front of them, to the east and between the mountains, flared the splendours of the dawn.

Something had struck Leonard heavily, so heavily that the blood ran down his face; he did not heed it, he scarcely felt it; he only clasped his brother in his arms and, for the first time for many years, he kissed him on the brow, staining it with the blood from his wound.

The dying man looked up. He saw the glory in the East. Now it ran along the mountain sides, now it burned upon their summits, to each summit a pillar of flame, a peculiar splendour of its own diversely shaped; and now the shapes of fire leaped from earth to heaven, peopling the sky with light. The dull clouds caught the light, but they could not hold it all: back it fell to earth again, and the forests lifted up their arms to greet it, and it shone upon the face of the waters.

Thomas Outram saw—and staggering to his knees he stretched out his arms towards the rising sun, muttering with his lips.

Then he sank upon Leonard's breast, and presently all his story was told.

CHAPTER 4

The Last Vigil

For a while Leonard sat by the body of his brother. The daylight grew and gathered about him, the round ball of the sun appeared above the mountains.

The storm was gone. Were it not for some broken fragments of the vanished hut, it would have been difficult to know even that it had been. Insects began to chirrup, lizards ran from the crevices of the rocks, yonder the rain-washed bud of a mountain lily opened before his eyes. Still Leonard sat on, his face stony with grief, till at length a shadow fell upon him from above. He looked up—it was cast by a vulture's wings, as they hurried to the place of death.

Grasping his loaded rifle Leonard sprang to his feet. Nearer and nearer came the bird, wheeling above him in lessening circles: it forgot the presence of the living in its desire for the dead. Leonard lifted the rifle, aimed and fired. The report rang out clearly on the silent air, and was echoed from *krantz* and *kloof* and mountain side, and from above answered the thud of the bullet. For a moment the smitten bird swayed upon its wide pinions, then they seemed to crumple beneath its weight, and it fell heavily and lay flapping and striking at the stones with its strong beak.

"I also can kill," said Leonard to himself as he watched it die. "Kill till you are killed—that is the law of life." Then he turned to the body of his brother and made it ready for burial as best he might, closing the eyes, tying up the chin with a band of twisted grass, and folding the thin toil-worn hands upon the quiet heart.

When all was finished he paused from his dreadful task, and a thought struck him.

"Where are those Kaffirs?" he said aloud—the sound of his voice seemed to dull the edge of solitude—"the lazy hounds, they ought to have been up an hour ago. Hi! Otter, Otter!"

The mountains echoed "Otter, Otter;" there was no other reply. Again he shouted without result. "I don't like to leave it," he said, "but I must go and see;" and, having covered the body with a red blanket to scare away the vultures, he started at a run round some projecting rocks that bordered the little plateau on which the hut had stood. Beyond them the plateau continued, and some fifty paces from the rocks was a hollow in the mountain side, where a softer vein of stone had been eaten away by centuries of weather.

It was here that the Kaffirs slept—four of them—and in front of this cave or grotto it was their custom to make a fire for cooking. But on that morning no fire was burning, and no Kaffirs were to be seen.

"Still asleep," was Leonard's comment as he strode swiftly towards the cave. In another moment he was in it shouting "Otter, Otter!" and saluting with a vigorous kick a prostrate form, of which he could just see the outline. The form did not move, which was strange, for such a kick should have suffered to wake even the laziest Basuto from his soundest sleep. Leonard stopped to examine it, and the next moment started back violently, exclaiming:

"Great heavens! it is Cheat, and he is dead."

At this moment a thick voice spoke from the corner of the cave in Dutch, the voice of Otter:

"I am here, Baas, but I am tied: the Baas must loosen me, I cannot stir."

Leonard advanced, striking a match as he came. Presently it burned up, and he saw the man Otter lying on his back, his legs and arms bound firmly with *rimpis* of hide, his face and body a mass of contusions. Drawing his hunting-knife Leonard cut the *rimpis* and brought the man from out the cave, carrying rather than leading him.

Otter was a knob-nosed Kaffir, that is of the Bastard Zulu race. The brothers had found him wandering about the country in a state of semi-starvation, and he had served them faithfully for some years. They had christened him Otter, his native patronymic being quite unpronounceable, because of his extraordinary skill in swimming, which almost equalled that of the animal after which he was named.

In face the man was hideous, though his ugliness was not unpleasant, being due chiefly to a great development of his tribal feature, the nose, and in body he was misshapen to the verge of monstrosity. In fact Otter was a dwarf, measuring little more than four feet in height. But what he lacked in height he made up in breadth; it almost seemed as though, intended by nature to be a man of many inches, he had been compressed to his present dimensions by art. His vast chest and limbs, indicating strength nearly superhuman, his long iron arms and massive head, all gave colour to this idea. Otter had one redeeming feature, however—his eyes, that when visible, which at this moment was not the case, were large, steady, and, like his skin, of a brilliant black.

"What has happened?" said Leonard, also speaking in Dutch.

"This, Baas! Last night those three Basuto villains, your servants, made up their minds to desert. They told me nothing, and they were so cunning that, though I watched even their thoughts, I never guessed. They knew better than to tell me, for I would have beaten them—yes, all! So they waited till I was sound asleep, then came behind me, the three of them, and tied me fast that I should not hinder them and that they might take away Baas Tom's gun which you lent me, and other things. Soon I found out their plans, and though I laughed in their faces, oh! my heart was black with rage.

"When the Basuto dogs had tied me they mocked me, calling me foul names and saying that I might stop and starve with the white fools, my masters, who always dug for yellow iron and found so little, being fools. Then they got together everything of value, yes, down to the kettle, and made ready to go, and each of them came and slapped me on the face, and one burnt me here upon the nose with a hot brand.

"All this I bore as a man must bear trouble which comes from the skies, but when Cheat took up Baas Tom's gun and the others came with a *reim* to tie me to the rock, I could bear it no more. So I shouted aloud and drove at Cheat, who held the gun. Ah! they had forgotten that if my arms are strong, my head is stronger! Butting like a bull I caught him fair in the middle, and his back was against the side of the cave. He made one noise, no more; he will never make another noise, for my head smashed him up inside and the rock hurt me through him. Then the other two hit me with *kerries*—great blows—and my arms being tied I could not defend myself, though I knew that they would soon kill me; so I groaned and dropped down, pretending to be dead—just like a stink-cat.

"At last, thinking that they had finished me, the Basutos ran away in a great hurry, for they feared lest you might hear the shouting and should come after them with rifles. They were so much afraid that they left the gun and most of the other things. After that I fainted; it was silly, but those *kerries* of theirs are of rhinoceros horn—I should not have minded so much had they been of wood, but the horn bites deep. That is all the story. It will please Baas Tom to know that I saved his gun. When he hears it he will forget his sickness and say 'Well done Otter! Ha! Otter, your head is hard.'"

"Make your heart hard also," said Leonard with a sad smile; "Baas Tom is dead. He died at daybreak in my arms. The fever killed him as it killed the other *Inkoosis* (chiefs)."

Otter heard, and, letting his bruised head fall upon his mighty chest, remained for a while in silence. At length he lifted it, and Leonard saw two tears wandering down the battered countenance. "*Wow*," he said, "is it so? Oh! my father, are you dead, you who were brave like a lion and gentle as a girl? Yes, you are dead, my ears have heard it, and were it not for your brother, the Baas Leonard, I think that I would kill myself and follow you. *Wow*, my father, are you indeed dead, who smiled upon me yesterday?"

"Come," said Leonard; "I dare not leave him long."

And he went, Otter following him with a reeling gait, for he was weak from his injuries. Presently they reached the spot, and Otter saw that the hut was gone.

"Certainly," he said, "our bad spirits were abroad last night. Well, next time it will be the turn of the good ones." Then he drew near to the corpse and saluted it with uplifted hand and voice.

"Chief and Father," he said in Zulu, for Otter had wandered long and knew many tongues, but he loved the Zulu best of all. "While you lived upon earth, you were a good man and brave, though somewhat quick of temper and quarrelsome like a woman. Now you have wearied of this world and flown away like an eagle towards the sun, and there where you live in the light of the sun you will be braver and better yet, and become more patient and not quarrel any more with those who are less clever than you. Chief and Father, I salute you! May he whom you named the Otter serve you and the *Inkoosi* your brother once more in the House of the Great-Great, if one so ugly and misshapen can enter there. As for the Basuto dog whom I slew and who would have stolen your gun, I see now that I killed him in a fortunate hour, that he might be the slave beneath your feet in the House of the Great-Great. Ah! had I known, I would have sent a better man, for there as here Cheat will still be Cheat. Hail, my father! Hail and farewell! Let your spirit watch over us and be gentle towards us, who love you yet."

And Otter turned away without further ado; and having washed his wounds, he set himself to the task of preparing such coarse food as they had in store.

When it was ready Leonard ate of it, and after he had finished eating, together they bore the body to the little cave for shelter. It was Leonard's purpose to bury his brother at sundown; he might not delay longer, but till then he would watch by him, keeping the last of many vigils. So all that remained of the Basuto Cheat having been dragged forth and thrust unceremoniously into an ant-bear hole by Otter, who while he disposed of the body did not spare to taunt the spirit of his late treacherous foe, the corpse of Thomas Outram was laid in its place, and Leonard sat himself by its side in the gloom of the cave.

About midday Otter, who had been sleeping off his sorrows, physical and mental, came into the cavern. They were short of meat, he said, and with the leave of the Baas he would take the gun of the dead Baas and try to shoot a buck.

Leonard bade him go, but to be back by sundown, as he should require his help.

"Where shall we dig a hole, Baas?" asked the dwarf.

"One is dug," answered Leonard; "he who is dead dug it himself as the others did. We will bury him in the last pit he made looking for gold, to the right of where the hut stood. It is deep and ready."

"Yes, Baas, a good place—though perhaps Baas Tom would not have worked at it so strongly had he known. *Wow!* Who knows to what end he labours? But perchance it is a little near the donga. Twice that hole has been flooded while Baas Tom was digging in it. Then he would jump out, but now——"

"I have settled it," said Leonard shortly; "go, and be back half an hour before sundown at latest. Stop! Bring some of those rock-lilies if you can. The Baas was fond of them."

The dwarf saluted and went. "Ah!" he said to himself as he waddled down the hill where he hoped to find game, "ah! you do not fear men dead or living—overmuch; yet, Otter, it is true that you are better here in the sun, though the sun is hot, than yonder in the cave. Say, Otter, why does Baas Tom look so awful now that he is dead—he who was so gentle while yet he lived? Cheat did not look awful, only uglier. But then you killed Cheat, and the Heavens killed Baas Tom and set their own seal upon him. And what will Baas Leonard do now that his brother is dead and the Basutos have run away? Go on digging for the yellow iron which is so hard to find, and of which, when it is found, no man can even make a spear? Nay, what is that to you, Otter? What the Baas does you do—and here be the spoor of an impala buck."

Otter was right. The day was fearfully hot. It was summer in East Africa, or rather autumn, the season of fever, thunder and rain, a time that none who valued their lives would care to spend in those latitudes searching for gold with poor food and but little shelter. But men who seek their fortunes are not chary of hazarding their own lives of those of others. They become fatalists, not avowedly perhaps, but unconsciously. Those who are destined to die must die, they think, the others will live. And, after all, it does not greatly matter which they do, for, as they know well, the world will never miss them.

When Leonard Outram, his brother, and two companions in adventure heard from the natives that at a particular spot on the mountains, nominally in the Portuguese territory near the lowest branch of the Zambezi, gold could be dug out like iron ore, and when, at the price of two Tower muskets and a half-bred greyhound, they received a concession from the actual chief of that territory to dig up and possess the gold without let or hindrance from any person whatsoever, they did not postpone their undertaking because the country was fever-stricken and the unhealthy season drew on. In the first place, their resources were not great at the moment; and in the second, they feared lest some other enterprising person with three Tower muskets and two grey-hounds should persuade the chief to rescind their concession in his favour.

So they journeyed laboriously to the place of hidden wealth, and with the help of such native labour as they could gather began their search. At first they were moderately successful; indeed, wherever they dug they found "colour," and once or twice stumbled upon pockets of nuggets. Their hopes ran high, but presently one of the four—Askew by name—sickened and died of fever. They buried him and persevered with varying luck. Then a second member of their party, Johnston, was taken ill. He lingered for a month and died also.

After this Leonard was for abandoning the enterprise, but, as fate would have it, on the day following Johnston's death they found gold in very promising quantities, and his brother, whose desire to win the wealth necessary was only increased by many disappointments, would not listen to such advice.

So they rebuilt the hut on a higher and healthier spot and stayed. But on one unfortunate day Thomas Outram went out shooting, and losing his path in the bush was forced to spend a night in the fever-fog. A week afterwards he complained of sickness and pains in the back and head—three weeks later he died as we have seen.

All these events and many others antecedent passed through Leonard's mind as he wore out the long hours seated by the side of his dead brother. Never before had he felt so lonely, so utterly desolate, so bankrupt of all love and hope. It was a fact that at this moment he had no friend in the wide world, unless he could call the knob-nosed native Otter a friend. He had been many years away from England, his few distant relations there troubled themselves no more about him or his brother, outcasts, wanderers in strange lands, and his school and college companions in all probability had forgotten his existence.

There was one indeed, Jane Beach. But since that night of parting, seven years ago, he had heard nothing of her. Twice he had written, but no answer came to his letters. Then he gave up writing, for Leonard was a proud man; moreover he guessed that she did not reply because she could not. As he had said to his brother, Jane might be dead by now, or more probably married to Mr. Cohen. And yet once they had loved each other, and to this hour he still loved her, or thought that he did. At least, through all the weary years of exile, labour, and unceasing search after the unattainable, her image and memory had been with him, a distant dream of sweetness, peace, and beauty, and they were with him yet, though nothing of her remained to him except the parting gift of her prayer-book and the lock of hair within it. The wilderness is not a place where men can forget their earliest love. No, he was alone, absolutely and utterly alone, a wanderer in wild lands, a sojourner with rough unlettered men and savages.

And now, what should he do? This place was played out. There was alluvial gold indeed, but Leonard knew today that it was not in the earth, but in the veins of quartz which permeated the mountains, that the real wealth must be sought for, and how could he extract it from the quartz without machinery or capital? Besides, his Kaffir servants had deserted him, worn out with hard work and fever, and there were no others to be had at this season. Well, it was only one more disappointment; he must go back to Natal and take his chance. At the worst he could always earn his living as a transport-rider, and at the best he wearied of this search for wealth which was to build up their family afresh.

Then of a sudden Leonard remembered what he had promised— to go on seeking till he died. Very good, he would keep the promise— till he died. And he remembered also that curious prophecy to which Thomas had given utterance on the previous night, that prophecy of wealth which should come to him.

Of course it was nothing but the distraught fancy of a dying man. For many years his brother had brooded over this possibility of gaining riches, not for their own sake indeed, but that it might be the means of restoring the ancient family, which their father had brought to shame and ruin. It was not wonderful in a man of his excitable temperament that at the hour of his death he should have grasped at some vision of attainment of the object of his life, though by the hand of another.

And yet how strangely he had looked at him! With what conviction he had spoken! But all this was beside the point; he, Leonard, had sworn an oath many years ago, and only last night he had promised to continue to observe that oath. Therefore, come good or ill, he must pursue it to the end.

Thus he mused till he grew weary as he sat hour after hour by the side of that rigid thing, which had been his playmate, his brother, and his friend. From time to time he rose and walked about the cave. As the afternoon waned the air grew hotter and stiller, while a great cloud gathered on the horizon.

"There will be thunder at sundown," said Leonard aloud; "I wish that Otter would come back, so that we might get the funeral over; otherwise we shall have to wait till tomorrow."

At length, about half an hour before nightfall, the dwarf appeared at the mouth of the cave, looking more like a gnome than a man against the lurid background of the angry sky. A buck was tied across his enormous shoulders, and in his hand he held a large bunch of the fragrant mountain lilies.

Then the two of them buried Thomas Outram, there in his lonely grave which he himself had dug by the gully, and the roll of the thunder was his requiem. It seemed a fitting termination to his stormy and laborious life.

CHAPTER 5

Otter Gives Counsel

When the burial was finished and Thomas Outram slept his last sleep beneath six feet of earth and stones, his brother took out the prayer-book that Jane Beach had given him, which in truth formed all his library, and read the funeral service over the grave, ending it by the glare of the lightning flashes. Then he and Otter went back to the cave and ate, speaking no word. After they had done their meal Leonard called to the dwarf, who took his food at a little distance.

"Otter," he said, setting the lantern between them, "you are a faithful man and clever in your way. I would tell you a story and ask you something. At the least," he added to himself in English, "in such a matter your judgment is as good as mine."

"Speak on, Baas," said the dwarf; "my ears are open;" and he squatted down on the further side of the lantern like some great toad, watching his master's face with his black eyes.

"Otter, the Baas who is dead and I journeyed to this country about seven years ago. Before we came here we had been rich men, chiefs in our own place, but we lost our kraals and cattle and lands; they were sold, others took them and we became poor. Yes, we who were fat grew lean as trek oxen at the end of winter. Then we said to each other, 'Here we have no longer any home, the shame of poverty has come upon us, we are broken vessels, empty men of no account; also we are chiefs by blood, and here we cannot let ourselves out to labour like the common people, lest both the common people and the nobles should make a mock of us. Our great stone kraal that has been ours for many generations is taken from us, others dwell in it, strange women order it, and their children shall move about the land. We will go away.'"

"The blood is the blood," broke in Otter, "the wealth is nothing;

that comes and goes, but the blood is always the blood. Why did you not gather an *impi*, my father, and put these strangers to the spear and take your kraal again?"

"In our land this may not be, Otter, for there wealth is more than race. So we should have been brought to still greater shame. Riches alone could give us back our home, and we had none left. Therefore we swore an oath together, the dead Baas and I, that we would journey to this far country and seek to win wealth that we might buy back our lands and kraal and rule over them as in past years, and our children after us."

"A good oath," said Otter, "but here we should have sworn it otherwise, and there would have been a ringing of steel about that kraal, not the chink of yellow iron."

"We came, Otter, and for seven years we have laboured harder than the lowest of our servants; we have travelled to and fro, mixing with many peoples, learning many tongues, and what have we found? The Baas yonder a grave in the wilderness—I the food that the wilderness gives, no more."

"A poor wage so far," said Otter. "Ah! the ways of my people are more simple and better. A red spear is brighter than the red gold, yes, and it is more honest."

"The wealth is unwon, Otter, and I have sworn to win the wealth or die. But last night I swore it again to him who lies dead."

"It is well, Baas; an oath is an oath and true men must keep it. But riches cannot be gathered here, for the gold, most of it, is hid in those rocks that are far too heavy to carry, and who may charm gold out of the rock? Not all the wizards in Zululand. At the least you and I cannot do it alone, even should the fever spare us. We must trek, Baas, and look elsewhere."

"Listen, Otter, the tale is yet to tell. The Baas who is dead dreamed before he died, he dreamed that I should win the gold, that I should win it by the help of a woman, and he bade me wait here a while after he was dead. Say now, Otter, you who come of a people learned in dreams and are the child of a dream-doctor, was this a true dream or a sick man's fancy?"

"Nay, Baas, who can tell for sure?" the dwarf answered; then pondered a while, and set himself to trace lines in the dust of the floor with his finger. "Yet I say," he went on, "that the words of the dead uttered on the edge of death shall come true. He promised that you should win the wealth: you will win it by this way or that, and the great kraal across the water shall be yours again, and the children of strangers shall wander there no more. Let us obey the words of the dead and bide here awhile as he commanded."

Seven days had passed, and on the night of the seventh Leonard Outram and Otter sat together once more in the little cave on Grave Mountain, for so they named this fatal spot. They did not speak, though each of them was speaking after his own fashion, and both had cause for thought. They had been hunting all day, but killed nothing except a guinea-fowl, most of which they had just eaten; it was the only food left to them. Game seemed to have abandoned the district—at least they could find none.

Since his brother's death Leonard had given up all attempt to dig for gold—it was useless. Time hung heavy on his hands, for a man cannot search all day for buck which are not. Gloom had settled on his mind also; he felt his brother's loss more acutely now than on the day he buried him. Moreover, for the first time he suffered from symptoms of the deadly fever which had carried off his three companions. Alas! he knew too well the meaning of this lassitude and nausea, and of the racking pain which from time to time shot through his head and limbs. That was how his brother's last sickness had begun.

Would his own days end in the same fashion? He did not greatly care, he was reckless as to his fate, for the hard necessities of life had left him little time or inclination to rack himself with spiritual doubts. And yet it was awful to think of. He rehearsed the whole scene in his mind again and yet again until it became a reality to him. He saw his own last struggle for life and Otter watching it. He saw the dwarf bearing him in his great arms to a lonely grave, there to cover him with earth, and then, with a sigh, to flee the haunted spot for ever. Why did he stop to die of fever? Because his brother had bidden him to do so with his dying breath; because of a superstition, a folly, which would move any civilised man to scorn.

Ah! there was the rub, he was no longer a civilised man; he had lived so long with nature and savages that he had come to be as nature makes the savage. His educated reason told him that this was folly, but his instinct—that faculty which had begun to take the place of edu- cated reason with him—spoke in another voice. He had gone back in the scale of life, he had grown primitive; his mind was as the mind of a Norseman or of an Aztec. It did not seem wonderful to him that his brother should have prophesied upon his dying bed; it did not strike him as strange even that he should believe in the prophecy and act upon it. And yet he knew that in all probability this obedience would result in his own death.

Those who have lived much with nature will in some degree be familiar with such sensations, for man and nature are ever at variance, and each would shape the other to its ends. In the issue nature wins. Man boasts continually of his conquests over her, her instincts, her terrors, and her hopes. But let him escape from out his cities and the fellowship of his kind, let him be alone with her for a while, and where is his supremacy? He sinks back on to her breast again and is lost there as in time to be all his labours shall be lost. The grass of the field and the sand of the desert are more powerful than Babylon; they were before her, they are after her; and so it is with everything physical and moral in their degrees, for here rules a nurse whom we human children must obey at last, however much we may defy her.

Thus brooded Leonard as he sat, his hands in his pockets and an empty pipe between his teeth. Their tobacco was done, and yet he drew at the pipe, perhaps from habit. And all the while Otter watched him.

"Baas," he said at length, "you are sick, Baas."

"No," he answered, "that is, perhaps a little."

"Yes, Baas, a little. You have said nothing, but I know, I who watch. The fever has touched you with his finger, by-and-by he will grip you with his whole hand, and then, Baas——"

"And then, Otter, good night."

"Yes, Baas, for you good night, and for me, what? Baas, you think too much and you have nothing to do, that is why you grow sick. Better that we should go and dig again."

"What for, Otter? Ant-bear holes make good graves."

"Evil talk, Baas. Rather let us go away and wait no more than that you should talk such talk, which is the beginning of death."

Then there was silence for a while.

"The truth is, Otter," said Leonard presently, "we are both fools. It is useless for us to stay here with nothing to eat, nothing to drink, nothing to smoke, and only the fever to look forward to, expecting we know not what. But what does it matter? Fools and wise men all come to one end. Lord! how my head aches and how hot it is! I wish that we had some quinine left. I am going out," and he rose impatiently and left the cave.

Otter followed him. He knew where he would go—to his brother's grave. Presently they were there, standing on the hither edge of a ravine. A cloud had hidden the face of the moon, and they could see nothing, so they stood awhile idly waiting for it to pass.

As they rested thus, suddenly a moaning sound came to their ears, or rather a sound which, beginning with a moan, ended in a long low wail.

"What is that?" asked Leonard, looking towards the shadows on the further side of the ravine, whence the cry seemed to proceed.

"I do not know," answered Otter, "unless it be a ghost, or the voice of one who mourns her dead."

"We are the only mourners here," said Leonard, and as he spoke once more the low and piercing wail thrilled upon the air. Just then the cloud passed, the moonlight shone out brilliantly, and they saw who it was that cried aloud in this desolate place. For there, not twenty paces from them, on the other side of the ravine, crouched upon a stone and rocking herself to and fro as though in an agony of despair and grief, sat a tall and withered woman.

With an exclamation of surprise Leonard started towards her, followed by the dwarf. So absorbed was the woman in her sorrow that she neither saw nor heard them. Even when they stood close to her she did not perceive them, for her face was hidden in her bony hands. Leonard looked at her curiously. She was past middle age, but he could see that once she had been handsome, and, for a native, very light in colour. Her hair was grizzled and crisp rather than woolly, and her hands and feet were slender and finely shaped. At the moment he could discern no more of the woman's personal appearance, for the face was covered, as has been said, and her body wrapped in a tattered blanket.

"Mother," he said, speaking in the Sisutu dialect, "what ails you that you weep here alone?"

The stranger let drop her hands and sprang up with a cry of fear. As it chanced, her gaze fell first upon the dwarf Otter, who was standing in front of her, and at the sight of him the cry died upon her lips, and her sunken cheeks, clear-cut features, and sullen black eyes became as those of one who is petrified with terror. So strange was her aspect indeed that the dwarf and his master neither spoke nor moved; they stood hushed and expectant. It was the woman who broke this silence, speaking in a low voice of awe and adoration and, as she spoke, sinking to her knees.

"And hast thou come to claim me at the last," she said, addressing Otter, "O thou whose name is Darkness, to whom I was given in marriage, and from whom I fled when I was young? Do I see thee in the flesh, Lord of the night, King of blood and terror, and is this thy priest? Or do I but dream? Nay, I dream not; slay on, thou priest, and let my sin be purged."

"Here it seems," said Otter, "that we have to do with one who is mad."

"Nay, Jal," the woman answered, "I am not mad, though madness has been nigh to me of late."

"Neither am I named Jal or Darkness," answered the dwarf with irritation; "cease to speak folly, and tell the White Lord whence you come, for I weary of this talk."

"If you are not Jal, Black One, the thing is strange, for as Jal is so you are. But perchance it does not please you, having put on the flesh, to avow yourself before me. At the least be it as you will. If you are not Jal, then I am safe from your vengeance, and if you are Jal I pray you forget the sins of my youth and spare me."

"Who is Jal?" asked Leonard curiously.

"Nay, I know not," answered the woman, with a sudden change of manner. "Hunger and weariness have turned my brain, and I spoke wandering words. Forget them and give me food, White Man," she added in a piteous tone, "give me food, for I starve."

"There is scant fare here," answered Leonard, "but you are welcome to it. Follow me, mother," and he led the way across the donga to the cave, the woman limping after him painfully.

There Otter gave her meat, and she ate as one eats who has gone hungry for long, greedily and yet with effort. When she had finished she looked at Leonard with her keen dark eyes and said:

"Say, White Lord, are you also a slave-trader?"

"No," he answered grimly, "I am a slave."

"Who is your master then—this Black One here?"

"Nay, he is but the slave of a slave. I have no master, mother; I have a mistress, and she is named Fortune."

"The worst of mistresses," said the old woman, "or the best, for she laughs ever behind her frown and mingles stripes with kisses."

"The stripes I know well, but not the kisses," answered Leonard gloomily; then added in another tone, "What is your errand, mother? How are you named, and what do you seek wandering alone in the mountains?"

"I am named Soa, and I seek succour for one whom I love and who is in sore distress. Will my lord listen to my tale?"

"Speak on," said Leonard.

Then the woman crouched down before him and told this story.

CHAPTER 6

The Tale of Soa

"My lord, I, Soa, am the servant of a white man, a trader who lives on the banks of the Zambezi some four days' march from hence, having a house there which he built many years ago."

"How is the white man named?" asked Leonard.

"The black people call him Mavoom, but his white name is Rodd. He is a good master and no common man, but he has this fault, that at times he is drunken. Twenty years ago or more Mavoom, my lord, married a white woman, a Portuguese whose father dwelt at Delagoa Bay, and who was beautiful, ah! beautiful. Then he settled on the banks of the Zambezi and became a trader, building the house where he is now, or rather where its ruins are. Here his wife died in childbirth; yes, she died in my arms, and it was I who reared her daughter Juanna, tending her from the cradle to this day.

"Now, after the death of his wife Mavoom became more drunken. Still, when he is not in liquor he is very clever and a good trader, and several times he has collected ivory and feathers and gold worth much money, and also has bred cattle by hundreds. Then he would say that he must leave the wilderness and go to another country across the water, I know not where, that country whence the Englishmen come.

"Twice he has started to go, and I with him and his daughter Juanna, my mistress, who is named the Shepherdess of Heaven by the black people, because they think that she has the gift of foretelling rain. But once Mavoom stopped in a town, at Durban in Natal, and getting drunk he gambled away all his money in a month, and once he lost it in a river, the boat being overset by a river-horse and the ivory and gold sinking out of sight. Still, the last time that he started he left his daughter, the Shepherdess, at Durban, and there she stayed for three years learning those things that the white women know, for she is very clever, as clever as she is beautiful and good. Now, for nearly two years she has been back at the Settlement, for she came to Delagoa Bay in a ship, and I with her, and Mavoom met us.

"But one month gone my mistress the Shepherdess spoke to her father Mavoom, telling him that she wearied of their lonely life in the wilderness and wished to sail across the waters to the land which is called Home. He listened to her, for Mavoom loves his daughter, and said that it should be so. But he said this also: that first he would go on a trading journey up the river to buy a store of ivory of which he knew. Now she was against this, saying, 'Let us start at once, we have tempted chance too long, and once again we are rich. Let us go to Natal and pass over the seas.'

"Still he would not listen, for he is a headstrong man. So on the morrow he started to search for the store of ivory, and the lady Juanna his daughter wept, for though she is fearless, it was not fitting that she should be left thus alone; also she hated to be apart from her father, for it is when she is not there to watch that he becomes drunken.

"Mavoom left, and twelve days went by while I and my mistress the Shepherdess sat at the Settlement waiting till he returned. Now it is the custom of my mistress, when she is dressed, to read each morning from a certain holy book in which are written the laws of that Great-Great whom she worships. On the thirteenth morning, therefore, she sat beneath the veranda of the house, reading in the book according to her custom, and I went about my work making food ready. Suddenly I heard a tumult, and looking over the wall which is round the garden and to the left of the house, I saw a great number of men, some of them white, some Arab, and some half-breeds, one mounted and the others on foot, and behind them a long caravan of slaves with the slave-sticks set upon their necks.

"As they came these men fired guns at the people of the Settlement, who ran this way and that. Some of the people fell, and more were made captive, but others of them got away, for they were at work in the fields and had seen the slave-traders coming.

"Now, as I gazed affrighted, I saw my mistress, the Shepherdess, flying towards the wall behind which I stood, the book she was reading being still in her hand. But as she reached it, the man mounted on the mule overtook her, and she turned about and faced him, setting her back against the wall. Then I crouched down and hid myself among some banana-trees, and watched what passed through a crack in the wall.

"The man on the mule was old and fat, his hair was white and his face yellow and wrinkled. I knew him at once, for often I have heard of him before, who has been the terror of this country for many years. He is named the Yellow Devil by the black people, but his Portuguese name is Pereira, and he has his place in a secret spot down by one of the mouths of the Zambezi. Here he collects the slaves, and here the traders come twice a year with their dhows to carry them to market.

"Now this man looked at my mistress as she stood terrified with her back against the wall; then he laughed and cried aloud in Portuguese, 'Here we have a pretty prize. This must be that Juanna of whose beauty I have heard. Where is your father, my dove? Gone trading up the river, has he not? Ah! I knew it, or perhaps I should not have ventured here. But it was wrong of him to leave one so pretty all alone. Well, well, he is about his business, and I must be about mine, for I am a merchant also, my dove, a merchant who trades in blackbirds. One with silver feathers does not often come my way, and I must make the most of her. There is many a young man in our part who will bid briskly for such eyes as yours. Never fear, my dove, we will soon find you a husband.'

"Thus the Yellow Devil spoke, White Man, while the Shepherdess my mistress crouched against the wall and stared at him with frightened eyes, and the slave-traders his servants laughed aloud at his evil words. Presently she seemed to understand, and I saw her slowly lift her hand towards her head. Then I knew her purpose.

"Now, there is a certain deadly poison, White Man, of which I have the secret, and that secret I taught long ago to my mistress. It is so deadly that a piece of it no larger than the smallest ant can kill a man—yes, the instant after it touches his tongue he will be dead. Living alone as she does in the wilds, it is the custom of my mistress to carry a portion of this poison hidden in her hair, since a time might come when she must use it to save herself from worse than death. Now it seemed to her that this hour was upon her, and I knew that she was about to take the poison. Then in my fear I whispered to her through the crack in the wall, speaking in an ancient tongue which I have taught her, the tongue of my own people, White Man, and saying: 'Hold your hand, Shepherdess; while you live you may escape, but from death there is no escape. It will be time to use the poison when the worst is with you.'

"She heard and understood, for I saw her bow her head slightly, and her hand fell to her side. Then Pereira spoke again:

"'And now, if you are ready,' he said, 'we will be moving, for it is eight days' journey to my little Nest on the coast, and who can tell when the dhows will come to fetch my blackbirds? Have you anything to say before you go, my dove?'

"Now my mistress spoke for the first time, answering, 'I am in your power, but I do not fear you, for if need be I can escape you. But I tell you this: that your wickedness shall bring your own death upon you;' and she glanced round at the bodies of those whom the slave-traders had murdered, at the captives upon whom they were setting chains and forks of wood, and the columns of smoke that were rising from her home, for the roof of the Settlement had been fired.

"For a moment the Portuguese looked frightened, then he laughed aloud and said with an oath, crossing himself after the fashion of his people as a protection against the curse, 'What! you prophesy, do you, my dove, and you can escape me at your will, can you? Well, we shall see. Bring the other mule for this lady, you fellows.'

"The mule was brought, and Juanna, my mistress, was set upon it. Then the slave-traders shot down such of the captives as they thought to be of no value, the drivers flogged the slaves with their three-thonged *sjambochs* of hippopotamus-hide, and the caravan moved on down the banks of the river.

"When all had gone I crept from my hiding-place and sought out those men of the Settlement who had escaped the slaughter, praying them to find arms and follow on the Yellow Devil's spoor, waiting for an opportunity to rescue the Shepherdess whom they loved. But they would not do this, for the heart was out of them, they were cowed by fear, and most of the head-men had been taken captive. No, they would do nothing except weep over their dead and the burnt kraals. 'You cowards,' I said, 'if you will not come, then I must go alone. At the least let some of you pass up the river and search for Mavoom, to tell him what has chanced here in his house.'

"The men said that they would do this, and taking a blanket and a little food, I followed upon the track of the slave-drivers. For four days I followed, sometimes coming in sight of them, till at length the meat was done and my strength left me. On the morning of the fifth day I could go no farther, so I crept to the top of a *koppie* and watched their long line winding across the plain. In its centre were two mules, and on one of these mules sat a woman. Then I knew that no harm had befallen my mistress as yet, for she still lived.

"Now from the *koppie* I saw a little kraal far away to the right, and to this kraal I came that same afternoon with my last strength. I told its people that I had escaped from the slave-drivers, and they treated me kindly. Here it was also I learnt that some white men from Natal were digging for gold in these mountains, and next day I travelled on in search of them, thinking perchance they would help me, for I know well that the English hate the slave-drivers. And here, my lord, I am come at last with much toil, and now I pray you deliver my mistress the Shepherdess from the hands of the Yellow Devil. Oh! my Lord, I seem poor and wretched; but I tell you that if you can deliver her you shall win a great reward. Yes, I will reveal to you that which I have kept hidden all my life, ay, even from Mavoom my master; *I will reveal to you the secret treasures of my people, 'The Children of the Mist.'*"

Now when Leonard, who all the while had been listening attentively and in silence to Soa's tale, heard her last words, he raised his head and stared at her, thinking that her sorrows had made her mad. There was no look of madness upon the woman's fierce face, however, but only one of the most earnest and indeed passionate entreaty. So, letting this matter go by for the while, he spoke to her:

"Are you then crazed, mother?" he said. "You see that I am alone here with one servant, for my three companions, of whom the people in the kraal told you, are dead through fever, and I myself am smitten with it. And yet you ask me, alone as I am, to travel to this slave-trader's camp that is you know not where, and there, single-handed, to rescue your mistress, if indeed you have a mistress, and your tale is true. Are you then mad, mother?"

"No, Lord, I am not mad, and that which I tell you is true, every word of it. I know that I ask a great thing, but I know also that you Englishmen can do great things when you are well paid. Strive to help me and you shall have your reward. Ay, should you fail, and live, I can still give you a reward; not much perhaps, but more than you have ever earned."

"Never mind the reward now, mother," broke in Leonard testily, for the veiled sarcasm of Soa's speech had stung him, "unless, indeed, you can cure me of the fever," he added with a laugh.

"I can do that," she answered quietly; "tomorrow morning I will cure you."

"So much the better," he said, with an incredulous smile. "And now of your wisdom tell me how am I to look for your mistress, to say nothing of rescuing her, when I do not know whither she has been taken? Probably this Nest of which the Portugee talked is a secret place. How long has she been carried off?"

"This will be the twelfth day, Lord. As for the Nest, it is secret; that I have discovered. It is to your wisdom that I look to find it."

Leonard mused awhile, then a thought struck him. Turning to the dwarf, who had been sitting by listening to all that was said in stolid silence, his great head resting upon his knees, he spoke to him in Dutch:

"Otter, were you not once taken as a slave?"

"Yes, Baas, once, ten years ago."

"How was it?"

"Thus Baas. I was hunting on the Zambezi with the soldiers of a tribe there—it was after my own people had driven me out because they said that I was too ugly to become their chief, as I was born to be. Then the Yellow Devil, that same man of whom the woman speaks, fell upon us with Arabs, and took us to his place, there to await the slave-dhows. He was a stout man, horrible to see, and elderly. The day the dhows came in I escaped by swimming; and all the others who remained alive were taken off in ships to Zanzibar."

"Could you find your way to that place again, Otter?"

"Yes, Baas. It is a hard spot to find, for the path runs through morasses; moreover the place is secret and protected by water. All of us slaves were blindfolded during the last day's march. But I worked up my bandage with my nose—ah! my big nose served me well that day—and watched the path from beneath it, and Otter never forgets a road over which his feet have travelled. Also I followed that path back."

"Could you find the spot from here?"

"Yes, Baas. I should go along these mountains, ten days' journey or more, till we struck the southernmost mouth of the Zambezi below Luabo. Then I should follow the river down a day's journey. Afterwards two or more days through the swamps and we come to the place. But it is a strong place, Baas, and there are many men armed with guns in it; moreover, there is a big cannon, a 'by-and-by'!"

Again Leonard thought a moment, then he turned to Soa and asked, "Do you understand Dutch? No? Well I have found out something of this Nest from my servant. Pereira said that it was eight days' journey from your master's settlement, so your mistress has been there some three or four days if she ever reached it. Now, from what I know of the habits of slave-traders on this coast, the dhows will not begin to take in their cargoes for another month, because of the monsoon. Therefore, if I am correct, there is plenty of time. Mind you, Mother, I am not saying that I will have anything to do with this business; I must think it over first."

"Yes, you will, White Man," she answered, "when you know the reward; but of that I will tell you tomorrow, after I have cured you of your fever. And now I pray, Black One, show me a place where I may sleep, for I am very weary."

CHAPTER 7

Leonard Swears on the Blood of Aca

On the morrow Leonard woke early from a troubled sleep, for his fever would scarcely let him rest. But, early as it was, the woman Soa had been up before him, and on coming out of the cave the first thing that he saw was her tall shape bending over a little fire, whereon a gourd was boiling, the contents of which she stirred from time to time.

"Good morning to you, White Man," she said; "here is that which shall cure you of your sickness as I promised to do;" and she lifted the gourd from the fire.

Leonard took it and sniffed at the liquor, which smelt abominably.

"It is more likely to poison me, mother," he said.

"No, no," she answered with a smile; "drink half of it now and half at midday, and the fever shall trouble you no more."

So soon as the stuff was cool enough Leonard obeyed, though with a doubting heart.

"Well, mother," he said, setting the gourd down with a gasp, "if nastiness is any proof of virtue your medicine should be good."

"It is good," she answered gravely; "many have been dragged from the edge of death by it."

And here it may be stated, whether it was owing to Soa's medicine or to other causes, that Leonard began to mend from that hour. By nightfall he felt a different man, and before three days were over he was as strong as he had ever been in his life. But into the ingredients of the draught he never found the courage to inquire, and perhaps it was as well.

Shortly after he had taken his dose Leonard observed Otter walking up the hill, bearing a huge lump of meat upon his shoulders.

"The old woman has brought us luck," said the dwarf as he loosed himself from his burden. "Once more the bush is full of game;

55

scarcely had I reached it when I killed a young koodoo, fat, ah! fat, and there are many of them about."

Then they prepared breakfast, and ate it, and when the meal was done once more they talked.

"Mother," began Leonard, "last night you asked me to undertake a great venture, and promised a reward in payment. Now, as you said, we Englishmen will do much for gold, and I am a poor man who seeks wealth. You demand of me that I should risk my life; now tell me of its price."

The woman Soa looked at him awhile, and answered:

"White Man, have you ever heard of the People of the Mist?"

"No," he said, "that is, except in London. I mean that I know nothing of such a people. What of them?"

"This: I, Soa, am one of that people. I was the daughter of their head-priest, and I fled from them many many years ago, because I was doomed to be offered up as a sacrifice to the god Jal, he who is shaped like the Black One yonder," and she pointed to Otter.

"This is rather interesting," said Leonard; "go on."

"White Man, that people is a great people. They live in a region of mist, upon high lands beneath the shadow of the tops of snow mountains. They are larger than other men in size, and very cruel, but their women are fair. Now of the beginning of my people I know nothing, for it is lost in the past. But they worship an ancient stone statue fashioned like a dwarf, and to him they offer the blood of men. Beneath the feet of the statue is a pool of water, and beyond the pool is a cave. In that cave, White Man, he dwells whom they adore in effigy above, he, Jal, whose name is Terror."

"Do you mean that a dwarf lives in the cave?" asked Leonard.

"No, White Man, not a dwarf, but a holy crocodile which they name the Snake, the biggest crocodile in the whole world, and the oldest, for he has dwelt there from the beginning. It is this Snake that devours the bodies of those who are offered to the Black One."

"As I remarked before," said Leonard, "all this is very romantic and interesting, but I cannot see that there is much profit to be made out of it."

"White Man, the lives of men are not the only things which the priests of the Children of the Mist offer to their god; they offer also such toys as *this*, White Man," and suddenly she unclosed her hand and exhibited to Leonard's astonished gaze a ruby, or what appeared to be a ruby, of such size and so lovely a colour, that his eyes were dazzled when he looked at it. The gem, though roughly polished, was uncut, but its dimensions were those of a small blackbird's egg, it was of the purest pigeon-blood colour, without a flaw, and worn almost round, apparently by the action of water. Now, as it chanced, Leonard knew something of gems, although unhappily he was less acquainted with the peculiarities of the ruby than with those of most other stones. Thus, although this magnificent specimen might be a true stone, as indeed appeared to be the case, it was quite possible that it was only a spinel, or a garnet, and alas! he had no means of setting his doubts at rest.

"Do your people find many of these pebbles, Soa?" he asked, "and if so, where do they find them?"

"Yes, White Man, they find many, though few of such a size as this. They dig them out of a dry river-bed in some spot that is known to the priests only, and with them other beautiful stones of a blue colour."

"Sapphires probably," said Leonard to himself: "they generally go together."

"Every year they dig them," she went on, "and the biggest of those that are found in their digging they bind upon the brow of her who is to be offered as a wife to the god Jal. Afterwards, before she dies, they take the gem from her brow and store it in a secret place, and there in that secret place are hidden all those that have been worn by the victims of countless years. Moreover the eyes of Jal are made of such stones, and there are others.

"This is the legend of my people, White Man, that Jal, God of Death and Evil, slew his mother, Aca, in the far past. There where the stones are found he slew her, and the red gems are her blood, and the blue gems are her tears which she shed praying to him for mercy. Therefore the blood of Aca is offered to Jal, and so it shall be offered till Aca comes again to drive his worship from the land."

"A nice bit of mythology, I am sure," said Leonard. "Our old friends the Darkness and the Dawn in an African shape, I suppose. But listen to me, mother. This stone, if it is genuine, is worth many ounces of gold, but there are other stones so like it that none who are not learned can tell the difference, and if it be one of these it is of little value. Still it may happen that this, and the others of which you speak, are true rubies; at any rate I should be willing to take my chance of that. But now, tell me, what is your plan? This is a very pretty story, and the rubies may be there, but how am I to get them?"

"I have a plan, White Man," she answered. "If you will help me, I offer to give you that stone, which I have borne hidden about me for many years, tellings its story to none, no, not even to Mavoom. I offer to give it to you now if you will promise to attempt the rescue of my mistress, for I know by your eyes that if once you promise you will not desert the quest;" and she paused, looking at him keenly.

"Very well," said Leonard, "but considering the risks the price does not seem quite good enough. As I told you, this stone may be worth nothing: you must make a better bid, mother."

"Truly, White Man, I have judged you well," answered Soa with a sneer; "also you are wise: little work for little wage. Listen now, this is the pay I proffer you.

"If you succeed, and the Shepherdess is saved alive from the grip of the Yellow Devil, I promise this on her behalf and on my own: that I will guide you to the land of the People of the Mist, and show you a way to win for yourself all those other countless stones that are hidden there."

"Good," said Leonard, "but why do you promise on behalf of your mistress and yourself? What has she got to do with it?"

"Without her nothing can be done, White Man. This people is great and strong, and we have no force with which to conquer them in war. Here craft must be your spear."

"You must speak more clearly, Soa. I cannot waste time in guessing riddles. How will you conquer this people by craft, and what has Miss Rodd, whom you name the Shepherdess, to do with the matter?"

"That you shall learn by-and-by, after you have rescued her, White Man; till then my lips are shut. I tell you that I have a plan, and this must be enough, for more I will not say. If you are not content, let me go to seek help elsewhere."

Leonard thought a moment, and seeing that she was determined not to be more explicit, said:

"Very well, then. And now how am I to know that your mistress will fall in with this scheme?"

"I answer for her," said Soa, "she will never go back upon my word. Look you, White Man, it is not for a little thing that I would have told you this tale. If you journey to the land of the People of the Mist, I must go with you, and there, should I be discovered, my death waits me. I tell you the tale, or some of it, and I offer you the bribe because I see that you need money, and I am sure that without the chance of winning money you will not hazard your life in this desperate search. But I love my mistress so well that I am ready to hazard mine; ay, I would give six lives, if I had them, to save her from the shame of the slave. Now, White Man, we have talked enough; is it a bargain?"

"What do you say, Otter?" asked Leonard, thoughtfully pulling at his beard, "you have heard all this wonderful tale and you are clever."

"Yes, Baas," said the dwarf, speaking for the first time, "I have heard the tale, and as for being clever, perhaps I am and perhaps I am not. My people said that I was clever, and that is one of the reasons why they would not have me for a chief. If I had been clever only, they could have borne it, they said, or if I had been ugly only, but being both ugly and clever I was no chief for them. They feared lest I should rule them too well and make all the people to be born ugly also. Ah! they were fools; they did not understand that it wants someone cleverer than I to make people so ugly."

"Never mind all that," said Leonard, who understood however that the dwarf was talking thus in order to give himself time to think before he answered. "Show me your mind, Otter."

"Baas, what can I say? I know nothing of the value of that red stone. I do not know whether this woman, of whom my heart tells me no good, speaks truth or lies about a distant people who live in a fog and worship a god shaped as I am. None have ever worshipped me, yet there may be a land where I should be deemed worthy of worship, and if so I should like to travel in that land. But as to the rescue of this Shepherdess from the Nest of the Yellow Devil, I do not know how it can be brought about. Say, mother, how many of the men of Mavoom were taken prisoners with your mistress?"

"Fifty of them perchance," answered Soa.

"Well now," went on the dwarf, "if we could loose those men and if they are brave we might do something, but there are many *ifs* about it, Baas. Still if you think the pay is good enough we can try. It will be better than sitting here, and it does not matter what happens. Every man to his fate, Baas, and fate to every man."

"A good motto," said Leonard. "Soa, I take your offer, though I am a fool for my pains. And now, with your leave, we will put the matter into writing so that there may be no mistake about it afterwards. Get a little blood from the buck's flesh, Otter, and mix *gunpo* water with it; that will do for ink if we add some hot water."

While the dwarf was compounding this ominous mixture Leonard sought of paper. He could find none; the last had been lost when the hut was blown away on the night of his brother's death. Then he bethought him of the prayer-book which Jane Beach had given him. He would not use the fly-leaf, because her name was on it, so he must write across the title-page. And thus he wrote in small, neat letters with his mixture of blood and gunpowder straight through the *Order of Common Prayer.*

59

Agreement between Leonard Outram and Soa, the native woman.

I. The said Leonard Outram agrees to use his best efforts to rescue Juanna, the daughter of Mr. Rodd, now reduced to a state of slavery and believed to be in the power of one Pereira, a slave-dealer.

II. In consideration of the services of the said Leonard Outram, the said Soa delivers to him a certain stone believed to be a ruby, of which the said Leonard Outram hereby acknowledges the receipt.

III. Should the rescue be effected, the said Soa hereby agrees, on behalf of herself and the said Juanna Rodd, to conduct the said Leonard Outram to a certain spot in central South Eastern Africa, inhabited by a tribe known as the People of the Mist, there to reveal to him and to help him to gain possession of the store of rubies used in the religious ceremonies of the said tribe. Further, the said Soa agrees, on behalf of the said Juanna Rodd, that she, the said Juanna, will accompany her upon the journey, and will play among the said People of the Mist any part that may be required of her as necessary to the success of this undertaking.

IV. It is mutually agreed that these enterprises be prosecuted until the said Leonard Outram is satisfied that they are fruitless.

Signed in the Manica Mountains, Eastern Africa, on the ninth day of May 18—

When he had finished this document, perhaps one of the most remarkable that were ever written since Pizarro drew up his famous agreement for the division of the prospective spoils of Peru, Leonard read it aloud and laughed heartily to himself. It was the first time that he had laughed for some months. Then he translated it to his companions, not without complaisancy, for it had a truly legal sound, and your layman loves to affect the lawyer.

"What do you think of that, Otter?" he asked when he had finished.

"It is fine, Baas, very fine," answered the dwarf. "Wonderful are the ways of the white man! But, Baas, how can the old woman promise things on behalf of another?"

Leonard pulled his beard reflectively. The dwarf had put his finger upon the weak spot in the document. But he was saved the necessity of answering by Soa herself, who said quietly, "Have no fear, White Man; that which I promise in her name, my mistress will certainly perform, if so be that you can save her. Give me the pen that I may make my mark upon the paper. But first do you swear upon the red stone that you will perform what you undertake in this writing."

So Leonard laughed, swore, and signed, and Soa made her mark. Then Otter affixed his, as witness to the deed, and the thing was finished. Laughing again at the comicality of the transaction, which indeed he had carried out more by way of joke than for any other reason, Leonard put the prayer-book in his pocket and the great ruby into a division of his belt. The old woman watched the stone vanish with an expression of triumph on her face, then she cried exultingly:

"Ah! White Man, you have taken my pay, and now you are my servant to the end. He who swears upon the blood of Aca swears an oath indeed, and woe be to him if he should break it."

"Quite so," answered Leonard; "I have taken your pay and I mean to earn it, so we need not enter into the matter of the blood of Aca. It seems to me more probable that our own blood will be in question before all is said and done. And now we had better make ready to start."

CHAPTER 8

The Start

Food was their first consideration, and to provide it Leonard bade Otter cut the lump of raw meat into strips and set them upon the rocks to dry in the broiling sun. Then they sorted their goods and selected such of them as they could carry.

Alas! they were but few. A blanket apiece—a spare pair of boots apiece—some calomel and sundries from the medicine-chest—a shot gun and the two best rifles and ammunition—a compass, a water bottle, three knives, a comb, and a small iron cooking-pot made up the total—a considerable weight for two men and a woman to drag across mountains, untravelled plains, and swamps. This baggage was divided into three loads, of which Soa's was the lightest, and that of Otter weighed as much as the other two put together.

"It was nothing," he said, "he could carry the three if need were;" and so great was the dwarf's strength that Leonard knew this to be no idle boast.

At length all was prepared, and the articles that remained were buried in the cave together with the mining tools. It was not likely that they would ever return to seek them; more probably they will lie there till, thousands of years hence, they are dug up and become priceless relics of the Anglo-African age. Still they hid them on the chance. Leonard had melted the fruits of their mining into little ingots. In all there were about a hundred ounces of almost pure gold—the price of three men's lives! Half of these ingots he placed with the ruby in the belt about his middle, and half he gave to Otter, who hid them in his bundle. Leonard's first idea was to leave the bullion, because it entailed the carrying of extra weight; but he remembered in time that gold is always useful, and nowhere more so than among Portuguese and Arab slave-drivers.

By evening everything was ready, and when the edge of the moon showed above the horizon, Leonard rose, and lifting his load, fastened it upon his shoulders with the loops of hide which had been prepared, Otter and Soa following his example. It was their plan to travel by night so long as the state of the moon served them, for thus they would escape the terrible heat and lessen the danger of being observed.

"Follow me in a few minutes," said Leonard to Otter; "you will find me by the donga."

The dwarf nodded. A quarter of an hour later he started also with Soa and found his master standing bareheaded by his brother's grave, taking a mute farewell of that which lay beneath before he left it for ever to its long sleep in the untrodden wilderness. It was a melancholy parting, but there have been many such in the African fever belt.

With one last look Leonard turned and joined his companions. Then, having taken counsel with them and with the compass, he set his face to the mountain and his heart to the new adventures, hopes, and fears that were beyond it. The past was done with, it lay buried in yonder grave, but by the mercy of God he was still a man, living beneath the sunlight, and the future stretched away before him. What would it bring? He cared little; experience had taught him the futility of anxieties as to the future. Perchance a grave like those which he had left, perchance wealth, love, and honour. Whatever the event he would strive to meet it with patience, dignity, and resignation. It was not his part to ask questions or to reason why; it was his part to struggle on and take such guerdon as it pleased Providence to send him.

Thus thought Leonard, and this is the right spirit for an adventurer to cultivate. It is the right spirit in which to meet the good and ill of life—that greatest of adventures which every one of us must dare. He who meets them thus and holds his heart pure and his hands clean will lay himself down to sleep without a sigh or a regret when mountain, swamp, river, and forest all are travelled, and the unknown innumerable treasure, buried from the olden time far out of reach of man's sight and knowledge, at last is opened to his gaze.

So Leonard started, and his hopes were high notwithstanding the desperate nature of their undertaking. For here it must be confessed that the undesirable element of superstition still held fast upon his mind, and now with some slight cause. Had not his brother spoken of wealth that he should win by the aid of a woman? And had not a woman come to him, bearing in her hand a jewel which, if real, was in itself worth a moderate fortune; promising also, with the help of another woman, to lead him to a land where many such might be found? Yes, these things were so, and it may be pardoned to Leonard if, setting aside the theory of coincidence, he began to believe that the end would be as the beginning had been, that the great adventure would be achieved and the wealth be won.

We shall not need to follow the footsteps of Leonard Outram and his companions day by day. For a week they travelled on, journeying mostly by night as they had proposed. They climbed mountains, they struggled through swamps and forests, they swam rivers. Indeed one of these was in flood, and they never could have crossed it had it not been for Otter's powers of natation. Six times did the dwarf face the torrent, bearing their goods and guns held above the water with one hand. On the seventh journey he was still more heavily weighted, for, with some assistance from Leonard, he must carry the woman Soa, who could swim but little. But he did it, and without any great fatigue. It was not until Otter was seen stemming a heavy current that his vast strength could be measured. Here, indeed, his stunted stature was a positive advantage, for it offered the less surface for the water to act upon.

So they travelled forward, sometimes hungry, sometimes full of meat, and even of what were better, of milk and corn. For the country was not entirely deserted; occasionally they came to scattered kraals, and were able to obtain provisions from their peaceful inhabitants in return for some such trifle as an empty cartridge of brass. At first Leonard was afraid lest Soa should tire, but notwithstanding her years and the hardships and sufferings which she had undergone, she showed wonderful endurance—endurance so wonderful that he came to the conclusion that it was her spirit which supported the frailty of her body, and the ever-present desire to rescue one whom she loved as a surly dog sometimes loves its master. However this might be, she pushed forward with the rest, rarely speaking except to urge them onwards.

On the eighth night of their journey they halted upon the crest of a high mountain. The moon had set, and it was impossible to go further; moreover, they were weary with long marching. Wrapping themselves up in their blankets—for here the air was piercingly cold— they lay down beneath the shelter of some bushes to sleep till dawn. It was Otter who woke them. "Look, Baas," he said to Leonard, "we have marched straight. There below us is the big river, and there far to the right is the sea."

They looked. Some miles from them, across the great plain of bush that merged gradually into swamp, lay that branch of the Zambezi which they would reach. They could not see it, indeed, for its face was hid by a dense cloak of soft white mist that covered it like a cloud. But there it was, won at last, and there away to the eastward shone the wide glitter of the sea, flecked with faint lines of broken billows whence the sun rose in glory.

"See, Baas," said Otter, when they had satisfied themselves with the beautiful sight, "yonder, some five hours' march from here, the mountains curve down to the edge of the river. Thither we must go, for it is on the further side of those hills that the great swamp lies where the Yellow Devil has his place. I know the spot well; I have passed it twice."

They rested till noonday; but that night, before the moon rose, they stood on the curve of the mountain, close down to the water's edge. At length she came up, and showed them a wonderful scene of desolation. Beyond the curve of hills the mountains trended out again to the south, gradually growing lower till at last they melted into the skyline. In the vast semicircle thus formed ran the river, spotted with green islands, while between it and the high ground, over a space which varied from one mile at the narrowest to twenty miles in width at the broadest of the curve, was spread a huge and dismal swamp, marked by patches of stagnant water, clothed with reeds which grew to the height of small trees, and exhaling a stench as of the rottenness of ages.

The loneliness of the place was dreadful, its waste and desolation were appalling. And yet it lived with a life of its own. Wild fowl flew in wedges from the sea to feed in its recesses, alligators and hippopotami splashed in the waters, bitterns boomed among the rushes, and from every pool and quagmire came the croaking of a thousand frogs.

"Yonder runs the slave road, or yonder it once ran," said Otter, pointing to the foot of a hill.

"Let us go and see," answered Leonard; "we can follow it for a while and camp."

They climbed down the hill. At its foot Otter cast backwards and forwards among the bushes like a hound. Then he held up his hand and whistled.

"I thought so," he said, as the others drew near; "the path is still the same. Look, Baas."

As he spoke he broke down the branches of a creeping bush with his strong foot. Among them lay the mouldering skeleton of a woman, and by her side that of a child.

"Not long dead," said Otter phlegmatically, "perhaps two weeks. Ah! the Yellow Devil leaves a spoor that all may follow."

Soa bent over the bones and examined them. "One of Mavoom's people," she said; "I know the fashion of the anklets."

Then they marched on for two hours or more, till at length they came to a spot where the trail ran to the edge of the water and stopped.

"What now, Otter?" said Leonard.

"Here the slaves are put on boats, Baas," the dwarf answered. "The boats should be hidden yonder," and he pointed to some thick reeds. "There too they 'weed the corn,' killing out the weakly ones, that they may not be burdened with them. Let us go and look."

They went, Otter leading the way. Presently he halted. "The boats are gone," he said, "all except one canoe; but the 'weeds' lie in a heap as of old."

He was right. Piled in a little open space lay the bodies of some thirty men, women, and children recently dead. In other spaces close by were similar heaps, but these were of bleached bones on which the moonlight shone brightly—mementoes of former sacrifices. Quite close to the first pile of dead was a mooring-place where at least a dozen flat-bottomed boats had been secured, for their impress could yet be seen in the sand. Now they were gone with the exception of the canoe, which was kept there, evidently to facilitate the loading and launching of the large boats.

Nobody made any comment. The sight was beyond comment, but a fierce desire rose in Leonard's heart to come face to face with this "Yellow Devil" who fattened on the blood and agony of helpless human beings, and to avenge them if he might.

"The light is going, we must camp here till the morning," he said after a while.

And there they camped in this Golgotha, this place of bones, every one of which cried to heaven for vengeance.

The night wind swept over them whispering in the giant reeds, fashioning the mists into fantastic shapes that threw strange shadows on the inky surface of the water as it crept slowly to the sea. From time to time the frogs broke into a sudden chorus of croaking, then grew silent again; the heron cried from afar as some alligator or river-horse disturbed its rest, and from high in air came the sound of the wings of wild-fowl that travelled to the ocean. But to Leonard's fancy all these various voices of nature were as one voice that spoke from the piles of skeletons gleaming faintly in the uncertain starlight and cried, "Oh! God, how long shall iniquity have power on the earth? Oh! God, how long shall thy Hand be stayed?"

The darkness passed, the sun shone out merrily, and the travellers arose, brushed the night-dew from their hair, and ate a scanty meal, for they must husband such food as they had with them. Then, as though by common consent, they went to the canoe, bailed her out, and started, Leonard and Otter using the paddles.

Now it was that the dwarf's marvellous memory for locality came into play. Without him they could not have gone a mile, for their course ran through numberless lagoons and canals, cut by nature and the current in the dense banks of reeds. There was nothing to enable them to distinguish one of these canals from another; in truth they all formed a portion of this mouth of the river. There were no landmarks to guide them; everywhere spread a sea of swamp diversified by rush-clothed islands, which to the inexperienced eye presented few points of difference. This was the road that Otter led them on unfalteringly; ten years had passed since he had travelled it, but he never even hesitated. Time upon time they came to new openings in the reeds leading this way and that. Then for a moment the dwarf would consider, and, lifting his hand, point out which water-way they should choose, and they followed it.

Thus they went on for the most part of that day, till towards evening they reached a place where the particular canal that they were following suddenly divided itself into two, one branch running north and one in a southerly direction.

"Which way, Otter?" asked Leonard.

"Nay, Baas, I know not. The water has changed; there was no land here, the cut went straight on."

This was a serious matter, for one false step in such a labyrinth meant that they would be lost utterly. For long they debated which stream to take, and at last decided to try that on the left hand, which Otter thought ran more nearly in the true direction. They had already started in pursuance of his advice when Soa, who had remained silent hitherto, suggested that they should first go a little way down the right-hand stream on the chance of finding a clue. Leonard demurred, but as the woman seemed bent upon it, he yielded, and turning the boat they paddled her some three hundred yards in this new direction. As there was nothing to be seen, however, Otter began to put her about again.

"Stay, White Man," said Soa, who had been searching the surface of the water with her quick eyes, "what is that thing yonder?" and she pointed to a clump of reeds about forty yards away, among which some small white object was just discernible.

"Feathers, I think," Leonard answered, "but we will go and see." In another moment they were there.

"It is paper, Baas," said Otter in a low voice, "paper stuck on a reed."

"Lift it carefully," answered Leonard in the same tone, for his anxiety was keen. How came it that they found paper fixed to a reed in such a place as this?

Otter obeyed, laying the sodden sheet on the thwart of the canoe before Leonard, who with Soa examined it closely.

"This is a leaf from that holy book in which my mistress reads," said the woman with conviction; "I know the shape of it well. She has torn the paper out and affixed it on the reed as a sign to any who might come after her."

"It looks like it," said Leonard; "that was a good thought of yours to turn up here, old lady." Then he bent down and read such verses as were still legible on the page; they ran thus:

"For he hath looked down from the height of his sanctuary; from heaven did the Lord behold the earth;"

"To hear the groaning of the prisoner; to loose those that are appointed to death;"

"The children of thy servants shall continue, and their seed shall be established before thee."

"Hum!" said Leonard to himself, "the quotation seems very appropriate. If one had faith in omens now, a man might say that this was a good one." And in his heart he believed it to be so.

Another hour's journey brought them to the point of the island along which they had been travelling.

"Ah," said Otter, "now I know the path again. This is the right stream, that to the left must be a new one. Had we taken it we should have lost our way, and perhaps have found it no more for days, or not at all."

"Say, Otter," said Leonard, "you escaped from this slave-camp. How did you do it—in a boat?"

"No, Baas. The Baas knows that I am strong, my Spirit who gave me ugliness gave me strength also to make up for it, and it is well, for had I been beautiful as you are, Baas, and not very strong, I should have been a slave now, or dead. With my chained hands I choked him who was set to watch me, and took his knife. Then by my strength I broke the irons—see, Baas, here are the scars of them to this day. When I broke them they cut into my flesh, but they were old irons that had been on many slaves, so I mastered them. Then as others came to kill me I threw myself into the water and dived, and they never saw me more. Afterwards I swam all the way, resting from

68

time to time on the islands and from time to time running along the shore where the reeds were not too thick, till at length I escaped into the open country. I travelled four days to reach it, and most of that time I was in the water."

"And what did you feed on?"

"Roots and the eggs of birds."

"And did not the alligators try to eat you?"

"Yes, one, Baas, but I am quick in the water. I got upon the water-snake's back—ah! my Spirit was with me then—and I drove the knife through his eye into his brain. Then I smeared myself over with his blood, and after that they did not touch me, for they knew the smell and thought that I was their brother."

"Say, Otter, are you not afraid of going back to this place?"

"Somewhat, Baas, for there is that hell of which you white people talk. But where the Baas goes there I can go also; Otter will not linger while you run. Also, Baas, I am not brave, no, no, yet I would look upon that Yellow Devil again, yes, if I myself must die to do it, and kill him with these hands."

And the dwarf dropped the paddle screaming "Kill him! kill him! kill him!" so loudly that the birds rose in affright from the marshes.

"Be quiet," said Leonard angrily; "do you want to bring the Arabs on us?"

But to himself he thought that he should be sorry for Pereira, alias the "Yellow Devil," if once Otter found a chance to fly at his throat.

Chapter 9

The Yellow Devil's Nest

Sundown came, and, as on the previous night, the three travellers camped upon an island waiting for the moon to rise. They had caught two flapper-ducks in some weeds, and there was a talk of lighting a fire to cook them by. Finally Leonard negatived this idea. "It is dangerous," he said, "for fires can be seen from afar." So they made a wretched meal off a little dried meat and some raw duck's eggs.

It was fortunate that his caution prevailed, since, as the twilight was dying into dark, they heard the stroke of paddles and made out the shapes of canoes passing them. There were several canoes, each of which towed something behind it, and the men in them shouted to one another from time to time, now in Portuguese and now in Arabic.

"Lie still, lie still," whispered Otter, "these are the slave-men taking back the big boats."

Leonard and Soa followed his advice to the letter, and the slavers, paddling furiously up stream, passed within thirty feet of where they crouched in the rushes.

"Give way, comrades," called one man to the captain of the next canoe; "the landing-place is near, and there is rum for those who earn it."

"I hope that they will not stop here," said Leonard beneath his breath.

"*Hist!*" answered Otter, "I hear them landing."

He was right; the party had disembarked about two hundred yards away. Presently they heard them collecting reeds for burning, and in ten minutes more two bright tongues of flame showed that they had lit their fires.

"We had better get out of this," said Leonard; "if they discover us——"

"They will not discover us, Baas, if we lie still," answered Otter; "let us wait awhile. I have another plan. Listen, Baas." And he whispered in his ear.

So they waited. From the fires below them came the sound of men eating and drinking—especially drinking. An hour passed, and Leonard rose, followed by Otter, who said:

"I will come too, Baas; I can move like a cat."

"Where are you going, White Man?" asked Soa.

"I am going to spy upon those men. I understand Portuguese, and wish to hear what they say. Otter, take your knife and revolver, but no gun."

"Good," said the woman, "but be careful. They are very clever."

"Yes, yes," put in Otter, "but the Baas is clever also, and I, I am clever. Do not fear for us, mother."

Then they started, creeping cautiously through the reeds. When they were within twenty yards of the fires, Leonard missed his footing and fell into a pool of water with a splash. Some of the slave-dealers heard the noise and sprang to their feet. Instantly Otter grunted in exact imitation of a hippopotamus-calf.

"A sea-cow," said a man in Portuguese. "She won't hurt us. The fire will frighten her."

Leonard and Otter waited awhile, then crept to a clump of reeds whence they could hear every word that was spoken. The men round the fire numbered twenty-two. One, their leader, appeared to be a pure-bred Portugee, some of the others were Bastards and the rest Arabs. They were drinking rum and water out of tin pannikins—a great deal of rum and very little water. Many of them seemed half-drunk already, at any rate their tongues were loosened.

"May a curse fall upon our father, the Devil!" said one, a half-breed; "why did he take it into his head to send us back with the boats just now? We shall miss the fun."

"What fun?" answered the leader of the party. "They won't cage the birds for another three or four days; the dhows are not ready, and there is talk of an English cruiser—may she sink to hell!—hanging about outside the river mouth."

"No, not that," said the man who had spoken first, "there is not much sport in driving a lot of stinking niggers on to a dhow. I mean the auction of the white girl, the English trader's daughter, whom we caught up the river yonder. There's a beauty for some lucky dog; I never saw such a one. What eyes she has, and what a spirit! why, most of the little dears would have cried themselves blind by now."

"You needn't think about her," sneered his leader; "she will go too dear for the likes of you; besides it is foolish to spend so much on one girl, white or black. When is the auction?"

"It was to have been the night before the dhows sail, but now the Devil says it shall be tomorrow night. I will tell you why—he is afraid of her. He thinks that she will bring misfortune to him, and wants to be rid of her. Ah! he is a wag, is the old man—he loves a joke, he does. 'All men are brothers,' he said yesterday, 'white or black; therefore all women are sisters.' So he is going to sell her like a nigger girl. What is good enough for them is good enough for her. Ha! ha! pass the rum, brother, pass the rum."

"Perhaps he will put it off and we may be back in time, after all," said the captain. "Anyhow, here is a health to her, the love. By the way, did some of you think to ask the password before we left this morning? I forgot to do so, myself."

"Yes," said a Bastard, "the old word, 'the Devil.'"

"There is none better, comrades, none better," hiccoughed the leader.

Then for an hour or more their talk went on—partly about Juanna, partly about other things. As they grew more drunk the conversation became more and more revolting, till Leonard could scarcely listen to it and lie still. At length it died away, and one by one the men sank into a sound and sodden sleep. They did not set a sentry, for here on the island they had no fear of foes.

Then Otter rose upon his hands and knees, and his face looked fierce in the faint light.

"Baas," he whispered, "shall we——" and he drew his hand across his throat.

Leonard thought awhile. His rage was deep, and yet he shrank from the slaughter of sleeping men, however wicked. Besides, could it be done without noise? Some of them would wake—fear would sober them, and they were many.

"No," he whispered back. "Follow me, we will cut loose the boats."

"Good, good," said Otter.

Then, stealthily as snakes, they crept some thirty yards to where the boats were tied to a low tree—three canoes and five large flat-bottomed punts, containing the arms and provisions of the slave-dealers. Drawing their knives they cut these loose. A gentle push set them moving, then the current caught them, and slowly they floated away into the night.

This done they crawled back again. Their path took them within five paces of where that half-breed ruffian lay who had begun the talk to which they had listened. Leonard looked at him and turned to creep away; already Otter was five paces ahead, when suddenly the edge of the moon showed for the first time and its light fell full upon the slaver's face. The sleeping man awoke, sat up, and saw them.

Now Leonard dared not hesitate, or they were lost. Like a tiger he sprang at the man's throat and had grasped it in his hand before he could even cry aloud. Then came a struggle short and sharp, and a knife flashed. Before Otter could get back to his side it was done—so swiftly and so silently that none of the band had wakened, though one or two of them stirred and muttered in their heavy sleep.

Leonard sprang up unhurt, and together they ran, rather than walked, back to the spot where they had left Soa.

She was watching for them, and pointing to Leonard's coat, asked "How many?"

"One," answered Otter.

"I would it had been all," Soa muttered fiercely, "but you are only two."

"Quick," said Leonard, "into the canoe with you. They will be after us presently."

In another minute they had pushed off and were clear of the island, which was not more than a quarter of a mile long. They paddled across the river, which at this spot ran rapidly and had a width of some eight hundred yards, so as to hide in the shadow of the opposite bank. When they reached it Otter rested on his paddles and gave vent to a suppressed chuckle, which was his nearest approach to laughter.

"Why do you laugh, Black One?" asked Soa.

"Look yonder," he answered, and he pointed to some specks on the surface of the river which were fast vanishing in the distance. "Yonder go the boats of the slave-dealers, and in them are their arms and food. We cut them loose, the Baas and I. There on the island sleep two-and-twenty men—all save one: there they sleep, and when they wake what will they find? They will find themselves on a little isle in the middle of great waters, into which, even if they could, they will not dare to swim because of the alligators. They can get no food on the island, for they have no guns and ducks do not stop to be caught, but outside the alligators will wait in hundreds to catch *them*. By-and-by they will grow hungry—they will shout and yell, but none will hear them—then they will become mad, and, falling on each other, they will eat each other and die miserably one by one. Some will take to the water, those will drown or be caught by the alligators, and so it shall go on till they are all dead, every one of them, dead, dead, dead!" and again Otter chuckled.

Leonard did not reprove him; with the talk of these wretches yet echoing in his ears he could feel little pity for the horrible fate which would certainly overtake them.

Hark! a faint sound stole across the quiet waters, a sound which grew into a clamour of fear and rage. The slavers had awakened, they had found the dead man in their midst mysteriously slain by an invisible foe. And now the clamour gathered to a yell, for they had learned that their boats were gone and that they were trapped.

From their shelter on the other side of the river, as they dropped leisurely down the stream, Leonard and Otter could catch distant glimpses of the frantic men rushing to and fro in the bright moonlight and seeking for their boats. But the boats had departed to return no more. By degrees the clamour lessened behind them, till at last it died away, swallowed in the silence of the night.

Then Leonard told Soa what he had heard by the slaver's fire.

"How far is the road, Black One?" she asked when he had finished.

"By sundown tomorrow we shall be at the Yellow Devil's gates!" answered Otter.

Two hours later they overtook the boats which they had cut adrift. Most of them were tied together, and they floated peacefully in a group.

"We had better scuttle them," said Leonard.

"No, Baas," answered Otter, "if we escape we may want them again. Yonder is the place where we must land," and he pointed to a distant tongue of marsh. "Let us go with the boats there and make them fast. Perhaps we may find food in them, and we need food."

The advice was good, and they followed it. Keeping alongside of the punts and directing them, when necessary, with a push of the paddles, they reached the point just as the dawn was breaking. Here in a sheltered bay they found a mooring-place to which they fastened all the boats with ropes that hung ready. Then they searched the lockers and to their joy discovered food in plenty, including cooked meat, spirits, biscuits, bread, and some oranges and bananas. Only those who have been forced to do without farinaceous food for days or weeks will know what this abundance meant to them. Leonard thought that he had never eaten a more delicious meal, or drunk anything so good as the rum and water with which they washed it down.

They found other things also: rifles, cutlasses and ammunition, and, better than all, a chest of clothes which had evidently belonged to the officer or officers of the party. One suit was a kind of uniform plentifully adorned with gold lace, having tall boots and a broad felt hat with a white ostrich feather in it to match. Also there were some long Arab gowns and turbans, the gala clothes of the slave-dealers, which they took with them in order to appear smart on their return.

But the most valuable find of all was a leather bag in the breeches of the uniform, containing the sum of the honest gains of the leader of the party, which he had preferred to keep in his own company even on his travels. On examination this bag was found to hold something over a hundred English sovereigns and a dozen or fifteen pieces of Portuguese gold.

"Now, Baas," said Otter, "this is my word, that we put on these clothes."

"What for?" asked Leonard.

"For this reason: that should we be seen by the slave-traders they will think us of their brethren."

The advantages of this step were so obvious that they immediately adopted it. Thus disguised, with a silk sash round his middle and a pistol stuck in it, Leonard might well have been mistaken for the most ferocious of slave-traders.

Otter too looked sufficiently strange, robed as an Arab and wearing a turban. Being a dwarf, the difficulty was that all the dresses proved too long for him. Finally it was found necessary to cut one down by the primitive process of laying it on a block of wood and chopping through it with a sabre.

When this change of garments had been effected, and their own clothes with the spare arms were hidden away in the rushes on the somewhat remote chance that they might be useful hereafter, they prepared for a start on foot across the marshes. By an afterthought Leonard fetched the bag of gold and put it in his pocket. He felt few scruples in availing himself of the money of the slave-driver, not for his own use indeed, but because it might help their enterprise.

Now their road ran along marshes and by secret paths that none save those who had travelled them could have found. But Otter had not forgotten. On they went through the broiling heat of the day, since linger they dared not. They met no living man on their path, though here and there they found the body of some wretched slave, whose corpse had been cast into the reeds by the roadside. But the road had been trodden, and recently, by many feet, among which were the tracks of two mules or donkeys.

At last, about an hour before sunset, they came to the home of the Yellow Devil. The Nest was placed thus. It stood upon an island having an area of ten or twelve acres. Of this, however, only about four and a half acres were available for a living space; the rest was a morass hidden by a growth of very tall reeds, which morass, starting from a great lagoon on the northern and eastern sides, ran up to the low enclosure of the buildings that, on these faces, were considered to be sufficiently defended by the swamp and the wide waters beyond. On the southern and western aspects of the camp matters were different, for here the place was strongly fortified both by art and nature. Firstly, a canal ran round these two faces, not very wide or deep indeed, but impassable except in boats, owing to the soft mud at its bottom. On the further side of this canal an earthwork had been constructed, having its crest stoutly palisaded and its steep sides planted with a natural defence of aloes and prickly-pears.

So much for the exterior of the place. Its interior was divided into three principal enclosures. Of these three the easternmost was the site of the Nest itself, a long low thatched building of wood, in front and to the west of which there was an open space or courtyard, with a hard floor. Herein were but two buildings, a shed supported on posts and open from the eaves to the ground, where sales of slaves were carried on, and further to the north, almost continuous with the line of the Nest itself, but separate from it, a small erection, very strongly built of brick and stone, and having a roof made from the tin linings of ammunition and other cases. This was a magazine. All round this enclosure stood rows of straw huts of a native build, evidently occupied as a camp by the Arabs and half-breed slave-traders of the baser sort.

The second enclosure, which was to the west of the Nest, comprised the slave camp. It may have covered an acre of ground, and the only buildings in it were four low sheds, similar in every respect to that where the slaves were sold, only much longer. Here the captives lay picketed in rows to iron bars which ran the length of the sheds, and were fixed into the ground at either end. This camp was separated from the Nest enclosure by a deep canal, thirty feet in width and spanned at one point by a slender and primitive drawbridge that led across the canal to the gate of the camp. Also it was protected on the Nest side by a low wall, and on the slave-camp side by an earthwork, planted as usual with prickly-pears. On this earthwork near the gate and little guard-house a six-pounder cannon was mounted, the muzzle of which frowned down upon the slave camp, a visible warning to its occupants of the fate that awaited the froward. Indeed, all the defences of this part of the island were devised as safeguards against a possible *emeute* of the slaves, and also to provide a second line of fortifications should the Nest itself chance to be taken by an enemy.

Beyond the slave camp, lay the garden that could only be approached through it. This also was fortified by water and earthworks, but not so strongly.

Such is a brief description of what was in those days the strongest slave-hold in Africa.

CHAPTER 10

Leonard Makes a Plan

The road which Leonard and his companions were following led them to the edge of the main and southernmost canal, debouching exactly opposite the water-gate that gave access to the Nest. But Otter did not venture to guide them to this point, for there they should be seen by the sentries, and, notwithstanding their masquerade dress, awkward questions might be asked which they could not answer. Therefore when they had arrived within five hundred yards of the gate, he struck off to the left into the thick bush that clothed the hither side of the canal. Through this they crawled as best they might till finally they halted near the water's edge, almost opposite to the south-west angle of the slave camp, and under the shadow of a dense clump of willows.

"See, Baas," said the dwarf in a low voice, "the journey is accomplished and I have brought you straight. Yonder is the house of the Yellow Devil—now it remains only to take it, or to rescue the maiden from it."

Leonard looked at the place in dismay. How was it possible that they—two men and a woman—could capture this fortified camp, filled as it was with scores of the most wicked desperadoes in Africa? How was it possible even that they could obtain access to it? Viewed from far off, the thing had seemed small—to be done somehow. But now! And yet they must do something, or all their labour would be in vain, and the poor girl they came to rescue must be handed over to her shameful fate, or, if she chose it in preference and could compass the deed, to self-murder.

"How on earth!" said Leonard aloud, then added, "Well, Otter, I can tell you one thing. I have come a long way on this business, and I am not going to turn my back to it now. I have never yet turned my back on a venture and I will not begin with this, though I dare say that my death lies in it."

"It is all in the hand of tomorrow," answered Otter; "but it is time that we made a plan, for the night draws on. Now, Baas, here is a thick tree shaded by other trees. Shall we climb it and look down into the camp?"

Leonard nodded, and climbing the tree with ease, they peeped down through the leafiest of its boughs. All the camp lay beneath them like a map, and Otter, clinging monkey-wise to a branch, pointed out its details to Leonard. He had been a prisoner there, and the memories of prisoners are long.

The place was peopled by numbers of men in strange costumes, and of different nationalities; dealers in "black ivory" of various degree. Perhaps there may have been more than a hundred of them. Some were strolling about in knots smoking and talking, some were gambling, others were going on their business. One group—captains, to judge from the richness of their attire—were standing round the arms-house and peeping through a grating in the wall, which they reached by sitting upon each other's shoulders. This amusement lasted them for some time, till at length a man, of whom at that distance they could see only that he was old and stout, came and drove them away, and they broke up laughing.

"That is the Yellow Devil," said Otter, "and those men were looking at the maid who is called the Shepherdess. She is locked up there until the hour comes for her to be sold. They will be the bidders."

Leonard made no reply; he was studying the place. Presently a drum was beaten, and men appeared carrying large tin pails of smoking stuff.

"Yonder is the food for the slaves," said Otter again. "See, they are going to feed them."

The men with the pails, accompanied by some of the officers having *sjambochs* or hide whips in their hands, advanced across the open space till they came to the moat which separated the slave camp from the Nest, whence they called to the sentry on the embankment to let down the drawbridge. He obeyed and they crossed. Each man with a bucket was followed by another who bore a wooden spoon, while a third behind them carried water in a large gourd. Having come to the first of the open sheds, they began their rounds, the man with the wooden spoon ladling out portions of the stiff porridge and throwing it down upon the ground before each slave in turn as food is thrown to a dog. Then the Arab with the gourd poured water into wooden bowls, that the captives might drink.

Presently there was a halt, and the officers gathered together to discuss something.

"A slave is sick," said Otter.

The knot separated, but a big white man with a hippopotamus-hide whip began to strike at a dark thing on the ground which did not seem to move.

The man ceased beating and called aloud. Then two of the Arabs went to the little guard-house that was by the drawbridge and brought tools with which they loosed the fetters on the limbs of the poor creature—apparently a woman—thus freeing her from the long iron bar. This done, some of the officers sauntering after them, they dragged the body to the high enclosure of earth and up a short ladder having a wooden platform at the top of it, that overhung the deep canal below.

"This is how the Yellow Devil buries his dead and cures his sick," said Otter.

"I have seen enough," answered Leonard, and began to descend the tree hastily, an example which Otter followed with more composure.

"Ah! Baas," he said when they reached the ground, "you are but a chicken. The hearts of those who have dwelt in slave camps are strong, and, after all, better the belly of a fish than the hold of a slave dhow. *Wow!* who do these things? Is it not the white men, your brothers, and do they not say many prayers to the Great Man up in the sky while they do them?"

"Be still," said Leonard, "and give me some brandy." He was in no mood to discuss the blessings of civilisation as they have often been put into practice in Africa. And to think that this fate might soon be his own!

Leonard drank the brandy and sat awhile in silence, pushing up his beard with his hand and gazing into the gathering gloom with his hawk-like eyes. Thus he had sat beside his dying brother's bed; it was a pose that he adopted unconsciously when lost in thought.

"Come, Soa," he said at length, "we have travelled here to please you; now give us the benefit of your suggestions. How are we going to get your mistress out of that camp?"

"Loose the slaves and let them kill their masters," Soa answered laconically.

"I doubt there is not much pluck in slaves," said Leonard.

"There should be fifty of Mavoom's men there," she replied, "and they will fight well enough if they have arms."

Then Leonard looked at Otter, seeking further ideas.

"My snake puts it into my head," said the dwarf, "that fire is a good friend when men are few and foes are many; also that the reeds yonder are dry, and the sea wind rises and will blow hard before midnight. Moreover all these houses are thatched, and in a wind fire jumps. But can a regiment have two generals? You are our captain, Baas; speak and we will do your bidding. Here one counsel is as good as another. Let fate speak through your mouth."

"Very well," said Leonard. "This is my plan; it goes a little further than yours, that is all. We must gain entrance to the Nest while it is still dark, before the moon rises. I know the watchword, 'Devil,' and disguised as we are, perhaps the sentry will let us pass unquestioned. If not, we must kill him, and silently."

"Good," said Otter, "but how about the woman here?"

"We will leave her hidden in the bush; she could be of no help in the camp and might hinder us."

"No, White Man," broke in Soa, "where you go I go also; moreover my mistress is yonder and I would seek her."

"As you like," answered Leonard, then went on: "we must get between the hut, there is only one, and the low wall that borders the canal separating the Nest from the slave camp, and, if the drawbridge is up and no other means can be found, we must swim the dike, dispose of the sentry there also and gain the slave camp. Then we must try to free some of the slaves and send them round through the garden into the morass to fire the reeds, should the wind blow strong enough. Meanwhile I propose to walk boldly into the camp, salute Pereira, pass myself off as a slaver with a dhow at the mouth of the river, and say that I have come to buy slaves, and above all to bid for the white girl. Luckily we have a good deal of gold. That is my plan so far as it goes, the rest we must leave to chance. If I can buy the Shepherdess I will. If not, I must try to get her off in some other way."

"So be it, Baas, and now let us eat, for we shall need all our strength tonight. Then we will go down to the landing-place and take our chance."

They ate of the food they had with them and drank sparingly of the slave-dealers' brandy, saying little the while, for the shadow of what was to come lay upon them. Even the phlegmatic and fatalistic Otter was depressed, perhaps because of the associations of the place, which, for him, were painful, perhaps because of the magnitude of their undertaking. Never had he known such a tale, never had he seen such an adventure as this—that two men and an old woman should attack an armed camp. Indeed, although he was not acquainted with the saying, Otter's feelings would have been correctly summed up in the well-known phrase, "*C'est magnifique, mais ce n'est pas la guerre.*"

As yet the night was intensely dark, and its gloom did not tend to improve their spirits; also, as Otter had predicted, the wind was rising and soughed through the reeds and willows in melancholy notes.

So the time passed till it was nine o'clock.

"We must move down to the landing-place," said Leonard; "there will soon be some light, enough for us to work by."

Then Otter took the lead and slowly, step by step, they crept back to the road and followed it down the shore of the canal opposite the water-gate. Here was a place where boats and canoes were tied, both for convenience in crossing the canal to and from the camp and for the use of the slave-dealers when they passed to the secret harbour six miles away, where the dhows embarked their cargoes.

They waited awhile. From the Nest came the sound of revelry, and from the slave camp there rose other sounds, the voice of groaning broken by an occasional wail wrung out of the misery of some lost creature who lay there in torment. Gradually the sky brightened a little.

"Perhaps we had better be making a start," said Leonard; "there is a canoe which will serve our turn."

Before the words were out of his mouth they heard the splash of oars, and a boat crept past them and made fast to the water-gate twenty yards away.

"Who goes there?" came the challenge of the sentry in Portuguese. "Speak quick or I fire."

"Don't be in such a hurry with your rifle, fool," answered a coarse voice. "The very best of friends goes here. An honest trader called Xavier who comes from his plantation on the coast to tell you all good news."

"Pardon, senor," said the sentry, "but how was a man to see in the dark, big as you are? What is the news then? Are the dhows in sight?"

"Come down and help us to tie up this cursed boat and I will tell you. You know where the post is, and we can't find it."

The sentry obeyed with alacrity, and the man called Xavier went on: "Yes, the dhows are in sight, but I don't think that they will get in tonight because of this wind, so you may look for a busy day tomorrow loading up the blackbirds. One *is* in by the way—a small one from Madagascar. The captain is a stranger, a big Frenchman named Pierre, or he may be an Englishman for anything I know. I hailed him and found that he is all right, but I didn't see him. However, I sent him a note to tell him that there was fun on here tonight, which was generous of me, as he may be a rival bidder."

"Is he coming, senor? I ask because, if so, I must look out for him."

"I don't know: he answered that he would if he could. But how is the English girl? She is to be put up tonight, isn't she?"

"Oh, yes, senor, there will be a great to-do at twelve, when the moon is high. So soon as she has been bought, the priest Francisco is to marry her to the lucky man, there and then. The old fellow insists on it; he has grown superstitious about the girl and says that she shall be properly married."

Xavier laughed aloud, "Has he now? He is getting into his dotage. Well, what does it matter? We have a good law of divorce in these parts, friend. I am going in for that girl; if I give a hundred ounces for her I will buy her, and I have brought the gold with me."

"A hundred ounces for one girl! It is a large sum, senor, but you are rich. Not like us poor devils who get all the risk and little profit."

By this time the men had finished tying up the boat and taking some baggage or provisions out of her, Leonard could not see which. Then Xavier and the sentry went up the steps together, followed by the two boatmen, and the gates were shut behind them.

"Well," whispered Leonard, "we have learnt something at any rate. Now, Otter, I am Pierre the French slave-trader from Madagascar, and, understand, you are my servant; as for Soa, she is the guide, or interpreter, or anyone you like. We must pass the gates, but the real Pierre must never pass them. There must be no sentry to let him in. Do you think that you can manage it, Otter, or must I?"

"It comes into my head, Baas, that we may learn a lesson from this Xavier. I might forget something in the canoe, and the sentry might help me to find it after you have passed the gates. For the rest I am quick and strong and silent."

"Quick and strong and silent you must be. A noise, and all is lost."

Then they crept to the canoe which they had selected and loosened her. They embarked and Otter took the paddle. First he let her float gently down stream and under cover of the shore for a distance of about fifty yards. Then he put about and the play began.

"Now, you fool, where are you paddling to?" said Leonard in a loud voice to Otter, speaking in the bastard Arabic which passes current for a language on this coast. "You will have us into the bank, I tell you. Curse this wind and the darkness! Steady now, you ugly black dog; those must be the gates the letter told of—are they not, woman? Hold on with the boat-hook, can't you?"

A wicket at the gate above rattled and the voice of the sentry challenged them.

"A friend—a friend!" answered Leonard in Portuguese; "one who is a stranger and would pay his respects to your leader, Dom Antonio Pereira, with a view to business."

"What is your name?" asked the guard suspiciously.

"Pierre is my name. Dog is the name of the dwarf my servant, and as for the old woman, you can call her anything you like."

"The password," said the sentry; "none come in here without the word."

"The word—Ah! what did the Dom Xavier say it was in his letter? 'Fiend!' No, I have it, 'Devil' is the word."

"Where do you hail from?"

"From Madagascar, where the goods you have to supply are in some demand just now. Come, let us in; we don't want to sit here all night and miss the fun."

The man began to unbar the door, and stopped, struck by a fresh doubt.

"You are not of our people," he said; "you speak Portuguese like a cursed Englishman."

"No, I should hope not; I am a 'cursed Englishman,' that is half—son of an English lord and a French Creole, born in the Mauritius at your service, and let me ask you to be a little more civil, for cross-bred dogs are fierce."

Now at length the sentry opened one side of the gate, grumbling, and Leonard swaggered up the steps followed by the other two. Already they were through it, when suddenly he turned and struck Otter in the face.

"Why, Dog," he said angrily, "you have forgotten to bring up the keg of brandy, my little present for the Dom. Go and fetch it. Quick, now."

"Pardon, Chief," answered Otter, "but I am a small man and the keg is heavy for me alone—if you will deign to help me, for the old woman is too weak."

"Do you take me for a porter that I should roll kegs of cognac up steps? Here, my friend," he went on addressing the sentry, "if you wish to earn a little present and a drink, perhaps you will give this fellow a hand with the cask. There is a spigot in it, and you can try the quality afterwards."

"Right, Senor," said the man briskly, and led the way down the steps.

A look of dreadful intelligence passed between the dwarf and his master. Then Otter followed, his hand upon the hilt of the Arab sabre which he wore, while Leonard and Soa waited above. They heard the man's heavily booted feet going down the steps followed by Otter's naked footfall.

"Where is your keg? I don't see it," said the sentry presently.

"Lean over, senor, lean over," answered Otter; "it is in the stern of the canoe. Let me help you."

There was a moment's pause, to the listeners it seemed hours. Then came the sound of a blow and a heavy splash. They hearkened on, but nothing more was to be heard except the beating of their hearts and the distant noise of revelry from the camp.

Three seconds passed and Otter stood beside them. In the dim light Leonard could see that his eyes stared wide and his nostrils twitched.

"Quick was the blow, strong was the blow, silent is the man for ever," whispered Otter. "So the Baas commanded, so it is."

Chapter 11

That Hero Otter

"Help me to secure the gate," said Leonard presently.

In another minute the great iron bar had been dropped into its place, and Leonard withdrew the key and put it in his pocket.

"Why do you secure the door, Baas?" whispered Otter.

"To keep the real Pierre out, in case he should come this way. Two Pierres would be one too many at this game. Now we must win or perish."

Then they crept along the embankment till they gained the shelter of the hut or barrack-shed which stood with its back to the dike that separated the Nest from the slave camp. Happily none saw them, and there were no dogs in the place. Dogs make a noise at inconvenient times, therefore slave-dealers do not love them.

The end of the shed behind which they were crouching was situated some eight or ten paces from the drawbridge, that formed the only path of entry to the slave camp.

"Baas," said Otter, "let me go forward and look. My eyes are the eyes of a cat; I can see in the dark. Perhaps the bridge is down."

Without waiting for an answer, he crept forward on his hands and knees so quietly that they could scarcely hear a movement. Notwithstanding his white dress, there was little chance of his being seen, for the shadow of the shed was dense and a fringe of rushes grew along the edge of the dike.

Five minutes passed—ten minutes passed, and Otter did not return. Leonard's anxiety grew very keen.

"Let us go and see what happened, mother," he whispered to Soa.

They crept along to the end of the shed. Within a yard of it they discovered the arms and clothes of Otter. But Otter! Where was he?

"The Black One has deserted us," said Soa beneath her breath.

"Never!" answered Leonard.

By now the clouds were breaking before the wind, which was rising steadily, and some stars shone out, giving a little light. The dike lay deep between its banks and was not more than twenty feet in width, so that the air did not ruffle it; moreover, as any observer of nature will have noticed, the surface of still water is never quite dark, even on much blacker nights than this.

Why had Otter taken off his clothes, Leonard wondered? Evidently that he might go into the water. And what could he want to go into the water for, unless it was that his heart failed him and, as Soa suggested, he had deserted. But this was impossible, for he knew well that the dwarf would die first. In his great perplexity Leonard stared at the dike. Now he could see that on its further side rose a flight of wooden steps, protected at the top by gates and that a man was seated on the lowest step, with a rifle beside him, his feet hanging down to within a few inches of the surface of the dike. It must be the sentry.

Next instant Leonard saw something else. Beneath the feet of the man a ripple grew on the face of the deep water, and something gleamed in the ripple like to the flash of steel. Then a small black object projected itself towards the feet of the sentry, who was half asleep and humming to himself drowsily. Suddenly he saw the man slide from his seat as though by magic. He said nothing, but making one ineffectual grasp at some rushes, he vanished into the deeps below. For a minute or more Leonard could distinguish a slight disturbance on the surface of the water, and that was all.

Now he guessed what had happened. Otter had dived, and rising beneath the feet of the man, he seized him, and with a sudden movement dragged him down to death by drowning. Either this, or an alligator had taken him, and that flash was the flash of his fangs.

As Leonard thought thus a dark form rose gasping at the foot of the steps; it drew itself out of the water and slipped stealthily up them. It was Otter, and he held a knife in his hand. Now the dwarf vanished through the gates into the little guard-house at the top of the embankment. Another minute, and ropes began to creak. Then the tall drawbridge, standing upright like a scaffold against the sky, was seen to bend itself forward. Down it came very softly, and the slave-camp was open to them. Again the black shape appeared, this time on the bridge.

"Come along," whispered Leonard to his companion; "that hero Otter has drowned the sentry and won the bridge. Stop, pick up his clothes and arms."

At that moment Otter himself arrived. "Quick," he said, "come over, Baas, before they see that the bridge is down. Give me my clothes and the gun."

"All right, here they are," answered Leonard, and in another minute they were over the bridge and standing on the parapet of the slave-camp.

"Into the guard-house, Baas; the windlass is there, but no man."

They entered: a lamp was burning in the place. Otter seized the handle of the windlass and began to wind. He was naked, and it was a wonderful sight to see the muscles starting out in knots on his huge but dwarfish frame as he strained at the weight of the bridge.

Presently it was up, and, leaning on the handle of the wheel, Otter chuckled aloud.

"Now we are safe for a time," he said, "and I will dress myself. Let the Baas forgive me for appearing thus before him—I, who am so ugly."

"Tell us the tale, Otter."

"It is short, Baas," the dwarf replied, as he put on his robe and turban. "When I left you I watched, I who can see in the dark, and in a little while I saw the guard come down the steps and sit by the edge of the water. He was sleepy, for he yawned and lit a roll of paper to smoke it. Presently it went out, and he had no more matches. He looked up to the house there, but was too lazy to fetch them; then I guessed that he was alone, for else he would have called to his companion for fire. Now he grew sleepier, and I said to myself, 'Otter, Otter, how can you kill this man silently? You must not shoot, because of the noise; and if you throw a knife or a spear, you may miss, or wound him only.' And my snake spoke in my heart and answered, 'Otter, Otter, dive, seize his feet, and drag him down swiftly and stamp him into the mud, you who are half a fish and can swim as no other man can swim. Do it at once, Otter, before the light comes and men can see the drawbridge move.'

"Well, and so I did it, Baas. *Wow!* I trod him deep into the mire, I trampled him as an ox tramples corn upon a threshing-floor. Never will he come up again. After that I rose and ran into the guard-house, fearing lest there might be another whom I must silence also, for when I was a slave two always kept watch. But the place was empty, so I let the bridge down. Ah! I remembered how it worked. And that is the tale, Baas."

"A great tale, Otter, but it is not finished yet. Now let us to the slaves. Come, take the light and lead the way. Here we are safe, is it not so?"

"Here, Baas, we are safe, for none can reach us except by storm, and yonder is the big gun which turns upon itself. Let us twist the gun round first, so that, if need be, we can fire into the camp."

"I don't know much of cannon," said Leonard doubtfully.

"But I know something, White Man," said Soa, speaking for the first time. "Mavoom, my master, has a small one up at the Settlement, and often I have helped to fire it for practice and as a signal to boats on the river, and so have many of the men who were carried away, if we can find them yonder."

"Good," said Leonard.

A path ran along the top of the embankment to the platform on which the gun was mounted. It was a six-pounder muzzle-loader. Leonard unhooked the rammer and ran it down the muzzle.

"She is loaded," he said; "now let us swing her round."

They did so easily enough, bringing the muzzle down upon the Nest camp; then they entered the little hut which stood alongside. Piled up in it, in case of emergency, were half-a-dozen rounds of grape-shot and powder.

"Lots of ammunition, if we should want to use it," said Leonard. "It never occurred to those gentlemen that a gun can shoot two ways. And now, Otter, lead us to the slaves, quick."

"This way, Baas, but first we must find the tools; they are in the guard-hut, I suppose."

So they crept back to the hut, holding their heads as low as possible, for the light was increasing, although the moon was not yet up, and they feared lest they should be seen against the sky-line. Here they found boxes containing nippers, chisels, and other instruments such as are used to undo the irons upon slaves. Also they found the keys of the padlocks that locked the iron bars to which the captives were tethered. Taking a lantern with them, but leaving another burning as before in the hut, lest its absence should excite suspicion, they passed through two strong gates and down the steps on the further side of the embankment. A few paces beyond stood the first slave-shed, a rough erection supported on posts, but without sides.

They entered the shed, Otter leading the way with the lantern. In the middle of it was a path, and on either side of this path ran the long bars to which the captives were fastened in a double row. Perhaps there might have been two hundred and fifty of them in this shed. Here the sights and scenes were such as need not be described. Of the miserable captives some lay on the wet ground, men and women together, trying to forget their sorrows in sleep; but the most part of them were awake, and the sound of moans ran up and down their lines like the moaning of trees in the wind.

When they saw the light the slaves ceased moaning, and crouched upon the ground like dogs that await the whip, for they thought that this was a visit from their captors. Some of them, indeed, stretched out their manacled hands imploring pity, but these were the exceptions; the most of them had abandoned hope and were sunk in dull despair. It was pitiful to see the glance of their terror-filled eyes and the answering quiver of their wealed frames whenever an arm was lifted or a sudden movement made.

Soa went down the line, rapidly examining the faces of the slaves.

"Do you see any of Mavoom's people?" asked Leonard anxiously.

"Not here, White Man; let us go to the next shed, unless you want to loose these."

"No good in that, mother," said Otter; "they would only betray us."

So they went to the next shed—in all there were four—and here at the second man who was sleeping, his head bowed on his chained hands, Soa stopped suddenly like a pointer dog when he scents game.

"Peter, Peter," she said.

The man awoke—he was a fine fellow about thirty years of age— and glared round wildly.

"Who called me by my old name?" he said hoarsely. "Nay, I dream, Peter is dead."

"Peter," said the woman again, "awake, child of Mavoom; it is I, Soa, who am come to save you."

The man cried aloud and began to tremble, but the other slaves took no notice, thinking only that he had been smitten with a scourge.

"Be silent," said Soa again, "or we are lost. Loose the bar, Black One; this is a head-man from the Settlement, a brave man."

Soon the bar was undone, then Otter bade Peter hold out his wrists while he twisted off the fetters. Presently they were gone, and in the ecstasy of his recovered liberty the man leaped high into the air, then fell at Otter's feet as though he would embrace them.

"Get up, you fool," said the dwarf roughly, "and if there are any more of the men of Mavoom here, show them to us: quick, or you will soon be fast again."

"There should be forty or more," Peter answered, recovering himself, "besides a few women and children. The rest of us are dead, except the Shepherdess alone, and she is yonder."

Then they went down the lines slipping the chains from the Settlement captives. Soon they had unmanacled ten or more men whom

Soa selected, and others stood round them with their hands still chained. As they went about the work Soa explained something of the position to Peter, who was fortunately a native of intelligence. He grasped the situation at once and earnestly seconded Leonard's efforts to preserve silence and to prevent confusion.

"Come," said Leonard to Soa, "we have got enough to begin with. I must be off. You can loose the rest at your leisure; the moon is rising, it is a quarter to twelve, and we have not a moment to lose. Now, Otter, before we go, how can we send men to fire the reeds—through the garden?"

"No, Baas, I have thought of a better way, the way by which I escaped myself—that is, if these men can swim."

"They can all swim," said Soa; "they were bred on the banks of a river."

"Good. Then they must swim down the dike where I killed the sentry, four of them. At the end are bars of wood, but in my day they were rotten; at the worst they can be climbed. Then they will find themselves in the morass among thick reeds. But they must not fire these till they have worked round to the place of the sunrise, whence the wind blows strongly. Then they must go from spot to spot and bend down the driest of the reeds, setting fire to them. Afterwards they can get to the back of the fire and wait till all is done one way or the other. If we win they will find us, if we are killed they can try to run away. But will the men go?"

Soa stepped forward and chose four of their number, but Peter she did not choose, for he also knew something of the working of cannon.

"Listen," she said, "you have heard the words of this Black One. Now, obey. And if you depart from them by one jot, may——" and she poured out so fearful a curse upon them that Leonard stared at her astonished.

"Ay!" added Otter, "and if I live through this I will cut your throats."

"No need to threaten," said one of the men; "we will do our best for our own sakes, as well as for yours and that of the Shepherdess. We understand the plan, but to light reeds we must have fire."

"Here are matches," said Otter.

"Wet matches will not light, and we must swim," answered the spokesman.

"Fool, do you then swim with your head under water? Tie them in your hair."

"Ah! he is clever," said the spokesman. "Now, if we live to reach them, when shall we fire the reeds?"

"As soon as you are ready," answered Otter. "You will not come easily to the back of them. Farewell, my children, and if you dare to fail, pray that you may die rather than look upon my face again."

"*Ou!* We have seen it once, is that not enough?" answered the spokesman, looking at Otter's huge nose with wonder not untouched by fear.

Two minutes later the four men were swimming swiftly down the dike, taking their chance of the alligators.

"Drop the bridge," said Leonard; "we must start."

Otter lowered it, at the same time explaining its mechanism, which was very simple, to Soa, Peter, and some of the other Settlement men.

"Now, mother, goodbye," said Leonard. "Loose all the men you can, and keep a keen look-out, so as to be ready to lower the bridge if you should see us or your mistress coming towards it. If we should not come by dawn, be ready also, for then we shall probably be dead, or prisoners, and you must act for yourself."

"I hear you, Lord," answered Soa, "and I say that you are a brave man. Whether you win or lose, the red stone is well earned already."

Another minute and they were gone.

Having crossed the bridge, which was instantly hoisted again, Leonard and Otter avoided observation by creeping back towards the water-gate as they had come—that is, behind the shelter of the shed. Emerging from this, they ran a few yards till they were opposite the gate, then walked leisurely across the open space, a distance of fifty paces or more, to the thatched hut where the sale of slaves was carried on.

There was nobody in this hut, but looking between the posts upon which it was supported, they could see by the light of the moon, now growing momentarily clearer, that a great and uproarious concourse of people was gathered beyond in front of the veranda of the Nest itself.

"Come on, Otter," whispered Leonard, "we must go among these gentry. Watch me closely, do what I do, keep your weapons ready, and if it comes to blows, get behind my back and fight like a fiend. Above all, don't be taken prisoner."

Leonard spoke calmly, but his heart was in his mouth, and his sensations were such as must have been known to Daniel when he went into the lions' den, for, as in the case of the prophet, he felt that nothing short of a special Providence could save them. They were round the shed now, and immediately in front of them was a mixed gathering of desperadoes—Portuguese, Arabs, Bastards, and black men of various tribes—such as Leonard had never seen in all his experience.

Villainy and greed were written on every countenance; it was a crew of human demons, and an extensive one. These wretches, most of whom had already drunk too freely and were drinking more, stood with their backs to them, looking towards the veranda of the Nest. On the steps of this veranda, surrounded by a choice group of companions, all of them gaudily dressed, a man was standing whom Leonard would have had no difficulty in identifying as the Dom Pereira, even without Otter's warning whisper of "See! The Yellow Devil!"

This remarkable person demands some description as he stood in glory that night, at the apex and, though he knew it not, the conclusion of his long career of infamy. He was old, perhaps seventy, his hair was white and venerable-looking, and his person obese. His black eyes were small, cunning, cold, and bright, and they had the peculiarity of avoiding the face of any person with whom he chanced to be in conversation, at least when that person was looking his way. Their glance passed over him, under him, round him, anywhere but at him.

As his sobriquet suggested, the colouring of Pereira's flesh was yellow, and the loose skin hung in huge wrinkles upon his cheeks. His mouth was large and coarse, and his fat hands twitched and grasped continually, as though with a desire of clutching money. For the rest he was gorgeously dressed, and, like his companions, somewhat in liquor.

Such was the outward appearance of Pereira, the fountain-head of the slave-trade on this part of the coast, who was believed in his day to be the very worst man in Africa, a pre-eminence to which few can hope to attain. Until his face had been seen, stamped as it was with the traces of long and unmentionable wickedness, few honest men could guess to what depths humanity can sink. Some indeed have declared that to see him was to understand the Evil One and all his works.

CHAPTER 12

A Choice Lot

At the moment of Leonard's and Otter's introduction to his society, the Yellow Devil was about to make a speech, and all eyes were fixed on him so intently that none saw or heard the pair approach.

"Now, my friends, make a path, if you please," said Leonard in a loud voice and speaking in Portuguese. "I wish to pay my respects to your chief."

A dozen men wheeled round at once.

"Who are you?" they cried, seeing a stranger.

"If you will be so kind as to let me pass, I shall be most happy to explain," Leonard answered, pushing his way through the throng.

"Who is that?" cried Pereira in coarse, thick tones. "Bring him here."

"There, you hear him—let us through, friends," said Leonard, "let us through!"

Thus adjured the throng opened a path, and Leonard and Otter passed down it, many suspicious eyes scanning them as they went.

"A greeting to you, senor," said Leonard when they had emerged in front of the veranda.

"Curse your greeting! Who in Satan's name are you?"

"A humble member of your honourable profession," said Leonard coolly, "come to pay his respects and do a little business."

"Are you? You don't look it. You look like an Englishman. And who is that abortion, pray?" and he pointed to Otter. "I believe that you are spies, and, by the Saints, if you are, I am the man to deal with you!"

"This is a likely story," said Leonard laughing, "that one man and a black dog should venture into the headquarters of gentlemen like you, not being of the cloth. But I think there is a noble gentleman among you—I mean the Senor Xavier—who can vouch for me. Did he not send a note to Captain Pierre, whose dhow lies in the harbour yonder, hailing from Madagascar? Well, Captain Pierre has the honour of accepting his invitation and arrives here, not without difficulty. Now he begins to think that he would have done better to stick to his ship."

"That is all right, Pereira," said Xavier, a huge Portuguese with a dash of negro blood and a villainous countenance, the same man whom they had followed through the gate. "I sent a note to the Senor. I told you of it."

"Then I wish you had left it alone," snarled Pereira for an answer. "I don't like your friend's looks. He might be the captain of an English man-of-war rigged up in our dress."

At the words "English man-of-war" a murmur of fear and anger went through the assembly. Some of those present had experience of these hated vessels and their bigoted crews, who loved not this honest commerce, and to all they were names of ill-omen. Things looked serious, and Leonard saw that he must do something, and quickly. So he lost his temper, or pretended to do so.

"Curse you all for a pack of suspicious curs!" he said; "I tell you that my dhow lies yonder. I am half an Englishman and half a Creole, and as good a man as any of you. Now look here, Dom Pereira, if you, or any of your crew, dare to doubt my word, just step out, and I will ram this down your lying throat;" and placing his hand on the hilt of his sabre, he took a pace forward and scowled.

The effect was instantaneous. Pereira turned a little pale beneath his yellow skin, for like most cruel men he was a great coward.

"Put up your pig-sticker," he said; "I see you are one of the right sort. I only wanted to try you. As you know, we must be careful in our business. Come and shake hands, brother, and be welcome. I trust you now, and old Antonio never does things by halves."

"Perhaps you had better try him a little further," said a young man who was standing near Pereira, as Leonard prepared to accept the invitation; "send for a slave and let us have the old test—there is none better."

Pereira hesitated and Leonard's blood turned cold.

"Look here, young man," he said more furiously than before, "I have cut the throats of more men than you have whipped, but if you want a test, I will give you one. Come down, my young cockerel, come down; there is plenty of light for comb-snipping."

The man turned white with rage, but stood a moment contemplating Leonard's athletic form and keen eyes. Apparently he found that in them which gave him pause, for instead of springing at him, he burst into a volume of threats and filthy abuse.

How the matter would have ended it is difficult to say, but at this juncture Pereira thought it well to interfere, and vigorously.

"Peace!" he thundered in his great voice, his white hair bristling with rage. "I have welcomed this man, and he is welcome. Is my word to be set aside by a drunken young brawler like you? Shut your ugly mouth or, by the Saints, I will have you clapped in irons."

The slave-driver obeyed; perhaps he was not sorry for an excuse to escape the quarrel. At any rate with a scowl at Leonard he dropped back and was silent.

Harmony being thus restored, Pereira proceeded with the business of the evening. First, however, he called Leonard to him, shook him by the hand, and bade a slave-girl bring him drink. Then he addressed the company thus:

"My lambs, my dear companions, my true and trusted friends, this is a sad moment for me, your old leader, for I stand here to bid you goodbye. Tomorrow the Nest will know the Yellow Devil no more, and you must find another captain. Alas! I grow old, I am no longer up to the work, and trade is not what it was, thanks to those infernal Englishmen and their cruisers, which prowl up and down our waters, seeking to rob honest men of the fruits of their enterprise. For nearly fifty years I have been connected with the business, and I think that the natives of these parts will remember me—not angrily, oh! no, but as a benefactor. For have not some twenty thousand of their young people passed through my hands, rescued by me from the curse of barbarism and sent to learn the blessings of civilisation and the arts of peace in the homes of kind and indulgent masters?

"Sometimes, not often, but now and again, there has been blood-shed in the course of our little expeditions. I regret it. But what will you? These people are so obstinate that they cannot see how well it is for them to come under my wing. And if they try to injure us in our good work, why, we must fight. We all know the bitterness of ingratitude, but we have to put up with it. It is a trial sent to us from Heaven, my lambs, always remember that. So I retire with such modest gains as I have won by a life of labour—indeed, they have gone before me, lest some of you might be put in the way of temptation—to spend the evening of my day in peace and prayer.

"And now there is one more little thing. As it chanced during our last journey, the daughter of an accursed Englishman fell into our hands. I took her and brought her here, and as her guardian I have asked you to meet me tonight, that I may choose her a husband, as it is my duty to do. I cannot keep her myself, for among the settled people near Mozambique, where I am going to live, her presence might lead to awkward questions. So I will be generous and pass her on to another.

"But to whom shall I give this prize, this pearl, this sweet and lovely maid? Among so many worthy gentlemen how can I set one above the others and declare him most deserving of the girl? I cannot, so I must leave it to chance, for I know that Heaven will choose better than I. Therefore to him who is ready to make the largest present to me I will give this maid, to comfort him with her love; to make a present, mind you, not to pay a price. Still, perhaps, it will be best that the amount of the donation should be ascertained in the usual way, by bidding—in ounces of gold, if you please!

"One condition more, there shall be nothing irregular in this matter, my friends. The Church shall have its say in it, and he whom I select must wed the maid, here, before us all. Have we not a priest at hand, and shall we find no work for him? Now, my children, time draws on. Ho! you, bring out the English girl."

This speech was not delivered quite so continuously as it is printed here. On the contrary, it was subject to many interruptions, mostly of an ironical nature, the allusions to "a present" to be given for the girl and to the proposed marriage ceremony being received with screams of ribald laughter.

Now the noise died away, for every eye watched for the appearance of Juanna.

In a few moments a figure clad in white and guarded by several men was seen advancing from the direction of the arms-house. This figure came on through the moonlight with a swift agile step, looking neither to the right nor to the left, till it arrived in front of the veranda and halted. Then it was that Leonard first saw Juanna Rodd. She was very tall and slight, her dark hair was twisted into a single knot at the back of her shapely head, her features were small, her face fair in colouring and somewhat rounded in form. So much he saw at a glance, but it was not until she looked up and round her that Leonard discovered the girl's peculiar glory, the glory of her eyes. Then and in that light he was unable to distinguish their colour, a difficult task at any time, for they varied from grey to blue according to the shadows which fell upon them, but he could see that they were wide and splendid, fearless and yet soft. For the rest she was clad in an Arab robe richly worked, and wore sandals upon her feet.

Juanna stopped in front of the veranda and searched it with her eyes. Presently they ceased their searching and she spoke in a clear, sweet voice.

"What do you want with me now, Dom Antonio Pereira?" she said.

"My dove," he answered in his coarse, mocking tones, "do not be angry with your slave. I promised you, my dove, that I would find a husband for you, and now all these gallant gentlemen are gathered for the choice. It is your marriage-hour, my dove."

"Dom Antonio Pereira," the girl answered, "for the last time I plead to you. I am helpless here among you, and I have done you no injury: let me go unharmed, I pray of you."

"Let you go unharmed? Why, who would hurt you, my dove?" answered the satyr. "Yes, that is what I mean to do. I will let you go to a husband."

"I shall never go to any husband of your choosing, Dom Antonio," Juanna said again in a low and steady voice. "Be assured of that, all of you. I have no fear of you, for God will help me in my need. And now, as I have pleaded to you for the last time, so for the last time I warn you, Dom Antonio, and your wicked companions also. Go on with this iniquity if you will, but a judgment awaits you. Death from Heaven above is near to you, you murderer, and after death, vengeance."

Thus she spoke, not loud indeed, but with conviction, a power, and a dignity of mien that carried terror to the hearts of the most hardened villains there. It was at the conclusion of her speech that her eyes first met those of Leonard Outram. He was bending forward to listen, and in his grief and anger he had forgotten to preserve the truculent expression which it was his part to wear. Once more Leonard's face was the face of an English gentleman, noble and open, if somewhat stern.

Their eyes met, and there was that in his which caused Juanna to pause. She looked at him swiftly as though she would read his very soul, and in answer he put all his will and heart's desire into his gaze, the will and the desire that she should know him to be her friend. They had never met before, she did not even dream of his existence, and there was little in Leonard's outward appearance to distinguish him from the ruffians by whom he was surrounded. Yet her quick sense, sharpened by despair, read what was written in his eyes, and read it aright. From that moment Juanna felt that she was not alone among these wolves, that there was one person at least who would save her if he could.

In an instant she had searched his face and dropped her eyes again, fearing lest she should awake suspicion. Then came a pause, for the minds of men were disturbed; she had aroused some remnant of conscience in them, she had called to life a lively terror of vengeance to come, of vengeance very near at hand. All were affected more or less, but chiefly was he affected to whom she had addressed her words. The Yellow Devil sank back into the chair from which he had risen to speak, a wonderful chair made of ebony inlaid with ivory, and string-seated, with a footstool attached to it. Superstitious dread took hold of him, and he shivered visibly.

The scene was one which Leonard never forgot. Above the bright moon shone in the heavens, before him were rank upon rank of evil faces, each marked with some new emotion, and standing alone in their midst was the beautiful girl, proud in the depth of her shame, defiant even in the power of foes gathered to destroy her.

For a while the wind had dropped and the silence was deep, so deep was it that Leonard could hear the mew of a kitten which had crept from the veranda, and was rubbing itself against Juanna's feet. She heard it also, and, stooping, lifted the little creature and held it to her breast.

"Let her go!" said a voice from the crowd. "She is a witch and will bring ill-luck upon us."

At the sound Pereira seemed to awake. With a hideous oath he flung himself from the chair and waddled down the steps towards his victim.

"Curse you, you slut!" he said, "do you think to frighten men with your threats? Let God help you if He can. The Yellow Devil is god here. You are as much in my power as this brute," and he snatched the kitten from her arms and dashed it to the ground. "You see, God does not help the kitten, and He will not help you. Here, let men see what they are going to buy," and gripping the breast of her white robe he rent it open.

With one hand Juanna gathered up the torn dress, and with the other she began to do something to her hair. An agony of fear took hold of Leonard. He knew the story of the poison which she carried: was she about to use it?

Once again their eyes met, and there was warning in his glance. Juanna loosed her hair indeed, and let it fall about her shoulders, covering her rent robe to the waist, but she did no more. Only after this Leonard saw that she kept her right hand closed, and knew that her death was hidden within it. Then she spoke once more to Pereira.

"In your last hour may you remember these two deeds!" she said, pointing to the writhing kitten and to her torn dress.

Now slaves drew near to do their master's bidding, but that audience would not suffer this.

"Leave her alone," they said; "we can see that the girl is fair and perfect."

Then the slaves hung back, nor did Pereira repeat his commands.

Returning to the veranda, he stood by the chair, and, taking an empty glass in his hand by way of an auctioneer's hammer, he began:

"Gentlemen, I am going to offer you a very choice lot, so choice that it makes up all the sale. The lot is a white girl, half English and half Portuguese by blood. She is well educated and devout; as to her docility I can say nothing, that will be for her husband to attend to. Of her beauty I need not speak; you can all see it yourselves. Look at that figure, that hair, those eyes; have any of you known their equal?

"Well, this lot will be sold to him among you who is inclined to make me the largest present in compensation; yes, he may take her this very hour, and my blessing with her. But there are conditions: he whom I approve must be lawfully married to the girl by the priest Francisco here," and turning he pointed to a small melancholy-looking man, with a womanish face and dark blue eyes, who stood in the background, clothed in a somewhat tattered priest's robe. "Then I shall have done my duty by her. One more thing, gentlemen: we are not going to waste time in little bids; the upset price will be thirty ounces."

"Silver?" said a voice.

"Silver? No, of course not. Do you think you are bidding for a nigger girl, fool? Gold, man, gold! Thirty ounces of gold, and payment to be made on the nail."

There was a groan of disappointment, and one ruffian cried out:

"What are we poor fellows to do? Thirty ounces for a beginning! Where is our chance?"

"What are you to do? Why, work hard at your profession, and grow rich, of course! Do you suppose that these prizes are for the poor? Now then, the fair is open. Who bids for the white girl Juanna? Thirty ounces is offered. What advance, what advance?"

"Thirty-five," said a wizened little man with a hectic cough, who looked fitter for a burial than a bridal.

"Forty!" cried another, a pure-bred Arab of stately appearance and saturnine expression, who wished to add to his harem.

"Forty-five," answered the wizened man.

Then the Arab bid fifty, and for a while it seemed that these two alone were competitors. When the bids had reached seventy ounces the Arab muttered "Allah!" and gave up. He preferred to wait for the *houris*.

"Knock her down," said the wizened man, "she is mine."

"Hold on a bit, my little friend," said the great Portugee, Xavier, who had passed the water-gate before Leonard and his companions. "I am going to begin now. Seventy-five."

"Eighty," said the little man.

"Eighty-five," answered Xavier.

"Ninety," screamed the other.

"Ninety-five," said Xavier.

"A hundred," yelled the small man, snapping his fingers.

"A hundred and five," replied Xavier, triumphantly capping his bid.

Then with a curse his antagonist gave up also, and the mob shouted, thinking that Xavier had won.

"Knock her down, Pereira," said Xavier in his turn, as he surveyed his prize with affected nonchalance.

"Wait a moment," put in Leonard, speaking for the first time. "I am going to begin now. A hundred and ten."

The multitude shouted again, the contest was growing exciting. Xavier glared at Leonard and bit his fingers with rage. He was very near his limit of possible expenditure.

"Now then," cried Pereira, licking his lips for joy, since the price had already run twenty ounces higher than he expected, "Now then, friend Xavier, am I to knock down this beauty to the stranger captain Pierre? It sounds a lot, but she is cheap at the price, dirt cheap. Look at her and bid up. But mind, it is cash down—no credit, no, not for an ounce."

"A hundred and fifteen," said Xavier, with the air of a man making his last throw for fortune.

"A hundred and twenty," replied Leonard quietly.

He had bid to the last ounce in his possession, and if Xavier went further he must give in, unless, indeed, he chose to offer Soa's ruby in payment. This, needless to say, he was not anxious to do; moreover, no one would believe a stone of that size to be genuine. Of all this, however, Leonard showed nothing in his face, but turning coolly he called to a slave-girl to bring him spirits and busied himself with filling his glass. His hand never trembled, for he knew well that his antagonist was watching for a cue, and if he showed uncertainty all might be lost. But in his heart, Leonard wondered what he should do if another ounce was bid.

Meanwhile the spectators were shouting encouragement, and Pereira was urging Xavier to increase his offer. For a while the Portugee hesitated, surveying Juanna, who stood pale and silent, her head bowed upon her breast. At this juncture Leonard turned, the glass still in his hand.

"Did you make any advance, senor?" he asked.

"No, curse you! Take her. I will not put down another ounce for her or any woman on the earth."

Leonard only smiled and looked at Pereira.

"Going!" said that worthy; "the white girl, Juanna, is going to the stranger Pierre for one hundred and twenty ounces of gold. Going! Come, Xavier, don't lose her. If you do you will only be sorry once, and that will be always. Now, for the last time," and he lifted his glass in his hand and paused.

Xavier made a step forward and opened his lips to speak.

Leonard's heart stood still, but presently the Portugee changed his mind and turned away.

"*Gone!*" screamed Pereira, bringing the glass down so heavily on the arm of his chair that it flew into fragments.

CHAPTER 13

A Midnight Marriage

"Gone," said Pereira again. "Now, friend Pierre, before we ratify this matter by the aid of holy Church, perhaps you will table the gold. This is a cash transaction, remember."

"Certainly," answered Leonard. "Where is that black dog of mine, the dwarf? Ah! there he is. Dog, weigh out the stuff; if you have not enough, here is more." And he unbuckled his belt, from which he had been careful to extract the ruby, and threw it to Otter.

"Now, gentlemen and companions," he went on, "for I hope that we may do business together by and by, drink my health and my bride's. I have paid pretty dear for her, but what of it? A gentleman of our profession should always be ready to back his fancy, for if his is apt to be a short life he may as well make it a merry one."

"She will think the better of you, and you of her for it," cried a voice. "Here is to Captain Pierre and the girl." And they drank, shouting aloud in their half-drunken merriment.

Meanwhile Otter, advancing with obsequious steps, was pouring handful after handful of gold coin and ingots into the large scales which Pereira caused to be held before him. At length all the gold was in, a shining heap.

"The balance does not turn," said Xavier; "I claim the girl."

"Baas," said Otter in a low voice, and speaking in Dutch, "have you more gold? The weight is short."

Leonard glanced carelessly at the scales: they were trembling on the turn.

"As much as you like," he said, "but here is what will do it."

And drawing off his signet ring he threw it on the pile. The ruby excepted, it was the last thing of value that he had about him. Then the scale vibrated and sank down.

"Good," said Pereira, rubbing his hands at the sight of so much

103

treasure. "Bring me the acid that I may test the stuff. No offence, stranger Pierre, but this is a wicked world, in which brass has passed for gold before today."

The acid was brought and the ingots were tested at hazard, Pereira holding them up to the light of a lamp.

"They are good," he said. "Now, Father, do your part."

The priest Francisco stepped forward. He was very pale and seemed terrified. Leonard, watching him, wondered what had brought him into such company, for the man's face was good and even refined.

"Dom Antonio," said the priest in a soft girlish voice, "I protest against this. Fate has brought me among you, though not of my own will, and I have been forced to bear the sight of much evil, but I have wrought none. I have shriven the dying, I have ministered to the sick, I have comforted the oppressed, but I have taken no share of the price of blood. I am a priest of our holy Church, and if I wed these two before the sight of men, they will be husband and wife till death, and I shall have set the seal of the blessing of the Church upon an act of shame. I will not do it."

"You will not do it, you shaveling traitor?" screamed Pereira in a voice hoarse with rage. "Do you want to follow your brother then? Look here, my friend, either you obey me and marry these two or——" and he hissed a horrible threat.

"*No, no,*" said Leonard, anxious to find an escape from this abominable mockery. "Let him be. What do the cheat's prayers matter? The lady and I can do without them."

"I tell you, stranger, that you shall marry the girl, and this sniveller must marry you. If you don't, I will keep both her and the gold. And as for him, he can choose. Here, slaves, bring the *sjamboch.*"

Francisco's delicate face flushed pink. "I am no hero that I can suffer thus," he said; "I will do your bidding, Dom Antonio, and may God forgive me the sin! For you, Pierre and Juanna, I am about to make you man and wife, to join you in a sacrament that is none the less holy and indissoluble because of the dreadful circumstances under which it is celebrated. I say to you, Pierre, abandon your wickedness, and love and cherish this woman, lest a curse from heaven fall upon you. I say to you, Juanna, put your trust in God, the God of the fatherless and oppressed, who will avenge your wrongs—and forgive me. Let water be brought, that I may consecrate it—water and a ring."

"Here, take this one," said Pereira, lifting Leonard's signet ring from the pile of gold. "I give it back for a luck-penny."

And he tossed the ring to the priest.

Water was brought in a basin, and the father consecrated it.

Then he bade Leonard stand by the girl and motioned to the crowd to fall back from them. All this while Leonard had been watching Juanna. She said no word, and her face was calm, but her eyes told him the terror and perplexity which tore her heart.

Once or twice she lifted her clenched right hand towards her lips, then dropped it without touching them. Leonard knew but too well what deed she meditated. He knew also the deadly nature of the drug she carried. If once it touched her tongue! The suspense was terrible. He could bear it no longer; even at the risk of discovery he must speak with her.

In obedience to the priest's direction he sauntered to her side laughing. Then, still laughing, with his hand he separated the tresses of dark hair, as though to look at the beauty of her side face, and bent down as if to kiss her.

She stood pale and rigid, but once more her hand was lifted towards her mouth.

"Stop," he whispered swiftly into her ear, speaking in English, "I have come to rescue you. Go through with this farce, it means nothing. Then, if I bid you, run for the drawbridge into the slave-camp."

She heard, a light of intelligence shone in her eyes, and her hand fell again.

"Come, stop that, friend Pierre," said Pereira suspiciously. "What are you whispering about?"

"I was telling the bride how beautiful I think her," he answered carelessly.

Juanna turned and flashed on him a well-simulated glance of hate and scorn. Then the service began.

The young priest was gifted with a low and beautiful voice, and by the light of the moon he read the ritual of marriage so solemnly that even the villains who stood round ceased their jokes and sneers and were silent. All things were done in order, though Juanna made no reply to the usual questions. With much sham courtesy the loathsome Pereira presided over the ceremony—their hands were joined, the ring was set upon Juanna's finger, the blessing was pronounced, and it was finished.

All this while Leonard stood like a man in a dream. He felt as though he were really being married; it even came into his mind, as he looked upon the loveliness of the mock bride at his side, that a worse fate might befall him. Then of a sudden he woke from his reverie— the farce was played, now they must strive to escape.

"There, that is done with, Dom Antonio," he said, "and I think I heard this lady whisper that with your permission we will bid you goodbye. My canoe——"

"Nonsense, you will stop here tonight," said Pereira.

"Thanks, I think not," answered Leonard. "Tomorrow I may return to do a little business of another kind. I have a commission for about fifty, at a good price for the right sort."

As Leonard spoke thus, glancing to the east, he saw dense masses of vapour rising into the air far away. The damp reeds were fired at last. The Settlement men had not failed in their task, and soon the flames would be discovered; he must be gone and swiftly.

"Well, if you must, you must," answered Pereira, and Leonard observed that he looked relieved as he said it. He did not know the reason at the time. It was this: Juanna had told him that the man who bought her would find his death in it. He had a superstitious fear of the girl, and believed her; therefore he was glad that her purchaser should go, lest it might be said that he had murdered him in order to retain both the woman and her price. So he bade him farewell, and Leonard turned to depart, followed by Otter and Juanna, whom he led by the hand.

All might have gone well for that time had it not been for an unlucky chance. Leonard's scheme was to walk towards the water-gate, but, if no better plan of reaching it should offer, to turn suddenly and run for the drawbridge, where Soa and the others would be waiting, and thence, with or without the people of Mavoom, to escape up the banks of the Zambezi.

Already he had started when the great Portuguese, Xavier, who was watching plunged in sullen thought, stepped forward. "At least I will have a kiss for my trouble," he said, and seizing Juanna round the waist, he drew her towards him.

Then it was that Leonard forgot his caution, as under such circumstances a man, with nerves already strained to breaking point, well might do. Doubling his fist, he struck the giant in the face with such force that Xavier fell headlong to the ground, dragging Juanna after him. Leonard would have done better had he suffered her to be insulted, but just then he remembered only that he was protecting a helpless girl.

Juanna was up in a moment and at his side. Xavier also sprang to his feet, cursing with fury and drawing his sabre as he rose.

"Follow me," said Leonard to Juanna and Otter. Then without more ado he took to his heels.

A shout of laughter went up from the mob.

"This is the brave man. This is the French fire-eater," they cried. "He strikes unawares and is afraid to fight." Nor did they stop at words. All of them were jealous of the stranger, and would have rejoiced to see him dead.

"Stop him!" they shouted, and many of the men started, running like dogs to turn a hare.

Still Leonard might have won through, for he was swift of foot. But neither Juanna nor Otter could run so fast as he, and his pace must be their pace. Before he had gone a hundred yards he found himself confronted by a dozen or more of the slavers, some of whom had knives in their hands.

"Stop, coward, stop and fight," they yelled in Portuguese and Arabic, waving their weapons in his face.

"Certainly," answered Leonard, wheeling round and glancing about him.

There, not thirty yards away, was the drawbridge of the slave camp, and he thought that he saw it tremble, as if it was about to fall. At his side were Otter and Juanna, and towards him, his hideous face red with blood, rushed the great Portugee, sabre aloft, and screaming imprecations.

"Otter," Leonard said quickly, as he drew his sword, "guard my back, for when I have killed this one the rest will spring. For you, young lady, reach the bridge if you can. Soa and your people are there."

Now Xavier was upon him with a rush. He struck furiously, and Leonard avoided the blow, springing backwards out of his reach. Twice more he rushed on thus and twice he smote, but each time Leonard ran backward towards the drawbridge, that now was not more than twenty yards away. A fourth time the Portugee came on, and the Englishman could not repeat his tactics, for the mob hemmed him in behind. On sped Xavier and smote his hardest: Leonard saw the steel gleam in the moonlight and lifted his sword to guard. The blow fell, fire sprang from it in sparks, and down rattled fragments of shattered steel. His sword was broken.

"Fight on, Baas," said the voice of Otter, "fight on! Both swords have gone."

Leonard looked up. It was true: the Portugee was casting aside his broken weapon and clutching at his knife. Now Leonard had no knife, and at the moment he never thought of his revolver. But he still held the hilt of his sword, and with it he sprang straight at Xavier, who rushed to meet him.

107

They met with a dull shock as bull meets bull. Leonard struck one blow with the broken sword-hilt, then dropped it—it was useless. But the stroke did him good service, for, falling on the right hand of the Portugee, it paralysed his arm for a second, causing him to let fall the dagger. Then they gripped each other, fighting desperately with their naked strength alone. Twice the huge Portugee lifted the Englishman from the ground, striving to throw him, while the crowd yelled with excitement, but twice he failed. Not for nothing had Leonard learnt wrestling as a lad and hardened his iron muscles by years of toil. Xavier may have weighed sixteen stone and Leonard did not weigh thirteen, but his arms were like bars of steel and he was struggling for dear life.

He waited awhile, letting the Portugee exhaust himself in efforts to hurl him to the ground. Then suddenly tightening his grip, Leonard put out all his strength. He could not hope to lift the man, that he knew, but he might throw him. With a sudden movement he hooked his right leg behind Xavier's left calf. Then he cast his weight forward and pushed with all his strength upon the great man's breast.

Xavier tottered, recovered himself, tottered again, and strove to shift his leg. Leonard felt the movement and met it with a supreme effort. Losing his balance, his foe swayed slowly backwards like a falling tree, then fell with a thud that shook the ground. It was a gallant throw, and even the "ranks of Tusculum" as represented by the slave-drivers "could scarce forbear to cheer." Now Leonard lay upon the breast of the man, for he was dragged to earth with him.

For a moment his enemy was still, breathing stertorously, for the shock of their fall had been great. Leonard looked round; there, some eight feet away, was the knife, and he who could grasp it must win this deadly game. But how could he grasp it? Xavier, whose strength and powers were coming back, still hugged him in his fearful grip; he also saw the knife, and would win it. Rapidly, by instinct almost, Leonard measured the distance with his eye. There was but one plan, to roll to it. The first roll would leave him undermost, but the dagger would still be out of Xavier's reach. Then, could he succeed in turning him upon his back once more, Leonard would be uppermost again, and if he was able to free his hand it might grasp the weapon. It was a terrible risk, but he must take it. He lay motionless awhile, husbanding his force, and the Portugee surged and heaved beneath him; he could feel the muscles of his mighty frame start up in knots as he struggled. At last Leonard let him have his way, and over they went, the two of them. Now Xavier was uppermost, and the mob yelled in triumph, for they thought that the stranger's strength was spent.

"The knife, the knife!" gasped Xavier, and one of his servants sprang forward to give it to him. But Otter was watching and started out of the press, naked sabre in hand: his fierce and ugly face was twitching with excitement, his black eyes shone, and his vast shoulders worked to and fro. To Juanna, fascinated by the fearful struggle, the dwarf looked like some black gnome, like a thing of supernatural power, half toad, half human.

"He who touches the knife dies!" he said in guttural Arabic, stretching his long arm and sabre over it. "Let these cocks fight it out, my masters."

The man shrank back: he also was afraid of Otter, deeming him uncanny; nor did any other interfere.

Now came the moment of death or victory. As he could not reach the weapon, with a sudden movement Xavier freed his right hand and grasped the Englishman's throat; but to do this he must lessen the pressure on his breast. Leonard felt the grip, and the knowledge that his end was at hand renewed his powers. Twice he writhed like a snake, gripping the ground with the muscles of his back and legs; once he swung his frame to the right, then a vast effort, and lo! Xavier turned slowly over like a log of wood, and again Leonard lay upon his breast.

Leonard lay upon his breast, and his right arm was free and within reach of the dagger. But the giant's grasp of his throat was cruel; the blood drummed in his ears and his senses began to fail. No, he would not die thus and leave the girl helpless. Where was it? He was blind, he could see nothing but her white face. He must get free—ah, he knew now!

They thought that he was spent: see! his head fell, when suddenly he lifted himself and heaved up his arm.

Crash it came full on the forehead of Xavier, that in its turn was pillowed on the stony earth. The grip slackened. Crash again, a fearful and despairing blow! Leonard's throat was free, and the air rushed into his bursting lungs. Now he could see and grasp the knife, but there was no need to use it. The great man beneath him flung his arms wide, shivered, and grew still.

Then it was, while men paused wondering at those awful blows, that Juanna, mindful of her deliverer's bidding, turned and fled, sick at heart but unhindered, to the edge of the ditch opposite the drawbridge. Otter also rushed up and dragged Leonard from the ground.

"*Wow!*" he cried, "a good fight and a great blow! Dead, by my mother's spirit, and no touch of steel. Awake, my father, awake! for if the boar is down the pigs remain!"

Leonard heard his words dimly and knew their import. With an effort he ceased to stagger and rested his weight upon the dwarf, much as a man might lean upon some sturdy post. His breath came back to him and his mind cleared. He looked round and saw Juanna standing near the bridge like one who hesitates whether to fly or stay.

"Sirs," gasped Leonard, "I have fought and I have won. Now let me go in peace with the girl. Is the man alive?"

A ring of men had crowded round the body of Xavier, and in their centre knelt the priest Francisco. At this moment he rose and said:

"It is useless to minister to him; he is no more."

The slavers looked at Leonard with awe not unmixed with admiration. Who had ever seen such a thing, that one whose strength had been a byword should be slain with the naked fist? They forgot that it is easy to kill the man whose head rests upon a stone.

Presently, however, their wonder gave way to rage. Xavier had been a favourite among them, and they were not minded that he should die unavenged. So they drew round Leonard scowling and cursing.

"Stand back," he said, "and let me pass. I fought your friend fairly; had I wished to take advantage of him, should I not have used this?" And for the first time he remembered and drew his Colt, the sight of which cooled their ardour somewhat, for they gave way. "Perhaps you will give me an arm, Father," Leonard went on, speaking to the priest, who was standing by. "I am much shaken."

Francisco complied, and they started towards Juanna, Otter guarding their rear with his sabre. Before they had gone ten yards, however, Pereira waddled towards them after a hasty consultation with one of his captains.

"Seize that man," he shouted; "he has killed the worthy Dom Xavier: having first insulted him, he has slain him by violence, and he must answer for it."

A dozen ruffians sprang forward at his bidding, only to be met by the sabre and pistol of Otter, with neither of which were they anxious to make a closer acquaintance. Leonard saw that the position was very grave, and a thought came into his mind. "You wish to escape from this place, Father?" he said rapidly to the priest.

"Yes," answered Francisco, "it is a hell."

"Then lead me as swiftly as you may to that bridge; I am hurt and weak, but there is succour beyond."

As he spoke the drawbridge, which was not ten yards away, fell with a crash.

"Run across, Juanna Rodd," cried Leonard in English.

She hesitated, then obeyed. It seemed to Leonard that the look upon her face said, "How can I leave you?"

"Now, Father," said Leonard, "make a rush for it," and leaning on the priest's shoulder he stumbled towards the bridge. But he would never have reached it had it not been for Otter.

"Treason!" roared Pereira; "stop him! Who let down the bridge?"

A man came on the attack; it was the same young captain that Leonard had offered to fight before the auction. In his hand was a knife already uplifted to fall on Leonard's back when Otter's sabre flashed and the man went down.

"Seize the bridge and hold it," roared Pereira again.

"Wind up! wind up!" yelled Otter in answer, as with sabre and pistol he held back the mob.

Those on the further side obeyed with such a will that Leonard and the priest rolled down the slanting planks.

"Otter!" cried Leonard—"good God! he will be killed!"

By way of answer Otter fired the last barrel of his pistol. Then with a yell, before his foes could close upon him he sprang like a wild cat straight at the iron chains of the bridge, which were used to secure it in its place when needful. At the moment they hung four feet or more above his head, but he grasped them and shouted to Soa to hoist away.

A man attempted to seize his legs, but Otter kicked him in the face and he fell into the water. Next second he was out of their reach and rapidly rising high into the air. Some threw knives and some fired pistol-shots after him, but none of these touched him.

"Ah! Yellow Devil," the dwarf cried as he swung, "look behind you: there is another devil, yellower and fiercer than you."

Pereira turned and all his company with him, and at that moment, with a crackling roar, a vast sheet of flame burst up from the morass. The reeds had caught at last in good earnest, and the strengthening wind was bringing the fire down upon them.

CHAPTER 14

Vengeance

"Treachery! treachery!" screamed Pereira. "The reeds are fired, and that witch has betrayed us."

"Ha! ha! ha! ha!" cried Otter again from his airy perch. "Treachery! treachery! And what if the slaves are loosed? And what if the gates be barred?"

Hitherto the mob had been silent in their fear and wonder. There they stood closely packed, a hundred or more of them, staring first at Otter, then at the advancing flames. Now they found tongue.

"He is a fiend! Kill him! Storm the slave camp! To the gates!" they yelled in this language and in that.

For many it was their last earthly cry, since at that moment a sheet of flame burst from the rampart of the camp, followed by the boom of the cannon, and six pounds of canister swept through the crowd. Right through them it swept, leaving a wide lane of dead and dying; and such a shriek went up to heaven as even that place of torment had never heard.

Then they broke and fled this way and that, screaming curses as they went.

When Leonard and the priest had rolled down the rising bridge they found Juanna standing safely by the guard-house, surrounded by some of the Settlement men.

"To the gun!" he cried, "to the gun! Fire into them! I will follow you."

Then it was that he saw Otter left to his death and called out in fear. But Otter saved himself as has been told, and clambered down the bridge safe and sound.

Leaning on the dwarf and Francisco, Leonard, followed by Juanna, staggered along the earthwork to the place where the gun was mounted. Before he had gone a step he caught sight of the figure of

Soa, outlined in bold relief against the background of the fire and surrounded by many of the freed Settlement men. At the instant when he saw her she was in the act of springing back from the breech of the gun, the lanyard in her hand. Then came the roar of the shot and the shriek of the smitten.

"*Wow!*" said Otter, "the old woman has not been idle. She is clever as a man, that one."

Another minute and they were helping to reload the piece, that is, except Soa, who was on her knees kissing Juanna's hands.

"Come, stop that!" said Leonard, sinking to the ground, for he was utterly exhausted. "Those devils have gone for their arms. They will try to storm us presently. Is the shot home, Peter? Then run her out, sharp; and you, Soa, screw her nose down." Next he bade the freed slaves arm themselves with stakes or anything that they could find, for of rifles they had but four, two of which they had found in the guard-house.

Presently the slavers came on with a yell, carrying long planks, by the help of which they hoped to cross the dike.

"Look out!" said Leonard, "they are going to open fire. Under the earthwork, every man of you!" And seizing Juanna who was standing near, he pulled her down into cover.

It was not too soon, for next instant a storm of bullets swept over them. Most of the men had understood and taken shelter, but some were too slow or too stupid. Of these one fell dead and two more were hit. Soa and Peter alone took no heed, and yet they remained unhurt. There stood the woman, while the bullets whistled round her, laying the gun as coolly as though she had served in the Royal Artillery, and with her was the head-man, Peter. Peter was shot through the waist-cloth and a ball cut its way through Soa's grizzled hair, but neither of them seemed to notice these trifles.

"They are mad, Baas," cried Otter, who was watching the enemy over the top of the embankment. "See! they are coming across the open."

Leonard looked. The dwarf was right: in their rage and hurry the slavers, half hidden in a cloud of smoke caused by their rapid firing, were advancing across the clear space instead of creeping along the edge of the dike. What was more, the necessity of carrying the planks caused them to pack in groups. Soa gave a final twist with her lever and waited, her hand on the lanyard. A bullet cut it in two, but without firing the gun, and she grasped the shortened cord.

"Now for it!" cried Leonard, as the first party came into the line of fire.

Soa sprang backwards with a yell: again the piece thundered out, and the canister screamed through the air. It tore along the advancing files, then, striking the beaten earth, rebounded and caught those who were following with the ricochet, and with awful effect. Whole groups were mowed down by this one discharge, the destruction being twice as large as that caused by the first shot, for at this greater range the canister found room to spread. Also the rebounding missiles flying hither and thither among the crowd did no little execution. Down went the men in heaps, and with them the planks they carried. They had no more wish to storm the slave camp; they had but one thought left, the thought of safety, and the survivors of them fled in all directions, yelling with fear and fury.

"Load up, load up!" cried Otter, lifting the charge of powder which lay at hand. "They will try to break open the gates and get out, then they will cut us off."

As he spoke they saw many men run from the auction-shed to the water-gate. But it could not be climbed, the key was gone, and the massive bolts and beams were not easy to break. So they brought hammers and a tree-trunk which had supported an angle of the shed, and battered at the gate. For two minutes or more it held, then it began to give.

"Swift! swift!" cried Otter again as he dragged at the cannon to turn it, "or all will yet be lost."

"Hurry no man's ox, Black One," said Soa, as she laid the gun with the help of Peter.

A cry went up from the slavers; the gate was tottering, but it still held by the upper hinges. A few more blows and it must surely fall. But those blows were never struck. Again Soa sprang backwards, and the roar of the gun was answered by the screams of the slavers as the shrapnel ploughed through them.

Of those who were left the most part fled for shelter to the auction-hut and to the Nest itself. Some ran across to the magazine, but appeared to be unable to enter it, for soon they were seen flying back again, while about a dozen of the boldest remained at the gate trying to complete its destruction. On these Leonard and Otter opened fire with rifles, but it was not until three or four of them had fallen that the rest fled to join their companions beneath the shelter of the sheds.

"Oh! look, look!" said Juanna, pointing to the east.

It was indeed a spectacle never to be forgotten.

The dense reeds, measuring twelve to fifteen feet in height, had been fired far to the east of the Nest, and as the wind gathered to a gale and the fire got firmer hold, it rolled down upon the doomed place in billows and sheets—a sea of flame that sometimes spouted high into the air and sometimes ran swiftly along the ground.

The reeds crackled and roared like musketry as the fire ate into them, giving out thick volumes of smoke. At first this smoke had passed above the spectators, now it blew into their faces, half choking them and blotting out the sky, and mixed up with it were showers of sparks and fragments of burning reeds brought forward on the wind.

"The house and sheds will soon catch now," said Leonard; "then they must take refuge in the open spaces, where we can deal with them," and he nodded towards the gun.

As he spoke tongues of flame darted into the air, first from the thatch of the shed, then from the roof of the Nest. They were afire.

"We must be careful, Baas," said Otter, "or the slave-shelters behind us will burn also, and all those in them."

"Heavens! I never thought of that," answered Leonard. "Here, Father, if you wish to do a good work, take some of these people and the buckets they use to water the slaves. Let three or four men get on to each roof and extinguish the sparks as they fall, while others bring them water from the moat."

The priest sprang up and set to the task, at which he laboured gallantly for two long hours. Had it not been for his efforts, the sheds and the slaves in them must have been burnt, for the sparks fell thick upon the dry thatch, which caught again and again.

Now the sights and sounds grew more and more fearful. Maddened with fear, the remainder of the slave-drivers and their servants rushed from the flaming buildings, striving to escape from the fire. Some flung themselves desperately into the aloes and prickly-pears on the inner rampart, and, climbing the palisade beyond, escaped into the marsh, while some collected on the open space, and at these the gun was fired from time to time when the smoke lifted. Others again ran to the dike of the slave camp begging for mercy, there to be shot by Otter, who never wearied in his task of revenge. From behind them also rose the hideous cries of the slaves, who believed that they were about to be burned alive, and screamed as they dragged at their manacles.

"Oh, it is like hell!" said Juanna to Leonard, as she buried her face in the grass that she might see no more, and to escape the suffocating smoke. She was right.

So the time went on. One by one the roofs of the various buildings fell in, and spouts of flame shot high into the air to descend about them in a rain of sparks. But at last the cries ceased, for even the slaves could yell no more; the fire grew less and less, and the wind dropped. Then the sun rose on the scene of death and desolation. The morass was swept bare to the depth of many hundred yards, and the camp was a smoking ruin strewn with the dead. The walls of the Nest still stood, however, and here and there a charred post remained. Everything else was gone, except the magazine, which had escaped the flames, being built of brick and stone, and roofed with tin.

The adventurers looked around them in silence, then they looked at each other. What a spectacle they presented in the clear light of the morning, as they stood by the gun which had done them such signal service! All were begrimed with smoke and powder, and their clothes were burnt by the falling sparks. Leonard's throat was a mass of bruises, his hands and face were bleeding, and he was so stiff and hurt that he could scarcely move. Soa's hair was singed and cut by the bullet which had shaved her head; the priest's robe hung in charred threads, and his hands were blistered with fire; Juanna's broidered Arab dress, torn by the brutal hand of Pereira, scarcely retained a trace of white, and her long dark locks were tangled and powdered with bits of blackened reed. All were utterly exhausted—that is, all except Otter, who advanced to speak to Leonard, begrimed and stripped to the waist, but fresh and fierce as ever.

"What is it, Otter?" he asked.

"Will the Baas let me take these men," and he nodded towards the freed slaves who had belonged to the Settlement, "and hunt through the camp yonder? Many of the devils still live, and wounded snakes strike hardest."

"As you like," answered Leonard. "Arm them with anything you can find, and search the camp thoroughly. But be careful."

In ten minutes Otter was gone with the men. Then Leonard and the others fetched water and washed as best they might, the guard-house being assigned to Juanna and Soa, who made their toilet with the help of a comb they found in it. There also they discovered food, the rations of the sentry, of which they ate with such appetite as they might, and a plentiful supply of meal for the slaves.

As they were finishing their breakfast Otter returned unharmed, though of the men who accompanied him five were missing. With him also were two of the four Settlement men who had been sent to fire the reeds on the previous night. They were much exhausted, for their task had been no easy one, and fortunately for Leonard it was only after long delay that they succeeded in it. Their two companions were dead: one had been taken by an alligator in the water, and the other had fallen into a deep hole in the morass, and, striking his head against a log, was drowned there.

"Is it finished?" said Leonard to the dwarf.

Otter nodded. "Some are dead and some are fled," he answered; "but from these last we have little to fear, for they believe that an army has come against them. Still that is not all the tale, Baas. We have taken one of them alive. Come and look at him, Baas."

Leonard clambered up the steps of the embankment, followed by the others. On its further side stood the group of Settlement men who had returned from scouring the camp, thin and haggard fellows, scarred by the slave-irons, but very fierce-looking. In their midst a white man crouched upon the ground, moaning with terror and misery. Just then he lifted his face—it was that of the Yellow Devil himself. There lay that aged Iniquity, that hoary Shame caught at last in his own snares.

"Where did you find him, Otter?" asked Leonard as they crossed the drawbridge.

"In the magazine, Baas, and your gold with him, also many rifles and much powder. He had locked himself up there, but he had not the heart to fire the powder and make an end."

Pereira did not see them as yet, but raising his head he begged for water.

"Give him blood," said one of the men sullenly. "He has drunk it all his days, let it be his last drink."

Leonard motioned to Francisco the priest to bring water, then Pereira saw them and began to pray for mercy.

"Antonio Pereira," Leonard answered sternly, "last night I and two companions, a woman and a black dwarf, set ourselves a task—to take this armed place of yours and rescue a white girl whom you had condemned to slavery. It did not seem possible that we should do it, but between sunset and sunrise we have done it. Who helped us then?— that we should have carried out this thing which was impossible. I will tell you; God helped us as He helped this lady when she called on Him. Cry to God, then, to do that which is still more impossible—to help you. From me you will have justice and no more."

For a moment Pereira ceased whining, and a flash of the old ferocity came into his eyes.

"Ah! my friend," he muttered, "if I had but known!" Then turning to Juanna he said: "My dove, have I not treated you kindly? Will you say no word for me, now that my enemies prevail against me?"

By way of answer Juanna looked first at the human reptile before

117

her, and next at the bosom of her torn dress, now roughly pinned up with the spikes of aloe leaves. Then she turned and went.

"Baas," said Otter, "may I speak?"

"Speak on," Leonard answered.

"Hearken, Yellow Devil," said the dwarf. "Ten years ago you took me, and I lay in this camp a slave; yes, in yonder shed. Here are the marks of the irons—your own seal. Ah! you have forgotten the black dwarf, or perhaps you never noticed him; but he remembers. Who could forget you, Yellow Devil, that once had slept beneath your roof? I escaped, but as I fled I swore that, if I might, I would bring vengeance upon you. The years went by, and the hour came at last. I led Baas to this place. I found you this morning, and we are not parted yet, Yellow Devil. What did you boast last night—that you had sent twenty thousand of us black people to slavery? Yes, and for every one that you have sold you have killed five—old men white with years, women with child, little children at the breast, you have murdered them all. Ah! yes, I have seen you laugh and kill them before the eyes of their mothers, as last night you killed the kitten.

"And now your time has come at last, Yellow Devil, and I, Otter the dwarf, will give you to drink of your own medicine. What! you cry for mercy, you who never gave it even in a dream? I tell you, did my chief yonder bid me loose you, I would disobey him even to force; I, who would rather die than put aside his word on any other matter.

"Look now at these men," and he pointed to the Settlement people, who glared hungrily at the crouching wretch, much as hounds glare at a fox that is held aloft by the huntsman; "look at them! Do you see mercy in their eyes? They, whose fathers and mothers you have murdered, whose little children you have stamped to death? *Wow!* Yellow Devil, the white men tell us of a hell, a place where dead people are tormented. We know nothing of that, it is for the white people, and they may keep it all to themselves. Now you are beginning to taste that hell of yours—only beginning, Yellow Devil.

"Baas Leonard, I demand this man to be tried by us and dealt with according to our customs, for it is against us black folk that he has sinned most of all, and we ask his blood in payment for our blood."

"What!" howled Pereira, "am I to be given over to these black dogs? Mercy! Mercy! Francisco, plead for me. Shrive me. I know I killed your brother, I had to do it. Plead for me!" and he rolled in the dust, trying to clasp Leonard's feet.

"I cannot shrive you," answered the priest shuddering, "but I will pray for you."

Then the hungry-eyed natives pounced upon Pereira to drag him thence, but Leonard broke through them saying:

"I will have none of your savage cruelties here. Let the man be shot if you will, but no more."

As it chanced, however, Pereira was not destined to die by the hand of man, for even as Otter gripped him he turned livid, threw up his arms, groaned, and fell to the earth.

Leonard looked at him; he was dead, dead through the fear of death, for terror had stopped the beating of his wicked heart.

"The Shepherdess prophesied truly," cried Otter presently, "for the Heavens above have robbed us of our vengeance. *Wow!* it is hard, but at least this one shall work no more evil."

"Carry it away," said Leonard with a shudder, for the dead man's face was ghastly to behold. Then turning to him as if nothing had happened, he added:

"Otter, take these men and loose the rest of the slaves; then get the ammunition, rifles, and stores from the arms-house and bring them to the water-gate. We must clear out of this place at once, or we shall have the escaped slavers and the crews of the dhows down upon us."

Thus then did fate at last find out Antonio Pereira, the Yellow Devil.

CHAPTER 15

Disillusion

Once more it was morning, and the travellers were encamped by that reedy point where they had left the big boats which they cut loose from the island. From the earliest dawn Leonard had been superintending the transport across the river of the hundreds of slaves whom they had released. They there were put on shore by the Settlement men, provided with a store of meal, and left to shift for themselves, it being found utterly impossible to take them any further.

"There, they are gone," said Otter, as the last boat-load set out under the charge of Peter. "Well, let them go, the silly sheep. So much the less trouble for us, who, although we have a Shepherdess, can scarcely lead so large a flock. Well, we have pulled the Missie yonder out of the Slave Nest, and the Yellow Devil—ah! we have talked with him and all his crew. And now are we to go on to win the gold—the real Yellow Devil, Baas?"

"I suppose so, Otter," answered Leonard—"that is, if Soa keeps her word. But it isn't gold, it is rubies. At any rate we must make for the Settlement below Sena, to take these men back and see if we can hear anything of Mavoom."

"So," said Otter after a pause. "Well, the Shepherdess, as these Settlement people call her, will want to find her father. Say, Baas, she is proud, is she not? She looks over our heads and speaks little."

"Yes, Otter, she is proud."

"And she is beautiful; no woman was ever so beautiful."

"Yes, Otter, she is beautiful."

"And she is cold, Baas; she does not say 'thank you' nicely for all that you have done."

"Perhaps she thinks it the more, Otter."

"Perhaps she thinks it the more. Still, she might say 'thank you' to you, Baas, who are her—husband."

"What do you mean by that?"

"I mean, Baas, that you bought her first, according to our custom, and married her afterwards according to your own, and if that does not make her your wife, nothing can."

"Stop that fool's talk," said Leonard angrily, "and never let me hear you repeat it. It was only a game that we played."

"As the Baas desires, so be it. I do but speak from my heart when I say that she is your wife, and some might think that not so ill, for she is fair and clever. Will the Baas rise and come to the river to bathe, that his soreness may leave him?"

Leonard took the suggestion, and came back from his bath a new man, for rest and the cold water had acted on him like magic. He was still stiff, indeed, and remained lame in one leg for ten days or more, but, with the exception of an aching of the throat where Xavier had gripped him, no other ill effects were left. Among the booty of the slave camp was a good supply of clothing, flannel shirts, corduroy suits, and hats. Casting aside the rags of the Portuguese uniform in which he had disguised himself, Leonard put on some of these articles and reappeared in the camp dressed like an ordinary English colonist, roughly indeed, but becomingly.

Meanwhile Juanna had also been making her toilet, with the help of Soa, who took this opportunity to tell her mistress the history of her meeting with Leonard Outram. But, either from design or because she forgot to do so, she did not at this time tell her about the agreement which had been entered into between them. As yet Soa had never spoken fully to her mistress of her early life or of the mysterious People of the Mist from whom she sprang, though she had taught her the language they spoke. Perhaps, for reasons of her own, she did not think this a favourable occasion on which to begin the story.

When Soa had finished Juanna fell into a reverie. She remembered that she had expressed no gratitude to Mr. Outram for his heroic rescue of her. Yet in her heart she was grateful enough. But for him she must now have been dead, and the world of light and love would have closed its gates upon her for ever. Still, mixed up with her gratitude and earnest admiration of the deed of heroism which had been wrought for her sake, was another feeling, a feeling of resentment and alarm. This stranger, this dark, keen-eyed, resolute man had bought her as a slave; more, he had gone through a form of marriage with her that was not all a form, for it had been solemnly celebrated by a priest, and there on her finger was the memorial of it. Of course it meant nothing, but the thought of it angered her and offended her pride.

Like other women, Juanna Rodd had not come to twenty years of age without dreaming of love, and, strange to say, her fancy had always chosen some such man as Leonard for the hero of the story. But that the hero should present himself in this ultra-heroic fashion, that he should buy her with gold, that he should go through a form of marriage with her within an hour of their first meeting—for these things she had not bargained. It was a fact—that marriage was an accomplished fact, although it might be null and void, and the female mind has a great respect for accomplished facts. To a woman of Juanna's somewhat haughty nature this was very galling. Already she felt it to be so, and as time went on the chain of its remembrance irked her more and more, a circumstance which accounts for much of her subsequent conduct.

Thinking such thoughts as these, Juanna strolled back towards the camp along a little pathway in the reeds, and suddenly came face to face with Leonard. She was clad in a white Arab robe, part of the loot, which she had adapted cleverly to the purposes of a dress, fastening it round her slender waist with an embroidered scarf. She wore no hat, and her rich dark hair was twisted into a great knot that shone in the sunlight. In her hand she held some crimson lilies which she had gathered, that made a spot of colour on the whiteness of her dress. The look of haunting terror was gone from her face, whose beauty had come back during her sleep; her changing eyes shone beneath their dark lashes, and she moved with the grace of a fawn.

Seen thus in that pure and pearly light against the green background of the feathered reeds, nothing could have seemed more sweet and lovely than did this girl, this child of the forest and the river, who mingled in herself the different beauty of the Saxon and the Spaniard, ripened by the African sun and dignified by the long companionship of Nature. There was a grace about her movements, a purity in her face, a mystery in the wide eyes and curved and smiling lips, such as Leonard had never seen before, and which overcame him utterly. Alas for the fickleness of the human heart! from that moment the adoration of his youth, the dream of his lonely years of wandering, Jane Beach, began to grow faint and fade away. But though this was so, as yet he did not admit it to himself; indeed, he scarcely knew it.

Juanna looked up and saw him standing before her, proud and handsome, an air of command upon his thoughtful face, deep-chested, bearded, vigorous, a man amongst men. She saw the admiration in his eyes and blushed, knowing that, do what she would to prevent it, it

122

was reflected in her own. She remembered all that this stranger had done for her, how he had risked his life a hundred times, how she would now have been dead and unlovely were it not for his intrepid deeds, and remembering, something stirred at her heart.

Was it gratitude that moved her thus? She did not know; but whatever it was, she turned her head that he might not read it on her face. Another moment, and she was holding out her hand to him and smiling pleasantly.

"Good morning," she said, "I hope that you have slept well, and that you have no bad news."

"I spent eight hours in a state of absolute stupor," he answered laughing, "and there is no news at all to speak of, except that I have got rid of those slaves, poor creatures. I fancy that our friends, the slave-dealers yonder, have had enough of our company, and are scarcely likely to follow us."

Juanna turned a shade paler, and answered:

"I trust so. At least I have had enough of them. By the way, Mr. Outram, I—I—have to thank you for a great deal;" here her eyes caught the gleam of the gold circlet on the third finger of her left hand—"this ring belongs to you, I will return it at once."

"Miss Rodd," said Leonard gravely, "we have passed through a very strange adventure together; will you not keep the ring in remembrance of it?"

Her strong impulse was to refuse. While she wore this ring the thought of that hateful scene and still more hateful mockery of marriage would be always with her. And yet, as the words of prompt refusal were on her lips, a feeling, an instinct, almost a superstition caused them to remain unspoken. "You are very kind," she said, "but this is your signet-ring—is not that what you call it? You cannot wish to give it to a chance acquaintance."

"Yes, it is my signet-ring, and if you will look at the crest and motto you will see that they are not inappropriate. And I do wish to give it even 'to a chance acquaintance,' Miss Rodd, if you will allow me no more intimate term."

"I have looked at them," she answered, as she examined the ring curiously. It was of plain and somewhat massive gold, and deeply cut into the shield-faced bezel was the Outram crest, a hand holding a drawn sword, beneath which the motto was engraved. "What is the last word of the motto?" she went on; "it is so rubbed that I cannot read it—'For Home, Honour——'"

"'And Heart,'" said Leonard.

Juanna blushed, though why the word "heart" should make her blush she knew not.

"Well, I will wear the ring, if you wish it, Mr. Outram, in memory of our adventure—that is, until you ask it back again," she said confusedly; then added with a change of tone: "There is one detail of the adventure that I hope you will not allude to more than you can avoid, for the recollection of it is most painful to me, probably more so even than to you."

"I suppose you mean the ceremony of marriage, Miss Rodd."

"I mean the wicked and abominable farce in which we were made to play a part," she answered passionately. "Most of the witnesses of that shameful scene are dead and cannot speak of it, and if you will keep your servant the dwarf silent I will do the same by Father Francisco. Let it be forgotten by both of us."

"Certainly, Miss Rodd," said Leonard, "that is, if anything so strange can be forgotten. And now, will you come to breakfast?"

She bowed her head in assent and swept past him, the red lilies in her hand.

"I wonder what hold she has over that priest," thought Leonard to himself, "that she talked of being able to keep him silent. By the way, I must find out whether we are to have the pleasure of his company. I would rather be without him myself. A strange girl! One can account for her beauty, she inherited that; but it is difficult to understand the manner. By rights she should be a half-wild hoyden, but I never saw an English lady with more grace and dignity. Perhaps I have forgotten; it is so long since I associated with ladies, or perhaps, like beauty, these are natural to her. After all, her father seems to have been a gentleman of birth, and people who live with nature may have every fault in the calendar, but they cannot be vulgar. That is the gift of civilisation."

When he reached the camp, Leonard found the priest talking confidentially to Juanna.

"By the way, Father," he said somewhat brusquely, "as you see, I have got rid of those slaves. It was impossible to take them with us, and now they must shift for themselves: at any rate, they are better off than they were yonder. What are your plans? You have behaved well to us, but I cannot forget that we found you in bad company. Perhaps you wish to return to it, and in that case your way lies eastward," and he nodded towards the Nest.

"I do not wonder that you distrust me, senor," said Francisco, his pale and girlish face colouring as he spoke, "for appearances are much against me. But I assure you that although I came into the company of Antonio Pereira by my own will, it was for no evil purpose. To be brief, senor, I had a brother who fled hither from Portugal because of a crime that he had committed, and joined Pereira's band. With much toil I tracked him out, and was welcomed at the Nest because I am a priest who can comfort the sick and shrive the dying, for wickedness does not console men at the last, senor. I persuaded my brother to return with me, and we made a plan to escape. But Pereira's ears were long: we were betrayed, and my brother was hanged. They did not hang me, because of my calling. Afterwards I was kept a prisoner and forced to accompany the band in their expeditions. That is all the story. Now, with your permission, I will follow you, for I have no money and nowhere else to go in this wilderness, though I fear that I am not strong enough to be of much service, and being of another faith you will scarcely need my ministrations."

"Very well, Father," answered Leonard coldly, "but please understand that we are still surrounded by many dangers, which any treachery might cause to overwhelm us. Therefore I warn you that should I detect anything of the sort my answer to it will be a quick one."

"I do not think that you need suspect the Father, Mr. Outram," said Juanna indignantly. "I owe him a great deal: had it not been for his kindness and counsel, I should not be alive today. I am most deeply grateful to him."

"If you vouch for him, Miss Rodd, that is enough. You have had the advantage of a closer acquaintance than I can boast," Leonard answered gravely, mentally contrasting the difference of her manner in acknowledging the priest's services and his own.

From that hour till a certain conversation opened his eyes, struggle as he would against it, Leonard disliked Francisco. He had a foolish British aversion to his class, and Juanna's marked partiality towards this particular individual did not lessen it in this instance. Prejudice is a strong thing, and when it is heightened by suspicion and jealousy, especially jealousy of the unacknowledged kind, it becomes formidable, both to him who entertains it and to him against whom it is entertained.

When their meal was done they proceeded up the river in the boats which they had captured from the slavers, each boat being rowed by the best oarsmen among the Settlement men. Including women and children their party numbered some sixty souls. At evening they passed the island where they had left the company of slavers, but could see no sign of life upon it, and never learned whether the men perished or escaped.

An hour later they encamped upon the bank of the river, and it was while they were sitting round the fire at night that Juanna told Leonard of the horrors which she had undergone during her dreadful sojourn with the slave caravan. She told him also how she had torn leaves from the Bible which she chanced to have with her, and fixed them upon the reeds whenever she could find an opportunity of so doing, in the hope that they might guide her father, should he return and attempt her rescue.

"It is all like a nightmare," she said; "and as for that hideous farce of marriage with which it ended, I can scarcely bear to think of it."

Then Francisco, who had been sitting silent, spoke for the first time. "You speak, senora," he said in his subdued voice, "of that 'hideous farce of marriage,' and I suppose you mean the ceremony which I performed between you and the Senor Outram, being forced to the act by Pereira. It is my duty to tell you both that, however irregular this marriage may have been, I do not believe it to be a farce. I believe that you are lawfully man and wife until death shall part you, unless indeed the Pope should annul the union, as he alone can do."

"Nonsense, nonsense," broke in Leonard; "you forget that there was no consent; that we are of another religion, and that the form was necessary to our plot."

"The Church knows nothing of the reasons which lead to the undertaking of wedlock," Francisco answered mildly. "They are various, and many of them would not bear investigation. But you were married without any open protest on your part, on Portuguese territory, according to Portuguese custom, and by a duly qualified priest. The fact that you are of the Protestant religion, and were united by the Catholic ritual, does not matter at all. For the purposes of the ceremony you accepted that ritual, as is customary when a Protestant marries a Catholic. It is disagreeable for me to have to tell you this, but the truth remains: I believe that you are man and wife before Heaven and the world."[1]

Here Juanna jumped to her feet, and even in that light Leonard could see that her breast was heaving and her eyes shone with anger.

"It is intolerable that I should be forced to listen to such false-hoods," she said, "and if you ever repeat them in my hearing, Father Francisco, I will not speak to you again. I utterly repudiate this marriage. Before the ceremony began, Mr. Outram whispered to me to go through with the 'farce,' and it was a farce. Had I thought otherwise I

---

1. The Editor does not hold himself responsible for Father Francisco's views on ecclesiastical marriage law.

should have taken the poison. If there is any foundation for what the Father says, I have been deceived and entrapped."

"Pardon, senora," replied the priest; "but you should not speak so angrily. The Senor Outram and I only did what we were forced to do."

"Supposing that Father Francisco is right, which I do not believe," said Leonard, with sarcasm, "do you think, Miss Rodd, that such a sudden undertaking would be more to my liking than to yours? Believe me, had I wished to 'deceive and entrap' you, I could not have done so without involving myself, since, if the marriage is binding, it is binding on both parties, and even such a humble individual as I am does not take a wife on the faith of a five minutes' acquaintance. To be frank, I undertook your rescue for purposes far other than those of matrimony."

"Might I ask what they were?" replied Juanna, in a tone of equal acerbity.

"Certainly, Miss Rodd. But first I must explain that I am no knight-errant. I am an almost penniless adventurer, and for urgent reasons of my own I seek to win fortune. Therefore, when the woman yonder," and he pointed to Soa, who was sitting watching them just out of range of the firelight, "came to me with a marvellous tale of a countless treasure of rubies, which she promised to reveal to me if I would undertake the little matter of your rescue, and when she even paid down a specimen stone of considerable value on account, having nothing better to do and nowhere to go, being in short desperate, I consented. Indeed, I did more, I took the precaution of reducing the matter to writing, I being one contracting party, and Soa, acting on her own behalf and as your attorney, being the other."

"I have not the least idea to what you allude, nor did I ever give Soa any authority to sign documents on my behalf. But may I see this writing?"

"Certainly," Leonard answered; and rising he went to the baggage, whence he returned presently with a lantern and the prayer-book.

Juanna placed the lantern beside her and opened the book. The first thing that she saw was a name on the fly-leaf, "Jane Beach," and beneath it this inscription, which evidently had been written by some one in a great hurry: "To dearest Leonard from Jane. 23 Jan."

"Turn over," he said hastily; "the document is on the other side."

She was not slow to note both the writing and the confusion which her perusal of it caused him. Who was Jane Beach, she wondered, and why did she call Mr. Outram "dearest Leonard"? In a moment, so strange are the hearts of women, Juanna felt herself much prepossessed against her, whoever she might be. But she turned the leaf and read the agreement. It was a pretty sight to see her bending over the cramped writing in the circle of the lantern light, but when at length she had finished and looked up, there was a smile upon her lovely face which had more of scorn in it than was pleasant.

"Come hither, Soa," she said, "and tell me what all this nonsense means about rubies and the People of the Mist."

"Shepherdess," answered Soa, squatting down on the ground before her, "it is not nonsense. The language which I taught you when you were little is that of this people. It is a true tale, though hitherto I have hid it from you and your father, Mavoom, lest Mavoom should seek to win the precious stones and come to his death through them. Listen, Shepherdess," and she repeated the outlines of the story with which she had already made Leonard acquainted, ending thus:

"I told this tale to the White Man because I saw that he was greedy, after the fashion of his race, and my strait was desperate. For this reason I bribed him with the red stone, and with the promise that I would lead him to the land of the People of the Mist, for had I not done so he would never have used his wit or put out his strength to rescue you from the Yellow Devil. Therefore it was also that I marked this paper on your behalf and my own, knowing well that I had no right to speak for you, and that by and by you could refuse to abide by it, though I am bound."

"Frank, at any rate," said Leonard to himself. "What an attorney the old lady would have made!"

"Say, Soa," asked Juanna, "to succeed in the search for these stones is it necessary that I should act a part among your people?"

"I can see no other way," she answered. "But what of that? You are free, and what I promised on your behalf is nothing. Let the White Man go without his reward, it will save him a long journey."

"Attorney!" murmured Leonard in admiration; "she ought to be Attorney-General."

"*Wow!* The wicked old cheat!" put in Otter. "If I had my way I would break her neck, though she is so clever with the big gun."

Juanna took no notice of these asides. For the moment she remained in thought, then looked up smiling.

"Really," she said, "this is a capital legal document. But oh! Mr. Outram, why did you dispel my illusions? You see, I had been making up such a romantic story out of this adventure. You were the knight-errant, and I was the Christian maiden in the hands of the ogre, and when you heard of it you buckled on your armour and started to the rescue. And now you bring me down to the nineteenth century with a run.

128

"It is not knight-errantry, but a commercial transaction: I am in difficulty, but by playing a certain undefined part you believe that I shall be able to help you to secure treasure; therefore you agree to undertake the risk. I am ignorant of what I am to do, for as yet nobody has explained it to me, but you need have no fear, I shall not repudiate, as Soa suggests with so much candour. Certainly I shall try my best to help you in this business, if I can, for you have worked hard and endangered your life, Mr. Outram, and I am sure that you have earned your money, or rather the prospect of it. Really it is all very amusing," and she laughed merrily.

As for Leonard, he sat before her, mad with secret wrath and burning with shame. What a fool he had been thus to expose himself to the shafts of this girl's tongue—this girl, whose beauty was only equalled by her malice! He wished that his hand had withered before he wrote that accursed document. But now the only thing to do was to face it out.

"I am glad that you see me in my true light at last, Miss Rodd," he said. "It simplifies matters. I entered into that agreement because it seemed to give me a remote chance of attaining my end, which is money. It does not quite follow, however, that I should not have attempted your rescue had there been no agreement; but, of course, I cannot expect you to believe that."

"I assure you, Mr. Outram, that I am deeply obliged to you for your caution. It has lifted a great weight from my mind, for if in any way I can help you to obtain possession of the valuables of this People of the Mist I shall have paid off an obligation which at present crushes me."

"We shall have to start early tomorrow morning, so with your permission I think that I will be turning in," said Leonard, springing up with singular alacrity.

Juanna watched him go with innocent eyes, and as he passed she saw by the firelight that his face was like a thunderstorm. "I have made him angry this time," she thought to herself, "and I am glad of it. What business had he to rescue *me* for money? But he is a strange man, and I don't think that I quite understand him. I wonder who Jane Beach is. I suppose that she wants the money. Women generally do, or at least they did in Durban."

Then she spoke aloud: "Soa, come here while I undress, and tell me again all about your meeting with Mr. Outram, and what he said, forgetting nothing. You have put me to shame, Soa, with your talk, and I will never forgive you. Tell me also how I can help to win the treasure of the People of the Mist!"

CHAPTER 16

Misunderstandings

For some days after the acrimonious conversation that has been reported, the relations between Leonard and Juanna were not a little strained, although the necessities of travel brought them into continual contact. Both felt that they had cause of complaint against the other, and both were at heart somewhat ashamed of the part which they had played. Leonard regretted ever having made the agreement with Soa, and Juanna, now that she had cooled down a little, regretted having spoken as she did upon the subject. Her pride was offended; but, after all, how could he know? Besides, he was an adventurer, and it was natural that he should make terms. Doubtless also his anxiety to win fortune had to do with the lady whose name was written in the prayer-book.

Perhaps this lady was only a maiden aunt, but a great desire seized Juanna to know about her; and when such a wish enters the heart of woman it is probable that she will find a means to satisfy it. Having no one else to ask, Juanna sounded Otter, with whom she was on friendly terms, only to find that the subject of Jane Beach did not interest the dwarf. He hazarded a remark, however, that doubtless she was one of the Baas's wives when he lived in his big kraal over the water.

This disgusted Juanna somewhat, but the allusion to a "big kraal" excited the curiosity, of which she had a certain share, and very adroitly she questioned the dwarf concerning it. He rose to the fly without hesitation, and told her that his master had been one of the greatest men in the world, and one of the richest, but that he lost his possessions through the wicked arts of foemen, and was come to this country to seek new ones.

Indeed Otter enlarged upon the theme, and, anxious to extol his beloved chief's worth in the eyes of the Shepherdess, it would not be too much to say that he drew upon his own imagination. Leonard, he declared, had owned country as wide as a horse could gallop across in a day; moreover, he had two hundred tribesmen, heads of families, who fed upon oxen killed for them—twenty oxen a week; and ten principal wives had called him husband. Juanna asked for the titles of the wives, whereon the undefeated Otter gave them all Kaffir names, not neglecting to describe their lineage, personal charms, and the number and sex of their children. The tale took about two hours to tell, and after hearing it Juanna conceived a great respect for Otter, but she saw clearly that if she wished for reliable information she must obtain it from Leonard himself.

It was not till the last day of their journey that Juanna found the opportunity she sought. The voyage had been most prosperous, and they expected to reach the ruined Settlement on the morrow, though whether or not they would find Mr. Rodd there was a matter of anxious conjecture, especially to his daughter. Day after day they rowed and sailed up the great river, camping at night upon its banks, which would have been pleasant had it not been for the mosquitoes. But all this while Leonard and Juanna saw little of each other, though they met often enough. On this particular occasion, however, it chanced that they were journeying in the same boat, alone, except for the rowers.

Possibly Juanna had contrived that it should be so, for as a general rule, in pursuit of his policy of avoiding a disagreeable young person, Leonard travelled with Otter in the first boat, while Juanna was accompanied by Francisco and Soa in the second. To the priest, indeed, she made herself very agreeable, perhaps to show Leonard how charming she could be when she chose. She conversed with him by the hour together as though he were a woman friend, and his melancholy eyes would lighten with pleasure at her talk. Indeed Francisco had something of the feminine in his nature; his very gentleness was womanly, and his slight stature, delicate hands and features heightened this impression. In face he was not unlike Juanna herself, and as time went on the resemblance seemed to grow. Had he been arrayed in a woman's loose attire, it would have been easy to mistake one for the other in the dusk, although she was the taller of the two.

The accident of his profession caused Juanna to admit Francisco to an intimacy which she would have withheld from any other man. She forgot, or did not understand, that she was playing a dangerous game—that after all he was a man, and that the heart of a man beat beneath his cassock. Nobody could be more charming in her manner or more subtle in her mind than Juanna, yet day by day she did not hesitate to display all her strength before the unfortunate young priest, which, in addition to her beauty, made her somewhat irresistible, at any rate on the Zambezi. Friendship and ignorance of the world were doubtless at the bottom of this reprehensible conduct, but it is also possible that unconscious pique had something to do with it. She was determined to show Leonard that she was not always a disagreeable person whom it was well to avoid, or at least that others did not think so. That all these airs and graces might have a tragic effect upon Francisco never occurred to her till too late.

Well, for once the order of things was changed; Leonard and Juanna sat side by side in the first boat. The evening was lovely, they glided slowly by the reed-fringed bank, watching the long lights play upon the surface of the lonely river, listening to the whistling wings of the countless wildfowl overhead, and counting the herds of various game that roamed upon the plains beyond.

For a while neither of them spoke much. Occasionally Juanna would call her companion's attention to some water-flower or to a great fish darting from the oars, and he would answer by a word or nod. His heart was wroth with the girl, as Otter would have said; he wondered why she had come with him—because she was tired of the priest perhaps. He wished her away, and yet he would have been sorry enough had she gone.

For her part Juanna desired to make him speak, and did not know how to break through his moody silence. Suddenly she leaned back in the boat and began to sing in a rich contralto voice that moved him. He had never heard her sing before, had never heard any good singing for many years indeed, and he was fond of singing. The song she sang was a Portuguese love-song, very tender and passionate, addressed by a bereaved lover to his dead mistress, and she put much expression into it. Presently she ceased, and he noticed that her beautiful eyes were full of tears. So she could feel!

"That is too sad," she said with a little laugh, and then burst into a Kaffir boat-song, of which the Settlement natives, joyous in the prospect of once more seeing their home, took up the chorus gleefully. Presently she wearied of the boat-chant. "I am tiring you," she said; "I dare say that you do not care for singing."

"On the contrary, Miss Rodd, I am very fond of it. Your voice is good, if you will allow me to say so, and it has been trained. I do not quite understand how you can have had the opportunity to learn so many things—music, for instance."

"I suppose, Mr. Outram, you think that I should be a sort of savage by rights; but as a matter of fact, although we have lived on the Zambezi, I have had some chances. There is always a certain amount of trade on the river, by means of which we often obtain books and other things, and are brought into occasional contact with European merchants, travellers, and missionaries. Then my father is a gently born and well-educated man, though circumstances have caused him to spend his life in these wild places. He was a scholar in his day and he has taught me a good deal, and I have picked up more by reading. Also, for nearly three years I was at a good school in Durban and did my best to improve myself there. I did not wish to grow up wild because I lived among wild people."

"Indeed, that explains the miracle. And do you like living among savages?"

"I have liked it well enough hitherto, but this last adventure has sickened me. Oh! it was dreadful. Had I not been very strong I could never have endured it; a nervous woman would have been driven mad. Yes, I have liked it well enough; I have always looked upon it as a preparation for life. I think that the society of nature is the best education for the society of man, since until you understand and are in sympathy with the one, you cannot really understand the other. Now I should like to go to Europe and see the world and its civilisations, for I know from what stuff they were evolved. But perhaps I never shall; at any rate, I have to find my dear father first," and she sighed.

Leonard made no answer; he was thinking.

"And you, Mr. Outram, do *you* care for this life?"

"I!" he exclaimed bitterly. "Like yourself, Miss Rodd, I am the victim of circumstances and must make the best of them. As I told you I am a penniless adventurer seeking my fortune in the rough places of the earth. Of course I might earn a livelihood in England, but that is of no use to me; I must win wealth, and a great deal of it."

"What is the good?" she said. "Is there any object in wearing out one's life by trying to grow rich?"

"That depends. I have an object, one which I have sworn to fulfil."

She looked at him inquiringly.

"Miss Rodd, I will tell you. My brother, who died of fever some weeks ago, and I were the last male survivors of a very ancient house. We were born to great prospects, or at least he was; but owing to the conduct of our father, everything was lost to us, and the old house, which had been ours for centuries, went to the hammer. That was some seven years ago, when I was a man of three-and-twenty. We swore that we would try to retrieve those fortunes—not for ourselves so much, but for the sake of the family—and came to Africa to do it. My brother is dead, but I inherit the oath and continue the quest, however hopeless it may be. And now, perhaps, you will understand why I signed a certain document."

"Yes," she said, "I understand now. It is a strange history. But tell me, have you no relations left?"

"One, I believe, if she still lives—a maiden aunt, my mother's sister."

"Is she Jane Beach?" she asked quickly. "Forgive me, but I saw that name in the prayer-book."

"No," he said, "she is not Jane Beach."

Juanna hesitated; then curiosity and perhaps other feelings overcame her, and she asked straight out—

"Who is Jane Beach?"

Leonard looked at Juanna and remembered all that he had suffered at her hands. It was impertinent of her to ask such a question, but since she chose to do so she should have an answer. Doubtless she supposed that he was in love with herself, doubtless her conduct was premeditated and aimed at the repression of his hopes. He would show her that there were other women in the world, and that one of them at any rate had not thought so poorly of him. It was foolish conduct on his part, but then people suffering under unmerited snubs, neglect, and mockery at the hands of a lady they admire are apt to lose their judgment and do foolish things. So he answered:

"Jane Beach is the lady to whom I was engaged."

"I guessed it," she replied with a smile and a shiver. "I guessed it when I saw that you always carried the prayer-book about with you."

"You forget, Miss Rodd, that the prayer-book contains an agreement which might become valuable."

Juanna took no heed of his sarcasm, she was too intent on other thoughts.

"And are you engaged to her now?"

"No, I suppose not. Her father broke off the match when we lost our fortunes."

"She must have been very sorry?"

"Yes, she was very sorry."

"How interesting! You must not think me curious, Mr. Outram, but I have never come across a love affair—that is a *white* love affair—out of a novel. Of course she often writes to you?"

"I have never heard from her since I left England."

"Indeed! Surely she might have written or sent a message?"

"I suppose that her father forbade it," Leonard answered; but in his heart he also thought that Jane might have written or sent a message, and could well guess why none had come.

"Ah! her father. Tell me, was she very beautiful?"

"She was the loveliest woman that I ever saw—except one who is sitting at my side," he added to himself.

"And do you love her very much?"

"Yes, I loved her very much."

If Juanna heard the change of tense she took no note of it; it was such a little thing, only one letter. And yet what a vast gulf there is between *love* and *loved*! It is measureless. Still, most people have crossed it in their lives, some of them more than once. He told her the exact truth, but after a woman's fashion she added to the truth. He said that he had loved Jane Beach, and she did not doubt that he still loved her more than ever. How was she to know that the image of this faraway and hateful Jane was fading from his mind, to be replaced by that of a certain present Juanna? She took it all for granted, and filled in the details with a liberal hand and in high colours.

Juanna took it all for granted. Again she shivered, and her lips turned grey with pain. She understood now that she had loved him ever since the night when they first met in the slave camp. It was her love, as yet unrecognised, which, transforming her, had caused her to behave so badly. It had been dreadful to her to think that she should be thrust upon this man in a mock marriage; it was worse to know that he had entered on her rescue not for her own sake, but in the hope of winning wealth. In the moment of her loss Juanna learned for the first time what she had gained. She had played and lost, and she could never throw those dice again; it was begun and finished.

So Juanna thought and felt. A little more experience of the world might have taught her differently. But she had no experience, and in such novels as she had read the hero seldom varied in the pursuit of his first love, or turned to look upon *another*. Ah! if all heroes and heroines acted up to this golden rule, what an uncommonly dull world it would be!

Juanna gathered her energies, and spoke in a low steady voice. "Mr. Outram," she said, "I am so much obliged to you for telling me all this. It interests me a great deal, and I earnestly hope that Soa's tale of treasure will turn out to be true, and that you may win it by my help. It will be some slight return for all that you have done for me. Yes, I hope that you will win it, and buy back your home, and after your years of toil and danger live there in honour, and happiness, and—love, as you deserve to do. And now I ask you to forgive me my behaviour, my rudeness, and my bitter speeches. It has been shameful, I know; perhaps you will make some excuse for me when you remember all that I have gone through. My nerves were shaken, I was not myself—I acted like a half-wild minx. There, that is all."

As she spoke Juanna began to draw the signet-ring from her left hand. But she never completed the act. It was his gift to her, the only outward link between her and the man whom she had lost—why should she part with it? It reminded her of so much. She knew now that this mock marriage was in a sense a true one; that is, so far as she was concerned, for from that hour she had indeed given her spirit into his keeping—not herself, but her better half and her love; and those solemn words over her in that dreadful place and time had consecrated the gift. It was nothing, it meant nothing; yet on her it should be binding, though not on him. Yes, all her life she would remain as true to him in mind and act as though she had indeed become his wife on that night of fear. To do so would be her only happiness, she thought, though it is strange that in her sorrow she should turn for comfort to this very event, the mere mention of which had moved her to scorn and bitterness. But so it was, and so let it be.

Leonard saw the look upon her face; he had never seen anything quite like it before. With astonishment he heard her gentle words, and something of the meaning of the look and words came home to him; at any rate he understood that she was suffering. She was changed in his sight, he no longer felt bitter towards her. He loved her; might it not be that she also loved him, and that here was the key to her strange conduct? Once and for all he would settle the matter; he would tell her that Jane Beach had ceased to be more than a tender memory to him, and that she had become all.

"Juanna," he said, addressing her by her Christian name for the first time.

But there, as it was fated, the sentence began and ended, for at that moment a canoe shot alongside of them, and Francisco's voice was heard hailing them through the fog.

"Peter says that you have passed the camping place, senora. He did not stop you because he thought that you knew it well."

"It was the mist, Father," Juanna answered with a little laugh. "We have lost ourselves in a mist."

A few minutes and they were on the bank, and Leonard's declaration remained unspoken. Nor did he make any attempt to renew it. It seemed to him that Juanna had built a wall between them which he could not climb. From that evening forward her whole attitude towards him changed. She no longer angered him by bitter words; indeed, she was gentleness itself, and nothing could be kindlier or more friendly and open than her manner, but there it began and ended. Once or twice, indeed, he attempted some small advance, with the result that instantly she seemed to freeze—to become cold and hard as marble. He could not understand her, he feared her somewhat, and his pride took alarm. At the least he could keep his feelings to himself, he need not expose them to be trampled upon by this incomprehensible girl.

So, although they were destined to live side by side for months, rarely out of each other's sight or thoughts, he went his way and she went hers. But the past and secret trouble left its mark on both. Leonard became sterner, more silent, watchful, and suspicious. Juanna grew suddenly from a girl into a woman of presence and great natural dignity. She did not often laugh during those months as had been her wont, she only smiled, sadly enough at times. Her thoughts would not let her laugh, for they were of what her life might have been had no such person as Jane Beach existed, and of what it must be because of Jane Beach. Indeed this unknown Jane took a great hold of her mind—she haunted her. Juanna pictured her in a dozen different shapes of beauty, endowed with many varying charms, and hated each phantasm worse than the last.

Still, for a while she would set it up as a rival, and try to outmatch its particular fancied grace or loveliness—a strange form of jealousy which at length led Otter to remark that the Shepherdess was not one woman but twenty women, and, therefore, bewitched and to be avoided. But these fits only took her from time to time. For the most part she moved among them a grave and somewhat stately young lady, careful of many things, fresh and lovely to look upon, a mystery to her white companions, and to the natives little short of a goddess.

But wherever Juanna moved two shadows went with her—her secret passion and the variable image of that far-off English lady who had robbed her of its fruit.

137

CHAPTER 17

The Death of Mavoom

One more day's journeying brought the party to the ruined Settlement, which they found in much the same condition as the Arabs had left it a few weeks before. Fortunately the destruction was not nearly so great as it appeared. The inside of the house, indeed, was burnt out, but its walls still remained intact, also many of the huts of the natives were still standing.

Messengers who left the canoes at dawn had spread the news of the rescue and return of the Shepherdess among the people of the neighbouring kraals, who flocked by scores to the landing-place. With these were at least a hundred of Mr. Rodd's own people, who had escaped the clutches of the slaver-traders by hiding, absence, and various other accidents, and now returned to greet his daughter and their own relatives as they would have greeted one risen from the grave. Indeed the welcome accorded to Juanna was most touching. Men, women, and children ran to her, the men saluting her with guttural voices and uplifted arms, the women and children gesticulating, chattering, and kissing her dress and hand.

Waving them aside impatiently, Juanna asked the men if anything had been seen or heard of her father. They answered, "No." Some of their number had started up the river to search for him on the same day when she was captured, but they had not returned, and no tidings had come from them or him.

"Do not be alarmed," said Leonard, seeing the distress and anxiety written on her face; "doubtless he has gone further than he anticipated, and the men have not been able to find him."

"I fear that something has happened to him," she answered; "he should have been back by now: he promised to return within the fortnight."

By this time the story of the capture and destruction of the slave camp was spread abroad among the people by the rescued men, and the excitement rose to its height. Otter, seeing a favourable opportunity to trumpet his master's fame, swaggered to and fro through the crowd shaking a spear and chanting Leonard's praises after the Zulu fashion.

"*Wow!*" he said, "*wow!* Look at him, ye people, and be astonished.

"Look at him, the White Elephant, and hear his deeds.

"In the night he fell upon them.

"He fell upon them, the armed men in a fenced place.

"He did it alone: no one helped him but a black monkey and a woman with a shaking hand.

"He beguiled them with a tongue of honey, he smote them with a spear of iron.

"He won the Shepherdess from the midst of them to be a wife to him.

"He satisfied the Yellow Devil, he satisfied him with gold.

"The praying man prayed over them, then strife arose.

"Their greatest warrior gave him battle, he broke him with his fist.

"Then the Monkey played his tricks, and the Shaking Hand made a great noise, a noise of thunder.

"They fell dead, they fell dead in heaps.

"The fire roared behind them, in front of them the bullets hailed.

"They cried like women, but the fire stayed not; it licked up their strength.

"Ashes are all that is left of them; they are dead, the armed men.

"No more shall they bring desolation; the day of slavery is gone by.

"Who did it? He did it, the terrible lion, the black-maned lion with the white face.

"He gave the slavers to the sword; he doomed their captain to death.

"He loosened the irons of the captives. Now they shall eat the bread of freedom.

"Praise him, ye people, who broke the strength of the oppressor.

"Praise him, the Shepherd of the Shepherdess, who led her from the house of the wicked.

"Praise him, ye Children of Mavoom, in whose hands are death and life.

"No such deeds have been told of in the land. Praise him, the Deliverer, who gives you back your children!"

"Ay, praise him!" said Juanna, who was standing by. "Praise him, children of my father, since but for him none of us would see the light today."

At this juncture Leonard himself arrived upon the scene, just in time to hear Juanna's words. All the people of the Settlement took up the cry, and hundreds of other natives collected there joined in it. They rushed towards him shouting: "Praise to thee, Shepherd of the Shepherdess! Praise to thee, Deliverer!"

Then Leonard, in a fury, caught hold of Otter, vowing that if he dared to say another word he would instantly break his neck, and the tumult ceased. But from that day forward he was known among the natives as "The Deliverer," and by no other name.

That evening, as Leonard, Juanna, and the priest sat at meat within the walls of the Settlement-house, with the plunder of the slave camp piled about them, talking anxiously of the fate of Mr. Rodd and wondering if anything could be done to discover his whereabouts, they heard a stir among the natives without. At this moment Otter rushed in, crying: "Mavoom has come!"

Instantly they sprang to their feet and ran outside the house, headed by Juanna. There, borne on the shoulders of six travel-worn men, and followed by a crowd of natives, they saw a litter, upon which lay the figure of a man covered with blankets.

"Oh! he is dead!" said Juanna, stopping suddenly, and pressing her hands to her heart.

For a moment Leonard thought that she was right. Before he could speak, however, they heard a feeble voice calling to the men who carried the litter to be more careful in their movements, and once more Juanna sprang forward, crying, "Father! Father!"

Then the bearers brought their burden into the house and set it down upon the floor. Leonard, looking, saw before him a tall and handsome man of about fifty years of age, and saw also by many unmistakable signs that he was at the point of death.

"Juanna," gasped her father, "is that you? Then you have escaped. Thank God! Now I can die happy."

It would serve little purpose to set out in detail the broken conversation which followed, but by degrees Leonard learnt the story. It seemed that Mr. Rodd was disappointed in his purpose of purchasing the hoard of ivory which he went out to seek, and, unwilling to return empty-handed, pushed on up the river with the hope of obtaining more. In this he failed also, and had just begun his homeward journey when he was met by the party which Soa despatched, and heard the terrible tidings of the abduction of his daughter by Pereira. It was nightfall when the messengers arrived, and too dark to travel.

For a while Mr. Rodd sat brooding over the news of this crush-ing disaster, perhaps the most fearful that could come to a father's ears; then he did what he was but too prone to do—flew for refuge to the bottle.

When he had drunk enough to destroy his judgment, he rose, and insisted upon continuing their march through the inky darkness of the night. In vain did his men remonstrate, saying that the road was rocky and full of danger. He would take no denial; indeed, he vowed that if they refused to come he would shoot them. So they started, Mr. Rodd leading the way, while his people stumbled after him through trees and over rocks as best they might.

The march was not a long one, however, for presently the men heard an oath and a crash, and their master vanished; nor could they find him till the dawn came to give them light. Then they discovered that they had halted upon the edge of a small but precipitous cliff, and at the bottom of the donga beneath lay Mavoom—not dead, indeed, but senseless, and with three ribs and his right ankle broken. For some days they nursed him there, till at length he decided upon being car-ried forward in a litter. So notwithstanding his sufferings, which were intense, they bore him homewards by short stages, till ultimately they reached the Settlement.

That night Leonard examined Mr. Rodd's injuries, and found that they were fatal; indeed, mortification had already set in about the re-gion of the broken ribs. Still he lived awhile.

On the following morning the dying man sent for Leonard. Enter-ing the room, he found him lying on the floor, his head supported in his daughter's lap, while the priest Francisco prayed beside him. He suffered no pain now, for when mortification begins pain passes, and his mind was quite clear.

"Mr. Outram," he said, "I have learnt all the story of the taking of the slave camp and your rescue of my daughter. It was the pluckiest thing that I ever heard of, and I only wish that I had been there to help in it."

"Don't speak of it!" said Leonard. "Perhaps you have heard also that I did it for a consideration."

"Yes, they told me that too, and small blame to you. If only that old fool Soa had let me into the secret of those rubies, I would have had a try for them years ago, as of course you will when I am gone. Well, I hope that you may get them. But I have no time to talk of rubies, for death has caught me at last, through my own fault as usual. If you ever take a drop, Outram, be warned by me and give it up; but you don't look as if you did; you look as I used to, before I learnt to tackle a bottle of rum at a sitting.

"Now listen, comrade, I am in a hole, not about myself, for that must have come sooner or later, and it does not much matter when the world is rid of a useless fellow like me; but about my girl here. What is to become of her? I have not got a cent; those cursed slavers have cleared me out, and she has no friend. How should she have, when I have been thirty years away from England?

"Look here, I am going to do the only thing I can do. I am going to leave my daughter in your charge, though it is rough on you, and as you deal with her, so may Heaven deal with you! I understand that there was some ceremony of marriage between you down yonder. I don't know how you take that, either of you, or how far the matter will go when I am dead. But if it goes any way at all, I trust to your honour, as an English gentleman, to repeat that ceremony the first time you come to a civilised country. If you do not care for each other, however, then Juanna must shift, as other women have to do, poor things. She can look after herself, and I suppose that her face will help her to a husband some time. There is one thing: though she hasn't a pound, she is the best girl that ever stepped, and of as good blood as you can be. There is no older family than the Rodds in Lincolnshire, and she is the last of them that I know of; also, her mother was well-born, although she was a Portugee.

"And now, do you accept the trust?"

"I would gladly," answered Leonard, "but how can I? I propose to go after these rubies. Would it not be better that Father Francisco here should take your daughter to the coast? I have a little money which is at her disposal."

"No," answered the dying man with energy, "I will only trust her to you. If you want to search for these rubies, and you would be a fool not to, she must accompany you—that is all. I know that you will look after her, and if the worst comes to the worst, she has a medicine to protect herself with, the same that she so nearly used in the slave camp. Now, what do you say?"

Leonard thought for a moment, while the dying man watched his face anxiously.

"It is a heavy responsibility," he said, "and the circumstances make it an awkward one. But I accept it. I will take care of her as though she were my wife, or—my daughter."

"Thank you for that," answered Rodd. "I believe you, and as to the relationship, you will settle that for yourselves. And now goodbye.

I like you. I wish that we had known one another before I got into trouble at home, became a Zambezi trader, and—a drunkard."

Leonard took the hand which Mr. Rodd lifted with a visible effort, and when he released it, it fell heavily, like the hand of a dead man. Then, as he turned to go, he glanced at Juanna's face, but could make nothing of it, for it was as the face of a sphinx.

There the girl sat, her back resting against the wall, her dying father's head pillowed upon her knee, motionless as if carved in stone. She was staring straight before her with eyes wide open and curved lips set apart, as though she were about to speak and suddenly had been stricken to silence. So still was she that Leonard could scarcely note any movement of her breast. Even her eyelids had ceased to quiver, and the very pallor of her face seemed fixed like that of a waxen image. He wondered what she was thinking of; but even had she been willing to bare her thoughts to him, it is doubtful whether she could have made them intelligible. Her mind was confused, but two things struggled one against the other within it, the sense of loss and the sense of shame.

The father whom, notwithstanding his faults, she loved dearly, who indeed had been her companion, her teacher, her playmate and her friend, the dearest she had known, lay dying before her eyes, and with his last breath he consigned her to the care of the man whom she loved, and from whom, as she believed, she was for ever separated. Would there, then, be no end to the obligations under which she laboured at the hands of this stranger, who had suddenly taken possession of her life? And what fate was on her that she should thus be forced into false positions, whence there was no escape?

Did she wish to escape even? Juanna knew not; but as she sat there with a sphinx-like face, trouble and doubt, and many another fear and feeling, took so firm a hold of her that at length her mind, bewildered with its own tumult, lost its grip of present realities, and sought refuge in dreams which he could not disentangle. No wonder, then, that Leonard failed to guess her thoughts, as she watched him go from the death-bed.

Mr. Rodd died peacefully that evening, and on the following afternoon they buried him, Francisco performing the service. Three more days passed before Leonard had any conversation with Juanna, who moved about the place, pale, self-contained, and silent. Nor would he have spoken to her then had she not taken the initiative.

"Mr. Outram," she said, "when do you propose to start upon this journey?"

"Really, I do not know. I am not sure that I shall start at all. It depends upon you. You see I am responsible for you now, and I can scarcely reconcile it with my conscience to take on you such a wild-goose chase."

"Please do not talk like that," she answered. "If it will simplify matters I may as well tell you at once that I have made up my mind to go."

"You cannot unless I go too," he answered smiling.

"You are wrong there," Juanna replied defiantly. "I can, and what is more, I will, and Soa shall guide me. It is you who cannot go without me—that is, if Soa tells the truth.

"For good or evil we are yoked together in this matter, Mr. Outram, so it is useless for us to try to pull different ways. Before he died, my dear father told you his views plainly, and even if there were no other considerations involved, such as that of the agreement—for, whatever you may think to the contrary, woman have some sense of honour, Mr. Outram—I would not disregard his wishes. Besides, what else are we to do? We are both adventurers now, and both penniless, or pretty nearly so. Perhaps if we succeed in finding this treasure, and it is sufficiently large, you will be generous and give me a share of it, say five per cent., on which to support my declining years," and she turned and left him.

"Beginning to show temper again," said Leonard to himself. "I will ask Francisco what he thinks of it."

Of late, things had gone a little better between Leonard and the priest. Not that the former had as yet any complete confidence in the latter. Still, he understood now that Francisco was a man of honest mind and gentle instincts, and naturally in this dilemma he turned to seek for counsel to his only white companion. Francisco listened to the story quietly; indeed, for the most part it was already known to him.

"Well," he said, when Leonard had finished, "I suppose that you must go. The Senora Juanna is not a young lady to change her mind when once she has made it up, and if you were to refuse to start, mark my words, she would make the expedition by herself, or try to do so. As to this story of treasure, and the possibility of winning it, I can only say that it seems strange enough to be true, and that the undertaking is so impracticable that it will probably be successfully accomplished."

"Hum!" said Leonard, "sounds a little paradoxical, but after that slave camp business, like you I am inclined to believe in paradoxes. And now, Father, what do you propose to do?"

"I? to accompany you, of course, if you will allow me. I am a priest and will play the part of chaperon, if I can do nothing else," he added with a smile.

Leonard whistled and asked, "Why on earth do you mix your-self up in such a doubtful business? You have all your life before you; you are able, and may make a career for yourself in religion; there is nothing for you to gain by this journey; on the contrary, it may bring you death—or," he added with meaning, "sorrow which cannot be forgotten."

"My life and death are in the hand of God," the priest answered humbly. "He appointed the beginning and He will appoint the end. As for that sorrow which cannot be forgotten, what if it is already with me?" And he touched his breast and looked up.

The eyes of the two men met, and they understood each other.

"Why don't you go away and try to forget her?" said Leonard.

The speech was blunt, but Francisco did not resent it.

"I do not go," he answered, "because it would be useless. So far as I am concerned the mischief is done; for her there is none to fear. While I stay it is possible that I may be able to do her some service, feeble as I am. I have sinned a great sin, but she does not know, and will never know it while I live, for you are a man of honour and will tell her nothing, and she has no eyes to see. What am I to her? I am a priest—no man. I am like a woman friend, and as such she is fond of me. No, I have sinned against Heaven, against myself, and her, and you. Alas! who could help it? She was like an angel in that Inferno, so kind, so sweet, so lovely, and the heart is evil."

"Why do you say that you sinned against me, Francisco? As to the rules of your Church, I have my own opinion of them. Still, there they are, and perhaps they prick your conscience. But what harm have you done to me?"

"I told you," he answered, "on the second night after the slave camp was burnt, that I believed you to be man and wife. I believe it yet, and have I not sinned doubly therefore in worshipping a woman who is wedded? Still, I pray that as you are one before Heaven and the Church, so you may become one in heart and deed. And when this is so, as I think that it will be, cherish her, Outram, for there is no such woman in the world, and for you she will turn the earth to heaven."

"She might turn it to the other place; such things have happened," said Leonard moodily. Then he stretched out his arm and grasped the priest's delicate hand. "You are a true gentleman," he added, "and I am a fool. I saw something of all this and I suspected you. As for the marriage, there is none, and the lady cares nothing for me; if anything, she dislikes me, and I do not wonder at it: most women would under the circumstances. But whatever befalls, I honour you and always shall honour you. I must go this journey, it is laid on me that I should, and she insists upon going also, more from perversity than for any other reason, I fancy. So you are coming too: well, we will do our best to protect her, both of us, and the future must look to itself."

"Thank you for your words," Francisco answered gently, and turned away, understanding that Leonard thought himself his companion in misfortune.

When the Father had gone, Leonard stood for a while musing upon the curiously tangled web in which he found himself involved. Here he was, committed to a strange and desperate enterprise. Nor was this all, for about him were other complications, totally different from those which might be expected in connection with such a mediaeval adventure, complications which, though they are frequent enough in the civilised life of men, were scarcely to be looked for in the wilds of Africa, and amidst savages. Among his companions were his ward, who chanced also to be the lady whom he loved and desired to make his wife, but who, as he thought, cared nothing for him; and a priest who was enamoured platonically of the same lady, and yet wished, with rare self-sacrifice, to bring about her union with another man. Here were materials enough for a romance, leaving the journey and the fabled treasure out of it; only then the scene should be laid elsewhere.

Leonard laughed aloud as he thought of these things; it was so curious that all this should be heaped upon him at once, so inartistic and yet so like life, in which the great events are frequently crowded together without sense of distance or proportion.

But even as he laughed, he remembered that this was no joking matter for anybody concerned, unless it were Juanna. Alas! already she was more to him than any treasure, and, as he thought, less attainable. Well, there it was, he accepted it as it stood. She had entered into his life, whether for good or for evil remained to be seen. He had no desire to repeat the experiment of his youth—to wear out his heart and exhaust himself in efforts to attain happiness, which might after all turn to wormwood on his lips. This time things should take their chance. The business of life remained to him, and he would follow it, for that is the mission of man. Its happiness must look to itself, for that is the gift of Heaven, after which it is useless to seek and to strive.

Meantime he could find time to pity Francisco, the priest with so noble a heart.

CHAPTER 18

Soa Shows Her Teeth

Three months had passed since that day, when Juanna declared her unalterable determination to accompany Leonard upon his search for the treasures of the People of the Mist. It was evening, and a party of travellers were encamped on the side of a river that ran through a great and desolate plain. They were a small party, three white people, namely, Leonard, Francisco, and Juanna, fifteen of the Settlement men under the leadership of Peter—that same headman who had been rescued from the slave camp—the dwarf, Otter, and Juanna's old nurse, Soa.

For twelve weeks they had travelled almost without intermission with Soa for their guide, steering continually northward and westward. First they followed the course of the river in canoes for ten days or more; then, leaving the main stream, they paddled for three weeks up that of a tributary called Mavuae, which ran for many miles along the foot of a great range of mountains named Manganja. Here they made but slow progress because of the frequent rapids, which necessitated the porterage of the canoes over broken ground, and for considerable distances. At length they came to a rapid which was so long and so continuous that regretfully enough they were obliged to abandon the canoes altogether and proceed on foot.

The dangers of their water journey had been many, but they were nothing compared with those that now environed them, and in addition to bodily perils, they must face the daily and terrible fatigue of long marches through an unknown country, cumbered as they were with arms and other absolutely necessary baggage. The country through which they were now passing was named Marengi, a land uninhabited by man, the home of herds of countless game.

On they went northward and upward through a measureless waste; plain succeeded plain in endless monotony, distance gave place to distance, and ever there were more beyond.

Gradually the climate grew colder: they were traversing a portion of the unexplored plateau that separates southern from central Africa. Its loneliness was awful, and the bearers began to murmur, saying that they had reached the end of the world, and were walking over its edge. Indeed they had only two comforts in this part of their undertaking; the land lay so high that none of them were stricken by fever, and they could not well miss the road, which, if Soa was to be believed, ran along the banks of the river that had its source in the territories of the People of the Mist.

The adventures that befell them were endless, but it is not proposed to describe them in detail. Once they starved for three days, being unable to find game. On another occasion they fell in with a tribe of bushmen who harassed them with poisoned arrows, killing two of their best men, and were only prevented from annihilating them through the terror inspired by their firearms, which they took for magical instruments.

Escaping from the bushmen, they entered a forest country which teemed with antelope and also with lions, that night by night they must keep at bay as best they could. Then came several days' march through a plain strewn with sharp stones which lamed most of the party; and after this eighty or a hundred miles of dreary rolling veldt, clothed with rank grass just now brown with the winter frosts, that caught their feet at every step.

Now at length they halted on the boundary of the land of the People of the Mist. There before them, not more than a mile away, towered a huge cliff or wall of rock, stretching across the plain like a giant step, far as the eye could reach, and varying from seven hundred to a thousand feet in height. Down the surface of this cliff the river flowed in a series of beautiful cascades.

Before they had finished their evening meal of buck's flesh the moon was up, and by its light the three white people stared hopelessly at this frowning natural fortification, wondering if they could climb it, and wondering also what terrors awaited them upon its further side. They were silent that night, for a great weariness had overcome them, and if the truth must be known, all three of them regretted that they had ever undertaken this mad adventure.

Leonard glanced to the right, where, some fifty paces away, the Settlement men were crouched round the fire. They also were silent, and it was easy to see that the heart was out of them.

"Won't somebody say something?" said Juanna at last with a rather pathetic attempt at playfulness. How could she be cheerful, poor girl, when her feet were sore and her head was aching, and she wished that she were dead, almost?

"Yes," answered Leonard, "I will say that I admire your pluck. I should not have thought it possible for any young lady to have gone through the last two months, and 'come out smiling' at the end of them."

"Oh, I am quite happy. Don't trouble about me," she said, laughing as merrily as though there were no such things as sore feet and headaches in the world.

"Are you?" said Leonard, "then I envy you, that is all. Here comes old Soa, and Otter after her. I wonder what is the matter now. Something disagreeable, I suppose."

Soa arrived and squatted down in front of them, her tall spare form and somewhat sullen face looking more formidable than usual in the moonlight. Otter was beside her, and though he stood and she sat, their heads were almost on a level.

"What is it, Soa?" said Leonard carelessly.

"Deliverer," she answered, for all the natives knew him now by this name, "some months ago, when you were digging for gold yonder, in the Place of Graves, I made a bargain with you, and we set the bargain down on paper. In that paper I promised that if you rescued my mistress I would lead you to the land were precious stones were to be won, and I gave you one of those stones in earnest. You saved my mistress, Mavoom her father died, and the time came when I must fulfil my promise. For my own part I would not have fulfilled it, for I only made it that promise hoping to deceive you. But my mistress yonder refused to listen to me.

"'No,' she said, 'that which you have sworn on my behalf and your own must be carried out. If you will not carry it out, go away, Soa, for I have done with you.'

"Then, Deliverer, rather than part with her whom I loved, and whom I had nursed from a babe, I yielded. And now you stand upon the borders of the country of my people. Say, are you minded to cross them, Deliverer?"

"What else did I come for, Soa?" he asked.

"Nay, I know not. You came out of the folly of your heart, to satisfy the desire of your heart. Listen, that tale I told you is true, and yet I did not tell you all the truth. Beyond that cliff live a people of great stature, and very fierce; a people whose custom it is to offer up strangers to their gods. Enter there, and they will kill you thus."

"What do you mean, woman?" asked Leonard.

"I mean that if you hold your life dear, or her life," and she pointed to Juanna, "you will turn with the first light and go back whence you came. It is true that the stones are there, but death shall be the reward of him who strives to steal them."

"I must say this is cheerful," replied Leonard. "What did you mean, then, by all that story you told me about a plan that you had to win the treasures of this people? Are you a liar, Soa?"

"I have said that all I told you was true," she answered sullenly.

"Very well, then, I have come a good many hundred miles to put it to the proof, nor am I going to turn back now. You can leave me one and all if you like, but I shall go on. I will not be made a fool of in this way."

"None of us have any wish to be made fools of, Mr. Outram," said Juanna gently; "and, speaking for myself, I would far rather die at once than attempt a return journey just at present. So now, Soa, perhaps you will stop croaking and tell us definitely what we must do to conciliate these charming countrymen of yours, whom we have come so far to spoil. Remember," she added with a flash of her grey eyes, "I am not to be played with by you, Soa. In this matter the Deliverer's interests are my interests, and his ends my ends. Together we stand or fall, together we live or die, and that shall be an unhappy hour for you, Soa, when you attempt to desert or betray us."

"It is well, Shepherdess," she answered, "your will is my will, for I love you alone in the world, and all the rest I hate," and she glared at Leonard and Otter. "You are my father, and my mother, and my child, and where you are, in death or in life, there is my home. Let us go then among this people of mine, there to perish miserably, so that the Deliverer may seek to glut himself with wealth.

"Listen; this is the law of my people, or this was their law when I left them forty years ago: That every stranger who passes through their gates should be offered as a sacrifice to Aca the mother if the time of his coming should be in summer, and to Jal the son if the time of his coming be in winter, for the Mist-dwellers do not love strangers. But there is a prophecy among my people which tells, when many generations have gone by, that Aca the mother, and Jal the son, shall return to the land which once they ruled, clothed in the flesh of men. And the shape of Aca shall be such a shape as yours, Shepherdess, and the shape of Jal shall be as is the shape of this black dog of a dwarf, whom when first I saw him in my folly I deemed immortal and divine. Then the mother and the son shall rule in the land, and its kings shall cease from kingship, and the priests of the Snake shall be their servants, and with them shall come peace and prosperity that do not pass away.

"Shepherdess, you know the tongue of the People of the Mist, for when you were little I taught it to you, because to me it is the most beautiful of tongues. You know the song also, the holy Song of Re-arising, that shall be on the lips of Aca when she comes again, and which I, being the daughter of the high-priest, learned, with many another secret, before I was doomed to be a bride to the Snake and fled, fearing my doom. Now come apart with me, Shepherdess, and you, Black One, come also, that I may teach you your lesson of what you shall do when we meet the squadrons of the People of the Mist."

Juanna rose to obey her, followed by Otter, grumbling, for he hated the old woman as much as she hated him, and, moreover, he did not take kindly to this notion of masquerading as a god, or, indeed, to the prospect of a lengthened sojourn amongst his adoring, but from all accounts somewhat truculent, worshippers. Before they went, however, Leonard spoke.

"I have heard you, Soa," he said, "and I do not like your words, for they show me that your heart is fierce and evil. Yes, though you love the Shepherdess, your heart is evil. Now hear me. Should you dare to play us false, whatever may befall us, be sure of this, that moment you die. Go!"

"Spare your threats, Deliverer," answered Soa haughtily. "I shall not betray you, because to do so would be to betray the Shepherdess. But are you then a fool that you think I should fear death at your hands, who tomorrow with a word could give you all to torment? Pray, Deliverer, that the hour may not be near when you shall rejoice to die by the bullet with which you threaten me, so that you may escape worse things." And she turned and went.

"I am not nervous," said Leonard to Francisco, "but that she-devil frightens me. If it were not for Juanna, she would cause us to be murdered on the first possible opportunity, and if only she can secure her safety, I believe that she will do it yet."

"And I believe that she is a witch, Outram," answered the priest with fervour, "a servant of the Evil One, such as are written of in the Scriptures. Last night I saw her praying to her gods; she did not know that I was near, for the place was lonely, but I saw her and I never wish to see anything so horrible again. I will tell you why she hates us all so much, Outram. She is jealous, because the senora— does not hate us. That woman's heart is wicked, wickedness was born in her, yet, as none are altogether evil, she has one virtue, her love of the senora. She is husbandless and childless, for even among the black people, as I have learnt from the Settlement men, all have

151

feared her and shrunk from her notwithstanding her good looks. Therefore, everything that is best in her has gone to nourish this love for the woman whom she nursed from a babe. It was because of her fierceness that the Senor Rodd, who is dead, chose her for his daughter's nurse, when he found that her heart was hungry with love for the child, for he knew that she would die before she suffered harm to come to her."

"He showed good judgment there," said Leonard. "Had it not been for Soa, Juanna would have been a slave-girl now, or dead."

"That is so, Outram, but whether we showed good judgment in trusting our lives to her tender mercies is quite another matter. Say, friend, do you think it well to go on with this business?"

"Oh, confound it all!" said Leonard with irritation, "how can we turn back now? Just think of the journey and how foolish we should look. Besides, we have none of us got anything to live upon; it took most of the gold that I had to bribe Peter and his men to accompany us. I dare say that we shall all be killed, that seems very probable, but for my part I really shan't be sorry. I am tired of life, Francisco; it is nothing but a struggle and a wretchedness, and I begin to feel that peace is all I can hope to win. I have done my best here according to my lights, so I don't know why I should be afraid of the future, especially as it has been taken out of me pretty well in the present, though of course I *am* afraid for all that, every man is. The only thing that troubles me is a doubt whether we ought to take Juanna into such a place. But really I do not know but what it would be as dangerous to go back as to proceed: those gentlemen with the poisoned arrows may have recovered from their fear of firearms by now."

"I wish we had nothing worse than the Hereafter to fear," said Francisco with a sigh. "It is the journey thither that is so terrible. As for our expedition, having undertaken it, I think on the whole that we had better persevere, especially as the senora wishes it, and she is very hard to turn. After all our lives are in the hands of the Almighty, and therefore we shall be just as safe, or unsafe, among the People of the Mist as in a European city. Those of us who are destined to live will live, and those whose hour is at hand must die. And now good night, for I am going to sleep."

Next morning, shortly before dawn, Leonard was awakened by a hubbub among the natives, and creeping out of his blankets, he found that some of them, who had been to the river to draw water, had captured two bushmen belonging to a nomadic tribe that lived by spearing fish. These wretched creatures, who notwithstanding the cold only wore a piece of bark tied round their shoulders, were screaming with fright, and it was not until they had been pacified by gifts of beads and empty brass cartridges that anything could be got out of them.

When confidence had at length been restored, Otter questioned them closely as to the country that lay beyond the wall of rock and the people who dwelt in it, through one of the Settlement men, who spoke a language sufficiently like their own to make himself understood. They replied that they had never been in that country themselves, because they dared not go there, but they had heard of it from others.

The land was very cold and foggy, they said, so foggy that sometimes people could not see each other for whole days, and in it dwelt a race of great men covered with hair, who sacrificed strangers to a snake which they worshipped, and married all their fairest maidens to a god. That was all they knew of the country and of the great men, for few who visited there ever returned to tell tidings. It was certainly a haunted land.

Finding that there was no more to be learnt from the bushmen, Leonard suffered them to depart, which they did at considerable speed, and ordered the Settlement men to make ready to march. But now a fresh difficulty arose. The interpreter had repeated all the bushmen's story to his companions, among whom, it is needless to say, it produced no small effect. Therefore when the bearers received their orders, instead of striking the little tent in which Juanna slept, and preparing their loads as usual, after a brief consultation they advanced upon Leonard in a body.

"What is it, Peter?" he asked of the headman.

"This, Deliverer: we have travelled with you and the Shepherdess for three full moons, enduring much hardship and passing many dangers. Now we learn that there lies before us a land of cold and darkness, inhabited by devils who worship a devil. Deliverer, we have been good servants to you, and we are not cowards, as you know, but it is true that we fear to enter this land."

"What do you wish to do then, Peter?" asked Leonard.

"We wish to return whence we came, Deliverer. Already we have nearly earned the money that you gave to us before we started, and we will take no more pay if we must win it by crossing yonder wall."

"The way back is far, Peter," answered Leonard, "and you know its perils. How many, think you, will reach their homes alive if I am not there to guide them? For know, Peter, I will not turn back now. Desert

153

me, if you wish, all of you, and still I will enter this country alone, or with Otter only. Alone we took the slave camp and alone we will visit the People of the Mist."

"Your words are true, Deliverer," said Peter, "the homeward way is far and its perils are many; mayhap but very few of us will live to see their huts again, for this is an ill-fated journey. But if we pass yonder," and he pointed to the wall of rock, "then we shall all of us certainly die, and be offered to a devil by devils."

Leonard pulled his beard thoughtfully and said: "It seems there is nothing else to say, Peter, except goodbye."

The headman saluted and was turning away with an abashed countenance when Juanna stopped him. Together with Otter and the others she had been listening to the colloquy in silence, and now spoke for the first time.

"Peter," she said gently, "when you and your companions were in the hands of the Yellow Devil and about to be sold as slaves, who was it that rescued you?"

"The Deliverer, Shepherdess."

"Yes. And now do my ears betray me, or do I hear you say that you and your brethren, who with many another were saved from shame and toil by the Deliverer, are about to leave him in his hour of danger?"

"You have heard aright, Shepherdess," the man answered sadly.

"It is well, Peter. Go, children of Mavoom, my father, who can desert me in my need. For learn, Peter, that where you fear to tread, there I, a white woman, will pass alone with the Deliverer. Go, children of my father, and may peace go with you. Yet, as you know, I, who foretold the doom of the Yellow Devil, am a true prophetess, and I tell you this, that but a very few of you shall live to see your kraal again, and *you* will not be of their number, Peter. As for those who come home safely, their names shall be a mockery, the little children shall call them coward, and traitor and jackal, and one by one they shall eat out their hearts and die, because they deserted him who saved them from the slave-ship and the scourge. Farewell, children of my father: may peace go with you, and may his ghost not come to haunt you on your path," and with one indignant glance she turned scornfully away.

"Brethren," said Peter after a moment's pause, "is it to be borne that the Shepherdess should mock us thus and tie such ropes of shame about our necks?"

"No," they answered, "we cannot bear it."

Then for a while they consulted together again, and presently Peter stood forward and said: "Deliverer, we will accompany you and the

Shepherdess into the country of devils, nor need you fear that we shall desert or betray you. We know well that we go to our death, every one of us; still it is better to die than to live bearing the burden of such bitter words as hide within the Shepherdess's lips."

"Very well," answered Leonard. "Get your loads and let us start."

"Ay! It is well indeed," put in Otter with a snort of indignation. "I tell you this, Peter, that before you left this place the words of the Shepherdess had come true for you and one or two others, for I should have fought you till I was killed, and though I have little wisdom yet I know how to fight."

Leonard smiled at the dwarf's rage, but his heart was heavy within him. He knew that these men had reason on their side, and he feared greatly lest their evil forebodings should come true and the lives of all of them pay forfeit for his rashness.

But it was too late to turn back now: things must befall as they were fated.

CHAPTER 19

The End of the Journey

An hour later the party began the ascent of the wall of rock, which proved to be an even more difficult business than they had anticipated. There was no path, for those who lived beyond this natural barrier never came down it, and few of the dwellers in the plains had ever ventured to go up. It was possible, for Soa herself had descended here in bygone years, and this was all that could be said for it.

In default of a better road they followed the course of the river, which thundered down the face of the precipice in four great waterfalls, connected by as many sullen pools, whose cavities had been hollowed out in the course of centuries from the rock. The second of these ledges proved so insurmountable that at one time Leonard thought that they would be obliged to abandon their attempt, and follow the foot of the cliff till they found some easier route. But at last Otter, who could climb like a cat, succeeded in passing the most dangerous part at the risk of his life, bearing a rope with him by means of which the rest of the party and the loads of goods were hauled up one by one. It was evening before the height was scaled, and they proceeded to encamp upon its summit, making a scanty meal of some meat which they had brought with them.

That night they passed in great discomfort, for it was mid-winter and here the climate proved to be very cold. Bitter winds swept across the vast plain before them and searched them through, all the clothing and blankets they had scarcely sufficing to keep them warm; indeed, the Settlement men and Francisco, who had been bred in a southern clime, suffered severely. Nor were matters improved when, on the breaking of the light, they woke from a troubled sleep to find the plain hidden in a dense mist. However, they rose, made a fire with reeds and dead wood which they gathered on the banks of the river, and ate, waiting for the fog to vanish.

But it did not vanish, so about nine o'clock they continued their journey under Soa's guidance, following the east bank of the river northwards. The ground proved easy to travel over, for, with the exception of isolated water-worn boulders of granite, the plain was perfectly smooth and covered with turf as fine as any that grows in northern lands.

All that day they marched on, wandering like ghosts through the mist, and guided in their path by the murmuring sound of the river. They met no man, but once or twice great herds of hairy creatures thundered past them. Leonard fired into one of these herds with an express rifle, for they wanted meat, and a prodigious snorting and bellowing told him that his shot had taken effect. Running to the spot whence the sounds came, he found a huge white bull kicking in its death struggle. The animal was covered with long white hair like that of the British breed of wild cattle, and measured at least seventeen hands in height. Round it stood others snorting with fear and wonder, that, when they saw Leonard, put down their heads threateningly, tearing up the turf with their great horns. He shouted aloud and fired another shot, whereon they turned and disappeared into the mist.

This happened towards nightfall, so they determined to camp upon the spot; but while they were engaged in skinning the bull an incident occurred that did not tend to raise their spirits. At sunset the sky cleared a little—at least the sinking sun showed red through the mist as it does in a London fog of the third density. Against this red ball of the sun, and some dozen yards away, suddenly there appeared the gigantic figure of a man, for, unless the fog deceived them, he must have been between six and seven feet high and broad in proportion. Of his face they could see nothing, but he was clad in goat-skins, and armed with a great spear and a bow slung upon his back.

Juanna was the first to see and point him out to Leonard with a start of fear, as he stood watching them in solemn silence. Obeying the impulse of the moment, Leonard stepped forward towards the vision holding his rifle ready, but before he reached the spot where it had stood the figure vanished.

Then he walked back again to Juanna. "I think we have heard so much of giants that we begin to believe we see them," he said laughing.

As he spoke something clove the air between them and stuck in the earth beyond. They went to it. It was a large arrow having a barbed point and flighted with red feathers.

"This is a very tangible fancy at any rate," Juanna answered, drawing the shaft out of the ground. "We have had a narrow escape."

Leonard did not speak, but raising his rifle he fired it at a venture in the direction whence the arrow had sped. Then he ran to put their little band in a position of defence, Juanna following him. But, as it chanced, he might have spared himself the trouble, for nothing further happened; indeed, the net outward and visible result of this mysterious apparition was that they spent a miserable night, waiting in the fog and wet—for it had come on to rain, or rather drizzle—for an enemy who, to their intense relief, never appeared.

But the inward and spiritual consequences were much greater, for now they knew that Soa spoke truth and that the legend of the bushmen as to "great men covered with hair" was no mere savage invention.

At length the morning came. It was damp and wretched, and they were all half starved with cold and oppressed by fears. Indeed some of the Settlement men were so terrified that they openly lamented having suffered their sense of shame and loyalty to overcome their determination to retreat. Now they could not do so, for the malcontents among them did not dare to retrace their steps alone; moreover, Leonard spoke plainly on the matter, telling them that he would drive away the first man who attempted any insubordination.

Soaked through, shivering, and miserable, they pursued their march across the unknown plain, Soa, who seemed to grow hourly grimmer now that she was in her own country, stalking ahead of them as guide. It was warmer walking than sitting still, and in one respect their lot was bettered, for a little wind stirring the mist from time to time revealed gleams of the watery sun. All that day they journeyed on, seeing no more of the man who had shot the arrow, or his fellows, till at length darkness drew near again.

Then they halted, and Leonard and Otter walked to and fro searching for a suitable place to make the camp and pitch their solitary tent. Presently Otter shouted aloud. Leonard ran towards him, and found him staring into the mist at something that loomed largely about a hundred yards away.

"Look, Baas," he said, "there is a house, a house of stone with grass growing on the roof."

"Nonsense," said Leonard, "it must be some more boulders. However, we can soon find out."

They crept cautiously towards the object, that, as soon became evident, was a house or a very good apology for one, built of huge undressed boulders, bedded in turf by way of mortar, and roofed with the trunks of small trees and a thick thatch of sods whereon the grass grew green. This building may have measured forty feet in length by twenty in depth, and seventeen from the ground-line to the wall-plate. Also it had a doorway of remarkable height and two window-places, but all these openings were unclosed, except by curtains of hide which hung before them. Leonard called Soa and asked her what the place was.

"Doubtless the house of a herdsman," she answered, "who is set here to watch the cattle of the king, or of the priests. It may chance that this is the dwelling of that man who shot the arrow yesterday."

Having assured themselves that here was a human habitation, it remained to be ascertained whether it was tenanted. After waiting awhile to see if anyone passed in or out, Otter undertook this task. Going down on his hands and knees he crept up to the wall, then along it to the doorway, and after listening there awhile he lifted a corner of the hide curtain and peeped into the interior. Presently he rose, saying:

"All right, Baas, the place is empty."

Then they both entered and examined the dwelling with curiosity. It was rude enough. The walls were unplastered, and the damp streamed down them; the floor was of trodden mud, and a hole in the roof served as a chimney; but, by way of compensation, the internal space was divided into two apartments, one of them a living room, and the other a sleeping chamber. It was evident that the place had not been long deserted, for fire still smouldered on the hearth, round which stood various earthen cooking dishes, and in the sleeping-room was a rough bedstead of wood whereon lay wrappings made from the hides of cattle and goats. When they had seen everything there was to be seen, they hurried back to the others to report their discovery, and just then the rain set in more heavily than before.

"A house!" said Juanna; "then for goodness' sake let us get into it. We are all half dead with the cold and wet."

"Yes," answered Leonard, "I think we had better take possession, though it may be a little awkward if the rightful owners come back."

The best that can be said for the night which they spent in this stone shanty, undisturbed by any visit from its lawful tenant, is that it passed a shade more comfortably than it would have done outside. They were dry, though the place was damp, and they had a fire. Still, until you are used to it, it is trying to sit in the company of a score of black people and of many thousand fleas, enveloped with a cloud of pungent smoke, according to the custom of our Norse ancestors.

Soon Juanna gave up the attempt and retired to the great bed in the inner chamber, wondering much who had occupied it last. A herdsman, she judged, as Soa had suggested, for in a corner of the room stood an ox-goad hugely fashioned. But it was a bed, and she slept as soundly in it as its numerous insect occupants would allow. The others were not so fortunate: they had the insects indeed, but no bed.

Again the morning came, wet, miserable, and misty, and through the mist and rain they pursued their course, whither they knew not. All day they wandered on by the banks of the river till night fell and they camped, this time without shelter. Now they had reached the extreme of wretchedness, for they had little or no food left, and could not find fuel to make a fire. Leonard took Soa aside and questioned her, for he saw clearly that a couple more days of this suffering would put an end to all of them.

"You say these people of yours have a city, Soa?"

"They have a city, Deliverer," she answered, "but whether they will allow you to enter it, except as a victim for sacrifice, is another matter."

"None of us will enter it unless we find shelter soon," he answered. "How far is the place away?"

"It should be a day's journey, Deliverer. Were the mist gone you could see it now. The city is built at the foot of great mountains, there are none higher, but the fog hides everything. Tomorrow, if it lifts, you will see that I speak truth."

"Are there any houses near where we can shelter?" he asked again.

"How can I tell?" she answered. "It is forty years since I passed this road, and here, where the land is barren, none dwell except the herdsmen. Perhaps there is a house at hand, or perhaps there is none for many miles. Who can say?"

Finding that Soa could give no further information, Leonard returned to the others, and they huddled themselves together for warmth on the wet ground as best they might, and sat out the hours in silence, not attempting to sleep. The Settlement men were numb with cold, and Juanna also was overcome for the first time, though she tried hard to be cheerful. Francisco and Leonard heaped their own blankets on her, pretending that they had found spare ones, but the wraps were wringing wet, and gave her little comfort. Soa alone did not appear to suffer, perhaps because it was her native climate, and Otter kept his spirits, which neither heat, nor cold, nor hunger seemed to affect.

"While my heart is warm I am warm," he said cheerfully, when Leonard asked him how he fared. As for Leonard himself, he sat silent listening to the moans of the Settlement men, and reflecting that twenty-four hours more of this misery would bring the troubles of most of them to an end. Without food or shelter it was very certain that few of those alive tonight would live to see a second dawn.

At last the light came and to their wonder and exceeding joy they found that the rain had ceased and the mist was melting.

Once more they beheld the face of the sun, and rejoiced in its warmth as only those can rejoice who for days and nights have lived in semi-darkness, wet to the skin and frozen to the marrow.

The worst of the mist was gone indeed, but it was not until they had breakfasted off a buck which Otter shot in the reeds by the river, that the lingering veils of vapour withdrew themselves from the more distant landscape. At last they had vanished, and for the first time the wanderers saw the land through which they were travelling. They stood upon a vast plain that sloped upwards gradually till it ended at the foot of a mighty range of snow-capped mountains named, as they learned in after-days, the Bina Mountains.

This range was shaped like a half-moon, or a bent bow, and the nearest point of the curve, formed by a soaring snowy peak, was exactly opposite to them, and to all appearance not more than five-and-twenty miles away. On either side of this peak the unbroken line of mountains receded with a vast and majestic sweep till the eye could follow them no more. The plain about them was barren and everywhere strewn with granite boulders, between which wandered herds of wild cattle, mixed with groups of antelopes; but the lower slopes of the mountains were clothed with dense juniper forests, and among them were clearings, presumably of cultivated land. Otter searched the scene with his eyes, that were as those of a hawk; then said quietly:

"Look yonder, Baas; the old hag has not lied to us. There is the city of the People of the Mist."

Following the line of the dwarf's outstretched hand, Leonard saw what had at first escaped him, that standing back in a wide bend at the foot of the great mountain in front of them were a multitude of houses, built of grey stone and roofed with green turf. Indeed, had not his attention been called to it, the town might well have missed observation until he was quite close to its walls, for the materials of which it was constructed resembled those of the boulders that lay about them in thousands, and the vivid green of its roofs gave it the appearance of a distant space of grassy land.

"Yes, there is the kraal of the Great People," said Otter again, "and it is a strong kraal. See, Baas, they know how to defend themselves. The mountain is behind them that none can climb, and all around their walls the river runs, joining itself together again on the plain beyond. It would go ill with the '*impi*' which tried to take that kraal."

For a while they all stood still and stared amazed. It seemed strange that they should have reached this fabled city; and now that they were there, how would they be received within its walls? This was the question which each one of them was asking of himself. There was but one way to find out—they must go and see; no retreat was now possible. Even the Settlement people felt this. "Better to die at the hands of the Great Men," said one of them aloud, "than to perish miserably in the mist and cold."

"Be of good cheer," Leonard answered; "you are not yet dead. The sun shines once more. It is a happy omen."

When they had rested and dried their clothes they marched on with a certain sense of relief. There before them was the goal they had travelled so far to win; soon they would know the worst that could befall, and anything was better than this long suspense.

By midday they had covered about fifteen miles of ground, and could now see the city clearly. It was a great town, surrounded by a Cyclopean wall of boulders, about which the river ran on every side, forming a natural moat. The buildings within the wall seemed to be arranged in streets, and to be build on a plan similar to that of the house in which they had slept two nights before, the vast conglomeration of grass-covered roofs giving the city the appearance of a broken field of turf hillocks supported upon walls of stone.

For the rest the place was laid out upon a slope, and at its head, immediately beneath the sheer steps of the mountain side stood two edifices very much larger in size than any of those below. One of these resembled the other houses in construction, and was surrounded by a separate enclosure; but the second, which was placed on higher ground, so far as they could judge at that distance, was roofless, and had all the characteristics of a Roman amphitheatre. At the far end of this amphitheatre stood a huge mass of polished rock, bearing a grotesque resemblance to the figure of a man.

"What are those buildings, Soa?" asked Leonard.

"The lower one is the house of the king, White Man, and that above is the Temple of Deep Waters, where the river rises from the bowels of the mountain."

"And what is the black stone beyond the temple?"

"That, White Man, is the statue of the god who sits there for ever, watching over the city of his people."

"He must be a great god," said Leonard, alluding to the size of the statue.

"He *is* great," she answered, "and my heart is afraid at the sight of him."

After resting for two hours they marched on again, and soon it became apparent that their movements were watched. The roadway which they were following—if a track beaten flat by the feet of men and cattle could be called a road—wound to and fro between boulders of rock, and here and there standing upon the boulders were men clad in goat-skins, each of them carrying a spear, a bow and a horn. So soon as their party came within five or six hundred yards of one of these men, he would shoot an arrow in their direction, which, when picked up, proved to be barbed with iron, and flighted with red feathers like the first that they had seen. Then the sentry would blow his horn, either as a signal or in token of defiance, bound from the rock, and vanish. This did not look encouraging, but there was worse to come. Presently, as they drew near to the city, they descried large bodies of armed men crossing the river that surrounded it in boats and on rafts, and mustering on the hither side. At length all of them were across, and the regiment, which appeared to number more than a thousand men, formed up in a hollow square and advanced upon them at the double.

The crisis was at hand.

CHAPTER 20

The Coming of Aca

Leonard turned and looked at his companions with something like dismay written on his face.

"What is to be done now?" he said.

"We must wait for them until they come near," answered Juanna, "then Otter and I are to meet them alone, and I will sing the song which Soa has taught me. Do not be afraid, I have learned my lesson, and, if things go right, they will think that we are their lost gods; or, at least, so Soa says."

"Yes, *if* things go right. But if they don't?"

"Then goodbye," answered Juanna, with a shrug of her shoulders. "At any rate, I must get ready for the experiment. Come, Soa, bring the bundle to those rocks over there—quick! Stop a minute—I forgot, Mr. Outram, you must lend me that ruby. I have to make use of it."

Leonard handed over the ruby, reflecting that he would probably never see it again, since it seemed almost certain that one of the Great People would steal it. However, at the moment he was thinking of that which was far above rubies, namely, of what chance they had of escaping with their lives.

So soon as she had possession of the stone, Juanna ran to a little ring of boulders that were scattered on the plain about fifty paces from them, followed by Soa, who carried a bundle in her hand.

Ten minutes passed, and Soa appeared from behind the shelter of the stones and beckoned to them. Advancing in obedience to her summons, they saw a curious sight. Standing in the ring of rocks was Juanna, but Juanna transformed. She wore a white robe cut low upon the neck and shoulders; indeed, it was the Arab dress in which she had escaped from the slave camp, that Soa had brought with them in preparation for this moment of trial. Nor was this all; for Juanna had loosened her dark hair—which was of great length and unusual beauty—so that it hung about her almost to her knees, and upon her forehead, gleaming like a red eye, was set the great ruby, ingeniously fastened thereto by Soa in a band of linen pierced in its centre to the size of the stone.

"Behold the goddess and do homage," said Juanna with mock solemnity, although Leonard could see that she was trembling with excitement.

"I do not quite understand what you are going to do, but you look the part well," he answered shortly. And, indeed, until that moment he had never known how beautiful she was.

Juanna blushed a little at the evident admiration in his eyes; then, turning to the dwarf, she said:

"Now, Otter, you must make ready too. And remember what Soa told you. Whatever you see or hear, you are not to open your mouth. Walk side by side with me and do as I do, that is all."

Otter grunted in assent, and proceeded to "make ready." The process was simple, consisting only in the shedding of his coat and trousers—an old pair of Leonard's, very much cut down—which left him naked, except for a *moocha* that he wore beneath them in accordance with native custom.

"What does all this mean?" asked the headman Peter, who, like his companions, was trembling with fear.

"It means," said Juanna, "that Otter and I are impersonating the gods of this people, Peter. If they receive us as gods, it is well; if not, we are doomed. Be careful, should we be so received, lest any of you betray the trick. Be wise and silent, I say, and do what we shall tell you from time to time, if you would live to look upon the sun."

Peter fell back astonished, while Leonard and Francisco turned their attention to the approaching soldiers of the People of the Mist.

They advanced slowly and in silence, but their measured tread shook the earth. At last they halted about a hundred and fifty yards away, presenting a truly terrifying spectacle to the little band among the rocks. So far as Leonard could see, there was not a man among them who stood less than six feet in height, and they were broad in proportion—hugely made. In appearance they were neither handsome nor repulsive, but solemn-looking, large-eyed, thick-haired—between black and yellow in hue—and wearing an expression of dreadful calm, like the calm of an archaic statue. For the rest they seemed to be well disciplined, each company being under the command of a captain, who, in addition to his arms, carried a trumpet fashioned from a wild bull's horn.

165

The regiment stood silent, gazing at the group of strangers, or, rather, at the boulders behind which they were concealed. In the centre of their hollow square was a knot of men, one of them young, and huge even in comparison with his companions. This man Leonard took to be a chief or king. Behind were orderlies and counsellors, and before him three aged persons of stately appearance and a cruel cast of countenance. These men were naked to the waist and unarmed, except for a knife or hanger fixed at the girdle. On their broad breasts, covering more than half the skin-surface, the head of a huge snake was tattooed in vivid blue. Evidently they were medicine-men or priests.

While the adventurers watched and wondered, the king or chief issued an order to his attendants, who ran to the corners of the square and called it aloud. Then he raised his great spear, and every captain blew upon his horn, making a deafening sound.

Now the enemy stood still for a while, staring towards the stones, and the three medicine-men drew near to the chief in the centre of the square and talked with him, as though debating what should be done.

"This is our chance," said Juanna excitedly. "If once they attack us it will be all over; a single volley of arrows would kill every one of us. Come, Otter."

"No, no!" said Leonard. "I am afraid of your venturing yourself among those savages. The danger is too great."

"Danger! Can the danger be more than it is here? In a minute we may all be dead. Nonsense! I *will* go! I know what to do and have made up my mind to it. Do not fear for me. Remember that, if the worst comes to the worst, I have the means to protect myself. You are not afraid to come, are you, Otter?"

"No, Shepherdess," said the dwarf. "Here all roads are alike."

Leonard thought awhile. Bitterly did he reproach himself in that he had been the cause of leading his ward into such a position. But now there was no help for it—she must go. And after all it could make no difference if she were killed or captured five minutes hence or half an hour later. But Francisco, who could not take such a philosophical view of the situation, implored her not to venture herself alone among those horrible savages.

"Go if you like, Juanna," said Leonard, not heeding the priest's importunities. "If anything happens I will try to avenge you before I follow. Go, but forgive me."

"What have I to forgive?" she said, looking at him with shining eyes. "Did you not once dare a greater danger for me?"

"Yes, go, Shepherdess," said Soa, who till now had been staring with all her eyes at the three aged men in the centre of the square; "there is little to fear, if this fool of a dwarf will but keep his tongue silent. I know my people, and I tell you that if you sing that song, and say the words which I have taught you, you and the black one here shall be proclaimed gods of the land. But be swift, for the soldiers are about to shoot."

As Soa spoke, Leonard saw that the conference in the square had come to an end. The messengers were calling commands to the captains, which the captains repeated to the soldiers, and then followed a mighty rattling of quivers. Another instant and the light shone upon many hundreds of arrow-heads, every one of which was pointed towards them.

Juanna saw also, and springing forward on to a rock, stood there for a moment in the full glare of the sun. Instantly a murmur went up from the host; a great voice called a command; the barbs of steel flickered like innumerable stars, and sank downwards.

Now Otter, naked except for his *moocha*, sprang on to the rock by Juanna's side, and the murmur of the soldiers of the Great People grew into a hoarse roar of astonishment and dismay. Wonder had turned to fear, though why this multitude of warriors should fear a lovely white girl and a black dwarf was not apparent.

For a moment the ill-assorted pair stood together on the rock; then Juanna leapt to the plain, Otter following her. For twenty yards or so she walked in silence, holding the dwarf by the hand; then suddenly she burst into singing wild and sweet. This was the refrain of the sacred song which she sang in the ancient language of the People of the Mist, the tongue that Soa had taught her as a child:

"I do but sleep. Have ye wept for me awhile? Hush! I did but sleep. I shall awake, my people! I am not dead, nor can I ever die. See, I have but slept! See, I come again, made beautiful! Have ye not seen me in the faces of the children? Have ye not heard me in the voices of the children? Look on me now, the sleeper arisen; Look on me, who wandered, whose name is the Dawning! Why have ye mourned me, the sleeper awakened?"

Thus she sang, ever more sweetly and louder, till her voice rang through the still air like the song of a bird in winter. Hushed were the companies of the Great Men as she drew towards them with slow gliding steps—hushed with fear and wonder, as though her presence awoke a memory or fulfilled a promise.

Now she was in front of their foremost rank, and, halting there, was silent for a moment. Then she changed her song.

167

"Will ye not greet me, children of my children? Have ye forgotten the promise of the dead? Shall I return to the dream-land whence I wander? Will ye refuse me, the Mother of the Snake?"

The soldiers looked upon one another and murmured each to each. Now she saw that they understood her words and were terror-stricken by them. For another moment there was silence, then suddenly the three priests or medicine-men, who had drawn near together, passed through the ranks and stood before her, accompanied by the warrior-chief.

Then one of them, the most aged, a man who must have numbered ninety years, spoke in the midst of an intense silence. To Juanna's joy, as they had understood her, so she understood him, for his language was the same that Soa taught her many years before, and in which, for the sake of practice, they had always conversed together for the last two months.

"Art thou woman, or spirit?" asked the ancient priest.

"I am both woman and spirit," she answered.

"And he with thee, he whom we know of"—went on the priest, pointing tremblingly to Otter—"is he god or man?"

"He is both god and man," she answered.

"And those yonder; who are they?"

"They are our ministers and servants, white for the white, and black for the black, the companions of our wanderings, men and not spirits."

The three priests consulted together, while the chief looked on Juanna's beauty with wondering eyes. Then the oldest of them spoke again: "Thou tellest us in our own tongue of things that have long been hidden, though perchance they are remembered. Either, O Beautiful, thou hast learned these things and liest to us, and then food are ye all for the Snake against whom thou dost blaspheme, or ye are gods indeed, and as gods ye shall be worshipped. Tell us now thy name, and the name of yonder dwarf, of whom we know."

"I am named the Shepherdess of Heaven among men. He is named Otter, Dweller in the Waters, among men. Once we had other names."

"Tell us the other names, O Shepherdess."

"Once in the far past I was named Brightness, I was named Dawn, I was named Daylight. Once in the far past he was named Silence, he was named Terror, he was named Darkness. Yet at the beginning we had other names. Perchance ye know them, Ministers of the Snake."

"Perchance we know them, O thou who art named Shepherdess of Heaven, O thou who wert named Brightness, and Dawn, and Daylight; O thou who art named Dweller in the Waters, and wert named

Silence, and Terror, and Darkness! Perchance we know them, although they be known to few, and are never spoken, save in utter gloom and with hidden head. But do ye know them, those names of the beginning? For if ye know them not, O Beautiful, ye lie and ye blaspheme, and ye are food for the Snake."

"Seldom through all the years have those holy names been spoken save in utter darkness and with covered heads," Juanna answered boldly; "but now is the new hour, the hour of the coming, and now they shall be called aloud in the light of day from open lips and with uplifted eyes. Hearken, Children of the Snake, these are the names by which we were known in the beginning: *Aca* is my name, the Mother of the Snake. *Jal* is he named, who is the Snake. Say, do ye know us now?"

As these words rang on her lips a groan of terror burst from every man who heard them. Then the aged priest cried aloud: "Down upon your faces, ye Children of the Snake; Worship, all ye People of the Spear, Dwellers in the Mist! Aca, the Queen immortal, has come home again: Jal, the god, has put on the flesh of men. Olfan, lay down thy kingship, it is his: ye priests, throw wide the temples, they are theirs. Worship the Mother, do honour to the god!"

The multitude heard and prostrated themselves like a single man, every one of them crying in a shout of thunder:

"Aca, the Queen of life, has come; Jal, the doom-god, has put on flesh. Worship the Mother, do honour to the god!"

It was as though the army had suddenly been smitten with death, and of the hundreds there, Juanna and Otter alone were left standing. There was one exception, however, and that was Olfan, the warrior chief, who remained upon his feet, not seeming to relish the command to abdicate his authority thus brusquely in favour of a dwarf, were he god or man.

Otter, who was utterly bewildered, not comprehending a word of what had been said, and being unable to fathom the meaning of these strange antics, pointed at the chief with his spear by way of calling Juanna's attention to the fact that he was still standing. But the great man interpreted the action otherwise; evidently he thought that the newly arrived god was invoking destruction on him. His pride yielded to his superstition, and he sank to his knees also.

When the sound of the worshipping had passed away Juanna spoke again, addressing the old priest.

"Rise, my child," she said—he might well have been her great-grandfather—"and rise all ye, soldiers of the Spear and servants of the Snake, and hear my words. Ye know me now, ye know me by the holy name, ye know me by the fashion of my face, and by the red stone that gleams upon my brow. In the beginning my blood fell yonder and was frozen into such gems as these, which today ye offer yearly to him who is my child, and slew me. Now the fate is accomplished and his reign is finished. I come with him indeed, and he is still a god, but he loves me as a son again, and bows the knee to me in service.

"Enough, ye know the ancient tale that is fulfilled this day. Now we pass on towards our city, there to sojourn with you awhile and to proclaim the law of the Ending, and we pass alone. There, in our city, let a place be made ready for us, a place apart, but nigh to the temple; and let food be brought to the place, that my servants may eat. At the gates of the city also let men be waiting to bear us to that dwelling. Let none spy upon us, lest an evil fate attend you all; and let none be disobedient, lest we pass from you back to the land of Death and Dreams. Perchance we shall not tarry here for long, perchance we come to bring a blessing and to depart again. Therefore hasten to do our bidding, and do it all. For this time farewell, my servants."

Having spoken thus with much dignity, accompanied by Otter, whose hand she held as before, Juanna withdrew herself, stepping backwards very slowly towards the circle of rocks, and singing as she went.

CHAPTER 21

The Folly of Otter

Juanna and Otter gained the circle of rocks where the little band lay watching and wonder-struck; that is, all except Soa, who sat apart brooding, her arms clasped upon her breast. Things had befallen as she expected, as they must befall indeed, provided that Juanna did not forget her lesson or show fear, and that the dwarf did nothing foolish. But Soa knew well enough that this was but the beginning of the struggle, and that, though it might be comparatively easy for Juanna and Otter to enter the city, and impose themselves upon its superstition-haunted people as the incarnations of their fabled gods, the maintenance of the imposture was a very different matter. Moreover, she knew, should they be discovered, that escape would be impossible, or at the best, that it must be most difficult. Therefore she sat apart and brooded, for, notwithstanding their present triumph, her heart foreboded evil.

But with the others it was different: they had heard the singing, they had seen the regiment of great men prostrate themselves, and the sound of worshipping had come to their ears like thunder; but of the why and wherefore of it all they could only guess.

"What has happened?" said Leonard eagerly; "your initiation seems to have come off well."

"Bid the men fall back and I will tell you," Juanna answered.

Leonard did so, but instead of speaking she broke into hysterical laughter. Her nerves had been over-strained, and now they sought relief thus.

"You must all be very respectful to Otter and myself," she said at length, "for we really are gods—don't look shocked, Francisco, I begin to believe in it myself. We have only just found it out, but I assure you it is a fact; they accepted us fully, and that after not more than five minutes' cross-examination. Listen!" And she told them all that had passed.

While she was speaking the regiment began to move, no longer in a square, but in a formation of companies. Company by company it rushed past them, shaking the earth with its footsteps, and as each section went by it tossed its spears into the air as a salute, crying: "Glory to the Mother! glory to the Snake!" and fled on towards the city.

At length the story was done and the regiment was gone.

"Well," said Leonard, "so far so good. Juanna, you are the bravest and cleverest girl in the whole world. Most young women would have forgotten everything and gone into hysterics at the critical point."

"I kept them till afterwards," she answered demurely. "And as for being brave and clever, I only repeated what Soa taught me like a parrot; you see I knew that I should be killed if I made any mistake, and such knowledge sharpens the memory. All I have to say is, if the Snake they talk so much about is anything like those which are tattooed upon the old priests' breasts, I have no wish to make a nearer acquaintance with it. I hate snakes. There, don't say any more"—for both Leonard and Francisco were breaking out into fresh protestations of gratitude and admiration; "if you want to thank anybody, thank Soa!"

"And so I do," said Leonard heartily, for his spirits had risen in a most wonderful manner. "Soa, you have told us the truth, and you have managed well and I thank you."

"Did you then take me for a liar?" the woman answered, fixing her gloomy eyes upon Leonard's face. "I told you the truth, Deliverer, when I said that my people would accept the Shepherdess and this black dog of yours as their gods. But did I not tell you also that the death of the rest of us lies in the matter? If not, I say so now. *You* have not been named a god, Deliverer, nor has yonder Bald-pate"—the natives called Francisco thus because of his tonsure—"and your black dog will betray you by his yapping. When you look down the jaws of the Snake, remember then that Soa told you the truth, Deliverer. Perchance you shall find the red stones you seek hidden in his belly, White Man."

"Be silent," said Juanna indignantly, and Soa slunk back like a whipped hound.

"Confound the old woman!" put in Leonard with a shiver. "She is a black Jonah, and if I have to go inside this snake I hope that it will be a case of ladies first, that is all."

"I am sure I don't know what has happened to Soa," said Juanna. "Her native air has a very bad effect upon her temper."

"Well, the future must look after itself," answered Leonard, "snake or no snake. At present we must follow our luck. Otter, listen to me. Do you understand that you are a god, the god of this people?"

172

"The god, Baas? What is a god?"

"Have I not told you, thickhead? You are not a man any more, you are a spirit. Once, so it seems, you ruled this people in the past, and now you will rule them again. You and the Shepherdess are both gods. She is your mother and you are her child."

"Yes, Baas, no doubt; but once I had another mother, a much uglier one."

"Otter, cease to talk folly, else when you are no more a god I will beat you. Now you are a god, and we are all your servants, except the Shepherdess. When you speak to us you must speak roughly, like a great chief to the lowest of his people, calling us dogs and slaves. If you name me 'Baas' in public, I will beat you privately when you are no more a god. You will do best to speak little or not at all, so that none can take hold of your words, which are always foolish."

"If you say that I am a god, Baas, it is enough, for doubtless you have met the gods and know their ways, though it is strange that none have told me this before. They must be an ugly people, the gods! But how will it be with the Settlement men when they hear that I am a great spirit? They will say: 'Does a spirit wait upon a man and call him chief? Does a spirit clean the guns and cook the food of a man?' They will ask many such things, and the Great people will hear them. And will they think then that I am a god? No, they will know me for a liar, and will kill me and all of us."

"That is true," said Leonard. Then he summoned Peter and the Settlement men and addressed them. He told them that the plot had succeeded, and that Otter and the Shepherdess were accepted as the gods of the People of the Mist. Because of this they were left alive and held in honour, who, but for it, would now be dead, riddled through with the arrows of the Great People. He explained to them for the second time that it was necessary to the safety of all that this delusion as to the divinity of Otter and the Shepherdess should be maintained, since, if the slightest suspicion of the fraud crossed the minds of the Great People, without doubt they would all be sacrificed as impostors.

This was the tale that they must tell:—They should say that all of them were hunting game in a far country with himself, Soa, and Francisco, when one night they heard a singing, and by the light of the moon they saw the Shepherdess and the dwarf Otter coming towards them. Then the Shepherdess and Otter commanded them to be their servants and travel with them to a new land, and they obeyed them, black and white together, for they saw that they were not mortals.—

This was the tale that they must tell; moreover, they must act up to their words if they would continue to look upon the sun.

But their first surprise was past, the Settlement men, who were quick-witted people, entered into the spirit of the plot readily enough; indeed, Peter caused them to repeat the story to him, so that he might be sure that they had its details by heart.

Then they continued their march towards the city on the hill. The two white men went first, next came Juanna and Otter followed by Soa, and last of all walked the Settlement men. An hour's journey brought them to the bank of the river, which, dividing above it, engirdled the town, to reunite near the roadway that they followed. Here canoes were ready to take them across to the island, or rather the peninsula, on which the city was built. On the other side of the river they found priests waiting in the great gateway with two litters that had been prepared for Juanna and Otter respectively. This, the further bank, was lined with some thousands of spectators, who, when the divine pair set their feet upon its shores, prostrated themselves, men, women, and children, and burst into a shout of welcome.

Juanna and Otter took no heed. With such dignity as they could command, and in the dwarf's case it was not much, they entered the litters, drew the hide curtains, and were borne forward swiftly. After them came Leonard, Francisco, and the others, while the population followed in silence.

Now the sun was sinking, but enough of daylight was left to show how strange were the place and the people among which they found themselves. The city, indeed, was rudely built of like materials and in similar fashion to the house in the plain that has been described already. But the streets were roughly paved; each habitation stood apart from the other in its own garden, and the gates were of wood, fastened together with primitive iron bolts. There were drinking-shops, or rather booths, and a large market-place, which they crossed as they ascended the hill, and where, as they afterwards discovered, this people carried on their trade, if trade it could be called, for they had no money, and conducted all transactions like other savages, upon a principle of barter.

As they went Leonard took note of these things, which, to his mind, showed clearly that the inhabitants of this city were the degenerate inheritors of some ancient and forgotten civilisation. Their fortifications, stone-built houses, drinking-shops, and markets indicated this, just as their rude system of theology, with its divinities of Light and Darkness, or of Death and Life, each springing from the other, engaged in an eternal struggle, and yet one, was probably the survival of some elaborate nature-myth of the early world.

But nothing struck him so much as the appearance of the people. In size they were almost giants, a peculiarity which was shared by the women, some of whom measured six feet in height. In common with other uncivilised races most of these women were little except a girdle and a goat-skin cloak that hung loosely upon their shoulders, displaying their magnificent proportions somewhat freely. They were much handsomer than the men, having splendid solemn eyes, very white teeth, and a remarkable dignity of gait. Their faces, however, wore the same sombre look as those of their husbands and brothers, and they did not chatter after the manner of their sex, but contented themselves with pointing out the peculiarities of the strangers in a few brief words to their children or to one another.

After crossing the market-place the party came to a long and gentle ascent, which terminated at a wall surrounding the lower of the two great buildings that they had seen from the plain. Passing its gates they halted at the doors of the first of these edifices. Here priests stood with torches—at least, they judged them to be priests from the symbol of the snake's head tattooed upon their naked breasts—ready to conduct them to their lodging, for now the night was closing in rapidly. Soon they found themselves within the walls of a great house, built in the usual way with rough boulders, but on three sides of a square, and enclosing a courtyard in which a fountain bubbled. The furniture of the house was rude but grotesquely carved, and in the courtyard stood a throne, sheltered by a roof of turf, and fashioned of black wood and ivory, with feet shaped like those of a human being. Indeed, as they afterwards discovered, this was the palace of the king, Olfan, who had been summarily ejected by the priests to make room for the newcomers.

Here in this strange dwelling the attendant priests assigned them all quarters, the Settlement men in one wing, Leonard, Francisco and Soa in the other, and Juanna and Otter in two separate apartments in the body of the building. This arrangement involved the separation of the party, but it was difficult to offer objections, so they were forced to acquiesce in it. Presently women entered bearing food, boiled corn, milk in bowls, and roasted flesh in plenty, of which Leonard and Francisco ate with thankfulness.

Before they went to sleep Leonard looked into the courtyard, and was somewhat alarmed to find that guards were stationed at every door, while in front of those leading to the apartments of Juanna and Otter stood a body of priests with torches in their hands. He made an effort to pass through these guards in order to visit Juanna, but without a word they lifted their great spears and stopped him, and for that time he abandoned the attempt.

"Why do the priests stand before the door of the Shepherdess, Soa?" asked Leonard.

"They guard the place of the gods," she answered. "Unless the gods will it, none may enter there."

"Say, Soa," Leonard asked again, "are you not afraid of being here in your own land?"

"I am much afraid, Deliverer, for if I am found out then I die. Yet many years have gone by since I fled; few live who knew me, and, perchance, none remember me. Also now I do not wear my hair after the fashion of my people, and therefore I may escape, unless the priests discover me by their magic. And now I would sleep."

On the following morning at dawn Leonard rose and, accompanied by Francisco, walked into the courtyard. This time the soldiers did not try to stop them, but the priests were still standing in front of Juanna's door, looking like spectres in the grey mist. They went to them and signified by signs that they would worship the Queen, but were sternly refused admission in words which they could not understand, but that Soa, who was listening, afterwards translated to them.

"The Mother had come to her home," said the spokesman, "and might be profaned no more by the eyes of the vulgar. The Snake also was in his home, and none should look upon him."

When arguments failed Leonard tried to force his way through, and was met by a huge spear pointed at his throat. How things would have ended it is difficult to say had not Juanna herself appeared at this juncture, standing between the curtains of the doorway. At the sight of her the priests and soldiers fell upon their faces, and Leonard had sufficient presence of mind to follow their example, dragging Francisco down beside him.

"What is this tumult?" she asked the guards in their own tongue.

"I tell you what it is, Juanna," said Leonard, rubbing his head upon the ground and speaking in English. "If you do not come to an understanding with these scoundrels, you will soon be cut of from all communication with us, and what is more, we shall be cut off too in another way. Will you be so good as to issue an order that we are to be admitted when we like?"

Juanna turned towards the priest and spoke angrily:

"Who has dared to forbid my servants to come before me and worship me? My will is my own, and I only make it known. It is my will that these white men and yonder black woman pass in before me at their pleasure."

"Your will is our will, Mother," said the priests humbly.

So they went in, and the curtains were closed behind them.

"I am so thankful to see you," said Juanna. "You don't know how dreadfully lonely it has been in this great room all night, and I am afraid of those solemn-eyed priests who stand round the doors. The women who brought me food last evening crawled about the place on all fours like dogs; it was horrible!"

"I am sorry that you have been left alone," said Leonard, "but you must try to make better arrangements. Soa might sleep with you, at any rate. Where is Otter? Let us pay him a visit; I want to see how the god is getting on."

Juanna went to the door and addressed the priests, saying that she desired to be led before the Snake, and her servants with her. They demurred a little, then gave way, and all four of them were conducted, first into the courtyard, in which no human being was to be seen, and thence to an adjoining chamber, where a curious sight awaited them. In a huge chair set upon a dais sat Otter, looking furious and by no means at ease; while stretched upon the ground in front of him lay four priests, who muttered prayers unceasingly.

"Welcome, Baas!" he cried in rapture at the sight of Leonard. "Welcome, Shepherdess!"

"You idiot!" answered Leonard in Dutch, but speaking in the most humble voice, and sinking to his knees. "If you will not remember that you are a god, I will pay you out so soon as we are alone. Bid these fellows begone; the Shepherdess will translate for you."

"Go, dogs!" said Otter, taking the hint; "go, and bring me food. I would speak with my servant, who is named Baas, and with my mother."

"These are the words of the Snake that he speaks in the holy tongue," said Juanna, and she translated them.

The four priests rose, and bowing to the earth, crept backwards from the room. So soon as they were gone, Otter leaped from his throne with an exclamation of rage that caused the others to burst out laughing.

"Laugh, Baas, laugh if you will!" said the dwarf, "for you have never been a god, and don't know what it is. What think you, Baas?—all night long I have sat upon that great stool, while those accursed dogs burnt stinking stuff beneath my nostrils and muttered nonsense. One hour more and I should have fallen on them and killed them, for I have had no meat, and hunger makes me mad."

"Hush!" said Leonard, "I hear footsteps! On to your throne, Otter! Quick, Juanna! stand by his side; we will kneel!"

They had barely time to obey when the curtains were drawn, and a priest entered, holding a vessel of wood covered with a cloth. Slowly he crept towards the throne, with his head bent almost to his knees; then, straightening himself suddenly, he lifted up the wooden vessel and cried aloud:

"We bring you food, O Snake. Eat and be satisfied."

Otter took the dish, and, lifting the cloth, gazed upon its contents hungrily, but with an ever-growing dissatisfaction.

"Son of a dog!" he cried in his own tongue, "is this food to set before a man?" And he held the platter downwards, exposing its contents.

They were simple, consisting of various sorts of vegetables and watercress—poor in quality, for the season was winter, and all of them uncooked. In the centre of this fodder—whether placed there in obedience to some religious tradition or by way of ornament, or perhaps to assist the digestive process of the god, as a tenpenny nail is said to assist that of an ostrich—was a fine ruby stone; not so big, indeed, as that which Soa had given to Leonard, but still of considerable size and value. Leonard saw it with delight, but not so the dwarf, the selfish promptings of whose stomach caused him to forget that his master had journeyed far to seek such gems as this. In the fury of his disappointed appetite he stood upon the footstool of the throne, and, seizing the ruby, he hurled it at the priest, hitting him fair between the eyes.

"Am I an eel?" he roared, "that I should live on water-grass, and red gravel?"

Then the priest, terrified at the behaviour of this strange divinity, picked up the offending gem—to the presence of which he attributed his anger—and fled, never looking behind him.

Juanna and Francisco were seized with uncontrollable laughter, while even Soa deigned to smile. But Leonard did not smile.

"Oh, you last descendant of generations of asses!" he said bitterly. "You ass with four ears and a tenfold bray! What have you done? You have hurled the precious stone at the head of him who brought it, and now he will bring no more. Had it not been for you, doubtless with every meal such stones would have been offered to you, and though you grew thin we should all of us have become rich, and that without trouble, tricks, or violence."

"Forgive me, Baas," lamented Otter, "but my rage took away my reason, and I forgot. See now what it is to be a god. It is to be fed upon stuff such as would gripe an ox. Oh, Baas, I would that these wild men had made you a god and left me your servant!" And again he gazed with disgust upon the watercress and rows of leathery vegetables resembling turnips.

"You had better eat them, Otter," said Juanna, who was still choking with laughter. "If you don't you may get nothing more for days. Evidently you are supposed to have a small appetite."

Then, driven to it by his ravening hunger, the wretched Otter fell upon the turnips and munched them sullenly, Leonard rating him all the while for his unequalled stupidity.

Scarcely had he finished his meal when there was a stir without, and once again priests entered, headed on this occasion by that same aged man who had acted as a spokesman when Juanna declared herself on the previous day, and who, as they had discovered, was named Nam. In fact he had many other and much longer names, but as this was the shortest ad most convenient of them, they adopted it.

It chanced that Leonard was standing by Soa, and when this priest entered, whom she now saw face to face for the first time, he noticed that she started, trembled, and then drew back into the shadow of the throne.

"Some friend of the old lady's youth," thought Leonard to himself. "I hope he won't recognise her, that is all."

Nam bent himself in adoration before the gods, then began an address, the substance of which Juanna translated from time to time. Bitterly did he grieve, he said, that such an insult had been offered to the Snake as the presenting to him among his food of the red stone, known as the Blood of Aca. That man who had done this folly was doomed to die, if, indeed, he were not already dead. Well could they understand that, the Mother and Snake having become reconciled, the proffering to Jal of that which reminded him of the sin of long ago was a wickedness that might bring a curse upon the land. Let the Snake be appeased. Command had been given that all such stones should be hidden in a secret place by him who had wrought the crime, and, as he had said, if the man returned alive from that place he should be slain. But he would not return alive, for to go thither was death, as it should be death henceforth even to mention that stone, of which but one should now be seen in the land, that which the Mother wore in memory of the past.

"O Otter, my friend," murmured Leonard to himself, "if I don't make you pay for this, my name is not Outram!"

But enough of the stones, went on Nam; he had come upon a more important matter. That night an assembly of all the tribe would be held in the great temple an hour before moonrise, that the Mother and the Snake might take up their royalty in the presence of the people. Thither they would come to lead them and their servants at the appointed time. Was this pleasing to the gods?

Juanna bent her head in assent, and the priest turned to go with many obeisances; but before he went he spoke again, asking if all things were as the gods desired.

"Not altogether, my servant," answered Juanna. "It is our will that these, our other servants, should have free access to us at all times and without question. Also, it is our will that their food should be brought to them with our food. Moreover, it is the desire of the Snake that no more grass should be given to him to eat; for now, in these latter days, having put on the flesh of men, he needs that which will support the flesh. One thing more, my servant; the Snake forgives the affront that was offered him, and I command that some of the greatest of the holy stones should be brought to me, that I may look on the blood which I shed so long ago."

"Alas! it may not be, Mother," answered the priest in tones of sorrow. "All the stones, both red and blue, have been placed in bags of hide and cast into that place whence they can be brought no more, together with him who offended. Nor can others be gathered at this season of the year, seeing that deep snow covers the place where they lie buried. In the summer, when the sun has melted the snow, more can be found, if your eyes still desire the sight of them."

Juanna made no reply, and the priest went.

"Here is a pretty business," said Leonard. "That idiot Otter has upset everything. We might have become millionaires for the asking, and now we must wait for months before we so much as get sight of a ruby or a sapphire."

Nobody answered. Indeed, the whole party were plunged into consternation at the fatal effects of this accident. As for Otter himself, when he understood fully what he had done, he almost wept for grief.

"Who could have known, Baas?" he groaned. "It was the sight of the green food that bewitched me, who have always hated the taste of grass. And now my folly has undone all, and it seems that I must be a god for many months, if, indeed, they do not find me out."

"Never mind, Otter," said Leonard, moved to pity by the dwarf's genuine grief. "You have lost the stones and you will have to find them again somehow. By the way, Soa, why did you start so when the old priest came in?"

"Because he is my father, Deliverer," she answered.

Leonard whistled; here was a new complication. What if Nam should recognise her?

CHAPTER 22

The Temple of Jal

In considerable agitation of mind Leonard bid goodbye to Juanna, promising to return soon, and went to visit the Settlement men, whom he had not seen since the previous evening.

He found them in good case enough, so far as their material comfort was concerned, for they were well supplied with food and warmly lodged. So much could not be said, however, of their mental state, for they were terrified by the multitude of solemn priests and warriors who watched them as cats watch mice. Crouching round him dejectedly they implored Leonard not to leave them, saying that they expected to be murdered every minute. He pacified them as well as he could and left them with the assurance that he would return presently, having first reminded them that the lives of all depended upon the maintenance of the delusion as to the divinity of Otter and the Shepherdess.

The remainder of that day passed heavily enough. After the first excitement of their strange position had gone by a reaction set in, and everybody was much depressed. As the hours drew on, the mist, which had lifted a little about ten o'clock, closed in very densely, throwing the ill-lighted chamber where they sat into a deep gloom. In such an atmosphere conversation languished; indeed, at times it died altogether, and the only sound to be heard was that of the monotonous voices of the priests without the curtains, as they muttered prayers unceasingly. At length Leonard could bear it no longer, but rose, declaring that he was going out to see whatever might be seen. Juanna tried faintly to dissuade him, and Otter wished to come too, which was impossible. The end of it was that he went alone.

First he revisited the Settlement men and tried to cheer them, and sadly did they need cheering. Then he passed to the great gates of the palace yard and looked through them. The mist had lifted a little, and

181

about a hundred paces away he could perceive the doors of the temple, on either side of which rose Cyclopean walls fifty feet or more in height. It was obvious that here preparations for some ceremony were in progress, and on a large scale, for immense crowds of people were gathered about the doors, through which bodies of priests and armed men passed continually. More he could not learn, for the gates of the palace yard were barred and guarded, and the soldiers would not let him through. He stood by them watching till sunset, then returning to the others, he told them what he had seen.

Another hour passed, and suddenly the curtains were drawn aside and a body of priests entered, twelve in number, bearing large candles of fat in their hands, and headed by their chief, Nam. Prostrating themselves before Juanna and Otter they remained plunged in silence.

"Speak on," said Juanna at length.

"We come, O Mother, and O Snake," said the priest Nam, "to lead you to the temple that the people may look upon their gods."

"It is well; lead on," Juanna answered.

"First you must be robed, Mother," said Nam, "for without the temple none may look upon your divinity, save your priests alone."

Rising as he spoke, he produced a black dress from a grass bag, which was carried by an attendant. This dress was very curious. It fastened in front with buttons of horn, and either was, or seemed to be, woven in a single piece from the softest hair of black-fleeced goats. Moreover, it had sleeves just long enough to leave the hands of the wearer visible, and beneath its peaked cap was a sort of mask with three slits, two for the eyes and one for the mouth.

Juanna retired to put on this hideous garment over her white robe, and reappeared presently, looking like the black ghost of a mediaeval monk. Then the priests gave her two flowers, a red lily and a white, to be held in either hand, and it appeared that her equipment was complete. Next they came to Otter and bound a scarlet fringe of hair about his forehead in such fashion that the fringe hid his eyes, at the same time placing in his hand a sceptre of ivory, apparently of very ancient workmanship, and fashioned in the shape of a snake standing on its tail.

"All is prepared," said Nam.

"Lead on," answered Juanna again. "But let our servants come with us, both those here and those without, save the woman only, who stays to make ready for our return."

Juanna spoke thus because Soa had announced her wish to be left behind when they went to the temple. Juanna had consulted Leonard on the subject, who gave it as his opinion that Soa had good reasons of her own for making this request. Also he pointed out that in case of disturbance she could scarcely help them, and might possibly prove an encumbrance.

"They wait," answered Nam; "all is prepared for *them* also": and as he spoke a sardonic smile flickered on his withered countenance that made Leonard feel very uncomfortable. What was prepared, he wondered?

They passed through the curtains into the courtyard, where soldiers, clad in goat-skin cloaks, waited with two litters. Here also were the Settlement men, armed, but in an extremity of fear, for they were guarded by about fifty of the Great People, also armed.

Juanna and Otter entered the litters, behind which Leonard formed up his little band, going in front of it himself with Francisco, both of them having rifles in their hands and revolvers at their girdles, of which no attempt was made to deprive them, for none knew their use.

Then they started, surrounded by the bare-breasted priests, who chanted and waved torches as they walked, and preceded and followed by the grim files of tall soldiers, on whose spears the torch-light flashed ominously. As they came the gates of the palace yard were opened. They passed them and across the space beyond until they reached the doors of the temple, which were thrown wide before them.

Here Otter and Juanna descended from the litters, and all the torches were extinguished, leaving them in darkness.

Leonard felt his hand seized and was led along, he knew not where, for the misty gloom was intense. He could scarcely see the face even of the priest who conducted them, but from the sounds he gathered that all their party were being guided in a similar fashion. Once or twice also he heard the voice of a Settlement man speaking in accents of fear or complaint, but such demonstrations were followed quickly by the sound of a heavy blow, dealt, no doubt, by the priest or soldier in charge of that individual. Evidently it was expected that all should be silent. Presently Leonard became aware that they had left the open space across which they were walking, for the air grew close and their footsteps rang hollow on the rocky floor.

"I believe that we are in a tunnel," whispered Francisco.

"Silence, dog," hissed a priest in his ear. "Silence, this place is holy."

They did not understand the meaning of the words at the moment, but the tone in which they were spoken made their purport sufficiently clear. Leonard took the hint, and at the same time clutched his rifle more tightly. He began to be afraid for their safety. Whither were they being led—to a dungeon? Well, they would soon know, and at the worst it was not probable that these barbarians would harm Juanna. They followed the tunnel or passage for about a hundred and fifty paces; at first it sloped downwards, then the floor became level till at length they began to ascend a stair. There were sixty-one stone steps in this stairway, for Leonard counted them, each about ten inches high, and when all were climbed they advanced eleven paces along a tunnel that echoed strangely to their steps, and was so low that they must bend their heads to pass it. Emerging from this tunnel through a narrow opening, they stood upon a platform also of stone, and once more the chill night air fanned their brows.

So dense was the gloom that Leonard could tell nothing of the place where they might be, but from far beneath them rose a hissing sound as of seething water, and combined with it another sound of faint murmuring, as though thousands of people whispered each to each. Also from time to time he heard a rustling like that of a forest when a gentle wind stirs its leaves, or the rustling of the robes of innumerable women.

This sense of the presence of hidden waters and of an unseen multitude was strange and terrifying in the extreme. It was as though, without perceiving them, their human faculties suddenly became aware of the spirits of the unnumbered dead, thronging, watching, following—there, but intangible; speaking without words, touching without hands.

Leonard was tempted to cry aloud, so great was the strain upon his nerves, which usually were strong enough; nor was he alone in this desire. Presently a sound arose from below him, as of some person in hysterics, and he heard a priest command silence in a fierce voice. The sobbing and laughter went on till it culminated in a shrill scream. After the scream came the thud of a blow, a heavy fall, a groan, and once again the invisible multitudes whispered and rustled.

"Someone has been killed," muttered Francisco in Leonard's ear; "who is it, I wonder?"

Leonard shuddered, but made no answer, for a great hand was placed upon his mouth in warning.

At length the portentous silence was broken and a voice spoke, the voice of Nam the priest. In the silence all that he uttered could be heard plainly, but his words came from far away, and the sound of them was still and small. This was what he said, as Juanna told it to them after the ceremony.

"Hear me, ye Children of the Snake, ye ancient People of the

Mist! Hearken to me, Nam, the priest of the Snake! Many a generation gone in the beginning of time, so runs the legend, the Mother goddess whom we worship from of old, descended from heaven and came hither to us, and with her came the Snake, her child. While she tarried in the land the crime of crimes was wrought, the Darkness slew the Daylight, and she passed hence, we know not how, or where; and from that hour the land has been a land of mist, and its people have wandered in the mist, for he whose name is Darkness has ruled over them, answering their prayers with death. But this doom was on the Snake, that because of his wickedness he must put off the flesh of men and descend into the holy place of waters, where, as we and our fathers have known, his symbol dwells eternally, taking tribute of the lives of men.

"Yet ere that crime was wrought the Mother gave a word of promise to her people. 'Now that I am about to die at the hands of him I bore, for so it is fated,' she said. 'But not for ever do I leave you, and not for ever shall the Snake be punished by putting off the flesh of men. Many generations shall go by and we will return again and rule over you, and the veil of mist shall be lifted from your land, and ye shall be great in the earth. Till then, choose you kings and let them govern you; moreover, forget not my worship, and see to it that throughout the ages the altar of the Snake is wet with blood, and that he lacks not the food he loves. And I will give you a sign by which we shall be known when at length the fate is accomplished, and the hour of forgiveness is at hand.

"'As a fair maid will I come again, a maid lovely and white, but because of his sin the Snake shall appear in the shape of that which sits within your temple, and his hue shall be black and his face hideous. Out of the earth will we arise, and we will call to you and ye shall know us, and we will tell you our holy names that shall not be spoken aloud from this hour to that hour of our coming. But beware lest ye be deceived and false gods set themselves up among you, for then shall the last evil fall upon you and the sun shall hide his face.'

"Thus, Children of the Mist, did the Mother speak to him who was her chief priest in the long ago, and he graved her words with iron on the stone of that whereon I stand, but none can read that writing, for its secret is lost to us, although the prophecy remains. And now the time is full, and it has been given to me, his successor, in my old age, to see the fulfilment of the saying.

"The time is full, and this night the promise of the past is accomplished, for, People of the Mist, the immortal gods, whose names are holy, have appeared to rule their children. Yesterday they came, ye saw them, and in your ears they called aloud the sacred names. As a maiden fair and white, and as a dwarf black and hideous, have they come, and *Aca* is the name of the maiden, and *Jal* is the name of the dwarf."

He ceased, and his voice died away in the echoes of the great place. Once again there was silence, broken only by the seething sound of waters and the indefinable murmur of an unseen throng beneath.

Leonard stood awhile, then edged himself gently forward with the design of discovering where and upon what they were standing. His curiosity soon met with a violent check, for before he had gone a yard he felt that his right foot was dangling in space, and it was only by a strong effort that he prevented himself from falling, whither he knew not.

Recovering his balance, he shuffled himself back again to the side of Francisco, and whispered a warning to him not to move if he valued his life. As Leonard spoke, he noticed that the blackness of the night was turning grey with the light of the unrisen moon. Already her rays, striking upwards, brightened the sky above and the mountains behind, and from them fell a pale reflection, which grew gradually stronger and clearer.

Now he could discover that close upon him to the left a black mass towered high into the air, and that far beneath him gleamed something like the foam on broken water. For a time he watched this water, or whatever it might be, until a smothered exclamation from Francisco caused him to look up again. As he looked, the edge of the moon rose above the temple wall, and by slow degrees a wonderful sight was revealed to him. Not till the moon was fully visible did he see everything, and to describe all as he discovered it, piecemeal, would be difficult. This was what Leonard saw at length.

Before him and underneath him lay a vast and roofless building, open to the east, covering some two acres of ground, and surrounded by Titanic walls, fifty feet or more in height. This building was shaped like a Roman amphitheatre, but, with the exception of the space immediately below him, its area was filled with stone seats, and round its wide circumference stone seats rose tier on tier. These were all occupied by men and women in hundreds, and, except at the further end, scarcely a place was empty. At the western extremity of the temple a huge statue towered seventy or eighty feet into the air, hewn, to all appearance, from a mass of living rock. Behind this colossus, and not more than a hundred paces from it, the sheer

186

mountain rose, precipice upon precipice, to the foot of a white peak clad in eternal snow. It was the peak that they had seen from the plain when the mist lifted, and the statue was the dark mass beneath it which had excited their curiosity.

This fearful colossus was fashioned to the shape of a huge dwarf of hideous countenance, seated with bent arms outstretched in a forward direction, and palms turned upwards as though to bear the weight of the sky. The statue stood, or rather sat, upon a platform of rock; and not more than four paces from its base, so that the outstretched hands and slightly bowed head overhung it indeed, was a circular gulf measuring, perhaps, thirty yards across, in which seething waters raged and boiled. Whence they came and whither they went it was impossible to see, but Leonard discovered afterwards that here was the source of the river which they had followed for so many days. Escaping from the gulf by underground passages that it had hollowed for itself through the solid rock, the two branches of the torrent passed round the walls of the town, to unite again in the plain below. How the pool itself was supplied Leonard was destined to learn in after days.

Between the steep polished sides of the rock basin and the feet of the statue was placed an altar, or sacrificial stone. Here on this ledge, which covered an area no greater than that of a small room, and in front of the altar, stood a man bound, in whom Leonard recognised Olfan, the king, while on either side of him were priests, naked to the waist, and armed with knives. Behind them again stood the little band of Settlement men, trembling with terror. Nor were their fears groundless, for there among them lay one of their number, dead. This was the man whose nerve had broken down, who shrieked aloud in the darkness, and in reward had been smitten into everlasting silence.

All this Leonard saw by degrees, but the first thing that he saw has not yet been told. Long before the brilliant rays of the moon lit the amphitheatre they struck upon the huge head of the dwarf idol, and there, on this giddy perch, some seventy feet from the ground, and nearly a hundred above the level of the pool of seething water, sat Juanna herself, enthroned in an ivory chair. She had been divested of her black cloak, and was clad in the robe of snowy linen cut low upon her breast, and fastened round her waist with a girdle. Her dark hair flowed about her shoulders; in either hand she held the lilies, red and white, and upon her forehead glowed the ruby like a blood-red star. She sat quite still, her eyes set wide in horror; and first the moonlight

187

gleamed upon the gem bound to her forehead, next it showed the pale and lovely face beneath, then her snowy arms and breast, the whiteness of her robes, and the hideous demon head whereon her throne was fixed.

No spirit could have seemed more beautiful than this woman set thus on high in that dark place of blood and fear. Indeed, in the unearthly light she looked like a spirit, the spirit of beauty triumphing over the hideousness of hell, the angel of light trampling the Devil and his works.

It was not wonderful that this fierce and barbarous people sighed like reeds before the wind when her loveliness dawned upon them, made ethereal by the moon, or that thenceforth Leonard could never think of her quite as he thought of any other woman. Under such conditions most well-favoured women would have appeared beautiful; Juanna did more, she seemed divine.

As the light grew downward and the shadows thinned before it, Leonard followed with his eyes, and presently he discovered Otter. The dwarf, naked except for his girdle and the fringe upon his head, was also enthroned, holding the ivory sceptre in his hand, but in a seat of ebony placed upon the knees of the colossus, nearly forty feet below Juanna.

Then Leonard turned to consider Francisco's position and his own, and found it terrible enough. Indeed, the moment that he discovered it was nigh to being his last. In company with two priests of the Snake, they were standing on the palm of the right hand of the idol, that formed a little platform some six feet square, which they had won in the darkness through a tunnel hewn in the arm of stone. There they stood unprotected by any railing or support, and before them and on either side of them was a sheer drop of some ninety feet to the water beneath or of fifty to the rock of the platform.

Leonard saw, and for a moment turned faint and dizzy, then, setting the butt of his rifle on to the stone, he leaned upon the barrel till his brain cleared. It was well for him that he had not known what lay beneath when, but now, he thrust his foot into vacancy, for then his senses might have failed him.

Suddenly he remembered Francisco, and opened his eyes, which he had closed to shut out the sight of the yawning gulf beneath. It was not too soon. The priest had seen also, and consciousness was deserting him; even as Leonard turned his knees gave way, and he sank forward and downward.

Quick as thought Leonard stretched out his right hand and caught

Francisco by the robe he wore, then, resting his weight upon the rifle, he strained at the priest's falling body with all his force in such a manner that its direction was turned, and it fell sideways upon the platform, not downwards into space. Leonard dragged at him again, and thrust him into the mouth of the little tunnel through which they had reached this dreadful eminence, where he lay quiet and safe, lost in blessed insensibility.

All this took place in a few seconds. The two priests of the Snake, who stood by them as calmly as though their feet were still on the solid earth, saw, but made no movement. Only Leonard thought that they smiled grimly, and a horrible fear struck his heart like a breath of ice. What if they waited a signal to cast him down? It might well be so. Already he had seen enough of their rites to enable him to guess that theirs was a religion of blood and human sacrifice.

He shivered, and again turned faint, so faint indeed that he did not dare to keep his feet, but sank into a sitting posture, resting his back against the stone of the idol's thumb.

CHAPTER 23

How Juanna Conquered Nam

Still the silence endured, and still the moonlight grew, creeping lower and lower till it shone upon the face of the seething waters, and, except in the immediate shadow of the walls, all the amphitheatre was full of it.

Then the voice of Nam spoke again from far away, and Leonard looked to see whence he spoke. Now he saw. Nam, attended by three priests, was perched like an eagle on the left palm of the colossus, and from this dizzy platform he addressed the multitude. Looking across the breast of the statue, Leonard could just see the outstretched arm and the fierce face of the high priest as he glared down upon the people.

"Hearken, ye Dwellers in the Mist, Children of the Snake! Ye have seen your ancient gods, your Father and your Mother, come back to rule you and to lead you on through war to peace, to wealth, to power, and to glory. Ye see them now by that light and in that place wherein only it is lawful that ye should look upon them. Say, do ye believe and do ye accept them? Answer, every one of you, answer with your voice!"

Then a mighty roar of sound went up from the gathered thousands, a roar that shaped itself into the words:

"We believe and we accept."

"It is well," said Nam when the tumult had died away. "Hearken, ye high gods! O Aca! and O Jal! Bend down your ears and deign to hearken to your priest and servant, speaking in the name of your children, the People of the Mist. Be ye kings to reign over us! Accept the power and the sacrifice, and sit in the place of kings. We give you rule through all the land; the life of every dweller in the land is yours; yours are their cattle and their goats, their city and their armies. For you the altars shall run red, the cry of the victim shall be music in your ears. Ye shall look upon him whom long ago ye set to guard the secret awful place, and he shall crawl beneath your feet. As ye ruled our fathers so ye shall rule us, according to the customs which ye laid down for ever. Glory be to you, O Aca, and to you, O Jal! immortal kings for evermore!"

And in a shout that rent the skies the great audience echoed: "Glory be to you, O Aca, and to you, O Jal, immortal kings for evermore!"

Then Nam spoke again, saying: "Bring forth the virgin, that fair maid who is destined to the Snake, that he may look upon her and accept her as his wife. Bring her forth also who, twelve months gone, was vowed in marriage to the Shape of stone, that she may bid her lord farewell."

As he spoke there was a stir behind the idol, and presently from each side of it a woman was led forward by two priests on to the little space of rock between its feet and the edge of the gulf, and placed one to the right of the altar, and one to the left. Both these women were tall and lovely with the dark and somewhat terrifying beauty of the People of the Mist, but there the resemblance between them ended. She to the right was naked except for a girdle of snake-skin and the covering of her abundant hair, which was crowned with a wreath of red lilies similar to the flower that the priests had given to Juanna. She to the left, on the contrary, was clothed in a black robe round which was broidered the shape of a blood-red snake, whose head rested upon her breast. Leonard noticed that the appearance of this woman was that of extreme terror, for she shrank and trembled, whereas that of the flower-crowned bride was jubilant and even haughty.

For a moment the two women stood still while the people gazed upon them. Then, at a signal from Nam, she who was crowned with flowers was led before the altar, and thrice she bowed the knee to the idol, or rather to Otter who sat upon it. Now all eyes were fixed on the dwarf, who stared at the girl but made no sign, which was not wonderful, seeing that he had no inkling of the meaning of the ceremony. As it chanced, he could not have acted more wisely, at least in the interests of the bride, for here, as elsewhere, silence was held to give consent.

"Behold, the god accepts," cried Nam, "the beauty of the maid is pleasing in his eyes. Stand aside, Saga, the blessed, that the people may look upon you and know you. Hail to you, wife of the Snake!"

Smiling triumphantly the girl moved back to her place by the altar, and turned her proud face to the people. Then the multitude shouted:

"Hail to you, bride of the Snake! Hail to you, the blessed, chosen of the god!"

While the tumult still lasted, the woman who was clad in the black robe was led forward, and when it had died away she also made her obeisance before the idol.

191

"Away with her that she may seek her Lord in his own place," cried Nam.

"Away with her, her day is done," echoed the multitude. Then, before Juanna could interfere, before she could even speak, for, be it remembered, she alone understood all that was said, the two priests who guarded the doomed woman rent the robe from her and with one swing of their strong arms hurled her backwards far into the pool of seething waters.

She fell with a shriek and lay floating on their surface, flung this way and that by the eddy of the whirlpool just where the moonlight beat most brightly. All who could of the multitude bent forward to see her end, and overcome by a fearful fascination, Leonard threw himself on his face, and, craning his head over the stone of the idol's hand, watched also, for the girl's struggling shape was almost immediately beneath him. Another minute and he would have foregone the hope of winning the treasure which he had come so far to seek, not to have yielded to the impulse.

For as he stared, the waters beneath the feet of the idol were agitated as a pond is agitated by the rush of a pike when he dashes at his prey. Then for an instant the light gleamed upon a dull enormous shape, and suddenly the head of a crocodile reared itself out of the pool. The head of a crocodile, but of such a crocodile as he had never heard or dreamed of, for this head alone was broader than the breast of the biggest man, its dull eyes were the size of a man's fist, its yellow fangs were like the teeth of a lion, and from its lower jaw hung tentacles or lumps of white flesh which at that distance gave it the appearance of being bearded like a goat. Also, the skin of this huge reptile, which could not have measured less than fifty feet in length by four feet in depth, was here and there corroded into rusty excrescences, as though some fungus or lichen had grown upon it like grey moss on an ancient wall. Indeed, its appearance seemed to point to extreme antiquity.[2]

Hearing the disturbance in the water, the reptile had emerged from the cave where it dwelt beneath the feet of the idol, to seek its accus-

---

2. Crocodiles are proverbially long-lived, but Leonard could never discover the age of this particular reptile. On enquiry he was able to trace it back for three hundred years, and tradition said that it had always dwelt among the People of the Mist from "the beginning of time." At least it was very old, and under the name of the Snake had been an object of worship for many generations. How it came among the People of the Mist is difficult to say, for no other specimen appeared to exist in the country. Perhaps it was captured in some distant age and placed in the cave by the priests, to figure as an incarnation of the Snake that was the object of their worship.

tomed food, which consisted of the human victims that were cast to it at certain intervals. It reared its hideous head and glared round, then of a sudden the monster and the victim vanished together into the depths.

Sick with horror Leonard drew himself back into a sitting posture, and glanced up at Juanna. She was crouched in her ivory chair overcome, and her eyes were closed, either through faintness or to shut out the sight of dread. Then he looked down at Otter. The dwarf, staring fixedly at the water, sat still as the stone effigy that supported him. Evidently in all his varied experience he had seen no such thing as this.

"The Snake has accepted the sacrifice," cried Nam again; "the Snake has taken her who was his bride to dwell with him in his holy house. Let the offerings be completed, for this is but the first-fruit. Take Olfan who was king, and offer him up. Cast down the white servants of the Mother, and offer them up. Seize the slaves who stood before her in the plain, and offer them up. Lead forth the captives, and offer them up. Let the sacrifice of the Crowning of Kings be accomplished according to custom, that the god whose name is Jal may be appeased; that he may listen to the pleadings of the Mother, that the sun may shine upon us, that fruitfulness may fill the land and peace be within its gates."

Thus he cried while Leonard felt his blood turn cold and his hair rise upon his head, for though he could not understand the words, he guessed their purport and his instinct told him that a great danger threatened them. He looked at the two priests who stood by, and they glared hungrily on him in answer. Then his courage came back to him; at least he had his rifle and would fight for his life. It must go hard if he could not put a bullet through one or both of them before they got a hold of him.

Meanwhile the priests below had seized the king Olfan, whose giant form they were dragging towards the stone of sacrifice. But of a sudden, for the first time Juanna spoke, and a deep silence fell upon the temple and all within it.

"Hearken, People of the Mist," she said; and her voice falling from that great height seemed small and far away, although so clear that every word was audible in the stillness of the night.

"Hear me, People of the Mist, and ye, priests of the Snake. Aca is come again and Jal is come again, and ye have given them back their rule after many generations, and in their hands lies the life of every one of you. As the old tradition told of them so they are, the Mother and the Child, and the one is clothed with beauty, the symbol of life and of the fruitful earth; and the other is black and hideous, the symbol of death and the evil that walks upon the earth. And ye would do sacrifice to Jal that he may be appeased according to the ancient law, and listen to the pleading of the Mother that fruitfulness may fill the land. Not so shall Jal be appeased, and not because of the sacrifice of men shall Aca plead with him that prosperity may reign in the land.

"Behold, the old law is done away, and we give you a new law. Now is the hour of reconciliation, now Life and Death walk hand in hand, and the hearts of Aca and Jal have grown gentle through the ages, and they no longer crave the blood of men as an offering to their majesty. Henceforth ye shall bring them fruits and flowers, and not the lives of men. See, in my hand I hold winter lilies, red and white, blood-red they are and white as snow. Now the red flower, token of sacrifice and slaughter, I crush and cast away, but the white bloom of love and peace I set upon my breast. It is done, gone is the old law; see, it falls into the place of the Snake, its home; but the new law blossoms above my heart and in it. Shall it not be so, my children, People of the Mist? Will ye not accept my mercy and my love?"

The multitude watched the red bloom as, bruised and broken, through the light and through the shadow, they fell slowly to the seething surface of the pool; then it looked up like one man and saw the white lily set upon Juanna's whiter breast. They saw, and, moved by a common impulse, they rose with a sound like the rush of the wind and shouted:

"Gone is the day of blood and sacrifice, come is the day of peace! We thank you, Mother, and we take your mercy and your love."

Then they were silent, and again there was a sound like that of the wind, as all their thousands sank back to the seats of stone.

Now Nam spoke again in a voice of fury that rang through the still air like a clarion.

"What is this that my ears hear?" he cried. "Are ye mad, O ye Dwellers in the Mist? Or does the Mother speak with a charmed voice? Shall the ancient worship be changed in an hour? Nay, not the gods themselves can alter their own worship. Slay on, ye priests, slay on, or ye yourselves shall die the dreadful death."

The priests below heard, and seizing the struggling king they cast him with difficulty down upon the stone.

"Leonard, Leonard," cried Juanna in English, addressing him for the first time by his Christian name, as even then he noticed, but looking straight before her that none might guess to whom she spoke.

"These priests are going to kill you and all of us, except Otter and myself. If you can, when you see me point with my hand, shoot that man who is about to sacrifice the king. Make no answer."

Leonard heard and understood all. Resting his back firmly against the thumb of the statue, he shifted his position a little so that the group below him came within his line of sight, and waited, watching Juanna, who now was speaking again in the language of the People of the Mist.

"This I promise you, ministers of blood," she said, "if ye obey me not ye shall indeed die the dreadful death, the death unknown. Hearken, my servant, who are named Deliverer," and she looked down upon Leonard, "and do my bidding. If one of these shall dare to lift his hand against yonder man, slay him swiftly as you know how."

"Smite on," screamed Nam, "smite on and fear not."

Most of the priests drew back affrighted; but one ruffian lifted his knife, and at that moment Juanna pointed with her hand. Then Leonard, stepping forward, covered the priest's great breast with his rifle as surely as the uncertain light would allow. Unconscious of his danger, the executioner muttered an invocation. Now the knife was about to fall upon the throat of Olfan, when fire and smoke sprang out far above him, the rifle rang, and, shot through the heart, the priest leaped high into the air and fell dead. Terror seized the witnesses of this unaccustomed and, to them, most awful sight.

"The gods speak with flame and thunder," one cried, "and death is in the flame."

"Silence, dogs!" screamed Nam, "ye are bewitched. Ho! you that stand on high, cast down the wizard who is named Deliverer, and let us see who will deliver him from death upon the stone."

Then one of the guards who stood by him made a movement to grasp Leonard and throw him down, but the other was terrified and could not stir. The first man stretched out his arm, but before it so much as touched its aim he himself was dead, for, seeing his purpose, Leonard had lifted the rifle, and once more its report rang through the temple. Suddenly the priest threw his arms wide, then fell backwards, and with a mighty rush dived into sheer space to crash lifeless on the stone floor below, where he lay, his head and hands hanging over the edge of the pool.

Now for the first time Otter's emotions overcame him. He stood up on the knees of the dwarf, and shaking the sceptre in his hand, he pointed with it to the dead men on the paving below, at the same time crying in stentorian tones:

195

"Well done, Baas, well done! Now tumble the old one yonder off his perch, for I weary of his howlings."

This speech of Otter's produced even a greater effect on the spectators, if that were possible, than the mysterious death of the priests. That he whose name was Silence should cry aloud in a strange tongue, of which they understood no single word, was a dread and ominous thing that showed his anger to be deep. But Leonard took no heed, he was too engaged in covering the second guard with the barrel of his repeater. This man, however, had no liking for such a dreadful death. Swiftly he flung himself on to his knees, imploring Leonard to spare him in humble accents, and with gestures that spoke more plainly than his words.

Taking advantage of the pause, again Juanna cried aloud: "Ye see, People of the Mist, I make no idle threats. Where are they now, the disobedient ones? The tongue of flame has licked them and they are dead, and as they have perished, so shall all perish who dare to gainsay my word, or the word of Jal. Ye know us for gods and ye have crowned us kings, and gods and kings we are indeed. Yet fear not, for on the rebellious only shall our anger fall. Answer you, Nam. Will you do our bidding? Or will you die also as your servants died?"

Nam glanced round desperately. He looked down on the multitude and found no help there. Long had they cowered beneath him; now hope was born in their breasts, and in the presence of a power greater than his, if only for a little while, they broke his yoke and the yoke of their red superstitions. He looked at the company of priests; their heart was out of them, they were huddled together like knots of frightened sheep, staring at the corpses of their two companions. Then he bethought him of Otter. Surely there was refuge in the god of blood and evil; and he cried to him:

"The Mother has spoken, but the Mother is not the child. Say, O Jal, what is your command?"

Otter made no answer, because he did not understand; but Juanna replied swiftly:

"I am the mouth of Jal, as Jal is my hand. When I speak I speak the words of Jal. Do his bidding and mine, or die, you disobedient servant."

This was the end of it. Nam was beaten; for the first time in his life he must own a master, and that master the gods whom he had himself discovered and proclaimed.

"So be it," he said suddenly. "The old order passes, and the new order comes. So be it! Let your will be done, O Aca and O Jal. I have striven for your glory, I have fed your altars, and ye threaten me with death and put away my gift. Priests, set free that man who was king. People, have your way, forget your ancient paths, pluck the white flower of peace—and perish! I have said."

So he spoke from on high, shaking his clenched fists above his hoary head, and was gone. Then the executioners unbound the limbs of the ex-king, and he rose from the stone of death.

"Olfan," cried Juanna from on high, "you that were the king, we, who have taken your kingship, give you life, and liberty, and honour; see that in reward you serve us well, lest again you should lie upon that bed of stone. Do you swear fealty to us?"

"For ever and for ever. I swear it by your holy heads," answered Olfan.

"It is well. Now under us once more we give you command of the armies of this people, our children. Summon your captains and your soldiers. Bid those that brought us hither lead us back whence we came, and there set guards about us, so that none trouble us. For you, our people, for this time fare you well. Go in peace to dwell in peace beneath the shadow of our strength."

CHAPTER 24

Olfan Tells of the Rubies

It was at this juncture that Francisco recovered his senses. "Oh!" he gasped, opening his eyes and sitting up, "is it done, and am I dead?"

"No, no, you are alive and safe," answered Leonard. "Stay where you are and don't look over the edge, or you will faint again. Here, take my hand. Now, you brute," and he made energetic motions to the surviving priest, indicating that he must lead them back along the path by which they had come, at the same time tapping his rifle significantly.

The man understood and started down the darksome tunnel as though he were glad to go, Leonard holding his robe with one hand, while with the other he pressed the muzzle of the loaded rifle against the back of his neck. Francisco followed, leaning on Leonard's shoulder, for he could not walk alone.

As they had come so they returned. They passed down the steps of stone which were hollowed in the body of the colossus; they traversed the long underground tunnel, and at length, to their intense relief, once more they stood upon the solid ground and in the open air. Now that the moon was up, and the mist which had darkened the night had melted, they could see their whereabouts. They had emerged upon a platform of rock within a bowshot of the great gates of the palace, from whence the secret subterranean passage used by the priests was gained, its opening being hidden cunningly among the stone-work of the temple.

"I wonder where the others are," asked Leonard anxiously of Francisco.

As he spoke, Juanna, wrapped in her dark cloak, appeared, apparently out of the stones of the wall, and with her Otter, the Settlement men bearing their dead companion, and a considerable company of priests, among whom, however, Nam was not to be seen.

"Oh, is that you, Leonard?" said Juanna in English, and in a voice broken with fear. "Thank Heaven that you are safe!"

"Thank Heaven that we are all safe," he answered. "Come, let us get on. No, we can walk, thank you," and he waved away the priests, who produced the litters from where they had hidden them under the wall.

The men fell back and they walked on. At the gate of the palace a welcome sight met their eyes, for here stood Olfan, and with him at least a hundred captains and soldiers, who lifted their spears in salute as they advanced.

"Olfan, hear our bidding," said Juanna. "Suffer no priest of the Snake to enter the palace gates. We give you command over them, even to death. Set guards at every doorway and come with us."

The ex-king bowed and issued some orders, in obedience to which the sullen priests fell back murmuring. Then they all passed the gates, crossed the courtyard, and presently stood in the torch-lit throne-room, where Juanna had slept on the previous night. Here food had been prepared for them by Soa, who looked at them curiously, especially at Leonard and Francisco, as though, indeed, she had never expected to see them again.

"Hearken, Olfan," said Juanna, "we have saved your life tonight and you have sworn fealty to us; is it not so?"

"It is so, Queen," the warrior answered. "And I will be faithful to my oath. This heart, that but for you had now been cold, beats for you alone. The life you gave back to me is yours, and for you I live and die."

As he spoke he glanced at her with an expression in which, as it seemed to Juanna, human feeling was mixed with supernatural awe. Was it possible, she wondered with a thrill of fear, that this savage king was mingling his worship of the goddess with admiration of the woman? And did he begin to suspect that she was no goddess after all? Time would show, but at least the look in his eyes alarmed her.

"Fear not," he went on; "a thousand men shall guard you night and day. The power of Nam is broken for a while, and now all this company may sleep in peace."

"It is well, Olfan. Tomorrow morning, after we have eaten, we will talk with you again, for we have much to say. Till then, watch!"

The great man bowed and went, and at last they were alone.

"Let us eat," said Leonard. "What is this? Spirit, or a very good imitation of it. Well, I never wanted a glass of brandy more in my life."

When they had finished their meal, at the request of Leonard Juanna translated all that had been said in the temple, and among her listeners there was none more interested than Soa.

199

"Say, Soa," said Leonard, when she had finished, "you did not expect to see us come back alive, did you? Is that why you stayed away?"

"No, Deliverer," she answered. "I thought that you would be killed, every one of you. And so it must have come about, had it not been for the Shepherdess. Also, I stayed away because those who have looked upon the Snake once do not desire to see him again. Many years ago I was bride to the Snake, Deliverer, and, had I not fled, my fate would have been the fate of her who died this night."

"Well, I do not wonder that you chose to go," said Leonard.

"Oh, Baas," broke in Otter, "why did you not shoot that old medicine-man as I told you? It would have been easy when you were about it, Baas, and now he would have been broken like an eggshell thrown from a house-top, and not alive and full of the meat of malice. He is mad with rage and wickedness, and I say that he will kill us all if he can."

"I rather wish I had," said Leonard, pulling his beard. "I thought of it, but could not do everything; and on future occasions, Otter, will you remember that your name is Silence? Luckily, these people do not understand you: if they did you would ruin us all. What is the matter, Soa?"

"Nothing, Deliverer," she answered; "only I was thinking that Nam is my father, and I am glad that you did not shoot him, as this black dog, who is named a god, suggests."

"Of gods I know nothing, you old cow," answered Otter angrily; "they are a far-off people, though it seems that I am one of them, at any rate among these fools, your kinsmen. But of dogs I can tell you something, and it is that they bite."

"Yes, and cows toss dogs," said Soa, showing her teeth.

"Here is another complication," thought Leonard to himself; "one day this woman will make friends with her venerable parent and betray us, and then where shall we be? Well, among so many dangers an extra one does not matter."

"I must go to bed," said Juanna faintly; "my head is swimming. I cannot forget those horrors and that giddy place. When first I saw where I was, I nearly fainted and fell, but after a while I grew more used to it. Indeed, while I was speaking to the people I quite forgot my fear, and the height seemed to exhilarate me. What a sight it was! When all is said and done, it is a grand thing to have lived through such an experience. I wonder if anyone has ever seen its like."

"You are a marvellous woman, Juanna," said Leonard, with admiration. "We owe our lives to your wit and courage."

"You see I was right in insisting on coming with you," she answered somewhat aggressively.

"For our sakes, yes; for your own I am not so sure. To tell you the truth, I think that we should have done better never to have started on this mad expedition. However, things look a little more promising now, though Nam and his company have still to be reckoned with, and we don't seem much nearer the rubies, which are our main object."

"No," said Juanna, "they are gone, and we shall be lucky if we do not follow them into the home of that hideous snake. Good night."

"Francisco," said Leonard, as he rolled himself up in his blanket, "you had a narrow escape tonight. If I had missed my hold!"

"Yes, Outram, it was lucky for me that your arm is strong and your mind quick. Ah, I am a dreadful coward, and I can see the place now;" and he shuddered. "Always from a child I have believed that I shall die by a fall from some height, and tonight I thought that my hour had come. At first I did not understand, for I was watching the Senora's face in the moonlight, and to me she looked like an angel. Then I saw, and my senses left me. It was as though hands were stretched up from the blackness to drag me down—yes, I saw the hands. But you saved me, Outram, though that will not help me, for I shall perish in some such way at last. So be it. It is best that I should die, who cannot conquer the evil of my heart."

"Nonsense, my friend," said Leonard; "don't talk like that about dying. We can none of us afford to die just at present—that is, unless we are obliged to do so. Your nerves are upset, and no wonder! As for 'the evil of your heart,' I wish that most men had as little—the world would be better. Come, go to sleep; you will feel very differently tomorrow."

Francisco smiled sadly and shook his head, then he knelt and began to say his prayers. The last thing that Leonard saw before his eyes closed in sleep was the rapt girlish face of the priest, round which the light of the taper fell like an aureole, as he knelt muttering prayer after prayer with his pale lips.

It was nine o'clock before Leonard awoke next morning—for they had not slept till nearly four—to find Francisco already up, dressed, and, as usual, praying. When Leonard was ready they adjourned to Juanna's room, where breakfast was prepared for them. Here they found Otter, looking somewhat disturbed.

"Baas, Baas," he said, "they have come and will not go away!"

"Who?" asked Leonard.

"The woman, Baas: she who was given to me to wife, and many other women—her servants—with her. There are more than twenty

201

of them outside, Baas, and all of them very big. Now, what shall I do with her, Baas? I came here to serve you and to seek the red stones that you desire, and not a woman tall enough to be my grandmother."

"I really don't know and don't care," answered Leonard. "If you will be a god you must take the consequences. Only beware, Otter: lock up your tongue, for this woman will teach you to speak her language, and she may be a spy."

"Yes, Baas, I will see to that. Is not my name Silence, and shall women make me talk—me, who have always hated them? But—the Baas would not like to marry her himself? I am a god, as you say, though it was you who made me one, Baas, not I, and my heart is large; I will give her to you, Baas."

"Certainly not," answered Leonard decidedly. "See if the breakfast is ready. No, I forgot, you are a god, so climb up into the throne and look the part, if you can."

As he spoke, Juanna came from her room, looking a little pale, and they sat down to breakfast. Before they had finished their meal, Soa announced that Olfan was waiting without. Juanna ordered him to be admitted, and presently he entered.

"Is all well, Olfan?" asked Juanna.

"All is well, Queen," he answered. "Nam and three hundred of his following held council at dawn in the house of the priests yonder. There is much stir and talk in the city, but the hearts of the people are light because their ancient gods have come back to us, bringing peace with them."

"Good," said Juanna. Then she began to question him artfully on many things, and by degrees they learnt more of the People of the Mist.

It seemed, as Leonard had already guessed, that they were a very ancient race, having existed for countless generations on the same misty upland plains. They were not, however, altogether isolated, for occasionally they made war with other savage tribes. But they never intermarried with these tribes, all the captives taken in their wars being offered in sacrifice at the religious festivals. The real governing power in the community was the Society of the Priests of the Snake, who held their office by hereditary tenure, outsiders being admitted to their body only under very exceptional circumstances. The council of this society chose the kings, and when they were weary of one of them, they sacrificed him and chose another, either from among his issue or elsewhere. This being the custom, as may be imagined, the relations between church and state were much strained, but hitherto, as Olfan explained with suppressed rage, the church had been supreme.

Indeed, the king for the time being was only its mouthpiece, or executive officer. He led the armies, but the superstitions of the people, and even of the soldiers themselves, prevented him from wielding any real power; and, unless he chanced to die naturally, his end was nearly always the same: to be sacrificed when the seasons were bad or "Jal was angry."

The country was large but sparsely populated, the fighting men numbered not more than four thousand, of whom about half lived in the great city, the rest occupying villages here and there on the mountain slopes. As a rule the people were monogamous, except the priests. It was the custom of sacrifice which kept down the population to its low level, made the power of the priests absolute, and their wealth greater than that of all the other inhabitants of the country put together, for they chose the victims that had offended against Jal or against the mother-goddess, and confiscated their possessions to "the service of the temple." Thus the great herds of half-wild cattle which the travellers had seen on the plains belonged to the priests, and the priests took a fourth of the produce of every man's field and garden—that is, when they did not take it all, and his life with it.

Twice in every year great festivals were held in the temple of Jal, at the beginning of the spring season and in the autumn after the ingathering of the crops. At each of these festivals many victims were offered in sacrifice, some upon the stone and some by being hurled into the boiling pool beneath the statue, there to be consumed by the Snake or swept down the secret course of the underground river. The feast celebrated in the spring was sacred to Jal, and that in the autumn to the mother-goddess. But there was this difference between them—that at the spring ceremony female victims only were sacrificed to Jal to propitiate him and to avert his evil influence, while at the autumn celebration males alone were offered up to the mother-goddess in gratitude for her gifts of plenty. Also criminals were occasionally thrown to the Snake that his hunger might be satisfied. The priests had other rites, Olfan added, and these they would have an opportunity of witnessing if the spring festival, which should be celebrated on the second day from that date, were held according to custom.

"It shall not be celebrated," said Juanna, almost fiercely.

Then Leonard, who had hitherto listened in silence, asked a question through Juanna. "How is it," he said, "that Nam and his fellows, being already in absolute power, were so willing to accept the gods Jal and Aca when they appeared in person, seeing that henceforth they must obey, not rule?"

203

"For two reasons, lord," Olfan answered; "first, because the gods are gods, and their servants know them; and secondly, because Nam has of late stood in danger of losing his authority. Of all the chief priests that have been told of, Nam is the most cruel and the most greedy. For three years he has doubled the tale of sacrifices, and though the people love these sights of death, they murmur, for none know upon whom the knife shall fall. Therefore he was glad to greet the gods come back, since he thought that they would confirm his power, and set him higher than he sat before. Now he is astonished because they proclaim peace and will have none of the sacrifice of men, for Nam does not love such gentle gods."

"Yet he shall obey them," said Otter, speaking for the first time by the mouth of Juanna, who all this while was acting as interpreter, "or drink his own medicine, for I myself will sacrifice him to myself."

When Juanna had translated the dwarf's bloodthirsty threat, Olfan bowed his head meekly and smiled; clearly the prospect of Nam's removal did not cause him unmixed grief. It was curious to see this stately warrior chief humbling his pride before the misshapen, knob-nosed Kaffir.

"Say, Olfan," asked Leonard, "who cut from the rock the great statue on which we sat last night, and what is that reptile we saw when the woman was thrown into the pool of troubled waters?"

"Ask the Water-dweller of the water-dweller, the Snake of the snake, and the Dwarf of his image," answered Olfan, nodding towards Otter. "How can I, who am but a man, tell of such things, lord? I only know that the statue was fashioned in the far past, when we, who are now but a remnant, were a great people; and as for the Snake, he has always lived there in his holy place. Our grandfather's grandfathers knew him, and since that day he has not changed."

"Interesting fact in natural history," said Leonard; "I wish I could get him home alive to the Zoological Gardens."

Then he asked another question. "Tell me, Olfan, what became of the red stones yesterday, and of him who offended in offering them to the god yonder?"

"The most of them were cast into the pit of waters, lord, there to be hidden for ever. There were three hide sacks full."

"Oh, heavens!" groaned Leonard when Juanna had translated this. "Otter, you have something to answer for!"

"But the choicest," went on Olfan, "were put in a smaller bag, and tied about the neck of the man who had sinned. There were not many, but among them were the largest stones, that until yesterday shone in the eyes of the idol, stones blue and red together. Also, there was that stone, shaped like a human heart, which hitherto has been worn by the high priest on the days of sacrifice, and with it the image of the Dwarf fashioned from a single gem, and that of the Water-dweller cut from the great blue stone, and other smaller ones chosen because of their beauty and also because they have been known for long in the land. For although many of these pebbles are found where the priests dig for them, but few are large and perfect, and the art of shaping them is lost."

"And what became of the man?" Leonard asked, speaking as quietly as he could, for his excitement was great.

"Nay, I do not know," answered Olfan. "I only know that he was let down with ropes into the home of the Snake, and that he gained that holy place, for it was told to me that he dragged rope after him, perhaps as he fled before the Snake.

"Now it was promised to the man that when he had laid the bag of stones in the place of the Snake, for the Snake to guard for ever, his sins would be purged, and, if it pleased the Water-dweller to spare him, that he should be drawn up again. Thus Nam swore to him, but he did not keep his oath, for when the man had entered the cave he bade those who held the ropes to cast them loose, and I know not what happened to him, but doubtless he is food for the Snake. None who look upon that holy place may live to see the sun again."

"I only hope that the brute did not swallow the rubies as well as their bearer," said Leonard to Juanna; "not that there is much chance of our getting them, anyway."

Then Olfan went, nor did he return till the afternoon, when he announced that Nam and his two principal priests waited without to speak with them. Juanna ordered that they should be admitted, and presently they came in. Their air was humble, and their heads were bowed; but Leonard saw fury gleaming in their sombre eyes, and was not deceived by this mask of humility.

"We come, O ye gods," said Nam, addressing Juanna and Otter, who sat side by side on the throne-like chairs: "we come to ask your will, for ye have laid down a new law which we do not understand. On the third day from now is the feast of Jal, and fifty women are made ready to be offered to Jal that his wrath may be appeased with their blood, and that he may number their spirits among his servants, and withhold his anger from the People of the Mist, giving them a good season. This has been the custom of the land for many a generation, and whenever that custom was broken then the sun has not shone, nor the corn grown, nor have the cattle and the goats multiplied after their kind. But now, O ye gods, ye have proclaimed a new law, and I, who am yet your servant, come hither to ask your will. How shall the feast go, and what sacrifice shall be offered unto you?"

"The feast shall go thus," answered Juanna. "Ye shall offer us a sacrifice indeed; to each of us shall ye offer an ox and a goat, and the ox and the goat shall be given to the Snake to feed him, but not the flesh of men; moreover, the feast shall be held at noon and not in the night-time."

"An ox and a goat—to each an ox and a goat!" said Nam humbly, but in a voice of bitterest sarcasm. "As ye will so let it be, O ye gentle-hearted gods. And the festival shall be held at noon, and not in the night season as of old. As ye will, O ye kind gods. Your word is my law, O Aca, and O Jal;" and bowing to the ground the aged man withdrew himself, followed by his satellites.

"That devilish priest makes my flesh creep," said Juanna, when she had translated his words.

"Oh! Baas, Baas," echoed Otter, "why did you not shoot him while you might? Now he will surely live to throw us to the Snake."

As he spoke Soa advanced from behind the thrones where she had taken refuge when Nam entered.

"It is not well for a dog who gives himself out as a god to threaten the life of one whom he has tricked," said she meaningly. "Perchance the hour shall come when the true god will avenge himself on the false, and by the hand of his faithful servant, whom you would do to death, you base-born dwarf." And before anyone could answer she left the chamber, casting a malevolent look at Otter as she went.

"That servant of yours makes *my* flesh creep, Juanna," said Leonard. "One thing is clear enough, we must not allow her to overhear any more of our plans; she knows a great deal too much already."

"I cannot understand what has happened to Soa," said Juanna; "she seems so changed."

"You made that remark before, Juanna; but for my part I don't think she is changed. The sight of her amiable parent has developed her hidden virtues, that is all."

CHAPTER 25

The Sacrifice After the New Order

The third day came, the day of sacrifice after the new order. Nothing particular had happened in the interval: Leonard and Francisco took some walks through the city, guarded by Peter and the Settlement men; that was all.

They did not see much there, except the exteriors of the houses built of stone and roofed with turves, and the cold stare of curiosity with which they were followed by hundreds of eyes gave them a sense of unrest that effectually checked their efforts at closer examination. Once indeed they halted in the market-place, which was thronged; whereon all business ceased, and seller, buyer, herdsmen, and presiding priests flocked around staring at them, half in fear and half in curiosity, for they had never seen white men before. This they could not bear, so they returned to the palace.

Of course Otter and Juanna, being divine, were not allowed to indulge in such recreations. They were gods and must live up to their reputation. For one day Otter endured it; on the second, in spite of Leonard's warnings, he sought refuge in the society of the bridge Saga. This was the beginning of evil, for if no man is a hero to his *valet de chambre*, much less can he remain a god for long in the eyes of a curious woman. Here, as in other matters, familiarity breeds contempt.

Leonard saw these dangers and spoke seriously to the dwarf on the subject. Still he could not conceal from himself that, putting aside the question of his *ennui*, which made his conduct natural, at any rate in a savage, Otter's position was a difficult one. So Leonard shrugged his shoulders and consoled himself as best he could with the reflection that, at least, his wife would teach the dwarf something of her language, which, by the way, he himself was practising assiduously under the tuition of Juanna and Soa.

At noon the party adjourned to the temple, escorted by a bevy of priests and soldiers, for in obedience to Juanna's commands the feast was to be celebrated in the daytime and not at night. As before, the vast amphitheatre was crowded with thousands of human beings, but there was a difference in the arrangements.

Juanna and Otter had declined to occupy their lofty thrones, and sat in chairs at the feet of the huge and hideous stone idol, almost on the edge of the pool, Nam alone standing before them, while Leonard, Francisco, and the Settlement men ranged themselves on either side. The day was cold and miserable, and snow fell from time to time in large flakes from an ashen sky.

Presently Nam addressed the multitude.

"People of the Mist," he cried, "ye are gathered here to celebrate the feast of Jal, according to ancient custom, but the gods have come back to you, as ye know, and the gods in their wisdom have changed the custom. Fifty women were prepared for the sacrifice; this morning they rose rejoicing, deeming that they were destined to the Snake, but now their joy is turned to sorrow, since the gods will not accept them, having chosen a new offering for themselves. Let it be brought forward."

At his word lads appeared from behind the idol, driving two lean bulls, and with them a pair of he-goats.

Whether by accident or design, they drove them so unskilfully that the animals blundered hither and thither over the rocky platform till they were finally despatched with blows from clubs and axes—that is, except one goat, which, escaping its pursuers, rushed down the amphitheatre and scrambled from seat to seat among the audience, uttering a succession of terrified "baa's." Indeed the scene was so comic that even that sombre and silent people began to laugh, accustomed as they were on these occasions to the hideous and impressive ceremonial of the midnight sacrifice of so many human beings.

The ancient feast was a fiasco; this was a fact which could not be concealed.

"Begone, ye People of the Mist," said Nam presently, pointing to the dead animals. "The sacrifice is sacrificed, the festival of Jal is done. May the Mother plead with the Snake that the sun may shine and fruitfulness bless the land!"

Now scarcely ten minutes had elapsed since the beginning of the ceremony, which in the ordinary course of events lasted through the greater part of the night, for it was the custom to slaughter each victim singly and with appropriate solemnities. A murmur of disapprobation arose from the far end of the amphitheatre, that swelled gradually to a roar. The people had been thankful to accept Juanna's message of peace, but, brutalised as they were by the continual sight of bloodshed, they were not willing to dispense with their carnivals of human sacrifice. A Roman audience gathered to witness a gladiatorial show, to find themselves treated instead to a donkey-race and a cock-fight, could scarcely have shown more fury.

"Bring out the women! Let the victims be offered up to Jal as of old," the multitude yelled in their rage, and ten minutes or more elapsed before they could be quieted.

Then Nam addressed them cunningly.

"People of the Mist," he said, "the gods have given us a new law, a law of the sacrifice of oxen and goats in the place of men and maids, and ye yourselves have welcomed that law. No longer shall the blood of victims flow to Jal beneath the white rays of the moon while the chant of his servants goes up to heaven. Nay, henceforth this holy place must be a shambles for the kine. So be it, my children; in my old age I hear the gods speaking in an altered voice and I obey them. It is nothing to me who am about to die, yet I tell you that rather would I myself be stretched upon the ancient stone than see the worship of our forefathers thus turned into a mockery. The sacrifice is sacrificed: now may the Maid intercede with the Snake that plenty may bless the land." And he smiled satirically and turned away.

Those of the audience who were near enough to hear his words cried them out to the ranks behind them, and when all understood there followed a scene of most indescribable tumult.

"Blood, give us blood!" roared the populace, their fierce faces alight with rage. "Shall we be mocked with the sacrifice of goats? Offer up the servants of the false gods. Give us blood! Lead forth the victims!"

In the midst of this uproar Juanna, clad in her white robes and with the red stone bound upon her brow, rose from her seat to speak.

"Silence!" cried Nam, "hear the voice of Aca;" and by degrees the shouting died away, and she spoke.

"Do ye dare thus to offer outrages to the gods?" she cried. "Be warned lest we bring death and famine upon you all. Men shall be offered up to us no more. I have spoken."

For a while there was silence, then the clamour broke out with redoubled violence, and a portion of the multitude made a rush round the edge of the pool towards the rock platform, which was repelled by the soldiers in a very half-hearted way.

"Now," said Olfan, "I think that these will do well to be going," and he pointed to Leonard, Francisco, and the Settlement men. "Doubtless the gods can defend themselves, but if the others do not fly this is sure, that presently they will be torn to pieces."

"Let us all go," said Juanna, whose nerve began to fail her; and suiting the action to the word she led the way towards the rock tunnel, followed by the others.

They were not allowed to reach it unmolested, however, for a number of the crowd, headed, as Leonard noticed, by two priests, forced their way through the cordon of guards and became mixed with the rear of their little party, the members of which they threatened and struck at savagely. This happened just as they were entering the mouth of the tunnel, behind the statue where the gloom was great.

This tunnel was protected by a door, which, so soon as they thought that all had passed, Olfan and Leonard made haste to close, leaving the mob howling without. Then they pressed on to the palace, which they reached in safety, Olfan remaining behind, however, to watch the movements of the mob.

"Oh! why would not you suffer them to sacrifice according to their wicked custom, Shepherdess?" said Otter. "What does it matter if they kill each other? So shall there be fewer of them. Now the end of it must be that the devils will find us out and murder us."

"No, no," said Francisco, "the senora was right. Let us trust in Providence and keep ourselves clean from such iniquity."

As he spoke the roars of wrath in the distance changed to a shout of triumph followed by silence.

"What is that?" said Juanna faintly. At this moment Olfan pushed the curtains aside and entered, and his face was heavy.

"Speak, Olfan," she said.

"The people sacrifice as of old, Queen," he answered. "All of us did not pass the gate; two of your black servants were mixed up with the crowd and left, and now they offer them to Jal, and others with them."

Leonard ran to the yard and counted the Settlement men, who were huddled together in their fear, staring towards the temple through the bars of the gate. Two were missing.

As he returned he met Olfan coming out.

"Where is he going?" he asked of Juanna.

"To guard the gates. He says that he cannot be sure of the soldiers. Is it true about the Settlement men?"

"Alas! yes. Two are gone."

She hid her face in her hands and shuddered.

"Poor creatures!" she said presently in a hoarse voice. "Why did we ever bring them here? Oh! Leonard, is there no escape from this land of demons?"

"I hope so," he answered; then added, "Come, Juanna, do not give way. Things look so bad that they are sure to mend."

"There is need of it," she sobbed.

All that evening and night they watched, hourly expecting to be attacked and dragged forth to sacrifice, but no attack was made. Indeed, on the morrow they learnt from Olfan that the people had dispersed after sacrificing about a score of human beings, and that quiet reigned in the city.

Now began the most dreadful of their trials, and the longest, for it endured five whole weeks. As has been said, the climate of these vast upland plains, backed by snow-clad mountains, that are the dwelling-place of the People of the Mist, is cold during the winter months to the verge of severity. But at a certain period of a year, almost invariably within a day or two of the celebration of the feast of Jal, the mists and frost vanish and warm weather sets in with bright sunshine.

This is the season of the sowing of crops, and upon the climatic conditions of the few following weeks depends the yield of the harvest. Should the spring be delayed even a week or two, a short crop would certainly result, but if its arrival is postponed for a month, it means something like a famine during the following winter. For although this people dwell on high lands they cultivate the same sorts of grain which are common in these latitudes, namely maize and sundry varieties of Kaffir corn, having no knowledge of wheat and the other hardy cereals. Therefore, it is all important to them that the corn should have a fair start, for if the autumn frosts catch it before it is fit to harvest the great proportion of the crop turns black and is rendered useless.

These agricultural details had no small bearing upon the fate of our adventurers. The feast of Jal was celebrated in order to secure a good seed-bed and springing time for the grain. Juanna and Otter had abolished the hideous ceremonies of that feast, and the People of the Mist watched for the results with a gloomy and superstitious eye. If the season proved more than ordinarily good, all might go well, but if it chanced to be bad——!

And, as was to be expected, seeing how much depended upon it, this spring proved the very worst which any living man could remember in that country. Day after day the face of the sun was hidden with mists that only yielded to the bitter winds which blew from the mountains at night, so that when the spring should have been a month old, the temperature was still that of mid-winter and the corn would not start at all.

Leonard and Juanna soon discovered what this meant for them, and never was the aspect of weather more anxiously scanned than by these two from day to day. In vain; every morning the blanket of cold mist fell like a cloud, blotting out the background of the mountains, and every night the biting wind swept down upon them from the fields of snow, chilling them to the marrow.

This state of things—wretched enough it itself—was only one of many miseries which afflicted them. Otter and Juanna were still treated as gods indeed, and considerable respect was shown to Leonard and Francisco, that is, within the walls of the palace. But if, wearied with the monotony of their life, they went out, which they did twice only during these five dreadful weeks, matters were different. Then they found themselves followed by a mob of men, women, and children, who glared at them ferociously and cursed them aloud, asking what they had their gods had done with the sunshine.

On the second occasion indeed they were forced to fly for their lives, and after this they gave up making the attempt to walk abroad, and sat in the palace with Juanna and Otter, who of course never dared to leave it.

It was a terrible life; there was nothing to do, nothing to read, and only anxieties to think on. The greater part of the day Leonard and Juanna occupied in talking, for practice, in the language of the People of the Mist. When their conversation was exhausted they told each other tales of their adventures in past years, or even invented stories like children and prisoners; indeed they were prisoners—prisoners, as they feared, under sentence of death.

They grew to know each other very well during those five weeks, so well indeed that each could almost guess the other's thoughts. But no tender word ever passed their lips. On this subject, whatever their hearts might feel, their tongues were sealed, and in their curious perversity the chief object of each was to disguise the truth from the other. Moreover, Leonard never for one moment forgot that Juanna was his ward, a fact that in itself would have sufficed to cause him to conceal any tender emotions he might have felt towards her.

So they lived side by side, lovers at heart, yet talking and acting as brother and sister might, and through it all were still happy after a fashion because they were together.

But Soa was not happy. She felt that her mistress no longer trusted her, and was at no loss to guess the cause. Day by day she stood behind them like a mummy at an Egyptian feast, and watched Leonard with ever-growing jealousy.

Francisco for his part did not attempt to conceal his fears. He was certain that they were about to perish and sought consolation in the constant practice of religion, which was edifying but scarcely improved him as a companion. As for Otter, he also believed that the hour of death was nigh, but being a fatalist this did not trouble him much. On the contrary, in spite of Leonard's remonstrances he began to live hard, betaking himself freely to the beer-pot. When Leonard remonstrated with him he turned somewhat sulky.

"Today I am a god, Baas," he answered, "tomorrow I may be carrion. While I am a god, let me drink and be merry. All my days also women have cursed me because I am ugly, but now my wife holds me great and beautiful. What is the good of thinking and looking sad? The end will come soon enough. Already Nam sharpens the knife for our hearts. Come and be merry with me, Baas, if the Shepherdess will let you."

"Do you take me for a pig like yourself?" said Leonard angrily. "Well, go your own way, foolish that you are, but beware of the beer and the spirits. Now you are beginning to know this language, and when you are drunk you talk, and do you think that there are no spies here? That girl, Saga, is great-niece to Nam, and you are besotted with her. Be careful lest you bring us all to death."

"Thither we shall come any way, so let us laugh before we weep, Baas," Otter replied sullenly. "Must I then sit here and do nothing till I die?"

Leonard shrugged his shoulders and went. He could not blame the dwarf, who after all was a savage and looked at things as a savage would, notwithstanding Francisco's earnest efforts to convert him. He sometimes wished, so deep was his depression, that he also was a savage and could do likewise.

But the worst of their trials is still to be told. For the first week the Settlement men stayed in the palace, their fears and the rumours that had reached them of the terrible fate of their two lost companions keeping them quiet. By degrees, however, this dread wore off, and one afternoon, wearied with the sameness of their life, they yielded to the solicitations of some men who spoke to them through the bars of the great gate, and went out in a body without obtaining Leonard's permission. That night they returned drunk—at least ten of them dead; the other two were missing. When they were sober again, Leonard questioned them as to the whereabouts of their companions, but they could give him no satisfactory information. They had been into various houses in the city, they said, where the people had plied them with beer, and they remembered nothing more.

These two men never reappeared, but the rest of them, now thoroughly frightened, obeyed Leonard's orders and stayed in the palace, although the decoy men still came frequently to the gates and called them. They passed the days in wandering about and drinking to drown their fears, and the nights huddled together for protection from an unseen foe, more terrible and craftier than the leopard of their native rocks. But these precautions were all in vain.

One morning, hearing a tumult among them, Leonard went to see what was the matter. Three more of the Settlement men were missing; they had vanished in the night, none could say how, vanished though the doors were barred and guarded. There where they had slept lay their guns and little possessions, but the men were gone, leaving no trace. When he was consulted Olfan looked very grave, but could throw no light upon the mystery beyond suggesting that there were many secret passages in the palace, of which the openings were known only to the priests, and that possibly the men had been let down them—terrible information enough for people in their position.

CHAPTER 26

The Last of the Settlement Men

On that day of the vanishing of the three Settlement men, Nam paid his weekly visit to "do honour to the gods," and Leonard, who by this time could make himself understood in the tongue of the People of the Mist, attacked him as to the whereabouts of their lost servants.

When he had finished, the priest answered with a cruel smile that he knew nothing of the matter. "Doubtless," he said, "the gods had information as to the fate of their own servants—it was not for him to seek those whom the gods had chosen to put away."

Then turning the subject, he went on to ask when it would please the Mother to intercede with the Snake that he might cause the sun to shine and the corn to spring, for the people murmured, fearing a famine in the land.

Of course Juanna was able to give no satisfactory answer to the priest's questions, and after this the quarters of the Settlement men were changed, and for a few days the survivors slept in safety. On the third night, however, two more of them were taken in the same mysterious manner, and one of those who remained swore that, hearing something stir, he woke and saw the floor open and a vision of great arms dragging his sleeping companions through the hole in it, which closed again instantly. Leonard hurried to the spot and made a thorough examination of the stone blocks of the pavement, but could find no crack in them. And yet, if the man had dreamed, how was the mystery to be explained?

After this, with the exception of Otter, who, sure of the fate that awaited them, took little heed of how or when it might fall, none of the party could even sleep because of their terror of the unseen foe who struck in silence and in darkness, dragging the victim to some unknown awful end. Leonard and Francisco took it in turns to watch each other's slumbers, laying themselves to rest outside the curtain of

215

Juanna's room. As for the survivors of the Settlement men, their state can scarcely be described. They followed Leonard about, upbraiding him bitterly for leading them into this evil land and cursing the hour when first they had seen his face. It would have been better, they said, that he should have left them to their fate in the slave camp than have brought them here to die thus; the Yellow Devil was at least a man, but these people were sorcerers and lost spirits in human shape.

Nor did the horror stop here, for at last the headman Peter, a man whom they all liked and respected, went mad with fear and ran to and fro in the palace yard while the guards and women watched him with curious eyes as he shrieked out curses upon Juanna and Leonard. This shocking scene continued for some hours, for his companions would not interfere with him, vowing that he was possessed by a spirit, till at length he put a period to it by suddenly committing suicide. In vain did Leonard caution the survivors to keep their heads and watch at night. They flew to the beer which was supplied to them in plenty, and drank till they were insensible. And still one by one they vanished mysteriously, till at length all were gone.

Never might Leonard forget his feelings when one day at dawn, in the fifth week of their incarceration, he hurried as usual to the chamber where the last two of the unfortunate men were accustomed to sleep, and found them not. There were their blankets, there was the place where they had been, and on it, laid carefully in the form of a St. Andrew's cross by some unknown hand, shone two huge sacrificial knives such as the priests wore at their girdles.

Sick and faint with fear he staggered back to the throne-room.

"Oh! what is it now?" said Juanna, who, early as it was, had risen already, looking at him with terrified eyes and trembling lips.

"Only this," he answered hoarsely; "the last two have been taken, and here is what was left in the place of them," and he cast down the knives on to the pavement.

Then at last Juanna gave way. "Oh! Leonard, Leonard," she said, weeping bitterly, "they were my father's servants whom I have known since I was a child, and I have brought them to this cruel end. Cannot you think of any way of getting out of this place? If not, I shall die of fear. I can sleep no more. I feel that I am watched at night, though I cannot tell by whom. Last night I thought that I heard some one moving near the curtain where you and Francisco lie, though Soa declares that it is fancy."

"It is impossible," said Leonard; "Francisco was on guard. Ah! here he comes."

As he spoke Francisco entered the room with consternation written on his face.

"Outram," he gasped, "some one must have been in the throne chamber where we slept last night. All the rifles have gone, ours and those of the Settlement men also."

"Great heavens!" said Leonard, "but you were watching."

"I suppose that I must have dozed for a few moments," answered the priest; "it is awful, awful; they are gone and we are weaponless."

"Oh! can we not escape?" moaned Juanna.

"There is no hope of it," answered Leonard gloomily. "We are friendless here except for Olfan, and he has little real power, for the priests have tampered with the captains and the soldiers who fear them. How can we get out of this city? And if we got out what would become of us, unarmed and alone? All that we can do is to keep heart and hope for the best. Certainly they are right who declare that no good comes of seeking after treasure; though I believe that we shall live to win it yet," he added.

"What! Deliverer," said a satirical voice behind him, "do you still desire the red stones, who whose heart's blood shall soon redden a certain stone yonder? Truly the greed of the white man is great."

Leonard looked round. It was Soa who spoke, Soa who had been listening to their talk, and she was glaring at him with an expression of intense hate in her sullen eyes. A thought came into his mind. "Was it not possible that this woman had something to do with their misfortunes? How came it about that the others were taken while she was left?"

"Who gave you leave, Soa," he said, looking her fixedly in the face, "to hearken to our words and thrust yourself into our talk?"

"You have been glad enough of my counsels hitherto, White Man," she answered furiously. "Who told you the tale of this people? And who led you to their land? Was it I or another?"

"You, I regret to say," said Leonard coolly.

"Yes, White Man, I led you here that you might steal the treasure of my people like a thief. I did it because the Shepherdess my mistress forced me to the deed, and in those days her will was my law. For her and you I came here to my death, and what has been my reward? I am put away from her, she has no kind word for me now; you are about her always, you hold her counsel, but to me her mind is as a shut door that I can no longer open. Ay! you have poisoned her against me, you and that black swine whom they call a god.

"Moreover, because she has learned to love you, white thief, wanderer without a kraal as you are, at your bidding she has also learned to hate me. Beware, White Man, I am of this people, and you know their temper, it is not gentle; when they hate they find a means to be revenged," and she ceased, gasping with rage.

Indeed, at that moment Soa would have made no bad model for a statue of one of the furies of Greek mythology.

Then Juanna attempted to interfere, but Leonard waved her back.

"So," he said, "as I thought, you are at the bottom of all this business. Perhaps you will not mind telling us what has become of your friends, the Settlement men, or, if you feel a delicacy on that point, how it is that you have escaped while they have vanished."

"I know nothing of the Settlement men," answered the Fury, "except that they have been taken and sacrificed as was their meed, and as yet I have lifted no hand and said no word against you, though a breath from me would have swept you all to doom. Hitherto I have been spared for the same reason that you and Bald-pate yonder have been spared—because we are the body-servants of the false gods, and are reserved to perish with them when the lie is discovered; or perhaps to live awhile, set in cages in the market-place, to be mocked by the passers-by and to serve as a warning to any whose monkey hearts should dare to plot sacrilege against the divinity of Aca and Jal.

"Now, Shepherdess, take your choice. As you know well, I have loved you from a babe and I love you yet, though you have scorned me for this man's sake. Take your choice, I say; cling to me and trust me, giving the Deliverer to the priests, and I will save you. Cling to him, and I will bring shame and death upon you all, for my love shall turn to hate."

At this juncture Leonard quietly drew his revolver, though at the time nobody noticed it except Francisco. Indeed by now Juanna was almost as angry as Soa herself.

"How dare you speak to me thus?" she said, stamping her foot, "you whom from a child I have thought good and have trusted. What do you say? That I must give him who saved me from death over to death, in order that I may buy back your love and protect myself. You evil woman, I tell you that first I will die as I would have died yonder in the slave camp," and she ceased, for her indignation was too great to allow her to say more.

"So be it, Shepherdess," said Soa solemnly, "I hear you. It was to be expected that you would prefer him whom you love to her who loves you. Yet, Shepherdess, was it not I after all who saved you yonder in the slave camp? Doubtless I dream, but it seems to me that when those men who are dead deserted you, running this way and that in their fear—and, Shepherdess, it is for this that I am glad they are dead, and lifted no hand to save them—I followed you alone. It seems to me that, having followed you far till I could walk no more for hunger and weariness, I used my wit and bribed a certain white man, of the sort who would sell their sisters and blaspheme their mothers for a reward, to attempt your rescue.

"I bribed him with a gem of great price—had there been ten of them, that gem would have bought them all—and with the gem I told him the secret of the treasure which is here. He took the bribe, and being brave and desperate, he drew you out of the clutches of the Yellow Devil, though in that matter also I had some part; and then you loved him. Ah! could I have foreseen it, Shepherdess, I had left you to die in the slave camp, for then you had died loving me who now hate me and cast me off for the sake of this white thief."

Leonard could bear it no longer, and in the interests of their common safety he came to a desperate resolve. With an exclamation, he lifted the pistol and covered Soa. Both Francisco and Juanna saw the act and sprang to him, the latter exclaiming, "Oh! what are you going to do?"

"I propose to kill this woman before she kills us, that is all," he answered coldly.

"No! no!" cried Juanna, "she has been faithful to me for many years. I cannot see her shot."

"Let the butcher do his work," mocked Soa; "it shall avail him little. Doubtless he is angry because I have spoken the truth about him," and she folded her arms upon her breast, awaiting the bullet.

"What is to be done?" said Leonard desperately. "If I do not shoot her, she will certainly betray us."

"Then let her betray," said Francisco; "it is written that you shall do no murder."

"If you fear to shoot a woman, send for your black dog, White Man," mocked Soa. "He would have killed my father, and doubtless this task also will be to his liking."

"I can't do it. Get a rope and tie her up, Francisco," said Leonard. "We must watch her day and night; it will be a pleasant addition to our occupations. After all it is only one more risk, which is no great matter among so many. I fancy the game is about played out, anyhow."

Francisco went for the rope and presently returned accompanied by Otter. A month of furious dissipation had left its mark even on the dwarf's iron frame. His bright black eyes were bloodshot and unsteady, his hand shook, and he did not walk altogether straight.

"You have been drinking again, you sot," said Leonard. "Go back to your drink; we are in sorrow here and want no drunkards in our company. Now then, Francisco, give me that rope."

"Yes, Baas, I have been drinking," answered the dwarf humbly; "it is well to drink before one dies, since we may not drink afterwards and I think that the hour of death is at hand. Oh! Shepherdess of the heavens, they said down yonder at the Settlement that you were a great rain-maker: now if you can make the rain to fall, can you not make the sun to shine? Wind and water are all very well, but we have too much of them here."

"Hearken," said Leonard, "while you revelled, the last of Mavoom's men vanished, and these are left in their place," and he pointed to the knives.

"Is it so, Baas?" answered Otter with a hiccough. "Well, they were a poor lot, and we shall not miss them. And yet I wish I were a man again and had my hands on the throat of that wizard Nam. *Wow!* but I would squeeze it."

"It is your throat that will be squeezed soon, Otter," said Leonard. "Look here, god or no god, get you sober or I will beat you."

"I am sober, Baas, I am indeed. Last night I was drunk, today nothing is left but a pain here," and he tapped his great head. "Why are you tying up that old cow Soa, Baas?"

"Because she threatens to use her horns, Otter. She says that she will betray us all."

"Indeed, Baas! Well, it is in my mind that she has betrayed us already. Why do you not kill her and have done?"

"Because the Shepherdess here will have none of it," answered Leonard; "also I do not like the task."

"I will kill her if you wish, Baas," said Otter with another hiccough. "She is wicked, let her die."

"I have told you that the Shepherdess will have none of it. Listen: we must watch this woman; we will guard her today and you must take your turn tonight—it will keep you from your drink."

"Yes, Baas, I will watch, though it would be better to kill her at once, for thus we should be spared trouble."

Then they bound Soa securely and set her in a corner of the throne chamber, and all that day Leonard and Francisco mounted guard over her alternately. She made no resistance and said nothing; indeed it seemed as if a certain lassitude had followed her outbreak of rage, for she leaned her head back and slept, or made pretence to sleep.

The day passed uneventfully. Olfan visited them as usual, and told them that the excitement grew in the city. Indeed the unprecedented prolongation of the cold weather was driving the people into a state of superstitious fury that must soon express itself in violence of one form or another, and the priests were doing everything in their power to foment the trouble. No immediate danger was to be apprehended, however.

After sundown Leonard and Francisco went out into the courtyard to inspect the weather according to their custom. There was no sign of a change; the wind blew as bitterly as ever from the mountains, the sky was ashen, and the stars seemed far off and cold.

"Will it never break?" said Leonard with a sigh, and re-entered the palace, followed by Francisco.

Then, having solemnly cautioned Otter to keep a strict guard over Soa, they wrapped themselves up in their blankets in order to get some rest, which both of them needed sadly. Juanna had retired already, laying herself to sleep immediately on the other side of the curtain, for she feared to be alone; indeed they could see the tips of her fingers appearing beneath the bottom of the curtain.

Very soon they were asleep, for even terror must yield at last to the necessities of rest, and a dense silence reigned over the palace, broken only by the tramp of the sentries without.

Once Leonard opened his eyes, hearing something move, and instantly stretched out his hand to assure himself of Juanna's safety. She was there, for in her sleep her fingers closed instinctively upon his own. Then he turned round and saw what had disturbed him. In the doorway of the chamber stood the bride of the Snake, Saga, a lighted torch in one hand and a gourd in the other, and very picturesque that handsome young woman looked with her noble figure illumined by the glare of the torchlight.

"What is the matter?" said Leonard.

"It is all right, Baas," answered Otter; "the old woman here is as safe as a stone statue yonder and quite as quiet. Saga brings me some water, that is all. I bade her do so because of the fire that rages inside me and the pain in my head. Fear not, Baas, I do not drink beer when I am on guard."

"Beer or water, I wish you would keep your wife at a distance," answered Leonard; "come, tell her to be off."

Then he looked at his watch, the hands of which he could just distinguish by the distant glare of the torch, and went to sleep again. This took place at ten minutes past eleven. When he awoke again dawn was breaking and Otter was calling to him in a loud, hoarse voice.

"Baas," he said, "come here, Baas."

Leonard jumped up and ran to him, to find the dwarf on his feet and staring vacantly at the wall against which Soa had been sitting. She was gone, but there on the floor lay the ropes with which she had been tied.

Leonard sprang at Otter and seized him by the shoulders.

"Wretched man!" he cried, "you have been sleeping, and now she has escaped and we are lost."

"Yes, Baas, I have been sleeping. Kill me if you wish, for I deserve it. And yet, Baas, never was I more wide-awake in my life until I drank that water. I am not wont to sleep on guard, Baas."

"Otter," said Leonard, "that wife of yours has drugged you."

"It may be so, Baas. At least the woman has gone, and, say, whither has she gone?"

"To Nam, her father," answered Leonard.

CHAPTER 27

Father and Daughter

While Leonard and Otter spoke thus in their amazement, had they but known it, a still more interesting conversation was being carried on some three hundred yards away. Its scene was a secret chamber hollowed in the thickness of the temple wall, and the *dramatis personae* consisted of Nam, the high priest, Soa, Juanna's servant, and Saga, wife of the Snake.

Nam was an early riser, perhaps because his conscience would not allow him to sleep, or because on this occasion he had business of importance to attend to. At any rate, on the morning in question, long before the break of dawn, he was seated in his little room alone, musing; and indeed his thoughts gave him much food for reflection. As has been said, he was a very aged man, and whatever may have been his faults, at least he was earnestly desirous of carrying on the worship of the gods according to the strict letter of the customs which had descended to him from his forefathers, and which he himself had followed all his life. In truth, from long consideration of them, their attributes, and the traditions concerning them, Nam had come to believe in the actual existence of these gods, although the belief was a qualified one and somewhat half-hearted. Or, to put it less strongly, he had never allowed his mind to entertain active doubt of the spiritual beings whose earthly worship was so powerful a factor in his own material rule and prosperity, and in that of his class. In its issues this half-faith of his had been sufficiently real to induce him to accept Otter and Juanna when they arrived mysteriously in the land.

It had been prophesied that they should arrive thus—that was a fact; and their outward appearance exactly fitted every detail of the prophecy—that was another fact; and these two facts together seemed to point to a conclusion so irresistible that, shrewd and experienced as

223

he was, Nam, was unable to set it down to mere coincidence. Therefore in the first rush of his religious enthusiasm he had accorded a hearty welcome to the incarnations of the divinities whom for some eighty years he had worshipped as powers spiritual.

But though pious zeal had much to do with this action, as Olfan informed Juanna, it was not devoid of worldly motives. He desired the glory of being the discoverer of the gods, he desired also the consolidation of the rule which his cruelties had shaken, that must result from their advent.

All this was well enough, but he had never even dreamed that the first step of these new-born divinities would be to discard the ancient ceremonial without which his office would become a sinecure and his power a myth, and even to declare an active hostility against himself.

Were they or were they not gods? This was the question that exercised his mind. If there was truth in prophesies they should be gods. On the other hand he could discover nothing particularly divine about their persons, characters, or attributes—that is to say, nothing sufficiently divine to deceive Nam himself, whatever impression they produced upon the vulgar. Thus Juanna might be no more than a very beautiful woman white in colour, and Otter only what he knew him to be through his spies, a somewhat dissolute dwarf.

That they had no great power was also evident, seeing that he, Nam, without incurring the heavenly vengeance, had been able to abstract, and afterwards to sacrifice comfortably, the greater number of their servants. Another thing which pleaded against their celestial origin was that so far, instead of peace and prosperity blessing the land as it should have done immediately on their arrival, the present season was proving itself the worst on record, and the country was face to face with a prospect of famine in the ensuing winter.

And yet, if they were not gods, who were they? Would any human beings in their senses venture among such people as the Children of the Mist, merely to play off a huge practical joke of which the finale was likely to be so serious to themselves? The idea was preposterous, since they had nothing to gain by so doing, for Nam, it may be observed, was ignorant of the value of rubies, which to him were only emblems employed in their symbolical ceremonies. Think as he would, he could come to no definite conclusion. One thing was clear, however, that it was now very much to his interest to demonstrate their non-celestial origin, though to do so would be to stultify himself and to prove that his judgment was not infallible. Otherwise, did the "gods" succeed in establishing their power, he and his authority seemed likely to come to a sudden end in the jaws of that monster, which his order had fostered for so many generations.

Thus reflected Nam in perplexity of soul, wishing to himself the while that he had retired from his office before he was called upon to face questions so difficult and so dangerous.

"I must be patient," he muttered to himself at last; "time will show the truth, or, if the weather does not change, the people will settle the matter for me."

As it chanced he had not long to wait, for just then there was a knock upon his door.

"Enter," he said, arranging his goat-skin robe about his broad shoulders.

A priest came in bearing a torch, for there was no window to the chamber, and after him two women.

"Who is this?" said Nam, pointing to the second of the women.

"This is she who is servant to Aca, Father," answered the priest.

"How comes she here?" said Nam again. "I gave no orders that she should be taken."

"She comes of her own free will, Father, having somewhat to say to you."

"Fool, how can she speak to me when she does not know our tongue? But of her presently; take her aside and watch her. Now, Saga, your report. First, what of the weather?"

"It is grey and pitiless, father. The mist is dense and no sun can be seen."

"I thought it, because of the cold," and he drew his robe closer round him. "A few more days of this——" and he stopped, then went on. "Tell me of Jal, your lord."

"Jal is as Jal was, merry and somewhat drunken. He speaks our language very ill, yet when he was last in liquor he sang a song which told of deeds that he, and he whom they name the Deliverer, had wrought together down in the south, rescuing the goddess Aca from some who had taken her captive. At least, so I understood that song."

"Perhaps you understood it wrong," answered Nam. "Say, niece, do you still worship this god?"

"I worship the god Jal, but the man, Dweller in the Waters, I hate," she said fiercely.

"Why, how is this? But two days gone you told me that you loved him, and that there was no such god as this man, and no such man as this god."

"That was so, father, but since then he has thrust me aside, saying

225

that I weary him, and courts a handmaid of mine own, and therefore I demand the life of that handmaiden."

Nam smiled grimly. "Perchance you demand the life of the god also?"

"Yes," she replied without hesitation, "I would see him dead if it can be brought about."

Again Nam smiled. "Truly, niece, your temper is that of my sister, your grandmother, who brought three men to sacrifice because she grew jealous of them. Well, well, these are strange times, and you may live to see your desire satisfied by the death of the god. Now, what of that woman? How comes she to be with you?"

"She was bound by the order of Aca, father, and Jal was set to watch her; but I drugged Jal, and loosing her bonds I led her down the secret way, for she desires to speak to you."

"How can that be, niece? Can I then understand her language?"

"Nay, father, but she understands ours. Had she been bred in the land she could not speak it better."

Nam looked astonished, and going to the door he called to the priest without to lead in the stranger.

"You have words to say to me," he said.

"Yes, lord, but not before these. That which I have to say is secret."

Nam hesitated.

"Have no fear, lord," said Soa, reading his thoughts. "See, I am unarmed."

Then he commanded the others to go, and when the door had closed behind them, he looked at her inquiringly.

"Tell me, lord, who am I?" asked Soa, throwing the wrapping from her head and turning her face to the glare of the torchlight.

"How can I know who you are, wanderer? Yet, had I met you by chance, I should have said that you were of our blood."

"That is so, lord, I am of your blood. Cast your mind back and think if you can remember a certain daughter whom you loved many years ago, but who through the workings of your foes was chosen to be a bride to the Snake," and she paused.

"Speak on," said Nam in a low voice.

"Perchance you can recall, lord, that, moved to it by love and pity, on the night of the sacrifice you helped that daughter to escape the fangs of the Snake."

"I remember something of it," he replied cautiously; "but tidings were brought to me that this woman of whom you speak was overtaken by the vengeance of the god, and died on her journey."

"That is not so, lord. I am your daughter, and you are none other than my father. I knew you when I first saw your face, though you did not know me."

"Prove it, and beware how you lie," he said. "Show me the secret sign, and whisper the hidden word into my ear."

Then, glancing suspiciously behind her, Soa came to him, and made some movements with her hands in the shadow of the table. Next bending forward, she whispered awhile into his ear. When she had finished, her father looked up, and there were tears in his aged eyes.

"Welcome, daughter," he said. "I thought that I was alone, and that none of my issue lived anywhere upon the earth. Welcome! Your life is forfeit to the Snake, but, forgetting my vows, I will protect you, ay, even at the cost of my own."

Then the two embraced each other with every sign of tenderness, a spectacle that would have struck anyone acquainted with their characters as both curious and interesting.

Presently Nam left the chamber, and having dismissed the attendant priest and his great-niece, Saga, who were waiting outside, he returned and prayed his daughter to explain the reason of her presence in the train of Aca.

"First, you shall swear an oath to me, my father," said Soa, "and if you swear it not, I will tell you no word of my story. You shall swear by the blood of Aca that you will do nothing against the life of that Queen with whom I journeyed hither. For the others, you may work your will upon them, but her you shall not harm."

"Why should I swear this, daughter?" he asked.

"You shall swear it because I, whom you love, love her, and also because so you shall gain the greater honour."

"Who am I that I should lift my hand against the gods, daughter? I swear it by the blood of Aca, and if I break my oath, then may Jal deal with me as once he dealt with Aca."

Then Soa went on freely, for she knew that this was a vow that could not be broken. Beginning at its commencement, she told him all the story of her life since, forty years ago, she had fled from among the People of the Mist, passing on rapidly, however, to that part of it which had to do with the capture and rescue of Juanna from the slave-traders, and with the promise that she had made to Leonard as the price of his assistance. This promise, she was careful to explain, she had not intended to fulfil until she was forced to do so by Juanna herself. Then she gave him a minute history of the object and details of their expedition, down to her final quarrel with Leonard and her mistress on the previous day.

To say that the old priest was thunderstruck at these extraordinary revelations would be too little; he was overwhelmed—so overwhelmed that for a while he could scarcely speak.

"It is fortunate for this jade of a mistress of yours, who dares to make a mockery of our goddess that she may steal her wealth, that I have sworn to save her from harm, daughter," he gasped at length, "else she had died, and swiftly. At least, the others remain to me," and he sprang to his feet.

"Stay awhile, father," said Soa, catching his cloak, "what is your plan?"

"My plan? To drag them to the temple and denounce them. What else is there to do?"

"And thereby denounce yourself also, who proclaimed them gods. I think I have a better."

"Tell it then, daughter."

"It is this. Do you pass in before the gods this day, speak humbly to the gods, praying them to change the face of the heavens that the sun may shine; telling them also that strange talk has come to your ears by the mouth of Saga and the other women, of words that have been spoken by the god Jal, which would seem to show that he is no god, but that of this you believe nothing as yet. Then say to them that if the face of the heavens remains grey on the morrow, you will know that this talk is true, and that they will be brought to the temple, there to be judged and dealt with according to the finding of the people, who have heard these things also."

"And what if the weather should change, daughter?"

"It will not change yet awhile; but if that should chance, we must make another plan."

"Just now I swore to you that I would not harm her whom you love, and yet, daughter, if she is proved to be a false goddess in the face of all the multitude, how shall she escape harm, for then her end must be quick and terrible?"

"She shall escape because she will not be there, father. You have seen the white man with her—not the Deliverer, the other. Were that man dressed in the robes of Aca, and sat on high upon the head of the statue when the light is low, who should say that he was not Aca?"

"Then you would give all the others to death, daughter?"

"Nay, I would save the Deliverer alive, for a while at least."

"And wherefore? You are too subtle for me."

"For this reason, father; he loves her who is named Aca, and trusts to marry her, to marry her fully according to the custom of his people: therefore I would that he should see her given to another."

"To another! To whom then?"

"To Olfan the king, who also loves her."

Now Nam held up his hands in perplexity, saying:

"Oh! my daughter, be plain, I pray of you, for I cannot understand your counsels. Were it not better to give to these people the red stones which they desire, and send them secretly from the land, saying that they had vanished into the earth again, for so it seems to me we should be rid of much shame and trouble?"

"Listen, my father, and I will tell you. Were she whom I love to leave this land, I should see her face no more, and this madness has come upon me that I cannot live without the sight of her. Also, how can these people escape the dangers of the road? But four of them are left alive, and even were they without our borders, they must journey for three months before they come to any place where white men live, passing through swamps and deserts and tribes of wild men. This they could hardly do with arms such as those whereby the Deliverer slew the priests, and now their arms are gone, you alone know where, my father."

"The instruments of which you speak lie in the deep waters of the temple pool, daughter, for there I caused them to be cast."

"Their arms are gone," said Soa, "they are alone, here they must live or die. Three of them I will give to death, and the fourth I would make the wife of the King, seeing that nothing better can be done for her. Let her be hidden awhile, and then let Olfan take her. As for the tale that we shall tell of the matter to the ears of the people, doubtless time will show it. I say that Olfan loves her and will buy her with a great price, and the price which you must ask shall be that henceforth he obeys you in everything."

"The scheme is good, daughter; at the least, bearing my oath in mind, I have none better, though were it not for my oath, either I should kill them all or set them free. Yet who can say that it shall succeed? It is in the hands of fate, let it go as fate wills. And now follow me, that I may place you where you shall dwell in comfort, then after we have eaten I will speak with these gods whom you have let loose upon us."

That morning passed heavily enough to the four wretched prisoners in the palace. For some hours they sat together in the throne-room almost silent, for they were crushed by misfortune and fear; the toils were closing on them, and they knew it, nor could they lift a finger to save themselves.

Francisco knelt and prayed, Leonard and Juanna sat hand in hand listening to him, while Otter wandered to and fro like an unquiet spirit, cursing Soa, Saga, and all women in many languages and with a resource and vigour that struck his hearers as unparalleled. At length he vanished through the curtains, to get drunk probably, Leonard reflected.

However, the dwarf sought not drink, but vengeance. A few minutes later, hearing screams in the courtyard, Leonard ran out to find himself witness to a curious scene. There on the ground, surrounded by a group of other women, her companions, who were laughing at her discomfiture, lay the stately Saga, bride of the Snake. Over her stood her lord and master, the god Jal, his left hand twisted in her long hair, while with his right, in which he grasped a leather thong, despite her screams and entreaties, he administered to her one of the soundest and, be it added, best deserved thrashings that ever fell to the lot of erring woman.

"What are you doing?" said Leonard.

"I am teaching this wife of mine that it is not well to drug a god, Baas," gasped Otter; then added with a final and most ferocious cut, "There, get you gone, witch, and let me see your ugly face no more."

The woman rose and went, cursing and weeping, while the dwarf followed Leonard back into the throne-room.

"You have done it now, Otter," said Leonard. "Well, it does not much matter. I fancy she is gone for good, any way."

"Yes, Baas, she has gone, and she has gone sore," replied Otter with a faint grin.

At that moment a messenger arrived announcing that Nam was without waiting for an audience.

"Let him be admitted," said Juanna with a sigh, and seated herself on one of the thrones, Otter clambering into the other.

They had scarcely taken their places when the curtains were thrown back and the ancient priest entered, attended by about a score of his fellows. He bowed himself humbly before Juanna and the dwarf and then spoke.

"Oh! ye gods," he said, "I come in the name of the People of the Mist to take counsel with you. Why it is we do not know, but things have gone amiss in the land: the sun does not shine as in past years before you came to bless us, neither does the grain spring. Therefore your people are threatened with a famine, and they pray that you may comfort them out of the store of your wisdom."

"And if we have no comfort to give, Nam?"

"Then, Queen, the people ask that you will be pleased to meet them tomorrow in the temple at the moon-rise, when the night is one hour old, that they may talk with you there through the mouth of me, your servant."

"And if we weary of your temple and will not come, Nam?" asked Juanna.

"Then this is the command of the people, O Aca: that we bring you thither, and it is a command that may not be disobeyed," answered the high priest slowly.

"Beware, Nam," replied Juanna; "strange things happen here that call for vengeance. Our servants pass away like shadows, and in their place we find such weapons as you carry," and she pointed to the priests' knives. "We will come tomorrow night at the rising of the moon, but again I say to you, beware, for now our mercy is but as a frayed rope, and it were well for you all that the cord should not break."

"Ye know best whither your servants have wandered, O Aca," said the priest, stretching out his hands in deprecation, and speaking in a tone of which the humility did not veil the insolence, "for true gods such as ye are can guard their servants. We thank you for your words, O ye gods, and we pray you to be merciful to us, for the threats of true gods are very terrible. And now one little word. I ask justice of you, O ye gods. She who was given to be bride of the Snake, my niece who is named Saga, has been cruelly beaten by some evil-doer here in the palace, as I know, for but now I met her bruised and weeping. I ask of you then that ye search out this evil-doer and punish him with death or stripes. Farewell, O ye high gods."

Leonard looked at the priest as he bowed humbly before the thrones, and a desire to take Otter's advice and kill him entered his heart, for he knew that he had come to drag them to their trial and perhaps to doom. He still had his revolver, and it would have been easy to shoot him, for Nam's broad breast was a target that few could miss. And yet, what could it help them to shed his blood? There were many to fill his place if he died, and violence would certainly be answered with violence. No, he would let him be, and they must bide their fate.

CHAPTER 28

Juanna Prevaricates

The morrow drew towards its evening. Like those that had gone before it, this day had been misty and miserable, only distinguished from its predecessors by the fall of some sharp showers of sleet. Now, as the afternoon waned, the sky began to clear in its accustomed fashion; but the bitter wind sweeping down the mountains, though it drove away the fog, gave no promise of any break in the weather. At sunset Leonard went to the palace gates and looked towards the temple, about the walls of which a number of people were already gathering, as though in anticipation of some great event. They caught sight of him, and drew as near to the gates of the palace as they dared, howling curses and shaking their fists.

"This is a foretaste of what we must expect tonight, I suppose," said Leonard to Francisco, who had followed him, as they retreated across the courtyard. "We are in trouble now, friend. I do not so much care for my own sake, but it breaks my heart to think of Juanna. What will be the end of it, I wonder?"

"For me, Outram, the end will be death, of that I am sure; well, I have long expected it, and I am ready to die. What your fate will be I cannot say; but as to the Senora, comfort yourself; for many weeks I have had a presentiment that she will escape safely."

"In that case I am ready enough to go," answered Leonard. "Life is as dear to me as to other men; but I tell you, Francisco, that I would pay mine down gladly tonight as the price of her deliverance."

"I know it, Outram; we are both of one mind there, and perhaps before many hours are over we shall be called upon to practise what we preach." By now they had reached the throne-room, where Otter, who for the last twenty hours had been quite sober, was squatted on the floor at the foot of his throne, a picture of repentant misery, while Juanna walked swiftly up and down the long room, lost in reflection.

"Any news, Leonard?" she said as they came in.

"None, except that there are great preparations going on yonder," and he nodded towards the temple; "also a mob is howling at the gates."

"Oh!" groaned Otter, addressing Juanna, "cannot you, who are named Shepherdess of the Heavens, prophesy to these people that the weather will break, and so save us from the Snake?"

"I can prophesy," she answered; "but it will not change tonight, nor, I think, tomorrow. However, I will try."

Then came a silence: nobody seemed to have anything to say. It was broken by the entrance of Olfan, whose face showed the disturbance of his mind.

"What passes, Olfan?" asked Juanna.

"Queen," he answered sadly, "there is great trouble at hand. The people rave for the blood of you, their gods. Nam told you that ye are summoned this night to confer with the people. Alas! I must tell you otherwise. This night ye will be put upon your trial before the Council of the Elders."

"That we guessed, Olfan, and if the verdict goes against us, what then?"

"Alas that I must say it! Then, Queen, you will be hurled, all of you, into the pool of the Snake, to be food for the Snake."

"Cannot you protect us, Olfan?"

"I cannot, O Queen, except with my own life. The soldiers are under my command indeed; but in this matter they will not obey me, for the priests have whispered in their ears, and if the sun does not shine they too must starve next winter. Pardon me, Queen, but if you are gods, how is it that you need help from me who am but a man? Cannot the gods then protect themselves and be avenged upon their enemies?"

Juanna looked despairingly at Leonard, who sat by her side pulling at his beard, as was his fashion when perplexed.

"I think that you had better tell him," he said in English. "Our situation is desperate. Probably in a few hours he will know us to be impostors; indeed, he guesses it already. It is better that he should learn the truth from our own lips. The man is honest; moreover, he owes his life to us, though it is true that were it not for us he would never have been in danger of his life. Now we must trust him and take our chance; if we make a mistake, it does not greatly matter—we have made so many already."

Juanna bowed her head and thought awhile, then she lifted it and spoke.

"Olfan," she said, "are we alone? That which I have to say must be overheard by none."

"We are alone, Queen," he answered, glancing round, "but these walls have ears."

"Olfan, draw near."

He obeyed, and leaning forward she spoke to him almost in a whisper, while the others clustered round to hear her words.

"You must call me Queen no more," she said in a voice broken with humiliation. "I am no goddess, I am but a mortal woman, and this man," and she pointed to Otter, "is no god, he is only a black dwarf."

She paused, watching the effect of her words. An expression of astonishment swept across the king's face, but it was her boldness rather than the purport of her speech that caused it. Then he smiled.

"Perhaps I have guessed as much," he answered. "And yet I must still call you by that name, seeing that you are the queen of all women, for say, where is there another so lovely, so brave, or so great? Here at least there are none," and he bowed before her with a stately courtesy that would have become any European gentleman.

Now it was Leonard's turn to look astonished. There was nothing in the king's words to which he could take objection, and yet he did not like their tone; it was too full of admiration. Moreover it seemed to him that Olfan was not in the least disappointed to discover as a fact that Juanna was only a woman—a supposition which was fully established by his next speech.

"I am glad to learn from your own lips, Queen, that you are no goddess, but a mortal lady, seeing that goddesses are far away and we men must worship them from afar, whereas women—we may love," and again he bowed.

"My word!" said Leonard to himself, "this king is setting himself up as my rival. I almost wish I had put things on a more satisfactory footing; but of course it is absurd. Poor Juanna!"

As for Juanna herself, she started and blushed; here was a new trouble, but however disagreeable it might prove to be, now was no time to show displeasure.

"Listen, Olfan," she said, "this is not an hour for pretty speeches which mean nothing, for it seems that before the light dawns again I may well be dead and far beyond all love and worship. This is our tale: we came to your land to seek adventures, and also to win those red stones that you name the blood of Aca, which among the white people are much prized as ornaments for their women. That is why I, who am a woman, urged the Deliverer to undertake this journey, and it is because of my folly that now we stand in danger of our lives."

"Your pardon, Queen," said Olfan bluntly, "but I would ask you one question before you tell me the end of your tale. What is this white man to you?"

Now Juanna was "in a cleft stick"; if she said that Leonard was nothing to her, it might possibly be better for him, though it was doubtful whether Olfan would believe her. If, on the other hand, she said that he was her husband, it might be better for herself, and protect her from the advances of this dignified savage; but against this course her pride revolted. Had she not always indignantly repudiated the validity of that hateful marriage, and though she loved him, were not she and Leonard in a sense at daggers drawn? Still she must decide, and quickly; her common-sense told her that under the circumstances it was her pride which must give way.

"He is my husband," she said boldly.

Olfan's face fell; then a look of doubt came into it, for Juanna's mode of life, every detail of which was known to him, seemed to contradict her statement.

Seeing that he did not believe her, Juanna plunged still deeper into the mire.

"He is my husband," she said again. "This man," and she pointed to Francisco, "who is a priest among us, married us according to our customs some six moons since, and Otter yonder was witness to the marriage."

"Is this so?" asked Olfan.

"It is so, King," replied Francisco. "I married them, and they are man and wife."

"Yes, yes, it is so," put in Otter, "for I saw it done, and we celebrated a great sacrifice in honour of that wedding feast. I would that we could have such another here tonight."

"Fear not, Dwarf," answered Olfan with a touch of irritation, "you will see enough of sacrifices before all is ended."

Then a new thought struck him, and he added, "You say that the Deliverer is your husband, Queen, and these men bear witness to it, all except your lord himself! Now tell me one thing more: do you love him and would you be sorry if he died?"

Juanna's brow burnt red as the ruby stone upon it, for with the exception of her black robe she was prepared to proceed to the temple. But there was no help for it now; she must speak clearly, however much it shamed her to do so, lest Olfan might take her silence as a hint, and the "husband" for whom she disavowed affection should be removed from her life for ever.

"You have little right to put such a question to me, King, yet I will answer it. I love him, and if he died I should die also."

Leonard suppressed an exclamation with difficulty, for here was Juanna appearing in a new light indeed.

"I am answered, Queen," said Olfan in tones of deep depression. "Now, if it pleases you, will you end your tale?"

"There is not much to tell," replied Juanna, heaving a sigh of relief, for this cross-examination as to her exact relations with Leonard had been somewhat trying. "The woman Soa, my servant, is of your people; indeed, she is a daughter to Nam the priest, and fled the land forty years ago because she was destined to the Snake."

"Where is she now?" interrupted Olfan, looking round.

"We do not know; last night she vanished as our other servants have vanished."

"Perhaps Nam knows, and if so you may see her again soon. Proceed, Queen."

"After the Deliverer and I were married, Soa, who had been my nurse for many years, told us of the Great People her brethren, among whom she wished to die."

"May her desire be gratified!" put in Otter.

"And said that if we would escort her thither we could buy many such stones as that upon my brow, which she had brought with her from this country and given to me. Then it was that I, desiring the playthings, tormented my husband till he consented to lead me hither, though his own heart spoke against it. So we came, and the journey was long and terrible, but at last we reached the cliff yonder which borders the Land of Mist, and it was then for the first time, when it was too late to go back, that Soa told us the tale of the gods of your people, and showed us that either we must do sacrilege and feign to be those gods come back, as the prophecy promised, or perish miserably. Indeed this was her plot, to set up false gods over you, having first told the secret to the priests that she might gain honour with them and save herself alive.

"And now, Olfan, that is all the tale. We have played the game and we have lost, or so it seems—that is, unless you help us;" and she clasped her hands and looked upon him pleadingly.

The king dropped his eyes as though he were not willing to contemplate the loveliness which, as he now learned, belonged to the white stranger at Juanna's side.

"Have I not said that my power is little, Queen?" he answered somewhat sullenly. "Also, why should I help those who came to this land to trick us, and who have brought the anger of the gods upon its children?"

"Because we saved your life, Olfan, and you swore to be loyal to us."

"Had it not been for you, Queen, my life would not have been in danger; moreover, I swore fealty to gods, and now the gods are mortals, upon whom the true gods will be avenged. Why then should I help you?"

"Because we have been friends, Olfan. You shall help us for my sake."

"For your sake, Queen," he said bitterly, "for your sake, who tell me that you are this man's wife and that you love him to the death. Nay, this is much to ask. Had it been otherwise, had you been unwed and willing to look upon me, the king of this land, with favour, then doubtless I had died for your sake if there were need. But now—! Have you then no better reasons to show why I should risk my life for you and for these men?"

"I have two more reasons, King, and if they are not enough, then leave us to our fate, and let us, who must prepare to die, waste no more breath in words. The first is that we are your friends and have trusted you, saving your life at the danger of our own and telling you this tale of our own free will. Therefore in the name of friendship, which you should hold sacred, who are no common man but a king, we demand your help, we who have put our lives in the hollow of your hand, knowing that you are of noble mind and will not betray us.

"The second is that our interest is your interest: we strive against Nam and the priests, and so do you. If Nam conquers us today, to-morrow it will be your turn, and the Snake, whose fangs we must feel, shall in days to come feed upon you also. Now is the hour of destiny for you and your descendants: cling to us and break the yoke of Nam and the priests, or desert us and bind that yoke upon your shoulders to your doom. I have spoken—choose."

Olfan thought awhile and answered:

"Truly your mind is great, Queen, and sees far into the darkness of things such as our women have no knowledge of. You should have ruled this country and not I, for then by now Nam, who is my master, would have begged his daily bread at the gates of your palace, and the priests his servants had become the hewers of your wood and the drawers of your water. But I will not talk to you of policy, for time is short. Nay, I will deal with your first reason and that alone.

"You have conjured me in the name of friendship and of my oath, and by the memory of service done, and not in vain. I am a man different from that race of men of whom you are, a wild chief of a wild tribe, having little wisdom; yet I have learned these things—never to break a promise, never to desert a friend, and never to forget a service. Therefore, because I swore fealty to you, because you are my friend, and because you saved my life, I will protect you to the last, though it may well chance that I can do nothing except die for you. For, Queen, although you can be nought to me while yonder man lives, still I am ready to give my life for you. As for the others I will say this only, that I will not harm them or betray them.

"Now I go to speak with certain of the great men who are friends to me and hate the priest, so that when this matter comes on for judgment they may lift up their voices in your favour, for nothing can be done except by policy—that is, not now. Shortly I will return to lead you to the temple. Till then, farewell," and he bowed and was gone.

When the curtain had swung to behind Olfan, Juanna sank back in her chair and sighed, but Leonard sprang up and said:

"Juanna, that savage is right, you should have been a queen. I know what it must have cost you to say what you did."

"Pray, to what do you refer, Leonard?" she said, interrupting him coldly.

"I mean about our being married and the rest."

"Oh! yes. Well, you see it is sometimes necessary to tell white lies, and I think that after tonight I am entitled to a prize for general proficiency in this respect. Of course," she added, dropping her sarcastic tone, "you will not misinterpret anything that I was forced to say to Olfan with reference to yourself, because you know that those statements were the biggest fibs of all. Just then, had it been needful, I should have been prepared to swear that I was married to Otter and deeply attached to him, or even to the king himself, who, by the way, strikes me as the most satisfactory savage that I have ever come across—in short, as a gentleman."

Leonard turned pale with anger.

"Really, Juanna," he said, "I think that you might wait until I seek to take some advantage of our friendship and accidental relations before you rebuke me as you think fit to do. It is little short of an insult, and were we in any civilised country I would never speak to you again."

"Don't get angry, Leonard," she said appealingly, for Juanna seemed to have every mood at her command and ready to be assumed at a moment's notice. Perhaps this gift was one of the secrets of her charm, since monotony is a thing to be avoided by women who seek to rule, even the monotony of sweetness. "It is very unkind of you," she went on, "to speak crossly to me when I am so tired with talking to that savage and we may all be dead and buried in a few hours," and she looked as though she were going to cry.

Leonard collapsed instantly, for Juanna's plaintive mood was the one that he could resist the least of any.

"You would make me angry if I were on my death-bed," he said, "that is, when you talk like that. But there it is, I cannot change you, so let us change the subject. Have you any of that poison to spare? If so, you might serve us out a little; we may want it before the evening is over."

Juanna put her hand to her hair and after some manipulation produced a tiny skin bag, from which she extracted a brown ball of about the size of a rifle bullet.

"I can afford to be generous," she said with a little laugh; "there is enough here to kill twenty of us."

Then Leonard took a knife and chipped off three fragments from the ball, taking one himself and presenting the other two to Francisco and Otter. The priest received it doubtfully, but the dwarf would have none of it.

"Keep it for yourself, Baas," he said, "keep it for yourself. Whatever way I die it shall not be thus. I do not love a medicine that causes men to tie themselves into knots and then turns them green. No, no; first I will face the jaws of the Snake."

So Leonard took that piece also.

CHAPTER 29

The Trial of the Gods

Juanna had scarcely restored the remainder of her deadly medicine to its hiding-place, when the curtains were drawn and Nam entered. After his customary salutations, which on this occasion were more copious than usual, he remarked blandly that the moon had risen in a clear sky.

"Which means, I suppose, that it is time for us to start," said Leonard gruffly.

Then they set out, Juanna in her monk-like robe, and Otter in his red fringe and a goat-skin cape which he insisted upon wearing.

"I may as well die warm as cold, Baas," he explained, "for of cold I shall know enough when I am dead."

At the palace gate Olfan and a guard were waiting, but they found no opportunity of speaking with him. Here also were gathered a great number of priests, who preceded and followed them.

The procession being formed, they were led solemnly to a different gate of the temple from that by which they had entered it on their previous visits. On this occasion the secret passages were avoided, and they passed up a broad avenue though the centre of the amphitheatre, to seats that had been prepared for them on that side of the pool which was furthest from the colossal idol. As before, the temple was crowded with human beings, and their advance through it was very impressive, for the priests chanted as they walked, while the multitude preserved an ominous silence.

At first Leonard was at a loss to know why they were placed on the hither side of the pool, but presently he saw the reason. In front of the chairs to be occupied by Juanna and Otter, an open space of rock was left, semicircular in shape, on which were set other seats to the number of thirty or more. These seats were allotted to elders of the people, who, as Leonard guessed rightly, had been chosen to act

240

as their judges. The position was selected for the convenience of these elders, and in order that the words they spoke might be heard by a larger proportion of their vast audience.

When Juanna and Otter were seated, and Leonard and Francisco had taken their places behind them, Nam came forward to address the Council and the multitude beyond.

"Elders of the People of the Mist," he said, "I have conveyed your wishes to the holy gods, who but lately have deigned to put on the flesh of men to visit us their people; namely, that they should meet you here and talk with you of the trouble which has come upon the land. And now the gracious gods have assented to your wish, and behold, they are face to face with you and with this great company of their children. Be pleased therefore to make known what you desire to the gods, that they may answer you, either with their own mouths or by the voice of me, their servant."

He ceased, and after a pause, during which the people murmured angrily, an elder rose and said:

"We would know of you how it is, O Aca and O Jal, that the summer has deserted the land. Now our strait is very sorry, for famine will come upon us with the winter snows. A while ago, O Aca and O Jal, you changed the worship of this people, forbidding the victims who had been prepared to be offered up at the spring festival, and lo! there has been no spring. Therefore we ask a word of you on this matter, for the people have consulted together, and say by our voice that they will have no gods who kill the spring. Speak, O ye gods, and you, Nam, speak also, for we would learn the reason of these evils; and from you, O Nam, we would learn how it comes that you have proclaimed gods in the land whose breath has destroyed the sunshine."

"Ye ask me, O People of the Mist," answered Juanna, "why it is that the winter stretches out his hand over the slumber of the spring, forbidding her to awake, and I will answer you in few words and short. It is because of your disobedience and the hardness of your hearts, O ye rebellious children. Did ye not do sacrifice when we forbade you to take the blood of men? Ay, and have not our servants been stolen secretly away and put to death to satisfy your lust for slaughter? It is for this reason, because of your disobedience, that the heavens have grown hard as your own hearts and will not bless you with their sunshine and their gentle rain. I have answered you."

Then again the spokesman of the elders rose and said:

"We have heard your words, O Aca, and they are words of little comfort, for to sacrifice is the custom of the land, and hitherto no evil has befallen us because of that ancient custom. Yet if there has been offence, it is not we who have offended, but rather the priests in whose hands these matters lie; and as for your servants, we know nothing of them, or of their fate. Now, Nam, make answer to the charges of the gods, and to the questions of the people, for you are the chief of their servants and you have proclaimed them to be true gods and set them over us to rule us."

Thus adjured, Nam stood forward, and his mien was humble and anxious, for he saw well that his accusers were not to be trifled with, and that his life, or at least his power, was at stake, together with those of the gods.

"Children of the Mist," he began, "your words are sharp, yet I do not complain of them, for, as ye shall learn, my fault has been grievous. Truly, I am the chief of the servants of the gods, and I am also the servant of the people, and now it would seem that I have betrayed both gods and people, though not of my own will.

"Listen: ye know the legend that has come down to us, that Aca and Jal should reappear in the land, wearing the shapes of a fair white maiden and of a black dwarf. Ye know also how they came as had been promised, and how I showed them to you here in this temple, and ye accepted them. Ye remember that then they put away the ancient law and forbade the sacrifices, and by the hand of their servant who is named Deliverer, they destroyed two of the priests, my brethren, in a strange and terrible fashion.

"Then I murmured, though they threatened me with death, but ye overruled my words and accepted the new law, and from that hour all things have gone ill. Now I took counsel with my heart, for it seemed wonderful to me that the gods should discard their ancient worship, and I said to my heart: Can these be true gods, or have I perchance been duped? Thenceforward I held my peace, and set myself to watch, and now after much watching—alas! I must say it to my shame—I have discovered that they are no true gods, but wicked liars who have sought to usurp the places of the gods."

He paused, and a roar of rage and astonishment went up from the assembled thousands.

"It has come at last," whispered Leonard into Juanna's ear.

"Yes, it has come," she answered. "Well, I expected it, and now we must face it out."

When the tumult had subsided, the spokesman of the elders addressed Nam, saying:

"These are heavy words, O Nam, and having uttered them you

242

must prove them, for until they are proved we will not believe readily that there are human beings so wicked that they dare to name themselves as gods. When you proclaimed these strangers to be Aca and Jal, we accepted them, perhaps too easily and after too short a search. Now you denounce them as liars, but we will not disclaim them whom we have once received till we are sure that there is no room for error. It may chance, Nam, that it would please you well to cast aside those gods who have threatened you with death and do not love you."

"I should be bold indeed," answered Nam, "if I dared to speak as I have spoken lacking testimony to establish a charge so dreadful as that which I bring against these wanderers. Nor should I seek to publish my own shame and folly were I not forced thereto by knowledge that, did I conceal it, would make me a partner of their crime. Listen, this is the tale of those whom we have worshipped: the fair woman, as she herself told us, is named Shepherdess of the Heavens, and she is the wife of the white man who is named Deliverer, and the dwarf Dweller in the Waters is their servant, together with the second white man and the others.

"Dwelling in a far country, these men and women chanced to learn the story of our people—how, I shall show you presently—and also that we find in the earth and use in the ceremonies of our temple certain red and blue stones which among the white people are of priceless value. These they determined to steal, being adventurers who seek after wealth. To this end the Shepherdess learned our language, also she learned how to play the part of Aca, while the dwarf, dog that he is, dared to take the holy name of Jal. I will be short: they accomplished their journey, and the rest you know. But, as it happened, none of the stones they covert have come into their hands, except that gem which the Shepherdess wears upon her forehead, and this she brought with her.

"Now, People of the Mist, when doubts of these gods had entered into me I made a plan: I set spies to watch them in the palace yonder, those spies being the wife who was given to the dwarf and her handmaidens. Also, I caused their black servants to be seized and thrown to the Snake, one or two of them at a time, for of this I was sure, that if they had the power they would protect their servants. But, as the Snake knows, those men were not protected. Meanwhile reports came to me from the women, and more especially from Saga, the granddaughter of my brother, who was given as a bride to Jal. And this was their report: that the dwarf behaved himself like a cur of low birth, and that when he was in liquor, which was often, he babbled of his doings with the Deliverer in other lands, though all that he said they could not tell me because even now he has little knowledge of our tongue.

"When these tales came to my ears, you may guess, O People of the Mist, that if I had doubted before, now my heart was shaken, and yet I had no proof. In my darkness I prayed to the gods for light, and lo! light came. Among the followers of these wanderers was a woman, and but yesterday this woman visited me and confessed all. Forty years ago she had fled from among our people—I know not why, but she took with her a knowledge of our secrets. It was she who told them of the gods and the story of the gods, and she instructed them how they should deceive us and win the red stones which they desired. But now her heart repents her of the evil, and I will summon her before you, that ye may judge between me and these liars who have brought me to this shame. Bring forth the woman."

There was a silence, and so intense was the interest that no sound came from the audience, which watched for the appearance of the witness. Presently Soa advanced from the shadows at the foot of the colossus, and escorted by two priests took her stand in the centre of the semicircle of judges.

"Speak, woman," said Nam.

Then Soa spoke. "I am of the People of the Mist," she said, "as ye may know by looking on me and hearing me. I was the daughter of a priest, and forty years ago, when I was young and fair, I fled this land for my own reasons, and travelled south for three months' journey, till I came to a village on a mighty river, where I dwelt for twenty years earning a livelihood as a doctoress of medicine. Then there came into that village a white man, whose wife gave birth to a daughter and died. I became the nurse of that daughter; she is the woman who sits before you, and her name is Shepherdess.

"Twenty years more went by, and I desired to return to my own land that I might die among my people. I told the tale of my land and of its wealth to the Shepherdess and to her husband the Deliverer, for I dared not travel alone. Therefore in my wickedness I showed them how they might feign to be the gods of the People of the Mist, come back according to the legend, for I saw that the dwarf, the Deliverer's servant, was shaped like to the shape of the statue of Jal, who sits in stone above you. Being greedy, they fell into the plan, for above all things they desired to win the precious stones. But when we were come hither the true gods visited me in a dream so that my heart was troubled because of the evil which I had done, and yesterday I escaped to Nam and told him all the tale which you have heard. That is the story, People of the Mist, and now I pray your mercy and your pardon."

Soa ceased, and Leonard, who had been watching the multitude, whispered to Juanna:

"Speak quickly if you can think of anything to say. They are silent now because of their astonishment, but in another minute they will break out, and then——"

"People of the Mist," cried Juanna, taking the hint, "you have heard the words of Nam and the words of her who was my servant. They dare to tell you that we are no gods. So be it: on this matter we will not reason with you, for can the gods descend to prove their godhead? We will not reason, but I will say this in warning: put us away if you wish,—and it may well chance that we shall suffer ourselves to be put away, since the gods do not desire to rule over those who reject them, but would choose rather to return to their own place.

"Yet for you it shall be a sad and an unlucky day when ye lift a hand against our majesty, for in going we will leave you that by which we shall be remembered. Ay, we will bequeath to you three things: famine and pestilence and civil war, which shall rage among you and destroy you till ye are no more a people. Ye have suffered our servants to be murdered, and disobeyed our commands, and it is for this reason, as I have told you, that the sun shines no more and the summer will not come. Complete your wickedness if ye will, and let the gods follow by the path that their servants trod. Then, People of the Mist, ye shall reap as ye have sown, and death and desolation shall be your harvest.

"Now for that base slave who has borne false witness against us. Among the many things she has told you, one thing she has left un-told: that she is daughter to Nam the priest; that she fled the land be-cause she was chosen bride to the Snake, and is therefore an apostate worthy of death. One word also as to Nam, her father; if his tale be true, then he himself is condemned by it, for doubtless he knew all at the beginning, from the lips of his daughter Soa.

"Yes, knowing the truth he dared to set up gods in the land whom he believed to be false, trusting thereby to increase his own power and glory, and when these failed him because of his wickedness, then he did not scruple to cry aloud his shame. I have spoken, People of the Mist. Now judge between us and let fate follow judgment, for we renounce you."

She ended, her face alight with anger and her eyes flashing with excitement, and so great was the power of her eloquence and beauty

245

that it seemed to throw a spell of silence over the hearts of her fierce and turbulent audience, while Soa slunk back into the shadow and Nam cowered visibly.

"It is false, O people," he cried in a voice that trembled with rage and fear. "My daughter told me the tale for the first time at dawn today."

His words awoke the audience as it were, and instantly there arose a babble of sounds that rent the very skies. "His daughter! He says that she is his daughter! Nam owns his crimes!" yelled some.

"Away with the false gods!" shouted others.

"Touch them not, they are true gods and will bring a curse upon us!" answered a third party, among whom Leonard recognised the voice of Olfan.

And so the clamour went on. For full ten minutes it raged, till the exhaustion of those that made it brought it to its end, and Juanna, who all this while sat silent as some lovely marble statue, became aware that the spokesman of the elders was once more addressing the multitude.

"People of the Mist," he said, "hold your peace, and hearken to me. We have been chosen judges of this matter, and now, having consulted together, we will give judgment, and you shall be bound by it. As to whether these strangers who are named Aca and Jal are true gods or false, we say no word. But if they are false gods, then surely Nam is guilty with them."

Here a shout of assent burst from the audience, and Leonard watching the high priest saw him tremble.

"Yet," he went on, "they have told us by the mouth of her who sits before you, that it is because of our offences that the sun has ceased to shine at their command. Therefore at their command it can be made to shine. Then let them give us a sign or let them die, if indeed they are mortal, for if they are not mortal we cannot kill them. And this shall be the sign which they must give: If tomorrow at the dawn the mists have vanished and the sun shines red and clear on the snows of yonder mountain, then it is well and we will worship them. But if the morning is cold and mist-laden, then, true gods or false, we will hurl them from the head of the statue into the pit of the Snake, there to be dealt with by the Snake, or to deal with him as it may chance. That is our judgment, People of the Mist, and Nam shall carry it out if need be, for he shall keep his power and his place until all these wonders are made clear, and then himself he shall be judged according to their issue."

Now the great mass of the people cried aloud that this was a wise and just saying, but others were silent, for though they did not agree with it they dared not dispute the sentence. Then Juanna rose and said:

"We have heard your words and we will withdraw to consider them, and by dawn ye shall see us seated on the Black One yonder. But whether we will cause the sun to shine or choose to pass to our own place by the path of boiling waters, we do not know, though it seems to me that the last thing is better than the first, for we weary of your company, People of the Mist, and it is not fitting that we should bless you longer with our presence. Nevertheless, should we choose that path, those evils which I have foretold shall fall upon you. Olfan, lead us hence."

The king stepped forward with his guards and the procession passed back towards the palace solemnly and in silence, for none attempted to bar their way. They reached it safely at exactly ten o'clock by Leonard's watch.

"Now let us eat and drink," said Leonard when they stood alone in the throne-room, "for we shall need all our strength tonight."

"Yes," answered Juanna with a sad smile, "let us eat and drink, for tomorrow we die."

CHAPTER 30

Francisco's Expiation

When they had finished their meal, which was about as sad an entertainment as can well be conceived, they began to talk.

"Do you see any hope?" asked Juanna of the other three.

Leonard shook his head and answered:

"Unless the sun shines at dawn tomorrow, we are dead men."

"Then there is little chance of that, Baas," groaned Otter, "for the night is as the nights have been for these five weeks. No wonder that this people are fierce and wicked who live in such a climate."

Juanna hid her face in her hands for a while, then spoke:

"They did not say that any harm was to come to you, Leonard, or to Francisco, so perhaps you will escape."

"I doubt it," he answered; "besides, to be perfectly frank, if you are going to die, I would rather die with you."

"Thank you, Leonard," she said gently, "but that will not help either of us much, will it? What will they do with us? Throw us from the head of the statue?" and she shuddered.

"That seems to be their amiable intention, but at any rate we need none of us go through with it alive. How long does your medicine take to work, Juanna?"

"Half a minute at the outside, I fancy, and sometimes less. Are you sure that you will take none, Otter? Think; the other end is dreadful."

"No, Shepherdess," said the dwarf, who now in the presence of imminent danger was as he had been before he sought comfort in the beer-pot, brave, ready, and collected, "it is not my plan to suffer myself to be hurled into the pit. Nay, when the time comes I shall spring there of my own free will, and if I am not killed—and an otter knows how to leap into a pool—then if I cannot avoid him I will make a fight for it with that great dweller in the water. Yes, and I go to make ready that with which I will fight," and he rose and departed to his sleeping-place.

Just then Francisco followed his example, seeking a quiet place in which to pursue his devotions, and thus Leonard and Juanna were left alone.

For some minutes he watched her as she sat beside him in her white temple dress, her beautiful face looking stern and sad against the dusky background of the torchlight, and a great shame and pity filled his heart. The blood of this girl was on his hands, and he could do nothing to help her. His selfishness had dragged her into this miserable enterprise, and now its inevitable end was at hand and he was her murderer, the murderer of the woman who was all the world to him, and who had been entrusted to his care with her father's dying breath.

"Forgive me," he said at length with something like a sob, and laying his hand upon hers.

"What have I to forgive, Leonard?" she replied gently. "Now that it is all finished and I look back upon the past few months, it seems to me that it is you who should forgive, for I have often behaved badly to you."

"Nonsense, Juanna, it was my wicked folly that led you into this, and now you are about to be cut off in the beginning of your youth and in the flower of your beauty. I am your murderer, Juanna," and dropping his voice he hesitated, then added: "It may as well out now, for time is short, though I have often sworn that nothing should make me say it: I love you."

She did not start or even stir at his words, but sat staring as before into the darkness: only a pink flush grew upon the pallor of her neck and cheek as she answered:

"You love me, Leonard? You forget—Jane Beach!"

"It is perfectly true, Juanna, that I was once attached to Jane Beach, and it is true that I still think of her with affection, but I have not seen her for many years, and I am certain that she has thrown me over and married another man. Most man pass through several affairs of the heart in their early days; I have had but one, and it is done with.

"When first I saw you in the slave camp I loved you, Juanna, and I have gone on loving you ever since, even after I became aware from your words and conduct that you did not entertain any such affection for myself. I know that your mind has not changed upon the matter, for had it done so, you would scarcely have spoken to me as you did today after Olfan left us. Indeed, I do not altogether understand why I have told you this, since it will not interest you very much and may possibly annoy you in your last hours. I suppose

249

it was because I wished to make a clean breast of it before I pass to where we lose all our loves and hopes."

"Or find them," said Juanna, still looking before her.

Then there was silence for a minute or more, till Leonard, believing that he had got his answer, began to think that he would do well to leave her for a while. Just as he was about to rise Juanna made a gentle movement; slowly, very slowly, she turned herself, slowly she stretched out her arms towards him, and laid her head upon his breast.

For a moment Leonard was astounded; he could scarcely believe the evidence of his senses. Then recovering himself, he kissed her tenderly.

Presently Juanna slipped from his embrace and said, "Listen to me, Leonard: are men all blind, I wonder, or are you an exception? I don't know and don't want to know, but certainly it does seem strange that what has been so painfully patent to myself for the last five or six months, should have been invisible to you. Leonard, you were not the only one who fell in love yonder in the slave camp. But you quickly checked my folly by telling me the story of Jane Beach, and of course after that, whatever my thoughts may have been, I did my utmost to hide them from you, with more success, it seems, than I expected. Indeed I am not sure that I am wise to let you see them now, for though you declare that Jane is dead and buried, she might re-arise at any moment. I do not believe that men forget their first loves, Leonard, though they may persuade themselves to the contrary—when they are a long way from them."

"Don't you think that we might drop Jane, dear?" he answered with some impatience, for Juanna's words brought back to his mind visions of another love-scene that had taken place amid the English snows more than seven years before.

"I am sure that I am quite ready to drop her now and for ever. But do not let us begin to spar when so little time is left to us. Let us talk of other things. Tell me that you love me, love me, love me, for those are the words that I would hear ringing in my years before they become deaf to this world and its echoes, and those are the words with which I hope that you will greet me some few hours hence and in a happier land. Leonard, tell me that you love me for today and for tomorrow, now and for ever."

So he told her that and much more, speaking to her earnestly, hopefully, and most tenderly, as a man might speak to the woman whom he worshipped and with whom is about to travel to that shore of which we know nothing, though day and night we hear the waves that bear us forward break yonder on its beach. They talked for long, and ever while they talked Juanna grew gentler and more human, as the barriers of pride melted in the fire of her passion and the shadow of death gathered thicker upon her and the man she loved. At length her strength gave way utterly and she wept upon Leonard's breast like some frightened child, and from weeping sank into deep slumber or swoon, he knew not which. Then he kissed her upon the forehead, and, carrying her to her bed, laid her down to rest awhile before she died, returning himself to the throne-room.

Here he found Francisco and Otter.

"Look, Baas," said the dwarf, producing from beneath his goat-skin cloak an article which he had employed the last hour in constructing. It was a fearful and a wonderful instrument, made out of the two sacrificial knives that had been left by the priests on the occasion of the kidnapping of the last of the Settlement men. The handles of these knives Otter had lashed together immovably with strips of hide, forming from them a weapon two feet or more in length, of which the curved points projected in opposite directions.

"What is that for, Otter?" said Leonard carelessly, for he was thinking of other things.

"This is for the Crocodile to eat, Baas; I have seen his brothers caught like that before in the marshes of the Zambezi," replied the dwarf with a grin. "Doubtless he thinks to eat me, but I have made another food ready for him. Ah! of one thing I am sure, that if he comes out there will be a good fight, whoever conquers in the end."

Then he proceeded to fix a hide rope to the handles of the knives, and having made it fast about his body with a running noose, he coiled its length, which may have measured some thirty feet, round and round his middle, artfully concealing its bulk together with the knives beneath his cloak and *moocha*.

"Now I am a man again, Baas," the dwarf said grimly. "I have done with drink and such follies to which I took in my hours of idleness, for the time has come to fight. Ay, and I shall win, Baas; the waters are my home, and I do not fear crocodiles however big—no, not one bit; for, as I told you, I have killed them before. You will see, you will see."

"I am afraid that I shall do nothing of the sort, Otter," answered Leonard sadly, "but I wish you luck, my friend. If you get out of this mess, they will think you a god indeed, and should you only find the sense to avoid drink, you may rule here till you die of old age."

"There would be no pleasure in that, Baas, if you were dead," answered the dwarf with a heavy sigh. "Alas! my folly has helped to bring

251

you into this trouble, but this I swear, that if I live—and my spirit tells me that I shall not die tonight—it will be to avenge you. Fear not, Baas; when I am a god again, one by one I will kill them all, and when they are dead, then I will kill myself and come to look for you."

"It is very kind of you, Otter, I am sure," said Leonard with something like a laugh, and at that moment the curtains swung aside and Soa stood before them accompanied by four armed priests.

"What do you want, woman?" exclaimed Leonard, springing towards her as though by instinct.

"Go back, Deliverer!" she said, holding up her hand and addressing him in the Sisutu tongue, which of course those with her did not understand. "I am guarded, and my death would be quickly followed by your own. Moreover, it would avail you little to kill me, since I come to bring you hope for the life of her you love and for your own. Listen: the sun will not shine tomorrow at the dawn; already the mist gathers thick and it will hold, therefore the Shepherdess and the Dwarf will be hurled from the head of the statue, while you and the Bald-pate, having witnessed their end, will be kept alive till the autumn sacrifice, then to be offered up with the other victims."

"Why do you come to tell us all this, woman?" said Leonard, "seeing that we knew it already—that is, except the news of the postponement of our own fate, which I for one do not desire. What hope is there in this story? If you have nothing better to say, get you gone, traitress, and let us see your hateful face no more."

"I have something more to say, Deliverer. I still love the Shepherdess as you love her, and," she added with emphasis, "as Bald-pate yonder also loves her. Now this is my plan: two must die at dawn, but of those two the Shepherdess need not be one. The morning will be misty, the statue of the god is high, and but few of the priests will see the victim shrouded in her black robe. What if a substitute can be found so like to her in shape and height and feature that, in the twilight and beneath the shadow of the hood, none shall know them apart?"

Leonard started. "Who can be found?"

Slowly Soa raised her thin hand and pointed to Francisco.

"*There stands the man!*" she said. "Were he wrapped in the cloak of Aca, who would know him from the Shepherdess? The pool and the Snake do not give back that which they have swallowed."

If Leonard had started before, now he fairly recoiled, as the full meaning of this terrible proposition possessed his mind. He looked at Francisco, who stood by wondering, for the priest did not understand the Sisutu dialect.

"Tell him," she said.

"Wait awhile," he answered hoarsely; "supposing that this were carried out, what would happen to the Shepherdess?"

"She would be concealed in the dungeons of the temple, in his dress and under his name," and again she pointed to Francisco, "until such time as a chance could be found for her to escape, or to return to rule this people unquestioned and with honour. My father alone knows of this plot, and because of his love for me he suffers me to try it, desperate as it seems. Also, for I will tell you all the truth, he is himself in danger, and he believes that by means of the Shepherdess—who, when she reappears having survived the sacrifice, will be held by the people to be immortal—he may save his life when the day of his own trial comes."

"And do you think," said Leonard, "that I will trust her alone to you, wicked and forsworn as you are, and to the tender mercies of your father? No, it is better that she should die and have done with her fears and torments."

"I did not ask you to do so, Deliverer," said Soa quietly. "You will be taken with her, and if she lives you will live also. Is that not enough? These men here come to bear you and Bald-pate to the dungeons: they will bear you and the Shepherdess, knowing no difference, that is all. Now tell him; perchance he may not be willing to accept."

"Francisco, come here," said Leonard in a low voice, speaking in Portuguese. Then he told him all, while Soa watched them with her glittering eyes. As the tale went on the priest turned ashen pale and trembled violently, but before it was finished he ceased to tremble, and Leonard, looking at his face, saw that it was alight as with a glory.

"I accept," he said in a clear voice, "for thus will it be given to me to save the life of the Senora, and to atone for my offence. Come, let me make ready."

"Francisco," muttered Leonard, for his emotion would not suffer him to speak aloud, "you are a saint and a hero. I wish that I could go through this in your stead, for most gladly would I do so, but it is not possible."

"It seems then that there are two saints and heroes," replied the priest gently. "But why talk thus? It is the bounden duty of either or both of us to die for her, yet it is far better that I should die leaving you alive to love and comfort her."

Leonard thought a moment. "I suppose it must be so," he said, "but Heaven knows, it is a terrible alternative. How can I trust that woman Soa? And yet if I do not trust her Juanna will be killed at once."

"You must take the chance of it," answered Francisco; "after all she is fond of her mistress, and it was because she grew jealous that she fled to Nam and betrayed us."

"There is another thing," said Leonard; "how are we to get Juanna away? If once she suspects the plot, there will be an end of it. Soa, come thither."

She came, and he put this question to her, telling her at the same time that Francisco consented to the scheme and that Juanna slept behind the curtain and might awake at any moment.

"I have that with me which shall overcome the difficulty, Deliverer," answered Soa, "for I foresaw it. See here," and she drew a small gourd from her dress, "this is that same water of which Saga gave your black dog to drink when I escaped you. Now mix it with some spirit, go to the Shepherdess, awake her, and bid her drink this to comfort her. She will obey, and immediately deep sleep will take her again that shall hold her fast for six hours."

"It is not a poison?" asked Leonard suspiciously.

"No, it is not a poison. What need would there be to poison one who must die at dawn?"

Then Leonard did as she told him. Taking a tin pannikin, one of their few possessions, he emptied the sleeping-draught into it and added enough native brandy to colour the water.

Next he went into Juanna's room and found her lying fast asleep upon the great bed. Going up to her he touched her gently on the shoulder, saying, "Wake, my love." She raised herself and opened her eyes.

"Is that you, Leonard?" she said. "I was dreaming that I was a girl again and at school at Durban, and that it was time to get up for early service at the church. Oh! I remember now. Is it dawn yet?"

"No, dear, but it soon will be," he answered; "here, drink this, it will give you courage."

"How horrid that spirit tastes!" she said, then sank back slowly on the cushion and in another minute fell sound asleep again. The draught was strong and it worked quickly.

Leonard went to the curtain and beckoned to Soa and the others. They all entered except the priests, who remained clustered together near the doorway of the great chamber talking in low tones and apparently taking no notice of what passed.

"Take off that robe, Bald-pate," said Soa; "I must give you another."

He obeyed, and while Soa was engaged in clothing Juanna's senseless form in the gown of the priest, Francisco drew his diary from the pocket in his vest where he kept it. Rapidly he wrote a few lines on a blank page, then shutting the book he handed it to Leonard together with his rosary, saying:

"Let the Senora read what I have written here, after I am dead, not before, and give her these beads in memory of me. Many is the time that I have prayed for her upon them. Perhaps she will wear them after I am gone, and, although she is a Protestant, sometimes offer up a prayer for me."

Leonard took the book and the rosary and placed them in an inner pocket. Then he turned to Otter and rapidly explained to him the meaning of all that was being done.

"Ah, Baas," said the dwarf, "put no faith in that she-devil. And yet perhaps she will try to save the Shepherdess, for she loves her as a lioness loves her young. But I am afraid for you, Baas, for you she hates."

"Never mind about me, Otter," answered Leonard. "Listen: they are going to hide us in the dungeons of the temple; if by any chance you escape, seek out Olfan and try to rescue us. If not, farewell, and may we meet again in another place."

"Oh! Baas, Baas," said Otter with a deep sob, "for myself I care nothing, nor whether I live or die, but it is sad to think that you will perish alone, and I not with you. Oh! why did Baas Tom dream that evil dream? Had it not been for him, we might have been transport-riding in Natal today. I would that I had been a better servant to you, Baas, but it is too late now." And as he spoke Leonard felt a great tear fall upon his hand.

"Never mind the servant, Otter," he answered; "you are the best friend, black or white, that ever I had, and Heaven reward you for it. If you can help the Baas yonder at the last, do so. At the least see that he swallows the medicine in time, for he is weak and gentle and not fitted to die such a death," and he turned away.

By this time Soa had arrayed Francisco in the black robe of Aca. The white dress worn in the temple ceremonies he did not put on, for it remained upon Juanna, completely hidden from sight, however, by the priest's gown.

"Who would know them apart now?" asked Soa triumphantly, then added, handing Leonard the great ruby which she had taken from Juanna's forehead, "Here, Deliverer, this belongs to you; do not lose the stone, for you have gone through much to win it."

Leonard took the gem and at first was minded to dash it into the old woman's sneering face, but remembering the uselessness of such a performance, he thrust it into his pocket together with the rosary.

"Come, let us be going," said Soa. "You must carry the Shepherdess, Deliverer; I will say that it is Bald-pate who has fainted with fear. Farewell, Bald-pate; after all you are a brave man, and I honour you for this deed. Keep the hood well about your face, and if you would preserve the Shepherdess alive, be silent, answering no word whoever addresses you, and uttering no cry however great your fear."

Francisco went to the bed where Juanna lay, and holding out his hand above her as though in blessing, he muttered some words of prayer or farewell. Then turning, he clasped Leonard in his arms, kissed him and blessed him also.

"Goodbye, Francisco," said Leonard in a choking voice; "surely the Kingdom of Heaven is made up of such as you."

"Do not weep, my friend," answered the priest, "for there in that kingdom I hope to greet you and her."

And so these friends parted.

CHAPTER 31

The White Dawn

Lifting Juanna in his arms, Leonard hurried from the sleeping apartment to the throne-room, where he halted hesitating, for he did not know what was to happen next. Soa, who had preceded him, surrounded by the four priests and with a torch in her hand, stood against that wall of the chamber where she had lain bound on the night of the drugging of Otter.

"Bald-pate has fainted with fear, he is a coward," she said to the priests, pointing to the burden in Leonard's arms; "open the secret way, and let us pass on."

Then a priest came forward, and pressed upon a stone in the wall, which gave way, leaving a space sufficiently large for him to insert his hand and pull upon some hidden mechanism with all his force. Thereon a piece of the wall swung outward as though upon a pivot, revealing a flight of steps, beyond which ran a narrow passage. Soa descended first, bearing the light, which she was careful to hold in such a way as to keep the figure of Leonard, and the burden that he bore, in comparative darkness. After her went two priests, followed by Leonard, carrying Juanna, the rear being brought up by the remaining priests, who closed the secret door behind them.

"So that is how it is done," thought Leonard to himself, turning his head to watch the process, no detail of which escaped him.

Otter, who had followed Leonard from Juanna's chamber, saw them go, though from some little distance, for, like a cat, the dwarf could see in the dark. When the rock had closed again, he returned to Francisco, who sat upon the bed lost in prayer or thought.

"I have seen how they make a hole in the wall," he said, "and pass through it. Doubtless our comrades, the Settlement men, went that way. Say, shall we try it?"

"What is the use, Otter?" answered the priest. "The road leads only to the dungeons of the temple; if we got so far we should be caught there, and everything would be discovered, including this trick," and he pointed to the robes of Aca, which he wore.

"That is true," said Otter. "Come, then, let us go and sit upon the thrones and wait till they fetch us."

So they went to the great chairs and sat themselves down in them, listening to the tramp of the guards outside the doorway. Here Francisco resumed his prayers, while Otter sang songs of the deeds that he had done, and more especially a very long one which he had composed upon the taking of the slave camp—"to keep his heart alive," as he explained to Francisco.

A quarter of an hour passed and the curtains were drawn aside, admitting a band of priests, headed by Nam, and bearing two litters.

"Now silence, Otter," whispered Francisco, drawing his hood over his face.

"Here sit the gods," said Nam, waving the torch that he carried towards the two quiet figures on the thrones. "Descend, ye gods, that we may bear you to the temple and seat you in a lofty place, whence ye shall watch the glories of the rising sun."

Then, without more ado, Otter and Francisco came down from their seats, and took their places in the litters. Presently they felt themselves being borne forward at a considerable speed. When they were outside the palace gates Otter peeped through the curtain in the hope of perceiving some change in the weather. In vain; the mist was denser than usual, although it grew grey with the light of the coming dawn. Now they were at those gates of the temple that were nearest to the colossal idol, and here, at the mouth of one of the numerous underground passages, guards assisted them to descend.

"Farewell, Queen," whispered the voice of Olfan into Francisco's ear; "I would have given my life to save you, but I have failed; as it is, I live to avenge you upon Nam and all his servants."

Francisco made no answer, but pressed on down the passage holding his head low. Soon they were at the foot of the idol, and, led by priests, began to ascend the stairway in the interior of the statue. Up they toiled slowly in the utter darkness; indeed, to Francisco this, the last journey of his life, seemed the longest.

At length they emerged upon the head of the colossus, where neither of them had been before. It formed a flat platform about eight feet square, quite unprotected at the edges, beneath which curved the sheer outlines of the sculptured head. The ivory throne whereon Juanna had sat when first she visited the temple was gone, and instead of it, placed at the very verge of the forehead, were two wooden stools upon which the victims must seat themselves. From this horrible elevation could be seen that narrow space of rock between the feet of the colossus and the wall of the pool where was the stone altar, although, owing to the slope of the bowed head, he who stood upon it almost overhung the waters of the well.

Otter and Francisco seated themselves on the stools, and behind them Nam and three other priests took their stand, Nam placing himself in such a position that his companions could not see anything of Francisco's slight form, which they believed to be that of the Shepherdess.

"Hold me, Otter," whispered Francisco. "My senses will leave me, and I shall fall."

"Shut your eyes and lean back, then you will see nothing," answered Otter. "Moreover, make ready your medicine, for the time is at hand."

"It is ready," he answered. "May I be forgiven the sin, for I cannot bear to be hurled living to the Snake!"

Otter made no answer, but set himself to watch the scene beneath him. The temple was filled with mist that from the great height looked like smoke, and through this veil he could just distinguish the black and moving mass of the vast assembly, who had sat the long night through waiting to witness the consummation of the tragedy, while the sound of their voices as they spoke together in hushed tones reached him like that of the murmuring of distant waters. Behind him stood the four priests or executioners in a solemn, silent line, their eyes fixed upon the grey mist, while above them, around them, and beneath them was nothing but sheer and giddy space.

It was a hideous position, heightened by every terror that man and nature can command, and even the intrepid dwarf, who feared neither death nor devil, and over whom religious doubts had no power, began to feel its chilling influence grip his heart. As for Francisco, such mind as he had left to him was taken up with fervent prayer, so it is possible that he did not suffer so much as might have been expected.

Five minutes or more passed thus; then a voice spoke from the mist below, saying:

"Are those who are named Aca and Jal on high, O priest?"

"They are on high," answered Nam.

"Is it the hour of dawn, O priest?" said the voice again, and this time Otter knew it for that of the spokesman of the elders.

"Not yet awhile," answered Nam, and he glanced at the snow peak that towered thousands of feet into the air behind and above the temple.

259

Indeed every eye in that assembly was staring at this peak, although its gigantic outline could only be seen dimly through the mist, dimly as the shape of a corpse buried in a winding-sheet of snow. Here, upon the loftiest precipices of the mountain the full light of morning struck first and struck always, for their pinnacles soared far above the level of the mist wreaths, and by the quality of that light this people judged the weather of the new-born day. If the snow was rosy-red, then they knew that ere long the sun would shine upon them. If, on the other hand, it gleamed cold and white, or, still worse, grey, it was a sign that the coming day would be misty in the city and on the plains. Therefore in this, the hour of the trial of the gods whom they had set up, all that company watched the mountain peak as they had never watched before, to see if it should show white or red.

Very gradually the light increased, and it seemed to Otter that the mist was somewhat thinner than was usual at this hour, though as yet it hung densely between them and the mountain snows. Now he could trace the walls of the amphitheatre, now he could see the black shimmer of the water beneath, and distinguish the glitter of many hundreds of upturned eyeballs as they glared at him and beyond him. The silence grew more and more intense, for none spoke or moved: all were waiting to see the dawn break upon the slope of snow, and wondering— would it be red or white? Must the gods die or live? So intense and fearful was the hush, unbroken by a breath of air or the calling of a bird, that Otter could bear it no longer, but suddenly burst into song.

He had a fine deep voice, and it was a Zulu war-song that he sang, a triumphant paean of the rush of conquering *impis* interspersed with the wails of women and the groans of the dying. Louder and louder he sang, stamping his naked feet upon the rock, while the people wondered at the marvel. Surely this was a god, they thought, who chanted thus exultingly in a strange tongue while men waited to see him cast into the jaws of the Snake. No mortal about to die so soon and thus terribly could find the heart to sing, and much less could he sing such a song as that they heard.

"He is a god," cried a voice far away, and the cry was echoed on every side till at length, suddenly, men grew silent, and Otter also ceased from his singing, for he had turned his head and seen. Lo! the veil of mist that hid the mountain's upper heights grew thin:—it was the moment of dawn, but would it be a red dawn or a white? As he looked the vapours disappeared from the peak, though they still lay thick upon the slopes below, and in their place were seen its smooth and shining outlines clothed in a cloak of everlasting snows.

The ordeal was ended. No touch of colour, no golden sunbeam or crimson shadow stained the ghastly surface of those snows, they were pallid as the faces of the dead.

"A white dawn! A white dawn!" roared the populace. "Away with the false gods! Hurl them to the Snake!"

"It is finished," whispered Otter again into Francisco's ear; "now take your medicine, and, friend, farewell!"

The priest heard and, clasping his thin hands together, turned his tormented face, in which the soft eyes shone, upwards towards the heavens. For some seconds he sat thus; then Otter, peering beneath his hood, saw his countenance change, and once more a glory seemed to shine upon it as it had shone when, some hours since, Francisco promised to do the deed that now he was about to dare.

Again there was silence below, for the spokesman of the Council of Elders had risen, and was crying the formal question to the priests above:

"Is the dawn white or red, ye who stand on high?"

Nam turned and looked upon the snow.

"The dawn is fully dawned and it is white!" he answered.

"Be swift," whispered Otter into Francisco's ear.

Then the priest raised his right hand to his lips, as though to partake of the sacrament of death.

A moment later and he let it fall with a sigh, whispering back to Otter: "I cannot, it is a deadly sin. They must kill me, for I will not kill myself."

Before the dwarf could answer, Nature, more merciful than his conscience, did that for Francisco which he refused to do for himself, for of a sudden he swooned. His face turned ashen and slowly he began to sink backwards, so that he would have fallen had not Nam, who saw that he had fainted with fear, caught him by the shoulders and held him upright.

"The dawn is white! We see it with our eyes," answered the spokesmen of the elders. "O ye who stand on high, cast down the false gods according to the judgment of the People of the Mist."

Otter heard and knew that the moment had come to leap, for now he need trouble himself with Francisco no more.

Swiftly he turned his head, looking at Nam, for he would know if he might carry out a purpose that he had formed. It was to seize the high priest and bear him to the depths below.

It was not possible, he was out of reach; moreover, were he to snatch Nam away, Francisco would fall backwards, and the others might see that this was not the Shepherdess. Otter stood up upon his feet, and kicking the stool on which he had sat off the platform, he watched its flight. It flew into the water, never touching the rock, and then the dwarf knew that he had planned well.

Now Nam and one priest seized the fainting form of Francisco and the other two stepped towards Otter. The dwarf waited till their hands were outstretched to grasp him, then suddenly he sprang at the man upon his right, and shouting "Come thou with me," he gripped him about the middle in his iron grasp, and, putting out all his strength, hurled himself and his burden into sheer space beneath.

The priest shrieked aloud, and a gasp of wonder went up from the watching thousands as the dwarf and his victim rushed downward like a stone. They cleared the edge of the pool by an inch or two—no more, and struck the boiling waters, sinking through them till Otter thought they would never rise again. But at last they did rise. Then Otter loosed the dead or senseless priest, and at that moment the body of Francisco, cast thither by Nam, struck the water beside him and straightway vanished for ever.

Otter loosed his grip, and diving beneath the surface swam hard for the north side of the pool, for there he had noticed that the current was least strong, and there also the rock bank overhung a little. He reached it safely, and rising once more grasped a knob of rock with one hand, and lay still where in the shadow and the swirl of waters he could not be discovered by any watching from above. He breathed deeply and moved his limbs; it was well, he was unhurt. The priest whom he had taken with him, being heaviest, had met the water first, so that though the leap was great the shock had been little.

"Ha!" said Otter to himself, "thus far my Spirit has been with me, and here I could lie for hours and never be seen. But there is still the Snake to contend with," and hastily he seized the weapon that he had constructed out of the two knives, and unwound a portion of the cord that was fast about his middle. Then again he looked across the surface of the waters. Some ten fathoms from him, in the exact centre of the whirlpool, the body of the priest was still visible, for the vortex bore it round and round, but of Francisco there was nothing to be seen. Only thirty feet above him Otter could see lines of heads bending over the rocky edges of the pool and gazing at the priest as he was tossed about like a straw in an eddy.

"Now, if he is still there and awake," thought Otter, "surely the father of crocodiles will take this bait; therefore I shall do best to be still awhile and see what happens."

As he reflected thus a louder shout than any he had heard before reached his ears from the multitude in the temple above him, so tumultuous a shout indeed, that for a few moments even the turmoil of the waters was lost in it.

"Now what chances up there, I wonder?" thought Otter again. Then his attention was diverted in a somewhat unpleasant fashion.

This was the cause of that shout: a miracle, or what the People of the Mist took to be a miracle, had come about; for suddenly, for the first time within the memory of man, the white dawn had changed to red. Blood-red was the snow upon the mountain, and lo! its peaks were turned to fire.

For a while all those who witnessed this phenomenon stood aghast, then there arose that babble of voices which had reached the ears of Otter as he lurked under the bank of rock.

"The gods have been sacrificed unjustly," yelled the people. "They are true gods; see, the dawn is red!"

The situation was curious and most unexpected, but Nam, who had been a high priest for more than fifty years, proved himself equal to it.

"This is a marvel indeed!" he cried, when silence had at length been restored; "for no such thing is told of in our history as that a white dawn upon the mountain should turn to red. Yet, O People of the Mist, those whom we thought gods have not been offered up wrongfully. Nay, this is the meaning of the sign: now are the true gods, Aca and Jal, appeased, because those who dared to usurp their power have gone down to doom. Therefore the curse is lifted from the land and the sunlight has come back to bless us."

As he finished speaking, again the tumult broke out, some crying this thing and some that. But no action was taken, for Nam's excuse was ready and plausible, and the minds of men were confused. So the assembly broke up in disorder; only the priests and as many more as could find place, Olfan among them, crowded round the edges of the pool to see what happened in its depths.

Meanwhile Otter had seen that which caused him to think no more of the shouting above him than of the humming of last year's gnats. Suffering his eyes to travel round the circumference of the rocky wall, he saw the mouth of a circular hole, situated immediately under the base of the idol, which may have measured some eight feet in diameter. The lower edge of this hole stood about six inches above the level of the pool, and water ran out of it in a thin stream. Passing down this stream, half swimming and half waddling, appeared that huge and ungainly reptile which was the real object of the worship of the People of the Mist.

Great as were its length and bulk, the dwarf saw it but for a few moments, so swift were its movements; then the creature vanished into the deep waters, to reappear presently by the side of the dead priest, who was now beginning to sink. Its horrible head rose upon the waters as on that night when the woman had been thrown to it; it opened its huge jaws, and, seizing the body of the man across the middle, it disappeared beneath the foam. Otter watched the mouth of the hole, and not in vain; for before he could have counted ten the monster was crawling through it, bearing its prey into the cave.

Now once more the dwarf felt afraid, for the Snake, or rather the crocodile, at close quarters was far more fearful than anything that his imagination had portrayed. Keeping his place beneath the ledge, which, except for the coldness of the water, he found himself able to do with little fatigue or difficulty, Otter searched the walls of the pool, seeking for some possible avenue of escape, since his ardour for personal conflict with this reptile had evaporated. But search as he would he could find nothing; the walls were full thirty feet high, and sloped inwards, like the sides of an inverted funnel. Wherever the exits from the pool might be, they were invisible; also, notwithstanding his strength and skill, Otter did not dare to swim into the furious eddy to look for them.

One thing he noticed, indeed: immediately above the entrance to the crocodile's den, and some twenty feet from the level of the water, two holes were pierced in the rock, six feet or so apart, each measuring about twelve inches square. But these holes were not to be reached, and even if reached they were too small to pass, so Otter thought no more of them.

Now the cold was beginning to nip him, and he felt that if he stayed where he was much longer he would become paralyzed by it, for it was fed from the ice and snow above. Therefore, it would seem that there was but one thing to do—to face the Water Dweller in his lair. To this, then, Otter made up his mind, albeit with loathing and a doubtful heart.

CHAPTER 32

How Otter Fought the Water Dweller

Keeping himself carefully under the overshadowing edge of the rock-bank, and holding his double-bladed knife ready in one hand, Otter swam to the mouth of the Snake's den. As he approached it he perceived by the great upward force of the water that the real body of the stream entered the pool from below, the hole where the crocodile lived being but a supplementary exit, which doubtless the river followed in times of flood.

Otter reached the mouth of the tunnel without any great difficulty, and, watching his chance, he lifted himself on his hands and slipped through it quickly, for he did not desire to be seen by those who were gathered above. Nor indeed was he seen, for his red head-dress and the goat-skin cloak had been washed away or cast off in the pool, and in that light his black body made little show against the black rock beneath.

Now he was inside the hole, and found himself crouching upon a bed of sand, or rather disintegrated rock, brought down by the waters. The gloom of the place was great, but the light of the white dawn, which had turned to red, was gathering swiftly on the surface of the pool without as the mist melted, and thence was reflected into the tunnel. So it came about that very soon Otter, who had the gift, not uncommon among savages, of seeing in anything short of absolute darkness, was able to make out his surroundings with tolerable accuracy. The place in a corner of which he squatted was a cave of no great height or width, hollowed in the solid rock by the force of water, as smoothly as though it had been hewn by the hand of man: in short, an enormous natural drain-pipe, but constructed of stone instead of earthenware.

In the bottom of this drain trickled a stream of water nowhere more than six inches in depth, on either side of which, for ten feet or more, lay a thick bed of debris ground small. How far the cave stretched of course he could not see, nor as yet could he discover the whereabouts of its hideous occupant, though traces of its presence were plentiful, for the sandy floor was marked with its huge footprints, and the air reeked with an abominable stink.

"Where has this evil spirit gone to?" thought Otter; "he must be near, and yet I can see nothing of him. Perhaps he lives further up the cave"; and he crept a pace or two forward and again peered into the gloom.

Now he perceived what had hitherto escaped him, namely, that some eight yards from the mouth of the tunnel a table-shaped fragment of stone rose from its floor to within six feet of the roof, having on the hither side a sloping plane that connected its summit with the stream-bed beneath. Doubtless this fragment or boulder, being of some harder material than the surrounding rock, had resisted the wear of the rushing river; the top of it, as was shown by the high-water marks on the sides of the cave, being above the level of the torrent, which, although it was now represented only by a rivulet, evidently at certain seasons of the year poured down with great force and volume.

"Here is a bed on which a crocodile might sleep," reflected Otter, creeping a little further forward and staring at the mass of rock, and more especially at a triangular-shaped object that was poised on the top of the sloping plane, and on something which lay beneath it.

"Now, if that thing be another stone," thought Otter again, "how comes it that it does not slip into the water as it should do, and what is that upon which it rests?" and he took a step to one side to prevent his body from intercepting any portion of the ray of light that momentarily shone clearer and pierced the darkness of the cave to a greater distance.

Then he looked again and almost fell in his horror, for now he could see all. The thing that he had taken for a stone set upon the rock-table was the head of the Dweller in the Waters, for there in it, as the light struck on them, two dreadful eyes gleamed with a dull and changing fire. Moreover, he discovered what was the object which lay under the throat of the reptile. It was the body of that priest whom Otter had taken with him in his leap from the statue, for he could see the dead face projecting on one side.

"Perhaps if I wait awhile he will begin to eat him," reflected the dwarf, remembering the habits of crocodiles, "and then I can attack him when he rests and sleeps afterwards"; and, acting on this idea, he stood still, watching the green fire as it throbbed and quivered, waxed and waned in the monster's eyes.

How long he remained thus Otter never knew; but after a time he became conscious that these eyes had taken hold of him and were drawing him towards them, though whether the reptile saw him or not he could not tell. For a space he struggled against this unholy fascination; then, overcome by dread, he strove to fly, back to the pool or anywhere out of reach of those devilish orbs. Alas! it was too late: no step could he move backwards, no, not to save his life.

Now he must go on. It was as though the Water Dweller had read his mind, and drew its foe towards itself to put the matter to the test. Otter took one step forward—rather would he have sprung again off the head of the colossus—and the eyes glowed more dreadfully than ever, as though in triumph.

Then in despair he sank to the ground, hiding his face in his hands and groaning in his heart.

"This is a devil that I have come to fight, a devil with magic in his eyes," he thought. "And how can I, who am but a common Knobnose dwarf, do battle against the king of evil spirits, clothed in the shape of a crocodile?"

Even now, when he could not see them, he felt the eyes drawing him. Yet, as they were no longer visible, his courage and power of mind came back to him sufficiently to enable him to think again.

"Otter," he said to himself, "if you stay thus, soon the magic will do its work. Your sense will leave you, and that devil will eat you up as a cobra devours a meer-cat. Yes, he will swallow you, and his inside will be your grave, and that is no end for one who has been called a god! Men, let alone gods, should die fighting, whether it be with other men, with wild beasts, with snakes, or with devils. Think now, if your master, the Deliverer, saw you crouch thus like a toad before an adder, how he would laugh and say, 'Ho! I thought this man brave. Ho! he talked very loud about fighting the Water Dweller, he who came of a line of warriors; but now I laugh at him, for I see that he is but a cross-bred cur and a coward.'

"Yes, yes, you can hear his words, Otter. Say now, will you bear their shame and sit here until you are snapped up and swallowed?"

Thus the dwarf addressed himself, and it seemed to his bewildered brain that the words which he had imagined were true, and that Leonard really stood by and mocked him.

At last he sprang to his feet, and crying, "Never, Baas!" so loudly that the cave rang with the echoes of his shout, he rushed straight at the foe, holding the two-bladed knife in his right hand.

The crocodile, that was waiting for him to fall insensible, as had ever been the custom of the living victims on whom it fixed its baneful glare, heard his cry and awoke from its seeming torpor. It lifted its head, fire seemed to flash from its dull eyes, its vast length began to stir. Higher and higher it reared its head, then of a sudden it leaped from the slope of rock, as alligators when disturbed leap from a river bank into the water, coming so heavily to the ground that the shock caused the cave to tremble, and stood before the dwarf with its tail arched upwards over its back.

Again Otter shouted, half in rage and half in terror, and the sound seemed to make the brute more furious.

It opened its huge mouth as though to seize him and waddled a few paces forward, halting within six feet of him. Now the dwarf's chance had come and he knew it, for with the opportunity all his courage and skill returned to him. It was he who sprang and not the crocodile. He sprang, he thrust his arm and the double knife far into the yawning mouth, and for a second held it there, one end pointing upwards to the brain and one to the tongue beneath. He felt the jaws close, but their rows of yellow fangs never touched his arm, for there was that between them which held them some little space apart. Then he cast himself on one side and to the ground, leaving the weapon in the reptile's throat.

For a few moments it shook its horrible head, while Otter watched gasping, for the reek of the brute's breath almost overpowered him. Twice it opened its great jaws and spat, and twice it strove to close them. Oh! what if it should rid itself of the knife, or drive it through the soft flesh of the throat? Then he was lost indeed! But this it might not do, for the lower blade caught upon the jawbone, and at each effort it drove the sharp point of the upper knife deeper towards its brain. Moreover, so good was the steel, and so firm were the hide bindings of the handles, shrunken as they were with the wet, that nothing broke or gave.

"Now he will trample me or dash me to pieces with his tail," said Otter; but as yet the Snake had no such mind—indeed, in its agony it seemed to have forgotten the presence of its foe. It writhed upon the floor of the cave, lashing the rock with its tail, and gasping horribly the while. Then suddenly it started forward past him, and the tough hide rope about Otter's middle ran out like the line from the bow of a whale-boat when the harpoon has gone home in the quarry.

Thrice the dwarf spun round violently, then he felt himself dragged in great jerks along the rocky floor, which, happily for him, was smooth. A fourth jerk, and once more he was in the waters of the pool, ay, and being carried to its remotest depths.

"Now, he is mad," thought Otter, "who ties himself to such a fish as this, for it will drown me ere it dies."

Had Otter been any other man, doubtless this would have been so. But he was as nearly amphibious as a human being can be, and could dive and swim and hold his breath, yes, and see beneath the surface as well as the animal from which he took his name. Never did such gifts stand their owner in better stead than during the minutes of this strange duel.

Twice the tortured reptile sank to the bottom of the pool—and its depth was great—dragging the dwarf after it, though, as it chanced, between dives it rose to the surface, giving him time to breathe. A third time it dived, and Otter must follow it—on this occasion to the mouth of one of the subterranean exits of the water, into which the dwarf was sucked. Then the brute turned, heading up the pool with the speed of a hooked salmon, and Otter, who had prayed that the line would break, now prayed that it might hold, for he knew that even he could never hope to swim against that undertow.

It held, and once more they rose to the surface, where the reptile lay lashing the waters in its pain, blood pouring from its mouth and nostrils. Very glad was Otter to be able to breathe again, for during that last rush he had gone near to suffocation. He lifted his head, inhaling the air with great gulps, and saw that the banks of the pool were lined with spectators who shouted and surged in their mad excitement. After that he did not see much more for a while, since just then it seemed to occur to the crocodile for the first time that the man alongside of him was the cause of his suffering; at least it wallowed round, causing the waters to boil about its horny sides, and charged him. With its fangs it could not bite, therefore it struck at him with its tail.

Twice Otter dived, avoiding the blows, but the third time he was not so successful, for the reptile followed him into the deep water and dealt him a fearful stroke before he could either sink or rise. He felt the rough scales cut into his flesh and a sensation as though every bone in his body was breaking and his eyes were starting from his head. Faintly and more faintly he struggled, but in vain, for now life and sense were leaving him together, and everything grew black.

But suddenly there came a change, and Otter knew vaguely that again he was being dragged through the water and over rock. Then darkness took him, and he remembered no more.

When the dwarf awoke it was to find himself lying on the floor of the cave, but not alone, for by his side, twisted into a last and hideous contortion, lay the Snake god—dead! The upper part of the double knife had worked itself into its brain, and, with a dying effort, it sought the den where it had lived for centuries, dragging Otter with it, and there expired, how or when he knew not. But the dwarf had triumphed. Before him was stretched the ancient terror of the People of the Mist, the symbol and, indeed, the object of their worship, slain by his skill and valour.

Otter saw, and, bruised and shaken as he was, his heart swelled with pride, for had he not done a deed single-handed such as was not told of in the stories of his land?

"Oh! that the Baas were here to see this sight!" he said, as he crawled along the length of his dead enemy, and seated himself upon its flat and loathsome snout. "Alas! he cannot," he added, "but I pray that my watching spirit may spare my life, that I may live to sing the song of the slaying of the Devil of the People of the Mist. *Wow!* that was a fight. When shall a man see another? And lo! save for many bruises and the cutting of the rope about my middle, I am not greatly hurt, for the water broke the weight of his tail when he smote me with it. After all, it is well that the line held, for it served to drag me from the pool as it had dragged me into it, otherwise I had surely drowned there.

"See, though, it is nearly done with," and grasping that end of the cord which hung from the jaws of the crocodile, he broke it with a jerk, for, with the exception of half a strand, it was frayed through by the worn fangs.

Then, having rested himself a little, and washed the worst of his hurts with water, Otter set himself to consider the position. First, however, he made an utterly ineffectual effort to extract the great knives. Ten men could not have moved them, for the upper blade was driven many inches deep into the bone and muscles of the reptile's massive head. But for this chance it would have soon shaken itself clear of them; but, as it was, every contortion and gnashing of its jaws had only served to drive the steel deeper—up to the hilt, indeed.

Abandoning this attempt, the dwarf crept cautiously to the mouth of the cave and peered at the further banks of the pool, whence he could hear shouts and see men moving to and fro, apparently in a state of great excitement.

"Now I am weary of that pool," he said to himself, "and if I am seen in it the Great People will surely shoot at me with arrows and kill me. What shall I do, then? I cannot stay in this place of stinks with the dead devil and the bones of those whom he has devoured, until I die of hunger. Yet this water must come from somewhere, therefore it seems best that I should follow it awhile, searching for the spot where it enters the cave. It will be dark walking, but the walls and the floor are smooth, so that I shall not hurt myself, and if I find nothing I can return again and strive to escape from the pool by night."

Having decided upon the adventure, Otter began to carry it out with characteristic promptness, the more readily, indeed, because his long immersion the water had chilled him, and he felt a weariness creeping over him as a result of the terrible struggle and emotions that he had passed through.

Coiling the hide ripe about his middle, which was sadly cut by its chafing, he started with an uncertain gait, for he was still very weak. A few steps brought him to that rock on which he had discovered the head of the reptile, and he paused to examine it. Climbing the sloping stone—no easy task, for it was smooth as ice—he came to the table-like top. On its edge lay the body of that priest who had shared his fall from the head of the colossus.

Then he inspected the surface of the rock, and for the first time understood how old that monster must have been which he had conquered in single combat. For there, where its body had lain from generation to generation, and perhaps from century to century, the hard material was worn away to the depth of two feet or more, while at the top of the sloping stone was a still deeper niche, wherein its head reposed as it lay keeping its sleepless watch on the waters of the pool.

Around this depression, and strewn about the floor of the cave itself, were the remains of many victims, a considerable number of whom had not been devoured. In every case, however, the larger bones were broken, and from this circumstance Otter judged that, although it was the custom of this dreadful reptile to crush the life out of all who were thrown to it with a bite of its fangs, yet, like that of other animals, its appetite was limited, and it was only occasionally that it consumed what it had killed.

The sight of these remains was so unpleasant and suggestive that even Otter, who certainly could not be called squeamish, hastened to descend the rock. As he passed round it his attention was attracted by the skeleton of a man who, from various indications, must have been alive within the last few weeks. The bones were clad in a priest's cloak, of which the dwarf, who was trembling with cold, hastened to possess himself. As he picked up the robe he observed beneath it a bag of tanned ox-hide that doubtless had once been carried by the owner of the cloak.

"Perhaps he kept food in this," thought Otter; "though what he who came to visit the Water Dweller should want with food I cannot guess. At the least it will be bad by now, so I will leave it and be gone. Only a vulture would stay for long in this house of the dead." Then he started forward.

For a few yards more he had light to guide his steps, but very soon the darkness became complete; still the cave was not difficult to travel, for everywhere the rock was smooth and the water shallow. All that he needed to do was to walk straight on, keeping touch of one side of the tunnel with one hand. Indeed he had but two things to fear, that he should fall into some pit and that he might suddenly encounter another crocodile, "for doubtless," thought Otter, "the devil was married."

But Otter fell into no hole and he saw no crocodile, since, as it chanced, the Water Dweller of the People of the Mist was a bachelor.

When the dwarf had travelled up a steep slope for rather more than half an hour, to his intense joy he saw light before him and hurried towards it. Presently he reached the further mouth of the cavern that was almost closed by blocks of ice, among which a little water trickled. Creeping through an aperture he found himself upon the crest of the impassable precipice at the back of the city, and that before him a vast glacier of green ice stretched upwards, whereon the sun shone gloriously.

CHAPTER 33

Trapped

It will be remembered that some hours before Otter found himself in the light of day, after his conquest of the reptile god, Leonard found himself in a very difference place, namely, in a secret passage bearing the senseless form of Juanna in his arms, and being guided by Soa, whither he knew not.

On they went through various tunnels, of the turnings of which Leonard tried to keep count in his mind, till at length Soa ushered him into a rock-hewn cell that evidently had been prepared for their reception, for on one side of it stood a bed covered with skin blankets, and on the other a table provided with the best food that the country could offer. At a sign from Soa he laid Juanna down upon the bed, whereon the woman instantly threw a blanket over her, so as to hide her face from the eyes of the curious. Then, of a sudden Leonard felt himself seized from behind, and while his arms were held by two of the priests, a third, under Soa's direction, removed his revolver and hunting knife, which weapons were carried away.

"You treacherous hag!" said Leonard to Soa, "be careful lest I kill you."

"To kill me, Deliverer, would be to kill yourself and another. These things are taken from you because it is not safe that you should have them; such toys are not for angry children. Stay," she said to a fourth priest, "search his pockets."

The man did as he was ordered, placing everything that Leonard had about him, such as his watch, Francisco's notebook and rosary, and the great ruby stone, in a little pile upon the table. Presently he came to the fragment of poison which was wrapped in a square of kid-skin. Soa took it, and after examination said:

"Why, Deliverer, you have been borrowing medicine that will bring you bad luck if you keep it," and going to a small aperture in the wall of the cell, she threw the tiny packet out of it, and after it a second packet which Leonard recognised as having been taken from Juanna's hair.

"There, now you cannot hurt yourself," she added in Portuguese. "Let me tell you something: so long as you remain quiet all will be well, but if you attempt violence or escape, then you shall be bound and placed by yourself, also you will bring about the death of the Shepherdess yonder. Be warned then by me, White Man, and turn gentle, for remember that my day has come at last and you are in my power."

"That is very clear, my estimable friend," answered Leonard, controlling his wrath as best he might. "But for your sake I hope that the hour will never come when you shall be in mine, for then I may remember more than you wish. I do not in the least understand what you are aiming at, nor do I much care so long as a certain person is protected."

"Do not fear, Deliverer, she shall be protected. As you know well, I hate you, and yet I keep you alive because without you she might die; therefore, for her sake be careful. Attempt no violence towards me or my father if we visit you alone, for we shall do so in order that she may not be discovered, and the moment that you lift a hand against us will be the beginning of her doom. And now I must leave you for a while, for something passes in the temple which I desire to see. If she awakes before I return, be careful not to frighten her. Farewell!"

Then Soa went taking the priests with her, and the massive timber door was closed upon them.

After he had restored his various belongings to his pockets, the revolver and the knife which had been removed excepted, Leonard turned down the rug and looked at Juanna, who appeared to be plunged in a deep and happy sleep, for there was a smile upon her face. Next he examined the place where they were confined. It had two doors, that by which they had entered and a second of equal solidity. The only other opening was the slit out of which Soa had dropped the poison. It was shaped like an inverted loophole, the narrow end facing inward. This aperture attracted Leonard's attention, both on account of its unusual form and because of the sounds that reached him through it. Of these, the first and most pervading was a noise of rushing water. Then after a while he distinguished a roar as of a multitude shouting, that was repeated again and again at intervals. Now he knew where they must be. They were hidden away in the rock of the temple, somewhere in the immediate neighbourhood of the raging pool that lay in front of the colossus, and these sounds which he heard were the clamour of the people who watched the fate of Otter and Francisco.

This conviction was terrible enough, but had he known that, as it entered his mind, the body of his friend the priest was travelling on its last journey within four feet of his eyes, Leonard might have been even more prostrated than he was.

For an hour or more the shouting continued, then followed a silence broken only by the everlasting murmur of the waters without.

When Soa departed she had left a fragment of dip made of goat-fat burning upon the floor, but very soon this expired, leaving them in darkness. Now, however, light began to flow into the dungeon through the slit in the rock, and it seemed to Leonard that the character of this light was clearer than that to which they had been accustomed in this gloomy land.

After a while Leonard sat down upon a stool, which he placed close to Juanna's bed, just where the beam of light pierced the shadows, and groaned aloud in the bitterness of his heart. It was over; the pure-hearted martyr, Francisco, was dead, and with him Otter, his faithful friend and servant. Except Soa, who had become an active enemy, at least so far as he was concerned, of all who travelled to this hellish country Juanna and he alone were left alive, and sooner or later fate must overtake them also. The greatest and last failure of his life was about to be consummated, and he would go down into a nameless grave, there to be lost, having for many years suffered and toiled to no purpose, pursuing a chimera.

Juanna still slept heavily under the influence of the drug, and he was glad of it, for when she woke it must be to a worse misery than any that had gone before. Partly for something to do, and partly because the cravings of nature made themselves felt even through his sorrows, Leonard turned to the table and ate and drank of the viands there, though not without fear that they might be doctored. As the food took effect upon him some share of hope and courage entered into his heart, for it is a true saying that a full stomach makes a brave man. After all they two still breathed and were unharmed in body, nor was it absolutely certain that they would be called upon to give up the ghost at present. This was much.

Moreover, he had lived long enough to win the love of the fearless and beautiful girl who slept beside him, and though perhaps under such circumstances love, however true and passionate, ceases to occupy a commanding place in a man's heart, even then he felt that this was more, and that happier days might dawn when it would be, if not everything, at least most of all.

As he thought thus, he saw colour creep into Juanna's pale face; then she sighed, opened her eyes, and sat up.

"Where am I?" she said, glancing round wildly. "This is not the bed on which I lay down. Oh!" she started, "is it over?"

"Hush, dear, hush! I am with you," said Leonard, taking her hand.

"So I see. But where are the others, and what is this dreadful place? Are we buried alive, Leonard? It looks like a tomb."

"No, we are only prisoners. Come, eat and drink something, and then I will tell you the story."

She rose to obey him, and for the first time her eyes fell upon the robe she wore.

"Why, this is Francisco's! Where is Francisco?"

"Eat and drink," he repeated.

She did his bidding mechanically, watching his face the while with wondering and frightened eyes.

"Now," she said, "tell me. I can bear this no longer. Where are Francisco and Otter?"

"Alas! Juanna, they are dead," he answered solemnly.

"Dead," she wailed, wringing her hand. "Francisco dead! Why then are we still live?"

"Have courage and listen, Juanna. After you went to sleep in the palace, Soa came to us with a plan which we accepted."

"What was the plan?" she asked hoarsely.

Twice he strove to tell her and twice he failed—the words would not come.

"Go on. Why do you torment me?"

"It was this, Juanna: that Francisco should be dressed in the robe of Aca, and offered up with Otter in your place, while you were hidden away."

"Has it been done?" she whispered.

"I believe so," Leonard replied, bowing his head to his breast. "We are prisoners in a secret cell beneath the feet of the statue. There has been great noise and confusion without, and now for some time silence."

Then Juanna sprang up and stood over him with flashing eyes.

"How dared you do this?" she said. "Who gave you leave to do it? I thought that you were a man, now I see that you are a coward."

"Juanna," said Leonard, "it is useless for you to talk like this. Whatever was done was done for your sake, not for that of anybody else."

"Oh, yes, you say so, but I believe that you made a plot with Soa to murder Francisco in order that you might save your own life. I have done with you. I will never speak to you again."

"You can please yourself about that," answered Leonard, who by now was thoroughly enraged, "but I am going to speak to you. Look here, you have said words to me for which, were you a man, I would do my best to be avenged upon you. But as you are a woman I can only answer them, and then wash my hands of you. As you must know, or will know when you come to your right mind, I would gladly have taken Francisco's place. But it was impossible, for had I attempted to dress myself up in the robe of Aca, I should instantly have been discovered, and *you* would have paid the price of my folly. We all knew this, and after we had consulted, things were arranged as I have told you. I only consented to your being brought here on the condition that I was allowed to accompany you for your protection. Now I wish that I had left it alone and gone with Francisco, then perhaps I should have found peace instead of bitter words and reproaches. However, do not be afraid, for I think it probable that I shall soon follow him. I know that you were very fond of this man—this hero—and also, either by accident or design, that you had succeeded in making him a great deal too fond of you for his peace of mind; therefore I make excuses for your conduct, which, with all such deductions, still remains perfectly intolerable."

He paused and looked at her as she sat on the edge of the couch, biting her lip and glancing towards him now and again with a curious expression on her beautiful face, in which grief, pride, and anger all had their share. Yet at that moment Juanna was thinking not of Francisco and his sacrifice, but of the man before her whom she had never loved so well as now, when he spoke to her thus bitterly, paying her back in her own coin.

"I cannot pretend to match you in scolding and violence," she said, "therefore I will give up argument. Perhaps, however, when *you* come to your right mind, you will remember that my life is my own, and that I gave nobody permission to save it at the cost of another person's."

"What is done, is done," answered Leonard moodily, for his anger had burnt out. "Another time I will not interfere without your express wish. By the way, my poor friend asked me to give you these," and he handed her the rosary and the notebook; "he has written something for you to read on the last sheet of the journal, and he bade me say that, should you live to escape, he hoped that you will

277

wear these in memory of him," and he touched the beads, "and also that you would not forget him in your prayers."

Juanna took the journal, and holding it to the light, opened it at hazard. The first thing that she saw was her own name, for in truth it contained, among many other matters, a record of the priest's unhappy infatuation from the first moment of their meeting, and also of his pious efforts to overcome it. Turning the pages rapidly she came to the last on which there was any writing. It ran as follows:

"Senora, of the circumstances under which I write these words you will learn in due course. The pages of this journal, should you deign to study them, will reveal to you my shameful weakness. But if I am a priest I am also a man—who soon shall be neither, but, as I hope, an immortal spirit—and the man in me, following those desires of the spirit that find expression through the flesh, has sinned and loved you. Forgive me this crime, as I trust it will be forgiven elsewhere, though myself I cannot pardon it. Be happy with that noble gentleman who has won your heart and who himself worships you as you deserve. May you be protected from all the dangers that now surround you, as I think you will, and may the blessing of Heaven be with you and about you for many peaceful years, till at length you come to the peace that passeth understanding! And when from time to time you think of me, may you in your heart couple my name with certain holy words: 'Greater love hath no man than this, that a man lay down his life for his friends.' Senora, pardon me and farewell."

Juanna read this touching and noble-hearted *adieu* with an ever-growing wonder, and when she had finished it, put down the book crying aloud,

"Oh! what have I done to deserve such devotion as this?" Then with a strange and bewildering inconsequence she flung herself into Leonard's arms, and burying her head upon his breast she began to weep.

When she was somewhat calmer he also read the letter and closed the book, saying:

"The world is poorer by a perfect gentleman. He was too good for any of us, Juanna."

"I think so," she answered.

Just then they heard a sound without the door; it opened, and Nam entered accompanied by Soa.

"Deliverer," said the aged priest, whose countenance and troubled eyes bore traces of many conflicting emotions, "and you, Shepherdess, I come to speak with you. As you see, I am alone, except for this woman, but should you attempt any violence towards her or me, that will be the signal for your deaths. With much toil and at no little risk to myself I have spared the life of the Shepherdess, causing the white man, your companion, to be offered up in her place."

"Has that offering been accomplished?" broke in Leonard, who could not restrain his anxiety to learn what had happened.

"I will be frank with you, Deliverer," answered the high-priest, when Juanna had translated his question, "since the truth cannot hurt me, for now we know too much of one another's secrets to waste time in bandying lies. I know, for instance, that the Shepherdess and the dwarf are no gods, but mortal like ourselves; and you know that I have dared to affront the true gods by changing the victim whom they had chosen. The sacrifice has been accomplished, but with so many signs and wonders that I am bewildered; the People of the Mist are bewildered also, so that none know what to think. The white man, your companion, was hurled fainting into the waters when the dawn had broken upon the mountain and was seen to be grey; but the dwarf, your servant, did not wait to have that office done for him, for he sprang thither himself, ay, and took one with him."

"Bravo, Otter!" cried Leonard; "I knew that you would die hard."

"Hard did he die indeed, Deliverer," said Nam with a sigh, "so hard that even now many swear that he was a god and not a man. Scarcely had they all vanished into the pool when a wonder chanced such as has not been told of in our records: Deliverer, the white dawn turned to red, perchance, as I cried to calm the people, because the false gods had met their doom."

"Then the true ones must be singularly blind," said Juanna, "seeing that I, whom you dare to call a false god, am still alive."

This argument silenced Nam for a moment, but presently he answered.

"Yes, Shepherdess, you are still alive," he said, laying a curious emphasis on the "still." "And, indeed," he added hastily, "if you are not foolish you may long remain so, both of you, for I have no desire to shed your blood who only seek to end my last days in peace. But listen to the end of the tale: While the people wondered at the omen of the changed dawn, it was seen that the dwarf, your servant, was not dead there in the pool. Yes! this was seen, Deliverer: to and fro in the troubled waters rushed the great Water Dweller, and after him, keeping pace with him, went that dwarf who was named Otter. Ay, round and round and down to the lowest depths, though how it could be that a man might swim with the Snake none can say."

"Oh, bravo, Otter!" said Leonard again, bethinking him of an explanation of the mystery which he did not reveal to Nam. "Well, what was the end of it?"

"That none know for certain, Deliverer," answered the priest perplexedly. "At last the Water Dweller, from whose mouth poured blood, was seen to sink with the dwarf; then he rose again and entered the cave, his home. But whether the dwarf entered with him, or no, I cannot say, for some swear one thing and some another, and in the foam and shadow it was hard to see; moreover, none will venture there to learn the truth."

"Well, dead or alive, he made a good fight for it," said Leonard. "And now, Nam, what is your business with us?"

This question appeared to puzzle the priest a little, for, to speak truth, he did not care to disclose the exact nature of his business, which was to separate Leonard from Juanna, without force if possible.

"I came here, Deliverer," he answered, "to tell you what had happened."

"Exactly," said Leonard, "to tell me that you have murdered my best friend, and one who was but lately your god. I thank you for your news, Nam, and now, if I might make bold to ask it, what are your plans with reference to ourselves—I mean until it suits you to send us after our companions?"

"Believe me, Deliverer, my plan is to save your lives. If the others have been sacrificed it was no fault of mine, for there are forces behind me that I cannot control even when I guide them. The land is in confusion and full of strange rumours. I know not what may happen during the next few days, but till they are over you must lie hid. This is a poor place in which to dwell, but there is none other safe and secret. Still, here is another chamber which you can use; perchance you have already seen it," and placing his hand upon what appeared to be a latch, he opened the second door which Leonard had noticed previously, revealing a cell of very similar construction to that in which they were, and of somewhat larger size.

"See, Deliverer," he went on, "here is the place," and he stepped forward to enter the cell, then drew back as though in courtesy to allow Leonard to pass in before him.

For once Leonard's caution forsook him, for at the moment he was thinking of other things. Almost mechanically he passed the threshold. Scarcely were his feet over it when he remembered the character of his host and the lodging, and turned quickly to come back.

It was too late, for even as he turned the heavy timber door closed in his face with a crash, and he was caged.

CHAPTER 34

Nam's Last Argument

For a moment Juanna stood stupefied; for the manoeuvre had been so sudden that at first she could scarcely realise its results.

"Now, Shepherdess," began Nam blandly, "we can talk in private, for I have words to say to you which it is not fitting that other ears should hear."

"You fiend," she answered fiercely; then comprehending that violence or remonstrance would be useless, she added, "Speak on, I hear you."

"Listen, Shepherdess, and for your own sake I implore you, do not give way to grief or rage. I swear to you that no harm shall come to yonder man if you will but do my bidding. Shepherdess, you are found out; I know, and the people know, that you are no goddess. It had been safer to sacrifice you today, but partly because of the pleading of my daughter who loves you, and partly for other reasons, I have caused you to be saved alive. Now, Shepherdess, from this country there is no escape; as you have chosen to come hither, here you must remain for life, and in this cell you cannot live and die. Therefore, for my daughter's sake I have cast about for a means to deliver you from bonds and to set you high in the land, ay, almost at its head," and he paused.

"Perhaps you will come to the point," said Juanna, who was trembling with fear and anger.

"It is this, Shepherdess," Nam answered bowing; "although you are dethroned as a goddess, you may still shine as a queen and rule over us as the wife of our king."

"Indeed," replied Juanna, turning suddenly cold; "and how shall I, who am held to be dead, appear again as a woman wedded to your king? Surely the people would find that strange, Nam?"

"No, Shepherdess, for I have prepared a tale which shall explain the wonder, and already its rumour runs from mouth to mouth. It will be said that you were a goddess and therefore immortal, but that for the sake of love you have put off your godhead and put on the flesh, that you might dwell for some years with him whom you desire."

"Indeed," said Juanna again. "And what if I refuse to consent to this scheme, which, as I think, can have come only from a woman's brain?" and she pointed to Soa.

"You are right, Shepherdess," answered Soa, "the plan is mine; I made it to save you, and also," she added coolly, "to be revenged upon that white thief who loves you, for he shall live to see you the wife of another man, a wild man."

"And have you never thought, Soa, that I may have wishes of my own in this matter?"

"Doubtless, yet the fairest women cannot always have what they may chance to wish. Know, Shepherdess, that this must be both for your own sake and for the sake of Nam, my father. Olfan loves you, and in these troubled times it is necessary that Nam and the priests should gain his support, which has been bought but now by the promise that you will be given to him in marriage on this very day. For you, Shepherdess, although you might have wished to wed one of your own race, at the least you will rule a queen, and that is better than to perish miserably."

"I think otherwise, Soa," Juanna answered calmly, for she saw that neither passion nor pleading would help her, "and of the two I choose to die," and she put her hand to her hair, then started, for she found the poison gone.

"You will choose to die, Shepherdess," said Soa with a cold smile, "but this is not always so easy. I have taken your medicine from you while you slept, and here there are no other means to compass death."

"I can starve, Soa," replied Juanna with dignity.

"That takes some time, Shepherdess, and today you will become the wife of Olfan. Still it is needful that you should yourself consent to marry him, for this chief is so foolish that he declares that he will not wed you till you have accepted him with your own mouth and in the presence of witnesses."

"Then I fear that the wedding will not be celebrated," said Juanna with a bitter laugh, for she could not refrain from giving some outward expression to all the loathing which she felt for this wicked woman, who in her fierce love would save the life of her mistress by selling her to shame.

"I think that it will, Shepherdess," answered Soa, "for it seems that we have a way by which we can win you to speak those words which Olfan desires to hear."

"There is no way, Soa."

"What, none, Shepherdess? Think now: he whom you name De-liverer is a prisoner beyond that door. What if his life hangs upon your choice? What if he were shown to you about to die a fearful death from which you alone could save him by speaking a certain word?"

Now for the first time Juanna fully understood the hideous nature of the plot whereby Soa purposed either to force her to become the wife of a savage, or to thrust upon her the guilt of causing the death of the man whom she loved, and she sank back upon the couch, saying:

"You would have done better to leave me yonder in the slave camp, Soa."

Then, abandoning the tone of forced calm in which she had spoken hitherto, Soa broke out bitterly:

"When you were in the slave camp, Shepherdess, you loved me who have loved you from a child, for then no white dog had come to sow mischief between us and to make you hate and distrust me. Then I would have died for you, ay, and this I would do now. But also I would be revenged upon the white dog, for I, who am husbandless and childless, had but this one thing, and he has taken it from me. You were to me as mother, and lover, and babe are to other women—my all, and now I am left desolate, and I will be revenged upon him before I die. But I still love you, Shepherdess, and could any other plan have been found to help you, I could not have forced this marriage on you. No such plan can be found; thus alone can you live and become great and happy; and thus alone can I continue to feast my eyes upon you, though it be from far."

She ceased, trembling with the strength of the passions that shook her, to which indeed her words had given but feeble expression.

"Go," said Juanna, "I would have time to think."

Then Nam spoke again.

"We go, Shepherdess, in obedience to your wish, but before evening we shall return to hear your answer. Do not attempt to work mischief upon yourself, for know that you will be watched though you cannot see the eyes that watch you. If you do but so much as lift a hand against your life, or even strive to cut off the light that flows through yonder hole, then at once you will be seized and bound, and my daughter will be set to guard you. Shepherdess, farewell."

And they went, leaving Juanna alone and a prey to such thoughts as can scarcely be written.

For several hours she sat there upon the couch, allowing no hint of what she felt to appear upon her face, for she was too proud to suffer the eyes which she knew were spying on her, though whence she could not tell, to read her secret anguish.

As she sat thus in her desolation several things grew clear to Juanna, and the first of them was that Soa must be mad. The love and hate that seethed in her fierce heart had tainted her brain, making her more relentless than a leopard robbed of its young. From the beginning she had detested Leonard and been jealous of him, and incautiously enough he had always shown his dislike and distrust of her. By slow degrees these feelings had hardened into insanity, and to gratify the vile promptings of her disordered mind she would hesitate at nothing.

From Soa, therefore, she could hope for no relenting. Nor had she better prospect with Nam, for it was evident that in his case political considerations operated as strongly as did those of a personal character with his daughter. He was so much involved, he had committed himself so deeply in this matter of the false gods, that, rightly or wrongly, he conceived Soa's plan to offer the only feasible chance of escape from the religious complications by which he was surrounded, that threatened to bring his life and power to a simultaneous end.

It was out of the question, therefore, to expect help from the high-priest, who was in the position of a man on a runaway horse with precipices on either side of him, unless, indeed, she could show him some safer path. Failing this, it would avail her nothing that he hated and feared Olfan, and only promoted this marriage in order to bribe the king into standing his friend during the expected political convulsions. Indeed, as she guessed rightly, Nam would much better like to know her safely over the borders of the Mist-land than to be called upon to greet her as its queen. This was obvious, seeing that should she return to power, religious or temporal, it was scarcely to be hoped that she would forget the wrongs which she had suffered at his hands. The marriage was merely a temporary expedient designed to ward off immediate evil, but should it come about and the crisis be tided over, it was plain that the struggle between the false goddess and the perjured priest must be carried on until it ended in the death of one or both of them. However, all these things lay in the future as Nam foretold it, a future which Juanna never meant to live to see.

There remained Leonard and Olfan. The former, of course, was powerless, at least for the present, having suffered himself to be entrapped, though his lack of caution mattered little, for doubtless if guile had failed, force would have been employed. It was she who must save Leonard, for he could do nothing to save her.

The more Juanna thought of the matter, the more she became

convinced that her only hope lay in Olfan himself, who had sworn friendship to her, and who certainly was no traitor. She remembered that in their conversation of the day before he had admitted that she could be nothing to him while Leonard lived. Probably Nam had told her that the Deliverer was dead, and then it was, actuated by his passion which she knew to be genuine enough, that he had entered into a bargain with the priest. These must be the terms of the compact, that the game of the false gods being played, Olfan undertook to support Nam and the rest of his party to the best of his power, for the consideration to be received of her hand in marriage, stipulating, however, that she should give it of her own free will.

This of course she would never do; therefore Olfan's proviso gave her a loophole of escape, though Juanna was well aware that it would not be wise to rely too implicitly on the generosity of the savage chief in matters upon which savages are apt to be neither generous nor delicate. On this she must fall back as a last resource, or rather as a last resource but one. Meanwhile, she would fight Nam and Soa step by step, yielding only when she saw that further obstinacy on her part would involve Leonard's destruction. It was possible, indeed it was probable, that everything might fail her, and in that event she must not fail herself; in other words, although the poison had been taken from her, she must find a means of death.

Having thought these problems out so far as it was in her power to do, Juanna rose and began to walk up and down the cell, noting its construction and peculiarities. Doubtless Leonard was behind yonder door, but it was so thick that she could hear nothing of his movements. For the rest, it seemed clear that escape was impossible. Excepting the doors, the shaft in the rock was the only other opening that she was able to see, but through this no child could pass, and if he might it would be to fall into the pool of raging water.

Had Otter lived through the fight with the snake god, she wondered? There was small chance of it, but at least he had made an end worthy of his reputation, and she felt proud of him. And the other—Francisco. Of him also she was proud indeed, but for herself she was ashamed, for she knew that she had been to blame, though not designedly. Who would have guessed that this frail timid man could prove himself such a hero, or who could estimate the power of the unsought and unhappy love which enabled him to conquer the fear of death?

She had been wrong to be angry with Leonard, for she knew well that, if it could have been so, he would gladly have given his own life for hers. Alas! it seemed that she was always wrong, for her temper was quick and the tongue is an unruly member. They had both of them been ready to die for her, and one of them had done so; well, now it was probable that the tables would be turned before many hours were over, and that she would be called upon to offer herself to save her lover. If this came about, she would not forget the example of Francisco, but would rather try to equal it in the heroism of her end.

The day passed slowly, and at length the gloom gathering in the little cell told her that night was near. Before it fell, however, Soa and Nam entered, bearing candles, which they fixed upon brackets in the walls.

"We come, Shepherdess, to hear your answer," said Nam. "Will you consent to take Olfan for a husband, or will you not?"

"I will not consent."

"Think again, Shepherdess."

"I have thought. You have my answer."

At the words Nam seized her arm, saying, "Come hither, Shepherdess; I would show you something," and he led her to that door in passing which Leonard had been entrapped. At the same time Soa extinguished one of the candles, and taking the other in her hand she left the cell, bolting the door behind her, so that Nam and Juanna stood in darkness.

"Shepherdess," said Nam sternly, "you are about to see him whom you name the Deliverer. Now remember this, if you cry out or speak above a whisper—he dies."

Juanna made no answer, although she felt her heart grow faint within her. Five minutes or more passed, and of a sudden a panel slid back in the upper part of the door which connected the two cells, so that Juanna could see through it, although those who stood on the further side could not see her, for they were in light and she was in darkness.

And this was what she saw: Ranged against the wall of the second prison, and opposite to her, were three priests holding candles in their hands, whereof the light shone upon their sullen, cruel faces, and the snake's head tattooed on their naked breasts. In front of these men stood two other priests, and between them was Leonard bound and gagged.

On the hither side of the cell, and not more than two feet from the open panel, stood Soa, on whom the eyes of the executioners were fixed, as though awaiting a command. Between Soa and these men yawned an open hole in the rock floor.

When Juanna had gazed upon this scene for some twenty seconds the sliding panel was closed, apparently by Soa, and Nam spoke:

"You have seen, Shepherdess," he said, "that the Deliverer is bound, and you have seen also that before him is a hole in the floor of the prison. He who falls down that hole, Shepherdess, finds himself in the den of the Snake beneath, from the visiting of whom no man has ever returned alive, for it is through it that we feed the Water-dweller at certain seasons of the year, and when there is no sacrifice. Now, Shepherdess, you must choose between two things; either to wed Olfan of your own free will this night, or to see the Deliverer thrown to the Snake before your eyes, and afterwards to wed Olfan whether you will it or not. What do you say, Shepherdess?"

Juanna took counsel with herself, and came to the conclusion that she would resist a little longer, for she thought that this scene might have been planned merely to try her fortitude.

"I refuse to marry Olfan," she answered.

Then Nam opened the panel and whispered a word into the ear of Soa, who uttered a command. Instantly the two executioner priests flung Leonard on to his back upon the ground, an easy task seeing that his legs were fastened with ropes, and dragged him forward until his head hung over the oubliette-like hole. Then they paused as though waiting for some further order. Nam drew Juanna some few paces away from the door.

"What is your word now, Shepherdess?" he said. "Is the man to die or be saved? Speak swiftly."

Juanna glanced through the opening and saw that now Leonard's head and shoulders had vanished down the oubliette, while one of the priests held him by the ankles, watching Soa for the sign to let him fall.

"Loose him," said Juanna faintly. "I will marry Olfan."

Stepping forward, Nam whispered to Soa, who issued another order. Thereupon the priests drew Leonard from his perilous position, and, unwillingly enough, rolled him to the side of the cell, for they would have preferred to be rid of him. At that moment also the shutter was closed.

"I said *loose him*," repeated Juanna; "now the man lies unable to move like a fallen tree, on the ground."

"No, Shepherdess," replied Nam; "perchance you may yet change your mind, and then it would be troublesome to bind him afresh, for he is very strong and violent. Listen, Shepherdess; when Olfan comes presently to ask your hand, you must say nothing of that man yonder, for he deems him to be dead, and the moment you speak of him he will be dead. Do you understand?"

"I understand," answered Juanna, "but at least the gag might be taken from his mouth."

"Fear not, Shepherdess, it shall be done—when you have spoken with Olfan. And now, at what hour will it be your pleasure to see him?"

"When you will. The sooner it is finished the better."

"Good. My daughter," he added to Soa, who just then entered the cell, "be pleased to make fire, and then summon the king Olfan, who waits without."

Soa departed upon her errand, and, overcome with terror which she would not show, Juanna sank upon the couch, hiding her face in her hands. For a while there was silence, then the door opened again and, heralded by Soa, Olfan, the king, stood before her.

"Be careful, Shepherdess," whispered Nam as they entered; "one word—and the Deliverer dies."

CHAPTER 35

Be Noble or Be Base

For a while there was silence, then Juanna looked up, searching Olfan's face with her eyes. Nothing was to be read there, for it was impossible to pierce the mask of solemn calm beneath which, in common with all his race, the king was accustomed to hide his thoughts. He leant on the shaft of his broad spear, his head bowed slightly as though in humility, his dark eyes fixed upon her face, immovable, impassive, a picture of savage dignity.

Indeed, Juanna was fain to confess to herself that she had never seen a grander specimen of the natural man than that presented by the chief of the People of the Mist, as he stood before her in her rock prison. The light of the candles fell full upon him, revealing his great girth and stature, beside which those of the finest men of her own race would have seemed insignificant. It shone upon the ivory torques, emblems of royalty, which were about his neck, wrists, and ankles, upon the glossy garments of black goat-skin that hung from his shoulders and middle, and the raven tresses of his hair bound back from his forehead by a narrow band of white linen, which showed in striking contrast against the clear olive colouring of his face and breast.

"Speak, Olfan," said Juanna at length.

"It was told to me, Queen," he answered in a low, full voice, "that you had words to say to me. Nevertheless, now as always, I obey you. Queen, I learn that your husband, he whom you loved, is dead, and believe me, I sorrow for you. In this shameful deed I had no hand; that, together with the end of the other white man and the dwarf, must be set down to the account of this priest, who swears that he was driven to it by the clamour of the people. Queen, they have all gone across the mountains and through the sky beyond, and you, like some weary dove, far travelled from a southern clime, are left a prey among the eagles of the People of the Mist.

"But a few hours since I thought you dead also, for with all the thousands in the temple I believed that it was your fair body which Nam hurled at dawn from the brow of the statue, and I tell you that when I saw it, I, who am a warrior, wept and cursed myself, because, although I was a king, I had no power to save you. Afterwards this man, the high priest, came to me, telling me the truth and a plan that he had made for his own ends, whereby you might be saved alive and lifted up among the people, and he also might be saved, and my rule be made sure in the land." And he ceased.

"What is this plan, Olfan?" asked Juanna, after a pause.

"Queen, it is that you should wed me, and appear before the people no longer as a goddess, but as a woman who has put on the flesh for her love's sake. I know well that I am all unworthy of such honour, moreover, that your heart must be sore with the loss of one who was dear to you, and little set upon the finding of another husband; also I remember certain words that passed between us and a promise which I made. All these things I told to Nam, and he answered me saying that the matter was urgent, that here you could not be hid away for long, and that if I did not take you to wife then you must die. Therefore, because my love towards you is great, I said to him, 'Go now and ask her if she will smile upon me if I come before her with such words.'

"Nam went, but before he went he made certain agreements with me on matters of policy, under which I must pay a heavy price for you, Lady, and forego revenge and forget many an ancient hate, all of which things I have promised to do should you smile upon me, so great is my love towards you. The hours went by, and Nam came back to me, saying that, having weighed the matter in your mind, your answer was favourable. To this I replied that I did not trust him, and would take it from your lips alone.

"And now, Queen, I am here to listen to your word, and to offer myself to you, to serve you all my life as your husband and your slave. I have little to give you who have been bred up in sunnier lands, and among a more gentle people; I who am but the wild chief of men whose hearts are rugged as our mountains, and gloomy as a winter's day that is heavy with snow to come,—only myself, the service of my soldiers' spears, and the first place among the Children of the Mist.

"Now let me hear your answer, and be it what it may, I will accept it without a murmur, for least of all things do I desire to force myself upon you in marriage. Still I pray you, speak to me plainly once and

290

for all, for if I must lose you I would know the worst; nor can I bear, when you have smiled upon me, to see you turn away. Nay, I would sooner die."

And once more he bowed his head, leaned upon his spear, and was silent.

Juanna considered the position rapidly. It was hopeless and cruel. Nam and Soa were on either side of her, the latter standing near the door with the sliding panel beyond which Leonard lay bound, and she knew well that did she speak a single word of the truth to Olfan, it would be the signal for her lover's death. It was possible that the king might be able to protect her own person from violence, but if Leonard died it mattered little what became of her. There was but one thing that she could do—declare herself willing to become the wife of Olfan. Yet it seemed shameless thus to treat this honourable man, the only friend that they had found among the People of the Mist. But of a truth, such necessities as hers cannot wait while those in their toils weigh scruples or the law of honour.

"Olfan," she said, "I have heard you, and this is my answer: I will take you as my husband. You know my story, you know that he who was my lord is but this day dead," here Soa smiled approvingly at the lie, "and that I loved him. Therefore of your gentleness, you will accord me some few weeks before I pass from him to you, in which I may mourn my widowhood. I will say no more, but surely you can guess the sorrow of my heart, and all that I have left unsaid."

"It shall be as you wish, Queen," replied Olfan, taking her hand and kissing it, while his sombre face grew radiant with happiness. "You shall pass into my keeping at that time which best pleases you, yet I fear that in one matter you must be troubled now, this very hour."

"What may that be, Olfan?" asked Juanna anxiously.

"Only this, Queen, that the rite of marriage as we practise it must be celebrated between us. It is necessary for many reasons which will be made clear to you tomorrow. Moreover, such was my bargain with Nam sealed by an oath sworn upon the blood of Aca, an oath that I do not dare to break."

"Oh, no, no!" said Juanna in acute distress. "Think, Olfan, how can I, whose husband is not six hours dead, vow myself to another man upon the altar of his grave? Give me some few days, I pray you."

"Most willingly would I do this, Lady, but I may not, it is against my oath. Also, what can it matter? You shall remain alone for so long as it shall please you."

Then Nam spoke for the first time, saying:

"Shepherdess, waste no breath in words, for learn that though this garment of modesty is becoming to one new widowed, yet you must put it from you. More depends upon this ceremony than you know of, the lives of many hang upon it, our own, perchance, among them, and especially the life of one of whom it does not become me to speak," and as though by accident Nam let his eyes rest upon the door of the adjoining cell.

Of his auditors Olfan thought that he was alluding to his own life, but Juanna and his daughter knew well that he spoke of that of Leonard, which would be sacrificed did the former persist in her objections to the instant celebration of the marriage.

"You hear his words, Queen," said Olfan, "and there is weight in them. The times are very dangerous, and if our plot is to be carried through, before midnight I must make oath to the captains and the Council of the Elders that you have come back from death to be my wife."

"Maybe," answered Juanna, catching at a straw in her despair, "but must I, who shall be set over this people as queen, be married thus in secret? At the least I will have witnesses. Let some of the captains whom you trust, Olfan, be brought here to see us wed, otherwise the time may come when I shall be held to be no true wife, and there are none to establish my honour by their words."

"There is little fear of such a thing, Queen," answered Olfan with a faint smile, "yet your demands are just. I will bring three of my captains here, men who will not betray us, and they shall be witness to this rite," and he turned as though he would go to seek them.

"Do not leave me," said Juanna, catching him by the wrist. "I trust you, but these two I do not trust. I fear to be left alone."

"There is no need for witnesses," exclaimed Nam in a threatening voice.

"The Shepherdess has asked for witnesses, and she shall have them," answered Olfan fiercely. "Old man, you have played with me long enough; hitherto I have been your servant, now I will be your master. Some hours ago your life was forfeit to me, for the white dawn had turned to red, and I meant to take it, but you bribed me with this bait," and he pointed to Juanna. "Nay, do not lay your hand upon your knife; you forget I have my spear. Your priests are without, I know it, but so are my captains, and I have told them where I am; if I vanish as many vanish here, my life will be required at your hands, for, Nam, your power is broken.

"Now, obey me. Bid that woman summon him who guards without. No, you do not stir," and he lifted the spear till its keen blue point quivered over the high priest's naked breast. "Bid her go to the door and summon the guard. I said to the door, but not beyond it, or beware!"

Nam was cowed: his tool had become his master.

"Obey," he said to Soa.

"Obey, but no more," echoed Olfan.

Snarling like a wolf, the woman slipped past them to the door, and opening it a little way, she whistled through the crack.

"Hide yourself, Lady," said Olfan.

Juanna retreated into the shadow behind the candle, and at that moment a voice spoke through the open door, saying, "I am here, father."

"Now, speak," said Olfan, advancing the spear an inch nearer Nam's heart.

"My son," said the priest, "go to the entrance by which the king entered, where you will find three captains, generals of the king. Lead them hither."

"And see that you speak to no one on the way," whispered Olfan in Nam's ear.

"And see that you speak to no one on the way," repeated Nam.

"I hear you, father," replied the priest, and went.

Some ten minutes passed and the door opened again. "The captains are here," whispered a voice.

"Let them enter," said Nam.

The order was obeyed, and three great men armed with spears stalked into the narrow chamber. One of them was brother to the king, and the two others were his chosen friends. Then the door closed.

"My brethren," said Olfan, "I have sent for you to acquaint you with a mystery and to ask you to witness a rite. The goddess Aca, who this day was hurled into the pool of the Snake, has returned to earth as a woman, and is about to become my wife,"—here the captains started—"nay, brethren, ask no questions; these things are so, it is enough. Now, priest, play your part."

After that, for a while all seemed a dream to Juanna, a dream of which she was never able to recover any exact memory. She could recollect standing side by side with Olfan, while Nam muttered prayers and invocations over them, administering to them terrible oaths, which they took, calling upon the names of Aca and of Jal, and swearing by the symbol of the Snake. Beyond that everything went blank. Indeed, her mind flew back to another marriage ceremony, when she stood beside Leonard in the slave camp, and the priest, Francisco, prayed over them and blessed them. It was that scene which she saw, and not the one enacting before her eyes, and with its visions were mixed up strange impersonal reflections on the irony of fate, which had brought it about that she should figure as the chief actor in two such dramas, the first of which Leonard had gone through to save her, and the second of which she must go through to save him.

At last it was done, and once more Olfan was bowing before her and kissing her hand.

"Greeting, Shepherdess. Hail! Queen of the People of the Mist," he said, and the captains repeated his words.

Juanna awoke from her stupor. What was to be done now? she wondered. What could be done? Everything seemed lost. Then of a sudden an inspiration took her.

"It is true that I am a queen, is it not, Olfan?"

"It is true, Lady."

"And as Queen of the People of the Mist I have power, have I not, Olfan."

"Even to life and death," he answered gravely; "though if you kill, you must answer to the Council of the Elders and to me. All in this land are your servants, Lady, and none dare to disobey you except on matters of religion."

"Good," said Juanna. Then addressing the captains in a tone of command, she added, "Seize that priest who is named Nam, and the woman with him."

Olfan looked astonished and the captains hesitated. As for Nam, he did not hesitate, but made a bound towards the door.

"Stay awhile, Nam," said the king, making a barrier before him with his spear; "doubtless the Queen has reasons, and you would wish to hear them. Hold them, my captains, since the Queen commands it."

Then the three men sprang upon them. Once Nam tried to draw his knife, but failing in his attempt he submitted without further struggle. With Soa it was different. She bit and tore like a wild-cat, and Juanna saw that she was striving to reach the panel and to speak through it.

"On your lives do not suffer her to come to that door," she said; "presently you shall know why."

Then the brother of the king dragged Soa to the couch, and throwing her down upon it stood over her, his spear-point at her throat.

"Now, Queen," said Olfan, "your will is done, and perhaps it may please you to explain."

"Listen, King, and listen, you, captains," she answered. "These liars told you that the Deliverer was dead, was it not so? He is not dead, he lies bound in yonder cell, but had I spoken a word to you, then he would have died. Olfan, do you know how my consent was won to be your wife? A shutter within that door was opened, and he, my husband, was shown to me, gagged and bound, and being held over the mouth of a hideous pit in the floor of his prison, that leads I know not whither.

"'Consent, or he dies,' they said, and for my love's sake I consented. This was the plot, Olfan: to marry me to you, partly because the woman yonder, who was my nurse, did not desire my death, and partly that Nam might use me to save himself from the anger of the people. But do not think that you would have kept me long, Olfan; for this was in the plot also, that when you had served their purpose you should die by secret means, as one who knew too much."

"It is a lie," said Nam.

"Silence!" answered Juanna. "Let that door be opened, and you shall see if I have lied."

"Wait awhile, Queen," said Olfan, who appeared utterly overcome. "If I understand you right, your husband lives, and therefore you say that the words which we have spoken and the oaths that we have sworn mean nothing, for you are not my wife."

"That is so, Olfan."

"Then now I am minded to turn wicked and let him die," said the king slowly, "for know this, Lady, I cannot give you up."

Juanna grew pale as death, understanding that this man's passions, now that once he had given them way, had passed beyond his control.

"I cannot give you up," he repeated. "Have I not dealt well with you? Did I not say to you, 'Consent or refuse, as it shall please you, but having once consented you must not go back upon your words'? What have I to do with the reasons that prompted them? My heart heard them and believed them. Queen, you are wed to me; those oaths that you have sworn may not be broken. It is too late; now you are mine, nor can I suffer you to pass from me back to another man, even though he was your husband before me."

"But the Deliverer! must I then become my husband's murderer?"

"Nay, I will protect him, and, if it may be, find means to send him from the land."

Juanna stood silent and despairing, and at this moment Soa, lying on the couch, broke into a shrill and mocking laugh that stung her like a whip and roused her from her lethargy.

"King," she said, "I am at your mercy, not through any wanton folly of my own, but because fate has made a sport of me. King, you have been hardly used, and, as you say, hitherto you have dealt well with me. Now I pray you let the end be as the beginning was, so that I may always think of you as the noblest among men, except one who died this day to save me. King, you say you love me; tell me then if my life hung upon a word of yours, would that word remain unspoken?

"Such was my case: I spoke the word and for one short hour I betrayed you. Will you, whose heart is great, bind me by such an oath as this, an oath wrung from me to save my darling from the power of those dogs? If this is so, then I have erred strangely in my reading of your mind, for till now I have held you to be a man who would perish ere he fell so low as to force a helpless woman to be his wife, one whose crime is that she deceived him to save her husband."

She paused, and, clasping her hands as though in prayer, looked up into his troubled face with beseeching eyes; then, as he did not speak, she went on:

"King, I have one more word to say. You are the strongest and you can take me, but you cannot hold me, for that hour would be my last, and you but the richer by your broken honour and a dead bride."

Olfan was about to answer when Soa, fearing lest Juanna's pleading should prevail against his passion, broke in saying, "Be not fooled, King, by a woman's pretty speeches, or by her idle threats that she will kill herself. She will not kill herself, I know her well, she loves her life too much; and soon, when you are wed, she will love you also, for it is the nature of us women to worship those who master us. Moreover, that man, the Deliverer, is not her husband, except in name; for months I have lived with them and I know it. Take her, King, take her now, this hour, or live to mourn her loss and your own folly all your life's days."

"I will not answer that slave's falsehoods," said Juanna, drawing herself up and speaking proudly, "and it were more worthy of you not to listen to them, King. I have spoken; now do your will. Be great or little, be noble or be base, as your nature teaches you."

And suddenly she sank to the ground and, shaking her long hair about her face and arms, she burst into bitter weeping.

Twice the King glanced at her, then he turned his head as though he dare look no more, and spoke keeping his eyes fixed upon the wall.

"Rise, Queen," he said hoarsely, "and cease your tears, since you are safe from me. Now as always I live to do your will, but I pray you, hide your face from me as much as may be, for, Lady, my heart is broken with love for you and I cannot bear to look on that which I have lost."

Still sobbing, but filled with admiration and wonder that a savage could be thus generous, Juanna rose and began to murmur thanks, while the captains stared, and Soa mocked and cursed them both.

"Thank me not," he said gently. "It seems that you, who can read all hearts, have read mine aright, or perchance you fashioned it as you would have it be. Now, having done with love, let us to war. Woman, what is the secret of that door?"

"Find it for yourself," snarled Soa. "It is easy to open when once you know the spring—like a woman's heart, Olfan. Or if you cannot find it, then it can be forced—like a woman's love, Olfan. Surely you who are so skilled in the winning of a bride need not seek my counsel as to the opening of a door, for when I gave it but now upon the first of these matters, you would not hearken, Olfan, but were melted by the sight of tears that you should have kissed away."

Juanna heard and from that moment made up her mind that whatever happened she had done with Soa. Nor was this wonderful, for few women could have pardoned what she had suffered at her hands.

"Drive the spear into her till she speaks, comrade," said Olfan.

Then at the touch of steel Soa gave up mocking and told the secret of the door.

CHAPTER 36

How Otter Came Back

After he had rested awhile at the bottom of the glacier, Otter set to work to explore the cliff on the top of which he found himself, with the view of descending it and hiding at its foot till nightfall, when he hoped to find means of re-entering the city and putting himself in communication with Olfan. Very soon, however, he discovered that if he was to return at all, he must follow the same route by which he had come.

Evidently the tunnel sloped upwards very sharply, for he was standing on the brow of a precipice cut into three steps, which, taken together, may have measured some three hundred feet in height, and, so far as he could see, it was utterly impossible to descend any of these cliffs without the aid of ropes. Nor could he continue his investigations over a wide area, for about four hundred paces to the left of the opening to the subterranean passage—whereof, by the way, he was very careful to note the exact position—the mountain pushed out a snowy shoulder, with declivities so precipitous that he dared not trust himself on them.

Then he tried the right-hand side, but with no better luck, for here he was stopped by a yawning rift in the rock. Now Otter sat down and considered the situation.

The day was still young, and he knew that it would be foolish to attempt escape from the pool before dark. In front of him the mountain rose steeply till, so far as he could judge, it reached a pass which lay some two miles off, at the base of that main peak, on whose snows the priests had watched the breaking of the dawn. Part of this declivity was covered with blocks of green ice, but here and there appeared patches of earth, on which grew stunted trees, shrubs, and even grass and flowers. Being very hungry, it occurred to Otter that he might find edible roots among this scanty vegetation.

With this hope he began to climb the slope, to be rewarded in due course by the discovery of a vegetable that he recognised, for it was the same which had been offered to him on the occasion of his unlucky outbreak that had resulted in the casting away of the rubies.

With this poor food the dwarf filled himself, and having found a bough that made him an excellent staff, he continued his climb, desiring to see what there might be on the other side of the neck.

Arriving there without any great difficulty, Otter stood astonished, although he was not much given to the study of scenery. Below him lay the City of the Mist, with its shining belt of rivers that, fed from the inexhaustible mountain snows, meandered across the vast plains—now no longer hidden in mist—which they had trodden on their journey. Above his head the mighty peak towered thousands of feet into the air, till it ended in a summit shaped like a human finger pointing eternally to the heavens. Before him the scene was even stranger, made up as it was of snowy fields broken by ridges of black rock, and laid one beneath the other like white sails drying upon the slopes of a sandhill.

Gradually, as the eye travelled downward, these snow-fields grew fewer and fewer, till at last they vanished altogether, and their place was taken, first by stretches of grass-land, and finally, at the foot of the mountain, by what seemed to be a rich and level country interspersed with clumps of bush and forest trees.

The first of these patches of snow lay within five furlongs of where the dwarf stood, but several hundred feet below him.

Between the neck of the pass and this snow stretched a mighty rift or chasm, with sides so sheer that no goat could have kept a footing on them. Yet this gulf was not without its bridge, for a rock wall rose from the bottom of the chasm, forming the bed of a glacier which spanned it from side to side. In some places the wall was comparatively level and in others it showed descents sharp as those of a waterfall. This remarkable bridge of ice—that varied from a hundred paces to a few yards in width—was bordered on either side by the most fearful precipices; while, just where its fall was sheerest and its width narrowest, it seemed to spring across a space of nothingness, like the arch of a bridge thrown from bank to bank of a river. Indeed, at this point its line became so attenuated that in the glittering sunlight Otter was doubtful whether it was not broken through for a distance of some yards.

Being of an inquiring mind, the dwarf decided to satisfy himself upon the matter. All around him lay slabs of rock, some of which were worn perfectly smooth and to the thinness of a tombstone, by centuries of polishing in the iron jaws of glaciers. Selecting one of these of convenient size, Otter approached the edge of the bridge, pushing the stone before him over the frozen snow. Here the ice was perfect, except for a slight hoar-frost that covered it, for the action of the wind prevented the snow from gathering on the bridge, and whenever the sun was strong enough to melt its surface, it froze again at night, so that no slide upon a parish pond could have been more slippery or free from inequalities.

Otter gave his stone a push, and away it went, sometimes swiftly and sometimes at a trifling speed, according to the nature of the angle down which it passed, leaving a bright green ribbon upon the ice in its wake, whence it swept the hoar-frost as it sped. Once or twice he thought that it was going to stop, but it never did stop. At length it approached the steepest and narrowest part of the descent, down which the stone rushed with fearful velocity.

"Now I shall see whether the bridge is broken," thought Otter; and just then the rock, travelling like an arrow, came to that portion of the glacier where, for a width difficult to estimate, it stretched unsupported over space, and measured only some few feet across. On it flew, then seemed to leap into the air, and once more sped forward till it reached the further slope of snow, up which it travelled for a distance, and stopped, appearing, even to Otter's keen sight, no larger than a midge upon a table-cloth.

"Now, if a man had been seated on that stone he might have passed this bridge in safety," said Otter to himself; "yet it is one that few would care to travel, unless sure death were behind them."

Then he determined on a second trial, and selecting another and somewhat lighter stone, he sent it upon its journey. It followed precisely the same course as its predecessor, but when it came to the knife-blade of the bridge it vanished.

"I am sorry for that stone," thought Otter, "for doubtless it, that has been whole for many years, is at this moment only little pieces."

A third time he repeated his experiment, choosing the heaviest rock that he could move. This messenger also leaped into the air at the narrowest portion of the bridge, then passed on in safety to the slope of snow beyond.

"A strange place," thought Otter; "and I pray that it may never be my lot to ride one of those stone horses."

Then he turned down the mountain again, for the afternoon was advancing. When he reached the entrance to the river-bed sunset was at hand. For a while he sat watching the fading light and eating some more roots which he had gathered. Now he crawled into the passage and commenced his darksome journey towards the home of the dead Water Dweller, though what he was to do when he got there he did not know. No accident befell him, and in due course he arrived safely in the den, his journey being much facilitated by the staff he bore, which enabled him to feel his way like a blind man.

Creeping to the edge of the pool he listened to its turmoil, for the shadows were gathering so fast that, with some ghostlike shapes of foam excepted, he could not even see the surface of the water.

"If I go in there how can I get out again?" Otter thought sadly. "After all, perhaps I should have done better to return while it was still light, for then, by the help of my staff and the rope, I might have made shift to climb the overhanging ledge of rock, but to try this now were madness. I will go back and sit in the cave with the ghosts of the god and his dead till the morning comes again, though I do not crave their company."

So he retreated a few paces and sat in silence near the tail of the dead Crocodile. After a while loneliness took hold of him; he tried to sleep and could not, for it seemed to Otter that he saw eyes staring at him from the depths of the cave, and heard dead men whispering to each other tales of their dreadful ends. Moment by moment his fears grew upon him, for Otter was very superstitious. Now he fancied that he could distinguish the head of the reptile limned in fire and resting on the edge of the rock as he had seen it that morning.

"Doubtless," he thought, "this monster is a devil and has come to life again to be revenged upon me. *Wow!* I liked him better when he was in the flesh than now that he has turned himself to fire." Then to comfort himself he began to talk aloud saying:

"Otter, unlucky that you are, why did you not die at once instead of living on to be tormented by ghosts? Perhaps your master, the Baas, whom alone you love, is dead already and waits for you to come to serve him. You are very tired; say now, Otter, would it not be well if you took that rope which is about your middle and hanged yourself? Thus you too would become a ghost and be able to do battle with them in their own fashion," and he groaned loudly.

Then of a sudden he grew fearful indeed, the short wool stood up upon his head, his teeth chattered, and, as he said afterwards, his very nose seemed to grow cold with terror. For as he sat he heard, or seemed to hear, a voice speaking to him from the air, and that voice his master's.

"*Otter, Otter,*" said the voice.

He made no answer, he was too frightened.

"Otter, is that you?" whispered the voice again.

Then he spoke. "Yes, Baas, it is I. I know that you are dead and call me. Give me one minute till I can undo my rope, and I will kill myself and come to you."

"Thank you, Otter," said the voice with a ghastly attempt at a laugh, "but if it is all the same, I would much rather that you came alive."

"Yes, Baas, and I too would rather stop alive, but being alive how can I join you who are dead?"

"You fool, I am not dead," said Leonard.

"Then, Baas, how is it that you speak out of the air? Come near to me that I may touch you and be comforted."

"I cannot, Otter; I am bound and in a prison above you. There is a hole in the floor, and if you have a rope, as I heard you say, perhaps you could climb up to me."

Now the dwarf began to understand. Rising, he stretched the long staff he had brought with him high above his head, and found to his delight that he could touch the roof of the cave. Presently the point of the staff ceased to press upon the rock.

"Is the place here, Baas?" said Otter.

"It is here, but you must throw the stick up like a spear through the hole, for I am tied, and cannot put out my hand to take it."

"Stay awhile, Baas; first I must make the line fast to it."

"Good, but be swift, for I am in danger."

Hurriedly Otter undid the hide rope from about his middle, knotting it securely to the centre of the stick. Then some five feet below the stick he made a loop large enough for a man to place his foot in, and having ascertained the exact situation of the opening in the roof of the cave, he hurled the staff upwards and jerked at the line.

"It is fixed," whispered Leonard from above. "Now come up if you can."

The dwarf required no second invitation. Seizing the rope as high as he could reach above his head, he began to drag himself up hand over hand—no easy task, for the hide cord was thin, and cut his fingers and his right leg, round which he had twisted it to get a better purchase. Presently, however, he succeeded in setting his foot in the loop he had prepared, when he found that his head and shoulders were in the hole, and that by reaching upwards he could grasp the staff which lay across it. The rest was easy, and within half a minute he lay gasping at his master's side.

"Have you a knife, Otter?"

"Yes, Baas, my small one, the big ones are down there; I will tell you that story by and by."

"Never mind the story now, Otter. My hands are tied behind my back. Feel for the lashings and cut them, then give me the knife that I may free my legs."

Otter obeyed, and presently Leonard rose and stretched himself with a sigh of relief.

"Where is the Shepherdess, Baas?"

"There, in the next cell. They separated me from her, and since then I have been dangled by the legs over that hole bound and gagged, I think in order to persuade her to consent to something or other by the sight of my danger, for doubtless she was placed where she could see all. Then they left me, and I managed to spit out the gag, but I could not undo the cords. I expect that they will soon be back again."

"Then had we not better fly, Baas? I have found a passage that leads to the mountains."

"How can we fly and leave the Shepherdess, Otter? Since I have been held down the hole, only two men have visited me from time to time, for they think me helpless. Let us seize these men when they come in and take their knives, for we are unarmed. Then we can think; also we shall have their keys."

"Yes, Baas, we may do that. You take the staff; it is stout."

"And what will you use?" asked Leonard.

"Fear not, Baas. Do these men bear lights?"

"Yes."

"Then in two minutes I will make me a weapon."

And, untying the hide rope from the stick, he began to fumble with it busily.

"Now I am ready, Baas," he said presently. "Where shall we stand?"

"Here," answered Leonard, leading him to the door. "We will crouch in the shadow, one on either side of this door, and when the priests have entered and closed it, and begin to look round for me, then we can spring upon them. Only, Otter, there must be no bungling and no noise."

"I think that there will be none, Baas; they will be too frightened to cry at first, and after that they will become dumb."

"Otter," whispered Leonard, as they stood in the dark, "did you kill the Water-Dweller?"

"Yes, yes, Baas," he chuckled in answer. "I caught him with the hook that I made ready. But he did not die easily, Baas, and if I had not been able to swim well he would have drowned me."

"I heard something of it from Nam," said Leonard. "You are a wonderful fellow, Otter."

"Oh, Baas! it was no valour of mine; when I saw his eyes I was horribly afraid, only I thought how gladly you would have attacked him had you been there, and what a coward you would hold me, could you have seen me shivering like a little girl before a big lizard, and these thoughts gave me courage."

"Oh, that is all very well!" replied Leonard, and suddenly added, "Hush! be ready!"

As he spoke the door opened, and two great priests came through it, one of them bearing a candle. He who bore the light turned to shut the door, for he suspected nothing. Then, at one and the same instant, Leonard, emerging from the shadow, dealt the first priest a blow upon the head with his staff, which stunned if it did not kill him, for he fell like an ox beneath the pole-axe, while Otter, standing where he was, dexterously cast his hide rope about the throat of the second man, and drew the noose tight with a jerk that brought him to the earth.

In twenty seconds it was all over. The men, who were the same that had held Leonard suspended in the oubliette, lay senseless or dead, and the dwarf and his master were engaged in possessing themselves of their knives and keys by the light of the candle, which, though it had fallen to the ground, fortunately remained burning.

"That was well done, Otter," said Leonard, "and I am not ashamed to have done it, for these devils kicked me when I was bound. Now we are armed, and have the keys. What next?"

Just then Otter sprang to his feet, crying, "Look out, Baas; here are more."

Leonard glanced up to see, and behold! the second door in the cell was opened, and through it came Juanna, Olfan, Nam, Soa, and three other men.

For a moment there was silence; till one of the captains cried out, "See! Jal the god has come back, and already he claims his victims!" And he pointed to the two priests.

Then followed a scene of confusion, for even Olfan and Nam were amazed at what seemed to them little short of a miracle, while Leonard and Juanna had eyes for each other only, and the three captains stared at Otter like men who think they see a ghost.

But one person in that company kept her head, and that person was Soa. The captain who guarded her had loosed his hold; silently she slunk back into the shadows, and, unseen of any, vanished through the doorway by which she had been led in. A minute passed, and Otter, thinking that he heard a noise without that door of the cell whereby the two priests had entered, which had been left ajar, went to it and tried to open it. Just then, also, Olfan missed Soa.

"Where is the woman, Nam's daughter?" he cried.

"It seems that she has escaped and shut us in, King," answered Otter, calmly.

Followed by the others, Olfan sprang first to the door of the cell where they were, and then through the connecting passage to that of Juanna's prison. It was true, both were closed.

"It matters nothing, here are the keys," said Leonard.

"They will not avail us, Deliverer," answered Olfan, "for these doors are made fast without by bars of stone thicker than my arm. Now this woman has gone to rouse the college of the priests, who will presently come to kill us like caged rats."

"Quick!" said Leonard, "waste no time, we must break down the doors."

"Yes, Deliverer," said Nam mockingly; "batter them in with your fists, cut through the stone-work with your spears; surely they are as nothing to your strength!"

CHAPTER 37

I Am Repaid, Queen

Their position was terrible. Soa had escaped, and Soa knew everything. Moreover, she was mad with hatred and longing for revenge on Leonard, Otter, and in a less degree on Olfan the king. Had they succeeded in revealing themselves to the people, all might have gone well, for Otter and Juanna would certainly have been accepted as true gods, who had passed and repassed the gates of death scatheless. But now the affair was different. Soa would tell the truth to the priests, who, even if they were inclined to desert her father in his extremity, must strike for their own sakes and for that of their order, which was the most powerful among the People of the Mist, and had no desire to be placed under the yoke of secular authority.

It was clear to all of them that if they could not escape, they must fall very shortly into the hands of the priests, who, knowing everything, would not dare to allow them to appeal to the army, or to the superstition of the outside public. The only good card they held was the possession of the person of Nam, though it remained to be seen how far this would help them.

To begin with, there are always some ready to step into the shoes of a high priest, also Nam had blundered so extensively in the matter of the false gods, that the greater part of the fraternity, whom he had involved in his mistakes, would not sorrow to see the last of him. These facts, which were perfectly well known to Olfan and guessed at by his companions, sharpened their sense of the danger in which they had been placed by Soa's resource and cunning. Indeed, their escape was a matter of life and death to them and to many hundreds of their adherents. If once they could reach the temple and proclaim the re-arisen gods to the people, all would go well, for the army would suffice to keep the priests from using violence. But if they failed in this, their death-warrant was already signed, for none of them would ever be heard of again.

No wonder, then, that they hurled themselves despairingly upon the stubborn doors. For an hour or more they laboured, but all in vain. The massive timbers of hard wood, six inches or more in thickness, could scarcely be touched by their knives and spears, nor might their united strength serve even to stir the stone bolts and bars that held them fast, and they had nothing that could be used as a battering-ram.

"It is useless," said Leonard at last, throwing down his knife in despair; "this wood is like iron, it would take us a week to cut through it."

"Why not try fire, Baas?" suggested Otter.

Accordingly they attempted to burn down the doors, with the result that they nearly stifled themselves in the smoke and made but little impression upon the woodwork.

At length they gave up the experiment—it was a failure—and sat looking blankly at each other as they listened to certain sounds which reached them from the passages without, telling them that their enemies were gathering there.

"Has anyone a suggestion to make?" said Leonard at last. "If not, I think that this game is about played."

"Baas," answered Otter, "I have a word to say. We can all go down through that hole by which I came up to you. The Water-Dweller is dead, I slew him with my own hand, so there is nothing to fear from him. Beneath the hole runs a tunnel, and that tunnel leads to the slope of the mountain above. At the top of this slope is an ice-bridge by which men may reach a fair country if they have a mind to."

"Then for heaven's sake let us cross it," put in Juanna.

"I have seen that bridge," said Olfan, while the captains stared wonderingly at the man whose might had prevailed against the ancient Snake, "but never yet have I heard of the traveller who dared to set his foot upon it."

"It is dangerous, but it can be crossed," replied Otter; "at the least, it is better to try it than to stay here to be murdered by the medicine-men."

"I think that we will go, Leonard," said Juanna; "if I am to die I wish to do so in the open air. Only what is to become of Nam? And perhaps Olfan and the captains would prefer to stop here?"

"Nam will go with us wherever we go," answered Leonard grimly; "we have a long score to settle with that gentleman. As for Olfan and his captains, they must please themselves."

"What will do you, Olfan?" asked Juanna, speaking to him for the first time since the scene in the other prison.

"It seems, Queen," he answered, with downcast eyes, "that I have sworn to defend you to the last, and this I will do the more readily

307

because now my life is of little value. As for my brethren here, I think, like you, that they will choose to die in the open, rather than wait to be murdered by the priests."

The three captains nodded an assent to his words. Then they all set to work.

First they took food and drink, of which there was an ample supply in the other cell, and hurriedly swallowing some of it, disposed the rest about their persons as best they could, for they foresaw that even if they succeeded in escaping, it was likely that they would go hungry for many days. Then Leonard wrapped Juanna in a goat-skin cloak which he took from one of the fallen priests, placing the second cloak over his own shoulders, for he knew that it would be bitterly cold on the mountains. Lastly, they tied Nam's arms behind him and deprived him of his knife, so that the old man might work none of them a sudden injury in his rage.

All being prepared, Otter made his rope fast to the staff and descended rapidly to the cave below. As his feet touched the ground, the priests began to batter upon the doors of the cell with beams of wood, or some such heavy instruments.

"Quick, Juanna!" said Leonard, "sit in this noose and hold the line, we will let you down. Hurry, those doors cannot stand for long."

Another minute and she was beside Otter, who stood beneath, a candle in his hand. Then Leonard came down.

"By the way, Otter," he said, "have you seen anything of the jewels that are supposed to be here?"

"There is a bag yonder by the Water-Dweller's bed, Baas," answered the dwarf carelessly, "but I did not trouble to look into it. What is the use of the red stones to us now?"

"None, but they may be of use afterwards, if we get away."

"Yes, Baas, *if* we get away," answered Otter, bethinking himself of the ice-bridge. "Well, we can pick it up as we go along."

Just then Nam arrived, having been let down by Olfan and the captains, and stood glaring round him, not without awe, for neither he nor any of his brethren had ever dared to visit the sacred home of the Snake-god. Then the captains descended, and last of all came Olfan.

"We have little time to spare, Deliverer," said the king; "the door is falling," and as he spoke they heard a great crash above. Otter jerked furiously at the rope, till by good luck one end of the stake slid over the edge of the hole and it fell among them.

"No need to leave this line for them to follow by," he said; "besides it may be useful." At that moment something appeared looking through the hole. It was the head of one of the pursuing priests. Nam saw it and took his opportunity.

"The false gods escape by the tunnel to the mountains," he screamed, "and with them the false king. Follow and fear not, the Water-Dweller is dead. Think not of me, Nam, but slay them."

With an exclamation Otter struck him heavily across the mouth, knocking him backwards, but the mischief was done, for a voice cried in answer:

"We hear you, father, and will find ropes and follow."

Then they started. One moment they paused to look at the huge bulk of the dead crocodile.

"This dwarf is a god in truth," cried one of the captains, "for no man could have wrought such a deed."

"Forward," said Leonard, "we have no time to lose."

Now they were by the crocodile's bed and among the broken bones of his victims.

"The bag, Otter, where is the bag?" asked Leonard.

"Here, Baas," answered the dwarf, dragging it from the mouldering skeleton of the unlucky priest who, having offended the new-found god, had been let down through the hole to lay it in its hiding-place and to perish in the jaws of the Water-Dweller.

Leonard took the bag, and opening its mouth, which was drawn tight with a running strip of hide, he peeped into it while Otter held down the candle that he might see. From its depths came a glimmer of red and blue light that glowed like the heart of some dull fire.

"It is the treasure," he said, in a low tone of exultation. "At last the luck has turned."

"How much does it weigh?" said Juanna, as they sped onwards.

"Some seven or eight pounds, I should say," he answered, still exultantly. "Seven or eight solid pounds of gems, the finest in the world."

"Then give it to me," she said; "I have nothing else to carry. You may have to use both your hands presently."

"True," he answered, and passed the string of the bag over her head.

Now they went on up the smooth sloping bed of the stream, suffering little inconvenience, except from the cold of the water that flowed about their ankles.

"The stream has risen a little, Baas, since I passed it this morning," said Otter. "Doubtless this day's sun has melted some snow at its source. Tomorrow we might not have been able to travel this road."

"Very likely," answered Leonard. "I told you that our luck had turned at last."

Twenty minutes more and they reached the mouth of the tunnel, and passing between the blocks of ice, found themselves upon the mountain side. But, as it chanced, the face of the moon was hidden by clouds, which is often the case in this country at the beginning of the spring season, for whereas in winter the days are almost invariably misty and the nights clear, in spring and summer these atmospheric conditions are frequently reversed. So dark was it indeed, that it proved impossible to attempt the ascent of the mountain until the day broke, since to do so would be to run the risk of losing themselves, and very possibly of breaking their necks among its numerous clefts and precipices.

After a minute's hasty discussion they set to work to fill up the mouth of the tunnel, or rather the cracks between the blocks of ice that already encumbered it, with such material as lay to hand, namely lumps of frozen snow, gravel, and a few large stones which they were fortunate enough to find in the immediate vicinity, for the darkness rendered it impossible to search for these at a distance. While they were thus engaged they heard the voices of priests speaking on the further side of their somewhat inefficient barrier, and worked harder than ever, thinking that the moment of attack had come.

To their astonishment, however, the sound of talking died away.

"Now where have they gone?" said Leonard—"to climb the cliff by another path and cut us off?"

"I think not, Deliverer," answered Olfan, "for I know of no such path. I think that they have gone to bring heavy beams by means of which they will batter down the ice wall."

"Still there is such a path, King," said one of the captains, "for I myself have often climbed it when I was young, searching for snow-flowers to bring to her whom I courted in those days."

"Can you find it now, friend?" asked Olfan eagerly.

"I do not forget a road that I have trod," said the captain, "but it is one not easy to follow."

"See now, Shepherdess," said Olfan after thinking awhile, "shall we take this man for a guide and return down the cliff to the city, for there, unless fate is against us, we may find friends among the soldiers and fight out this battle with the priests."

"No, no," answered Juanna almost passionately, "I would rather die than go back to that dreadful place to be murdered at last. Do you go if you will, Olfan, and leave us to take our chance."

"That I cannot do, Queen, for I am sworn to a certain service," he said proudly. "But hearken, my friend; follow this path of which you speak, if you can do so in the darkness, and find help. Then return swiftly to this spot where I and your two comrades will hold the priests at bay. Perchance you will not find us living, but this I charge you, if we are dead give it out that the gods have left the land because they were so evilly dealt with, and rouse up the people to fall upon the priests and make an end of them once and for ever, for thus only shall they win peace and safety."

Making no reply, the man shook Olfan and the other two captains by the hand, saluted Juanna, and vanished into the darkness. Then they all sat down in front of the mouth of the tunnel to wait and watch, and very glad were they of the goat-skin cloaks which had belonged to the priests, for as the night drew towards the dawn, the cold became so bitter that they could scarcely bear it, but were obliged to rise and stamp to and fro to keep their wet feet from freezing.

"Leonard," said Juanna, "you do not know what passed after Nam trapped you," and she told him all the tale.

When she had finished he rose and, taking Olfan by the hand, said: "King, I thank you. May fortune deal as well with you as you have dealt by me and mine!"

"Say no more, Deliverer," answered Olfan hastily; "I have but done my duty and fulfilled my oath, though at times the path of duty is hard for a man to follow." And he looked towards Juanna and sighed.

Leonard sat down and was silent, but many a time both then and in after-days did he wonder at the nobleness of mind of this savage king, which enabled him, under circumstances so cruel, to conquer his own passion and show himself willing to lay down life and throne together, that he might carry out his vow to protect the woman who had brought him so much pain and now left him for ever with his successful rival.

At length, looking at the mountain peak above them, they saw its snows begin to blush red with the coming of the dawn, and just then also they heard many voices talking within the tunnel, and caught glimpses of lights flashing through the openings in their rude fortifications. The priests, who no doubt had been delayed by the procuring of the timbers which were to serve as battering-rams, and the labour necessary to drag them up the steep incline of the tunnel, had returned, and in force. A few more minutes and a succession of dull thuds on the further side of the ice wall told the little band of defenders that their enemies were at work.

"The light grows quickly, Deliverer," said Olfan quietly; "I think that now you may begin to ascend the mountain and take no harm."

"What shall we do with this man?" asked Leonard, pointing to Nam.

"Kill him," said Otter.

"No, not yet awhile," answered Olfan. "Take this," and he handed Leonard the spear of the third captain, who had left it when he started down the mountain, fearing that it might encumber him, "and drive him along with you at its point. Should we be overpowered, you may buy your lives as the price of his. But should we hold them back and you escape, then do with him what you will."

"I know well what I would do," muttered Otter, glowering at the priest.

"And now, farewell," went on Olfan in the same calm voice. "Bring more ice, comrades, or stone if you can see any; the wall cracks."

Leonard and Otter wrung the king's hand in silence, but Juanna could not leave him thus, for her heart was melted at the thought of all his goodness.

"Forgive me," she murmured, "that I have brought you grief, and, as I fear, death to follow grief."

"The grief you could not help, Queen, and be sure I shall welcome death if he should choose me. Go now, and happiness go with you. May you escape in safety with the bright pebbles which you desire! May you and your husband, the Deliverer, be blessed for many years in each other's love, and when you grow old together, from time to time think kindly of that wild man, who worshipped you while you were young and laid down his life to save you."

Juanna listened, and tears sprang to her eyes; then of a sudden she seized the great man's hand and kissed it.

"I am repaid, Queen," he said, "and perchance your husband will not be jealous. Now go, and swiftly."

As he spoke a small portion of the wall fell outwards and the fierce face of a priest appeared at the opening. With a shout Olfan lifted his broad spear and thrust. The priest fell backwards, and just then the captains arrived with stones and stopped the hole.

Then the three turned and fled up the mountain side, Otter driving Nam before him with blows and curses, till at length the old man fell and lay on his face groaning. Nor could the dwarf's blows, which were not of the softest, force him to rise.

"Get up, you treacherous dog," said Leonard, threatening him with the spear.

"Then you must loose my arms, Deliverer," answered the priest; "I am very weak, and I cannot travel up this mountain with my hands bound behind me. Surely you have nothing to fear from one aged and unarmed man."

"Not much at present, I suppose," muttered Leonard, "though we have had enough to fear from you in the past." And taking his knife he cut loose the lashings.

While he did so, Juanna turned and looked behind her. Far below them she could see the forms of Olfan and his companions standing shoulder to shoulder, and even catch the gleams of light reflected from their spears, for now the sun was rising. Beneath them again she saw the grass-grown roofs of that earthly hell, the City of the People of the Mist, and the endless plain beyond through which the river wandered like a silver serpent. There also was the further portion of the huge wall of the temple built by unknown hands in forgotten years, and rising above the edge of that gap in the cliff through which she was looking, appeared a black mass which she knew to be the head and shoulders of the hideous colossus, on whose dizzy brow she had sat in that strange hour when the shouting thousands thundered a welcome to her as their goddess, and whence her most beloved friend, Francisco, had been hurled to his cruel death.

"Oh, what I have suffered in that place!" she thought to herself. "How have I lived through it, I wonder? And yet I have won something," and she glanced at Leonard who was driving Nam towards her, "and if only we survive and I am the means of enabling him to fulfil his vow and buy back his home with these jewels, I shall not regret all that I have endured to win them. Yes, even when he is no longer so very much in love, he must always be grateful to me, for few women will have done as much for their husbands."

Then Nam staggered past her, hissing curses, while the untiring Otter rained blows upon his back, and losing sight of Olfan and his companions they went on in safety, till they reached the neck and saw the ice-bridge glittering before them and the wide fields of snow beyond.

CHAPTER 38

The Triumph of Nam

"Which way are we to go now?" said Juanna; "must we climb down this great gulf?"

"No, Shepherdess," answered Otter; "see, before you is a bridge," and he pointed to the band of ice and rock which traversed the wide ravine.

"A bridge?" gasped Juanna, "why it is as slippery as a slide and steep as the side of a house. A fly could not keep its footing on it."

"Look here, Otter," put in Leonard, "either you are joking or you are mad. How can we cross that place? We should be dashed to pieces before we had gone ten yards."

"Thus, Baas: we must sit each of us on one of the flat stones that lie round here, then the stone will take us across of itself. I know, for I have tried it."

"Do you mean to tell me that you have been over there on a rock?"

"No, Baas, but I have sent three stones over. Two crossed safely, I watched them go the whole way, and one vanished in the middle. I think that there is a hole there, but we must risk that. If the stone is heavy enough it will jump it, if not, then we shall go down the hole and be no more troubled."

"Great heavens!" said Leonard, wiping his forehead with the back of his hand, "this is practical tobogganing with a vengeance. Is there no other way?"

"I can see none, Baas, except for the birds, and I think that we had better stop talking and make ready, for the priests are still behind us. If you will watch on the neck here so that we are not surprised, I will seek stones to carry us."

"How about this man?" said Leonard, pointing to Nam, who lay face downwards on the snow, apparently in a dead faint.

314

"Oh! we must keep him a while, Baas; he may be useful if those priests come. If not, I will talk with him before we start. He is asleep and cannot run away."

Then Leonard went to the top of the neck, which was distant some twenty yards, and Otter began to search for stones suitable to his purpose.

As for Juanna, she turned her back to the ice-bridge, at which she scarcely dared to look, and sat herself upon a rock. In doing so the jewels in the bag struck against her knee and jingled, and the thought came into her mind that she would examine them while she waited, partly because she desired to distract her thoughts from the vision of this new and terrible ordeal which lay before her, and partly to gratify a not unnatural curiosity.

Opening the mouth of the bag, she thrust her fingers into it, and one by one drew out the biggest gems which were jumbled together there, placing them on the rock beside her. In less than a minute she was feasting her eyes upon such a collection of priceless jewels as had never before gladdened the sight of any white woman, even in her wildest dreams; indeed, till now Juanna had not thought it possible that stones so splendid could exist on the hither side of the walls of heaven.

First there were great sapphires roughly squared, and two enormous round star rubies: these had formed the eyes of the colossus, which were removed on the morrow of their arrival, the star rubies representing the blood-red pupils. Then there was a heart-shaped ruby of perfect colour and without flaw, almost as large as a jackdaw's egg, which on the days of sacrifice had adorned the breasts of the chief priests of the People of the Mist for many generations. Next came the greatest wonders of this treasure, two marvellous stones, one a sapphire and one a ruby, fashioned respectively into models of the statue of the Dwarf and of the hideous shape of the Water-Dweller. Then there were others—dozens of them—some rudely cut and polished, and some as they came from the earth, but every one of them singled out for its remarkable size and flawlessness, or its perfect fire and beauty.

Juanna arranged them in rows and stared at them with ecstasy—where is the woman who would not have done so?—till in contemplating them she even forgot the present terrors of her position—forgot everything except the gorgeous loveliness and infinite value of the wealth of gems, which she had been the means of winning for Leonard.

Among other things that passed from her mind at this moment was the presence of Nam, who, overcome by rage and exhaustion, lay in a seeming faint upon the snow within twelve paces of her. She never saw him lift his head and look at her with an expression as cold and cruel as that which Otter had seen in the eyes of the Water-Dweller, when he lifted *his* head from its bed of rock. She never saw him roll slowly over and over across the snow towards her, pausing a while between each turn of his body, for now she was occupied in replacing the jewels one by one into their bag of leather.

At last all were in, and with a sigh—for it was sad to lose sight of objects so beautiful—Juanna drew the mouth of the bag tight and prepared to place it round her neck.

At this moment it was that a hand, withered and lean with age, passed beneath her eyes, and, swiftly as the snatch of an eagle's talon, seized the bag and rent it from her grasp. She sprang up with a cry of dismay, and well might she be dismayed, for there, running from her with incredible speed, was Nam, the jewels in his hand.

Otter and Leonard heard her cry, and, thinking that the priest was escaping, sped to cut him off. But he had no idea of escape, at least not of such escape as they expected. Some forty yards from where Juanna had been sitting, a little promontory of rock jutted out over the unclimbable gulf below them and towards this spot Nam directed his steps. Running along the ridge he halted at its end: indeed he must do, unless he would fall a thousand feet or more to the bottom of the ravine beneath. Then he turned and faced his pursuers, who by now had reached the edge of the cliff.

"Come one step nearer," he cried, "and I let this bag fall whence you shall never recover it, for no foot can tread these walls of rock, and there is water at the bottom of the gulf."

Leonard and Otter stopped, trembling for the fate of the jewels.

"Listen, Deliverer," cried Nam; "you came to this land to seek these trinkets, is it not so? And now you have found them and would be gone with them? But before you go you wish to kill me for vengeance' sake, because I have shown you to be cheats, and have sought to offer you up to those gods whom you have blasphemed. But the red stones you desire are in my hands, and if I unclasp my fingers they will be lost to you and all the world for ever. Say now, if I bring them back to you in safety, will you swear to give me my life and suffer me to go my ways in peace?"

"Yes, we will swear it," answered Leonard, who could not conceal the anguish of his anxiety. "Come back, Nam, and you shall depart unharmed; but if you let the stones fall, then you shall follow them."

"You swear it," said the priest contemptuously: "you are come to this, that you will sacrifice your revenge to satisfy your greed, O White

316

Man with a noble heart! Now I will outdo you, for I, who am not noble, will sacrifice my life to disappoint you of your desires. What! shall the ancient holy treasure of the People of the Mist be stolen by two white thieves and their black hound? Never! I would have killed you all had time been granted to me, but in that I failed, and I am glad that I have failed, for now I will deal you a bitterer blow than any death. May the curse of Jal and Aca cleave to you, you dogs without a kennel! May you live outcasts and die in the dirt, and may your fathers and your mothers and your children spit upon your bones as I do! Farewell!"

And shaking his disengaged hand at them he spat towards them; then with a sudden motion Nam hurled himself backwards off the point of rock and vanished into space, bearing the treasure with him.

For a while the three stood aghast and stared at each other and the point of rock which had been occupied by the venerable form of the late high priest; then Juanna sank upon the snow sobbing.

"It is my fault," she wailed, "all my fault. Just now I was boasting to myself that I had won wealth for you, and I have lost everything. And we have suffered for nothing, and, Leonard, you are a beggar. Oh! it is too much—too much!"

"Go out there, Otter," said Leonard in a hoarse voice, pointing to the place where Nam had hurled himself, "and see whether there is any chance of our being able to climb down into the gulf."

The dwarf obeyed and presently returned shaking his head.

"It is impossible, Baas," he said; "the walls of rock are sheer as though they had been cut with a knife; moreover there is water at the bottom of them, as the old wizard said, for I can hear the sound of it. Oh! Baas, Baas, why did you not kill him at first, or let me kill him afterwards? Surely I told you that he would bring evil on us. Well, they are gone and we can never find them again, so let us save our lives if we may, for after all these are more to us than bright stones. Come now and help me, Baas, for I have found two flat rocks that will serve our turn, a big one for you and the Shepherdess, since doubtless she will fear to make this journey alone, and a smaller one for myself."

Leonard followed him without a word; he was too heart-broken to speak, while Juanna rose and returned to the spot where Nam had robbed her. Looking up presently, her eyes still blurred with tears, she saw Leonard and the dwarf laboriously pushing two heavy stones across the snow towards her.

"Come, do not cry, Juanna," said Leonard, ceasing from his labours and laying his hand kindly upon her shoulder, "they are gone and there is an end of it. Now we must think of other things."

"Oh!" she answered, "if only you had seen them, you would never stop crying all your life."

"Then I dare say that the fit will be a short one," replied Leonard grimly, glancing at the awful bridge which stretched between them and safety.

"Listen, Juanna, you and I must lie upon this stone, and it will—so says Otter—carry us across to the other side of the ravine."

"I cannot, I cannot," she gasped, "I shall faint and fall off. I am sure that I shall."

"But you must, Juanna," answered Leonard. "At least you must choose between this and returning to the City of the Mist."

"I will come," she said. "I know that I shall be killed, but it is better than going back to those horrible priests; and besides, it does not matter now that I have lost the jewels."

"Jewels are not everything, Juanna."

"Listen, Shepherdess," put in Otter, "the thing is easy, though it looks difficult. All that you have to do is to shut your eyes and lie still, then the stone will carry you over. I am not afraid. I will go first to show you the way, and where a black dwarf can pass, there you white people who are so much braver can follow. But before I start, I will tie you and the Deliverer together with my cord, for so you will feel safer."

Then Otter dragged both stones to the very verge of the incline, and having passed the rope about the waists of Juanna and Leonard, he prepared himself for the journey.

"Now, Deliverer," he said, "when I am safe across, all that you must do it to lie flat upon the stone, both of you, and to push a little with the spear. Then before you know it, you will be by my side."

"All right," said Leonard doubtfully. "Well, I suppose that you had better start; waiting won't make the matter any easier."

"Yes, Baas, I will go now. Ah! little did I think that I should ever be forced to take such a ride as this. Well, it will be something to make songs about afterwards."

And Otter laid himself face downwards on the stone with a little laugh, though Leonard noticed that, however brave his spirit might be, he could not prevent his flesh from revealing its natural weakness, for it quivered pitifully.

"Now, Baas," he said, gripping the edges of the stone with his large hands, "when I give the word do you push gently, and then you will see how a black bird can fly. Put your head lower, Baas."

Leonard obeyed, and the dwarf whispered in his ear:

"I only want to say, Baas, in case we should not meet again, for accidents will happen even on the safest roads, that I am sorry that I made such a pig of myself yonder; it was so dull down there in that hole of a palace, and the fog made me see all things wrong. Moreover, drink and a wife have corrupted many a better man. Don't answer, Baas, but start me, for I am growing afraid."

Placing his hand at the back of the stone, Leonard gave it a slight push. It began to move, very slowly at first, then more fast and faster yet, till it was rushing over the smooth ice pathway with a whirring sound like that produced by the flight of a bird. Presently it had reached the bottom of the first long slope and was climbing the gentle rise opposite, but so slowly that for a while Leonard thought that it was going to stop. It crossed its brow, however, and vanished for a few seconds into a dip where the watchers could not see it, then it appeared again at the head of the second and longest slope, of which the angle was very steep. Down this the stone rushed like an arrow from a bow, till it reached the narrow waist of the bridge, whereof the general conformation bore some resemblance to that of a dead wasp lying on its back. Indeed, from where Leonard and Juanna stood, the span of ice at this point seemed to be no thicker than a silver thread, while Otter and the stone might have been a fly upon the thread. Now of a sudden Leonard distinctly saw the rock sledge and its living burden, which just then was travelling its swiftest, move upwards as though it had leaped into the air and then continue its course along the rising place which represented the throat of the wasp, till at length it stopped.

Leonard looked at his watch; the time occupied by the transit was just fifty seconds, and the distance could not have been much less than half a mile.

"See," he cried to Juanna, who all this while had sat with her hand before her eyes to shut out the vision of the dwarf's dreadful progress, "he has crossed safely!" and he pointed to a figure that appeared to be dancing with glee upon the breast of the snow slope.

As he spoke a faint sound reached their ears, for in those immense silences sound can travel far. It was Otter shouting, and his words seemed to be, "Come on, Baas; it is easy."

"I am glad he is safe," said Juanna faintly, "but now we must follow him. Take my handkerchief, Leonard, and tie it over my eyes, please, for I cannot bear to look. The idol's head was nothing to this."

Leonard obeyed her, bidding her not to be afraid.

"Oh! but I am terribly afraid," she said. "I never was so much frightened in all my life, and I—I have lost the jewels! Leonard, do forgive me for behaving so badly to you. I know that I have behaved badly in many ways, though I have been too proud to admit it before. But now, when I am going to die, I want to beg your pardon. I hope you will think kindly of me, Leonard, when I am dead, for I do love you with all my heart, indeed I do." And tears began to roll down beneath the bandage.

"Dearest," he answered, kissing her tenderly, "as we are tied together, it seems that if you die I must die too. Do not break down now after you have borne so much."

"It is the jewels," she sobbed, "the jewels; I feel as though I had committed a murder."

"Oh! bother the jewels!" said Leonard. "We can think about them afterwards." And he advanced towards the flat stone, Juanna feeling the while as though they were two of Carrier's victims about to know the Marriage of the Loire.

As they came to the stone Leonard heard a sound behind him, a sound of footsteps muffled by the snow, and glancing round he saw Soa rushing towards them, almost naked, a spear-wound in her side, and the light of madness shining in her eyes.

"Get back," he said sternly, "or——" and he lifted the great spear.

"Oh! Shepherdess," she wailed, "take me with you, Shepherdess, for I cannot live without you."

"Tell her to go away," said Juanna, recognising the voice; "I never want to see her any more."

"You hear, Soa," answered Leonard. "Stay, how has it gone yonder? Speak truly."

"I know not, Deliverer; when I left, Olfan and his brother still held the mouth of the tunnel and were unhurt, but the captain was dead. I slipped past them and got this as I went," and she pointed to the gash in her side.

"If he can hold out a little longer, help may reach him," muttered Leonard. Then without more words, he laid himself and Juanna face downwards on the broad stone.

"Now, Juanna," he said, "we are going to start. Grip fast with your right hand, and see that you do not leave go of the edge of the stone, or we shall both slip off it."

"Oh! take me with you, Shepherdess, take me with you, and I will be wicked no more, but serve you as of old," shrilled the voice of Soa in so despairing a cry that the rocks rang.

"Hold fast," said Leonard through his set teeth, as, disengaging his right hand from about Juanna's waist, he seized the handle of the spear and pressed its broad blade against a knob of rock behind them. Now the stone, that was balanced on the very verge of the declivity, trembled beneath them, and now, slowly and majestically as a vessel starting from her slips when the launching cord is severed, it began to move down the icy way.

For the first second it scarcely seemed to stir, then the motion grew palpable, and at that instant Leonard heard a noise behind him and felt his left foot clasped by a human hand. There was a jerk that nearly dragged them off their sledge, but he held fast to the front edge of the stone, and though he could still feel the hand upon his ankle, the strain became almost imperceptible.

CHAPTER 39

The Passing of the Bridge

Lifting his head very cautiously, Leonard looked over his shoulder and the mystery was explained. In her madness and the fury of her love for the mistress whom she had outraged and betrayed, Soa had striven to throw herself upon the stone with them so soon as she saw it commence to move. She was too late, and feeling herself slipping forward, she grasped despairingly at the first thing that came to her hand, which chanced to be Leonard's ankle. Now she must accompany them upon their awesome journey; only, while they rode upon the stone, she was dragged after them upon her breast.

A flash of pity passed through Leonard's brain as he realised her fearful plight. Then for a while he forgot all about her, since his attention was amply occupied with his own and Juanna's peril. Now they were rushing down the long slope with an ever-increasing velocity, and now they breasted the first rise, during the last ten yards of which, as in the case of Otter, the pace of the stone slowed down so much in proportion to the progressive exhaustion of its momentum, that Leonard thought they were coming to a standstill. Then it was that he kicked out viciously, striving to free himself from the weight of Soa, which threatened to bring them to a common ruin. But she clung to him like ivy to a tree, and he desisted from his efforts, fearing lest he should cause their sledge to alter its course.

On the very top of the rise the motion of the stone decreased almost to nothingness, then little by little increased once more as they traversed a short sharp dip, the same in which they had lost sight of Otter, to be succeeded by a gentle rise. So far, though exciting and novel, their journey had been comparatively safe, for the path was broad and the ice perfectly smooth. Its terrors were to come.

Looking forward, Leonard saw that they were at the commencement of a decline measuring four or five hundred yards in length, and so steep that, even had it offered a good foothold, human beings could scarcely have stood upon it. As yet the tongue of ice was fifty paces or more in width, but it narrowed rapidly as it fell, till at length near the opposite shore of the ravine, it fined away to a point like that of a great white needle, and then seemed to break off altogether.

Now they were well under way, and now they sped down the steep green ice at a pace that can hardly be imagined, though perhaps it is sometimes equalled by an eagle rushing on its quarry from some vast height of air. Indeed it is possible that the sensations of an eagle making his headlong descent and those of Leonard may have been very similar, with the important exception that the bird feels no fear, whereas absolute terror are the only words wherewith to describe the mental state of the man. So smooth was the ice and so precipitous its pitch that he felt as though he were falling through space, unsupported by anything, for travelling at that speed the friction of the stone was imperceptible. Only the air shrieked as they clove it, and Juanna's long tresses, torn by it from their fastenings, streamed out behind her like a veil.

Down they went, still down; half—two-thirds of the distance was done, then he looked again and saw the horror that lay before them. Already the bridge was narrow, barely the width of a small room; sixty yards further on it tapered to so fine a point that their stone would almost cover its breadth, and beneath it on either side yawned that unmeasured gulf wherein Nam was lost with the jewels. Nor was this all, for at its narrowest *the ice band was broken away for a space of ten or twelve feet*, to continue on the further side of the gap for a few yards at a somewhat lower level, and then run upwards at a steep incline to the breast of snow where Otter sat in safety.

On they whizzed, ice beneath them and before them, and ice in Leonard's heart, for he was frozen with fear. His breath had left him because of the rush of their progress, but his senses remained painfully acute. Involuntarily he glanced over the edge of the stone, saw the sheer depths below him, and found himself wondering what was the law that kept their sledge upon this ribbon of ice, when it seemed so easy for it to whirl off into space.

Now the gap was immediately in front of them. "God help us!" he murmured, or rather thought, for there was no time for words, and they had left the road of ice and were flying through the air as though the stone which carried them were a living thing, that, seeing the peril, had gathered up its energies and sprung forward for its life.

What happened? Leonard never knew for certain, and Otter

swore that his heart leaped from his bosom and stood in front of his eyes so that he could not see. Before they touched the further point of ice—while they were in the air, indeed—they, or rather Leonard, heard a hideous scream, and felt a jerk so violent that his hold of the stone was loosened, and it passed from beneath them. Then came a shock, less heavy than might have been expected, and lo! they were spinning onwards down the polished surface of the ice, while the stone which had borne them so far sped on in front like a horse that has thrown its rider.

Leonard felt the rubbing of the ice burn him like hot iron. He felt also that his ankle was freed from the hand that had held it, then for some minutes he knew no more, for his senses left him. When they returned, it was to hear the voice of Otter crying, "Lie still, lie still, Baas, do not stir for your life; I come."

Instantly he was wide awake, and, moving his head ever so little, saw their situation. Then he wished that he had remained asleep, for it was this:

The impetus of their rush had carried them almost to the line where the ice stopped and the rock and snow began, within some fifteen feet of it, indeed. But those fifteen feet were of the smoothest ice and very sheer, so smooth and sheer that no man could hope to climb them. Below them the slope continued for about thirteen or fourteen yards, till it met the corresponding incline that led to the gap in the bridge.

On this surface of ice they were lying spread-eagled. For a moment Leonard wondered how it was that they did not slide back to the bottom of the slope, there to remain till they perished, for without ropes and proper implements no human being could scale it. Then he saw that a chance had befallen them, which in after-days he was wont to attribute to the direct intervention of Providence.

It will be remembered that when they started, Leonard had pushed the rock off with a spear which Olfan had given them. This spear he drew in again as they began to move, placing it between his chest and the stone, for he thought that it might be of service to him should they succeed in crossing the gulf. When they were jerked from the sledge, and left to slide along the ice on the further side of the gap, in obedience to the impetus given to them by the frightful speed at which they were travelling, the spear, obeying the same laws of motion, accompanied them, but, being of a less specific gravity, lagged behind in the race, just as the stone, which was heaviest, outstripped them.

As it happened, near the top of the rise there was a fissure in the ice, and in this fissure the weapon had become fixed, its weighted blade causing it to assume an upright position. When the senseless bodies of Leonard and Juanna had slid as far up the slope as the unexpended energy of their impetus would allow, naturally enough they began to move back again in accordance with the laws of gravity. Then it was, as luck would have it, that the spear, fixed in the crevice of the ice, saved them from destruction; for it chanced that the descent of their two forms, passing on either side of it, was checked by the handle of the weapon, which caught the hide rope whereby they were bound together.

All of this Leonard took in by degrees; also he discovered that Juanna was either dead or senseless, at the time he could not tell which.

"What are you going to do?" he asked of Otter, who by now was on the verge of the ice fifteen feet above them.

"Cut steps and pull you up, Baas," answered the dwarf cheerfully.

"It will not be easy," said Leonard, glancing over his shoulder at the long slope beneath, "and if we slip or the rope breaks——"

"Do not talk of slipping, Baas," replied Otter, as he began to hack at the ice with the priest's heavy knife, "and as for the rope, if it was strong enough for the Water-Dweller to drag me round the pool by, it is strong enough to hold you two, although it has seen some wear. I only wish I had such another, for then this matter would be simple."

Working furiously, Otter hacked at the hard surface of the ice. The first two steps he hollowed from the top of the slope lying on his stomach. After this difficulties presented themselves which seemed insuperable, for he could not chip at the ice when he had nothing by which to support himself.

"What is to be done now?" said Leonard.

"Keep cool, Baas, and give me time to think," and for a moment Otter squatted down and was silent.

"I have it," he said presently, and rising he took off his goat-skin cloak and cut it into strips, each strip measuring about two inches in width by two feet six inches in length. These strips he knotted together firmly, making a serviceable rope of them, long enough to reach to where Leonard and Juanna were suspended on the stout handle of the spear.

Then he took the stake which had already done him such good service, and, sharpening its point, fixed it as deeply as he could into the snow and earth on the border of the ice belt, and tied the skin rope to it.

"Now, Baas," he said, "all is well, for I can begin from the bottom." And, without further words, he let himself down till he hung beside them.

"Is the Shepherdess dead, Baas?" he asked, glancing at Juanna's pale face and closed eyes, "or does she only sleep?"

"I think that she is in a swoon," answered Leonard; "but for heaven's sake be quick, Otter, for I am being frozen on this ice. What is your plan now?"

"This, Baas: to tie about your middle the end of the rope that I have made from the cloak, then to undo the cord that binds you and the Shepherdess together, and return to the top of the slope. Once there I can pull her up by the hide line, for it is strong, and she will slip easily over the ice, and you can follow."

"Good!" said Leonard.

Then hanging by one hand the dwarf managed, with such assistance as Leonard could give him, to knot beneath Leonard's arms the end of the rope which he had constructed from the skin garment. Next he set to work to untie the hide cord, thereby freeing him from Juanna. And now came the most difficult and dangerous part of the task, for Leonard, suspended from the shaft of the spear by one hand, must support Juanna's senseless form with the other, while Otter made shift to drag himself to the summit of the ice, holding the hide line in his teeth. The spear bent dreadfully, and Leonard did not dare to put any extra strain upon the roughly fastened cord of goat-skin, by which the dwarf was hauling himself up the ice, for if it gave they must all be precipitated to the dip below, there to perish miserably. Faint and frozen as he was, it seemed hours to him before Otter reached the top and called to him to get go of Juanna.

Leonard obeyed, and seating himself on the snow, his feet supported by the edge of the ice, the dwarf put out his strength and began to pull her up. Strong as he was, it proved as much as he was able to do; indeed, had Juanna lain on any other material than ice, he could not have done it at all. But in the end he succeeded, and with a gasp of gratitude Leonard saw her stretched safe upon the snow.

Now Otter, hastily undoing the cord from Juanna's waist, made it into a running noose which he threw down to Leonard, who placed it over his shoulders. Having lifted the spear from the cleft in which it stood, he commenced his ascent. His first movements cost him a pang of agony, and no wonder, for the blood from wounds that had been caused by the friction of his flesh as he was hurled along the surface of the slide, had congealed, freezing his limbs to the ice, whence they could not easily be loosened. The pain, sharp as it was, did him good, however, for it aroused his benumbed energies and enabled him to drag on the goat-skin cord with all his strength, while Otter tugged at that which was beneath his arms.

Well for him was it that the dwarf had taken the precaution of throwing down this second line, for presently Otter's stake, which had no firm hold in the frozen earth, came out and slid away, striking Leonard as it passed and bearing the knotted lengths of the cloak with it. The dwarf cried aloud and bent forward as though he were about to fall. By a fearful effort he recovered himself and held fast the rope in his hand, while Leonard, suspended by it, swung to and fro on the surface of the ice like the pendulum of a clock.

Then followed the most terrible moments of all their struggle against the difficulties of this merciless place. The dwarf held fast above, and Leonard, ceasing to swing, lay with hands and legs outstretched on the face of the ice.

"Now, Baas," said Otter, "be brave, and when I pull, do you wriggle forward."

He tugged till the thin hide rope stretched, while Leonard clawed and kicked at the ice with his toes, knees, and disengaged hand.

Alas! it gave no hold—he might as well have tried to climb a dome of plate glass at an angle of sixty degrees.

"Rest awhile, Baas," said the dwarf, whose breath was coming in great sobs, "then make a little nick in the ice with the blade of the spear, and when next I pull, try to set some of your weight upon it."

Leonard did as he was bid without speaking.

"Now," said the dwarf, and with a push and a struggle Leonard was two feet higher up the incline. Again the process was repeated, and this time he got his left hand into the lowest of the two steps that Otter had hacked with the knife, and once more they paused for breath. A third effort, the fiercest of them all, a clasping of hands, and he was lying trembling like a frightened child above the glacier's lip.

The ordeal was over, that danger was done with, but at what a cost! Leonard's nerves were completely shattered, he could not stand, his face was bleeding, his nails were broken, and the bone of one knee was exposed by the friction of the ice, to say nothing of the shock to the system and the bruises which he had received when he was hurled from the stone. Otter's condition was a little better, but his hands were cut by the rope and he was utterly exhausted with toil and the strain of suspense. Indeed, of the three Juanna had come off by far the best, for she swooned at the very beginning of the passage of the bridge, and when they were jerked from the stone, being lighter than Leonard, she had fallen upon him. Moreover, the thick goat-skin cloak which was wrapped about her had protected her from all hurt beyond a few trifling cuts and bruises. Of their horrible position when they were hanging to the spear, and the rest of the adventure, including the death of Soa, she knew nothing, and it was well for her reason that this was so.

"Otter," murmured Leonard in a shaking voice, "have you lost that gourd of spirit?"

"No, Baas, it is safe."

"Thank Heaven!" he said; "hold it to my lips if you can."

The dwarf lifted it with a trembling hand, and Leonard gulped down the fiery liquor.

"That's better," he said; "take some yourself."

"Nay, Baas, I have sworn to touch drink no more," Otter answered, looking at the gourd longingly; "besides you and the Shepherdess will want it all. I have some food here and I will eat."

"What happened to Soa, Otter?"

"I could not see rightly, Baas, I was too frightened, much more frightened than I had been when I rode the stone myself; but I think that her legs caught in the ice on this side of the hole, and so she fell. It was a good end for her, the vicious old cow!" he added, with a touch of satisfaction.

"It was very near being a bad end for us," answered Leonard, "but we have managed to come out of it alive somehow. Not for all the rubies in the world would I cross that place again."

"Nor I, Baas. *Wow!* it was awful. Now my stomach went through my head, and now my head went through my stomach, and the air was red and green and blue, and devils shouted at me out of it. Yes, and when I came to the hole, there I saw the Water-Dweller all fashioned in fire waiting with an open mouth to eat me. It was the drink that made me think of these things, Baas, and that is why I have sworn to touch it no more. Yes, I swore it as I flew through the air and saw the flaming Water-Dweller beneath me. And now, Baas, I am a little rested, so let us try and wake up the Shepherdess, and get us gone."

"Yes," said Leonard, "though I am sure I do not know where we are to go to. It can't be far, for I am nearly spent."

Then crawling to where Juanna lay wrapped in her cloak, Otter poured some of the native spirit down her throat while Leonard rubbed her hands. Presently this treatment produced its effect, for she sat up with a start, and seeing the ice before her, began to shriek, saying, "Take me away; I can't do it, Leonard, I can't indeed."

"All right, dear," he answered, "you have done it. We are over."

"Oh!" she said, "I *am* thankful. But where is Soa? I thought that I heard her throw herself down behind us."

"Soa is dead," he answered. "She fell down the gulf and nearly pulled us with her. I will tell you all about it afterwards; you are not fit to hear it now. Come, dear, let us be going out of this accursed place."

Juanna staggered to her feet.

"I am so stiff and sore that I can hardly stand," she said, "but, Leonard, what is the matter with you? You are covered with blood."

"I will tell you afterwards," he replied again.

Then Otter collected their baggage, which consisted chiefly of the hide line and the spear, and they crawled forward up the snow-slope. Some twenty or thirty yards ahead of them, and almost side by side, lay the two glacier stones on which they had passed the bridge, and near them those which Otter had despatched as pioneers on the previous morning. They looked at them wondering. Who could have believed that these inert things, not an hour before, had been speeding down the icy way quicker than any express train that ever travelled, and they with them?

One thing was certain: did they remain unbroken for another two or three million years, and that is a short life for a stone, they would never again make so strange a journey.

Then the three toiled on to the top of the snow-slope, which was about four hundred yards away.

"Look, Baas," said Otter, who had turned to gaze a fond farewell at the gulf behind; "there are people yonder on the further side."

He was right. On the far brink of the crevasse were the forms of men, who seemed to be waving their arms in the air and shouting. But whether these were the priests who, having overcome the resistance of Olfan, had pursued the fugitives to kill them, or the soldiers of the king who had conquered the priests, the distance would not allow them to see. The fate of Olfan and the further domestic history of the People of the Mist were now sealed books to them, for they never heard any more of these matters, nor are they likely to do so.

Then the travellers began to descend from field to field of snow, the great peak above alone remaining to remind them that they were near to the country of the Mist. Once they stopped to eat a little of such food as they had with them, and often enough to rest, for their strength was small. Indeed, as they dragged themselves wearily forward, each of the men holding Juanna by the hand, Leonard found himself wondering how it came about, putting aside the bodily perils from which they had escaped, that they had survived the exhaustion and the horrors, physical and mental, of the last forty-eight hours.

But there they were still alive, though in a sorry plight, and before evening they found themselves below the snow line in a warm and genial climate.

"I must stop," said Juanna as the sun began to set; "I can drag myself no further."

Leonard looked at Otter in despair.

"There is a big tree yonder, Baas," said the dwarf with an attempt at cheerfulness, "and water by it. It is a good place to camp, and here the air is warm, we shall not suffer from cold. Nay, we are lucky indeed; think how we passed last night."

They reached the tree, and Juanna sank down half fainting against its bole. With difficulty Leonard persuaded her to swallow a little meat and a mouthful of spirit, and then, to his relief, she relapsed into a condition with partook more of the nature of stupor than of sleep.

CHAPTER 40

Otter's Farewell

The night which followed, Leonard is wont to declare, proved to be the very worst that he ever spent in his life. Notwithstanding his intense weariness, he could not sleep, his nerves were too shattered to allow of it. Whenever he shut his eyes, he saw himself hanging head downwards over the oubliette in the cell beneath the idol, or flying through the air across the dreadful gap in the ice-bridge, or in some other position of terror, similar to those with which they had made such intimate acquaintance of late. Did these visions cease, from time to time he seemed to hear the voice of Francisco bidding him farewell, the yell of Soa falling to her dreadful death, or Nam raving his last defiance at them. Also his hurts, which were many, gave him great pain, and though the climate here was mild, the breeze from the snow heights chilled him through, and they had not even a match wherewith to light a fire and scare the wild beasts that roared about them.

Rarely have three human beings been in a position more desolate and desperate than that in which they found themselves this night, exhausted, unarmed, almost without food or clothing, and wandering they knew not where through the vastness of Central Africa. Unless some help found them, as Leonard was aware, they must perish of starvation, by the fangs of lions, or the spears of natives. It was impossible that they could live through another week, and the thought came into his mind that it would be well for them if they died that night and had done with it.

It would be well; yes, and it would have been better if he had been laid by the side of his brother Tom before ever he listened to Soa's accursed tale of the People of the Mist and their treasure of rubies. Only then he would never have known Juanna, for she must have died in the slave camp.

This was the fruit of putting faith in the visions of dying men. And yet, it was strange, he had *nearly* got the money and "by the help of a woman," for those rubies would have sufficed to buy back Outram ten times over. But, alas! nearly is not quite. That dream was done with, and even if they escaped, it would be to find himself more utterly beggared than before, for now he would be a married beggar.

At last the night wore away and the dawn came, but Juanna did not wake until the sun was high. Leonard, who had crept to a little distance—for now he was quite unable to walk—saw her sit up and crawled back to her. She stared at him vacantly and said something about Jane Beach. Then he knew that she was wandering. There was nothing to be done. What could be done in that wilderness with a woman in delirium, except wait for death?

Accordingly Leonard and Otter waited for some hours. Then the dwarf, who was in far the best condition of the three, took the spear—Olfan's gift—and said that he would go and seek for food, since their store was exhausted. Leonard nodded, though he knew that there was little chance of a man armed with a spear alone being able to kill game, and Otter went.

Towards evening he returned, reporting that he had seen plenty of buck, but could not get near them, which was just what his master expected. That night they passed hungry, by turns watching Juanna, who was still delirious. At dawn Otter started out again, leaving Leonard, who had been unable to sleep as on the previous night, crouched at Juanna's side, his face buried in his hands.

Before noon Leonard chanced to look up, and saw the dwarf reeling towards him, for he also was faint with want of food. Indeed his great head and almost naked body, through the skin of which the misshapen bones seemed to start in every direction, presented so curious a spectacle that his master, whose brain was shaken by weakness, began to laugh.

"Don't laugh, Baas," gasped the dwarf; "either I am mad, or we are saved."

"Then I think that you must be mad, Otter, for we shall take a deal of saving," he answered wearily, for he had ceased to believe in good fortune. "What is it?"

"This, Baas. There is a white man coming this way and more than a hundred servants with him; they are marching up the mountain slope."

"You are certainly mad, Otter," Leonard replied. "What in the names of Jal and Aca is a white man doing here? I am the only one of that species who have been fool enough to penetrate these regions, I and Francisco," and he shut his eyes and dozed off.

Otter looked at him for a while, then he tapped his forehead significantly and started down the slope again. An hour later, Leonard, still dozing, was awakened by a sound of many voices, and by a hand that shook him not too gently.

"Awake, Baas," said the dwarf, for the hand was his; "I have caught the white man and brought him here."

Leonard staggered to his feet and saw before him, surrounded by gun-bearers and other attendants, an English gentleman, rather under than over middle age, with a round and kindly face tanned by the sun, and somewhat deep-set dark eyes having an eyeglass fixed in one of them, through which its wearer regarded him with much commiseration.

"How do you do, sir?" said the stranger in a pleasant voice. "So far as I can make out from your servant you seem to be in a baddish way. By George! there is a lady."

"How do you do?" answered Leonard. "Capital sun-helmet that of yours. I envy it, but you see I have had to go bare-headed lately," and he ran his fingers through his matted hair. "Who is the maker of that eight-bore? Looks a good gun!"

"Achmet," said the stranger, turning to an Arab at his side, "go to the first donkey and fetch this lord of the earth a pint of champagne and some oatmeal cakes; he seems to want them. Tell the bearers also to bring up my tent and to pitch it there by the water. Quick, now."

Forty-eight hours had passed, and the benevolent stranger was sitting on a camp-stool in the door of his tent, looking at two forms that lay wrapped in blankets and comfortably asleep within it.

"I suppose that they will wake some time," he murmured, dropping his eyeglass and taking the pipe from his mouth. "The quinine and champagne have done them a lot of good: there is nothing like quinine and champagne. But what an unconscionable liar that dwarf must be! There is only one thing he can do better, and that is eat. I never saw a chap stow away so much grub, though I must say that he looks as though he needed it. Still, allowing for all deductions, it is a precious queer story. Who are they, and what the deuce are they doing here? One thing is clear: I never saw a finer-looking man nor a prettier girl." And he filled his pipe again, replaced the eyeglass in his eye, and began smoking.

Ten minutes later Juanna sat up suddenly, whereupon the stranger withdrew out of sight. She looked round her wildly, then, seeing Leonard lying at the further side of the tent, she crept to him and began kissing him, saying: "Leonard! Thank God that you are still alive, Leonard! I dreamed that we both were dead. Thank God that you are alive!"

Then the man who had been thus adjured woke up also and returned her caresses.

"By George! this is quite affecting," said the traveller. "I suppose that they are married; if not, they ought to be. Any way, I had better clear out for a while."

An hour later he returned to find that the pair had made themselves as presentable as soap and water, and some few spare garments which he had sent to Leonard, would allow, and were now sitting in the sun outside the tent. He advanced, lifting his helmet, and they rose to meet him.

"I suppose that I had better introduce myself," he said with some hesitation, for he was a shy man. "I am an English traveller, doing a little exploring on my own account, for lack of any other occupation, and my name is Sydney Wallace."

"Mine is Leonard Outram," answered Leonard, "and this young lady is Miss Juanna Rodd."

Mr. Wallace started and bowed again. So they were *not* married!

"We are deeply indebted to you, sir," went on Leonard; "for you have rescued us from death."

"Not at all," answered Mr. Wallace. "You must thank that servant of yours, the dwarf, and not me, for if he had not seen us, I should have passed a mile or more to the left of you. The fact is that I am rather fond of mountaineering, and seeing this great peak above us—I am told that it is the highest in the Bisa-Mushinga Mountains—I thought that I might as well have a try at it before I turn homewards, *via* Lake Nyassa, Livingstonia, Blantyre, and Quilimane. But perhaps you will not mind telling me how you came to be here. I have heard something from the dwarf, but his tale seems a little too steep."

"I am afraid you will think ours rather steeper, Mr. Wallace," said Leonard, and he proceeded to give him a short outline of their adventures.

When he came to their arrival among the People of the Mist, and described the inauguration of Otter and Juanna as gods in the temple of the colossus, he noticed that his auditor had let the eyeglass fall from his round eye, and was regarding him with mild amazement.

"I am afraid that all this does not interest you," said Leonard stiffly.

"On the contrary, Mr. Outram, it interests me very much. I am exceedingly fond of romances, and this is rather a good one."

"As I thought; it is scarcely worth while to go on," said Leonard again. "Well, I cannot wonder that you do not believe me."

"Leonard," interposed Juanna quietly, "you still have the star ruby; show it to Mr. Wallace!"

He did so, somewhat sulkily, and then, as he seemed disinclined to say anything more, Juanna took up the tale, showing in evidence of its truth the spear, the frayed rope, and the tattered white robe which she had worn in her character of Aca, and, indeed, still wore beneath poor Francisco's cassock—for she had no other.

Mr. Wallace heard her out, then, without making any comment, he rose, saying that he must try to shoot some meat for the camp, and begged that they would make themselves comfortable until his return that evening.

Before sundown he reappeared, and, coming straight to the tent, asked their pardon for his incredulity.

"I have been up yonder," he said, "following your spoor backwards. I have seen the snow-bridge and the stones, and the nicks which the dwarf cut in the ice. All is just as you told me, and it only remains for me to congratulate you upon having escaped from the strangest series of dangers that ever I heard of"; and he held out his hand, which both Leonard and Juanna shook warmly.

"By the way," he added, "I sent men to examine the gulf for several miles, but they report to me that they found no spot where it would be possible to descend it, and I fear, therefore, that the jewels are lost for ever. I confess that I should have liked to try to penetrate into the Mist country, but my nerves are not strong enough for the ice-bridge, and if they were, stones won't slide uphill. Besides, you must have had about enough of roughing it, and will be anxious to turn your faces towards civilisation. So after you have rested another couple of days I think that we had better start for Quilimane, which, barring accidents, is about three months' march from here."

Shortly afterwards they started accordingly, but with the details of their march we need not concern ourselves. An exception must be made, however, in the case of a single event which happened at the mission-station of Blantyre. That event was the wedding of Leonard and Juanna in conformance with the ceremonies of their own church.

No word of marriage had been spoken between them for some weeks, and yet the thought of it was never out of the minds of either. Indeed, had their feelings been much less tender towards each other than was the case, it would still have been desirable, in view of the extraordinary intimacy into which they had been thrown during the past months, that they should become man and wife. Leonard felt that alone as she was in the wide world, nothing short of mutual aversion would have justified him in separating from Juanna, and as it was love and not aversion that he entertained towards her, this argument came home to him with overmastering force.

"Juanna," he said to her on the day of their arrival at Blantyre, "you remember some words that passed between your father and myself when he lay upon his death-bed, to the effect that, should we both wish it, he trusted to my honour to remarry you formally as soon as an opportunity might arise.

"Now the opportunity is here, and I ask you if you desire to take me for your husband, as, above everything in the world, I desire to make you my beloved wife."

She coloured to her beautiful eyes and answered in a voice that was almost a whisper:

"If you wish it and think me worthy of you, Leonard, you know that I wish it also. I have always loved you, dear, yes, even when I was behaving worst to you; but there is—Jane Beach!"

"I have told you before, Juanna," he answered with some little irritation, "and now I tell you again, that Jane Beach and I have done with each other."

"I am sure that I am very glad to hear it," Juanna replied, still somewhat dubiously. The rest of that conversation, being of a private character, will scarcely interest the public.

When he spoke thus, Leonard little knew after what fashion Jane Beach and he had wound up their old love affair.

Two days later Leonard Outram took Juanna Rodd to wife, "to have and to hold, for better, for worse, for richer, for poorer, in sickness and in health, to love and to cherish till death did them part," and their rescuer, Sydney Wallace, who by now had become their fast friend, gave her away.

Very curious were the memories that passed through Juanna's mind as she stood by her husband's side in the little grass-roofed chapel of Blantyre, for was this not the third time that she had been married, and now only of her own free will? She bethought her of that wild scene in the slave camp; of Francisco who died to save her, and of the blessing which he had called down upon her and this very man; of that other scene in the rock prison, when, to protect Leonard's life, she was wed, according to the custom of the Children of the Mist, to that true-hearted gentleman and savage, Olfan, their king. Then she awoke with a happy sigh to know that the lover at her side could never be taken from her again until death claimed one of them.

"We shall be dreadfully poor, Leonard," she said to him afterwards; "it would have been much better for you, dear, if I had fallen into the gulf instead of the rubies."

"I am not of your opinion, love," he answered with a smile for he was very happy. "Hang the rubies! Your price is far above rubies, and no man may struggle against fate. I have always been able to make a living for myself heretofore, and I do not doubt that I shall continue to do so for both of us, and we will leave the rest to Providence. You are more to me, Juanna, than any wealth—more even than Outram."

That evening Mr. Wallace found Otter gazing disconsolately at the little house in which Leonard and Juanna were staying.

"Are you sad because your master is married, Otter?" he asked.

"No," answered the dwarf, "I am glad. For months he has been running after her and dreaming of her, and now at last he has got her. Henceforth she must dream of him and run after him, and he will have time to think about other people, who love him quite as well."

Another month or so went by while the party journeyed in easy stages towards the coast, and never had wedded lovers a happier honeymoon, or one more unconventional, than that passed by Leonard and Juanna, though perhaps Mr. Wallace and Otter did not find the contemplation of their raptures a very exhilarating occupation.

At last they reached Quilimane in safety, and pitched their camp on some rising ground outside of the settlement, which is unhealthy. Next morning at daybreak Mr. Wallace started to the post-office, where he expected to find letters. Leonard and Juanna did not accompany him, but went for a walk before the sun grew hot. Then it was, as they walked, that a certain fact came home to them; namely, that they could not avail themselves of their host's kindness any longer, and, further, that they were quite penniless. When one is moving slowly across the vast African wilds, and living on the abounding game, love and kisses seem an ample provision for all wants. But the matter strikes the mind in a different light after the trip is done, and civilisation with its necessities looms large in the immediate future.

"What are we to do, Juanna?" asked Leonard in dismay. "We have no money to enable us to reach Natal or anywhere, and no credit on which to draw."

"I suppose that we must sell the great ruby," she answered, with a sigh, "though I shall be sorry to part with it."

"Nobody will buy such a stone here, Juanna, and it may not be a real ruby after all. Perhaps Wallace might be willing to advance me a trifle on it, though I hate having to ask him."

Then they went back to breakfast, which they did not find an altogether cheerful meal. As they were finishing, Mr. Wallace returned from the town.

"I have got good news," he said; "the British India mail will be here in two days, so I shall pay off my men and go up to Aden in her, and thence home. Of course you will come too, for, like me, I expect you have had enough of Africa for the present. Here are some copies of the weekly edition of the 'Times'; look through them, Mrs. Outram, and see the news while I read my letters."

Leonard turned aside moodily and lit his pipe. How was he to find money to take even a third-class passage on the British India mail? But Juanna, obeying the instinct that prompts a woman to keep up appearances at all hazards, took one of the papers and opened it, although the tears which swam in her eyes would scarcely suffer her to see the print. Thus things went on for ten minutes or more, as she idly turned the pages of two or three issues of the weekly "Times," trying to collect her thoughts and pick up the thread of current events.

But it is wonderful how uninteresting and far-away those events appear after the reader has been living a life to herself for a year or so, and Juanna, preoccupied as she was with her own thoughts, was about to give up the attempt as a failure, when the name of *Outram* started to her eyes.

A minute later her two companions heard a sharp exclamation and turned round.

"What is the matter, Mrs. Outram?" said Wallace. "Has France declared war against Germany, or is Mr. Gladstone dead?"

"Oh! no, something much more important than that. Listen to this advertisement, Leonard:—

"'If Leonard Outram, second son of Sir Thomas Outram, Bart., late of Outram Hall, who was last heard of in the territory to the north of Delagoa Bay, Eastern Africa, or, in the event of his death, his lawful heirs, will communicate with the undersigned, he or they will hear of something very greatly to his or their advantage. Thomson & Turner, 2 Albert Court, London, E.C.'"

"Are you joking, Juanna?" said Leonard after a pause.

"Look for yourself," she answered.

He took the paper, and read and reread the notice.

"Well, there is one thing certain," he said, "that no one ever stood in greater need of hearing something to his advantage than I do at this moment, for excepting the ruby, which may not be a true stone, we haven't a *stiver* to bless ourselves with in the world. Indeed, I don't know how I am to avail myself of Messrs. Thomson & Turner's kind invitation, unless I write them a letter and go to live in a Kaffir hut till the answer comes."

"Don't let that trouble you, my dear fellow," said Wallace; "I can get plenty of cash here, and it is very much at your service."

"I am ashamed to take further advantage of your kindness," answered Leonard, flushing. "This advertisement may mean nothing, or perhaps a legacy of fifty pounds, though I am sure I don't know who would leave me even that sum. And then, how should I repay you?"

"Stuff!" said Wallace.

"Well," replied Leonard, "beggars must put their pride in their pockets. If you will lend me a couple of hundred pounds and take the ruby in pledge, I shall be even more grateful to you than I am at present, and that is saying a good deal."

On this business basis the matter was ultimately arranged, though within half an hour Wallace handed back the great stone into Juanna's keeping, bidding her "keep it dark"; an injunction which she obeyed in every sense of the word, for she hid the ruby where once the poison had lain—in her hair.

Two busy days went by, and on the third morning a messenger came running from the town to announce that the northward mail was in sight. Then it was that Otter, who all this while had said nothing, advanced solemnly towards Leonard and Juanna, holding his hand outstretched.

"What is the matter, Otter?" asked Leonard, who was engaged in helping Wallace to pack his hunting trophies.

"Nothing, Baas; I have come to say goodbye to you and the Shepherdess, that is all. I wish to go now before I see the Steam-fish carry you away."

"Go!" said Leonard; "you wish to go?"

Somehow Otter had become so much a part of their lives, that, even in their preparations to leave for England, neither of them had ever thought of parting from him.

"Why do you wish to go?" he added.

"Because I am an ugly old black dog, Baas, and can be of no further use to you out yonder," and he nodded towards the sea.

"I suppose you mean that you do not want to leave Africa, even for a while," said Leonard, with ill-concealed grief and vexation. "Well, it is hard to part with you like this. Also," he added with a little laugh, "it is awkward, for I owe you more than a year's wages, and have not the money to spare to pay you. Moreover, I had taken your passage on the ship."

"What does the Baas say?" asked Otter slowly; "that he has bought me a place in the Steam-fish?"

Leonard nodded.

"Then I beg your pardon, Baas. I thought that you had done with me and were going to throw me away like a worn-out spear."

"So you wish to come, Otter?" said Leonard.

"Wish to come!" he answered wonderingly. "Are you not my father and my mother, and is not the place where you may be my place? Do you know what I was going to do just now, Baas? I was going to climb to the top of a tree and watch the Steam-fish till it vanished over the edge of the world; then I would have taken this rope, which already has served me well among the People of the Mist, and set it about my throat and hanged myself there in the tree, for that is the best end for old dogs, Baas."

Leonard turned away to hide the tears which started to his eyes, for the dwarf's fidelity touched him more than he cared to show. Seeing his trouble, Juanna took up the talk to cover his confusion.

"I fear that you will find it cold over yonder, Otter," she said. "It is a land of fog, they tell me, and there are none of your own people, no wives or Kaffir beer. Also, we may be poor and have to live hardly."

"Of fog I have seen something lately, Shepherdess," answered the dwarf; "and yet I was happy in the fog, because I was near the Baas. Of hard living I have seen something also, and still I was happy, because I was near the Baas. Once I had a wife and beer in plenty, more than a man could want, and then I was unhappy, because they estranged me from the Baas, and he knew that I had ceased to be Otter, his servant whom he trusted, and had become a beast. Therefore, Shepherdess, I would see no more of wives and beer."

"Otter, you idiot," broke in Leonard brusquely, "you had better stop talking and get something to eat, for it will be the last meal that you will wish to see for many a day."

"The Baas is right," replied the dwarf; "moreover, I am hungry, for sorrow has kept me from food for these two days. Now I will fill myself full, that I may have something to offer to the Black Water when he shakes me in his anger."

ENVOI

The End of the Adventure

Six weeks or so had passed when a four-wheeled cab drew up at the door of 2 Albert Court, London, E.C.

The progress of this vehicle had excited some remark among the more youthful and lighter-minded denizens of the City, for on its box, arrayed in an ill-fitting suit of dittoes and a brown hat some sizes to small for him, sat a most strange object, whose coal-black countenance, dwarfed frame, and enormous nose and shoulders attracted their ribald observance.

"Look at him, Bill," said one youth to an acquaintance; "he's escaped from Madame Tussaud's, he has. Painted hisself over with Day & Martin's best, and bought a second-hand Guy Fawkes nose."

Just then his remarks were cut short, for Otter, having been made to understand by the driver that they had arrived at their destination, descended from the box in a manner so original, that it is probably peculiar to the aborigines of Central Africa, and frightened that boy away.

From the cab emerged Leonard and Juanna, looking very much the better for their sea journey. Indeed, having recovered her health and spirits, and being very neatly dressed in a grey frock, with a wide black hat trimmed with ostrich feathers, Juanna looked what she was, a very lovely woman. Entering an outer office Leonard asked if Messrs. Thomson & Turner were to be seen.

"Mr. Turner is within, sir," answered a clerk of venerable appearance. "Mr. Thomson"—here his glance fell upon Otter and suddenly he froze up, then added with a jerk—"has been dead a hundred years! Thomson, sir," he explained, recovering his dignity, but with his eyes still fixed on Otter, "was the founder of this firm; he died in the time of George III. That is his picture over the door—the person with a harelip and a snuffbox."

341

"Indeed!" said Leonard. "As Mr. Thomson is not available, perhaps you will tell Mr. Turner that a gentleman would like to speak to him."

"Certainly, sir," said the old clerk, still staring fixedly at Otter, whose aspect appeared to fascinate him as much as that worthy had been fascinated by the eyes of the Water-Dweller. "Have you an appointment, sir?"

"No," answered Leonard. "Tell him that it is in reference to an advertisement which his firm inserted in the 'Times' some months ago."

The clerk started, wondering if this could be the missing Mr. Outram. That much-sought-for individual was understood to have resided in Africa, which is the home of dwarfs and other oddities. Once more he stared at Otter and vanished through a swing door.

Presently he returned. "Mr. Turner will see you, sir, if you and the lady will please to step in. Does this—gentleman—wish to accompany you?"

"No," said Leonard, "he can stop here."

Thereupon the clerk handed Otter a tall stool, on which the dwarf perched himself disconsolately. Then he opened the swing door and ushered Leonard and his wife into Mr. Turner's private room.

"Whom have I the pleasure of addressing?" said a bland, stout gentleman, rising from before a table strewn with papers. "Pray be seated, madam."

Leonard drew from his pocket a copy of the weekly "Times" and handed it to him, saying:

"I understand that you inserted this advertisement."

"Certainly we did," answered the lawyer after glancing at it. "Do you bring me any news of Mr. Leonard Outram?"

"Yes, I do. I am he, and this lady is my wife."

The lawyer bowed politely. "This is most fortunate," he said; "we had almost given up hope—but, of course, some proofs of identity will be required."

"I think that they can be furnished to your satisfaction," answered Leonard briefly. "Meanwhile, for the sake of argument, perhaps you will assume that I am the person whom I state myself to be, and inform me to what this advertisement refers."

"Certainly," answered the lawyer, "there can be no harm in that. Sir Thomas Outram, the late baronet, as you are doubtless aware, had two sons, Thomas and Leonard. Leonard, the second son, as a young man was engaged to, or rather had some love entanglement with, a lady—really I forget her maiden name, but perhaps you can inform me of it——"

"Do you happen to mean Miss Jane Beach?" said Leonard quietly.

At this point Juanna turned in her chair and became extraordinarily, indeed almost fiercely, interested in the conversation.

"Quite so; Beach was the name. You must excuse my forgetfulness. Well, Sir Thomas's affairs fell into confusion, and after their father's death Mr. Leonard Outram, with his elder brother Thomas, emigrated to South Africa. In that same year Miss Jane—eh—Beach married a client of ours, Mr. Cohen, whose father had purchased the estate of Outram from the trustees in bankruptcy."

"Indeed!" said Leonard.

"Shortly afterwards," went on the lawyer, "Mr. Cohen, or rather Sir Jonas Cohen, succeeded to the estate on the death of his father. Two years ago he died leaving all his property, real and personal, to his only child, a daughter named Jane, with reversion to his widow in fee simple. Within a month of his death the child Jane died also, and nine months later her mother, Lady Cohen, *nee* Jane Beach, followed her to the grave."

"Yes," said Leonard in a dull voice, and hiding his face in his hand; "go on, sir."

"Lady Cohen made a somewhat peculiar will. Under the terms of that will she bequeaths the mansion house and estates of Outram, together with most of her personal property, amounting in all to something over a hundred thousand pounds, to her old friend Leonard Outram and the heirs of his body, with reversion to her brother. This will has not been disputed; therefore, if you are Leonard Outram, I may congratulate you upon being once more the owner of your ancestral estate and a considerable fortune in cash."

For a while Leonard was too agitated to speak.

"I will prove to you," he said at last, "that I am this person, that is, I will prove it *prima facie*; afterwards you can satisfy yourself of the truth of my statements by the usual methods." And he proceeded to adduce a variety of evidence as to his identity which need not be set out here. The lawyer listened in silence, taking a note from time to time.

"I think," he said when Leonard had finished, "that, subject to those inquiries of which you yourself have pointed out the necessity in so grave a matter, I may accept it as proved that you are none other than Mr. Leonard Outram, or rather," he added, correcting himself, "if, as I understand, your elder brother Thomas is dead, than Sir Leonard Outram. Indeed you have so entirely convinced me that this is the case, that I have no hesitation in placing in your hands a letter addressed to you by the late Lady Cohen, and deposited with me together with the

343

executed will; though, when you have read it, I shall request you to leave that letter with me for the present.

"By the way, it may interest you to learn," Mr. Turner added, as he went to a safe built into the wall and unlocked its iron door, "that we have been hunting for you for a year or more. We even sent a man to South Africa, and he tracked you to a spot in some mountains somewhere north of Delagoa Bay, where it was reported that you, with your brother Thomas and two friends, were digging for gold. He reached the spot on the night of the ninth of May last year."

"The very day that I left it," broke in Leonard.

"And found the site of your camp and three graves. At first our representative thought that you were all dead, but afterwards he fell in with a native who appears to have deserted from your service, and who told him that one of the brothers was dying when he left the camp, but one was still in good health, though he did not know where he had gone."

"My brother Thomas died on the first of May—this day year," said Leonard.

"After that all trace of you was lost, but I still kept on advertising, for missing people have a wonderful way of turning up to claim fortunes, and you see the result. Here is the letter, Sir Leonard."

Leonard took the document and looked at it, while strange feelings crowded into his mind. This was the first letter that he had ever received from Jane Beach; also it was the last that he ever could receive.

"Before I open this, Mr. Turner," he said, "for my own satisfaction I may as well ask you to compare the handwriting of the address with another specimen of it that chances to be in my possession"; and producing the worn prayer-book from his pocket—Jane's parting gift—he opened it at the fly-leaf, and pointed out the inscription to the lawyer, placing the envelope beside it.

Mr. Turner took a reading-glass and examined first one writing and then the other. "These words appear to have been written by the same hand," he said presently. "Lady Cohen's writing was peculiar, and it is difficult to be mistaken on the point, though I am no expert. To free you from responsibility, with your consent I myself will open this letter," and he slit the envelope at the top with an ivory paper-knife, and, drawing out its contents, he handed them to Leonard. They ran thus:

My Dearest Leonard,—For so I, who am no longer a wife, may call you without shame, seeing that you are in truth the dearest to my heart, whether you be still living, or dead like my husband and my child.

344

The will which I am to sign tomorrow will prove to you if you are yet alive, as I believe to be the case, how deep is my anxiety that that you should re-enter into possession of the ancestral home of which fortune has deprived you. It is with the greatest pleasure that I make you this bequest, and I can do so with a clear conscience, for my late husband has left everything at my absolute disposal—being himself without near relations—in the sad event which has occurred, of the death of his daughter, our only child. May you live long enough to enjoy the lands and fortune which I am enabled thus to return to your family, and may your children and their descendants sit at Outram for many a generation to come!

And now I will talk no more of this matter, for I have an explanation to make and a pardon to ask. It may well be, Leonard, that when your eyes fall upon these lines, you will have forgotten me—most deservedly—and have found some other woman to love you. No, as I set this down I feel that it is not true; you will never forget me altogether, Leonard—your first love—and no other woman will ever be quite the same to you as I have been; or, at least, so I believe in my foolishness and vanity.

You will ask what explanation is possible after the way in which I have treated you, and the outrage that I have done to my own love. Such as it is, however, I offer it to you.

I was driven into this marriage, Leonard, by my late father, who could be very cruel when he chose. To admit this is, as I know, a proof of weakness. So be it, I have never concealed from myself that I am weak. Yet, believe me, I struggled while I could; I wrote to you even, but they intercepted my letter; and I told all the truth to Mr. Cohen, but he was self-willed and passionate, and would take no heed of my pleading. So I married him, Leonard, and was fairly happy with him, for he was kindness itself to me, but from that hour I began to die.

And now more than six years have passed since the night of our parting in the snow, and the end is at hand, for I am really dying. It has pleased God to take my little daughter, and this last shock proved more than I can bear, and so I go to join her and to wait with her till such time as I shall once more see your unforgotten face.

That is all that I have to say, dear Leonard.

Pardon me, and I am selfish enough to add—do not forget me.

Jane

P.S.—Why is it that an affection like ours, which has never borne fruit even, should in the end prove stronger than any other earthly tie? Heaven knows, and Heaven alone, how passionately I loved and love my dead child; and yet, now that my own hour is at hand, it is of *you* that I think the most, you who are neither child nor husband. I suppose that I shall understand ere long, but, O Leonard, Leonard, Leonard, if, as I believe, my nature is immortal, I swear that such love as mine for you, however much it be dishonoured and betrayed, is still the most immortal part of it!—*J.*

Leonard put down the letter on the table, and again he covered his face with his hand to hide his emotion, for his feelings overcame him as a sense of the depth and purity of this dead woman's undying love sank into his heart.

"May I read that letter, Leonard?" asked Juanna in a quiet voice.

"Yes, I suppose so, dear, if you like," he answered, feeling dully that it was better to make a clean breast of the matter at once, and thus to prevent future misunderstandings.

Juanna took the letter and perused it twice, by which time she knew it as well as she did the Lord's Prayer, nor did she ever forget a single word of it. Then she handed it back to the lawyer, saying nothing.

"I understand," said Mr. Turner, breaking in on a silence which he felt to be painful, "that you will be able to produce the necessary proofs of identity within the next few days, and then we can get the will proved in the usual form. Meanwhile, you must want money, which I will take the risk of advancing you," and he wrote a cheque for a hundred pounds and gave it to Leonard.

Half an hour later Leonard and Juanna were alone in a room at their hotel, but as yet scarcely a word had passed between them since they left the lawyer's office.

"Don't you see, Leonard," his wife said almost fiercely, "it is most amusing, you made a mistake. Your brother's dying prophecy was like a Delphic oracle—it could be taken two ways, and, of course, you adopted the wrong interpretation. You left Grave Mountain a day too soon. It was by *Jane Beach's* help that you were to recover Outram, not by mine," and she laughed sadly.

"Don't talk like that, dear," said Leonard in a sad voice; "it pains me."

"How else am I to talk after reading that letter?" she answered, "for what woman can hold her own against a dead rival? Now also I must be indebted to her bounty all my days. Oh! if I had not lost the jewels—if only I had not lost the jewels!"

History does not relate how Leonard dealt with this unexpected and yet natural situation.

A week had passed and Leonard, with Juanna at his side, found himself once more in the great hall at Outram, where, on a bygone night, many years ago, he and his dead brother had sworn their oath. All was the same, for in this hall nothing had been changed—Jane had seen to that. There chained to its stand was the Bible, upon which they had registered their vow; there were the pictures of his ancestors gazing down calmly upon him, as though they cared little for the story of his struggles and of his strange triumph over fortune "by the help of a woman." There was the painted window, with its blazoned coats of arms and its proud mottoes—"*For Heart, Home, and Honour*," and "*Per ardua ad astra*." He had won the heart and home, and he had kept his honour and his oath. He had endured the toils and dangers and the crown of stars was his.

And yet, was Leonard altogether happy as he stood looking on these familiar things? Perhaps not quite, for yonder in the churchyard there was a grave, and within the church a monument in white marble, that was wonderfully like one who had loved him and whom he had loved, though time and trouble had written a strange difference on her face. Also, he had failed: he had kept his oath indeed and fought on till the end was won, but himself he had not won it. What now was his had once belonged to his successful rival, who doubtless little dreamed of the payment that would be exacted from him by the decree of fate.

And was Juanna happy? She knew well that Leonard loved her truly; but oh! it was cruel that she who had shared the struggles should be deprived of her reward—that it should be left to another, who if not false had at least been weak, to give to her husband that which she had striven so hard to win—that which she had won—and lost. And harder still was it that in this ancient place which would henceforth be her home, by day and by night she must feel the presence of the shadow of a woman, a woman sweet and pale, who, as she believed, stood between her and that which she desired above all things—the complete and absolute possession of her husband's heart.

Doubtless she overrated the trouble; men and women do not spend their lives in brooding upon the memories of their first loves—if they did, this would be a melancholy world. But to Juanna it was real enough, and remained so for some years. And if a thing is true to the heart, it avails little that reason should give it the lie.

In short, now in the hour of their full property, Leonard and Juanna were making acquaintance with the fact that fortune never gives with both hands, as the French say, but loves to rob with one while she bestows with the other. To few is it allowed to be completely miserable, to none to be completely happy. Their good luck had been so overwhelming in many ways, that it would have partaken of the unnatural, and might well have excited their fears for the future, had its completeness been unmarred by these drawbacks which, such as they were, probably they learned to disremember as the years passed over them bringing them new trials and added blessings.

Perhaps a peep into the future will tell us the rest of the story of Leonard and Juanna Outram better and more truly than any further chronicling of events.

Ten years or so have gone by and Sir Leonard, now a member of Parliament and the Lord-Lieutenant of his county, comes out of church on the first Sunday in May accompanied by his wife, the stateliest matron in the country-side, and some three or four children, boys and girls together, as healthy as they are handsome. After a glance at a certain grave that lies near to the chancel door, they walk homewards across the budding park in the sweet spring afternoon, till, a hundred yards or more from the door of Outram Hall, they pause at the gates of a dwelling known as "The Kraal," shaped like a beehive, fashioned of straw and sticks, and built by the hands of Otter alone.

Basking in the sunshine in front of this hut sits the dwarf himself, cutting broom-sticks with a knife out of the straightest of a bundle of ash saplings that lie beside him. He is dressed in a queer mixture of native and European costume, but otherwise time has wrought no change in him.

"Greeting, Baas," he says as Leonard comes up. "Is Baas Wallace here yet?"

"No, he will be down in time for dinner. Mind that you are there to wait, Otter."

"I shall not be late, Baas, on this day of all days."

"Otter," cries a little maid, "you should not make brown-sticks on Sunday, it is very wrong."

The dwarf grins by way of answer, then speaks to Leonard in a tongue that none but he can understand.

"What did I tell you many years ago, Baas?" he says. "Did I not tell you that by this way or by that you should win the wealth, and that the great kraal across the water should be yours again, and that the children of strangers should wander there no more? See, it has come true," and he points to the happy group of youngsters. "*Wow!* I, Otter, who am a fool in most things, have proved to be the best of prophets. Yet I will rest content and prophesy no more, lest I should lose my name for wisdom."

A few hours later and dinner is over in the larger hall. All the servants have gone except Otter, who dressed in a white smock stands behind his master's chair. There is no company present save Mr. Wallace, who has just returned from another African expedition, and sits smiling and observant, his eyeglass fixed in his eye as of yore. Juanna is arrayed in full evening dress, however, and a great star ruby blazes upon her breast.

"Why have you got the red stone on tonight, mother?" asks her eldest son Thomas, who with his two sisters has come down to desert.

"Hush, dear," she answers, as Otter advances to that stand on which the Bible is chained, holding a glass filled with port in his hand.

"Deliverer and Shepherdess," he says, speaking in Sisutu, "on this day eleven years gone Baas Tom died out yonder; I, who drink wine but once a year, drink to the memory of Baas Tom, and to our happy meeting with him in the gold House of the Great-Great"; and swallowing the port with a single gulp Otter throws the glass behind him, shattering it on the floor.

"Amen," says Leonard. "Now, love, your toast."

"I drink to the memory of Francisco who died to save me," says Juanna in a low voice.

"Amen," repeats her husband.

For a moment there is silence, for Leonard gives no toast; then the boy Thomas lifts his glass and cries,

"And I drink to Olfan, the king of the People of the Mist, and to Otter, who killed the Snake-god, and whom I love the best of all of them. Mother, may Otter get the spear and the rope and tell us the story of how he dragged you and father up the ice-bridge?"

Black Heart and
White Heart

CHAPTER 1

Philip Hadden and King Cetywayo

At the date of our introduction to him, Philip Hadden was a transport-rider and trader in "the Zulu." Still on the right side of forty, in appearance he was singularly handsome; tall, dark, upright, with keen eyes, short-pointed beard, curling hair and clear-cut features. His life had been varied, and there were passages in it which he did not narrate even to his most intimate friends. He was of gentle birth, however, and it was said that he had received a public school and university education in England. At any rate he could quote the classics with aptitude on occasion, an accomplishment which, coupled with his refined voice and a bearing not altogether common in the wild places of the world, had earned for him among his rough companions the *soubriquet* of "The Prince."

However these things may have been, it is certain that he had emigrated to Natal under a cloud, and equally certain that his relatives at home were content to take no further interest in his fortunes. During the fifteen or sixteen years which he had spent in or about the colony, Hadden followed many trades, and did no good at any of them. A clever man, of agreeable and prepossessing manner, he always found it easy to form friendships and to secure a fresh start in life. But, by degrees, the friends were seized with a vague distrust of him; and, after a period of more or less application, he himself would close the opening that he had made by a sudden disappearance from the locality, leaving behind him a doubtful reputation and some bad debts.

Before the beginning of this story of the most remarkable episodes in his life, Philip Hadden was engaged for several years in transport-riding—that is, in carrying goods on ox wagons from Durban or Maritzburg to various points in the interior. A difficulty such as had more than once confronted him in the course of his career, led to his temporary abandonment of this means of earning a livelihood.

On arriving at the little frontier town of Utrecht in the Transvaal, in charge of two wagon loads of mixed goods consigned to a storekeeper there, it was discovered that out of six cases of brandy five were missing from his wagon. Hadden explained the matter by throwing the blame upon his Kaffir "boys," but the storekeeper, a rough-tongued man, openly called him a thief and refused to pay the freight on any of the load. From words the two men came to blows, knives were drawn, and before anybody could interfere the storekeeper received a nasty wound in his side. That night, without waiting till the matter could be inquired into by the *landdrost* or magistrate, Hadden slipped away, and trekked back into Natal as quickly as his oxen would travel. Feeling that even here he was not safe, he left one of his wagons at Newcastle, loaded up the other with Kaffir goods—such as blankets, calico, and hardware—and crossed into Zululand, where in those days no sheriff's officer would be likely to follow him.

Being well acquainted with the language and customs of the natives, he did good trade with them, and soon found himself possessed of some cash and a small herd of cattle, which he received in exchange for his wares. Meanwhile news reached him that the man whom he had injured still vowed vengeance against him, and was in communication with the authorities in Natal. These reasons making his return to civilisation undesirable for the moment, and further business being impossible until he could receive a fresh supply of trade stuff, Hadden like a wise man turned his thoughts to pleasure. Sending his cattle and wagon over the border to be left in charge of a native headman with whom he was friendly, he went on foot to Ulundi to obtain permission from the king, Cetywayo, to hunt game in his country. Somewhat to his surprise, the *Indunas* or headmen, received him courteously—for Hadden's visit took place within a few months of the outbreak of the Zulu war in 1878, when Cetywayo was already showing unfriendliness to the English traders and others, though why the king did so they knew not.

On the occasion of his first and last interview with Cetywayo, Hadden got a hint of the reason. It happened thus. On the second morning after his arrival at the royal *kraal*, a messenger came to inform him that "the Elephant whose tread shook the earth" had signified that it was his pleasure to see him. Accordingly he was led through the thousands of huts and across the Great Place to the little enclosure where Cetywayo, a royal-looking Zulu seated on a stool, and wearing a *kaross* of leopard skins, was holding an *indaba*, or conference, surrounded by his counsellors. The *Induna* who had conducted him to

354

the august presence went down upon his hands and knees, and, uttering the royal salute of *Bayéte*, crawled forward to announce that the white man was waiting.

"Let him wait," said the king angrily; and, turning, he continued the discussion with his counsellors.

Now, as has been said, Hadden thoroughly understood Zulu; and, when from time to time the king raised his voice, some of the words he spoke reached his ear.

"What!" Cetywayo said, to a wizened and aged man who seemed to be pleading with him earnestly; "am I a dog that these white hyenas should hunt me thus? Is not the land mine, and was it not my father's before me? Are not the people mine to save or to slay? I tell you that I will stamp out these little white men; my *impis* shall eat them up. I have said!"

Again the withered aged man interposed, evidently in the character of a peacemaker. Hadden could not hear his talk, but he rose and pointed towards the sea, while from his expressive gestures and sorrowful mien, he seemed to be prophesying disaster should a certain course of action be followed.

For a while the king listened to him, then he sprang from his seat, his eyes literally ablaze with rage.

"Hearken," he cried to the counsellor; "I have guessed it for long, and now I am sure of it. You are a traitor. You are Sompseu's[1] dog, and the dog of the Natal Government, and I will not keep another man's dog to bite me in my own house. Take him away!"

A slight involuntary murmur rose from the ring of *indunas*, but the old man never flinched, not even when the soldiers, who presently would murder him, came and seized him roughly. For a few seconds, perhaps five, he covered his face with the corner of the *kaross* he wore, then he looked up and spoke to the king in a clear voice.

"O King," he said, "I am a very old man; as a youth I served under Chaka the Lion, and I heard his dying prophecy of the coming of the white man. Then the white men came, and I fought for Dingaan at the battle of the Blood River. They slew Dingaan, and for many years I was the counsellor of Panda, your father. I stood by you, O King, at the battle of the Tugela, when its grey waters were turned to red with the blood of Umbulazi your brother, and of the tens of thousands of his people. Afterwards I became your counsellor, O King, and I was with you when Sompseu set the crown upon your head and you made promises to Sompseu—promises that you have not kept. Now you

1. Sir Theophilus Shepstone's.

are weary of me, and it is well; for I am very old, and doubtless my talk is foolish, as it chances to the old. Yet I think that the prophecy of Chaka, your great-uncle, will come true, and that the white men will prevail against you and that through them you shall find your death. I would that I might have stood in one more battle and fought for you, O King, since fight you will, but the end which you choose is for me the best end. Sleep in peace, O King, and farewell. *Bayéte!*"[2]

For a space there was silence, a silence of expectation while men waited to hear the tyrant reverse his judgment. But it did not please him to be merciful, or the needs of policy outweighed his pity.

"Take him away," he repeated. Then, with a slow smile on his face and one word, "Good-night," upon his lips, supported by the arm of a soldier, the old warrior and statesman shuffled forth to the place of death.

Hadden watched and listened in amazement not unmixed with fear. "If he treats his own servants like this, what will happen to me?" he reflected. "We English must have fallen out of favour since I left Natal. I wonder whether he means to make war on us or what? If so, this isn't my place."

Just then the king, who had been gazing moodily at the ground, chanced to look up. "Bring the stranger here," he said.

Hadden heard him, and coming forward offered Cetywayo his hand in as cool and nonchalant a manner as he could command.

Somewhat to his surprise it was accepted. "At least, White Man," said the king, glancing at his visitor's tall spare form and cleanly cut face, "you are no '*umfagozan*' (low fellow); you are of the blood of chiefs."

"Yes, King," answered Hadden, with a little sigh, "I am of the blood of chiefs."

"What do you want in my country, White Man?"

"Very little, King. I have been trading here, as I daresay you have heard, and have sold all my goods. Now I ask your leave to hunt buffalo, and other big game, for a while before I return to Natal."

"I cannot grant it," answered Cetywayo, "you are a spy sent by Sompseu, or by the Queen's *Induna* in Natal. Get you gone."

"Indeed," said Hadden, with a shrug of his shoulders; "then I hope that Sompseu, or the Queen's *Induna*, or both of them, will pay me when I return to my own country. Meanwhile I will obey you because I must, but I should first like to make you a present."

"What present?" asked the king. "I want no presents. We are rich here, White Man."

"So be it, King. It was nothing worthy of your taking, only a rifle."

2. The royal salute of the Zulus.

"A rifle, White Man? Where is it?"

"Without. I would have brought it, but your servants told me that it is death to come armed before the 'Elephant who shakes the Earth.'"

Cetywayo frowned, for the note of sarcasm did not escape his quick ear.

"Let this white man's offering be brought; I will consider the thing."

Instantly the *Induna* who had accompanied Hadden darted to the gateway, running with his body bent so low that it seemed as though at every step he must fall upon his face. Presently he returned with the weapon in his hand and presented it to the king, holding it so that the muzzle was pointed straight at the royal breast.

"I crave leave to say, O Elephant," remarked Hadden in a drawling voice, "that it might be well to command your servant to lift the mouth of that gun from your heart."

"Why?" asked the king.

"Only because it is loaded, and at full cock, O Elephant, who probably desires to continue to shake the Earth."

At these words the "Elephant" uttered a sharp exclamation, and rolled from his stool in a most unkingly manner, whilst the terrified *Induna*, springing backwards, contrived to touch the trigger of the rifle and discharge a bullet through the exact spot that a second before had been occupied by his monarch's head.

"Let him be taken away," shouted the incensed king from the ground, but long before the words had passed his lips the *Induna*, with a cry that the gun was bewitched, had cast it down and fled at full speed through the gate.

"He has already taken himself away," suggested Hadden, while the audience tittered. "No, King, do not touch it rashly; it is a repeating rifle. Look——" and lifting the Winchester, he fired the four remaining shots in quick succession into the air, striking the top of a tree at which he aimed with every one of them.

"*Wow*, it is wonderful!" said the company in astonishment.

"Has the thing finished?" asked the king.

"For the present it has," answered Hadden. "Look at it."

Cetywayo took the repeater in his hand, and examined it with caution, swinging the muzzle horizontally in an exact line with the stomachs of some of his most eminent *Indunas*, who shrank to this side and that as the barrel was brought to bear on them.

"See what cowards they are, White Man," said the king with indignation; "they fear lest there should be another bullet in this gun."

"Yes," answered Hadden, "they are cowards indeed. I believe that if they were seated on stools they would tumble off them just as it chanced to your Majesty to do just now."

"Do you understand the making of guns, White Man?" asked the king hastily, while the *Indunas* one and all turned their heads, and contemplated the fence behind them.

"No, King, I cannot make guns, but I can mend them."

"If I paid you well, White Man, would you stop here at my *kraal*, and mend guns for me?" asked Cetywayo anxiously.

"It might depend on the pay," answered Hadden; "but for awhile I am tired of work, and wish to rest. If the king gives me the permission to hunt for which I asked, and men to go with me, then when I return perhaps we can bargain on the matter. If not, I will bid the king farewell, and journey to Natal."

"In order to make report of what he has seen and learned here," muttered Cetywayo.

At this moment the talk was interrupted, for the soldiers who had led away the old *Induna* returned at speed, and prostrated themselves before the king.

"Is he dead?" he asked.

"He has travelled the king's bridge," they answered grimly; "he died singing a song of praise of the king."

"Good," said Cetywayo, "that stone shall hurt my feet no more. Go, tell the tale of its casting away to Sompseu and to the Queen's *Induna* in Natal," he added with bitter emphasis.

"*Baba!* Hear our Father speak. Listen to the rumbling of the Elephant," said the *Indunas* taking the point, while one bolder than the rest added: "Soon we will tell them another tale, the white Talking Ones, a red tale, a tale of spears, and the regiments shall sing it in their ears."

At the words an enthusiasm caught hold of the listeners, as the sudden flame catches hold of dry grass. They sprang up, for the most of them were seated on their haunches, and stamping their feet upon the ground in unison, repeated:—

Indaba ibomvu—indaba ye mikonto Lizo dunyiswa nge impi ndhlebeni yaho. (A red tale! A red tale! A tale of spears, And the *impis* shall sing it in their ears.)

One of them, indeed, a great fierce-faced fellow, drew near to Hadden and shaking his fist before his eyes—fortunately being in the royal presence he had no *assegai*—shouted the sentences at him.

The king saw that the fire he had lit was burning too fiercely.

"Silence," he thundered in the deep voice for which he was remarkable, and instantly each man became as if he were turned to stone, only the echoes still answered back: "And the *impis* shall sing it in their ears—in their ears."

"I am growing certain that this is no place for me," thought Hadden; "if that scoundrel had been armed he might have temporarily forgotten himself. Hullo! who's this?"

Just then there appeared through the gate of the fence a splendid specimen of the Zulu race. The man, who was about thirty-five years of age, was arrayed in a full war dress of a captain of the Umcityu regiment. From the circlet of otter skin on his brow rose his crest of plumes, round his middle, arms and knees hung the long fringes of black oxtails, and in one hand he bore a little dancing shield, also black in colour. The other was empty, since he might not appear before the king bearing arms. In countenance the man was handsome, and though just now they betrayed some anxiety, his eyes were genial and honest, and his mouth sensitive. In height he must have measured six foot two inches, yet he did not strike the observer as being tall, perhaps because of his width of chest and the solidity of his limbs, that were in curious contrast to the delicate and almost womanish hands and feet which so often mark the Zulu of noble blood. In short the man was what he seemed to be, a savage gentleman of birth, dignity and courage.

In company with him was another man plainly dressed in a *moocha* and a blanket, whose grizzled hair showed him to be over fifty years of age. His face also was pleasant and even refined, but the eyes were timorous, and the mouth lacked character.

"Who are these?" asked the king.

The two men fell on their knees before him, and bowed till their foreheads touched the ground—the while giving him his *sibonga* or titles of praise.

"Speak," he said impatiently.

"O King," said the young warrior, seating himself Zulu fashion, "I am Nahoon, the son of Zomba, a captain of the Umcityu, and this is my uncle Umgona, the brother of one of my mothers, my father's youngest wife."

Cetywayo frowned. "What do you here away from your regiment, Nahoon?"

"May it please the king, I have leave of absence from the head captains, and I come to ask a boon of the king's bounty."

"Be swift, then, Nahoon."

"It is this, O King," said the captain with some embarrassment: "A while ago the king was pleased to make a *keshla* of me because of certain service that I did out yonder——" and he touched the black ring which he wore in the hair of his head. "Being now a ringed man and a captain, I crave the right of a man at the hands of the king—the right to marry."

"Right? Speak more humbly, son of Zomba; my soldiers and my cattle have no rights."

Nahoon bit his lip, for he had made a serious mistake.

"Pardon, O King. The matter stands thus: My uncle Umgona here has a fair daughter named Nanea, whom I desire to wife, and who desires me to husband. Awaiting the king's leave I am betrothed to her and in earnest of it I have paid to Umgona a *lobola* of fifteen head of cattle, cows and calves together. But Umgona has a powerful neighbour, an old chief named Maputa, the warden of the Crocodile Drift, who doubtless is known to the king, and this chief also seeks Nanea in marriage and harries Umgona, threatening him with many evils if he will not give the girl to him. But Umgona's heart is white towards me, and towards Maputa it is black, therefore together we come to crave this boon of the king."

"It is so; he speaks the truth," said Umgona.

"Cease," answered Cetywayo angrily. "Is this a time that my soldiers should seek wives in marriage, wives to turn their hearts to water? Know that but yesterday for this crime I commanded that twenty girls who had dared without my leave to marry men of the Undi regiment, should be strangled and their bodies laid upon the cross-roads and with them the bodies of their fathers, that all might know their sin and be warned thereby. Ay, Umgona, it is well for you and for your daughter that you sought my word before she was given in marriage to this man. Now this is my award: I refuse your prayer, Nahoon, and since you, Umgona, are troubled with one whom you would not take as son-in-law, the old chief Maputa, I will free you from his importunity. The girl, says Nahoon, is fair—good, I myself will be gracious to her, and she shall be numbered among the wives of the royal house. Within thirty days from now, in the week of the next new moon, let her be delivered to the *Sigodhla*, the royal house of the women, and with her those cattle, the cows and the calves together, that Nahoon has given you, of which I fine him because he has dared to think of marriage without the leave of the king."

CHAPTER 2

The Bee Prophesies

"'A Daniel come to judgment' indeed," reflected Hadden, who had been watching this savage comedy with interest; "our love-sick friend has got more than he bargained for. Well, that comes of appealing to Caesar," and he turned to look at the two suppliants.

The old man, Umgona, merely started, then began to pour out sentences of conventional thanks and praise to the king for his goodness and condescension. Cetywayo listened to his talk in silence, and when he had done answered by reminding him tersely that if Nanea did not appear at the date named, both she and he, her father, would in due course certainly decorate a cross-road in their own immediate neighbourhood.

The captain, Nahoon, afforded a more curious study. As the fatal words crossed the king's lips, his face took an expression of absolute astonishment, which was presently replaced by one of fury—the just fury of a man who suddenly has suffered an unutterable wrong. His whole frame quivered, the veins stood out in knots on his neck and forehead, and his fingers closed convulsively as though they were grasping the handle of a spear. Presently the rage passed away—for as well might a man be wroth with fate as with a Zulu despot—to be succeeded by a look of the most hopeless misery. The proud dark eyes grew dull, the copper-coloured face sank in and turned ashen, the mouth drooped, and down one corner of it there trickled a little line of blood springing from the lip bitten through in the effort to keep silence. Lifting his hand in salute to the king, the great man rose and staggered rather than walked towards the gate.

As he reached it, the voice of Cetywayo commanded him to stop. "Stay," he said, "I have a service for you, Nahoon, that shall drive out of your head these thoughts of wives and marriage. You see this white man here; he is my guest, and would hunt buffalo and big game in the bush country. I put him in your charge; take men with you, and see that he comes to no hurt. So also that you bring him before me within a month, or your life shall answer for it. Let him be here at my royal *kraal* in the first week of the new moon—when Nanea comes—and then I will tell you whether or no I agree with you that she is fair. Go now, my child, and you, White Man, go also; those who are to accompany you shall be with you at the dawn. Farewell, but remember we meet again at the new moon, when we will settle what pay you shall receive as keeper of my guns. Do not fail me, White Man, or I shall send after you, and my messengers are sometimes rough."

"This means that I am a prisoner," thought Hadden, "but it will go hard if I cannot manage to give them the slip somehow. I don't intend to stay in this country if war is declared, to be pounded into *mouti* (medicine), or have my eyes put out, or any little joke of that sort."

****

Ten days had passed, and one evening Hadden and his escort were encamped in a wild stretch of mountainous country lying between the Blood and Unvunyana Rivers, not more than eight miles from that "Place of the Little Hand" which within a few weeks was to become famous throughout the world by its native name of Isandhlwana. For three days they had been tracking the spoor of a small herd of buffalo that still inhabited the district, but as yet they had not come up with them. The Zulu hunters had suggested that they should follow the Unvunyana down towards the sea where game was more plentiful, but this neither Hadden, nor the captain, Nahoon, had been anxious to do, for reasons which each of them kept secret to himself. Hadden's object was to work gradually down to the Buffalo River across which he hoped to effect a retreat into Natal. That of Nahoon was to linger in the neighbourhood of the *kraal* of Umgona, which was situated not very far from their present camping place, in the vague hope that he might find an opportunity of speaking with or at least of seeing Nanea, the girl to whom he was affianced, who within a few weeks must be taken from him, and given over to the king.

A more eerie-looking spot than that where they were encamped Hadden had never seen. Behind them lay a tract of land—half-swamp and half-bush—in which the buffalo were supposed to be hiding. Beyond, in lonely grandeur, rose the mountain of Isandhlwana, while in front was an amphitheatre of the most gloomy forest, ringed round in the distance by sheer-sided hills. Into this forest there ran a river which drained the swamp, placidly enough upon the level. But it was not al-

362

ways level, for within three hundred yards of them it dashed suddenly over a precipice, of no great height but very steep, falling into a boiling rock-bound pool that the light of the sun never seemed to reach.

"What is the name of that forest, Nahoon?" asked Hadden.

"It is named *Emagudu*, The Home of the Dead," the Zulu replied absently, for he was looking towards the *kraal* of Nanea, which was situated at an hour's walk away over the ridge to the right.

"The Home of the Dead! Why?"

"Because the dead live there, those whom we name the *Esemkofu*, the Speechless Ones, and with them other Spirits, the *Amahlosi*, from whom the breath of life has passed away, and who yet live on."

"Indeed," said Hadden, "and have you ever seen these ghosts?"

"Am I mad that I should go to look for them, White Man? Only the dead enter that forest, and it is on the borders of it that our people make offerings to the dead."

Followed by Nahoon, Hadden walked to the edge of the cliff and looked over it. To the left lay the deep and dreadful-looking pool, while close to the bank of it, placed upon a narrow strip of turf between the cliff and the commencement of the forest, was a hut.

"Who lives there?" asked Hadden.

"The great *Isanusi*—she who is named *Inyanga* or Doctoress; she who is named Inyosi (the Bee), because she gathers wisdom from the dead who grow in the forest."

"Do you think that she could gather enough wisdom to tell me whether I am going to kill any buffalo, Nahoon?"

"Mayhap, White Man, but," he added with a little smile, "those who visit the Bee's hive may hear nothing, or they may hear more than they wish for. The words of that Bee have a sting."

"Good; I will see if she can sting me."

"So be it," said Nahoon; and turning, he led the way along the cliff till he reached a native path which zigzagged down its face.

By this path they climbed till they came to the sward at the foot of the descent, and walked up it to the hut which was surrounded by a low fence of reeds, enclosing a small court-yard paved with ant-heap earth beaten hard and polished. In this court-yard sat the Bee, her stool being placed almost at the mouth of the round opening that served as a doorway to the hut. At first all that Hadden could see of her, crouched as she was in the shadow, was a huddled shape wrapped round with a greasy and tattered cat-skin *kaross*, above the edge of which appeared two eyes, fierce and quick as those of a leopard. At her feet smouldered a little fire, and ranged around it in a semi-circle were a number of human skulls, placed in pairs as though they were talking together, whilst other bones, to all appearance also human, were festooned about the hut and the fence of the courtyard.

"I see that the old lady is set up with the usual properties," thought Hadden, but he said nothing.

Nor did the witch-doctoress say anything; she only fixed her beady eyes upon his face. Hadden returned the compliment, staring at her with all his might, till suddenly he became aware that he was vanquished in this curious duel. His brain grew confused, and to his fancy it seemed that the woman before him had shifted shape into the likeness of colossal and horrid spider sitting at the mouth of her trap, and that these bones were the relics of her victims.

"Why do you not speak, White Man?" she said at last in a slow clear voice. "Well, there is no need, since I can read your thoughts. You are thinking that I who am called the Bee should be better named the Spider. Have no fear; I did not kill these men. What would it profit me when the dead are so many? I suck the souls of men, not their bodies, White Man. It is their living hearts I love to look on, for therein I read much and thereby I grow wise. Now what would you of the Bee, White Man, the Bee that labours in this Garden of Death, and—what brings *you* here, son of Zomba? Why are you not with the Umcityu now that they doctor themselves for the great war—the last war—the war of the white and the black—or if you have no stomach for fighting, why are you not at the side of Nanea the tall, Nanea the fair?"

Nahoon made no answer, but Hadden said:—

"A small thing, mother. I would know if I shall prosper in my hunting."

"In your hunting, White Man; what hunting? The hunting of game, of money, or of women? Well, one of them, for a-hunting you must ever be; that is your nature, to hunt and be hunted. Tell me now, how goes the wound of that trader who tasted of your steel yonder in the town of the Maboon (Boers)? No need to answer, White Man, but what fee, Chief, for the poor witch-doctoress whose skill you seek," she added in a whining voice. "Surely you would not that an old woman should work without a fee?"

"I have none to offer you, mother, so I will be going," said Hadden, who began to feel himself satisfied with this display of the Bee's powers of observation and thought-reading.

"Nay," she answered with an unpleasant laugh, "would you ask a question, and not wait for the answer? I will take no fee from you at present, White Man; you shall pay me later on when we meet again," and once more she laughed. "Let me look in your face, let me look in your face," she continued, rising and standing before him.

Then of a sudden Hadden felt something cold at the back of his neck, and the next instant the Bee had sprung from him, holding between her thumb and finger a curl of dark hair which she had cut from his head. The action was so instantaneous that he had neither time to avoid nor to resent it, but stood still staring at her stupidly.

"That is all I need," she cried, "for like my heart my magic is white. Stay—son of Zomba, give me also of your hair, for those who visit the Bee must listen to her humming."

Nahoon obeyed, cutting a little lock from his head with the sharp edge of his *assegai*, though it was very evident that he did this not because he wished to do so, but because he feared to refuse.

Then the Bee slipped back her *kaross*, and stood bending over the fire before them, into which she threw herbs taken from a pouch that was bound about her middle. She was still a finely-shaped woman, and she wore none of the abominations which Hadden had been accustomed to see upon the persons of witch-doctoresses. About her neck, however, was a curious ornament, a small live snake, red and grey in hue, which her visitors recognised as one of the most deadly to be found in that part of the country. It is not unusual for Bantu witch-doctors thus to decorate themselves with snakes, though whether or not their fangs have first been extracted no one seems to know.

Presently the herbs began to smoulder, and the smoke of them rose up in a thin, straight stream, that, striking upon the face of the Bee, clung about her head enveloping it as though with a strange blue veil. Then of a sudden she stretched out her hands, and let fall the two locks of hair upon the burning herbs, where they writhed themselves to ashes like things alive. Next she opened her mouth, and began to draw the fumes of the hair and herbs into her lungs in great gulps; while the snake, feeling the influence of the medicine, hissed and, uncoiling itself from about her neck, crept upwards and took refuge among the black *saccaboola* feathers of her head-dress.

Soon the vapours began to do their work; she swayed to and fro muttering, then sank back against the hut, upon the straw of which her head rested. Now the Bee's face was turned upwards towards the light, and it was ghastly to behold, for it had become blue in colour, and the open eyes were sunken like the eyes of one dead, whilst above her forehead the red snake wavered and hissed, reminding Hadden of the Uraeus crest on the brow of statues of Egyptian kings. For ten seconds or more she remained thus, then she spoke in a hollow and unnatural voice:—

"O Black Heart and body that is white and beautiful, I look into your heart, and it is black as blood, and it shall be black with blood. Beautiful white body with black heart, you shall find your game and hunt it, and it shall lead you into the House of the Homeless, into the Home of the Dead, and it shall be shaped as a bull, it shall be shaped as a tiger, it shall be shaped as a woman whom kings and waters cannot harm. Beautiful white body and black heart, you shall be paid your wages, money for money, and blow for blow. Think of my word when the spotted cat purrs above your breast; think of it when the battle roars about you; think of it when you grasp your great reward, and for the last time stand face to face with the ghost of the dead in the Home of the Dead.

"O White Heart and black body, I look into your heart and it is white as milk, and the milk of innocence shall save it. Fool, why do you strike that blow? Let him be who is loved of the tiger, and whose love is as the love of a tiger. Ah! what face is that in the battle? Follow it, follow it, O swift of foot; but follow warily, for the tongue that has lied will never plead for mercy, and the hand that can betray is strong in war. White Heart, what is death? In death life lives, and among the dead you shall find the life you lost, for there awaits you she whom kings and waters cannot harm."

As the Bee spoke, by degrees her voice sank lower and lower till it was almost inaudible. Then it ceased altogether and she seemed to pass from trance to sleep. Hadden, who had been listening to her with an amused and cynical smile, now laughed aloud.

"Why do you laugh, White Man?" asked Nahoon angrily.

"I laugh at my own folly in wasting time listening to the nonsense of that lying fraud."

"It is no nonsense, White Man."

"Indeed? Then will you tell me what it means?"

"I cannot tell you what it means yet, but her words have to do with a woman and a leopard, and with your fate and my fate."

Hadden shrugged his shoulders, not thinking the matter worth further argument, and at that moment the Bee woke up shivering, drew the red snake from her head-dress and coiling it about her throat wrapped herself again in the greasy *kaross*.

"Are you satisfied with my wisdom, *Inkoos*?" she asked of Hadden.

"I am satisfied that you are one of the cleverest cheats in Zululand, mother," he answered coolly. "Now, what is there to pay?"

The Bee took no offence at this rude speech, though for a second or two the look in her eyes grew strangely like that which they had seen in those of the snake when the fumes of the fire made it angry.

"If the white lord says I am a cheat, it must be so," she answered, "for he of all men should be able to discern a cheat. I have said that I ask no fee;—yes, give me a little tobacco from your pouch."

Hadden opened the bag of antelope hide and drawing some tobacco from it, gave it to her. In taking it she clasped his hand and examined the gold ring that was upon the third finger, a ring fashioned like a snake with two little rubies set in the head to represent the eyes.

"I wear a snake about my neck, and you wear one upon your hand, *Inkoos*. I should like to have this ring to wear upon my hand, so that the snake about my neck may be less lonely there."

"Then I am afraid you will have to wait till I am dead," said Hadden.

"Yes, yes," she answered in a pleased voice, "it is a good word. I will wait till you are dead and then I will take the ring, and none can say that I have stolen it, for Nahoon there will bear me witness that you gave me permission to do so."

For the first time Hadden started, since there was something about the Bee's tone that jarred upon him. Had she addressed him in her professional manner, he would have thought nothing of it; but in her cupidity she had become natural, and it was evident that she spoke from conviction, believing her own words.

She saw him start, and instantly changed her note.

"Let the white lord forgive the jest of a poor old witch-doctoress," she said in a whining voice. "I have so much to do with Death that his name leaps to my lips," and she glanced first at the circle of skulls about her, then towards the waterfall that fed the gloomy pool upon whose banks her hut was placed.

"Look," she said simply.

Following the line of her outstretched hand Hadden's eyes fell upon two withered mimosa trees which grew over the fall almost at right angles to its rocky edge. These trees were joined together by a rude platform made of logs of wood lashed down with *riems* of hide. Upon this platform stood three figures; notwithstanding the distance and the spray of the fall, he could see that they were those of two men and a girl, for their shapes stood out distinctly against the fiery red of the sunset sky. One instant there were three, the next there were two—for the girl had gone, and something dark rushing down the

367

face of the fall, struck the surface of the pool with a heavy thud, while a faint and piteous cry broke upon his ear.

"What is the meaning of that?" he asked, horrified and amazed.

"Nothing," answered the Bee with a laugh. "Do you not know, then, that this is the place where faithless women, or girls who have loved without the leave of the king, are brought to meet their death, and with them their accomplices. Oh! they die here thus each day, and I watch them die and keep the count of the number of them," and drawing a tally-stick from the thatch of the hut, she took a knife and added a notch to the many that appeared upon it, looking at Nahoon the while with a half-questioning, half-warning gaze.

"Yes, yes, it is a place of death," she muttered. "Up yonder the quick die day by day and down there"—and she pointed along the course of the river beyond the pool to where the forest began some two hundred yards from her hut—"the ghosts of them have their home. Listen!"

As she spoke, a sound reached their ears that seemed to swell from the dim skirts of the forests, a peculiar and unholy sound which it is impossible to define more accurately than by saying that it seemed beastlike, and almost inarticulate.

"Listen," repeated the Bee, "they are merry yonder."

"Who?" asked Hadden; "the baboons?"

"No, *Inkoos*, the *Amatongo*—the ghosts that welcome her who has just become of their number."

"Ghosts," said Hadden roughly, for he was angry at his own tremors, "I should like to see those ghosts. Do you think that I have never heard a troop of monkeys in the bush before, mother? Come, Nahoon, let us be going while there is light to climb the cliff. Farewell."

"Farewell *Inkoos*, and doubt not that your wish will be fulfilled. Go in peace *Inkoos*—to sleep in peace."

CHAPTER 3

The End of the Hunt

The prayer of the Bee notwithstanding, Philip Hadden slept ill that night. He felt in the best of health, and his conscience was not troubling him more than usual, but rest he could not. Whenever he closed his eyes, his mind conjured up a picture of the grim witch-doctoress, so strangely named the Bee, and the sound of her evil-omened words as he had heard them that afternoon. He was neither a superstitious nor a timid man, and any supernatural beliefs that might linger in his mind were, to say the least of it, dormant. But do what he might, he could not shake off a certain eerie sensation of fear, lest there should be some grains of truth in the prophesy-ings of this hag. What if it were a fact that he was near his death, and that the heart which beat so strongly in his breast must soon be still for ever—no, he would not think of it. This gloomy place, and the dreadful sight which he saw that day, had upset his nerves. The domestic customs of these Zulus were not pleasant, and for his part he was determined to be clear of them so soon as he was able to escape the country.

In fact, if he could in any way manage it, it was his intention to make a dash for the border on the following night. To do this with a good prospect of success, however, it was necessary that he should kill a buffalo, or some other head of game. Then, as he knew well, the hunters with him would feast upon meat until they could scarcely stir, and that would be his opportunity. Nahoon, however, might not suc-cumb to this temptation; therefore he must trust to luck to be rid of him. If it came to the worst, he could put a bullet through him, which he considered he would be justified in doing, seeing that in reality the man was his jailor. Should this necessity arise, he felt indeed that he could face it without undue compunction, for in truth he disliked Nahoon; at times he even hated him. Their natures were antagonistic, and he knew that the great Zulu distrusted and looked down upon him, and to be looked down upon by a savage "nigger" was more than his pride could stomach.

At the first break of dawn Hadden rose and roused his escort, who were still stretched in sleep around the dying fire, each man wrapped in his *kaross* or blanket. Nahoon stood up and shook himself, looking gigantic in the shadows of the morning.

"What is your will, *Umlungu* (white man), that you are up before the sun?"

"My will, *Muntumpofu* (yellow man), is to hunt buffalo," answered Hadden coolly. It irritated him that this savage should give him no title of any sort.

"Your pardon," said the Zulu reading his thoughts, "but I cannot call you *Inkoos* because you are not my chief, or any man's; still if the title 'white man' offends you, we will give you a name."

"As you wish," answered Hadden briefly.

Accordingly they gave him a name, *Inhlizin-mgama*, by which he was known among them thereafter, but Hadden was not best pleased when he found that the meaning of those soft-sounding syllables was "Black Heart." That was how the *inyanga* had addressed him—only she used different words.

An hour later, and they were in the swampy bush country that lay behind the encampment searching for their game. Within a very little while Nahoon held up his hand, then pointed to the ground. Hadden looked; there, pressed deep in the marshy soil, and to all appearance not ten minutes old, was the spoor of a small herd of buffalo.

"I knew that we should find game today," whispered Nahoon, "because the Bee said so."

"Curse the Bee," answered Hadden below his breath. "Come on."

For a quarter of an hour or more they followed the spoor through thick reeds, till suddenly Nahoon whistled very softly and touched Hadden's arm. He looked up, and there, about two hundred yards away, feeding on some higher ground among a patch if mimosa trees, were the buffaloes—six of them—an old bull with a splendid head, three cows, a heifer and a calf about four months old. Neither the wind nor the nature of the *veldt* were favourable for them to stalk the game from their present position, so they made a detour of half a mile and very carefully crept towards them up the wind, slipping from trunk to trunk of the mimosas and when these failed them, crawling on their stomachs under cover of the tall *tambuti* grass. At last they were within forty yards, and a further advance seemed impracticable; for although he could not smell them, it was evident from his movements that the old bull heard some unusual sound and was growing suspicious. Nearest to Hadden, who alone of the party had a rifle, stood the heifer broadside on—a beautiful shot. Remembering that she would make the best beef, he lifted his Martini, and aiming at her immediately behind the shoulder, gently squeezed the trigger. The rifle exploded, and the heifer fell dead, shot through the heart. Strangely enough the other buffaloes did not at once run away. On the contrary, they seemed puzzled to account for the sudden noise; and, not being able to wind anything, lifted their heads and stared round them.

The pause gave Hadden space to get in a fresh cartridge and to aim again, this time at the old bull. The bullet struck him somewhere in the neck or shoulder, for he came to his knees, but in another second was up and having caught sight of the cloud of smoke he charged straight at it. Because of this smoke, or for some other reason, Hadden did not see him coming, and in consequence would most certainly have been trampled or gored, had not Nahoon sprung forward, at the imminent risk of his own life, and dragged him down behind an antheap. A moment more and the great beast had thundered by, taking no further notice of them.

"Forward," said Hadden, and leaving most of the men to cut up the heifer and carry the best of her meat to camp, they started on the blood spoor.

For some hours they followed the bull, till at last they lost the trail on a patch of stony ground thickly covered with bush, and exhausted by the heat, sat down to rest and to eat some *biltong* or sun-dried flesh which they had with them. They finished their meal, and were preparing to return to the camp, when one of the four Zulus who were with them went to drink at a little stream that ran at a distance of not more than ten paces away. Half a minute later they heard a hideous grunting noise and a splashing of water, and saw the Zulu fly into the air. All the while that they were eating, the wounded buffalo had been lying in wait for them under a thick bush on the banks of the streamlet, knowing—cunning brute that he was—that sooner or later his turn would come. With a shout of consternation they rushed forward to see the bull vanish over the rise before Hadden could get a chance of firing at him, and to find their companion dying, for the great horn had pierced his lung.

"It is not a buffalo, it is a devil," the poor fellow gasped, and expired.

"Devil or not, I mean to kill it," exclaimed Hadden. So leaving the others to carry the body of their comrade to camp, he started on accompanied by Nahoon only. Now the ground was more open and the chase easier, for they sighted their quarry frequently, though they could not come near enough to fire. Presently they travelled down a steep cliff.

"Do you know where we are?" asked Nahoon, pointing to a belt of forest opposite. "That is *Emagudu*, the Home of the Dead—and look, the bull heads thither."

Hadden glanced round him. It was true; yonder to the left were the Fall, the Pool of Doom, and the hut of the Bee.

"Very well," he answered; "then we must head for it too."

Nahoon halted. "Surely you would not enter there," he exclaimed.

"Surely I will," replied Hadden, "but there is no need for you to do so if you are afraid."

"I am afraid—of ghosts," said the Zulu, "but I will come."

So they crossed the strip of turf, and entered the haunted wood. It was a gloomy place indeed; the great wide-topped trees grew thick there shutting out the sight of the sky; moreover, the air in it which no breeze stirred, was heavy with the exhalations of rotting foliage. There seemed to be no life here and no sound—only now and again a loathsome spotted snake would uncoil itself and glide away, and now and again a heavy rotten bough fell with a crash.

Hadden was too intent upon the buffalo, however, to be much impressed by his surroundings. He only remarked that the light would be bad for shooting, and went on.

They must have penetrated a mile or more into the forest when the sudden increase of blood upon the spoor told them that the bull's wound was proving fatal to him.

"Run now," said Hadden cheerfully.

"Nay, *hamba gachle*—go softly—" answered Nahoon, "the devil is dying, but he will try to play us another trick before he dies." And he went on peering ahead of him cautiously.

"It is all right here, anyway," said Hadden, pointing to the spoor that ran straight forward printed deep in the marshy ground.

Nahoon did not answer, but stared steadily at the trunks of two trees a few paces in front of them and to their right. "Look," he whispered.

Hadden did so, and at length made out the outline of something brown that was crouched behind the trees.

"He is dead," he exclaimed.

"No," answered Nahoon, "he has come back on his own path and is waiting for us. He knows that we are following his spoor. Now if you stand there, I think that you can shoot him through the back between the tree trunks."

Hadden knelt down, and aiming very carefully at a point just below the bull's spine, he fired. There was an awful bellow, and the next instant the brute was up and at them. Nahoon flung his broad spear, which sank deep into its chest, then they fled this way and that. The buffalo stood still for a moment, its fore legs straddled wide and its head down, looking first after the one and then the other, till of a sudden it uttered a low moaning sound and rolled over dead, smashing Nahoon's *assegai* to fragments as it fell.

"There! he's finished," said Hadden, "and I believe it was your *assegai* that killed him. Hullo! what's that noise?"

Nahoon listened. In several quarters of the forest, but from how far away it was impossible to tell, there rose a curious sound, as of people calling to each other in fear but in no articulate language. Nahoon shivered.

"It is the *Esemkofu*," he said, "the ghosts who have no tongue, and who can only wail like infants. Let us be going; this place is bad for mortals."

"And worse for buffaloes," said Hadden, giving the dead bull a kick, "but I suppose that we must leave him here for your friends, the *Esemkofu*, as we have got meat enough, and can't carry his head."

So they started back towards the open country. As they threaded their way slowly through the tree trunks, a new idea came into Hadden's head. Once out of this forest, he was within an hour's run of the Zulu border, and once over the Zulu border, he would feel a happier man than he did at that moment. As has been said, he had intended to attempt to escape in the darkness, but the plan was risky. All the Zulus might not over-eat themselves and go to sleep, especially after the death of their comrade; Nahoon, who watched him day and night, certainly would not. This was his opportunity—there remained the question of Nahoon.

Well, if it came to the worst, Nahoon must die: it would be easy—he had a loaded rifle, and now that his *assegai* was gone, Nahoon had only a *kerry*. He did not wish to kill the man, though it was clear to him, seeing that his own safety was at stake, that he would be amply justified in so doing. Why should he not put it to him—and then be guided by circumstances?

Nahoon was walking across a little open space about ten spaces ahead of him where Hadden could see him very well, whilst he himself was under the shadow of a large tree with low horizontal branches running out from the trunk.

"Nahoon," he said.

The Zulu turned round, and took a step towards him.

"No, do not move, I pray. Stand where you are, or I shall be obliged to shoot you. Listen now: do not be afraid for I shall not fire without warning. I am your prisoner, and you are charged to take me back to the king to be his servant. But I believe that a war is going to break out between your people and mine; and this being so, you will understand that I do not wish to go to Cetywayo's *kraal*, because I should either come to a violent death there, or my own brothers will believe that I am a traitor and treat me accordingly. The Zulu border is not much more than an hour's journey away—let us say an hour and a half's: I mean to be across it before the moon is up. Now, Nahoon, will you lose me in the forest and give me this hour and a half's start—or will you stop here with that ghost people of whom you talk? Do you understand? No, please do not move."

"I understand you," answered the Zulu, in a perfectly composed voice, "and I think that was a good name which we gave you this morning, though, Black Heart, there is some justice in your words and more wisdom. Your opportunity is good, and one which a man named as you are should not let fall."

"I am glad to find that you take this view of the matter, Nahoon. And now will you be so kind as to lose me, and to promise not to look for me till the moon is up?"

"What do you mean, Black Heart?"

"What I say. Come, I have no time to spare."

"You are a strange man," said the Zulu reflectively. "You heard the king's order to me: would you have me disobey the order of the king?"

"Certainly, I would. You have no reason to love Cetywayo, and it does not matter to you whether or no I return to his *kraal* to mend guns there. If you think that he will be angry because I am missing, you had better cross the border also; we can go together."

"And leave my father and all my brethren to his vengeance? Black Heart, you do not understand. How can you, being so named? I am a soldier, and the king's word is the king's word. I hoped to have died fighting, but I am the bird in your noose. Come, shoot, or you will not reach the border before moonrise," and he opened his arms and smiled.

"If it must be, so let it be. Farewell, Nahoon, at least you are a brave man, but every one of us must cherish his own life," answered Hadden calmly.

Then with much deliberation he raised his rifle and covered the Zulu's breast.

Already—whilst his victim stood there still smiling, although a twitching of his lips betrayed the natural terrors that no bravery can banish— already his finger was contracting on the trigger, when of a sudden, as instantly as though he had been struck by lightning, Hadden went down backwards, and behold! there stood upon him a great spotted beast that waved its long tail to and fro and glared down into his eyes.

It was a leopard—a tiger as they call it in Africa—which, crouched upon a bough of the tree above, had been unable to resist the temptation of satisfying its savage appetite on the man below. For a second or two there was silence, broken only by the purring, or rather the snoring sound made by the leopard. In those seconds, strangely enough, there sprang up before Hadden's mental vision a picture of the *inyanga* called *Inyosi* or the Bee, her death-like head resting against the thatch of the hut, and her death-like lips muttering "think of my word when the great cat purrs above your face."

Then the brute put out its strength. The claws of one paw it drove deep into the muscles of his left thigh, while with another it scratched at his breast, tearing the clothes from it and furrowing the flesh beneath. The sight of the white skin seemed to madden it, and in its fierce desire for blood it drooped its square muzzle and buried its fangs in its victim's shoulder. Next moment there was a sound of running feet and of a club falling heavily. Up reared the leopard with an angry snarl, up till it stood as high as the attacking Zulu. At him it came, striking out savagely and tearing the black man as it had torn the white. Again the *kerry* fell full on its jaws, and down it went backwards. Before it could rise again, or rather as it was in the act of rising, the heavy knob-stick struck it once more, and with fearful force, this time as it chanced, full on the nape of the neck, and paralysing the brute. It writhed and bit and twisted, throwing up the earth and leaves, while blow after blow was rained upon it, till at length with a convulsive struggle and a stifled roar it lay still—the brains oozing from its shattered skull.

Hadden sat up, the blood running from his wounds.

"You have saved my life, Nahoon," he said faintly, "and I thank you."

"Do not thank me, Black Heart," answered the Zulu, "it was the king's word that I should keep you safely. Still this tiger has been hardly dealt with, for certainly *he* has saved *my* life," and lifting the Martini he unloaded the rifle.

At this juncture Hadden swooned away.

Twenty-four hours had gone by when, after what seemed to him to be but a little time of troubled and dreamful sleep, through which he could hear voices without understanding what they said, and feel himself borne he knew not whither, Hadden awoke to find himself lying upon a *kaross* in a large and beautifully clean Kaffir hut with a bundle of furs for a pillow. There was a bowl of milk at his side and tortured as he was by thirst, he tried to stretch out his arm to lift it to his lips, only to find to his astonishment that his hand fell back to his side like that of a dead man. Looking round the hut impatiently, he found that there was nobody in it to assist him, so he did the only thing which remained for him to do—he lay still. He did not fall asleep, but his eyes closed, and a kind of gentle torpor crept over him, half obscuring his recovered senses. Presently he heard a soft voice speaking; it seemed far away, but he could clearly distinguish the words.

"Black Heart still sleeps," the voice said, "but there is colour in his face; I think that he will wake soon, and find his thoughts again."

"Have no fear, Nanea, he will surely wake, his hurts are not dangerous," answered another voice, that of Nahoon. "He fell heavily with the weight of the tiger on top of him, and that is why his senses have been shaken for so long. He went near to death, but certainly he will not die."

"It would have been a pity if he had died," answered the soft voice, "he is so beautiful; never have I seen a white man who was so beautiful."

"I did not think him beautiful when he stood with his rifle pointed at my heart," answered Nahoon sulkily.

"Well, there is this to be said," she replied, "he wished to escape from Cetywayo, and that is not to be wondered at," and she sighed. "Moreover he asked you to come with him, and it might have been well if you had done so, that is, if you would have taken me with you!"

"How could I have done it, girl?" he asked angrily. "Would you have me set at nothing the order of the king?"

"The king!" she replied raising her voice. "What do you owe to this king? You have served him faithfully, and your reward is that within a few days he will take me from you—me, who should have been your wife, and I must—I must——" And she began to weep softly, adding between her sobs, "if you loved me truly, you would think more of me and of yourself, and less of the Black One and his orders. Oh! let us fly, Nahoon, let us fly to Natal before this spear pierces me."

"Weep not, Nanea," he said; "why do you tear my heart in two between my duty and my love? You know that I am a soldier, and that I must walk the path whereon the king has set my feet. Soon I think I shall be dead, for I seek death, and then it will matter nothing."

"Nothing to you, Nahoon, who are at peace, but to me? Yet, you are right, and I know it, therefore forgive me, who am no warrior, but a woman who must also obey—the will of the king." And she cast her arms about his neck, sobbing her fill upon his breast.

CHAPTER 4

Nanea

Presently, muttering something that the listener could not catch, Nahoon left Nanea, and crept out of the hut by its bee-hole entrance. Then Hadden opened his eyes and looked round him. The sun was sinking and a ray of its red light streaming through the little opening filled the place with a soft and crimson glow. In the centre of the hut—supporting it—stood a thorn-wood roof-tree coloured black by the smoke of the fire; and against this, the rich light falling full upon her, leaned the girl Nanea—a very picture of gentle despair.

As is occasionally the case among Zulu women, she was beautiful—so beautiful that the sight of her went straight to the white man's heart, for a moment causing the breath to catch in his throat. Her dress was very simple. On her shoulders, hanging open in front, lay a mantle of soft white stuff edged with blue beads, about her middle was a buck-skin *moocha*, also embroidered with blue beads, while round her forehead and left knee were strips of grey fur, and on her right wrist a shining bangle of copper. Her naked bronze-hued figure was tall and perfect in its proportions; while her face had little in common with that of the ordinary native girl, showing as it did strong traces of the ancestral Arabian or Semitic blood. It was oval in shape, with delicate aquiline features, arched eyebrows, a full mouth, that drooped a little at the corners, tiny ears, behind which the wavy coal-black hair hung down to the shoulders, and the very loveliest pair of dark and liquid eyes that it is possible to imagine.

For a minute or more Nanea stood thus, her sweet face bathed in the sunbeam, while Hadden feasted his eyes upon its beauty. Then sighing heavily, she turned, and seeing that he was awake, started, drew her mantle over her breast and came, or rather glided, towards him.

"The chief is awake," she said in her soft Zulu accents. "Does he need aught?"

378

"Yes, Lady," he answered; "I need to drink, but alas! I am too weak."

She knelt down beside him, and supporting him with her left arm, with her right held the gourd to his lips.

How it came about Hadden never knew, but before that draught was finished a change passed over him. Whether it was the savage girl's touch, or her strange and fawn-like loveliness, or the tender pity in her eyes, matters not—the issue was the same. She struck some cord in his turbulent uncurbed nature, and of a sudden it was filled full with passion for her—a passion which if, not elevated, at least was real. He did not for a moment mistake the significance of the flood of feeling that surged through his veins. Hadden never shirked facts.

"By Heaven!" he said to himself, "I have fallen in love with a black beauty at first sight—more in love than I have ever been before. It's awkward, but there will be compensations. So much the worse for Nahoon, or for Cetywayo, or for both of them. After all, I can always get rid of her if she becomes a nuisance."

Then, in a fit of renewed weakness, brought about by the turmoil of his blood, he lay back upon the pillow of furs, watching Nanea's face while with a native salve of pounded leaves she busied herself dressing the wounds that the leopard had made.

It almost seemed as though something of what was passing in his mind communicated itself to that of the girl. At least, her hand shook a little at her task, and getting done with it as quickly as she could, she rose from her knees with a courteous "It is finished, *Inkoos*," and once more took up her position by the roof-tree.

"I thank you, Lady," he said; "your hand is kind."

"You must not call me lady, *Inkoos*," she answered, "I am no chieftainess, but only the daughter of a headman, Umgona."

"And named Nanea," he said. "Nay, do not be surprised, I have heard of you. Well, Nanea, perhaps you will soon become a chieftainess—up at the king's *kraal* yonder."

"Alas! and alas!" she said, covering her face with her hands.

"Do not grieve, Nanea, a hedge is never so tall and thick but that it cannot be climbed or crept through."

She let fall her hands and looked at him eagerly, but he did not pursue the subject.

"Tell me, how did I come here, Nanea?"

"Nahoon and his companions carried you, *Inkoos*."

"Indeed, I begin to be thankful to the leopard that struck me down. Well, Nahoon is a brave man, and he has done me a great service. I trust that I may be able to repay it—to you, Nanea."

****

This was the first meeting of Nanea and Hadden; but, although she did not seek them, the necessities of his sickness and of the situation brought about many another. Never for a moment did the white man waver in his determination to get into his keeping the native girl who had captivated him, and to attain his end he brought to bear all his powers and charm to detach her from Nahoon, and win her affections for himself. He was no rough wooer, however, but proceeded warily, weaving her about with a web of flattery and attention that must, he thought, produce the desired effect upon her mind. Without a doubt, indeed, it would have done so—for she was but a woman, and an untutored one—had it not been for a simple fact which dominated her whole nature. She loved Nahoon, and there was no room in her heart for any other man, white or black. To Hadden she was courteous and kindly but no more, nor did she appear to notice any of the subtle advances by which he attempted to win a foothold in her heart. For a while this puzzled him, but he remembered that the Zulu women do not usually permit themselves to show feeling towards an undeclared suitor. Therefore it became necessary that he should speak out.

His mind once made up, he had not to wait long for an opportunity. He was now quite recovered from his hurts, and accustomed to walk in the neighbourhood of the *kraal*. About two hundred yards from Umgona's huts rose a spring, and thither it was Nanea's habit to resort in the evening to bring back drinking-water for the use of her father's household. The path between this spring and the *kraal* ran through a patch of bush, where on a certain afternoon towards sundown Hadden took his seat under a tree, having first seen Nanea go down to the little stream as was her custom. A quarter of an hour later she reappeared carrying a large gourd upon her head. She wore no garment now except her *moocha*, for she had but one mantle and was afraid lest the water should splash it. He watched her advancing along the path, her hands resting on her hips, her splendid naked figure outlined against the westering sun, and wondered what excuse he could make to talk with her. As it chanced fortune favoured him, for when she was near him a snake glided across the path in front of the girl's feet, causing her to spring backwards in alarm and overset the gourd of water. He came forward, and picked it up.

"Wait here," he said laughing; "I will bring it to you full."

"Nay, *Inkoos*," she remonstrated, "that is a woman's work."

"Among my people," he said, "the men love to work for the women," and he started for the spring, leaving her wondering.

Before he reached her again, he regretted his gallantry, for it was necessary to carry the handleless gourd upon his shoulder, and the contents of it spilling over the edge soaked him. Of this, however, he said nothing to Nanea.

"There is your water, Nanea, shall I carry it for you to the *kraal*?"

"Nay, *Inkoos*, I thank you, but give it to me, you are weary with its weight."

"Stay awhile, and I will accompany you. Ah! Nanea, I am still weak, and had it not been for you I think that I should be dead."

"It was Nahoon who saved you—not I, *Inkoos*."

"Nahoon saved my body, but you, Nanea, you alone can save my heart."

"You talk darkly, *Inkoos*."

"Then I must make my meaning clear, Nanea. I love you."

She opened her brown eyes wide.

"You, a white lord, love me, a Zulu girl? How can that be?"

"I do not know, Nanea, but it is so, and were you not blind you would have seen it. I love you, and I wish to take you to wife."

"Nay, *Inkoos*, it is impossible. I am already betrothed."

"Ay," he answered, "betrothed to the king."

"No, betrothed to Nahoon."

"But it is the king who will take you within a week; is it not so? And would you not rather that I should take you than the king?"

"It seems to be so, *Inkoos*, and I would rather go with you than with the king, but most of all I desire to marry Nahoon. It may be that I shall not be able to marry him, but if that is so, at least I will never become one of the king's women."

"How will you prevent it, Nanea?"

"There are waters in which a maid may drown, and trees upon which she can hang," she answered with a quick setting of the mouth.

"That were a pity, Nanea, you are too fair to die."

"Fair or foul, yet I die, *Inkoos*."

"No, no, come with me—I will find a way—and be my wife," and he put her arm about her waist, and strove to draw her to him.

Without any violence of movement, and with the most perfect dignity, the girl disengaged herself from his embrace.

"You have honoured me, and I thank you, *Inkoos*," she said quietly, "but you do not understand. I am the wife of Nahoon—I belong to Nahoon; therefore, I cannot look on any other man while Nahoon lives. It is not our custom, *Inkoos*, for we are not as the white women, but ignorant and simple, and when we vow ourselves to a man, we abide by that vow till death."

"Indeed," said Hadden; "and so now you go to tell Nahoon that I have offered to make you my wife."

"No, *Inkoos*, why should I tell Nahoon your secrets? I have said 'nay' to you, not 'yea,' therefore he has no right to know," and she stooped to lift the gourd of water.

Hadden considered the situation rapidly, for his repulse only made him the more determined to succeed. Of a sudden under the emergency he conceived a scheme, or rather its rough outline. It was not a nice scheme, and some men might have shrunk from it, but as he had no intention of suffering himself to be defeated by a Zulu girl, he decided—with regret, it is true—that having failed to attain his ends by means which he considered fair, he must resort to others of more doubtful character.

"Nanea," he said, "you are a good and honest woman, and I respect you. As I have told you, I love you also, but if you refuse to listen to me there is nothing more to be said, and after all, perhaps it would be better that you should marry one of your own people. But, Nanea, you will never marry him, for the king will take you; and, if he does not give you to some other man, either you will become one of his 'sisters,' or to be free of him, as you say, you will die. Now hear me, for it is because I love you and wish your welfare that I speak thus. Why do you not escape into Natal, taking Nahoon with you, for there as you know you may live in peace out of reach of the arm of Cetywayo?"

"That is my desire, *Inkoos*, but Nahoon will not consent. He says that there is to be war between us and you white men, and he will not break the command of the king and desert from his army."

"Then he cannot love you much, Nahoon, and at least you have to think of yourself. Whisper into the ear of your father and fly together, for be sure that Nahoon will soon follow you. Ay! and I myself with fly with you, for I too believe that there must be war, and then a white man in this country will be as a lamb among the eagles."

"If Nahoon will come, I will go, *Inkoos*, but I cannot fly without Nahoon; it is better I should stay here and kill myself."

"Surely then being so fair and loving him so well, you can teach him to forget his folly and to escape with you. In four days' time we must start for the king's *kraal*, and if you win over Nahoon, it will be easy for us to turn our faces southwards and across the river that lies between the land of the Amazulu and Natal. For the sake of all of us, but most of all for your own sake, try to do this, Nanea, whom I have loved and whom I now would save. See him and plead with him as you know how, but as yet do not tell him that I dream of flight, for then I should be watched."

"In truth, I will, *Inkoos*," she answered earnestly, "and oh! I thank you for your goodness. Fear not that I will betray you—first would I die. Farewell."

"Farewell, Nanea," and taking her hand he raised it to his lips.

****

Late that night, just as Hadden was beginning to prepare himself for sleep, he heard a gentle tapping at the board which closed the entrance to his hut.

"Enter," he said, unfastening the door, and presently by the light of the little lantern that he had with him, he saw Nanea creep into the hut, followed by the great form of Nahoon.

"*Inkoos*," she said in a whisper when the door was closed again, "I have pleaded with Nahoon, and he has consented to fly; moreover, my father will come also."

"Is it so, Nahoon?" asked Hadden.

"It is so," answered the Zulu, looking down shamefacedly; "to save this girl from the king, and because the love of her eats out my heart, I have bartered away my honour. But I tell you, Nanea, and you, White Man, as I told Umgona just now, that I think no good will come of this flight, and if we are caught or betrayed, we shall be killed every one of us."

"Caught we can scarcely be," broke in Nanea anxiously, "for who could betray us, except the *Inkoos* here——"

"Which he is not likely to do," said Hadden quietly, "seeing that he desires to escape with you, and that his life is also at stake."

"That is so, Black Heart," said Nahoon, "otherwise I tell you that I should not have trusted you."

Hadden took no notice of this outspoken saying, but until very late that night they sat there together making their plans.

****

On the following morning Hadden was awakened by sounds of violent altercation. Going out of his hut he found that the disputants were Umgona and a fat and evil-looking Kaffir chief who had arrived at the *kraal* on a pony. This chief, he soon discovered, was named Maputa, being none other than the man who had sought Nanea in

383

marriage and brought about Nahoon's and Umgona's unfortunate appeal to the king. At present he was engaged in abusing Umgona furiously, charging him with having stolen certain of his oxen and bewitched his cows so that they would not give milk. The alleged theft it was comparatively easy to disprove, but the wizardry remained a matter of argument.

"You are a dog, and a son of a dog," shouted Maputa, shaking his fat fist in the face of the trembling but indignant Umgona. "You promised me your daughter in marriage, then having vowed her to that *umfagozan*—that low lout of a soldier, Nahoon, the son of Zomba—you went, the two of you, and poisoned the king's ear against me, bringing me into trouble with the king, and now you have bewitched my cattle. Well, wait, I will be even with you, Wizard; wait till you wake up in the cold morning to find your fence red with fire, and the slayers standing outside your gates to eat up you and yours with spears——"

At this juncture Nahoon, who till now had been listening in silence, intervened with effect.

"Good," he said, "we will wait, but not in your company, Chief Maputa. *Hamba!* (go)——" and seizing the fat old ruffian by the scruff of his neck, he flung him backwards with such violence that he rolled over and over down the little slope.

Hadden laughed, and passed on towards the stream where he proposed to bathe. Just as he reached it, he caught sight of Maputa riding along the footpath, his head-ring covered with mud, his lips purple and his black face livid with rage.

"There goes an angry man," he said to himself. "Now, how would it be——" and he looked upwards like one seeking an inspiration. It seemed to come; perhaps the devil finding it open whispered in his ear, at any rate—in a few seconds his plan was formed, and he was walking through the bush to meet Maputa.

"Go in peace, Chief," he said; "they seem to have treated you roughly up yonder. Having no power to interfere, I came away for I could not bear the sight. It is indeed shameful that an old and venerable man of rank should be struck into the dirt, and beaten by a soldier drunk with beer."

"Shameful, White Man!" gasped Maputa; "your words are true indeed. But wait a while. I, Maputa, will roll that stone over, I will throw that bull upon its back. When next the harvest ripens, this I promise, that neither Nahoon nor Umgona, nor any of his *kraal* shall be left to gather it."

"And how will you manage that, Maputa?"

"I do not know, but I will find a way. Oh! I tell you, a way shall be found."

Hadden patted the pony's neck meditatively, then leaning forward, he looked the chief in the eyes and said:—

"What will you give me, Maputa, if I show you that way, a sure and certain one, whereby you may be avenged to the death upon Nahoon, whose violence I also have seen, and upon Umgona, whose witchcraft brought sore sickness upon me?"

"What reward do you seek, White Man?" asked Maputa eagerly.

"A little thing, Chief, a thing of no account, only the girl Nanea, to whom as it chances I have taken a fancy."

"I wanted her for myself, White Man, but he who sits at Ulundi has laid his hand upon her."

"That is nothing, Chief; I can arrange with him who 'sits at Ulundi.' It is with you who are great here that I wish to come to terms. Listen: if you grant my desire, not only will I fulfil yours upon your foes, but when the girl is delivered into my hands I will give you this rifle and a hundred rounds of cartridges."

Maputa looked at the sporting Martini, and his eyes glistened.

"It is good," he said; "it is very good. Often have I wished for such a gun that will enable me to shoot game, and to talk with my enemies from far away. Promise it to me, White Man, and you shall take the girl if I can give her to you."

"You swear it, Maputa?"

"I swear it by the head of Chaka, and the spirits of my fathers."

"Good. At dawn on the fourth day from now it is the purpose of Umgona, his daughter Nanea, and Nahoon, to cross the river into Natal by the drift that is called Crocodile Drift, taking their cattle with them and flying from the king. I also shall be of their company, for they know that I have learned their secret, and would murder me if I tried to leave them. Now you who are chief of the border and guardian of that drift, must hide at night with some men among the rocks in the shallows of the drift and await our coming. First Nanea will cross driving the cows and calves, for so it is arranged, and I shall help her; then will follow Umgona and Nahoon with the oxen and heifers. On these two you must fall, killing them and capturing the cattle, and afterwards I will give you the rifle."

"What if the king should ask for the girl, White Man?"

"Then you shall answer that in the uncertain light you did not recognise her and so she slipped away from you; moreover, that at first you feared to seize the girl lest her cries should alarm the men and they should escape you."

"Good, but how can I be sure that you will give me the gun once you are across the river?"

"Thus: before I enter the ford I will lay the rifle and cartridges upon a stone by the bank, telling Nanea that I shall return to fetch them when I have driven over the cattle."

"It is well, White Man; I will not fail you."

So the plot was made, and after some further conversation upon points of detail, the two conspirators shook hands and parted.

"That ought to come off all right," reflected Hadden to himself as he plunged and floated in the waters of the stream, "but somehow I don't quite trust our friend Maputa. It would have been better if I could have relied upon myself to get rid of Nahoon and his respected uncle—a couple of shots would do it in the water. But then that would be murder and murder is unpleasant; whereas the other thing is only the delivery to justice of two base deserters, a laudable action in a military country. Also personal interference upon my part might turn the girl against me; while after Umgona and Nahoon have been wiped out by Maputa, she *must* accept my escort. Of course there is a risk, but in every walk of life the most cautious have to take risks at times."

As it chanced, Philip Hadden was correct in his suspicions of his coadjutor, Maputa. Even before that worthy chief reached his own *kraal*, he had come to the conclusion that the white man's plan, though attractive in some ways, was too dangerous, since it was certain that if the girl Nanea escaped, the king would be indignant. Moreover, the men he took with him to do the killing in the drift would suspect something and talk. On the other hand he would earn much credit with his majesty by revealing the plot, saying that he had learned it from the lips of the white hunter, whom Umgona and Nahoon had forced to participate in it, and of whose coveted rifle he must trust to chance to possess himself.

****

An hour later two discreet messengers were bounding across the plains, bearing words from the Chief Maputa, the Warden of the Border, to the "great Black Elephant" at Ulundi.

CHAPTER 5

The Doom Pool

Fortune showed itself strangely favourable to the plans of Nahoon and Nanea. One of the Zulu captain's perplexities was as to how he should lull the suspicions and evade the vigilance of his own companions, who together with himself had been detailed by the king to assist Hadden in his hunting and to guard against his escape. As it chanced, however, on the day after the incident of the visit of Maputa, a messenger arrived from no less a person than the great military *Induna*, Tvingwayo ka Marolo, who afterwards commanded the Zulu army at Isandhlwana, ordering these men to return to their regiment, the Umcityu Corps, which was to be placed upon full war footing. Accordingly Nahoon sent them, saying that he himself would follow with Black Heart in the course of a few days, as at present the white man was not sufficiently recovered from his hurts to allow of his travelling fast and far. So the soldiers went, doubting nothing.

Then Umgona gave it out that in obedience to the command of the king he was about to start for Ulundi, taking with him his daughter Nanea to be delivered over into the *Sigodhla*, and also those fifteen head of cattle that had been *lobola'd* by Nahoon in consideration of his forthcoming marriage, whereof he had been fined by Cetywayo. Under pretence that they required a change of veldt, the rest of his cattle he sent away in charge of a Basuto herd who knew nothing of their plans, telling him to keep them by the Crocodile Drift, as there the grass was good and sweet.

All preparations being completed, on the third day the party started, heading straight for Ulundi. After they had travelled some miles, however, they left the road and turning sharp to the right, passed unobserved of any through a great stretch of uninhabited bush. Their path now lay not far from the Pool of Doom, which, indeed, was close to Umgona's *kraal*, and the forest that was called Home of the

387

Dead, but out of sight of these. It was their plan to travel by night, reaching the broken country near the Crocodile Drift on the following morning. Here they proposed to lie hid that day and through the night; then, having first collected the cattle which had preceded them, to cross the river at the break of dawn and escape into Natal. At least this was the plan of his companions; but, as we know, Hadden had another programme, whereon after one last appearance two of the party would play no part.

During that long afternoon's journey Umgona, who knew every inch of the country, walked ahead driving the fifteen cattle and carrying in his hand a long travelling stick of black and white *umzimbeet* wood, for in truth the old man was in a hurry to reach his journey's end. Next came Nahoon, armed with a broad *assegai*, but naked except for his *moocha* and necklet of baboon's teeth, and with him Nanea in her white bead-bordered mantle. Hadden, who brought up the rear, noticed that the girl seemed to be under the spell of an imminent apprehension, for from time to time she clasped her lover's arm, and looking up into his face, addressed him with vehemence, almost with passion.

Curiously enough, the sight touched Hadden, and once or twice he was shaken by so sharp a pang of remorse at the thought of his share in this tragedy, that he cast about in his mind seeking a means to unravel the web of death which he himself had woven. But ever that evil voice was whispering at his ear. It reminded him that he, the white *Inkoos*, had been refused by this dusky beauty, and that if he found a way to save him, within some few hours she would be the wife of the savage gentleman at her side, the man who had named him Black Heart and who despised him, the man whom he had meant to murder and who immediately repaid his treachery by rescuing him from the jaws of the leopard at the risk of his own life. Moreover, it was a law of Hadden's existence never to deny himself of anything that he desired if it lay within his power to take it—a law which had led him always deeper into sin. In other respects, indeed, it had not carried him far, for in the past he had not desired much, and he had won little; but this particular flower was to his hand, and he would pluck it. If Nahoon stood between him and the flower, so much the worse for Nahoon, and if it should wither in his grasp, so much the worse for the flower; it could always be thrown away. Thus it came about that, not for the first time in his life, Philip Hadden discarded the somewhat spasmodic prickings of conscience and listened to that evil whispering at his ear.

About half-past five o'clock in the afternoon the four refugees passed the stream that a mile or so down fell over the little precipice into the Doom Pool; and, entering a patch of thorn trees on the further side, walked straight into the midst of two-and-twenty soldiers, who were beguiling the tedium of expectancy by the taking of snuff and the smoking of *dakka* or native hemp. With these soldiers, seated on his pony, for he was too fat to walk, waited the Chief Maputa.

Observing that their expected guests had arrived, the men knocked out the *dakka* pipe, replaced the snuff boxes in the slits made in the lobes of their ears, and secured the four of them.

"What is the meaning of this, O King's soldiers?" asked Umgona in a quavering voice. "We journey to the *kraal* of U'Cetywayo; why do you molest us?"

"Indeed. Wherefore then are your faces set towards the south. Does the Black One live in the south? Well, you will journey to another *kraal* presently," answered the jovial-looking captain of the party with a callous laugh.

"I do not understand," stammered Umgona.

"Then I will explain while you rest," said the captain. "The Chief Maputa yonder sent word to the Black One at Ulundi that he had learned of your intended flight to Natal from the lips of this white man, who had warned him of it. The Black One was angry, and despatched us to catch you and make an end of you. That is all. Come on now, quietly, and let us finish the matter. As the Doom Pool is near, your deaths will be easy."

Nahoon heard the words, and sprang straight at the throat of Hadden; but he did not reach it, for the soldiers pulled him down. Nanea heard them also, and turning, looked the traitor in the eyes; she said nothing, she only looked, but he could never forget that look. The white man for his part was filled with a fiery indignation against Maputa.

"You wicked villain," he gasped, whereat the chief smiled in a sickly fashion, and turned away.

Then they were marched along the banks of the stream till they reached the waterfall that fell into the Pool of Doom.

Hadden was a brave man after his fashion, but his heart quailed as he gazed into that abyss.

"Are you going to throw me in there?" he asked of the Zulu captain in a thick voice.

"You, White Man?" replied the soldier unconcernedly. "No, our orders are to take you to the king, but what he will do with you I do not know. There is to be war between your people and ours, so perhaps he means to pound you into medicine for the use of the witch-doctors, or to peg you over an ant-heap as a warning to other white men."

Hadden received this information in silence, but its effect upon his brain was bracing, for instantly he began to search out some means of escape.

By now the party had halted near the two thorn trees that hung over the waters of the pool.

"Who dives first," asked the captain of the Chief Maputa.

"The old wizard," he replied, nodding at Umgona; "then his daughter after him, and last of all this fellow," and he struck Nahoon in the face with his open hand.

"Come on, Wizard," said the captain, grasping Umgona by the arm, "and let us see how you can swim."

At the words of doom Umgona seemed to recover his self-command, after the fashion of his race.

"No need to lead me, soldier," he said, shaking himself loose, "who am old and ready to die." Then he kissed his daughter at his side, wrung Nahoon by the hand, and turning from Hadden with a gesture of contempt walked out upon the platform that joined the two thorn trunks. Here he stood for a moment looking at the setting sun, then suddenly, and without a sound, he hurled himself into the abyss below and vanished.

"That was a brave one," said the captain with admiration. "Can you spring too, girl, or must we throw you?"

"I can walk my father's path," Nanea answered faintly, "but first I crave leave to say one word. It is true that we were escaping from the king, and therefore by the law we must die; but it was Black Heart here who made the plot, and he who has betrayed us. Would you know why he has betrayed us? Because he sought my favour, and I refused him, and this is the vengeance that he takes—a white man's vengeance."

"*Wow!*" broke in the chief Maputa, "this pretty one speaks truth, for the white man would have made a bargain with me under which Umgona, the wizard, and Nahoon, the soldier, were to be killed at the Crocodile Drift, and he himself suffered to escape with the girl. I spoke him softly and said 'yes,' and then like a loyal man I reported to the king."

"You hear," sighed Nanea. "Nahoon, fare you well, though presently perhaps we shall be together again. It was I who tempted you from your duty. For my sake you forgot your honour, and I am repaid. Farewell, my husband, it is better to die with you than to enter the house of the king's women," and Nanea stepped on to the platform.

Here, holding to a bough of one of the thorn trees, she turned and addressed Hadden, saying:—

"Black Heart, you seem to have won the day, but me at least you lose and—the sun is not yet set. After sunset comes the night, Black Heart, and in that night I pray that you may wander eternally, and be given to drink of my blood and the blood of Umgona my father, and the blood of Nahoon my husband, who saved your life, and whom you have murdered. Perchance, Black Heart, we may yet meet yonder—in the House of the Dead."

Then uttering a low cry Nanea clasped her hands and sprang upwards and outwards from the platform. The watchers bent their heads forward to look. They saw her rush headlong down the face of the fall to strike the water fifty feet below. A few seconds, and for the last time, they caught sight of her white garment glimmering on the surface of the gloomy pool. Then the shadows and mist-wreaths hid it, and she was gone.

"Now, husband," cried the cheerful voice of the captain, "yonder is your marriage bed, so be swift to follow a bride who is so ready to lead the way. *Wow!* but you are good people to kill; never have I had to do with any who gave less trouble. You——" and he stopped, for mental agony had done its work, and suddenly Nahoon went mad before his eyes.

With a roar like that of a lion the great man cast off those who held him and seizing one of them round the waist and thigh, he put out all his terrible strength. Lifting him as though he had been an infant, he hurled him over the edge of the cliff to find his death on the rocks of the Pool of Doom. Then crying:—

"Black Heart! your turn, Black Heart the traitor!" he rushed at Hadden, his eyes rolling and foam flying from his lips, as he passed striking the chief Maputa from his horse with a backward blow of his hand. Ill would it have gone with the white man if Nahoon had caught him. But he could not come at him, for the soldiers sprang upon him and notwithstanding his fearful struggles they pulled him to the ground, as at certain festivals the Zulu regiments with their naked hands pull down a bull in the presence of the king.

"Cast him over before he can work more mischief," said a voice. But the captain cried out, "Nay, nay, he is sacred; the fire from Heaven has fallen on his brain, and we may not harm him, else evil would overtake us all. Bind him hand and foot, and bear him tenderly to where he can be cared for. Surely I thought that these evil-doers were giving us too little trouble, and thus it has proved."

So they set themselves to make fast Nahoon's hands and wrists, using as much gentleness as they might, for among the Zulus a lunatic is accounted holy. It was no easy task, and it took time.

Hadden glanced around him, and saw his opportunity. On the ground close beside him lay his rifle, where one of the soldiers had placed it, and about a dozen yards away Maputa's pony was grazing. With a swift movement, he seized the Martini and five seconds later he was on the back of the pony, heading for the Crocodile Drift at a gallop. So quickly indeed did he execute this masterly retreat, that occupied as they all were in binding Nahoon, for half a minute or more none of the soldiers noticed what had happened. Then Maputa chanced to see, and waddled after him to the top of the rise, screaming:—

"The white thief, he has stolen my horse, and the gun too, the gun that he promised to give me."

Hadden, who by this time was a hundred yards away, heard him clearly, and a rage filled his heart. This man had made an open murderer of him; more, he had been the means of robbing him of the girl for whose sake he had dipped his hands in these iniquities. He glanced over his shoulder; Maputa was still running, and alone. Yes, there was time; at any rate he would risk it.

Pulling up the pony with a jerk, he leapt from its back, slipping his arm through the rein with an almost simultaneous movement. As it chanced, and as he had hoped would be the case, the animal was a trained shooting horse, and stood still. Hadden planted his feet firmly on the ground and drawing a deep breath, he cocked the rifle and covered the advancing chief. Now Maputa saw his purpose and with a yell of terror turned to fly. Hadden waited a second to get the sight fair on his broad back, then just as the soldiers appeared above the rise he pressed the trigger. He was a noted shot, and in this instance his skill did not fail him; for, before he heard the bullet tell, Maputa flung his arms wide and plunged to the ground dead.

Three seconds more, and with a savage curse, Hadden had remounted the pony and was riding for his life towards the river, which a while later he crossed in safety.

CHAPTER 6

The Ghost of the Dead

When Nanea leapt from the dizzy platform that overhung the Pool of Doom, a strange fortune befell her. Close in to the precipice were many jagged rocks, and on these the waters of the fall fell and thundered, bounding from them in spouts of spray into the troubled depths of the *foss* beyond. It was on these stones that the life was dashed out from the bodies of the wretched victims who were hurled from above. But Nanea, it will be remembered, had not waited to be treated thus, and as it chanced the strong spring with which she had leapt to death carried her clear of the rocks. By a very little she missed the edge of them and striking the deep water head first like some practised diver, she sank down and down till she thought that she would never rise again. Yet she did rise, at the end of the pool in the mouth of the rapid, along which she sped swiftly, carried down by the rush of the water. Fortunately there were no rocks here; and, since she was a skilful swimmer, she escaped the danger of being thrown against the banks.

For a long distance she was borne thus till at length she saw that she was in a forest, for trees cut off the light from the water, and their drooping branches swept its surface. One of these Nanea caught with her hand, and by the help of it she dragged herself from the River of Death whence none had escaped before. Now she stood upon the bank gasping but quite unharmed; there was not a scratch on her body; even her white garment was still fast about her neck.

But though she had suffered no hurt in her terrible voyage, so exhausted was Nanea that she could scarcely stand. Here the gloom was that of night, and shivering with cold she looked helplessly to find some refuge. Close to the water's edge grew an enormous yellow-wood tree, and to this she staggered—thinking to climb it, and seek shelter in its boughs where, as she hoped, she would be safe from wild beasts. Again fortune befriended her, for at a distance of a few feet from the ground there was a great hole in the tree which, she discovered, was hollow. Into this hole she crept, taking her chance of its being the home of snakes or other evil creatures, to find that the interior was wide and warm. It was dry also, for at the bottom of the cavity lay a foot or more of rotten tinder and moss brought there by rats or birds. Upon this tinder she lay down, and covering herself with the moss and leaves soon sank into sleep or stupor.

How long Nanea slept she did not know, but at length she was awakened by a sound as of guttural human voices talking in a language that she could not understand. Rising to her knees she peered out of the hole in the tree. It was night, but the stars shone brilliantly, and their light fell upon an open circle of ground close by the edge of the river. In this circle there burned a great fire, and at a little distance from the fire were gathered eight or ten horrible-looking beings, who appeared to be rejoicing over something that lay upon the ground. They were small in stature, men and women together, but no children, and all of them were nearly naked. Their hair was long and thin, growing down almost to the eyes, their jaws and teeth protruded and the girth of their black bodies was out of all proportion to their height. In their hands they held sticks with sharp stones lashed on to them, or rude hatchet-like knives of the same material.

Now Nanea's heart shrank within her, and she nearly fainted with fear, for she knew that she was in the haunted forest, and without a doubt these were the *Esemkofu*, the evil ghosts that dwelt therein. Yes, that was what they were, and yet she could not take her eyes off them—the sight of them held her with a horrible fascination. But if they were ghosts, why did they sing and dance like men? Why did they wave those sharp stones aloft, and quarrel and strike each other? And why did they make a fire as men do when they wish to cook food? More, what was it that they rejoiced over, that long dark thing which lay so quiet upon the ground? It did not look like a head of game, and it could scarcely be a crocodile, yet clearly it was food of some sort, for they were sharpening the stone knives in order to cut it up.

While she wondered thus, one of the dreadful-looking little creatures advanced to the fire, and taking from it a burning bough, held it over the thing that lay upon the ground, to give light to a companion who was about to do something to it with the stone knife. Next instant Nanea drew back her head from the hole, a stifled shriek upon her lips. She saw what it was now—it was the body of a man. Yes, and these were no ghosts; they were cannibals of whom when she was little, her mother had told her tales to keep her from wandering away from home.

But who was the man they were about to eat? It could not be one of themselves, for his stature was much greater. Oh! now she knew; it must be Nahoon, who had been killed up yonder, and whose dead body the waters had brought down to the haunted forest as they had brought her alive. Yes, it must be Nahoon, and she would be forced to see her husband devoured before her eyes. The thought of it overwhelmed her. That he should die by order of the king was natural, but that he should be buried thus! Yet what could she do to prevent it? Well, if it cost her her life, it should be prevented. At the worst they could only kill and eat her also, and now that Nahoon and her father were gone, being untroubled by any religious or spiritual hopes and fears, she was not greatly concerned to keep her own breath in her.

Slipping through the hole in the tree, Nanea walked quietly towards the cannibals—not knowing in the least what she should do when she reached them. As she arrived in line with the fire this lack of programme came home to her mind forcibly, and she paused to reflect. Just then one of the cannibals looked up to see a tall and stately figure wrapped in a white garment which, as the flame-light flickered on it, seemed now to advance from the dense background of shadow, and now to recede into it. The poor savage wretch was holding a stone knife in his teeth when he beheld her, but it did not remain there long, for opening his great jaws he uttered the most terrified and piercing yell that Nanea had ever heard. Then the others saw her also, and presently the forest was ringing with shrieks of fear. For a few seconds the outcasts stood and gazed, then they were gone this way and that, bursting their path through the undergrowth like startled jackals. The *Esemkofu* of Zulu tradition had been routed in their own haunted home by what they took to be a spirit.

Poor *Esemkofu*! they were but miserable and starving bushmen who, driven into that place of ill omen many years ago, had adopted this means, the only one open to them, to keep the life in their wretched bodies. Here at least they were unmolested, and as there was little other food to be found amid that wilderness of trees, they took what the river brought them. When executions were few in the Pool of Doom, times were hard for them indeed—for then they were driven to eat each other. That is why there were no children.

As their inarticulate outcry died away in the distance, Nanea ran forward to look at the body that lay on the ground, and staggered back with a sigh of relief. It was not Nahoon, but she recognised the face for that of one of the party of executioners. How did he come here? Had Nahoon killed him? Had Nahoon escaped? She could not tell, and at the best it was improbable, but still the sight of this dead soldier lit her heart with a faint ray of hope, for how did he come to be dead if Nahoon had no hand in his death? She could not bear to leave him lying so near her hiding-place, however; therefore, with no small toil, she rolled the corpse back into the water, which carried it swiftly away. Then she returned to the tree, having first replenished the fire, and awaited the light.

At last it came—so much of it as ever penetrated this darksome den—and Nanea, becoming aware that she was hungry, descended from the tree to search for food. All day long she searched, finding nothing, till towards sunset she remembered that on the outskirts of the forest there was a flat rock where it was the custom of those who had been in any way afflicted, or who considered themselves or their belongings to be bewitched, to place propitiatory offerings of food wherewith the *Esemkofu* and *Amahlosi* were supposed to satisfy their spiritual cravings. Urged by the pinch of starvation, to this spot Nanea journeyed rapidly, and found to her joy that some neighbouring *kraal* had evidently been in recent trouble, for the Rock of Offering was laden with cobs of corn, gourds of milk, porridge and even meat. Helping herself to as much as she could carry, she returned to her lair, where she drank of the milk and cooked meat and mealies at the fire. Then she crept back into the tree, and slept.

For nearly two months Nanea lived thus in the forest, since she could not venture out of it—fearing lest she should be seized, and for a second time taste of the judgment of the king. In the forest at least she was safe, for none dared enter there, nor did the *Esemkofu* give her further trouble. Once or twice she saw them, but on each occasion they fled from her presence—seeking some distant retreat, where they hid themselves or perished. Nor did food fail her, for finding that it was taken, the pious givers brought it in plenty to the Rock of Offering.

But, oh! the life was dreadful, and the gloom and loneliness coupled with her sorrows at times drove her almost to insanity. Still she lived on, though often she desired to die, for if her father was dead, the corpse she had found was not the corpse of Nahoon, and in her heart there still shone that spark of home. Yet what she hoped for she could not tell.

When Philip Hadden reached civilised regions, he found that war was about to be declared between the Queen and Cetywayo, King of the Amazulu; also that in the prevailing excitement his little adventure with the Utrecht store-keeper had been overlooked or forgotten. He was the owner of two good buck-wagons with spans of salted oxen, and at that time vehicles were much in request to carry military stores for the columns which were to advance into Zululand; indeed the transport authorities were glad to pay £90 a month for the hire of each wagon and to guarantee the owners against all loss of cattle. Although he was not desirous of returning to Zululand, this bait proved too much for Hadden, who accordingly leased out his wagons to the Commissariat, together with his own services as conductor and interpreter.

He was attached to No. 3 column of the invading force, which it may be remembered was under the immediate command of Lord Chelmsford, and on the 20th of January, 1879, he marched with it by the road that runs from Rorke's Drift to the Indeni forest, and encamped that night beneath the shadow of the steep and desolate mountain known as Isandhlwana.

That day also a great army of King Cetywayo's, numbering twenty thousand men and more, moved down from the Upindo Hill and camped upon the stony plain that lies a mile and a half to the east of Isandhlwana. No fires were lit, and it lay there in utter silence, for the warriors were "sleeping on their spears."

With that *impi* was the Umcityu regiment, three thousand five hundred strong. At the first break of dawn the *Induna* in command of the Umcityu looked up from beneath the shelter of the black shield with which he had covered his body, and through the thick mist he saw a great man standing before him, clothed only in a *moocha*, a gaunt wild-eyed man who held a rough club in his hand. When he was spoken to, the man made no answer; he only leaned upon his club looking from left to right along the dense array of innumerable shields.

"Who is this *Silwana* (wild creature)?" asked the *Induna* of his captains wondering.

The captains stared at the wanderer, and one of them replied, "This is Nahoon-ka-Zomba, it is the son of Zomba who not long ago held rank in this regiment of the Umcityu. His betrothed, Nanea, daughter of Umgona, was killed together with her father by order of the Black One, and Nahoon went mad with grief at the sight of it, for the fire of Heaven entered his brain, and mad he has wandered ever since."

"What would you here, Nahoon-ka-Zomba?" asked the *Induna*.

Then Nahoon spoke slowly. "My regiment goes down to war against the white men; give me a shield and a spear, O Captain of the king, that I may fight with my regiment, for I seek a face in the battle."

So they gave him a shield and a spear, for they dared not turn away one whose brain was alight with the fire of Heaven.

****

When the sun was high that day, bullets began to fall among the ranks of the Umcityu. Then the black-shielded, black-plumed Umcityu arose, company by company, and after them arose the whole vast Zulu army, breast and horns together, and swept down in silence upon the doomed British camp, a moving sheen of spears. The bullets pattered on the shields, the shells tore long lines through their array, but they never halted or wavered. Forward on either side shot out the horns of armed men, clasping the camp in an embrace of steel. Then as these began to close, out burst the war cry of the Zulus, and with the roar of a torrent and the rush of a storm, with a sound like the humming of a billion bees, wave after wave the deep breast of the *impi* rolled down upon the white men. With it went the black-shielded Umcityu and with them went Nahoon, the son of Zomba. A bullet struck him in the side, glancing from his ribs, he did not heed; a white man fell from his horse before him, he did not stab, for he sought but one face in the battle.

He sought—and at last he found. There, among the wagons where the spears were busiest, there standing by his horse and firing rapidly was Black Heart, he who had given Nanea his betrothed to death. Three soldiers stood between them, one of them Nahoon stabbed, and two he brushed aside; then he rushed straight at Hadden.

But the white man saw him come, and even through the mask of his madness he knew Nahoon again, and terror took hold of him. Throwing away his empty rifle, for his ammunition was spent, he leaped upon his horse and drove his spurs into its flanks. Away it went among the carnage, springing over the dead and bursting through the lines of shields, and after it came Nahoon, running long and low with head stretched forward and trailing spear, running as a hound runs when the buck is at view.

Hadden's first plan was to head for Rorke's Drift, but a glance to the left showed him that the masses of the Undi barred that way, so he fled straight on, leaving his path to fortune. In five minutes he was over a ridge, and there was nothing of the battle to be seen,

398

in ten all sounds of it had died away, for few guns were fired in the dread race to Fugitive's Drift, and the *assegai* makes no noise. In some strange fashion, even at this moment, the contrast between the dreadful scene of blood and turmoil that he had left, and the peaceful face of Nature over which he was passing, came home to his brain vividly. Here birds sang and cattle grazed; here the sun shone undimmed by the smoke of cannon, only high up in the blue and silent air long streams of vultures could be seen winging their way to the Plain of Isandhlwana.

The ground was very rough, and Hadden's horse began to tire. He looked over his shoulder—there some two hundred yards behind came the Zulu, grim as Death, unswerving as Fate. He examined the pistol in his belt; there was but one undischarged cartridge left, all the rest had been fired and the pouch was empty. Well, one bullet should be enough for one savage: the question was should he stop and use it now? No, he might miss or fail to kill the man; he was on horseback and his foe on foot, surely he could tire him out.

A while passed, and they dashed through a little stream. It seemed familiar to Hadden. Yes, that was the pool where he used to bathe when he was the guest of Umgona, the father of Nanea; and there on the knoll to his right were the huts, or rather the remains of them, for they had been burnt with fire. What chance had brought him to this place, he wondered; then again he looked behind him at Nahoon, who seemed to read his thoughts, for he shook his spear and pointed to the ruined *kraal*.

On he went at speed for here the land was level, and to his joy he lost sight of his pursuer. But presently there came a mile of rocky ground, and when it was past, glancing back he saw that Nahoon was once more in his old place. His horse's strength was almost spent, but Hadden spurred it forward blindly, whither he knew not. Now he was travelling along a strip of turf and ahead of him he heard the music of a river, while to his left rose a high bank. Presently the turf bent inwards and there, not twenty yards away from him, was a Kaffir hut standing on the brink of a river. He looked at it, yes, it was the hut of that accursed *inyanga*, the Bee, and standing by the fence of it was none other than the Bee herself. At the sight of her the exhausted horse swerved violently, stumbled and came to the ground, where it lay panting. Hadden was thrown from the saddle but sprang to his feet unhurt.

"Ah! Black Heart, is it you? What news of the battle, Black Heart?" cried the Bee in a mocking voice.

"Help me, mother, I am pursued," he gasped.

"What of it, Black Heart, it is but by one tired man. Stand then and face him, for now Black Heart and White Heart are together again. You will not? Then away to the forest and seek shelter among the dead who await you there. Tell me, tell me, was it the face of Nanea that I saw beneath the waters a while ago? Good! bear my greetings to her when you two meet in the House of the Dead."

Hadden looked at the stream; it was in flood. He could not swim it, so followed by the evil laugh of the prophetess, he sped towards the forest. After him came Nahoon, his tongue hanging from his jaws like the tongue of a wolf.

Now he was in the shadow of the forest, but still he sped on following the course of the river, till at length his breath failed, and he halted on the further side of a little glade, beyond which a great tree grew. Nahoon was more than a spear's throw behind him; therefore he had time to draw his pistol and make ready.

"Halt, Nahoon," he cried, as once before he had cried; "I would speak with you."

The Zulu heard his voice, and obeyed.

"Listen," said Hadden. "We have run a long race and fought a long fight, you and I, and we are still alive both of us. Very soon, if you come on, one of us must be dead, and it will be you, Nahoon, for I am armed and as you know I can shoot straight. What do you say?"

Nahoon made no answer, but stood still at the edge of the glade, his wild and glowering eyes fixed on the white man's face and his breath coming in short gasps.

"Will you let me go, if *I* let *you* go?" Hadden asked once more. "I know why you hate me, but the past cannot be undone, nor can the dead be brought to earth again."

Still Nahoon made no answer, and his silence seemed more fateful and more crushing than any speech; no spoken accusation would have been so terrible in Hadden's ear. He made no answer, but lifting his *assegai* he stalked grimly toward his foe.

When he was within five paces Hadden covered him and fired. Nahoon sprang aside, but the bullet struck him somewhere, for his right arm dropped, and the stabbing spear that he held was jerked from it harmlessly over the white man's head. But still making no sound, the Zulu came on and gripped him by the throat with his left hand. For a space they struggled terribly, swaying to and fro, but Hadden was unhurt and fought with the fury of despair, while Nahoon had been twice wounded, and there remained to him but one sound arm wherewith to strike. Presently forced to earth by the white man's iron strength, the soldier was down, nor could he rise again.

"Now we will make an end," muttered Hadden savagely, and he turned to seek the *assegai*, then staggered slowly back with starting eyes and reeling gait. For there before him, still clad in her white robe, a spear in her hand, stood the spirit of Nanea!

"Think of it," he said to himself, dimly remembering the words of the *inyanga*, "when you stand face to face with the ghost of the dead in the Home of the Dead."

There was a cry and a flash of steel; the broad spear leapt towards him to bury itself in his breast. He swayed, he fell, and presently Black Heart clasped that great reward which the word of the Bee had promised Him.

****

"Nahoon! Nahoon!" murmured a soft voice, "awake, it is no ghost, but I—Nanea—I, your living wife, to whom my *Ehlose*[3] has given it me to save you."

Nahoon heard and opened his eyes to look and his madness left him.

"Welcome, wife," he said faintly, "now I will live since Death has brought you back to me in the House of the Dead."

****

Today Nahoon is one of the *Indunas* of the English Government in Zululand, and there are children about his *kraal*. It was from the lips of none other than Nanea his wife that the teller of this tale heard its substance.

The Bee also lives and practises as much magic as she dares under the white man's rule. On her black hand shines a golden ring shaped like a snake with ruby eyes, and of this trinket the Bee is very proud.

---

3. Guardian Spirit.

The Wizard

CHAPTER 1

The Deputation

Has the age of miracle quite gone by, or is it still possible to the Voice of Faith calling aloud upon the earth to wring from the dumb heavens an audible answer to its prayer? Does the promise uttered by the Master of mankind upon the eve of the end—"Whoso that believeth in Me, the works that I do he shall do also. . . . and whatsoever ye shall ask in My name, that will I do;"—still hold good to such as do ask and do believe?

Let those who care to study the history of the Rev. Thomas Owen, and of that strange man who carried on and completed his work, answer this question according to their judgment.

****

The time was a Sunday afternoon in summer, and the place a church in the Midland counties. It was a beautiful church, ancient and spacious; moreover, it had recently been restored at great cost. Seven or eight hundred people could have found sittings in it, and doubtless they had done so when Busscombe was a large manufacturing town, before the failure of the coal supply and other causes drove away its trade. Now it was much what it had been in the time of the Normans, a little agricultural village with a population of 300 souls. Out of this population, including the choir boys, exactly thirty-nine had elected to attend church on this particular Sunday; and of these, three were fast asleep and four were dozing.

The Rev. Thomas Owen counted them from his seat in the chancel, for another clergyman was preaching; and, as he counted, bitterness and disappointment took hold of him. The preacher was a "Deputation," sent by one of the large missionary societies to arouse the indifferent to a sense of duty towards their unconverted black brethren in Africa, and incidentally to collect cash to be spent in the conversion of the said brethren. The Rev. Thomas Owen himself suggested the visit of the Deputation, and had laboured hard to secure him a good audience. But the beauty of the weather, or terror of the inevitable subscription, prevailed against him. Hence his disappointment.

"Well," he thought, with a sigh, "I have done my best, and I must make it up out of my own pocket."

Then he settled himself to listen to the sermon.

The preacher, a battered-looking individual of between fifty and sixty years of age, was gaunt with recent sickness, patient and unimaginative in aspect. He preached extemporarily, with the aid of notes; and it cannot be said that his discourse was remarkable for interest, at any rate in its beginning. Doubtless the sparse congregation, so prone to slumber, discouraged him; for offering exhortations to empty benches is but weary work. Indeed he was meditating the advisability of bringing his argument to an abrupt conclusion when, chancing to glance round, he became aware that he had at least one sympathetic listener, his host, the Rev. Thomas Owen.

From that moment the sermon improved by degrees, till at length it reached a really high level of excellence. Ceasing from rhetoric, the speaker began to tell of his own experience and sufferings in the Cause amongst savage tribes; for he himself was a missionary of many years standing. He told how once he and a companion had been sent to a nation, who named themselves the Sons of Fire because their god was the lightning, if indeed they could be said to boast any gods other than the Spear and the King. In simple language he narrated his terrible adventures among these savages, the murder of his companion by command of the Council of Wizards, and his own flight for his life; a tale so interesting and vivid that even the bucolic sleepers awakened and listened open-mouthed.

"But this is by the way," he went on; "for my Society does not ask you to subscribe towards the conversion of the Children of Fire. Until that people is conquered—which very likely will not be for generations, seeing that they live in Central Africa, occupying a territory that white men do not desire—no missionary will dare again to visit them."

At this moment something caused him to look a second time at Thomas Owen. He was leaning forward in his place listening eagerly, and a strange light filled the large, dark eyes that shone in the pallor of his delicate, nervous face.

"There is a man who would dare, if he were put to it," thought the Deputation to himself. Then he ended his sermon.

That evening the two men sat at dinner in the rectory. It was a very fine rectory, beautifully furnished; for Owen was a man of taste which he had the means to gratify. Also, although they were alone, the dinner was good—so good that the poor broken-down missionary, sipping his unaccustomed port, a vintage wine, sighed aloud in admiration and involuntary envy.

"What is the matter?" asked Owen.

"Nothing, Mr. Owen;" then, of a sudden thawing into candour, he added: "that is, everything. Heaven forgive me; but I, who enjoy your hospitality, am envious of you. Don't think too hardly of me; I have a large family to support, and if only you knew what a struggle my life is, and has been for the last twenty years, you would not, I am sure. But you have never experienced it, and could not understand. 'The labourer is worthy of his hire.' Well, my hire is under two hundred a year, and eight of us must live—or starve—on it. And I have worked, ay, until my health is broken. A labourer indeed! I am a very hodman, a spiritual Sisyphus. And now I must go back to carry my load and roll my stone again and again among those hopeless savages till I die of it—till I die of it!"

"At least it is a noble life and death!" exclaimed Owen, a sudden fire of enthusiasm burning in his dark eyes.

"Yes, viewed from a distance. Were you asked to leave this living of two thousand a year—I see that is what they put it at in Crockford—with its English comforts and easy work, that *you* might lead that life and attain that death, then you would think differently. But why should I bore you with such talk? Thank Heaven that your lines are cast in pleasant places. Yes, please, I will take one more glass; it does me good."

"Tell me some more about that tribe you were speaking of in your sermon, the 'Sons of Fire' I think you called them," said Owen, as he passed him the decanter.

So, with an eloquence induced by the generous wine and a quickened imagination, the Deputation told him—told him many strange things and terrible. For this people was an awful people: vigorous in mind and body, and warriors from generation to generation, but superstition-ridden and cruel. They lived in the far interior, some months' journey by boat and ox-wagon from the coast, and of white men and their ways they knew but little.

"How many of them are there?" asked Owen.

"Who can say?" he answered. "Nearly half-a-million, perhaps; at least they pretend that they can put sixty thousand men under arms."

"And did they treat you badly when you first visited them?"

"Not at first. They received us civilly enough; and on a given day we were requested to explain to the king and the Council of Wizards the religion which we came to teach. All that day we explained and all the next—or rather my friend did, for I knew very little of the language—and they listened with great interest. At last the chief of the wizards and the first prophet to the king rose to question us. He was named Hokosa, a tall, thin man, with a spiritual face and terrible calm eyes.

"'You speak well, son of a White Man,' he said, 'but let us pass from words to deeds. You tell us that this God of yours, whom you desire that we should take as our God, so that you may become His chief prophets in the land, was a wizard such as we are, though grater than we are; for not only did He know the past and the future as we do, but also He could cure those who were smitten with hopeless sickness, and raise those who were dead, which we cannot do. You tell us, moreover, that by faith those who believe on Him can do works as great as He did, and that you do believe on Him. Therefore we will put you to the proof. Ho! there, lead forth that evil one.'

"As he spoke a man was placed before us, one who had been convicted of witchcraft or some other crime.

"'Kill him!' said Hokosa.

"There was a faint cry, a scuffle, a flashing of spears, and the man lay still before us.

"'Now, followers of the new God,' said Hokosa, 'raise him from the dead as your Master did!'

"In vain did we offer explanations.

"'Peace!' said Hokosa at length, 'your words weary us. Look now, either you have preached to us a false god and are liars, or you are traitors to the King you preach, since, lacking faith in Him, you cannot do such works as He gives power to do to those who have faith in Him. Out of your own mouths are you judged, White Men. Choose which horn of the bull you will, you hang to one of them, and it shall pierce you. This is the sentence of the king, I speak it who am the king's mouth: That you, White Man, who have spoken to us and cheated us these two weary days, be put to death, and that you, his companion who have been silent, be driven from the land.'

"I can hardly bear to tell the rest of it, Mr. Owen. They gave my poor friend ten minutes to 'talk to his Spirit,' then they speared him before my face. After it was over, Hokosa spoke to me, saying:—

"'Go back, White Man, to those who sent you, and tell them the words of the Sons of Fire: That they have listened to the message of peace, and though they are a people of warriors, yet they thank them for that message, for in itself it sounds good and beautiful in their ears, if it be true. Tell them that having proved you liars, they dealt with you as all honest men seek that liars should be dealt with. Tell them that they desire to hear more of this matter, and if one can be sent to them who has no false tongue; who in all things fulfils the promises of his lips, that they will hearken to him and treat him well, but that for such as you they keep a spear.'"

"And who went after you got back?" asked Owen, who was listening with the deepest interest.

"Who went? Do you suppose that there are many mad clergymen in Africa, Mr. Owen? Nobody went."

"And yet," said Owen, speaking more to himself than to his guest, "the man Hokosa was right, and the Christian who of a truth believes the promises of our religion should trust to them and go."

"Then perhaps you would like to undertake the mission, Mr. Owen," said the Deputation briskly; for the reflection stung him, unintentional as it was.

Owen started.

"That is a new idea," he said. "And now perhaps you wish to go to bed; it is past eleven o'clock."

CHAPTER 2

Thomas Owen

Thomas Owen went to his room, but not to bed. Taking a Bible from the table, he consulted reference after reference.

"The promise is clear," he said aloud presently, as he shut the book; "clear and often repeated. There is no escape from it, and no possibility of a double meaning. If it is not true, then it would seem that nothing is true, and that every Christian in the world is tricked and deluded. But if it *is* true, why do we never hear of miracles? The answer is easy: Because we have not faith enough to work them. The Apostles worked miracles; for they had seen, therefore their faith was perfect. Since their day nobody's faith has been quite perfect; at least I think not. The physical part of our nature prevents it. Or perhaps the miracles still happen, but they are spiritual miracles."

Then he sat down by the open window, and gazing at the dreamy beauty of the summer night, he thought, for his soul was troubled. Once before it had been troubled thus; that was nine years ago, for now he was but little over thirty. Then a call had come to him, a voice had seemed to speak to his ears bidding him to lay down great possessions to follow whither Heaven should lead him. Thomas Owen had obeyed the voice; though, owing to circumstances which need not be detailed, to do so he was obliged to renounce his succession to a very large estate, and to content himself with a younger son's portion of thirty thousand pounds and the reversion to the living which he had now held for some five years.

Then and there, with singular unanimity and despatch, his relations came to the conclusion that he was mad. To this hour, indeed, those who stand in his place and enjoy the wealth and position that were his by right, speak of him as "poor Thomas," and mark their disapprobation of his peculiar conduct by refusing with an unvarying steadiness to subscribe even a single shilling to a missionary society. How "poor

Thomas" speaks of them in the place where he is we may wonder, but as yet we cannot know—probably with the gentle love and charity that marked his every action upon earth. But this is by the way.

He had entered the Church, but what had he done in its shadow? This was the question which Owen asked himself as he sat that night by the open window, arraigning his past before the judgment-seat of conscience. For three years he had worked hard somewhere in the slums; then this living had fallen to him. He had taken it, and from that day forward his record was very much of a blank. The parish was small and well ordered; there was little to do in it, and the Salvation Army had seized upon and reclaimed two of the three confirmed drunkards it could boast.

His guest's saying echoed in his brain like the catch of a tune— "that *you* might lead that life and attain that death." Supposing that he were bidden so to do now, this very night, would he indeed "think differently"? He had become a priest to serve his Maker. How would it be were that Maker to command that he should serve Him in this extreme and heroic fashion? Would he flinch from the steel, or would he meet it as the martyrs met it of old?

Physically he was little suited to such an enterprise, for in appearance he was slight and pale, and in constitution delicate. Also, there was another reason against the thing. High Church and somewhat ascetic in his principles, in the beginning he had admired celibacy, and in secret dedicated himself to that state. But at heart Thomas was very much a man, and of late he had come to see that which is against nature is presumably not right, though fanatics may not hesitate to pronounce it wrong. Possibly this conversion to more genial views of life was quickened by the presence in the neighbourhood of a young lady whom he chanced to admire; at least it is certain that the mere thought of seeing her no more for ever smote him like a sword of sudden pain.

****

That very night—or so it seemed to him, and so he believed—the Angel of the Lord stood before him as he was wont to stand before the men of old, and spoke a summons in his ear. How or in what seeming that summons came Thomas Owen never told, and we need not inquire. At the least he heard it, and, like the Apostles, he arose and girded his loins to obey. For now, in the hour of trial, it proved that this man's faith partook of the nature of their faith. It was utter and virgin; it was not clogged with nineteenth-century qualifications; it had never dallied with strange doctrines, or kissed the feet of pinchbeck substitutes for God. In his heart he believed that the Almighty, without intermediary, but face to face, had bidden him to go forth into the wilderness there to perish. So he bowed his head and went.

On the following morning at breakfast Owen had some talk with his friend the Deputation.

"You asked me last night," he said quietly, "whether I would undertake a mission to that people of whom you were telling me—the Sons of Fire. Well, I have been thinking it over, and come to the conclusion that I will do so——"

At this point the Deputation, concluding that his host must be mad, moved quietly but decidedly towards the door.

"Wait a moment," went on Owen, in a matter-of-fact voice, "the dog-cart will not be round for another three-quarters of an hour. Tell me, if it were offered to you, and on investigation you proved suitable, would you care to take over this living?"

"Would I care to take over this living?" gasped the astonished Deputation. "Would I care to walk down that garden and find myself in Heaven? But why are you making fun of me?"

"I am not making fun of you. If I go to Africa I must give up the living, of which I own the *advowson*, and it occurred to me that it might suit you—that is all. You have done your share; your health is broken, and you have many dependent upon you. It seems right, therefore, that you should rest, and that I should work. If I do no good yonder, at the least you and yours will be a little benefited."

****

That same day Owen chanced to meet the lady who has been spoken of as having caught his heart. He had meant to go away without seeing her, but fortune brought them together. Hitherto, whilst in reality leading him on, she had seemed to keep him at a distance, with the result that he did not know that it was her fixed intention to marry him. To her, with some hesitation, he told his plans. Surprised and frightened into candour, the lady reasoned with him warmly, and when reason failed to move him she did more. By some subtle movement, with some sudden word, she lifted the veil of her reserve and suffered him to see her heart. "If you will not stay for aught else," said her troubled eyes, "then, love, stay for me."

For a moment he was shaken. Then he answered the look straight out, as was his nature.

"I never guessed," he said. "I did not presume to hope—now it is

412

too late! Listen! I will tell you what I have told no living soul, though thereafter you may think me mad. Weak and humble as I am, I believe myself to have received a Divine mission. I believe that I shall execute it, or bring about its execution, but at the ultimate cost of my own life. Still, in such a service two are better than one. If you—can care enough—if you——"

But the lady had already turned away, and was murmuring her farewell in accents that sounded like a sob. Love and faith after this sort were not given to her.

Of all Owen's trials this was the sharpest. Of all his sacrifices this was the most complete.

CHAPTER 3

The Temptation

Two years have gone by all but a few months, and from the rectory in a quiet English village we pass to a scene in Central, or South Central, Africa.

On the brow of a grassy slope dotted over with mimosa thorns, and close to a gushing stream of water, stands a house, or rather a hut, built of green brick and thatched with grass. Behind this hut is a fence of thorns, rough but strong, designed to protect all within it from the attacks of lions and other beasts of prey. At present, save for a solitary mule eating its provender by the wheel of a tented ox-wagon, it is untenanted, for the cattle have not yet been kraaled for the night. Presently Thomas Owen enters this enclosure by the back door of the hut, and having attended to the mule, which whinnies at the sight of him, goes to the gate and watches there till he sees his native boys driving the cattle up the slope of the hill. At length they arrive, and when he has counted them to make sure that none are missing, and in a few kind words commended the herds for their watchfulness, he walks to the front of the house and, seating himself upon a wooden stool set under a mimosa tree that grows near the door, he looks earnestly towards the west.

The man has changed somewhat since last we saw him. To begin with, he has grown a beard, and although the hot African sun has bronzed it into an appearance of health, his face is even thinner than it was, and therein the great spiritual eyes shine still more strangely.

At the foot of the slope runs a wide river, just here broken into rapids where the waters make an angry music. Beyond this river stretches a vast plain bounded on the horizon by mountain ranges, each line of them rising higher than the other till their topmost and more distant peaks melt imperceptibly into the tender blue of the heavens. This is the land of the Sons of Fire, and yonder amid the slopes of the nearest hills is the great *kraal* of their king, Umsuka, whose name, being interpreted, means The Thunderbolt.

In the very midst of the foaming rapids, and about a thousand yards from the house lies a space of rippling shallow water, where, unless it chances to be in flood, the river can be forded. It is this ford that Owen watches so intently.

"John should have been back twelve hours ago," he mutters to himself. "I pray that no harm has befallen him at the Great Place yonder."

Just then a tiny speck appears far away on the plain. It is a man travelling towards the water at a swinging trot. Going into the hut, Owen returns with a pair of field-glasses, and through them scrutinises the figure of the man.

"Heaven be praised! It is John," he mutters, with a sigh of relief. "Now, I wonder what answer he brings?"

Half an hour later John stands before him, a stalwart native of the tribe of the Amasuka, the People of Fire, and with uplifted hand salutes him, giving him titles of honour.

"Praise me not, John," said Owen; "praise God only, as I have taught you to do. Tell me, have you seen the king, and what is his word?"

"Father," he answered, "I journeyed to the great town, as you bade me, and I was admitted before the majesty of the king; yes, he received me in the courtyard of the House of Women. With his guards, who stood at a distance out of hearing, there were present three only; but oh! those three were great, the greatest in all the land after the king. They were Hafela, the king that is to come, the prince Nodwengo, his brother, and Hokosa the terrible, the chief of the wizards; and I tell you, father, that my blood dried up and my heart shrivelled when they turned their eyes upon me, reading the thoughts of my heart."

"Have I not told you, John, to trust in God, and fear nothing at the hands of man?"

"You told me, father, but still I feared," answered the messenger humbly. "Yet, being bidden to it, I lifted my forehead from the dust and stood upon my feet before the king, and delivered to him the message which you set between my lips."

"Repeat the message, John."

"'O King,' I said, 'beneath those footfall the whole earth shakes, whose arms stretch round the world and whose breath is the storm, I, whose name is John, am sent by the white man whose name is Messenger'—for by that title you bade me make you known—'who for a year has dwelt in the land that your spears have wasted beyond the banks of the river. These are the words which he spoke to me, O

King, that I pass on to you with my tongue: "To the King Umsuka, lord of the Amasuka, the Sons of Fire, I, Messenger, who am the servant and the ambassador of the King of Heaven, give greeting. A year ago, King, I sent to you saying that the message which was brought by that white man whom you drove from your land had reached the ears of Him whom I serve, the High and Holy One, and that, speaking in my heart, He had commanded me to take up the challenge of your message. Here am I, therefore, ready to abide by the law which you have laid down; for if guile or lies be found in me, then let me travel from your land across the bridge of spears. Still, I would dwell a little while here where I am before I pass into the shadow of your rule and speak in the ears of your people as I have been bidden. Know, King, that first I would learn your tongue, and therefore I demand that one of your people may be sent to dwell with me and to teach me that tongue. King, you heard my words and you sent me a man to dwell with me, and that man has taught me your tongue, and I also have taught him, converting him to my faith and giving him a new name, the name of John. King, now I seek your leave to visit you, and to deliver into your ears the words with which I, Messenger, am charged. I have spoken."'

"Thus I, John, addressed the great ones, my father, and they listened in silence. When I had done they spoke together, a word here and a word there. Then Hokosa, the king's mouth, answered me, telling the thought of the king: 'You are a bold man, you whose name is John, but who once had another name—you, my servant, who dare to appear before me, and to make it known to me that you have been turned to a new faith and serve another king than I. Yet because you are bold, I forgive you. Go back now to that white man who is named Messenger and who comes upon an embassy to me from the Lord of Heaven, and bid him come in peace. Yet warn him once again that here also we know something of the Powers that are not seen, here also we have our wizards who draw wisdom from the air, who tame the thunderbolt and compel the rain, and that he must show himself greater than all of these if he would not pass hence by the bridge of spears. Let him, therefore, take counsel with his heart and with Him he serves, if such a One there is, and let him come or let him stay away as it shall please him.'"

"So be it," said Owen; "the words of the king are good, and tomorrow we will start for the Great Place."

John heard and assented, but without eagerness.

"My father," he said, in a doubtful and tentative voice, "would it not perhaps be better to bide here awhile first?"

416

"Why?" asked Owen. "We have sown, and now is the hour to reap."

"It is so, my father, but as I ran hither, full of the king's words, it came into my mind that now is not the time to convert the Sons of Fire. There is trouble brewing at the Great Palace, father. Listen, and I will tell you; as I have heard, so I will tell you. You know well that our King Umsuka has two sons, Hafela and Nodwengo; and of these Hafela is the heir-apparent, the fruit of the chief wife of the king, and Nodwengo is sprung from another wife. Now Hafela is proud and cruel, a warrior of warriors, a terrible man, and Nodwengo is gentle and mild, like to his mother whom the king loves. Of late it has been discovered that Hafela, weary of waiting for power, has made a plot to depose his father and to kill Nodwengo, his brother, so that the land and those who dwell in it may become his without question. This plot the king knows—I had it from one of his women, who is my sister— and he is very wroth, yet he dare do little, for he grows old and timid, and seeks rest, not war. Yet he is minded, if he can find the heart, to go back upon the law and to name Nodwengo as his heir before all the army at the feast of the first-fruits, which shall be held on the third day from tonight. This Hafela knows, and Nodwengo knows it also, and each of them has summoned his following, numbering thousands and tens of thousands of spears, to attend this feast of the first-fruits. That feast may well be a feast of vultures, my father, and when the brothers and their regiments rush together fighting for the throne, what will chance to the white man who comes at such a moment to preach a faith of peace, and to his servant, one John, who led him there?"

"I do not know," answered Owen, "and it troubles me not at all. I go to carry out my mission, and in this way or in that it will be carried out. John, if you are fearful or unbelieving leave me to go alone."

"Nay, father, I am not fearful; yet, father, I would have you understand. Yonder there are men who can work wizardry. *Wow!* I know, for I have seen it, and they will demand from you magic greater than their magic."

"What of it, John?"

"Only this, my father, that if they ask and you fail to give, they will kill you. You teach beautiful things, but say, are you a wizard? When the child of a woman yonder lay dead, you could not raise it as did the Christ; when the oxen were sick with the pest, you could not cure them; or at least, my father, you did not, although you wept for the child and were sorry at the loss of the oxen. Now, my father, if perchance they ask you to do such things as these yonder, or die, say what will happen?"

"One of two things, John: either I shall die or I shall do the things."

"But"—hesitated John—"surely you do not believe that——" and he broke off.

Owen turned round and looked at his disciple with kindling eyes. "I do believe, O you of little faith!" he said. "I do believe that yonder I have a mission, and that He Whom I serve will give me power to carry out that mission. You are right, I can work no miracles; but He can work miracles Whom everything in heaven and earth obeys, and if there is need He will work them through me, His instrument. Or perhaps He will not work them, and I shall die, because thus His ends will best be forwarded. At the least I go in faith, fearing nothing, for what has he to fear who knows the will of God and does it? But to you who doubt, I say—leave me!"

The man spread out his hands in deprecation; his thick lips trembled a little, and something like a tear appeared at the corners of his eyes.

"Father," he said, "am I a coward that you should talk to me thus? I, who for twenty years have been a soldier of my king and for ten a captain in my regiment? These scars show whether or no I am a coward," and he pointed to his breast, "but of them I will not speak. I am no coward, else I had not gone upon that errand of yours. Why, then, should you reproach me because my ears are not so open as yours, as my heart has not understanding? I worship that God of Whom you have taught me, but He never speaks to me as He does to you. I never meet Him as I walk at night; He leaves me quite alone. Therefore it is that I fear that when the hour of trial comes He may desert you; and unless He covers you with His shield, of this I am sure, that the spear is forged which shall blush red in your heart, my father. It is for you that I fear, who are so gentle and tender; not for myself, who am well accustomed to look in the eyes of Death, and who expect no more than death."

"Forgive me," said Owen hastily, for he was moved; "and be sure that the shield will be over us till the time comes for us to pass whither we shall need none."

****

That night Owen rose from the task at which he was labouring slowly and painfully—a translation of passages from the Gospel of St. John into the language of the Amasuka—and going to the open window-place of the hut, he rested his elbows upon it and thought, staring with empty eyes into the blackness of the night. Now it was as he sat thus that a great agony of doubt took possession of his soul. The strength which hitherto had supported him seemed to be withdrawn, and he was left, as John had said, "quite alone." Strange voices seemed to whisper in his ears, reproaching and reviling him; temptations long ago trampled under foot rose again in might, alluring him.

"Fool," said the voices, "get you hence before it is too late. You have been mad; you who dreamed that for your sake, to satisfy your pride, the Almighty will break His silence and strain His law. Are you then better, or greater, or purer than millions who have gone before you, that for you and you alone this thing should be done? Why, were it not that you are mad, you would be among the chief of sinners; you who dare to ask that the Powers of Heaven should be set within your feeble hand, that the Angels of Heaven should wait upon your mortal breath. Worm that you are, has God need of such as you? If it is His will to turn the heart of yonder people He will do it, but not by means of *you*. You and the servant whom you are deluding to his death will perish miserably, and this alone shall be the fruit of your presumptuous sin. Get you back out of this wilderness before the madness takes you afresh. You are still young, you have wealth; look where She stands yonder whom you desire. Get you back, and forget your folly in her arms."

These thoughts, and many others of like nature, tore Owen's soul in that hour of strange and terrible temptation. He seemed to see himself standing before the thousands of the savage nation he went to save, and to hear the mocking voices of their witch-finders commanding him, if he were a true man and the servant of that God of Whom he prated, to give them a sign, only a little sign; perhaps to move a stone without touching it with his hand, or to cause a dead bough to blossom.

Then he would beseech Heaven with frantic prayers, and in vain, till at length, amidst a roar of laughter, he, the false prophet and the liar, was led out to his doom. He saw the piteous wondering look of the believer whom he had betrayed to death; he saw the fierce faces and the spears on high. Seeing all this his spirit broke, and, just as the little clock in the room behind him struck the first stroke of midnight, with a great and bitter cry to God to give him back the faith and strength that he had lost, Owen's head fell forward and he sank into a swoon there upon the window-place.

CHAPTER 4

The Vision

Was it swoon or sleep?

At least it seemed to Owen that presently once again he was gazing into the dense intolerable blackness of the night. Then a marvel came to pass, for the blackness opened, or rather on it, framed and surrounded by it, there appeared a vision. It was the vision of a native town, having a great bare space in the centre of it encircled by hundreds or thousands of huts. But there was no one stirring about the huts, for it was night—not this his night of trial indeed, since now the sky was strewn with innumerable stars. Everything was silent about that town, save that now and again a dog barked or a fretful child wailed within a hut, or the sentries as they passed saluted each other in the name of the king.

Among all those hundreds of huts, to Owen it seemed that his attention was directed to one which stood apart surrounded with a fence. Now the interior of the hut opened itself to him. It was not lighted, yet with his spirit sense he could see its every detail: the polished floor, the skin rugs, the beer gourds, the shields and spears, the roof-tree of red wood, and the dried lizard hanging from the thatch, a charm to ward off evil. In this hut, seated face to face halfway between the centre-post and the door-hole, were two men. The darkness was deep about them, and they whispered to each other through it; but in his dream this was no bar to Owen's sight. He could discern their faces clearly.

One of them was that of a man of about thirty-five years of age. In stature he was almost a giant. He wore a *kaross* of leopard skins, and on his wrists and ankles were rings of ivory, the royal ornaments. His face was fierce and powerful; his eyes, which were set far apart, rolled so much that at times they seemed all white; and his fingers played nervously with the handle of a spear that he carried in his right hand. His companion was of a different stamp; a person of more than fifty years, he was tall and spare in figure, with delicately shaped hands and feet. His hair and little beard were tinged with grey, his face was strikingly handsome, nervous and expressive, and his forehead both broad and high. But more remarkable still were his eyes, which shone with a piercing brightness, almost grey in colour, steady as the flame of a well-trimmed lamp, and so cold that they might have been precious stones set in the head of a statue.

"Must I then put your thoughts in words?" said this man in a clear quick whisper. "Well, so be it; for I weary of sitting here in the dark waiting for water that will not flow. Listen, Prince; you come to talk to me of the death of a king—is it not so? Nay do not start. Why are you affrighted when you hear upon the lips of another the plot that these many months has been familiar to your breast?"

"Truly, Hokosa, you are the best of wizards, or the worst," answered the great man huskily. "Yet this once you are mistaken," he added with a change of voice. "I came but to ask you for a charm to turn my father's heart——"

"To dust? Prince, if I am mistaken, why am I the best of wizards, or the worst, and why did your jaw drop and your face change at my words, and why do you even now touch your dry lips with your tongue? Yes, I know that it is dark here, yet some can see in it, and I am one of them. Ay, Prince, and I can see your mind also. You would be rid of your father: he has lived too long. Moreover his love turns to Nodwengo, the good and gentle; and perhaps—who can say?—it is even in his thought, when all his regiments are about him two days hence, to declare that you, Prince, are deposed, and that your brother, Nodwengo, shall be king in your stead. Now, Nodwengo you cannot kill; he is too well loved and too well guarded. If he died suddenly, his dead lips would call out 'Murder!' in the ears of all men; and, Prince, all eyes would turn to you, who alone could profit by his end. But if the king should chance to die—why he is old, is he not? and such things happen to the old. Also he grows feeble, and will not suffer the regiments to be doctored for war, although day by day they clamour to be led to battle; for he seeks to end his years in peace."

"I say that you speak folly," answered the prince with vehemence.

"Then, Son of the Great One, why should you waste time in listening to me? Farewell, Hafela the Prince, first-born of the king, who in a day to come shall carry the shield of Nodwengo; for he is good and gentle, and will spare your life—if I beg it of him."

Hafela stretched out his hand through the darkness, and caught Hokosa by the wrist.

"Stay," he whispered, "it is true. The king must die; for if he does not die within three days, I shall cease to be his heir. I know it through my spies. He is angry with me; he hates me, and he loves Nodwengo and the mother of Nodwengo. But if he dies before the last day of the festival, then that decree will never pass his lips, and the regiments will never roar out the name of Nodwengo as the name of the king to come. He must die, I tell you, Hokosa, and—by your hand."

"By *my* hand, Prince! Nay; what have you to offer me in return for such a deed as this? Have I not grown up in Umsuka's shadow, and shall I cut down the tree that shades me?"

"What have I to offer you? This: that next to myself you shall be the greatest in the land, Hokosa."

"That I am already, and whoever rules it, that I must always be. I, who am the chief of wizards; I, the reader of men's hearts; I, the hearer of men's thoughts! I, the lord of the air and the lightning; I, the invulnerable. If you would murder, Prince, then do the deed; do it knowing that I have your secret, and that henceforth you who rule shall be my servant. Nay, you forget that I can see in the dark; lay down that assegai, or, by my spirit, prince as you are, I will blast you with a spell, and your body shall be thrown to the kites, as that of one who would murder his king and father!"

The prince heard and shook, his cheeks sank in, the muscles of his great form seemed to collapse, and he grovelled on the floor of the hut.

"I know your magic," he groaned; "use it for me, not against me! What is there that I can offer you, who have everything except the throne, whereon you cannot sit, seeing that you are not of the blood-royal?"

"Think," said Hokosa.

For a while the prince thought, till presently his form straightened itself, and with a quick movement he lifted up his head.

"Is it, perchance, my affianced wife?" he whispered; "the lady Noma, whom I love, and who, according to our custom, I shall wed as the queen to be after the feast of first-fruits? Oh! say it not, Hokosa."

"I say it," answered the wizard. "Listen, Prince. The lady Noma is the only child of my blood-brother, my friend, with whom I was brought up, he who was slain at my side in the great war with the tribes of the north. She was my ward: she was more; for through her— ah! you know not how—I held my converse with the things of earth and air, the very spirits that watch us now in this darkness, Hafela. Thus it happened, that before ever she was a woman, her mind grew greater than the mind of any other woman, and her thought became my thought, and my thought became her thought, for I and no other am her master. Still I waited to wed her till she was fully grown; and while I waited I went upon an embassy to the northern tribes. Then it was that you saw the maid in visiting at my *kraal*, and her beauty and her wit took hold of you; and in the council of the king, as you have a right to do, you named her as your head wife, the queen to be.

"The king heard and bowed his head; he sent and took her, and placed her in the House of the Royal Women, there to abide till this feast of the first-fruits, when she shall be given to you in marriage. Yes, he sent her to that guarded house wherein not even I may set my foot. Although I was afar, her spirit warned me, and I returned, but too late; for she was sealed to you of the blood-royal, and that is a law which may not be broken.

"Hafela, I prayed you to return her to me, and you mocked me. I would have brought you to your death, but it could not have availed me: for then, by that same law, which may not be broken, she who was sealed to you must die with you; and though thereafter her spirit would sit with me till I died also, it was not enough, since I who have conquered all, yet cannot conquer the fire that wastes my heart, nor cease to long by night and day for a woman who is lost to me. Then it was, Hafela, that I plotted vengeance against you. I threw my spell over the mind of the king, till he learnt to hate you and your evil deeds; and I, even I, have brought it about that your brother should be preferred before you, and that you shall be the servant in his house. This is the price that you must pay for her of whom you have robbed me; and by my spirit and her spirit you shall pay! Yet listen. Hand back the girl, as you may do—for she is not yet your wife—and choose another for your queen, and I will undo all that I have done, and I will find you a means, Hafela, to carry out your will. Ay, before six suns have set, the regiments rushing past you shall hail you King of the Nation of the Amasuka, Lord of the ancient House of Fire!"

"I cannot," groaned the prince; "death were better than this!"

"Ay, death were better; but you shall not die, you shall live a servant, and your name shall become a mockery, a name for women to make rhymes on."

Now the prince sprang up.

"Take her!" he hissed; "take her! you, who are an evil ghost; you, beneath whose eyes children wail, and at whose passing the hairs on the backs of hounds stand up! Take her, priest of death and ill; but take my curse with her! Ah! I also can prophecy; and I tell you that this woman whom you have taught, this witch of many spells, whose glance can shrivel the hearts of men, shall give you to drink of your own medicine; ay, she shall dog you to the death, and mock you while you perish by an end of shame!"

"What," laughed the wizard, "have I a rival in my own arts? Nay, Hafela, if you would learn the trade, pay me well and I will give you lessons. Yet I counsel you not; for you are flesh, nothing but flesh, and he who would rule the air must cultivate the spirit. Why, I tell you, Prince, that even the love for her who is my heart, the lady whom we both would wed, partaking of the flesh as, alas! it does, has cost me half my powers. Now let us cease from empty scoldings, and strike our bargain.

"Listen. On the last day of the feast, when all the regiments are gathered to salute the king there in his Great Place according to custom, you shall stand forth before the king and renounce Noma, and she shall pass back to the care of my household. You yourself shall bring her to where I stand, and as I take her from you I will put into your hand a certain powder. Then you shall return to the side of the king, and after our fashion shall give him to drink the bowl of the first-fruits; but as you stir the beer, you will let fall into it that powder which I have given you. The king will drink, and what he leaves undrunk you will throw out upon the dust.

"Now he will rise to give out to the people his royal decree, whereby, Prince, you are to be deposed from your place as heir, and your brother, Nodwengo, is to be set in your seat. But of that decree never a word shall pass his lips; if it does, recall your saying and take back the lady Noma from where she stands beside me. I tell you that never a word will pass his lips; for even as he rises a stroke shall take him, such a stroke as often falls upon the fat and aged, and he will sink to the ground snoring through his nostrils. For a while thereafter—it may be six hours, it may be twelve—he shall lie insensible, and then a cry will arise that the king is dead!"

"Ay," said Hafela, "and that I have poisoned him!"

"Why, Prince? Few know what is in your father's mind, and with those, being king, you will be able to deal. Also this is the virtue of the poison which I choose, that it is swift, yet the symptoms of it are the symptoms of a natural sickness. But that your safety and mine may be assured, I have made yet another plan, though of this there will be little need. You were present two days since when a runner came from the white man who sojourns beyond our border, he who seeks to teach us, the Children of Fire, a new faith, and gives out that he is the messenger of the King of heaven. This runner asked leave for the white man to visit the Great Place, and, speaking in the king's name, I gave him leave. But I warned his servant that if his master came, a sign should be required of him to show that he was a true man, and had of the wisdom of the King of Heaven; and that if he failed therein, then that he should die as that white liar died who visited us in bygone years.

"Now I have so ordered that this white man, passing through the Valley of Death yonder, shall reach the Great Place not long before the king drinks of the cup of the first-fruits. Then if any think that something out of nature has happened to the king, they will surely think also that this strange prayer-doctor has wrought the evil. Then also I will call for a sign from the white man, praying of him to recover the king of his sickness; and when he fails, he shall be slain as a worker of spells and the false prophet of a false god, and so we shall be rid of him and his new faith, and you shall be cleared of doubt. Is not the plan good, Prince?"

"It is very good, Hokosa—save for one thing only."

"For what thing?"

"This: the white man who is named Messenger might chance to be a true prophet of a true God, and to recover the king."

"Oho, let him do it, if he can; but to do it, first he must know the poison and its antidote. There is but one, and it is known to me only of all men in this land. When he has done that, then I, yes, even I, Hokosa, will begin to inquire concerning this God of his, who shows Himself so mighty in person of His messenger." And he laughed low and scornfully.

"Prince, farewell! I go forth alone, whither you dare not follow at this hour, to seek that which we shall need. One word—think not to play me false, or to cheat me of my price; for whate'er betides, be sure of this, that hour shall be the hour of your dooming. Hail to you, Son of the King! Hail! and farewell." Then, removing the door-board, the wizard passed from the hut and was gone.

****

The vision changed. Now there appeared a valley walled in on either side with sloping cliffs of granite; a desolate place, sandy and, save for a single spring, without water, strewn with boulders of rock, some of them piled fantastically one upon the other. At a certain spot this valley widened out, and in the mouth of the space thus formed, midway between the curved lines of the receding cliffs, stood a little hill or *koppie*, also built up of boulders. It was a place of death; for all around the hill, and piled in hundreds between the crevices of its stones, lay the white bones of men.

Nor was this all. Its summit was flat, and in the midst of it stood a huge tree. Even had it not been for the fruit which hung from its branches, the aspect of that tree must have struck the beholder as uncanny, even as horrible. The bark on its great bole was leprous white; and from its gaunt and spreading rungs rose branches that subdivided themselves again and again, till at last they terminated in round green fingers, springing from grey, flat slabs of bark, in shape not unlike that of a human palm. Indeed, from a little distance this tree, especially if viewed by moonlight, had the appearance of bearing on it hundreds or thousands of the arms and hands of men, all of them stretched imploringly to Heaven.

Well might they seem to do so, seeing that to its naked limbs hung the bodies of at least twenty human beings who had suffered death by order of the king or his captains, or by the decree of the company of wizards, whereof Hokosa was the chief. There on the Hill of Death stood the Tree of Death; and that in its dank shade, or piled upon the ground beneath it, hung and lay the pitiful remnants of the multitudes who for generations had been led thither to their doom.

Now, in Owen's vision a man was seen approaching by the little pathway that ran up the side of the mount—the Road of Lost Footsteps it was called. It was Hokosa the wizard. Outside the circle of the tree he halted, and drawing a tanned skin from a bundle of medicines which he carried, he tied it about his mouth; for the very smell of that tree is poisonous and must not be suffered to reach the lungs.

Presently he was under the branches, where once again he halted; this time it was to gaze at the body of an old man which swung to and fro in the night breeze.

"Ah! friend," he muttered, "we strove for many years, but it seems that I have conquered at the last. Well, it is just; for if you could have had your way, your end would have been my end."

Then very leisurely, as one who is sure that he will not be interrupted, Hokosa began to climb the tree, till at length some of the green fingers were within his reach. Resting his back against a bough, one by one he broke off several of them, and averting his face so that the fumes of it might not reach him, he caused the thick milk-white juice that they contained to trickle into the mouth of a little gourd which was hung about his neck by a string. When he had collected enough of the poison and carefully corked the gourd with a plug of wood, he descended the tree again. At the great fork where the main branches sprang from the trunk, he stood a while contemplating a creeping plant which ran up them. It was a plant of naked stem, like the tree it grew upon; and, also like the tree, its leaves consisted of bunches of green spikes having a milky juice.

"Strange," he said aloud, "that Nature should set the bane and the antidote side by side, the one twined about the other. Well, so it is in everything; yes, even in the heart of man. Shall I gather some of this juice also? No; for then I might repent and save him, remembering that he has loved me, and thus lose her I seek, her whom I must win back or be withered. Let the messenger of the King of Heaven save him, if he can. This tree lies on his path; perchance he may prevail upon its dead to tell him of the bane and of the antidote." And once more the wizard laughed mockingly.

****

The vision passed. At this moment Thomas Owen, recovering from his swoon, lifted his head from the window-place. The night before him was as black as it had been, and behind him the little American clock was still striking the hour of midnight. Therefore he could not have remained insensible for longer than a few seconds.

A few seconds, yet how much he had seen in them. Truly his want of faith had been reproved—truly he also had been "warned of God in a dream,"—truly "his ears had been opened and his instruction sealed." His soul had been "kept back from the pit," and his life from "perishing by the sword;" and the way of the wicked had been made clear to him "in a dream, in a vision of the night when deep sleep falleth upon men."

Not for nothing had he endured that agony, and not for nothing had he struggled in the grip of doubt.

427

CHAPTER 5

The Feast of the First-Fruits

On the third morning from this night whereof the strange events have been described, an ox-wagon might have been seen outspanned on the hither side of those ranges of hills that were visible from the river. These mountains, which although not high are very steep, form the outer barrier and defence of the kingdom of the Amasuka. Within five hundred yards of where the wagon stood, however, a sheer cliffed gorge, fire-riven and water-hewn, pierced the range, and looking on it, Owen knew it for the gorge of his dream. Night and day the mouth of it was guarded by a company of armed soldiers, whose huts were built high on outlook places in the mountains, whence their keen eyes could scan the vast expanses of plain. A full day before it reached them, they had seen the white-capped wagon crawling across the *veldt*, and swift runners had reported its advent to the king at his Great Place.

Back came the word of the king that the white man, with the wagon and his servant, were to be led on towards the Great Place at such speed as would bring him there in time for him to behold the last ceremony of the feast of first-fruits; but, for the present, that the wagon itself and the oxen were to be left at the mouth of the gorge, in charge of a guard, who would be answerable for them.

Now, on this morning the captain of the guard and his orderlies advanced to the wagon and stood in front of it. They were splendid men, armed with great spears and shields, and adorned with feather head-dresses and all the wild finery of their regiment. Owen descended from the wagon and came to meet them, and so for a few moments they remained, face to face, in silence. A strange contrast they presented as they stood there; the bare-headed white man frail, delicate, spiritual of countenance, and the warriors great, grave, powerful, a very embodiment of the essence of untamed humanity, an incarnate presentation of the spirit of savage warfare.

"How are you named, White Man?" asked the captain.

"Chief, I am named Messenger."

"The peace of the king be with you, Messenger," said the captain, lifting his spear.

"The peace of God be with you, Chief," answered Owen, holding up his hands in blessing.

"Who is God?" asked the captain.

"Chief, He is the King I serve, and His word is between my lips."

"Then pass on, Messenger of God, and deliver the word of God your King into the ears of my king, at his Great Place yonder. Pass on riding the beast you have brought with you, for the way is rough; but your wagon, your oxen, and your servants, save this man only who is of the Children of Fire, must stay here in my keeping. Fear not, Messenger, I will hold them safe."

"I do not fear, Chief, there is honour in your eyes."

****

Some hours later, Owen, mounted on his mule, was riding through the gorge, a guard in front of and behind him, and with them carriers who had been sent to bear his baggage. At his side walked his disciple John, and his face was sad.

"Why are you still afraid?" asked Owen.

"Ah! father, because this is a place of fear. Here in this valley men are led to die; presently you will see."

"I have seen," answered Owen. "Yonder where we shall halt is a mount, and on that mount stands a tree; it is called the Tree of Death, and it stretches a thousand hands to Heaven, praying for mercy that does not come, and from its boughs there hangs fruit, a fruit of dead men—yes, twenty of them hang there this day."

"How know you these things, my father," asked the man amazed, "seeing that I have never spoken to you of them?"

"Nay," he answered, "God has spoken to me. My God and your God."

Another hour passed, and they were resting by the spring of water, near to the shadow of the dreadful tree, for in that gorge the sun burned fiercely. John counted the bodies that swung upon it, and again looked fearfully at Owen, for there were twenty of them.

"I desire to go up to that tree," Owen said to the guard.

"As you will, Messenger," answered their leader; "I have no orders to prevent you from so doing. Still," he added with a solemn smile, "it is a place that few seek of their own will, and, because I

429

like you well, Messenger, I pray it may never be my duty to lead you there of the king's will."

Then Owen went up to the tree and John with him, only John would not pass beneath the shadow of its branches; but stood by wondering, while his master bound a handkerchief about his mouth.

"How did he know that the breath of the tree is poisonous?" John wondered.

Owen walked to the bole of the tree, and breaking off some of the finger-like leaves of the creeper that twined about it, he pressed their milky juice into a little bottle that he had made ready. Then he returned quickly, for the sights and odours of the place were not to be borne.

Outside the circle of the branches he halted, and removed the handkerchief from his mouth.

"Be of good cheer," he said to John, "and if it should chance that I am called away before my words come true, yet remember my words. I tell you that this Tree of Death shall become the Tree of Life for all the children of your people. Look! there above you is its sign and promise."

John lifted his eyes, following the line of Owen's outstretched hand, and saw this. High up upon the tree, and standing clear of all the other branches, was one straight, dead limb, and from this dead limb two arms projected at right angles, also dead and snapped off short. Had a carpenter fashioned a cross of wood and set it there, its proportions could not have been more proper and exact. It was very strange to find this symbol of the Christian hope towering above that place of human terror, and stranger still was the purpose which it must serve in a day to come.

Owen and John returned to the guard in silence, and presently they set forward on their journey. At length, passing beneath a natural arch of rock, they were out of the Valley of Death, and before them, not five hundred paces away, appeared the fence of the Great Place.

This Great Place stood upon a high plateau, in the lap of the surrounding hills, all of which were strongly fortified with *schanses*, pitfalls, and rough walls of stone. That plateau may have measured fifteen miles in circumference, and the fence of the town itself was about four miles in circumference. Within the fence and following its curve, for it was round, stood thousands of dome-shaped huts carefully set out in streets. Within these again was a stout stockade of timber, enclosing a vast arena of trodden earth, large enough to contain all the cattle of the People of Fire in times of danger, and to serve as a review ground for their *impis* in times of peace or festival.

At the outer gate of the *kraal* there was a halt, while the keepers of the gate despatched a messenger to their king to announce the advent of the white man. Of this pause Owen took advantage to array himself in the surplice and hood which he had brought with him in readiness for that hour. Then he gave the mule to John to lead behind him.

"What do you, Messenger?" asked the leader of the guard, astonished.

"I clothe myself in my war-dress," he answered.

"Where then is your spear, Messenger?"

"Here," said Owen, presenting to his eyes a crucifix of ivory, most beautifully carved.

"I perceive that you are of the family of wizards," said the man, and fell back.

Now they entered the *kraal* and passed for three hundred yards or more through rows of huts, till they reached the gate of the stockade, which was opened to them. Once within it, Owen saw a wonderful sight, such a sight as few white men have seen. The ground of the enormous oval before him was not flat. Either from natural accident or by design it sloped gently upwards, so that the spectator, standing by the gate or at the head of it before the house of the king, could take in its whole expanse, and, if his sight were keen enough, could see every individual gathered there.

On the particular day of Owen's arrival it was crowded with regiments, twelve of them, all dressed in their different uniforms and bearing shields to match, not one of which was less than 2500 strong. At this moment the regiments were massed in deep lines, each battalion by itself, on either side of the broad roadway that ran straight up the *kraal* to where the king, his sons, his advisers and guards, together with the company of wizards, were placed in front of the royal house.

There they stood in absolute silence, like tens of thousands of bronze statues, and Owen perceived that either they were resting or that they were gathered thus to receive him. That the latter was the case soon became evident, for as he appeared, a white spot at the foot of the slope, countless heads turned and myriads of eyes fastened themselves upon him. For an instant he was dismayed; there was something terrifying in this numberless multitude of warriors, and the thought of the task that he had undertaken crushed his spirit. Then he remembered, and shaking off his fear and doubt, alone, save for his disciple John, holding the crucifix aloft, he walked slowly up the wide road towards the place where he guessed that the king must be. His arm was weary ere ever he reached it, but at length he found himself standing before a thickset old man, who was clad in leopard skins and seated upon a stool of polished wood.

"It is the king," whispered John behind him.

"Peace be to you," said Owen, breaking the silence.

"The wish is good, may it be fulfilled," answered the king in a deep voice, sighing as he said the words. "Yet yours is a strange greeting," he added. "Whence came you, White Man, how are you named, and what is your mission to me and to my people?"

"King, I come from beyond the sea; I am named Messenger, and my mission is to deliver to you the saying of God, my King and—yours."

At these words a gasp of astonishment went up from those who stood within hearing, expecting as they did to see them rewarded by instant death. But Umsuka only said:—

"'My King and yours'? Bold words, Messenger. Where then is this King to whom I, Umsuka, should bow the knee?"

"He is everywhere—in the heavens, on the earth, and below the earth."

"If He is everywhere, then He is here. Show me the likeness of this King, Messenger."

"Behold it," Owen answered, thrusting forward the crucifix.

Now all the great ones about the king stared at this figure of a dying man crowned with thorns and hanging on a cross, and then drew up their lips to laugh. But that laugh never left them; a sudden impulse, a mysterious wave of feeling choked it in their throats. A sense of the strangeness of the contrast between themselves in their armed multitudes and this one white-robed man in his loneliness took hold of them, and with it another sense of something not far removed from fear.

"A wizard indeed," they thought in their hearts, and what they thought the king uttered.

"I perceive," he said, "that you are either mad, White Man, or you are a prince of wizards. Mad you do not seem to be, for your eyes are calm, therefore a wizard you must be. Well, stand behind me: by-and-by I will hear your message and ask of you to show me your powers; but before then there are things which I must do. Are the lads ready? Ho, you, loose the bull!"

At the command a line of soldiers moved from the right, forming itself up in front of the king and his attendants, revealing a number of youths, of from sixteen to seventeen years of age, armed with sticks only, who stood in companies outside a massive gate. Presently this gate was opened, and through it, with a mad bellow, rushed a wild buffalo bull. On seeing them the brute halted, and for a few moments stood pawing the earth and tearing it with its great horns. Then it put down its head and charged. Instead of making way for it, uttering a shrill whistling sound, the youths rushed at the beast, striking with their sticks.

Another instant, and one of them appeared above the heads of his companions, thrown high into the air, to be followed by a second and a third. Now the animal was through the throng and carrying a poor boy on its horn, whence presently he fell dead; through and through the ranks of the regiments it charged furiously backward and forward.

Watching it fascinated, Owen noted that it was a point of honour for no man to stir before its rush; there they stood, and if the bull gored them, there they fell. At length, exhausted and terrified, the brute headed back straight up the lane where the main body of the youths were waiting for it. Now it was among them, and, reckless of wounds or death, they swarmed about it like bees, seizing it by legs, nose, horns and tail, till with desperate efforts they dragged it to the ground and beat the life out of it with their sticks. This done, they formed up before the king and saluted him.

"How many are killed?" he asked.

"Eight in all," was the answer, "and fifteen gored."

"A good bull," he said with a smile; "that of last year killed but five. Well, the lads fought him bravely. Let the dead be buried, the hurt tended, or, if their harms are hopeless, slain, and to the rest give a double ration of beer. Ho, now, fall back, men, and make a space for the Bees and the Wasps to fight in."

Some orders were given and a great ring was formed, leaving an arena clear that may have measured a hundred and fifty yards in diameter. Then suddenly, from opposite sides, the two regiments, known as the Bees and the Wasps respectively, rushed upon each other, uttering their war-cries.

"I put ten head of cattle on the Bees; who wagers on the Wasps?" cried the king.

"I, Lord," answered the Prince Hafela, stepping forward.

"You, Prince!" said the king with a quick frown. "Well, you are right to back them, they are your own regiment. Ah! they are at it."

By this time the scene was that of a hell broken loose upon the earth. The two regiments, numbering some 5000 men in all, had come together, and the roar of their meeting shields was like the roar of thunder. They were armed with *kerries* only, and not with spears, for the fight was supposed to be a mimic one; but these weapons they used with such effect that soon hundreds of them were down dead or with shattered skulls and bruised limbs. Fiercely they fought, while the whole army watched, for their rivalry was keen and for many months they had known that they were to be pitted one against the other on this day. Fiercely they fought, while the captains cried their orders, and the dust rose up in clouds as they swung to and fro, breast thrusting against breast. At length the end came; the Bees began to give, they fell back ever more quickly till their retreat was a rout, and, leaving many stretched upon the ground, amid the mocking cries of the army they were driven to the fence, by touching which they obtained peace at the hands of their victors.

The king saw, and his somewhat heavy, quiet face grew alive with rage.

"Search and see," he said, "if the captain of the Bees is alive and unhurt."

Messengers went to do his bidding, and presently they returned, bringing with them a man of magnificent appearance and middle age, whose left arm had been broken by a blow from a *kerry*. With his right hand he saluted first the king, then the Prince Nodwengo, a kindly-faced, mild-eyed man, in whose command he was.

"What have you to say?" asked the king, in a cold voice of anger. "Know you that you have cost me ten head of the royal white cattle?"

"King, I have nothing to say," answered the captain calmly, "except that my men are cowards."

"That is certainly so," said the king. "Let all the wounded among them be carried away; and for you, captain, who turn my soldiers into cowards, you shall die a dog's death, hanging tomorrow on the Tree of Doom. As for your regiment, I banish it to the fever country, there to hunt elephants for three years, since it is not fit to fight with men."

"It is well," replied the captain, "since death is better than shame. Only King, I have done you good service in the past; I ask that it may be presently and by the spear."

"So be it," said the king.

"I crave his life, father," said the Prince Nodwengo; "he is my friend."

"A prince should not choose cowards for his friends," replied the king; "let him be killed, I say."

Then Owen, who had been watching and listening, his heart sick with horror, stood forward and said:—

434

"King, in the name of Him I serve, I conjure you to spare this man and those others that are hurt, who have done no crime except to be driven back by soldiers stronger than themselves."

"Messenger," answered the king, "I bear with you because you are ignorant. Know that, according to our customs, this crime is the greatest of crimes, for here we show no mercy to the conquered."

"Yet you should do so," said Owen, "seeing that you also must ere long be conquered by death, and then how can you expect mercy who have shown none?"

"Let him be killed!" said the king.

"King!" cried Owen once more, "do this deed, and I tell you that before the sun is down great evil will overtake you."

"Do you threaten me, Messenger? Well, we will see. Let him be killed, I say."

Then the man was led away; but, before he went he found time to thank Owen and Nodwengo the prince, and to call down good fortune upon them.

CHAPTER 6

The Drinking of the Cup

Now the king's word was done, the anger went out of his eyes, and once more his countenance grew weary. A command was issued, and, with the most perfect order, moving like one man, the regiments changed their array, forming up battalion upon battalion in face of the king, that they might give him the royal salute so soon as he had drunk the cup of the first-fruits.

A herald stood forward and cried:—

"Hearken, you Sons of Fire! Hearken, you Children of Umsuka, Shaker of the Earth! Have any of you a boon to ask of the king?"

Men stood forward, and having saluted, one by one asked this thing or that. The king heard their requests, and as he nodded or turned his head away, so they were granted or refused.

When all had done, the Prince Hafela came forward, lifted his spear, and cried:—

"A boon, King!"

"What is it?" asked his father, eyeing him curiously.

"A small matter, King," he replied. "A while ago I named a certain woman, Noma, the ward of Hokosa the wizard, and she was sealed to me to fill the place of my first wife, the queen that is to be. She passed into the House of the Royal Women, and, by your command, King, it was fixed that I should marry her according to our customs tomorrow, after the feast of the first-fruits is ended. King, my heart is changed towards that woman; I no longer desire to take her to wife, and I pray that you will order that she shall now be handed back to Hokosa her guardian."

"You blow hot and cold with the same mouth, Hafela," said Umsuka, "and in love or war I do not like such men. What have you to say to this demand, Hokosa?"

Now Hokosa stepped forward from where he stood at the head

436

of the company of wizards. His dress, like that of his companions, was simple, but in its way striking. On his shoulders he wore a cloak of shining snakeskin; about his loins was a short kilt of the same material; and round his forehead, arms and knees were fillets of snakeskin. At his side hung his pouch of medicines, and in his hand he held no spear, but a wand of ivory, whereof the top was roughly carved so as to resemble the head of a cobra reared up to strike.

"King," he said, "I have heard the words of the prince, and I do not think that this insult should have been put upon the Lady Noma, my ward, or upon me, her guardian. Still, let it be, for I would not that one should pass from under the shadow of my house whither she is not welcome. Without my leave the prince named this woman as his queen, as he had the right to do; and without my leave he unnames her, as he has the right to do. Were the prince a common man, according to custom he should pay a fine of cattle to be held by me in trust for her whom he discards; but this is a matter that I leave to you, King."

"You do well, Hokosa," answered Umsuka, "to leave this to me. Prince, you would not wish the fine that you should pay to be that of any common man. With the girl shall be handed over two hundred head of cattle. More, I will do justice: unless she herself consents, she shall not be put away. Let the Lady Noma be summoned."

Now the face of Hafela grew sullen, and watching, Owen saw a swift change pass over that of Hokosa. Evidently he was not certain of the woman. Presently there was a stir, and from the gates of the royal house the Lady Noma appeared, attended by women, and stood before the king. She was a tall and lovely girl, and the sunlight flashed upon her bronze-hued breast and her ornaments of ivory. Her black hair was fastened in a knot upon her neck, her features were fine and small, her gait was delicate and sure as that of an antelope, and her eyes were beautiful and full of pride. There she stood before the king, looking round her like a stag. Seeing her thus, Owen understood how it came about that she held two men so strangely different in the hollow of her hand, for her charm was of a nature to appeal to both of them—a charm of the spirit as well as of the flesh. And yet the face was haughty, a face that upon occasion might even become cruel.

"You sent for me and I am here, O King," she said, in a slow and quiet voice.

"Listen, girl," answered the king. "A while ago the Prince Hafela, my son, named you as her who should be his queen, whereon you were taken and placed in the House of the Royal Women, to abide the day of your marriage, which should be tomorrow."

"It is true that the prince has honoured me thus, and that you have been pleased to approve of his choice," she said, lifting her eyebrows. "What of it, O King?"

"This, girl: the prince who was pleased to honour you is now pleased to dishonour you. Here, in the presence of the council and army, he prays of me to annul his sealing to you, and to send you back to the house of your guardian, Hokosa the wizard."

Noma started, and her face grew hard.

"Is it so?" she said. "Then it would seem that I have lost favour in the eyes of my lord the prince, or that some fairer woman has found it."

"Of these matters I know nothing," replied the king; "but this I know, that if you seek justice you shall have it. Say but the word, and he to whom you were promised in marriage shall take you in marriage, whether he wills or wills it not."

At this speech, the face of Hafela was suddenly lit up as with the fire of hope, while over that of Hokosa there passed another subtle change. The girl glanced at them both and was silent for a while. Her breast heaved and her white teeth bit upon her lip. To Owen, who noted all, it was clear that rival passions were struggling in her heart: the passion of power and the passion of love, or of some emotion which he did not understand. Hokosa fixed his calm eyes upon her with a strange intensity of gaze, and while he gazed his form quivered with a suppressed excitement, much as a snake quivers that is about to strike its prey. To the careless eye there was nothing remarkable about his look and attitude; to the observer it was evident that both were full of extraordinary purpose. He was talking to the girl, not with words, but in some secret language that he and she understood alone. She started as one starts who catches the tone of a well-remembered voice in a crowd of strangers, and lifting her eyes from the ground, whither she had turned them in meditation, she looked up at Hokosa.

Instantly her face began to change. The haughtiness and anger went out of it, it grew troubled, the lips parted in a sigh. First she bent her head and body towards him, then without more ado she walked to where he stood and took him by the hand. Here, at some whispered word or sign, she seemed to recover herself, and again resuming the character of a proud offended beauty, she curtseyed to Umsuka, and spoke:

"O King, as you see, I have made my choice. I will not force myself upon a man who scorns me, no, not even to share his place and power, though it is true that I love them both. Nay, I will return to Hokosa my guardian, and to his wife, Zinti, who has been as my mother, and with them be at peace."

"It is well," said the king, "and perhaps, girl, your choice is wise; perhaps your loss is not so great as you have thought. Hafela, take you the hand of Hokosa and release the girl back to him according to the law, promising in the ears of men before the first month of winter to pay him two hundred head of cattle as forfeit, to be held by him in trust for the girl."

In a sullen voice, his lips trembling with rage, Hafela did as the king commanded; and when the hands of the conspirators unclasped, Owen perceived that in that of the prince lay a tiny packet.

"Mix me the cup of the first-fruits, and swiftly," said the king again, "for the sun grows low in the heavens, and ere it sinks I have words to say."

Now a polished gourd filled with native beer was handed to Nodwengo, the second son of the king, and one by one the great councillors approached, and, with appropriate words, let fall into it offerings emblematic of fertility and increase. The first cast in a grain of corn; the second, a blade of grass; the third, a shaving from an ox's horn; the fourth, a drop of water; the fifth, a woman's hair; the sixth, a particle of earth; and so on, until every ingredient was added to it that was necessary to the magic brew.

Then Hokosa, as chief of the medicine men, blessed the cup according to the ancient forms, praying that he whose body was the heavens, whose eyes were lightning, and whose voice was thunder, the spirit whom they worshipped, might increase and multiply to them during the coming year all those fruits and elements that were present in the cup, and that every virtue which they contained might comfort the body of the king. His prayer finished, it was the turn of Hafela to play his part as the eldest born of the king. Kneeling over the cup which stood upon the ground, a spear was handed to him that had been made red hot in the fire. Taking the spear, he stabbed with it towards the four quarters of the horizon; then, muttering some invocation, he plunged it into the bowl, stirring its contents till the iron grew black. Now he threw aside the spear, and lifting the bowl in both hands, he carried it to his father and offered it to him.

Although he had been unable to see him drop the poison into the cup, a glance at Hafela told Owen that it was there; for though he kept his face under control, he could not prevent his hands from twitching or the sweat from starting upon his brow and breast.

The king rose, and taking the bowl, held it on high, saying:—

"In this cup, which I drink on behalf of the nation, I pledge you, my people."

It was the signal for the royal salute, for which each regiment had been prepared. As the last word left the king's lips, every one of the thirty thousand men present in that great place began to rattle his *kerry* against the surface of his ox-hide shield. At first the sound produced resembled that of the murmur of the sea; but by slow and just degrees it grew louder and ever louder, till the roar of it was like the deepest voice of thunder, a sound awe-inspiring, terrible.

Suddenly, when its volume was most, four spears were thrown into the air, and at this signal every man ceased to beat upon his shield. In the place itself there was silence, but from the mountains around the echoes still crashed and volleyed. When the last of them had died away, the king brought the cup to the level of his lips. Owen saw, and knowing its contents, was almost moved to cry out in warning. Indeed, his arm was lifted and his mouth was open, when by chance he noted Hokosa watching him, and remembered. To act now would be madness, his time had not yet come.

The cup touched the king's lips, and at the sign from every throat in that countless multitude sprang the word *"King!"* and every foot stamped upon the ground, shaking the solid earth. Thrice the monarch drank, and thrice this tremendous salute, the salute of the whole nation to its ruler, was repeated, each time more loudly than the last. Then pouring the rest of the liquor on the ground, Umsuka set aside the cup, and in the midst of a silence that seemed deep after the crash of the great salute, he began to address the multitude:—

"Hearken, Councillors and Captains, and you, my people, hearken. As you know, I have two sons, calves of the Black Bull, princes of the land—my son Hafela, the eldest born, and my son Nodwengo, his half-brother——"

At this point the king began to grow confused. He hesitated, passing his hand over his eyes, then slowly and with difficulty repeated those words which he had already said.

"We hear you, Father," cried the councillors in encouragement, as for the second time he paused. While they still spoke, the veins in the king's neck were seen to swell suddenly, foam flecked with blood burst from his lips, and he fell headlong to the ground.

CHAPTER 7

The Recovery of the King

For a moment there was silence, then a great cry arose—a cry of "Our father is dead!" Presently with it were mingled other and angrier shouts of "The king is murdered!" and "He is bewitched, the white wizard has bewitched the king! He prophesied evil upon him, and now he has bewitched him!"

Meanwhile the captains and councillors formed a ring about Umsuka, and Hokosa bending over him examined him.

"Princes and Councillors," he said presently, "your father yet lives, but his life is like the life of a dying fire and soon he must be dead. This is sure, that one of two things has befallen him: either the heat has caused the blood to boil in his veins and he is smitten with a stroke from heaven, such as men who are fat and heavy sometimes die of; or he has been bewitched by a wicked wizard. Yonder stands one," and he pointed to Owen, "who not an hour ago prophesied that before the sun was down great evil should overtake the king. The sun is not yet down, and great evil has overtaken him. Perchance, Princes and Councillors, this white prophet can tell us of the matter."

"Perchance I can," answered Owen calmly.

"He admits it!" cried some. "Away with him!"

"Peace!" said Owen, holding the crucifix towards those whose spears threatened his life.

They shrank back, for this symbol of a dying man terrified them who could not guess its significance.

"Peace," went on Owen, "and listen. Be sure of this, Councillors, that if I die, your king will die; whereas if I live, your king may live. You ask me of this matter. Where shall I begin? Shall I begin with the tale of two men seated together some nights ago in a hut so dark that no eyes could see in it, save perchance the eyes of a wizard? What did they talk of in that hut, and who were those men? They talked, I think,

441

of the death of a king and of the crowning of a king. They talked of a price to be paid for a certain medicine; and one of them had a royal air, and one——"

"Will ye hearken to this wild babbler while your king lies dying before your eyes?" broke in Hokosa, in a shrill, unnatural voice; for almost palsied with fear as he was at Owen's mysterious words, he still retained his presence of mind. "Listen now: what is he, and what did he say? He is one who comes hither to preach a new faith to us; he comes, he says, on an embassy from the King of Heaven, who has power over all things, and who, so these white men preach, can give power to His servants. Well, let this one cease prating and show us his strength, as he has been warned he would be called upon to do. Let him give us a sign. There before you lies your king, and he is past the help of man; even I cannot help him. Therefore, let this messenger cure him, or call upon his God to cure him; that seeing, we may know him to be a true messenger, and one sent by that King of whom he speaks. Let him do this now before our eyes, or let him perish as a wizard who has bewitched the king. Do you hear my words, Messenger, and can you draw this one back from between the Gates of Death?"

"I hear them," answered Owen quietly; "and I can—or if I cannot, then I am willing to pay the penalty with my life. You who are a doctor say that your king is as one who is already dead, so that whatever I may do I cannot hurt him further. Therefore I ask this of you, that you stand round and watch, but molest me neither by word nor deed while I attempt his cure. Do you consent?"

"It is just; we consent," said the councillors. "Let us see what the white man can do, and by the issue let him be judged." But Hokosa stared at Owen wondering, and made no answer.

"Bring some clean water to me in a gourd," said Owen.

It was brought and given to him. He looked round, searching the faces of those about him. Presently his eye fell upon the Prince Nodwengo, and he beckoned to him, saying:—

"Come hither, Prince, for you are honest, and I would have you to help me, and no other man."

The prince stepped forward and Owen gave him the gourd of water. Then he drew out the little bottle wherein he had stored the juice of the creeper, and uncorking it, he bade Nodwengo fill it up with water. This done, he clasped his hands, and lifting his eyes to heaven, he prayed aloud in the language of the Amasuka.

"O God," he prayed, "upon whose business I am here, grant, I beseech Thee, that by Thy Grace power may be given to me to work this miracle in the face of these people, to the end that I may win them to cease from their iniquities, to believe upon Thee, the only true God, and to save their souls alive. Amen."

Having finished his prayer, he took the bottle and shook it; then he commanded Nodwengo to sit upon the ground and hold his father's head upon his knee. Now, as all might see by many signs, the king was upon the verge of death, for his lips were purple, his breathing was rare and stertorous, and his heart stood well-nigh still.

"Open his mouth and hold down the tongue," said Owen.

The prince obeyed, pressing down the tongue with a snuff spoon. Then placing the neck of the bottle as far into the throat as it would reach, Owen poured the fluid it contained into the body of the king, who made a convulsive movement and instantly seemed to die.

"He is dead," said one; "away with the false prophet!"

"It may be so, or it may not be so," answered Owen. "Wait for the half of an hour; then, if he shows no sign of life, do what you will with me."

"It is well," they said; "so be it."

Slowly the minutes slipped by, while the king lay like a corpse before them, and outside of that silent ring the soldiers murmured as the wind. The sun was sinking fast, and Hokosa watched it, counting the seconds. At length he spoke:—

"The half of the hour that you demanded is dead, White Man, as dead as the king; and now the time has come for you to die also," and he stretched out his hand to take him.

Owen looked at his watch and replied:—

"There is still another minute; and you, Hokosa, who are skilled in medicines, may know that this antidote does not work so swiftly as the bane."

The shot was a random one, but it told, for Hokosa fell back and was silent.

The seconds passed on as the minute hand of the watch went round from ten to twenty, from twenty to thirty, from thirty to forty. A few more instants and the game was played. Had that dream of his been vain imagining, and was all his faith nothing but a dream wondered Owen? Well, if so, it would be best that he should die. But he did not believe that it was so; he believed that the Power above him would intervene to save—not him, indeed, but all this people.

"Let us make an end," said Hokosa, "the time is done."

"Yes," said Owen, "the time is done—and *the king lives!*"

Even as he spoke the pulses in the old man's forehead were seen

443

to throb, and the veins in his neck to swell as they had swollen after he had swallowed the poison; then once more they shrank to their natural size. Umsuka stirred a hand, groaned, sat up, and spoke:—

"What has chanced to me?" he said. "I have descended into deep darkness, now once again I see light."

No one answered, for all were staring, terrified and amazed, at the Messenger—the white wizard to whom had been given power to bring men back from the gate of death. At length Owen said:—

"This has chanced to you, King: that evil which I prophesied to you if you refused to listen to the voice of mercy has fallen upon you. By now you would have been dead, had it not pleased Him Whom I serve, working through me, His messenger, to bring you back to look upon the sun. Thank Him, therefore, and worship Him, for He alone is Master of the Earth," and he held the crucifix before his eyes.

The humbled monarch lifted his hand—he who for many years had made obeisance to none—and saluted the symbol, saying:—

"Messenger, I thank Him and I worship Him, though I know Him not. Say now, how did His magic work upon me to make me sick to death and to recover me?"

"By the hand of man, King, and by the virtues that lie hid in Nature. Did you not drink of a cup, and were not many things mixed in the draught? Was it not but now in your mind to speak words that should bring down the head of pride and evil, and lift up the head of truth and goodness?"

"O White Man, how know you these things?" gasped the king.

"I know them, it is enough. Say, who was it that stirred the bowl, King, and who gave you to drink?"

Now Umsuka staggered to his feet, and cried aloud in a voice that was thick with rage:—

"By my head and the heads of my fathers I smell the plot! My son, the Prince Hafela, has learned my counsel, and would have slain me before I said words that should set him beneath the feet of Nodwengo. Seize him, captains, and let him be brought before me for judgment!"

Men looked this way and that to carry out the command of the king, but Hafela was gone. Already he was upon the hillside, running as a man has rarely run before—his face set towards that fastness in the mountains where he could find refuge among his mother's tribesmen and the regiments which he commanded. Of late they had been sent thither by the king that they might be far from the Great Place when their prince was disinherited.

"He is fled," said one; "I saw him go."

"Pursue him and bring him back, dead or alive!" thundered the king. "A hundred head of cattle to the man who lays hand upon him before he reaches the *impi* of the North, for they will fight for him!"

"Stay!" broke in Owen. "Once before this day I prayed of you, King, to show mercy, and you refused it. Will you refuse me a second time? Leave him his life who has lost all else."

"That he may rebel against me? Well, White Man, I owe you much, and for this time your wisdom shall be my guide, though my heart speaks against such gentleness. Hearken, councillors and people, this is my decree: that Hafela, my son, who would have murdered me, be deposed from his place as heir to my throne, and that Nodwengo, his brother, be set in that place, to rule the People of Fire after me when I die."

"It is good, it is just!" said the council. "Let the king's word be done."

"Hearken again," said Umsuka. "Let this white man, who is named Messenger, be placed in the House of Guests and treated with all honour; let oxen be given him from the royal herds and corn from the granaries, and girls of noble blood for wives if he wills them. Hokosa, into your hand I deliver him, and, great though you are, know this, that if but a hair of his head is harmed, with your goods and your life you shall answer for it, you and all your house."

"Let the king's word be done," said the councillors again.

"Heralds," went on Umsuka, "proclaim that the feast of the first-fruits is ended, and my command is that every regiment should seek its quarters, taking with it a double gift of cattle from the king, who has been saved alive by the magic of this white man. And now, Messenger, farewell, for my head grows weary. Tomorrow I will speak with you."

Then the king was led away into the royal house, and save those who were quartered in it, the regiments passed one by one through the gates of the *kraal*, singing their war-songs as they went. Darkness fell upon the Great Place, and through it parties of men might be seen dragging thence the corpses of those who had fallen in the fight with sticks, or been put to death thereafter by order of the king.

"Messenger," said Hokosa, bowing before Owen, "be pleased to follow me." Then he led him to a little *kraal* numbering five or six large and beautifully made huts, which stood by itself, within its own fence, at the north end of the Great Place, not far from the house of the king. In front of the centre hut a fire was burning, and by its light women appeared cleaning out the huts and bringing food and water.

445

"Here you may rest in safety, Messenger," said Hokosa, "seeing that night and day a guard from the king's own regiment will stand before your doors."

"I do not need them," answered Owen, "for none can harm me till my hour comes. I am a stranger here and you are a great man; yet, Hokosa, which of us is the safest this night?"

"Your meaning?" said Hokosa sharply.

"O man!" answered Owen, "when in a certain hour you crept up the valley yonder, and climbing the Tree of Death gathered its poison, went I not with you? When, before that hour, you sat in yonder hut bargaining with the Prince Hafela—the death of a king for the price of a girl—was I not with you? Nay, threaten me not—in your own words I say it—'lay down that assegai, or by my spirit your body shall be thrown to the kites, as that of one who would murder the king'— and the king's guest!"

"White Man," whispered Hokosa throwing down the spear, "how can these things be? I was alone in the hut with the prince, I was alone beneath the Tree of Doom, and you, as I know well, were beyond the river. Your spies must be good, White Man."

"My spirit is my only spy, Hokosa. My spirit watched you, and from your own lips he learned the secret of the bane and of the antidote. Hafela mixed the poison as you taught him; I gave the remedy, and saved the king alive."

Now the knees of Hokosa grew weak beneath him, and he leaned against the fence of the *kraal* for support.

"I have skill in the art," he said hoarsely; "but, Messenger, your magic is more than mine, and my life is forfeit to you. Tomorrow morning, you will tell the king all, and tomorrow night I shall hang upon the dreadful Tree. Well, so be it; I am overmatched at my own trade, and it is best that I should die. You have plotted well and you have conquered, and to you belong my place and power."

"It was you who plotted, and not I, Hokosa. Did you not contrive that I should reach the Great Place but a little before the poison was given to the king, so that upon me might be laid the crime of his bewitching? Did you not plan also that I should be called upon to cure him—a thing you deemed impossible—and when I failed that I should be straightway butchered?"

"Seeing that it is useless to lie to you, I confess that it was so," answered Hokosa boldly.

"It was so," repeated Owen; "therefore, according to your law your life is forfeit, seeing that you dug a pit to snare the innocent feet. But

I come to tell you of a new law, and that which I preach I practise. Hokosa, I pardon you, and if you will put aside your evil-doing, I promise you that no word of all your wickedness shall pass my lips."

"It has not been my fashion to take a boon at the hand of any man, save of the king only," said the wizard in a humble voice; "but now it seems that I am come to this. Tell me, White Man, what is the payment that you seek of me?"

"None, Hokosa, except that you cease from evil and listen with an open heart to that message which I am sworn to deliver to you and to all your nation. Also you would do well to put away that fair woman whose price was the murder of him that fed you."

"I cannot do it," answered the wizard. "I will listen to your teaching, but I will not rob my heart of her it craves alone. White Man, I am not like the rest of my nation. I have not sought after women; I have but one wife, and she is old and childless. Now, for the first time in my days, I love this girl—ah, you know not how!—and I will take her, and she shall be the mother of my children."

"Then, Hokosa, you will take her to your sorrow," answered Owen solemnly, "for she will learn to hate you who have robbed her of royalty and rule, giving her wizardries and your grey hairs in place of them."

And thus for that night they parted.

CHAPTER 8

The First Trial by Fire

On the following day, while Owen sat eating his morning meal with a thankful heart, a messenger arrived saying that the king would receive him whenever it pleased him to come. He answered that he would be with him before noon, for already he had learned that among natives one loses little by delay. A great man, they think, is rich in time, and hurries only to wait upon his superiors.

At the appointed hour a guard came to lead him to the royal house, and thither Owen went, followed by John bearing a Bible. Umsuka was seated beneath a reed roof supported by poles and open on all sides; behind him stood councillors and attendants, and by him were Nodwengo the prince, and Hokosa, his mouth and prophet. Although the day was hot, he wore a *kaross* or rug of wild cat-skins, and his face showed that the effects of the poisoned draught were still upon him. At the approach of Owen he rose with something of an effort, and, shaking him by the hand, thanked him for his life, calling him "doctor of doctors."

"Tell me, Messenger," he added, "how it was that you were able to cure me, and who were in the plot to kill me? There must have been more than one," and he rolled his eyes round with angry suspicion.

"King," answered Owen, "if I knew anything of this matter, the Power that wrote it on my mind has wiped it out again, or, at the least, has forbidden me to speak of its secret. I saved you, it is enough; for the rest, the past is the past, and I come to deal with the present and the future."

"This white man keeps his word," thought Hokosa to himself, and he looked at him thanking him with his eyes.

"So be it," answered the king; "after all, it is wise not to stir a dung-heap, for there we find little beside evil odours and the nests of snakes. Now, what is your business with me, and why do you come

448

from the white man's countries to visit me? I have heard of those countries, they are great and far away. I have heard of the white men also—wonderful men who have all knowledge; but I do not desire to have anything to do with them, for whenever they meet black people they eat them up, taking their lands and making them slaves. Once, some years ago, two of you white people visited us here, but perhaps you know that story."

"I know it," answered Owen; "one of those men you murdered, and the other you sent back with a message which he delivered into my ears across the waters; thousands of miles away."

"Nay," answered the king, "we did not murder him; he came to us with the story of a new God who could raise the dead and work other miracles, and gave such powers to His servants. So a man was slain and we begged of him to bring him back to life; and since he could not, we killed him also because he was a liar."

"He was no liar," said Owen; "since he never told you that he had power to open the mouth of the grave. Still, Heaven is merciful, and although you murdered him that was sent to you, his Master has chosen me to follow in his footsteps. Me also you may murder if you will, and then another and another; but still the messengers shall come, till at last your ears are opened and you listen. Only, for such deeds your punishment must be heavy."

"What is the message, White Man?"

"A message of peace, of forgiveness, and of life beyond the grave, of life everlasting. Listen, King. Yesterday you were near to death; say now, had you stepped over the edge of it, where would you be this day?"

Umsuka shrugged his shoulders. "With my fathers, White Man."

"And where are your fathers?"

"Nay, I know not—nowhere, everywhere: the night is full of them; in the night we hear the echo of their voices. When they are angry they haunt the thunder-cloud, and when they are pleased they smile in the sunshine. Sometimes also they appear in the shape of snakes, or visit us in dreams, and then we offer them sacrifice. Yonder on the hillside is a haunted wood; it is full of their spirits, White Man, but they cannot talk, they only mutter, and their footfalls sound like the dropping of heavy rain, for they are strengthless and unhappy, and in the end they fade away."

"So you say," answered Owen, "who are not altogether without understanding, yet know little, never having been taught. Now listen to me," and very earnestly he preached to him and those about him of peace, of forgiveness, and of life everlasting.

"Why should a God die miserably upon a cross?" asked the king at length.

"That through His sacrifice men might become as gods," answered Owen. "Believe in Him and He will save you."

"How can we do that," asked the king again, "when already we have a god? Can we desert one god and set up another?"

"What god, King?"

"I will show him to you, White Man. Let my litter be brought."

The litter was brought and the king entered it with labouring breath. Passing through the north gate of the Great Place, the party ascended a slope of the hill that lay beyond it till they reached a flat plain some hundreds of yards in width. On this plain vegetation grew scantily, for here the bed rock of ironstone, denuded with frequent and heavy rains, was scarcely hidden by a thin crust of earth. On the further side of the plain, however, and separated from it by a little stream, was a green bank of deep soft soil, beyond which lay a gloomy valley full of great trees, that for many generations had been the burying-place of the kings of the Amasuka.

"This is the house of the god," said the king.

"A strange house," answered Owen, "and where is he that dwells in it?"

"Follow me and I will show you, Messenger; but be swift, for already the sky grows dark with coming tempest."

Now at the king's command the bearers bore him across the sere plateau towards a stone that lay almost in its centre. Presently they halted, and, pointing to this mass, the king said:—

"Behold the god!"

Owen advanced and examined the object. A glance told him that this god of the Amasuka was a meteoric stone of unusual size. Most of such stones are mere shapeless lumps, but this one bore a peculiar resemblance to a seated human being holding up one arm towards the sky. So strange was this likeness that, other reasons apart, it seemed not wonderful that savages should regard the thing with awe and veneration. Rather would it have been wonderful had they not done so.

"Say now," said Owen to the king when he had inspected the stone, "what is the history of this dumb god of yours, and why do you worship him?"

"Follow me across the stream and I will tell you, Messenger," answered the king, again glancing at the sky. "The storm gathers, and when it breaks none are safe upon this plain except the heaven doctors such as Hokosa and his companions who can bind the lightning."

So they went and when they reached the further side of the stream Umsuka descended from his litter.

"Messenger," he said, "this is the story of the god as it has come down to us. From the beginning our land has been scourged with lightning above all other lands, and with the floods of rain that accompany the lightning. In the old days the Great Place of the king was out yonder among the mountains, but every year fire from heaven fell upon it, destroying much people: and at length in a great tempest the house of the king of that day was smitten and burned, and his wives and children were turned to ashes. Then that king held a council of his wizards and fire-doctors, and these having consulted the spirits of their forefathers, retired into a place apart to fast and pray; yes, it was in yonder valley, the burying ground of kings, that they hid themselves. Now on the third night the God of Fire appeared to the chief of the doctors in his sleep, and he was shaped like a burning brand and smoke went up from him. Out of the smoke he spoke to the doctor, saying: 'For this reason it is that I torment your people, that they hate me and curse at me and pay me little honour.'

"In his dream the doctor answered: 'How can the people honour a god that they do not see?' Then the god said: 'Rise up now in the night, all the company of you, and go take your stand upon the banks of yonder stream, and I will fall down in fire from heaven, and there on the plain you shall find my image. Then let your king move his Great Place into the valley beneath the plain, and henceforth my bolts shall spare it and him. Only, month by month you shall make prayers and offerings to me; moreover, the name of the people shall be changed, for it shall be called the People of Fire.'

"Now the doctor rose, and having awakened his companions, he told them of his vision. Then they all of them went down to the banks of this stream where we now stand. And as they waited there a great tempest burst over them, and in the midst of that tempest they saw the flaming figure of a man descend from heaven, and when he touched the earth it shook. The morning came and there upon the plain before them, where there had been nothing, sat the likeness of the god as it sits today and shall sit for ever. So the name of this people was changed, and the king's Great Place was built where it now is.

"Since that day, Messenger, no hut has been burned and no man killed in or about the Great Place by fire from heaven, which falls only here where the god is, though away among the mountains and elsewhere men are sometimes killed. But wait a while and you shall see with your eyes. Hokosa, do you, whom the lightning will not touch, take that pole of dead wood and set it up yonder in the crevice of the rock not far from the figure of the god."

"I obey," said Hokosa, "although I have brought no medicines with me. Perhaps," he added with a faint sneer, "the white man, who is so great a wizard, will not be afraid to accompany me."

Now Owen saw that all those present were looking at him curiously. It was evident they believed that he would not dare to accept the challenge. Therefore he answered at once and without hesitation:—

"Certainly I will come; the pole is heavy for one man to carry, and where Hokosa goes, there I can go also."

"Nay, nay, Messenger," said the king, "the lightning knows Hokosa and will turn from him, but you are a stranger to it and it will eat you up."

"King," answered Owen, "I do not believe that Hokosa has any power over the lightning. It may strike him or it may strike me; but unless my God so commands, it will strike neither of us."

"On your head be it, White Man," said Hokosa, with cold anger. "Come, aid me with the pole."

Then they lifted the dead tree, and between them carried it into the middle of the plain, where they set it up in a crevice of the rock. By this time the storm was almost over them, and watching it Owen perceived that the lightnings struck always along the bank of the stream, doubtless following a hidden line of the bed of ironstone.

"It is but a very little storm," said Hokosa contemptuously, "such as visit us almost every afternoon at this period of the year. Ah! White Man, I would that you could see one of our great tempests, for these are worth beholding. This I fear, however, that you will never do, seeing it is likely that within some few minutes you will have passed back to that King who sent you here, with a hole in your head and a black mark down your spine."

"That we shall learn presently, Hokosa," answered Owen; "for my part, I pray that no such fate may overtake you."

Now Hokosa moved himself away, muttering and pointing with his fingers, but Owen remained standing within about thirty yards of the pole. Suddenly there came a glare of light, and the pole was split into fragments; but although the shock was perceptible, they remained unhurt. Almost immediately a second flash leaped from the cloud, and Owen saw Hokosa stagger and fall to his knees. "The man is struck," he thought to himself, but it was not so, for recovering his balance, the wizard walked back to the stream.

Owen never stirred. From boyhood courage had been one of his good qualities, but it was a courage of the spirit rather than of the flesh. For instance, at this very moment, so far as his body was concerned, he was much afraid, and did not in the least enjoy standing upon an ironstone plateau at the imminent risk of being destroyed by lightning. But even if he had not had an end to gain, he would have scorned to give way to his human frailties; also, now as always, his faith supported him. As it happened the storm, which was slight, passed by, and no more flashes fell. When it was over he walked back to where the king and his court were standing.

"Messenger," said Umsuka, "you are not only a great doctor, you are also a brave man, and such I honour. There is no one among us here, not being a lord of the lightning, who would have dared to stand upon that place with Hokosa while the flashes fell about him. Yet you have done it; it was Hokosa who was driven away. You have passed the trial by fire, and henceforth, whether we refuse your message or accept it, you are great in this land."

"There is no need to praise me, King," answered Owen. "The risk is something; but I knew that I was protected from it, seeing that I shall not die until my hour comes, and it is not yet. Listen now: your god yonder is nothing but a stone such as I have often seen before, for sometimes in great tempests they come to earth from the clouds. You are not the first people that have worshipped such a stone, but now we know better. Also this plain before you is full of iron, and iron draws the lightning. That is why it never strikes your town below. The iron attracts it more strongly than earth and huts of straw. Again, while the pole stood I was in little danger, for the lightning strikes the highest thing; but after the pole was shattered and Hokosa wisely went away, then I was in some danger, only no flashes fell. I am not a magician, King, but I know some things that you do not know, and I trust in One whom I shall lead you to trust also."

"We will talk of this more hereafter," said the king hurriedly, "for one day, I have heard and seen enough. Also I do not believe your words, for I have noted ever that those who are the greatest wizards of all say continually that they have no magic power. Hokosa, you have been famous in your day, but it seems that henceforth you who have led must follow."

"The battle is not yet fought, King," answered Hokosa. "Today I met the lightnings without my medicines, and it was a little storm; when I am prepared with my medicines and the tempest is great, then I will challenge this white man to face me yonder, and then in that hour *my* god shall show his strength and *his* God shall not be able to save him."

453

"That we shall see when the time comes," answered Owen, with a smile.

That night as Owen sat in his hut working at the translation of St. John, the door was opened and Hokosa entered.

"White Man," said the wizard, "you are too strong for me, though whence you have your power I know not. Let us make a bargain. Show me your magic and I will show you mine, and we will rule the land between us. You and I are much akin—we are great; we have the spirit sight; we know that there are things beyond the things we see and hear and feel; whereas, for the rest, they are fools, following the flesh alone. I have spoken."

"Very gladly will I show you my magic, Hokosa," answered Owen cheerfully, "since, to speak truth, though I know you to be wicked, and guess that you would be glad to be rid of me by fair means or foul; yet I have taken a liking for you, seeing in you one who from a sinner may grow into a saint.

"This then is my magic: To love God and serve man; to eschew wizardry, wealth, and power; to seek after holiness, poverty and humility; to deny your flesh, and to make yourself small in the sight of men, that so perchance you may grow great in the sight of Heaven and save your soul alive."

"I have no stomach for that lesson," said Hokosa.

"Yet you shall live to hunger for it," answered Owen. And the wizard went away angered but wondering.

CHAPTER 9

The Crisis

Now, day by day for something over a month Owen preached the Gospel before the king, his councillors, and hundreds of the head men of the nation. They listened to him attentively, debating the new doctrine point by point; for although they might be savages, these people were very keen-witted and subtle. Very patiently did Owen sow, and at length to his infinite joy he also gathered in his first-fruit. One night as he sat in his hut labouring as usual at the work of translation, wherein he was assisted by John whom he had taught to read and write, the Prince Nodwengo entered and greeted him. For a while he sat silent watching the white man at his task, then he said:—

"Messenger, I have a boon to ask of you. Can you teach me to understand those signs which you set upon the paper, and to make them also as does John your servant?"

"Certainly," answered Owen; "if you will come to me at noon tomorrow, we will begin."

The prince thanked him, but he did not go away. Indeed, from his manner Owen guessed that he had something more upon his mind. At length it came out.

"Messenger," he said, "you have told us of baptism whereby we are admitted into the army of your King; say, have you the power of this rite?"

"I have."

"And is your servant here baptised?"

"He is."

"Then if he who is a common man can be baptised, why may not I who am a prince?"

"In baptism," answered Owen, "there is no distinction between the highest and the lowest; but if you believe, then the door is open and through it you can join the company of Heaven."

455

"Messenger, I do believe," answered the prince humbly.

Then Owen was very joyful, and that same night, with John for a witness, he baptised the prince, giving him the new name of Constantine, after the first Christian emperor.

On the following day Nodwengo, in the presence of Owen, who on this point would suffer no concealment, announced to the king that he had become a Christian. Umsuka heard, and for a while sat silent. Then he said in a troubled voice:—

"Truly, Messenger, in the words of that Book from which you read to us, I fear that you have come hither to bring, 'not peace but a sword.' Now when the witch-doctors and the priests of fire learn this, that he whom I have chosen to succeed me has become the servant of another faith, they will stir up the soldiers and there will be civil war. I pray you, therefore, keep the matter secret, at any rate for a while, seeing that the lives of many are at stake."

"In this, my father," answered the prince, "I must do as the Messenger bids me; but if you desire it, take from me the right of succession and call back my brother from the northern mountains."

"That by poison or the spear he may put all of us to death, Nodwengo! Be not afraid; ere long when he learns all that is happening here, your brother Hafela will come from the northern mountains, and the spears of his *impis* shall be countless as the stars of the sky. Messenger, you desire to draw us to the arms of your God—and myself, I am at times minded to follow the path of my son Nodwengo and seek a refuge there—but say, will they be strong enough to protect us from Hafela and the warriors of the north? Already he gathers his clans, and already my captains desert to him. By-and-by, in the springtime—may I be dead before the day—he will roll down upon us like a flood of water——"

"To fall back like waters from a wall of rock," answered Owen. "'Let not your heart be troubled,' for my Master can protect His servants, and He will protect you. But first you must confess Him openly, as your son has done."

"Nay, I am too old to hurry," said the king with a sigh. "Your tale seems full of promise to one who is near the grave; but how can I know that it is more than a dream? And shall I abandon the worship of my fathers and change, or strive to change, the customs of my people to follow after dreams? Nodwengo has chosen his part, and I do not blame him; yet, for the present I beseech you both to keep silence on this matter, lest to save bloodshed I should be driven to side against you."

"So be it, King," said Owen; "but I warn you that Truth has a loud voice, and that it is hard to hide the shining of a light in a dark place, nor does it please my Lord to be denied by those who confess Him."

"I am weary," replied the old king, and they saluted him and went.

In obedience to the wish of Umsuka his father, the conversion of Nodwengo was kept secret, and yet—none knew how—the thing leaked out. Soon the women in their huts, and the soldiers by their watch-fires, whispered it in each other's ears that he who was appointed to be their future ruler had become a servant of the unknown God. That he had forsworn war and all the delights of men; that he would take but one wife and appear before the army, not in the uniform of a general, but clad in a white robe, and carry, not the broad spear, but a cross of wood. Swiftly the strange story flew from mouth to mouth, yet it was not altogether believed till it chanced that one day when he was reviewing a regiment, a soldier who was drunk with beer openly insulted the prince, calling him "a coward who worshipped a coward."

Now men held their breaths, waiting to see this fool led away to die by torture of the ant-heap or some other dreadful doom. But the prince only answered:

"Soldier, you are drunk, therefore I forgive you your words. Whether He Whom you blaspheme will forgive you, I know not. Get you gone!"

The warriors stared and murmured, for by those words, wittingly or unwittingly, their general had confessed his faith, and that day they made ribald songs about him in the camp. But on the morrow when they learned how that the man whom the prince spared had been seized by a lion and taken away as he sat at night with his companions in the bivouac, his mouth full of boasting of his own courage in offering insult to the prince and the new faith, then they looked at each other askance and said little more of the matter. Doubtless it was chance, and yet this Spirit Whom the Messenger preached was one of Whom it seemed wisest not to speak lightly.

But still the trouble grew, for by now the witch-doctors, with Hokosa at the head of them, were frightened for their place and power, and fomented it both openly and in secret. Of the women they asked what would become of them when men were allowed to take but one wife? Of the heads of *kraals*, how they would grow wealthy when their daughters ceased to be worth cattle? Of the councillors and generals, how the land could be protected from its foes when they were commanded to lay down the spear? Of the soldiers, whose only trade was war, how it would please them to till the fields like girls? Dismay took hold of the nation, and although they were much loved, there was open talk of killing or driving away the king and Nodwengo who favoured the white man, and of setting up Hafela in their place.

At length the crisis came, and in this fashion. The Amasuka, like many other African tribes, had a strange veneration for certain varieties of snakes which they declared to be possessed by the spirits of their ancestors. It was a law among them that if one of these snakes entered a *kraal* it must not be killed, or even driven away, under pain of death, but must be allowed to share with the human occupants any hut that it might select. As a result of this enforced hospitality deaths from snake-bite were numerous among the people; but when they happened in a *kraal* its owners met with little sympathy, for the doctors explained that the real cause of them was the anger of some ancestral spirit towards his descendants. Now, before John was despatched to instruct Owen in the language of the Amasuka a certain girl was sealed to him as his future wife, and this girl, who during his absence had been orphaned, he had married recently with the approval of Owen, who at this time was preparing her for baptism. On the third morning after his marriage John appeared before his master in the last extremity of grief and terror.

"Help me, Messenger!" he cried, "for my ancestral spirit has entered our hut and bitten my wife as she lay asleep."

"Are you mad?" asked Owen. "What is an ancestral spirit, and how can it have bitten your wife?"

"A snake," gasped John, "a green snake of the worst sort."

Then Owen remembered the superstition, and snatching bluestone and spirits of wine from his medicine chest, he rushed to John's hut. As it happened, he was fortunately in time with his remedies and succeeded in saving the woman's life, whereby his reputation as a doctor and a magician, already great, was considerably enlarged.

"Where is the snake?" he asked when at length she was out of danger.

"Yonder, under the *kaross*," answered John, pointing to a skin rug which lay in the corner.

"Have you killed it?"

"No, Messenger," answered the man, "I dare not. Alas! we must live with the thing here in the hut till it chooses to go away."

"Truly," said Owen, "I am ashamed to think that you who are a Christian should still believe so horrible a superstition. Does your faith teach you that the souls of men enter into snakes?"

Now John hung his head; then snatching a *kerry*, he threw aside the *kaross*, revealing a great green serpent seven or eight feet long. With fury he fell upon the reptile, killed it by repeated blows, and hurled it into the courtyard outside the house.

"Behold, father," he said, "and judge whether I am still superstitious." Then his countenance fell and he added: "Yet my life must pay for this deed, for it is an ancient law among us that to harm one of these snakes is death."

"Have no fear," said Owen, "a way will be found out of this trouble."

That afternoon Owen heard a great hubbub outside his *kraal*, and going to see what was the matter, he found a party of the witch-doctors dragging John towards the place of judgment, which was by the king's house. Thither he followed to discover that the case was already in course of being opened before the king, his council, and a vast audience of the people. Hokosa was the accuser. In brief and pregnant sentences, producing the dead snake in proof of his argument, he pointed out the enormity of the offence against the laws of the Amasuka wherewith the prisoner was charged, demanding that the man who had killed the house of his ancestral spirit should instantly be put to death.

"What have you to say?" asked the king of John.

"This, O King," replied John, "that I am a Christian, and to me that snake is nothing but a noxious reptile. It bit my wife, and had it not been for the medicine of the Messenger, she would have perished of the poison. Therefore I killed it before it could harm others."

"It is a fair answer," said the king. "Hokosa, I think that this man should go free."

"The king's will is the law," replied Hokosa bitterly; "but if the law were the king's will, the decision would be otherwise. This man has slain, not a snake, but that which held the spirit of an ancestor, and for the deed he deserves to die. Hearken, O King, for the business is larger than it seems. How are we to be governed henceforth? Are we to follow our ancient rules and customs, or must we submit ourselves to a new rule and a new custom? I tell you, O King, that the people murmur; they are without light, they wander in the darkness, they cannot understand. Play with us no more, but let us hear the truth that we may judge of this matter."

Umsuka looked at Owen, but made no reply.

"I will answer you, Hokosa," said Owen, "for I am the spring of all this trouble, and at my command that man, my disciple, killed yonder snake. What is it? It is nothing but a reptile; no human spirit ever dwelt within it as you imagine in your superstition. You ask to hear the truth; day by day I have preached it in your ears and you have not listened, though many among you have listened and understood. What is it that you seek?"

"We seek, Messenger, to be rid of you, your fantasies and your religion; and we demand that our king should expel you and restore the ancient laws, or failing this, that you should prove your power openly before us all. Your word, O King!"

Umsuka thought for a while and answered:—

"This is my word, Hokosa: I will not drive the Messenger from the land, for he is a good man; he saved my life, and there is virtue in his teaching, towards which I myself incline. Yet it is just that he should be asked to prove his power, so that an end may be put to doubt and all of us may learn what god we are to worship."

"How can I prove my power," asked Owen, "further than I have proved it already? Does Hokosa desire to set up his god against my God—the false against the true?"

"I do," answered the wizard with passion, "and according to the issue let the judgment be. Let us halt no longer between two opinions, let us become wholly Christian or rest wholly heathen, for to be divided is to be destroyed. The magic of the Messenger is great; once and for all let us learn if it is more than our magic. Let us put him and his doctrines to the trial by fire."

"What is the trial by fire?" asked Owen.

"You have seen something of it, White Man, but not much. This is the trial by fire: to stand yonder before the face of the god of thunder when a great tempest rages—not such a storm as you saw, but a storm that splits the heavens—and to come thence unscathed. Listen: I who am a 'heaven-herd,' I who know the signs of the weather, tell you that within two days such a tempest as this will break upon us. Then White Man, I and my companions will be ready to meet you on the plain. Take the cross by which you swear and set it up yonder and stand by it, and with you your converts, Nodwengo the prince, and this man whom you have named John, if they dare to go. Over against you, around the symbol of the god by which we swear, will stand I and my company, and we will pray our god and you shall pray your God. Then the storm will break upon us, and when it is ended we shall learn which of us remain alive. If you and your cross are shattered, to us will be the victory; if we are laid low, take it for your own. Your judgment, King!"

Again Umsuka thought and answered:—

"So be it. Messenger, hear me. There is no need for you to accept

460

this challenge; but if you will not accept it, then go from my country in peace, taking with you those who cleave to you. If on the other hand you do accept it, these shall be the stakes: that if you pass the trial unharmed, and the fire-doctors are swept away, your creed shall be my creed and the creed of the land; but if the fire-doctors prevail against you, then it shall be death or banishment to any who profess that creed. Now choose!"

"I have chosen," said Owen. "I will meet Hokosa and his company on the Place of fire whenever he may appoint, but for the others I cannot say."

"We will come with you," said Nodwengo and John, with one voice; "where you go, Messenger, we will surely follow."

CHAPTER 10

The Second Trial by Fire

When this momentous discussion was finished, as usual Owen preached before the king, expounding the Scriptures and taking for his subject the duty of faith. As he went back to his hut he saw that the snake which John had killed had been set upon a pole in that part of the Great Place which served as a market, and that hundreds of natives were gathered beneath it gesticulating and talking excitedly.

"See the work of Hokosa," he thought to himself. "Moses set up a serpent to save the people; yonder wizard sets up one to destroy them."

That evening Owen had no heart for his labours, for his mind was heavy at the prospect of the trial which lay before him. Not that he cared for his own life, for of this he scarcely thought; it was the prospects of his cause which troubled him. It seemed much to expect that Heaven again should throw over him the mantle of its especial protection, and yet if it did not do so there was an end of his mission among the People of Fire. Well, he did not seek this trial—he would have avoided it if he could, but it had been thrust upon him, and he was forced to choose between it and the abandonment of the work which he had undertaken with such high hopes and pushed so far toward success. He did not choose the path, it had been pointed out to him to walk upon; and if it ended in a precipice, at least he would have done his best. As he thought thus John entered the hut, panting.

"What is the matter?" Owen asked.

"Father, the people saw and pursued me because of the death of that accursed snake. Had I not run fast and escaped them, I think they would have killed me."

"At least you have escaped, John; so be comforted and return thanks."

"Father," said the man presently, "I know that you are great, and can do many wonderful things, but have you in truth power over lightning?"

"Why do you ask?"

"Because a great tempest is brewing, and if you have not we shall certainly be killed when we stand yonder on the Place of Fire."

"John," he said, "I cannot speak to the lightning in a voice which it can hear. I cannot say to it 'go yonder,' or 'come hither,' but He Who made it can do so. Why do you tempt me with your doubts? Have I not told you the story of Elijah the prophet and the priests of Baal? Did Elijah's Master forsake him, and shall He forsake us? Also this is certain, that all the medicine of Hokosa and his wizards will not turn a lightning flash by the breadth of a single hair. God alone can turn it, and for the sake of His cause among these people I believe that He will do so."

Thus Owen spoke on till, in reproving the weakness of another, he felt his own faith come back to him and, remembering the past and how he had been preserved in it, the doubt and trouble went out of his mind to return no more.

The third day—the day of trial—came. For sixty hours or more the heat of the weather had been intense; indeed, during all that time the thermometer in Owen's hut, notwithstanding the protection of a thick hatch, had shown the temperature to vary between a maximum of 113 and a minimum of 101 degrees. Now, in the early morning, it stood at 108.

"Will the storm break today?" asked Owen of Nodwengo, who came to visit him.

"They say so, Messenger, and I think it by the feel of the air. If so, it will be a very great storm, for the heaven is full of fire. Already Hokosa and the doctors are at their rites upon the plain yonder, but there will be no need to join them till two hours after midday."

"Is the cross ready?" asked Owen.

"Yes, and set up. It is a heavy cross; six men could scarcely carry it. Oh! Messenger, I am not afraid—and yet, have you no medicine? If not, I fear that the lightning will fall upon the cross as it fell upon the pole and then——"

"Listen, Nodwengo," said Owen, "I know a medicine, but I will not use it. You see that wagon chain? Were one end of it buried in the ground and the other with a spear blade made fast to it hung to the top of the cross, we could live out the fiercest storm in safety. But I say that I will not use it. Are we witch doctors that we should take refuge in tricks? No, let faith be our shield, and if it fail us, then let us die. Pray now with me that it may not fail us."

****

It was afternoon. All round the Field of Fire were gathered thousands upon thousands of the people of the Amasuka. The news of this duel between the God of the white man and their god had travelled far and wide, and even the very aged who could scarcely crawl and the little ones who must be carried were collected there to see the issue. Nor had they need to fear disappointment, for already the sky was half hidden by dense thunder-clouds piled ridge on ridge, and the hush of the coming tempest lay upon the earth. Round about the meteor stone which they called a god, each of them stirring a little gourd of medicine that was placed upon the ground before him, but uttering no word, were gathered Hokosa and his followers to the number of twenty. They were all of them arrayed in their snakeskin dresses and other wizard finery. Also each man held in his hand a wand fashioned from a human thigh-bone. In front of the stone burned a little fire, which now and again Hokosa fed with aromatic leaves, at the same time pouring medicine from his bowl upon the holy stone. Opposite the symbol of the god, but at a good distance from it, a great cross of white wood was set up in the rock by a spot which the witch-doctors themselves had chosen. Upon the banks of the stream, in the place apart, were the king, his councillors and the regiment on guard, and with them Owen, the Prince Nodwengo and John.

"The storm will be fierce," said the king uneasily, glancing at the western sky, upon whose bosom the blue lightnings played with an incessant flicker. Then he bade those about him stand back, and calling Owen and the prince to him, said: "Messenger, my son tells me that your wisdom knows a plan whereby you may be preserved from the fury of the tempest. Use it, I pray of you, Messenger, that your life may be saved, and with it the life of the only son who is left to me."

"I cannot," answered Owen, "for thus by doubting Him I should tempt my Master. Still, it is not laid upon the prince to accompany through this trial. Let him stay here, and I alone will stand beneath the cross."

"Stay, Nodwengo," implored the old man.

"I did not think to live to hear my father bid me, one of the royal blood of the Amasuka, to desert my captain in the hour of battle and hide myself in the grass like a woman," answered the prince with a bitter smile. "Nay, it may be that death awaits me yonder, but nothing except death shall keep me back from the venture."

"It is well spoken," said the king; "be it as you will."

464

Now the company of wizards, leaving their medicine-pots upon the ground, formed themselves in a treble line, and marching to where the king stood, they saluted him. Then they sang the praises of their god, and in a song that had been prepared, heaped insult upon the God of the white man and upon the messenger who preached Him. To all of this Owen listened in silence.

"He is a coward!" cried their spokesman; "he has not a word to say. He skulks there in his white robes behind the majesty of the king. Let him go forth and stand by his piece of wood. He dare not go! He thinks the hillside safer. Come out, little White Man, and we will show you how we manage the lightnings. Ah! they shall fly about you like spears in battle. You shall throw yourself upon the ground and shriek in terror, and then they will lick you up and you shall be no more, and there will be an end of you and the symbol of your God."

"Cease your boastings," said the king shortly, "and get you back to your place, knowing that if it should chance that the white man conquers you will be called upon to answer for these words."

"We shall be ready, O King," they cried; and amidst the cheers of the vast audience they marched back to their station, still singing the blasphemous mocking song.

Now to the west all the heavens were black as night, though the eastern sky still showed blue and cloudless. Nature lay oppressed with silence—silence intense and unnatural; and so great was the heat that the air danced visibly above the ironstone as it dances about a glowing stove. Suddenly the quietude was broken by a moaning sound of wind; the grass stirred, the leaves of the trees began to shiver, and an icy breath beat upon Owen's brow.

"Let us be going," he said, and lifting the ivory crucifix above his head, he passed the stream and walked towards the wooden cross. After him came the Prince Nodwengo, wearing his royal dress of leopard skin, and after him, John, arrayed in a linen robe.

As the little procession appeared to their view some of the soldiers began to mock, but almost instantly the laughter died away. Rude as they were, these savages understood that here was no occasion for their mirth, that the three men indeed seemed clothed with a curious dignity. Perhaps it was their slow and quiet gait, perhaps a sense of the errand upon which they were bound; or it may have been the strange unearthly light that fell upon them from over the edge of the storm cloud; at the least, as the multitude became aware, their appearance was impressive. They reached the cross and took up their stations there, Owen in front of it, Nodwengo to the right, and John to the left.

Now a sharp squall of strong wind swept across the space, and with it came a flaw of rain. It passed by, and the storm that had been muttering and growling in the distance began to burst. The great clouds seemed to grow and swell, and from the breast of them swift lightnings leapt, to be met by other lightnings rushing upwards from the earth. The air was filled with a tumult of uncertain wind and a hiss as of distant rain. Then the batteries of thunder were opened, and the world shook with their volume. Down from on high the flashes fell blinding and incessant, and by the light of them the fire-doctors could be seen running to and fro, pointing now here and now there with their wands of human bones, and pouring the medicines from their gourds upon the ground and upon each other. Owen and his two companions could be seen also, standing quietly with clasped hands, while above them towered the tall white cross.

At length the storm was straight over head. Slowly it advanced in its awe-inspiring might as flash after flash, each more fantastic and horrible than the last, smote upon the floor of ironstone. It played about the shapes of the doctors, who in the midst of it looked like devils in an inferno. It crept onwards towards the station of the cross, but—*it never reached the cross.*

One flash struck indeed within fifty paces of where Owen stood. Then of a sudden a marvel happened, or something which to this day the People of Fire talk of as a marvel, for in an instant the rain began to pour like a wall of water stretching from earth to heaven, and the wind changed. It had been blowing from the west, now it blew from the east with the force of a gale.

It blew and rolled the tempest back upon itself, causing it to return to the regions whence it had gathered. At the very foot of the cross its march was stayed; there was the water-line, as straight as if it had been drawn with a rule. The thunder-clouds that were pressed forward met the clouds that were pressed back, and together they seemed to come to earth, filling the air with a gloom so dense that the eye could not pierce it. To the west was a wall of blackness towering to the heavens; to the east, light, blue and unholy, gleamed upon the white cross and the figures of its watchers.

For some seconds—twenty or more—there was a lull, and then it seemed as though all hell had broken loose upon the world. The wall of blackness became a wall of flame, in which strange and ardent shapes appeared ascending and descending; the thunder bellowed till the mountains rocked, and in one last blaze, awful and indescribable, the skies melted into a deluge of fire. In the flare of it Owen thought that he saw the figures of men falling this way and that, then he staggered against the cross for support and his senses failed him.

****

When they returned again, he perceived the storm being drawn back from the face of the pale earth like a pall from the face of the dead, and he heard a murmur of fear and wonder rising from ten thousand throats.

****

Well might they fear and wonder, for of the twenty and one wizards eleven were dead, four were paralysed by shock, five were flying in their terror, and one, Hokosa himself, stood staring at the fallen, a very picture of despair. Nor was this all, for the meteor stone with a human shape which for generations the People of Fire had worshipped as a god, lay upon the plain in fused and shattered fragments.

The people saw, and a sound as of a hollow groan of terror went up from them. Then they were silent. For a while Owen and his companions were silent also, since their hearts were too full for speech. Then he said:—

"As the snake fell harmless from the hand of Paul, so has the lightning turned back from me, who strive to follow in his footsteps, working death and dismay among those who would have harmed us. May forgiveness be theirs who were without understanding. Brethren, let us return and make report to the king."

Now, as they had come, so they went back; first Owen with the crucifix, next to him Nodwengo, and last of the three John. They drew near to the king, when suddenly, moved by a common impulse, the thousands of the people upon the banks of the stream with one accord threw themselves upon their knees before Owen, calling him God and offering him worship. Infected by the contagion, Umsuka, his guard and his councillors followed their example, so that of all the multitude Hokosa alone remained upon his feet, standing by his dishonoured and riven deity.

"Rise!" cried Owen aghast. "Would you do sacrilege, and offer worship to a man? Rise, I command you!"

Then the king rose, saying:—

"You are no man, Messenger, you are a spirit."

"He is a spirit," repeated the multitude after him.

"I am *not* a spirit, I am yet a man," cried Owen again, "but the Spirit Whom I serve has made His power manifest in me His servant,

467

and your idols are smitten with the sword of His power, O ye Sons of Fire! Hokosa still lives, let him be brought hither."

They fetched Hokosa, and he stood before them.

"You have seen, Wizard," said the king. "What have you to say?"

"Nothing," answered Hokosa, "save that victory is to the Cross, and to the white man who preaches it, for his magic is greater than our magic. By his command the tempest was stayed, and the boasts we hurled fell back upon our heads and the head of our god to destroy us."

"Yes," said the king, "victory is to the Cross, and henceforth the Cross shall be worshipped in this land, or at least no other god shall be worshipped. Let us be going. Come with me, Messenger, Lord of the Lightning."

CHAPTER 11

The Wisdom of the Dead

On the morrow Owen baptised the king, many of his councillors, and some twenty others whom he considered fit to receive the rite. Also he despatched his first convert John, with other messengers, on a three months' journey to the coast, giving them letters acquainting the bishop and others with his marvellous success, and praying that missionaries might be sent to assist him in his labours.

Now day by day the Church grew till it numbered hundreds of souls, and thousands more hovered on its threshold. From dawn to dark Owen toiled, preaching, exhorting, confessing, gathering in his harvest; and from dark to midnight he pored over his translation of the Scriptures, teaching Nodwengo and a few others how to read and write them. But although his efforts were crowned with so signal and extraordinary a triumph, he was well aware of the dangers that threatened the life of the infant Church. Many accepted it indeed, and still more tolerated it; but there remained multitudes who regarded the new religion with suspicion and veiled hatred. Nor was this strange, seeing that the hearts of men are not changed in an hour or their ancient customs easily overset.

On one point, indeed, Owen had to give way. The Amasuka were a polygamous people; all their law and traditions were interwoven with polygamy, and to abolish that institution suddenly and with violence would have brought their social fabric to the ground. Now, as he knew well, the missionary Church declares in effect that no man can be both a Christian and a polygamist; therefore among the followers of that custom the missionary Church makes but little progress. Not without many qualms and hesitations, Owen, having only the Scriptures to consult, came to a compromise with his converts. If a man already married to more than one wife wished to become a Christian, he permitted him to do so upon the condition that he took no more wives; while a man unmarried at the time of his conversion might take one wife only. This decree, liberal as it was, caused great dissatisfaction among both men and women. But it was as nothing compared to the feeling that was evoked by Owen's preaching against all war not undertaken in self-defence, and against the strict laws which he prevailed upon the king to pass, suppressing the practice of wizardry, and declaring the chief or doctor who caused a man to be "smelt out" and killed upon charges of witchcraft to be guilty of murder.

At first whenever Owen went abroad he was surrounded by thousands of people who followed him in the expectation that he would work miracles, which, after his exploits with the lightning, they were well persuaded that he could do if he chose. But he worked no more miracles; he only preached to them a doctrine adverse to their customs and foreign to their thoughts.

So it came about that in time, when the novelty was gone off and the story of his victory over the Fire-god had grown stale, although the work of conversion went on steadily, many of the people grew weary of the white man and his doctrines. Soon this weariness found expression in various ways, and in none more markedly than by the constant desertions from the ranks of the king's regiments. At first, by Owen's advice, the king tolerated these desertions; but at length, having obtained information that an entire regiment purposed absconding at dawn, he caused it to be surrounded and seized by night. Next morning he addressed that regiment, saying:—

"Soldiers, you think that because I have become a Christian and will not permit unnecessary bloodshed, I am also become a fool. I will teach you otherwise. One man in every twenty of you shall be killed, and henceforth any soldier who attempts to desert will be killed also!"

The order was carried out, for Owen could not find a word to say against it, with the result that desertions almost ceased, though not before the king had lost some eight or nine thousand of his best soldiers. Worst of all, these soldiers had gone to join Hafela in his mountain fastnesses; and the rumour grew that ere long they would appear again, to claim the crown for him or to take it by force of arms.

Now too a fresh complication arose. The old king sickened of his last illness, and soon it became known that he must die. A month later die he did, passing away peacefully in Owen's arms, and with his last breath exhorting his people to cling to the Christian religion; to take Nodwengo for their king and to be faithful to him.

The king died, and that same day was buried by Owen in the gloomy resting-place of the blood-royal of the People of Fire, where a Christian priest now set foot for the first time.

On the morrow Nodwengo was proclaimed king with much ceremony in face of the people and of all the army that remained to him. One captain raised a cry for Hafela his brother. Nodwengo caused him to be seized and brought before him.

"Man," he said, "on this my coronation day I will not stain my hand with blood. Listen. You cry upon Hafela, and to Hafela you shall go, taking him this message. Tell him that I, Nodwengo, have succeeded to the crown of Umsuka, my father, by his will and the will of the people. Tell him it is true that I have become a Christian, and that Christians follow not after war but peace. Tell him, however, that though I am a Christian I have not forgotten how to fight or how to rule. It has reached my ears that it is his purpose to attack me with a great force which he is gathering, and to possess himself of my throne. If he should choose to come, I shall be ready to meet him; but I counsel him against coming, for it will be to find his death. Let him stay where he is in peace, and be my subject; or let him go afar with those that cleave to him, and set up a kingdom of his own, for then I shall not follow him; but let him not dare to lift a spear against me, his sovereign, since if he does so he shall be treated as a rebel and find the doom of a rebel. Begone, and show your face here no more!"

The man crept away crestfallen; but all who heard that speech broke into cheering, which, as its purport was repeated from rank to rank, spread far and wide; for now the army learned that in becoming a Christian, Nodwengo had not become a woman. Of this indeed he soon gave them ample proof. The old king's grip upon things had been lax, that of Nodwengo was like iron. He practised no cruelties, and did injustice to none; but his discipline was severe, and soon the regiments were brought to a greater pitch of proficiency than they had ever reached before, although they were now allowed to marry when they pleased, a boon that hitherto had been denied to them. Moreover, by Owen's help, he designed an entirely new system of fortification of the *kraal* and surrounding hills, which would, it was thought, make the place impregnable. These and many other acts, equally vigorous and far-seeing, put new heart into the nation. Also the report of them put fear into Hafela, who, it was rumoured, had now given up all idea of attack.

Some there were, however, who looked upon these changes with little love, and Hokosa was one of them. After his defeat in the duel by fire, for a while his spirit was crushed. Hitherto he had more or less been a believer in the protecting influence of his own god or fetish, who would, as he thought, hold his priests scatheless from the lightning. Often and often had he stood in past days upon that plain while the great tempests broke around his head, and returned thence unharmed, attributing to sorcery a safety that was really due to chance. From time to time indeed a priest was killed; but, so his companions held, the misfortune resulted invariably from the man's neglect of some rite, or was a mark of the anger of the heavens.

Now Hokosa had lived to see all these convictions shattered: he had seen the lightning, which he pretended to be able to control, roll back upon him from the foot of the Christian cross, reducing his god to nothingness and his companions to corpses.

At first Hokosa was dismayed, but as time went on hope came back to him. Stripped of his offices and power, and from the greatest in the nation, after the king, become one of small account, still no harm or violence was attempted towards him. He was left wealthy and in peace, and living thus he watched and listened with open eyes and ears, waiting till the tide should turn. It seemed that he would not have long to wait, for reasons that have been told.

"Why do you sit here like a vulture on a rock," asked the girl Noma, whom he had taken to wife, "when you might be yonder with Hafela, preparing him by your wisdom for the coming war?"

"Because I am a king-vulture, and I wait for the sick bull to die," he answered, pointing to the Great Place beneath him. "Say, why should I bring Hafela to prey upon a carcase I have marked down for my own?"

"Now you speak well," said Noma; "the bull suffers from a strange disease, and when he is dead another must lead the herd."

"That is so," answered her husband, "and, therefore, I am patient."

It was shortly after this conversation that the old king died, with results very different from those which Hokosa had anticipated. Although he was a Christian, to his surprise Nodwengo showed that he was also a strong ruler, and that there was little chance of the sceptre slipping from his hand—none indeed while the white teacher was there to guide him.

"What will you do now, Hokosa?" asked Noma his wife upon a certain day. "Will you turn to Hafela after all?"

"No," answered Hokosa; "I will consult my ancient lore. Listen. Whatever else is false, this is true: that magic exists, and I am its master. For a while it seemed to me that the white man was greater at the art

472

than I am; but of late I have watched him and listened to his doctrines, and I believe that this is not so. It is true that in the beginning he read my plans in a dream, or otherwise; it is true that he hurled the lightning back upon my head; but I hold that these things were accidents. Again and again he has told us that he is not a wizard; and if this be so, he can be overcome."

"How, husband?"

"How? By wizardry. This very night, Noma, with your help I will consult the dead, as I have done in bygone time, and learn the future from their lips which cannot lie."

"So be it; though the task is hateful to me, and I hate you who force me to it."

Noma answered thus with passion, but her eyes shone as she spoke: for those who have once tasted the cup of magic are ever drawn to drink of it again, even when they fear the draught.

****

It was midnight, and Hokosa with his wife stood in the burying-ground of the kings of the Amasuka. Before Owen came upon his mission it was death to visit this spot except upon the occasion of the laying to rest of one of the royal blood, or to offer the annual sacrifice to the spirits of the dead. Even beneath the bright moon that shone upon it the place seemed terrible. Here in the bosom of the hills was an amphitheatre, surrounded by walls of rock varying from five hundred to a thousand feet in height. In this amphitheatre grew great mimosa thorns, and above them towered pillars of granite, set there not by the hand of man but by nature. It would seem that the Amasuka, led by some fine instinct, had chosen these columns as fitting memorials of their kings, at the least a departed monarch lay at the foot of each of them.

The smallest of these unhewn obelisks—it was about fifty feet high—marked the resting-place of Umsuka; and deep into its granite Owen with his own hand had cut the dead king's name and date of death, surmounting his inscription with a symbol of the cross.

Towards this pillar Hokosa made his way through the wet grass, followed by Noma his wife. Presently they were there, standing one upon each side of a little mound of earth more like an ant-heap than a grave; for, after the custom of his people, Umsuka had been buried sitting. At the foot of each of the pillars rose a heap of similar shape, but many times as large. The kings who slept there were accompanied to their resting-places by numbers of their wives and servants, who

473

had been slain in solemn sacrifice that they might attend their Lord whithersoever he should wander.

"What is that you desire and would do?" asked Noma, in a hushed voice. Bold as she was, the place and the occasion awed her.

"I desire wisdom from the dead!" he answered. "Have I not already told you, and can I not win it with your help?"

"What dead, husband?"

"Umsuka the king. Ah! I served him living, and at the last he drove me away from his side. Now he shall serve me, and out of the nowhere I will call him back to mine."

"Will not this symbol defeat you?" and Noma pointed at the cross hewn in the granite. At her words a sudden gust of rage seemed to shake the wizard. His still eyes flashed, his lips turned livid, and with them he spat upon the cross.

"It has no power," he said. "May it be accursed, and may he who believes therein hang thereon! It has no power; but even if it had, according to the tale of that white liar, such things as I would do have been done beneath its shadow. By it the dead have been raised—ay! dead kings have been dragged from death and forced to tell the secrets of the grave. Come, come, let us to the work."

"What must I do, husband?"

"You shall sit you there, even as a corpse sits, and there for a little while you shall die—yes, your spirit shall leave you—and I will fill your body with the soul of him who sleeps beneath; and through your lips I will learn his wisdom, to whom all things are known."

"It is terrible! I am afraid!" she said. "Cannot this be done otherwise?"

"It cannot," he answered. "The spirits of the dead have no shape or form; they are invisible, and can speak only in dreams or through the lips of one in whose pulses life still lingers, though soul and body be already parted. Have no fear. Ere his ghost leaves you it shall recall your own, which till the corpse is cold stays ever close at hand. I did not think to find a coward in you, Noma."

"I am not a coward, as you know well," she answered passionately, "for many a deed of magic have we dared together in past days. But this is fearsome, to die that my body may become the home of the ghost of a dead man, who perchance, having entered it, will abide there, leaving my spirit houseless, or perchance will shut up the doors of my heart in such fashion that they never can be opened. Can it not be done by trance as aforetime? Tell me, Hokosa, how often have you thus talked with the dead?"

"Thrice, Noma."

"And what chanced to them through whom you talked?"

"Two lived and took no harm; the third died, because the awakening medicine lacked power. Yet fear nothing; that which I have with me is of the best. Noma, you know my plight: I must win wisdom or fall for ever, and you alone can help me; for under this new rule, I can no longer buy a youth or maid for purposes of witchcraft, even if one could be found fitted to the work. Choose then: shall we go back or forward? Here trance will not help us; for those entranced cannot read the future, nor can they hold communion with the dead, being but asleep. Choose, Noma."

"I have chosen," she answered. "Never yet have I turned my back upon a venture, nor will I do so now. Come life, come death, I will submit me to your wish, though there are few women who would dare as much for any man. Nor in truth do I do this for you, Hokosa; I do it because I seek power, and thus only can we win it who are fallen. Also I love all things strange, and desire to commune with the dead and to know that, if for some few minutes only, at least my woman's breast has held the spirit of a king. Yet, I warn you, make no fault in your magic; for should I die beneath it, then I, who desire to live on and to be great, will haunt you and be avenged upon you!"

"Oh! Noma," he said, "if I believed that there was any danger for you, should I ask you to suffer this thing?—I, who love you more even than you love power, more than my life, more than anything that is or ever can be."

"I know it, and it is to that I trust," the woman answered. "Now begin, before my courage leaves me."

"Good," he said. "Seat yourself there upon the mound, resting your head against the stone."

She obeyed; and taking thongs of hide which he had made ready, Hokosa bound her wrists and ankles, as these people bind the wrists and ankles of corpses. Then he knelt before her, staring into her face with his solemn eyes and muttering: "Obey and sleep."

Presently her limbs relaxed, and her head fell forward.

"Do you sleep?" he asked.

"I sleep. Whither shall I go? It is the true sleep—test me."

"Pass to the house of the white man, my rival. Are you with him?"

"I am with him."

"What does he?"

"He lies in slumber on his bed, and in his slumber he mutters the name of a woman, and tells her that he loves her, but that duty is more than love. Oh! call me back I cannot stay; a Presence guards him, and thrusts me thence."

"Return," said Hokosa starting. "Pass through the earth beneath you and tell me what you see."

"I see the body of the king; but were it not for his royal ornaments none would know him now."

"Return," said Hokosa, "and let the eyes of your spirit be open. Look around you and tell me what you see."

"I see the shadows of the dead," she answered; "they stand about you, gazing at you with angry eyes; but when they come near you, something drives them back, and I cannot understand what it is they say."

"Is the ghost of Umsuka among them?"

"It is among them."

"Bid him prophesy the future to me."

"I have bidden him, but he does not answer. If you would hear him speak, it must be through the lips of my body; and first my body must be emptied of my ghost, that his may find a place therein."

"Say, can his spirit be compelled?"

"It can be compelled, or that part of it which still hover near this spot, if you dare to speak the words you know. But first its house must be made ready. Then the words must be spoken, and all must be done before a man can count three hundred; for should the blood begin to clot about my heart, it will be still for ever."

"Hearken," said Hokosa. "When the medicine that I shall give does its work, and the spirit is loosened from your body, let it not go afar, no, whatever tempts or threatens it, and suffer not that the death-cord be severed, lest flesh and ghost be parted for ever."

"I hear, and I obey. Be swift, for I grow weary."

Then Hokosa took from his pouch two medicines: one a paste in a box, the other a fluid in a gourd. Taking of the paste he knelt upon the grave before the entranced woman and swiftly smeared it upon the mucous membrane of the mouth and throat. Also he thrust pellets of it into the ears, the nostrils, and the corners of the eyes.

The effect was almost instantaneous. A change came over the girl's lovely face, the last awful change of death. Her cheeks fell in, her chin dropped, her eyes opened, and her flesh quivered convulsively. The wizard saw it all by the bright moonlight. Then he took up his part in this unholy drama.

All that he did cannot be described, because it is indescribable. The Witch of Endor repeated no formula, but she raised the dead; and so did Hokosa the wizard. But he buried his face in the grey dust of the grave, he blew with his lips into the dust, he clutched at the dust with his hands, and when he raised his face again, lo! it was grey like the dust. Now began the marvel; for, though the woman before him remained a corpse, from the lips of that corpse a voice issued, and its sound was horrible, for the accent and tone of it were masculine, and the instrument through which it spoke—Noma's throat—was feminine. Yet it could be recognised as the voice of Umsuka the dead king.

"Why have you summoned me from my rest, Hokosa?" muttered the voice from the lips of the huddled corpse.

"Because I would learn the future, Spirit of the king," answered the wizard boldly, but saluting as he spoke. "You are dead, and to your sight all the Gates are opened. By the power that I have, I command you to show me what you see therein concerning myself, and to point out to me the path that I should follow to attain my ends and the ends of her in whose breast you dwell."

At once the answer came, always in the same horrible voice:—

"Hearken to your fate for this world, Hokosa the wizard. You shall triumph over your rival, the white man, the messenger; and by your hand he shall perish, passing to his appointed place where you must meet again. By that to which you cling you shall be betrayed, ah! you shall lose that which you love and follow after that which you do not desire. In the grave of error you shall find truth, from the deeps of sin you shall pluck righteousness. When these words fall upon your ears again, then, Wizard, take them for a sign and let your heart be turned. That which you deem accursed shall lift you up on high. High shall you be set above the nation and its king, and from age to age the voice of the people shall praise you. Yet in the end comes judgment; and there shall the sin and the atonement strive together, and in that hour, Wizard, you shall——"

Thus the voice spoke, strongly at first, but growing ever more feeble as the sparks of life departed from the body of the woman, till at length it ceased altogether.

"What shall chance to me in that hour?" Hokosa asked eagerly, placing his ears against Noma's lips.

No answer came; and the wizard knew that if he would drag his wife back from the door of death he must delay no longer. Dashing the sweat from his eyes with one hand, with the other he seized the gourd of fluid that he had placed ready, and thrusting back her head, he poured of its contents down her throat and waited a while. She did not move. In an extremity of terror he snatched a knife, and with a single cut severed a vein in her arm, then taking some of the fluid

477

that remained in the gourd in his hand, he rubbed it roughly upon her brow and throat and heart. Now Noma's fingers stirred, and now, with horrible contortions and every symptom of agony, life returned to her. The blood flowed from her wounded arm, slowly at first, then more fast, and lifting her head she spoke.

"Take me hence," she cried, "or I shall go mad; for I have seen and heard things too terrible to be spoken!"

"What have you seen and heard?" he asked, while he cut the thongs which bound her wrists and feet.

"I do not know," Noma answered weeping; "the vision of them passes from me; but all the distances of death were open to my sight; yes, I travelled through the distances of death. In them I met him who was the king, and he lay cold within me, speaking to my heart; and as he passed from me he looked upon the child which I shall bear and cursed it, and surely accursed it shall be. Take me hence, O you most evil man, for of your magic I have had enough, and from this day forth I am haunted!"

"Have no fear," answered Hokosa; "you have made the journey whence but few return; and yet, as I promised you, you have returned to wear the greatness you desire and that I sent you forth to win; for henceforth we shall be great. Look, the dawn is breaking—the dawn of life and the dawn of power—and the mists of death and of disgrace roll back before us. Now the path is clear, the dead have shown it to me, and of wizardry I shall need no more."

"Ay!" answered Noma, "but night follows dawn as the dawn follows night; and through the darkness and the daylight, I tell you, Wizard, henceforth I am haunted! Also, be not so sure, for though I know not what the dead have spoken to you, yet it lingers on my mind that their words have many meanings. Nay, speak to me no more, but let us fly from this dread home of ghosts, this habitation of the spirit-folk which we have violated."

So the wizard and his wife crept from that solemn place, and as they went they saw the dawn-beams lighting upon the white cross that was reared in the Plain of Fire.

CHAPTER 12

The Message of Hokosa

The weeks passed by, and Hokosa sat in his *kraal* weaving a great plot. None suspected him any more, for though he did not belong to it, he was heard to speak well of the new faith, and to acknowledge that the god of fire which he had worshipped was a false god. He was humble also towards the king, but he craved to withdraw himself from all matters of the State, saying that now he had but one desire— to tend his herds and garden, and to grow old in peace with the new wife whom he had chosen and whom he loved. Owen, too, he greeted courteously when he met him, sending him gifts of corn and cattle for the service of his church. Moreover, when a messenger came from Hafela, making proposals to him, he drove him away and laid the matter before the council of the king. Yet that messenger, who was hunted from the *kraal*, took back a secret word for Hafela's ear.

"It is not always winter," was the word, "and it may chance that in the springtime you shall hear from me." And again, "Say to the Prince Hafela, that though my face towards him is like a storm, yet behind the clouds the sun shines ever."

At length there came a day when Noma, his wife, was brought to bed. Hokosa, her husband, tended her alone, and when the child was born he groaned aloud and would not suffer her to look upon its face. Yet, lifting herself, she saw.

"Did I not tell you it was accursed?" she wailed. "Take it away!" and she sank back in a swoon. So he took the child, and buried it deep in the cattle-yard by night.

After this it came about that Noma, who, though her mind owned the sway of his, had never loved him over much, hated her husband Hokosa. Yet he had this power over her that she could not leave him. But he loved her more and more, and she had this power over him that she could always draw him to her. Great as her beauty had ever been, after the birth of the child it grew greater day by day, but it was an evil beauty, the beauty of a witch; and this fate fell upon her, that she feared the dark and would never be alone after the sun had set.

When she was recovered from her illness, Noma sat one night in her hut, and Hokosa sat there also watching her. The evening was warm, but a bright fire burned in the hut, and she crouched upon a stool by the fire, glancing continually over her shoulder.

"Why do you bide by the fire, seeing that it is so hot, Noma?" he asked.

"Because I fear to be away from the light," she answered; adding, "Oh, accursed man! for your own ends you have caused me to be bewitched, ah! and that which was born of me also, and bewitched I am by those shadows that you bade me seek, which now will never leave me. Nor, is this all. You swore to me that if I would do your will I should become great, ay! and you took me from one who would have made me great and whom I should have pushed on to victory. But now it seems that for nothing I made that awful voyage into the deeps of death; and for nothing, yet living, am I become the sport of those that dwell there. How am I greater than I was—I who am but the second wife of a fallen witch-doctor, who sits in the sun, day by day, while age gathers on his head like frost upon a bush? Where are all your high schemes now? Where is the fruit of wisdom that I gathered for you? Answer, Wizard, whom I have learned to hate, but from whom I cannot escape!"

"Truly," said Hokosa in a bitter voice, "for all my sins against them the heavens have laid a heavy fate upon my head, that thus with flesh and spirit I should worship a woman who loathes me. One comfort only is left to me, that you dare not take my life lest another should be added to those shadows who companion you, and what I bid you, that you must still do. Ay, you fear the dark, Noma; yet did I command you to rise and go stand alone through the long night yonder in the burying-place of kings, why, you must obey. Come, I command you—go!"

"Nay, nay!" she wailed in an extremity of terror. Yet she rose and went towards the door sideways, for her hands were outstretched in supplication to him.

"Come back," he said, "and listen: If a hunter has nurtured up a fierce dog, wherewith alone he can gain his livelihood, he tries to tame that dog by love, does he not? And if it will not become gentle, then, the brute being necessary to him, he tames it by fear. I am the hunter and, Noma, you are the hound; and since this curse is on me that I cannot live without you, why I must master you as best I may. Yet, believe me, I would not cause you fear or pain, and it saddens me that you should be haunted by these sick fancies, for they are nothing more. I have seen such cases before today, and I have noted that they can be cured by mixing with fresh faces and travelling in new countries. Noma, I think it would be well that, after your late sickness, according to the custom of the women of our people, you should part from me a while, and go upon a journey of purification."

"Whither shall I go and who will go with me?" she asked sullenly.

"I will find you companions, women discreet and skilled. And as to where you shall go, I will tell you. You shall go upon an embassy to the Prince Hafela."

"Are you not afraid that I should stop there?" she asked again, with a flash of her eyes. "It is true that I never learned all the story, yet I thought that the prince was not so glad to hand me back to you as you would have had me to believe. The price you paid for me must have been good, Hokosa, and mayhap it had to do with the death of a king."

"I am not afraid," he answered, setting his teeth, "because I know that whatever your heart may desire, my will follows you, and while I live that is a cord you cannot break unless I choose to loose it, Noma. I command you to be faithful to me and to return to me, and these commands you must obey. Hearken: you taunted me just now, saying that I sat like a dotard in the sun and advanced you nothing. Well, I will advance you, for both our sakes, but mostly for your own, since you desire it, and it must be done through the Prince Hafela. I cannot leave this *kraal*, for day and night I am watched, and before I had gone an hour's journey I should be seized; also here I have work to do. But the Place of Purification is secret, and when you reach it you need not bide there, you can travel on into the mountains till you come to the town of the Prince Hafela. He will receive you gladly, and you shall whisper this message in his ear:—

"'These are the words of Hokosa, my husband, which he has set in my mouth to deliver to you, O Prince. Be guided by them and grow great; reject them and die a wanderer, a little man of no account. But first, this is the price that you shall swear by the sacred oath to pay to Hokosa, if his wisdom finds favour in your sight and through it you come to victory: That after you, the king, he, Hokosa, shall be the first man in our land, the general of the armies, the captain of the council, the head of the doctors, and that to him shall be given half the cattle of Nodwengo, who now is king. Also to him shall be given power to stamp out the new faith which overruns the land like a foreign weed, and to deal as he thinks fit with those who cling thereto.'

"Now, Noma, when he has sworn this oath in your ear, calling

481

down ruin upon his own head, should he break one word of it, and not before, you shall continue the message thus: 'These are the other words that Hokosa set in my mouth: "Know, O Prince, that the king, your brother, grows very strong, for he is a great soldier, who learned his art in bygone wars; also the white man that is named Messenger has taught him many things as to the building of forts and walls and the drilling and discipline of men. So strong is he that you can scarcely hope to conquer him in open war—yet snakes may crawl where men cannot walk. Therefore, Prince, let your part be that of a snake. Do you send an embassy to the king, your brother and say to him:—

"'My brother, you have been preferred before me and set up to be king in my place, and because of this my heart is bitter, so bitter that I have gathered my strength to make war upon you. Yet, at the last, I have taken another council, bethinking me that, if we fight, in the end it may chance that neither of us will be left alive to rule, and that the people also will be brought to nothing. To the north there lies a good country and a wide, where but few men live, and thither I would go, setting the mountains and the river between us; for there, far beyond your borders, I also can be a king. Now, to reach this country, I must travel by the pass that is not far from your Great Place, and I pray you that you will not attack my *impis* or the women and children that I shall send, and a guard before them, to await me in the plain beyond the mountains, seeing that these can only journey slowly. Let us pass by in peace, my brother, for so shall our quarrel be ended; but if you do so much as lift a single spear against me, then I will give you battle, setting my fortune against your fortune and my god against your God!'

"Such are the words that the embassy shall deliver into the ears of the king, Nodwengo, and it shall come about that when he hears them, Nodwengo, whose heart is gentle and who seeks not war, shall answer softly, saying:—

"'Go in peace, my brother, and live in peace in that land which you would win.'

"Then shall you, Hafela, send on the most of your cattle and the women and the children through that pass in the mountains, bidding them to await you in the plain, and after a while you shall follow them with your *impis*. But these shall not travel in war array, for carriers must bear their fighting shields in bundles and their stabbing spears shall be rolled up in mats. Now, on the sixth day of your journey you shall camp at the mouth of the pass which the cattle and the women have already travelled, and his outposts and spies will bring it to the ears of the king that your force is sleeping there, purposing to climb the pass on the morrow.

482

"But on that night, so soon as the darkness falls, you must rise up with your captains and your regiments, leaving your fires burning and men about your fires, and shall travel very swiftly across the valley, so that an hour before the dawn you reach the second range of mountains, and pass it by the gorge which is the burying-place of kings. Here you shall light a fire, which those who watch will believe to be but the fire of a herdsman who is cold. But I, Hokosa, also shall be watching, and when I see that fire I will creep, with some whom I can trust, to the little northern gate of the outer wall, and we will spear those that guard it and open the gate, that your army may pass through. Then, before the regiments can stand to their arms or those within it are awakened, you must storm the inner walls and by the light of the burning huts, put the dwellers in the Great Place to the spear, and the rays of the rising sun shall crown you king.

"Follow this counsel of mine, O Prince Hafela, and all will go well with you. Neglect it and be lost. There is but one thing which you need fear—it is the magic of the Messenger, to whom it is given to read the secret thoughts of men. But of him take no account, for he is my charge, and before ever you set a foot within the Great Place he shall have taken his answer back to Him Who sent him."

Hokosa finished speaking.

"Have you heard?" he said to Noma.

"I have heard."

"Then speak the message."

She repeated it word for word, making no fault. "Have no fear," she added, "I shall forget nothing when I stand before the prince."

"You are a woman, but your counsel is good. What think you of the plan, Noma?"

"It is deep and well laid," she answered, "and surely it would succeed were it not for one thing. The white man, Messenger, will be too clever for you, for as you say, he is a reader of the thoughts of men."

"Can the dead read men's thoughts, or if they can, do they cry them on the market-place or into the ears of kings?" asked Hokosa. "Have I not told you that, before I see the signal-fire yonder, the Messenger shall sleep sound? I have a medicine, Noma, a slow medicine that none can trace."

"The Messenger may sleep sound, Hokosa, and yet perchance he may pass on his message to another and, with it, his magic. Who can say? Still, husband, strike on for power and greatness and revenge, letting the blow fall where it will."

483

CHAPTER 13

The Basket of Fruit

Three days later it was announced that according to the custom of the women of the People of Fire, Noma having given birth to a still-born child, was about to start upon a journey to the Mount of Purification. Here she would abide awhile and make sacrifice to the spirits of her ancestors, that they might cease to be angry with her and in future protect her from such misfortunes. This not unusual domestic incident excited little comment, although it was remarked that the four matrons by whom she was to be accompanied, in accordance with the tribal etiquette, were all of them the wives of soldiers who had deserted to Hafela. Indeed, the king himself noticed as much when Hokosa made the customary formal application to him to sanction the expedition.

"So be it," he said, "though myself I have lost faith in such rites. Also, Hokosa, I think it likely that although your wife goes out with company, she will return alone."

"Why, King?" asked Hokosa.

"For this reason—that those who travel with her have husbands yonder at the town of the Prince Hafela, and the Mount of Purification is on the road thither. Having gone so far, they may go farther. Well, let them go, for I desire to have none among my people whose hearts turn otherwhere, and it would not be wonderful if they should choose to seek their lords. But perchance, Hokosa, there are some in this town who may use them as messengers to the prince"—and he looked at him keenly.

"I think not, King," said Hokosa. "None but a fool would make use of women to carry secret words or tidings. Their tongues are too long and their memories too bad, or too uncertain."

"Yet I have heard, Hokosa, that you have made use of women in many a strange work. Say now, what were you doing upon a night a

484

while ago with that fair witch-wife if yours yonder in the burying-place of kings, where it is not lawful that you should set your foot? Nay, deny it not. You were seen to enter the valley after midnight and to return thence at the dawn, and it was seen also that as she came homewards your wife walked as one who is drunken, and she, whom it is not easy to frighten, wore a face of fear. Man, I do not trust you, and were I wise I should hunt you hence, or keep you so close that you could scarcely move without my knowledge.

"Why should I trust you?" Nodwengo went on vehemently. "Can a wizard cease from wizardry, or a plotter from his plots? No, not until the waters run upward and the sun shines at night; not until repentance touches you and your heart is changed, which I should hold as much a marvel. You were my father's friend and he made you great; yet you could plan with my brother to poison him, your king. Nay, be silent; I know it, though I have said nothing of it because one that is dear to me has interceded for you. You were the priest of the false god, and with that god are fallen from your place, yet you have not renounced him. You sit still in your *kraal* and pretend to be asleep, but your slumber is that of the serpent which watches his time to strike. How do I know that you will not poison me as you would have poisoned my father, or stir up rebellion against me, or bring my brother's *impis* on my head?"

"If the King thinks any of these things of his servant," answered Hokosa in a humble voice, but with dignity, "his path is plain: let him put me to death and sleep in peace. Who am I that I should full the ears of a king with my defence against these charges, or dare to wrangle with him?"

"Long ago I should have put you to death, Hokosa," answered Nodwengo sternly, "had it not been that one has pleaded for you, declaring that in you there is good which will overcome the evil, and that you who now are an axe to cut down my throne, in time to come shall be a roof-tree for its support. Also, the law that I obey does not allow me to take the blood of men save upon full proof, and against you as yet I have no proof. Still, Hokosa, be warned in time and let your heart be turned before the grave claims your body and the Wicked One your soul."

"I thank you, King, for your gentle words and your tender care for my well-being both on earth and after I shall leave it. But I tell you, King, that I had rather die as your father would have killed me in the old days, or your brother would kill me now, did either of them hate or fear me, than live on in safety, owing my life to a new law and a new mercy that do not befit the great ones of the world. King, I am your servant," and giving him the royal salute, Hokosa rose and left his presence.

"At the least there goes a man," said Nodwengo, as he watched him depart.

"Of whom do you speak, King?" asked Owen, who at that moment entered the royal house.

"Of him whom you must have touched in the door-way, Messenger, Hokosa the wizard," answered the king, and he told him of what had passed between them. "I said," he added, "that he was a man, and so he is; yet I hold that I have done wrong to listen to your pleading and to spare him, for I am certain that he will bring bloodshed upon me and trouble on the Faith. Think now, Messenger, how full must be that man's heart of secret rage and hatred, he who was so great and is now so little! Will he not certainly strive to grow great again? Will he not strive to be avenged upon those who humbled him and the religion they have chosen?"

"It may be," answered Owen, "but if so, he will not conquer. I tell you, King, that like water hidden in a rock there is good in this man's heart, and that I shall yet find a rod wherewith to cause it to gush out and refresh the desert."

"It is more likely that he will find a spear wherewith to cause your blood to gush out and refresh the jackals," answered the king grimly; "but be it as you will. And now, what of your business?"

"This, King: John, my servant, has returned from the coast countries, and he brings me a letter saying that before long three white teachers will follow him to take up the work which I have begun. I pray that when they come, for my sake and for the sake of the truth that I have taught you, you will treat them kindly and protect them, remembering that at first they can know little of your language or your customs."

"I will indeed," said the king, with much concern. "But tell me, Messenger, why do you speak of yourself as of one who soon will be but a memory? Do you purpose to leave us?"

"No, King, but I believe that ere long I shall be recalled. I have given my message, my task is well-nigh ended and I must be turning home. Save for your sakes I do not sorrow at this, for to speak truth I grow very weary," and he smiled sadly.

****

Hokosa went home alarmed and full of bitterness, for he had never

486

guessed that the "servant of the Messenger," as he called Nodwengo the King, knew so much about him and his plans. His fall was hard to him, but to be thus measured up, weighed, and contemptuously forgiven was almost more than he could bear. It was the white prophet who had done this thing; he had told Nodwengo of his, Hokosa's, share in the plot to murder the late King Umsuka, though how he came to know of that matter was beyond guessing. He had watched him, or caused him to be watched, when he went forth to consult spirits in the place of the dead; he had warned Nodwengo against him. Worst of all, he had dared to treat him with contempt; had pleaded for his life and safety, so that he was spared as men spare a snake from which the charmer has drawn the fangs. When they met in the gate of the king's house yonder this white thief, who had stolen his place and power, had even smiled upon him and greeted him kindly, and doubtless while he smiled, by aid of the magic he possessed, had read him through and gone on to tell the story to the king. Well, of this there should be an end; he would kill the Messenger, or himself be killed.

When Hokosa reached his *kraal* he found Noma sitting beneath a fruit tree that grew in it, idly employed in stringing beads, for the work of the household she left to his other wife, Zinti, an old and homely woman who thought more of the brewing of the beer and the boiling of the porridge than of religions or politics or of the will of kings. Of late Noma had haunted the shadow of this tree, for beneath it lay that child which had been born to her.

"Does it please the king to grant leave for my journey?" she asked, looking up.

"Yes, it pleases him."

"I am thankful," she answered, "for I think that if I bide here much longer, with ghosts and memories for company, I shall go mad," and she glanced at a spot near by, where the earth showed signs of recent disturbance.

"He gives leave," Hokosa went on, taking no notice of her speech, "but he suspects us. Listen——" and he told her of the talk that had passed between himself and the king.

"The white man has read you as he reads in his written books," she answered, with a little laugh. "Well, I said that he would be too clever for you, did I not? It does not matter to me, for tomorrow I go upon my journey, and you can settle it as you will."

"Ay!" answered Hokosa, grinding his teeth, "it is true that he has read me; but this I promise you, that all books shall soon be closed to him. Yet how is it to be done without suspicion or discovery? I know many poisons, but all of them must be administered, and let him work never so cunningly, he who gives a poison can be traced."

"Then cause some other to give it and let him bear the blame," suggested Noma languidly.

Hokosa made no answer, but walking to the gate of the *kraal*, which was open, he leaned against it lost in thought. As he stood thus he saw a woman advancing towards him, who carried on her head a small basket of fruit, and knew her for one of those whose business it was to wait upon the Messenger in his huts, or rather in his house, for by now he had built himself a small house, and near it a chapel. This woman saw Hokosa also and looked at him sideways, as though she would like to stop and speak to him, but feared to do so.

"Good morrow to you, friend," he said. "How goes it with your husband and your house?"

Now Hokosa knew well that this woman's husband had taken a dislike to her and driven her from his home, filling her place with one younger and more attractive. At the question the woman's lips began to tremble, and her eyes swam with tears.

"Ah! great doctor," she said, "why do you ask me of my husband? Have you not heard that he has driven me away and that another takes my place?"

"Do I hear all the gossip of this town?" asked Hokosa, with a smile. "But come in and tell me the story; perchance I may be able to help you, for I have charms to compel the fancy of such faithless ones."

The woman looked round, and seeing that there was no one in sight, she slipped swiftly through the gate of the *kraal*, which he closed behind her.

"Noma," said Hokosa, "here is one who tells me that her husband has deserted her, and who comes to seek my counsel. Bring her milk to drink."

"There are some wives who would not find that so great an evil," replied Noma mockingly, as she rose to do his bidding.

Hokosa winced at the sarcasm, and turning to his visitor, said:—

"Now tell me your tale; but say first, why are you so frightened?"

"I am frightened, master," she answered, "lest any should have seen me enter here, for I have become a Christian, and the Christians are forbidden to consult the witch-doctors, as we were wont to do. For my case, it is——"

"No need to set it out," broke in Hokosa, waving his hand. "I see it written on your face; your husband has put you away and loves another woman, your own half-sister whom you brought up from a child."

"Ah! master, you have heard aright."

"I have not heard, I look upon you and I see. Fool, am I not a wizard? Tell me——" and taking dust into his hand, he blew the grains this way and that, regarding them curiously. "Yes, it is so. Last night you crept to your husband's hut—do you remember, a dog growled at you as you passed the gate?—and there in front of the hut he sat with his new wife. She saw you coming, but pretending not to see, she threw her arms about his neck, kissing and fondling him before your eyes, till you could bear it no longer, and revealed yourself, upbraiding them. Then your rival taunted you and stirred up the man with bitter words, till at length he took a stick and beat you from the door, and there is a mark of it upon your shoulder."

"It is true, it is too true!" she groaned.

"Yes, it is true. And now, what do you wish from me?"

"Master, I wish a medicine to make my husband hate my rival and to draw his heart back to me."

"That must be a strong medicine," said Hokosa, "which will turn a man from one who is young and beautiful to one who is past her youth and ugly."

"I am as I am," answered the poor woman, with a touch of natural dignity, "but at least I have loved him and worked for him for fifteen long years."

"And that is why he would now be rid of you, for who cumbers his *kraal* with old cattle?"

"And yet at times they are the best, Master. Wrinkles and smooth skin seem strange upon one pillow," she added, glancing at Noma, who came from the hut carrying a bowl of milk in her hand.

"If you seek counsel," said Hokosa quickly, "why do you not go to the white man, that Messenger in whom you believe, and ask him for a potion to turn your husband's heart?"

"Master, I have been to him, and he is very good to me, for when I was driven out he gave me work to do and food. But he told me that he had no medicine for such cases, and that the Great Man in the sky alone could soften the breast of my husband and cause my sister to cease from her wickedness. Last night I went to see whether He would do it, and you know what befell me there."

"That befell you which befalls all fools who put their trust in words alone. What will you pay me, woman, if I give you the medicine which you seek?"

"Alas, master, I am poor. I have nothing to offer you, for when I would not stay in my husband's *kraal* to be a servant to his new wife, he took the cow and the five goats that belonged to me, as, I being childless, according to our ancient law he had the right to do."

"You are bold who come to ask a doctor to minister to you, bearing no fee in your hand," said Hokosa. "Yet, because I have pity on you, I will be content with very little. Give me that basket of fruit, for my wife has been sick and loves its taste."

"I cannot do that, Master," answered the woman, "for it is sent by my hand as a present to the Messenger, and he knows this and will eat of it after he has made prayer today. Did I not give it to him, it would be discovered that I had left it here with you."

"Then begone without your medicine," said Hokosa, "for I need such fruit."

The woman rose and said, looking at him wistfully:—

"Master, if you will be satisfied with other fruits of this same sort, I know where I can get them for you."

"When will you get them?"

"Now, within an hour. And till I return I will leave these in pledge with you; but these and no other I must give to the Messenger, for he has already seen them and might discover the difference; also I have promised so to do."

"As you will," said Hokosa. "If you are with the fruit within an hour, the medicine will be ready for you, a medicine that shall not fail."

CHAPTER 14

The Eating of the Fruit

The woman slipped away secretly. When she had gone Hokosa bade his wife bring the basket of fruit into the hut.

"It is best that the butcher should kill the ox himself," she answered meaningly.

He carried in the basket and set it on the floor.

"Why do you speak thus, Noma?" he asked.

"Because I will have no hand in the matter, Hokosa. I have been the tool of a wizard, and won little joy therefrom. The tool of a murderer I will not be!"

"If I kill, it is for the sake of both of us," he said passionately.

"It may be so, Hokosa, or for the sake of the people, or for the sake of Heaven above—I do not know and do not care; but I say, do your own killing, for I am sure that even less luck will hang to it than hangs to your witchcraft."

"Of all women you are the most perverse!" he said, stamping his foot upon the ground.

"Thus you may say again before everything is done, husband; but if it be so, why do you love me and tie me to you with your wizardry? Cut the knot, and let me go my way while you go yours."

"Woman, I cannot; but still I bid you beware, for, strive as you will, my path must be your path. Moreover, till I free you, you cannot lift voice or hand against me." Then, while she watched him curiously, Hokosa fetched his medicines and took from them some powder fine as dust and two tiny crow quills. Placing a fruit before him, he inserted one of these quills into its substance, and filling the second with the powder, he shook its contents into it and withdrew the tube. This process he repeated four times on each of the fruits, replacing them one by one in the basket. So deftly did he work upon them, that however closely they were scanned none could guess that they had been tampered with.

"Will it kill at once?" asked Noma.

"No, indeed; but he who eats these fruits will be seized on the third day with dysentery and fever, and these will cling to him till within seven weeks—or if he is very strong, three months—he dies. This is the best of poisons, for it works through nature and can be traced by none."

"Except, perchance, by that Spirit Whom the white man worships, and Who also works through nature, as you learned, Hokosa, when He rolled the lightning back upon your head, shattering your god and beating down your company."

Then of a sudden terror seized the wizard, and springing to his feet, he cursed his wife till she trembled before him.

"Vile woman, and double-faced!" he said, "why do you push me forward with one hand and with the other drag me back? Why do you whisper evil counsel into one ear and into the other prophesy of misfortunes to come? Had it not been for you, I should have let this business lie; I should have taken my fate and been content. But day by day you have taunted me with my fall and grieved over the greatness that you have lost, till at length you have driven me to this. Why cannot you be all good or all wicked, or at the least, through righteousness and sin, faithful to my interest and your own?"

"Because I hate you, Hokosa, and yet can strike you only through my tongue and your mad love for me. I am fast in your power, but thus at least I can make you feel something of my own pain. Hark! I hear that woman at the gate. Will you give her back the basket, or will you not? Whatever you may choose to do, do not say in after days that I urged you to the deed."

"Truly you are great-hearted!" he answered, with cold contempt; "one for whom I did well to enter into treachery and sin! So be it: having gone so far upon it, come what may, I will not turn back from this journey. Let in that fool!"

Presently the woman stood before them, bearing with her another basket of fruit.

"These are what you seek, Master," she said, "though I was forced to win them by theft. Now give me my own and the medicine and let me go."

He gave her the basket, and with it, wrapped in a piece of kidskin, some of the same powder with which he had doctored the fruits.

"What shall I do with this?" she asked.

"You must find means to sprinkle it upon your sister's food, and thereafter your husband shall come to hate even the sight of her."

"But will he come to love me again?"

Hokosa shrugged his shoulders.

"I know not," he answered; "that is for you to see to. Yet this is sure, that if a tree grows up before the house of a man, shutting it off from the sunlight, when that tree is cut down the sun shines upon his house again."

"It is nothing to the sun on what he shines," said the woman.

"If the saying does not please you, then forget it. I promise you this and no more, that very soon the man shall cease to turn to your rival."

"The medicine will not harm her?" asked the woman doubtfully. "She has worked me bitter wrong indeed, yet she is my sister, whom I nursed when she was little, and I do not wish to do her hurt. If only he will welcome me back and treat me kindly, I am willing even that she should dwell on beneath my husband's roof, bearing his children, for will they not be of my own blood?"

"Woman," answered Hokosa impatiently, "you weary me with your talk. Did I say that the charm would hurt her? I said that it would cause your husband to hate the sight of her. Now begone, taking or leaving it, and let me rest. If your mind is troubled, throw aside that medicine, and go soothe it with such sights as you saw last night."

On hearing this the woman sprang up, hid away the poison in her hair, and taking her basket of fruit, passed from the *kraal* as secretly as she had entered it.

"Why did you give her death-medicine?" asked Noma of Hokosa, as he stood staring after her. "Have you a hate to satisfy against the husband or the girl who is her rival?"

"None," he answered, "for they have never crossed my path. Oh, foolish woman! cannot you read my plan?"

"Not altogether, Husband."

"Listen then: this woman will give to her sister a medicine of which in the end she must die. She may be discovered or she may not, but it is certain that she will be suspected, seeing that the bitterness of the quarrel between them is known. Also she will give to the Messenger certain fruits, after eating of which he will be taken sick and in due time die, of just such a disease as that which carries off the woman's rival. Now, if any think that he is poisoned, which I trust none will, whom will they suppose to have poisoned him, though indeed they can never prove the crime?"

"The plan is clever," said Noma with admiration, "but in it I see a flaw. The woman will say that she had the drug from you, or, at the least, will babble of her visit to you."

"Not so," answered Hokosa, "for on this matter the greatest talker in the world would keep silence. Firstly, she, being a Christian, dare not own that she has visited a witch-doctor. Secondly, the fruit she brought in payment was stolen, therefore she will say nothing of it. Thirdly, to admit that she had medicine from me would be to admit her guilt, and that she will scarcely do even under torture, which by the new law it is not lawful to apply. Moreover, none saw her come here, and I should deny her visit."

"The plan is very clever," said Noma again.

"It is very clever," he repeated complacently; "never have I made a better one. Now throw those fruits to the she goats that are in the *kraal*, and burn the basket, while I go and talk to some in the Great Place, telling them that I have returned from counting my cattle on the mountain, whither I went after I had bowed the knee in the house of the king."

****

Two hours later, Hokosa, having made a wide detour and talked to sundry of his acquaintances about the condition of his cattle, might have been seen walking slowly along the north side of the Great Place towards his own *kraal*. His path lay past the chapel and the little house that Owen had built to dwell in. This house was furnished with a broad veranda, and upon it sat the Messenger himself, eating his evening meal. Hokosa saw him, and a great desire entered his heart to learn whether or no he had partaken of the poisoned fruit. Also it occurred to him that it would be wise if, before the end came, he could contrive to divert all possible suspicion from himself, by giving the impression that he was now upon friendly terms with the great white teacher and not disinclined even to become a convert to his doctrine.

For a moment he hesitated, seeking an excuse. One soon suggested itself to his ready mind. That very morning the king had told him not obscurely that Owen had pleaded for his safety and saved him from being put upon his trial on charges of witchcraft and murder. He would go to him, now at once, playing the part of a grateful penitent, and the White Man's magic must be keen indeed if it availed to pierce the armour of his practised craft.

So Hokosa went up and squatted himself down native fashion among a little group of converts who were waiting to see their teacher upon one business or another. He was not more than ten paces from the veranda, and sitting thus he saw a sight that interested him strangely. Having eaten a little of a dish of roasted meat, Owen put out

494

his hand and took a fruit from a basket that the wizard knew well. At this moment he looked up and recognised Hokosa.

"Do you desire speech with me, Hokosa?" he asked in his gentle voice. "If so, be pleased to come hither."

"Nay, Messenger," answered Hokosa, "I desire speech with you indeed, but it is ill to stand between a hungry man and his food."

"I care little for my food," answered Owen; "at the least it can wait," and he put down the fruit.

Then suddenly a feeling to which the wizard had been for many years a stranger took possession of him—a feeling of compunction. That man was about to partake of what would cause his death—of what he, Hokosa, had prepared in order that it should cause his death. He was good, he was kindly, none could allege a wrong deed against him; and, foolishness though it might be, so was the doctrine that he taught. Why should he kill him? It was true that never till that moment had he hesitated, by fair means or foul, to remove an enemy or rival from his path. He had been brought up in this teaching; it was part of the education of wizards to be merciless, for they reigned by terror and evil craft. Their magic lay chiefly in clairvoyance and powers of observation developed to a pitch that was almost superhuman, and the best of their weapons was poison in infinite variety, whereof the guild alone understood the properties and preparation. Therefore there was nothing strange, nothing unusual in this deed of devilish and cunning murder that the sight of its doing should stir him thus, and yet it did stir him. He was minded to stop the plot, to let things take their course.

Some sense of the futility of all such strivings came home to him, and as in a glass, for Hokosa was a man of imagination, he foresaw their end. A little success, a little failure, it scarcely mattered which, and then—that end. Within twenty years, or ten, or mayhap even one, what would this present victory or defeat mean to him? Nothing so far as he was concerned; that is, nothing so far as his life of today was concerned. Yet, if he had another life, it might mean everything. There was another life; he knew it, who had dragged back from its borders the spirits of the dead, though what might be the state and occupations of those dead he did not know. Yet he believed—why he could not tell—that they were affected vitally by their acts and behaviour here; and his intelligence warned him that good must always flow from good, and evil from evil. To kill this man was evil, and of it only evil could come.

What did he care whether Hafela ruled the nation or Nodwengo, and whether it worshipped the God of the Christians or the god of Fire—who, by the way, had proved himself so singularly inefficient in the hour of trial. Now that he thought of it, he much preferred Nod-wengo to Hafela, for the one was a just man and the other a tyrant; and he himself was more comfortable as a wealthy private person than he had been as a head medicine-man and a chief of wizards. He would let things stand; he would prevent the Messenger from eating of that fruit. A word could do it; he had but to suggest that it was unripe or not wholesome at this season of the year, and it would be cast aside.

All these reflections, or their substance, passed through Hokosa's mind in a few instants of time, and already he was rising to go to the veranda and translate their moral into acts, when another thought occurred to him—How should he face Noma with this tale? He could give up his own ambitions, but could he bear her mockery, as day by day she taunted him with his faint-heartedness and reproached him with his failure to regain greatness and to make her great? He forgot that he might conceal the truth from her; or rather, he did not contemplate such concealment, of which their relations were too peculiar and too intimate to permit. She hated him, and he worshipped her with a half-inhuman passion—a passion so unnatural, indeed, that it suggested the horrid and insatiable longings of the damned—and yet their souls were naked to each other. It was their fate that they could hide nothing each from each—they were cursed with the awful necessity of candour.

It would be impossible that he should keep from Noma anything that he did or did not do; it would be still more impossible that she should conceal from him even such imaginings and things as it is common for women to hold secret. Her very bitterness, which it had been policy for her to cloak or soften, would gush from her lips at the sight of him; nor, in the depth of his rage and torment, could he, on the other hand, control the ill-timed utterance of his continual and overmastering passion. It came to this, then: he must go forward, and against his better judgment, because he was afraid to go back, for the whip of a woman's tongue drove him on remorselessly. It was better that the Messenger should die, and the land run red with blood, than that he should be forced to endure this scourge.

So with a sigh Hokosa sank back to the ground and watched while Owen ate three of the poisoned fruits. After a pause, he took a fourth and bit into it, but not seeming to find it to his taste, he threw it to a child that was waiting by the veranda for any scraps which might be left over from his meal. The child caught it, and devoured it eagerly.

Then, smiling at the little boy's delight, the Messenger called to Hokosa to come up and speak with him.

CHAPTER 15

Noma Comes to Hafela

Hokosa advanced to the veranda and bowed to the white man with grave dignity.

"Be seated," said Owen. "Will you not eat? though I have nothing to offer you but these," and he pushed the basket of fruits towards him, adding, "The best of them, I fear, are already gone."

"I thank you, no, Messenger; such fruits are not always wholesome at this season of the year. I have known them to breed dysentery."

"Indeed," said Owen. "If so, I trust that I may escape. I have suffered from that sickness, and I think that another bout of it would kill me. In future I will avoid them. But what do you seek with me, Hokosa? Enter and tell me," and he led the way into a little sitting-room.

"Messenger," said the wizard, with deep humility, "I am a proud man; I have been a great man, and it is no light thing to me to humble myself before the face of my conqueror. Yet I am come to this. Today when I was in audience with the king, craving a small boon of his graciousness, he spoke to me sharp and bitter words. He told me that he had been minded to put me on trial for my life because of various misdoings which are alleged against me in the past, but that you had pleaded for me and that for this cause he spared me. I come to thank you for your gentleness, Messenger, for I think that had I been in your place I should have whispered otherwise in the ear of the king."

"Say no more of it, friend," said Owen kindly, "We are all of us sinners, and it is my place to push back your ancient sins, not to drag them into the light of day and clamour for their punishment. It is true I know that you plotted with the Prince Hafela to poison Umsuka the King, for it was revealed to me. It chanced, however, that I was able to recover Umsuka from his sickness, and Hafela is fled, so why should I bring up the deed against you? It is true that you still practise witchcraft, and that you hate and strive against the holy Faith which I preach; but you were brought up to wizardry and have been the priest of another creed, and these things plead for you.

"Also, Hokosa, I can see the good and evil struggling in your soul, and I pray and I believe that in the end the good will master the evil; that you who have been pre-eminent in sin will come to be pre-eminent in righteousness. Oh! be not stubborn, but listen with your ear, and let your heart be softened. The gate stands open, and I am the guide appointed to show you the way without reward or fee. Follow them ere it be too late, that in time to come when my voice is stilled you also may be able to direct the feet of wanderers into the paths of peace. It is the hour of prayer; come with me, I beg of you, and listen to some few words of the message of my lips, and let your spirit be nurtured with them, and the Sun of Truth arise upon its darkness."

Hokosa heard, and before this simple eloquence his wisdom sank confounded. More, his intelligence was stirred, and a desire came upon him to investigate and examine the canons of a creed that could produce such men as this. He made no answer, but waiting while Owen robed himself, he followed him to the chapel. It was full of new-made Christians who crowded even the doorways, but they gave place to him, wondering. Then the service began—a short and simple service. First Owen offered up some prayer for the welfare of the infant Church, for the conversion of the unbelieving, for the safety of the king and the happiness of the people. Then John, the Messenger's first disciple, read aloud from a manuscript a portion of the Scripture which his master had translated. It was St. Paul's exposition of the resurrection from the dead, and the grandeur of its thoughts and language were by no means lost upon Hokosa, who, savage and heathen though he might be, was also a man of intellect.

The reading over, Owen addressed the congregation, taking for his text, "Thy sin shall find thee out." Being now a master of the language, he preached very well and earnestly, and indeed the subject was not difficult to deal with in the presence of an audience many of whose pasts had been stepped in iniquities of no common kind. As he talked of judgment to come for the unrepentant, some of his hearers groaned and even wept; and when, changing his note, he dwelt upon the blessed future state of those who earned forgiveness, their faces were lighted up with joy.

But perhaps among all those gathered before him there were none more deeply interested than Hokosa and one other, that woman to whom he had sold the poison, and who, as it chanced, sat next to him.

Hokosa, watching her face as he was skilled to do, saw the thrusts of the preacher go home, and grew sure that already in her jealous haste she had found opportunity to sprinkle the medicine upon her rival's food. She believed it to be but a charm indeed, yet knowing that in using such charms she had done wickedly, she trembled beneath the words of denunciation, and rising at length, crept from the chapel.

"Truly, her sin will find her out," thought Hokosa to himself, and then in a strange half-impersonal fashion he turned his thoughts to the consideration of his own case. Would *his* sin find him out? he wondered. Before he could answer that question, it was necessary first to determine whether or no he had committed a sin. The man before him—that gentle and yet impassioned man—bore in his vitals the seed of death which he, Hokosa, had planted there. Was it wrong to have done this? It depended by which standard the deed was judged. According to his own code, the code on which he had been educated and which hitherto he had followed with exactness, it was not wrong. That code taught the necessity of self-aggrandisement, or at least and at all costs the necessity of self-preservation. This white preacher stood in his path; he had humiliated him, Hokosa, and in the end, either of himself or through his influences, it was probable that he would destroy him. Therefore he must strike before in his own person he received a mortal blow, and having no other means at his command, he struck through treachery and poison.

That was his law which for many generations had been followed and respected by his class with the tacit assent of the nation. According to this law, then, he had done no wrong. But now the victim by the altar, who did not know that already he was bound upon the altar, preached a new and a very different doctrine under which, were it to be believed, he, Hokosa, was one of the worst of sinners. The matter, then, resolved itself to this: which of these two rules of life was the right rule? Which of them should a man follow to satisfy his conscience and to secure his abiding welfare? Apart from the motives that swayed him, as a mere matter of ethics, this problem interested Hokosa not a little, and he went homewards determined to solve it if he might. That could be done in one way only—by a close examination of both systems. The first he knew well; he had practised it for nearly forty years. Of the second he had but an inkling. Also, if he would learn more of it he must make haste, seeing that its exponent in some short while would cease to be in a position to set it out.

"I trust that you will come again," said Owen to Hokosa as they left the chapel.

"Yes, indeed, Messenger," answered the wizard; "I will come every day, and if you permit it, I will attend your private teachings also, for I accept nothing without examination, and I greatly desire to study this new doctrine of yours, root and flower and fruit."

****

On the morrow Noma started upon her journey. As the matrons who accompanied her gave out with a somewhat suspicious persistency, its ostensible object was to visit the Mount of Purification, and there by fastings and solitude to purge herself of the sin of having given birth to a stillborn child. For amongst savage peoples such an accident is apt to be looked upon as little short of a crime, or, at the least, as indicating that the woman concerned is the object of the indignation of spirits who need to be appeased. To this Mount, Noma went, and there performed the customary rites.

"Little wonder," she thought to herself, "that the spirits were angry with her, seeing that yonder in the burying-ground of kings she had dared to break in upon their rest."

From the Place of Purification she travelled on ten days' journey with her companions till they reached the mountain fastness where Hafela had established himself. The town and its surroundings were of extraordinary strength, and so well guarded that it was only after considerable difficulty and delay that the women were admitted. Hearing of her arrival and that she had words for him, Hafela sent for Noma at once, receiving her by night and alone in his principal hut. She came and stood before him, and he looked at her beauty with admiring eyes, for he could not forget the woman whom the cunning of Hokosa had forced him to put away.

"Whence come you, pretty one?" he asked, "and wherefore come you? Are you weary of your husband, that you fly back to me? If so, you are welcome indeed; for know, Noma, that I still love you."

"Ay, Prince, I am weary of my husband sure enough; but I do not fly to you, for he holds me fast to him with bonds that you cannot understand, and fast to him while he lives I must remain."

"What hinders, Noma, that having got you here I should keep you here? The cunning and magic of Hokosa may be great, but they will need to be still greater to win you from my arms."

"This hinders, Prince, that you are playing for a higher stake than that of a woman's love, and if you deal thus by me and my husband, then of a surety you will lose the game."

"What stake, Noma?"

"The stake of the crown of the People of Fire."

"And why should I lose if I take you as a wife?"

"Because Hokosa, seeing that I do not return and learning from his spies why I do not return, will warn the king, and by many means bring all your plans to nothing. Listen now to the words of Hokosa that he has set between my lips to deliver to you"—and she repeated to him all the message without fault or fail.

"Say it again," he said, and she obeyed.

Then he answered:—

"Truly the skill of Hokosa is great, and well he knows how to set a snare; but I think that if by his counsel I should *springe* the bird, he will be too clever a man to keep upon the threshold of my throne. He who sets one snare may set twain, and he who sits by the threshold may desire to enter the house of kings wherein there is no space for two to dwell."

"Is this the answer that I am to take back to Hokosa?" asked Noma. "It will scarcely bind him to your cause, Prince, and I wonder that you dare to speak it to me who am his wife."

"I dare to speak it to you, Noma, because, although you be his wife, all wives do not love their lords; and I think that, perchance in days to come, you would choose rather to hold the hand of a young king than that of a witch-doctor sinking into *eld*. Thus shall you answer Hokosa: You shall say to him that I have heard his words and that I find them very good, and will walk along the path which he has made. Here before you I swear by the oath that may not be broken—the sacred oath, calling down ruin upon my head should I break one word of it—that if by his aid I succeed in this great venture, I will pay him the price he asks. After myself, the king, he shall be the greatest man among the people; he shall be general of the armies; he shall be captain of the council and head of the doctors, and to him shall be given half the cattle of Nodwengo. Also, into his hand I will deliver all those who cling to this faith of the Christians, and, if it pleases him, he shall offer them as a sacrifice to his god. This I swear, and you, Noma, are witness to the oath. Yet it may chance that after he, Hokosa, has gathered up all this pomp and greatness, he himself shall be gathered up by Death, that harvest-man whom soon or late will garner every ear;" and he looked at her meaningly.

"It may be so, Prince," she answered.

"It may be so," he repeated, "and when——"

"When it is so, then, Prince, we will talk together, but not till then. Nay, touch me not, for were he to command me, Hokosa has this power over me that I must show him all that you have done, keeping nothing back. Let me go now to the place that is made ready for me, and afterwards you shall tell me again and more fully the words that I must say to Hokosa my husband."

****

On the morrow Hafela held a secret council of his great men, and the next day an embassy departed to Nodwengo the king, taking to him that message which Hokosa, through Noma his wife, had put into the lips of the prince. Twenty days later the embassy returned saying that it pleased the king to grant the prayer of his brother Hafela, and bringing with it the tidings that the white man, Messenger, had fallen sick, and it was thought that he would die.

So in due course the women and children of the people of Hafela started upon their journey towards the new land where it was given out that they should live, and with them went Noma, purposing to leave them as they drew near the gates of the Great Place of the king. A while after, Hafela and his *impis* followed with carriers bearing their fighting shields in bundles, and having their stabbing spears rolled up in mats.

CHAPTER 16

The Repentance of Hokosa

Hokosa kept his promise. On the morrow of his first attendance there he was again to be seen in the chapel, and after the service was over he waited on Owen at his house and listened to his private teaching. Day by day he appeared thus, till at length he became master of the whole doctrine of Christianity, and discovered that that which at first had struck him as childish and even monstrous, now presented itself to him in a new and very different light. The conversion of Hokosa came upon him through the gate of reason, not as is usual among savages—and some who are not savage—by that of the emotions. Given the position of a universe torn and groaning beneath the dual rule of Good and Evil, two powers of well-nigh equal potency, he found no great difficulty in accepting this tale of the self-sacrifice of the God of Good that He might wring the race He loved out of the conquering grasp of the god of Ill. There was a simple majesty about this scheme of redemption which appealed to one side of his nature. Indeed, Hokosa felt that under certain conditions and in a more limited fashion he would have been capable of attempting as much himself.

Once his reason was satisfied, the rest followed in a natural sequence. Within three weeks from the hour of his first attendance at the chapel Hokosa was at heart a Christian.

He was a Christian, although as yet he did not confess it; but he was also the most miserable man among the nation of the Sons of Fire. The iniquities of his past life had become abominable to him; but he had committed them in ignorance, and he understood that they were not beyond forgiveness. Yet high above them all towered one colossal crime which, as he believed, could never be pardoned to him in this world or the next. He was the treacherous murderer of the Messenger of God; he was in the very act of silencing the Voice that had proclaimed truth in the dark places of his soul and the dull ears of his countrymen.

The deed was done; no power on earth could save his victim. Within a week from the day of eating that fatal fruit Owen began to sicken, then the dysentery had seized him which slowly but surely was wasting out his life. Yet he, the murderer, was helpless, for with this form of the disease no medicine could cope. With agony in his heart, an agony that was shared by thousands of the people, Hokosa watched the decrease of the white man's strength, and reckoned the days that would elapse before the end. Having such sin as thus upon his soul, though Owen entreated him earnestly, he would not permit himself to be baptised. Twice he went near to consenting, but on each occasion an ominous and terrible incident drove him from the door of mercy.

Once, when the words "I will" were almost on his lips, a woman broke in upon their conference bearing a dying boy in her arms.

"Save him," she implored, "save him, Messenger, for he is my only son!"

Owen looked at him and shook his head.

"How came he like this?" he asked.

"I know not, Messenger, but he has been sick ever since he ate of a certain fruit which you gave to him;" and she recalled to his mind the incident of the throwing of a fruit to the child, which she had witnessed.

"I remember," said Owen. "It is strange, but I also have been sick from the day that I ate of those fruits; yes, and you, Hokosa, warned me against them."

Then he blessed the boy and prayed over him till he died; but when afterwards he looked round for Hokosa, it was to find that he had gone.

Some eight days later, having to a certain extent recovered from this shock, Hokosa went one morning to Owen's house and talked to him.

"Messenger," he said, "is it necessary to baptism that I should confess all my sins to you? If so, I can never be baptised, for there is wickedness upon my hands which I am unable to tell into the ear of living man."

Owen thought and answered:—

"It is necessary that you should repent all of your sins, and that you should confess them to heaven; it is not necessary that you should confess them to me, who am but a man like yourself."

"Then I will be baptised," said Hokosa with a sigh of relief.

At this moment, as it chanced, their interview was again interrupted, for runners came from the king requesting the immediate presence of the Messenger, if he were well enough to attend, upon a matter connected with the trial of a woman for murder. Thinking that he might be of service, Owen, leaning on the shoulder of Hokosa, for already he was too weak to walk far, crept to the litter which was waiting for him, and was borne to the place of judgment that was before the house of the king. Hokosa followed, more from curiosity than for any other reason, for he had heard of no murder being committed, and his old desire to be acquainted with everything that passed was still strong on him. The people made way for him, and he seated himself in the first line of spectators immediately opposite to the king and three other captains who were judges in the case. So soon as Owen had joined the judges, the prisoner was brought before them, and to his secret horror Hokosa recognised in her that woman to whom he had given the poison in exchange for the basket of fruit.

Now it seemed to Hokosa that his doom was on him, for she would certainly confess that she had the drug from him. He thought of flight only to reject the thought, for to fly would be to acknowledge himself an accessory. No, he would brazen it out, for after all his word was as good as hers. With the prisoner came an accuser, her husband, who seemed sick, and he it was who opened the case against her.

"This woman," he said, "was my wife. I divorced her for barrenness, as I have a right to do according to our ancient law, and I took another woman to wife, her half-sister. This woman was jealous; she plagued me continually, and insulted her sister, so that I was forced to drive her away. After that she came to my house, and though they said nothing of it at the time, she was seen by two servants of mine to sprinkle something in the bowl wherein our food was cooking. Subsequently my wife, this woman's half-sister, was taken ill with dysentery. I also was taken ill with dysentery, but I still live to tell this story before you, O King, and your judges, though I know not for how long I live. My wife died yesterday, and I buried her this morning. I accuse the woman of having murdered her, either by witchcraft or by means of a medicine which she sprinkled on the food, or by both. I have spoken."

"Have you anything to say?" asked the king of the prisoner. "Are you guilty of the crime whereof this man who was your husband charges you, or does he lie?"

Then the woman answered in a low and broken voice:—

"I am guilty, King. Listen to my story:" and she told it all as she told it to Hokosa. "I am guilty," she added, "and may the Great Man in the sky, of Whom the Messenger has taught us, forgive me. My sister's blood is upon my hands, and for aught I know the blood of my hus-

505

band yonder will also be on my hands. I seek no mercy; indeed, it is better that I should die; but I would say this in self-defence, that I did not think to kill my sister. I believed that I was giving to her a potion which would cause her husband to hate her and no more."

Here she looked round and her eyes met those of Hokosa.

"Who told you that this was so?" asked one of the judges.

"A witch-doctor," she answered, "from whom I bought the medicine in the old days, long ago, when Umsuka was king."

Hokosa gasped. Why should this woman have spared him?

No further question was asked of her, and the judges consulted together. At length the king spoke.

"Woman," he said, "you are condemned to die. You will be taken to the Doom Tree, and there be hanged. Out of those who are assembled to try you, two, the Messenger and myself, have given their vote in favour of mercy, but the majority think otherwise. They say that a law has been passed against murder by means of witchcraft and secret medicine, and that should we let you go free, the people will make a mock of that law. So be it. Go in peace. Tomorrow you must die, and may forgiveness await you elsewhere."

"I ask nothing else," said the woman. "It is best that I should die."

Then they led her away. As she passed Hokosa she turned and looked him full in the eyes, till he dropped his head abashed. Next morning she was executed, and he learned that her last words were: "Let it come to the ears of him who sold me the poison, telling me that it was but a harmless drug, that as I hope to be forgiven, so I forgive him, believing that my silence may win for him time for repentance, before he follows on the road I tread."

Now, when Hokosa heard these words he shut himself up in his house for three days, giving out that he was sick. Nor would he go near to Owen, being altogether without hope, and not believing that baptism or any other rite could avail to purge such crimes as his. Truly his sin had found him out, and the burden of it was intolerable. So intolerable did it become, that at length he determined to be done with it. He could live no more. He would die, and by his own hand, before he was called upon to witness the death of the man whom he had murdered. To this end he made his preparations. For Noma he left no message; for though his heart still hungered after her, he knew well that she hated him and would rejoice at his death.

When all was ready he sat down to think a while, and as he thought, a man entered his hut saying that the Messenger desired to see him. At first he was minded not to go, then it occurred to him that it would be well if he could die with a clean heart. Why should he not tell all to the white man, and before he could be delivered up to justice take that poison which he had prepared? It was impossible that he should be forgiven, yet he desired that his victim should learn how deep was his sorrow and repentance, before he proved it by preceding him to death. So he rose and went.

He found Owen in his house, lying in a rude chair and propped up by pillows of bark. Now he was wasted almost to a shadow, and in the pale pinched face his dark eyes, always large and spiritual, shone with unnatural lustre, while his delicate hands were so thin that when he held them up in blessing the light showed through them.

"Welcome, friend," he said. "Tell me, why have you deserted me of late? Have you been ill?"

"No, Messenger," answered Hokosa, "that is, not in my body. I have been sick at heart, and therefore I have not come."

"What, Hokosa, do your doubts still torment you? I thought that my prayers had been heard, and that power had been given me to set them at rest for ever. Man, let me hear the trouble, and swiftly, for cannot you who are a doctor see that I shall not be here for long to talk with you? My days are numbered, Hokosa, and my work is almost done."

"I know it," answered Hokosa. "And, Messenger, *my* days are also numbered."

"How is this?" asked Owen, "seeing that you are well and strong. Does an enemy put you in danger of your life?"

"Yes, Messenger, and I myself am that enemy; for today I, who am no longer fit to live, must die by my own hand. Nay, listen and you will say that I do well, for before I go I would tell you all. Messenger, you are doomed, are you not? Well, it was I who doomed you. That fruit which you ate a while ago was poisoned, and by my hand, for I am a master of such arts. From the beginning I hated you, as well I might, for had you not worsted me and torn power from my grasp, and placed the people and the king under the rule of another God? Therefore, when all else failed, I determined to murder you, and I did the deed by means of that woman who not long ago was hung for the killing of her sister, though in truth she was innocent." And he told him what had passed between himself and the woman, and told him also of the plot which he had hatched to kill Nodwengo and the Christians, and to set Hafela on the throne.

"She was innocent," he went on, "but I am guilty. How guilty you and I know alone. Do you remember that day when you ate the fruit, how after it I accompanied you to the church yonder and listened to your preaching? 'Your sin shall find you out,' you said, and of a surety mine has found me out. For, Messenger, it came about that in listening to you then and afterwards, I grew to love you and to believe the words you taught, and therefore am I of all men the most miserable, and therefore must I, who have been great and the councillor of kings, perish miserably by the death of a dog.

"Now curse me, and let me go."

Chapter 17

The Loosing of Noma

When Owen heard that it was Hokosa who had poisoned him, he groaned and hid his face in his hands, and thus he remained till the evil tale was finished. Now he lifted his head and spoke, but not to Hokosa.

"O God," he said, "I thank Thee that at the cost of my poor life Thou hast been pleased to lead this sinner towards the Gate of Righteousness, and to save alive those whom Thou hast sent me to gather to Thy Fold."

Then he looked at Hokosa and said:—

"Unhappy man, is not your cup full enough of crime, and have you not sufficiently tempted the mercy of Heaven, that you would add to all your evil deeds that of self-murder?"

"It is better to die today by my own hand," answered Hokosa, "than tomorrow among the mockery of the people to fall a victim to your vengeance, Messenger."

"Vengeance! Did I speak to you of vengeance? Who am I that I should take vengeance upon one who has repented? Hokosa, freely do I forgive you all, even as in some few days I hope to be forgiven. Freely and fully from my heart do I forgive you, nor shall my lips tell one word of the sin that you have worked against me."

Now, when Hokosa heard those words, for a moment he stared stupefied; then he fell upon his knees before Owen, and bowing his head till it touched the teacher's feet, he burst into bitter weeping.

"Rise and hearken," said Owen gently. "Weep not because I have shown kindness to you, for that is my duty and no more, but for your sins in your own heart weep now and ever. Yet for your comfort I tell you that if you do this, of a surety they shall be forgiven to you. *Hokosa, you have indeed lost that which you loved, and henceforth you must follow after that which you did not desire. In the very grave of error you have found truth, and from the depths of sin you shall pluck righteousness. Ay, that Cross which you deemed accursed shall lift you up on high, for by it you shall be saved."*

Hokosa heard and shivered.

"Who set those words between your lips, Messenger?" he whispered.

"Who set them, Hokosa? Nay, I know not—or rather, I know well. He set them Who teaches us to speak all things that are good."

"It must be so, indeed," replied Hokosa. "Yet I have heard them before; I have heard them from the lips of the dead, and with them went this command: that when they fell upon my ears again I should 'take them for a sign, and let my heart be turned.'"

"Tell me that tale," said Owen.

So he told him, and this time it was the white man who trembled.

"Horrible has been your witchcraft, O Son of Darkness!" said Owen, when he had finished; "yet it would seem that it was permitted to you to find truth in the pit of sorcery. Obey, obey, and let your heart be turned. The dead told you that you should be set high above the nation and its king, and that saying I cannot read, though it may be fulfilled in some fashion of which today you do not think. At the least, the other saying is true, that in the end comes judgment, and that there shall the sin and the atonement strive together; therefore for judgment prepare yourself. And now depart, for I must talk with the king as to this matter of the onslaught of Hafela."

"Then, that will be the signal for my death, for what king can forgive one who has plotted such treachery against him?" said Hokosa.

"Fear not," answered Owen, "I will soften his heart. Go you into the church and pray, for there you shall be less tempted; but before you go, swear to me that you will work no evil on yourself."

"I swear it, Messenger, since now I desire to live, if only for awhile, seeing that death shuts every door."

Then he went to the church and waited there. An hour later he was summoned, and found the king seated with Owen.

"Man," said Nodwengo, "I am told by the Messenger here that you have knowledge of a plot which my brother the Prince Hafela has made to fall treacherously upon me and put me and my people to the spear. How you come to be acquainted with the plot, and what part you have played in it, I will not now inquire, for so much have I promised to the Messenger. Yet I warn you it will be well that you should tell me all you know, and that should you lie to me or attempt to deceive me, then you shall surely die."

"King, hear all the truth," answered Hokosa in a voice of desper-

510

ate calm. "I have knowledge of the plot, for it was I who wove it; but whether or not Hafela will carry it out altogether I cannot say, for as yet no word has reached me from him. King, this was the plan that I made." And he told him everything.

"It is fortunate for you, Hokosa," said Nodwengo grimly when he had finished, "that I gave my word to the Messenger that no harm should come to you, seeing that you have repented and confessed. This is certain, that Hafela has listened to your evil counsels, for I gave my consent to his flight from this land with all his people, and already his women and children have crossed the mountain path in thousands. Well, this I swear, that their feet shall tread it no more, for where they are thither he shall go to join them, should he chance to live to do so. Hokosa, begone, and know that day and night you will be watched. Should you so much as dare to approach one of the gates of the Great Place, that moment you shall die."

"Have no fear, O King," said Hokosa humbly, "for I have emptied all my heart before you. The past is the past, and cannot be recalled. For the future, while it pleases you to spare me, I am the most loyal of your servants."

"Can a man empty a spring with a pitcher?" asked the king contemptuously. "By tomorrow this heart of yours may be full again with the blackest treachery, O master of sin and lies. Many months ago I spared you at the prayer of the Messenger; and now at his prayer I spare you again, yet in doing so I think that I am foolish."

"Nay, I will answer for him," broke in Owen. "Let him stay here with me, and set your guard without my gates."

"How do I know that he will not murder you, friend?" asked the king. "This man is a snake whom few can nurse with safety."

"He will not murder me," said Owen smiling, "because his heart is turned from evil to good; also, there is little need to murder a dying man."

"Nay, speak not so," said the king hastily; "and as for this man, be it as you will. Come, I must take counsel with my captains, for our danger is near and great."

So it came about that Hokosa stayed in the house of Owen.

On the morrow the Great Place was full of the bustle of preparation, and by dawn of the following day an *impi* of some seventeen thousand spears had started to ambush Hafela and his force in a certain wooded defile through which he must pass on his way to the mountain pass where his women and children were gathered. The army was not large, at least in the eyes of the People of Fire who, before the death of Umsuka and the break up of the nation, counted their warriors by tens of thousands. But after those events the most of the regiments had deserted to Hafela, leaving to Nodwengo not more than two-and-twenty thousand spears upon which he could rely. Of these he kept less than a third to defend the Great Place against possible attacks, and all the rest he sent to fall upon Hafela far away, hoping there to make an end of him once and for all. This counsel the king took against the better judgment of many of his captains, and as the issue proved, it was mistaken.

When Owen told Hokosa of it, that old general shrugged his shoulders.

"The king would have done better to keep his regiments at home," he said, "and fight it out with Hafela here, where he is well prepared. Yonder the country is very wide, and broken, and it may well chance that the *impi* will miss that of Hafela, and then how can the king defend this place with a handful, should the prince burst upon him at the head of forty thousand men? But who am I that I should give counsel for which none seek?"

"As God wills, so shall it befall," answered Owen wearily; "but oh! the thought of all this bloodshed breaks my heart. I trust that its beatings may be stilled before my eyes behold the evil hour."

On the evening of that day Hokosa was baptised. The ceremony took place, not in the church, for Owen was too weak to go there, but in the largest room of his house and before some few witnesses chosen from the congregation. Even as he was being signed with the sign of the cross, a strange and familiar attraction caused the convert to look up, and behold, before him, watching all with mocking eyes, stood Noma his wife. At length the rite was finished, and the little audience melted away, all save Noma, who stood silent and beautiful as a statue, the light of mockery still gleaming in her eyes. Then she spoke, saying:—

"I greet you, Husband. I have returned from doing your business afar, and if this foolishness is finished, and the white man can spare you, I would talk with you alone."

"I greet you, Wife," answered Hokosa. "Say out your say, for none are present save us three, and from the Messenger here I have no secrets."

"What, Husband, none? Do you ever talk to him of certain fruit that you ripened in a garden yonder?"

"From the Messenger I have no secrets," repeated Hokosa in a heavy voice.

"Then his heart must be full of them indeed, and it is little wonder that he seems sick," replied Noma, gibing. "Tell me, Hokosa, is it true that you have become a Christian, or would you but fool the white man and his following?"

"It is true."

At the words her graceful shape was shaken with a little gust of silent laughter.

"The wizard has turned saint," she said. "Well, then, what of the wizard's wife?"

"You were my wife before I became Christian; if the Messenger permits it, you can still abide with me."

"If the Messenger permits it! So you have come to this, Hokosa, that you must ask the leave of another man as to whether or no you should keep your own wife! There is no other thing that I could not have thought of you, but this I would never have believed had I not heard it from your lips. Say now, do you still love me, Hokosa?"

"You know well that I love you, now and always," he answered, in a voice that sounded like a groan; "as you know that for love of you I have done many sins from which otherwise I should have turned aside."

"Grieve not over them, Hokosa; after all, in such a count as yours they will make but little show. Well, if you love me, I hate you, though through your witchcraft your will yet has the mastery of mine. I demand of you now that you should loose that bond, for I do not desire to become a Christian; and surely, O most good and holy man, having one wife already, it will not please you henceforth to live in sin with a heathen woman."

Now Hokosa turned to Owen:—

"In the old days," he said, "I could have answered her; but now I am fallen; or raised up—at the least I am changed and cannot. O prophet of Heaven, tell me what I shall do."

"Sever the bond that you have upon her and let her go," answered Owen. "This love of yours is unnatural, unholy and born of witchcraft; have done with it, or if you cannot, at the least deny it, for such a woman, a woman who hates you, can work you no good. Moreover, since she is a second wife, you being a Christian, are bound to free her should she so desire."

"She can work me no good, Messenger, that I know; but I know also that while she struggles in the net of my will she can work me no evil. If I loose the net and the fish swims free, it may be otherwise."

"Loose it," answered Owen, "and leave the rest to Providence. Henceforth, Hokosa, do right, and take no thought for the morrow, for the morrow is with God, and what He decrees, that shall befall."

"I hear you," said Hokosa, "and I obey." For a while he rocked himself to and fro, staring at the ground, then he lifted his head and spoke:—

"Woman," he said, "the knot is untied and the spell is broken. Begone, for I release you and I divorce you. Flesh of my flesh have you been, and soul of my soul, for in the web of sorceries are we knit together. Yet be warned and presume not too far, for remember that which I have laid down I can take up, and that should I choose to command, you must still obey. Farewell, you are free."

Noma heard, and with a sigh of ecstasy she sprang into the air as a slave might do from whom the fetters have been struck off.

"Ay," she cried, "I am free! I feel it in my blood, I who have lain in bondage, and the voice of freedom speaks in my heart and the breath of freedom blows in my nostrils. I am free from you, O dark and accursed man; but herein lies my triumph and revenge—*you* are not free from me. In obedience to that white fool whom you have murdered, you have loosed me; but you I will not loose and could not if I would. Listen now, Hokosa: you love me, do you not?—next to this new creed of yours, I am most of all to you. Well, since you have divorced me, I will tell you, I go straight to another man. Now, look your last on me; for you love me, do you not?" and she slipped the mantle from her shoulders and except for her girdle stood before him naked, and smiled.

"Well," she went on, resuming her robe, "the last words of those we love are always dear to us; therefore, Hokosa, you who were my husband, I leave mine with you. You are a coward and a traitor, and your doom shall be that of a coward and a traitor. For my sake you betrayed Umsuka, your king and benefactor; for your own sake you betrayed Nodwengo, who spared you; and now, for the sake of your miserable soul, you have betrayed Hafela to Nodwengo. Nay, I know the tale, do not answer me, but the end of it—ah! that is yet to learn. Lie there, snake, and lick the hand that you have bitten, but I, the bird whom you have loosed, I fly afar—taking your heart with me!" and suddenly she turned and was gone.

Presently Hokosa spoke in a thick voice:—

"Messenger," he said, "this cross that you have given me to bear is heavy indeed."

"Yes, Hokosa," answered Owen, "for to it your sins are nailed."

CHAPTER 18

The Passing of Owen

Once she was outside of Owen's house, Noma did not tarry. First she returned to Hokosa's *kraal*, where she had already learnt from his head wife, Zinti, and others the news of his betrayal of the plot of Hafela, of his conversion to the faith of the Christians, and of the march of the *impi* to ambush the prince. Here she took a little spear, and rolling up in a skin blanket as much dried meat as she could carry, she slipped unnoticed from the *kraal*. Her object was to escape from the Great Place, but this she did not try to do by any of the gates, knowing them to be guarded. Some months ago, before she started on her embassy, she had noted a weak spot in the fence, where dogs had torn a hole through which they passed out to hunt at night. To this spot she made her way under cover of the darkness—for though she still greatly feared to be alone at night, her pressing need conquered her fears—and found that the hole was yet there, for a tall weed growing in its mouth had caused it to be overlooked by those whose duty it was to mend the fence. With her assegai she widened it a little, then drew her lithe shape through it, and lying hidden till the guard had passed, climbed the two stone walls beyond. Once she was free of the town, she set her course by the stars and started forward at a steady run.

"If my strength holds I shall yet be in time to warn him," she muttered to herself. "Ah! friend Hokosa, this new madness of yours has blunted your wits that once were sharp enough. You have set me free, and now you shall learn how I can use my freedom. Not for nothing have I been your pupil, Hokosa the fox."

Before the dawn broke Noma was thirty miles from the Great Place, and before the next dawn she was a hundred. At sunset on that second day she stood among mountains. To her right stretched a great defile, a rugged place of rocks and bush, wherein she knew that the

515

regiments of the king were hid in ambush. Perchance she was too late, perchance the *impi* of Hafela had already passed to its doom in yonder gorge. Swiftly she ran forward on to the trail which led to the gorge, to find that it had been trodden by many feet and recently. Moving to and fro she searched the spoor with her eyes, then rose with a sigh of joy. It was old, and marked the passage of the great company of women and children and their thousands of cattle which, in execution of the plot, had travelled this path some days before. Either the *impi* had not yet arrived, or it had gone by some other road. Weary as she was, Noma followed the old spoor backwards. A mile or more away it crossed the crest of a hog-backed mountain, from whose summit she searched the plain beyond, and not in vain, for there far beneath her twinkled the watch-fires of the army of Hafela.

Three hours later a woman, footsore and utterly exhausted, staggered into the camp, and waving aside the spears that were lifted to stab her, demanded to be led to the prince. Presently she was there.

"Who is this woman?" asked the great warrior; for, haggard as she was with travel, exhaustion, and the terror of her haunted loneliness, he did not know her in the uncertain firelight.

"Hafela," she said, "I am Noma who was the wife of Hokosa, and for whole nights and days I have journeyed as no woman ever journeyed before, to tell you of the treachery of Hokosa and to save you from your doom."

"What treachery and what doom?" asked the prince.

"Before I answer you that question, Hafela, you must pay me the price of my news."

"Let me hear the price, Noma."

"It is this, Prince: First, the head of Hokosa, who has divorced me, when you have caught him."

"That I promise readily. What more?"

"Secondly, the place of your chief wife today; and a week hence, when I shall have made you king, the name and state of Queen of the People of Fire with all that hangs thereto."

"You are ambitious, woman, and know well how to drive a bargain. Well, if you can ask, I can give, for I have ever loved you, and your mind is great as your body is beautiful. If through your help I should become King of the People of Fire, you shall be their Queen, I swear it by the spirits of my fathers and by my own head. And now—your tidings."

"These are they, Hafela. Hokosa has turned Christian and betrayed the plot to Nodwengo; and the great gorge yonder but three hours march away is ambushed. Tomorrow you and your people would have

516

been cut off there had I not run so fast and far to warn you, after which the *impis* of Nodwengo were commanded to follow your women and cattle over the mountain pass and capture them."

"This is news indeed," said the prince. "Say now, how many regiments are hidden in the gorge?"

"Eight."

"Well, I have fourteen; so, being warned, there is little to fear. I will catch these rats in their own hole."

"I have a better plan," said Noma; "it is this: leave six regiments posted upon the brow of yonder hill and let them stay there. Then when the generals of Nodwengo see that they do not enter the gorge, they will believe that the ambush is discovered, and, after waiting one day or perhaps two, will move out to give battle, thinking that before them is all your strength. But command your regiments to run and not to fight, drawing the army of Nodwengo after them. Meanwhile, yes, this very night, you yourself with all the men that are left to you must march upon the Great Place, which, though it be strong, can be stormed, for it is defended by less than five thousand soldiers. There, having taken it, you shall slay Nodwengo, proclaiming yourself king, and afterwards, by the help of the *impi* that you leave here which will march onward to your succour, you can deal with yonder army."

"A great scheme truly," said Hafela in admiration; "but how do I know whether all this tale is true, or whether you do but set a snare for me?"

"Bid scouts go out and creep into yonder gully," answered Noma, "and you will see whether or no I have spoken falsely. For the rest, I am in your hands, and if I lie you can take my life in payment."

"If I march upon the Great Place, it must be at midnight when none see me go," said Hafela, "and what will you do then, Noma, who are too weary to travel again so soon?"

"I will be borne in a litter till my strength comes back to me," she answered. "And now give me to eat and let me rest while I may."

****

Five hours later, Hafela with the most of his army, a force of something over twenty thousand men, was journeying swiftly but by a circuitous route towards the Great Place of the king. On the crest of the hill facing the gorge, as Noma had suggested, he left six regiments with instructions to fly before Nodwengo's generals, and when they had led them far enough, to follow him as swiftly as they were able. These orders, or rather the first part of them, they carried out, for as

517

it chanced after two days' flight, the king's soldiers got behind them by a night march, and falling on them at dawn, killed half of them and dispersed the rest. Then it was that Nodwengo's generals learned for the first time that they were following one wing of Hafela's army only, while the main body was striking at the heart of the kingdom, and turned their faces homewards in fear and haste.

****

On the morning after the flight of Noma, Owen passed into the last stage of his sickness, and it became evident, both to himself and to those who watched him, that at the most he could not live for more than a few days. For his part, he accepted his doom joyfully, spending the time which was left to him in writing letters that were to be forwarded to England whenever an opportunity should arise. Also he set down on paper a statement of the principal events of his strange mission, and other information for the guidance of his white successors, who by now should be drawing near to the land of the Amasuka. In the intervals of these last labours, from time to time he summoned the king and the wisest and trustiest of them whom he had baptised to his bedside, teaching them what they should do when he was gone, and exhorting them to cling to the Faith.

On the afternoon of the fourth day from that of the baptism of Hokosa he fell into a quiet sleep, from which he did not wake till sundown.

"Am I still here?" he asked wondering, of John and Hokosa who watched at his bedside. "From my dreams I thought that it was otherwise. John, send a messenger to the king and ask of him to assemble the people, all who care to come, in the open place before my house. I am about to die, and first I would speak with them."

John went weeping upon his errand, leaving Owen and Hokosa alone.

"Tell me know what shall I do?" said Hokosa in a voice of despair, "seeing that it is I and no other who have brought this death upon you."

"Fret not, my brother," answered Owen, "for this and other things you did in the days of your blindness, and it was permitted that you should do them to an end. Kneel down now, that I may absolve you from your sins before I pass away; for I tell you, Hokosa, I believe that ere many days are over you must walk on the same path which I travel tonight."

"Is it so?" Hokosa answered. "Well, I am glad, for I have no longer any lust of life."

518

Then he knelt down and received the absolution.

Now John returned and Nodwengo with him, who told him that the people were gathering in hundreds according to his wish.

"Then clothe me in my robes and let us go forth," he said, "for I would speak my last words in the ears of men."

So they put the surplice and hood upon his wasted form and went out, John preceding him holding on high the ivory crucifix, while the king and Hokosa supported him, one on either side.

Without his gate stood a low wooden platform, whence at times Owen had been accustomed to address any congregation larger than the church would contain. On this platform he took his seat. The moon was bright above him, and by it he could see that already his audience numbered some thousands of men, women and children. The news had spread that the wonderful white man, Messenger, wished to take his farewell of the nation, though even now many did not understand that he was dying, but imagined that he was about to leave the country, or, for aught they knew, to vanish from their sight into Heaven. For a moment Owen looked at the sea of dusky faces, then in the midst of an intense stillness, he spoke in a voice low indeed but clear and steady:—

"My children," he said, "hear my last words to you. More than three years ago, in a far, far land and upon such a night as this, a Voice spoke to me from above commanding me to seek you out, to turn you from your idolatry and to lighten your darkness. I listened to the Voice, and hither I journeyed across sea and land, though how this thing might be done I could not guess. But to Him Who sent me all things are possible, and while yet I lingered upon the threshold of your country, in a dream were revealed to me events that were to come. So I appeared before you boldly, and knowing that he had been poisoned and that I could cure him, I drew back your king from the mouth of death, and you said to yourselves: 'Behold a wizard indeed! Let us hear him.' Then I gave battle to your sorcerers yonder upon the plain, and from the foot of the Cross I teach, the lightnings were rolled back upon them and they were not. Look now, their chief stands at my side, among my disciples one of the foremost and most faithful. Afterwards troubles arose: your king died a Christian, and many of the people fell away; but still a remnant remained, and he who became king was converted to the truth. Now I have sown the seed, and the corn is ripe before my eyes, but it is not permitted that I should reap the harvest. My work is ended, my task is done, and I, the Messenger, return to make report to Him Who sent the message.

"Hear me yet a little while, for soon shall my voice be silent. 'I come not to bring peace, but a sword,'—so said the Master Whom I preach, and so say I, the most unworthy of His servants. Salvation cannot be bought at a little price; it must be paid for by the blood and griefs of men, and in blood and griefs must you pay, O my children. Through much tribulation must you also enter the kingdom of God. Even now the heathen is at your gates, and many of you shall perish on his spears, but I tell you that he shall not conquer. Be faithful, cling to the Cross, and do not dare to doubt your Lord, for He will be your Captain and you shall be His people. Cleave to your king, for he is good; and in the day of trial listen to the counsel of this Hokosa who once was the first of evil-doers, for with him goes my spirit, and he is my son in the spirit.

"My children, fare you well! Forget me not, for I have loved you; or if you will, forget me, but remember my teaching and hearken to those who shall tread upon the path I made. The peace of God be with you, the blessing of God be upon you, and the salvation of God await you, as it awaits me tonight! Friends, lead me hence to die."

They turned to him, but before their hands touched him Thomas Owen fell forward upon the breast of Hokosa and lay there a while. Then suddenly, for the last time, he lifted himself and cried aloud:—

"I have fought a good fight! I have finished my course! I have kept the faith! Henceforth there is laid up for me a crown of righteousness. . . . and not to me only, but to all those who love His appearing."

Then his head fell back, his dark eyes closed, and the Messenger was dead.

Hokosa, the man who had murdered him, having lifted him up to show him to the people, amidst a sound of mighty weeping, took the body in his arms and bore it thence to make it ready for burial.

CHAPTER 19

The Fall of the Great Place

On the morrow at sundown all that remained of Thomas Owen was laid to rest before the altar of the little church, Nodwengo the king and Hokosa lowering him into the grave, while John, his first disciple, read over him the burial service of the Christians, which it had been one of the dead man's last labours to translate into the language of the Amasuka.

Before the ceremony was finished, a soldier, carrying a spear in his hand, pushed his way through the dense and weeping crowd, and having saluted, whispered something into the ear of the king. Nodwengo started, and, with a last look of farewell at the face of his friend, left the chapel, accompanied by some of his generals who were present, muttering to Hokosa that he was to follow when all was done. Accordingly, some few minutes later, he went and was admitted into the Council Hut, where captains and messengers were to be seen arriving and departing continuously.

"Hokosa," said the king, "you have dealt treacherously with me in the past, but I believe now that your heart is true; at the least I follow the commands of our dead master and trust you. Listen: the outposts have sighted an *impi* of many regiments advancing towards the Great Place, though whether or no it be my own *impi* returning victorious from the war with my brother, I cannot say. There is this against it, however, that a messenger has but just arrived reporting that the generals have perceived the host of Hafela encamped upon a ridge over against the gorge where they awaited him. If that be so, they can scarcely have given him battle, for the messenger is swift of foot and has travelled night and day. Yet how can this be the *impi* of Hafela, who, say the generals, is encamped upon the ridge?"

"He may have left the ridge, King, having been warned of the ambush."

"It cannot be, for when the runner started his fires burned there and his soldiers were gathered round them."

"Then perhaps his captains sit upon the ridge with some portion of his strength to deceive those who await him in the gorge; while, knowing that here men are few, he himself swoops down on you with the main body of his *impi*."

"At least we shall learn presently," answered the king; "but if it be as I fear and we are outwitted, what is there that we can do against so many?"

Now one of the captains proposed that they should stay where they were and hold the place.

"It is too large," answered the king, "they will burst the fences and break our line."

Another suggested that they should fly and, avoiding the regiments of Hafela in the darkness of the night, should travel swiftly in search of the main army that had been sent to lie in ambush.

"What," said Nodwengo, "leaving the aged and the women and children to perish, for how can we take such a multitude? No, I will have none of this plan."

Then Hokosa spoke. "King," he said, "listen to my counsel: Command now that all the women and the old men, taking with them such cattle and food as are in the town, depart at once into the Valley of Death and collect in the open space that lies beyond the Tree of Doom, near the spring of water that is there. The valley is narrow and the cliffs are steep, and it may chance that by the help of Heaven we shall be able to hold it till the army returns to relieve us, to seek which messengers must be sent at once with these tidings."

"The plan is good," said the king, though none had thought of it; "but so we shall lose the town."

"Towns can be rebuilt," answered Hokosa, "but who may restore the lives of men?"

As the words left his lips, a runner burst into the council, crying: "King, the *impi* is that of Hafela, and the prince heads it in person. Already his outposts rest upon the Plain of Fire."

Then Nodwengo rose and issued his orders, commanding that all the ineffective population of the town, together with such food and cattle as could be gathered, should retreat at once into the Valley of Death. By this time the four or five thousand soldiers who were left in the Great Place had been paraded on the open ground in front of the king's house, where they stood, still and silent, in the moonlight. Nodwengo and the captains went out to them, and as they saw him

522

come they lifted their spears like one man, giving him the royal salute of "King!" He held up his hand and addressed them.

"Soldiers," he said, "we have been outwitted. My *impi* is afar, and that of Hafela is at our gates. Yonder in the valley, though we be few, we can defend ourselves till succour reaches us, which already messengers have gone out to seek. But first we must give time for the women and children, the sick and the aged, to withdraw with food and cattle; and this we can do in one way only, by keeping Hafela at bay till they have passed the archway, all of them. Now, soldiers, for the sake of your own lives, of your honour and of those you love, swear to me, in the holy Name which we have been taught to worship, that you will fight out this great fight without fear or faltering."

"We swear it in the holy Name, and by your head, King," roared the regiments.

"Then victory is already ours," answered Nodwengo. "Follow me, Children of Fire!" and shaking his great spear, he led the way towards that portion of the outer fence upon which Hafela was advancing.

By now the town behind them was a scene of almost indescribable tumult and confusion, for the companies detailed to the task were clearing the numberless huts of their occupants, and collecting women, children and oxen in thousands, preparatory to driving them into the defile. Panic had seized many of these poor creatures, who, in imagination, already saw themselves impaled upon the cruel spears of Hafela's troops, and indeed in not a few instances believed those who were urging them forward to be the enemy. Women shrieked and wrung their hands, children wailed piteously, oxen lowed, and the infirm and aged vented their grief in groans and cries to Heaven, or their ancient god, for mercy. In truth, so difficult was the task of marshalling this motley array at night, numbering as it did ten or twelve thousand souls, that a full hour went by before the mob even began to move, slowly and uncertainly, towards the place of refuge, whereof the opening was so narrow that but few of them could pass it at a time.

Meanwhile Hafela was developing the attack. Forming his great army into the shape of a wedge he raised his battle-cry and rushed down on the first line of fortifications, which he stormed without difficulty, for they were defended by a few skirmishers only. Next he attacked the second line, and carried it after heavy fighting, then hurled himself upon the weakest point of the main fence of the vast *kraal*. Here it was that the fray began in earnest, for here Nodwengo was waiting for him. Thrice the thousands rolled on in the face of a storm of spears, and thrice they fell back from the wide fence of thorns and the wall of stone behind it. By now the battle had raged for about an hour and a half, and it was reported to the king that the first of the women and children had passed the archway into the valley, and that nearly all of them were clear of the eastern gate of the town.

"Then it is time that we follow them," said the king, "for if we wait here until the warriors of Hafela are among us, our retreat will become a rout and soon there will be none left to follow. Let one company," and he named it, "hold the fence for a while to give us time to withdraw, taking the wounded with us."

"We hear you, king," said one of that company, "but our captain is killed."

"Who among you will take over the command of these men and hold the breach?" asked Nodwengo of the group of officers about him.

"I, King," answered old Hokosa, lifting his spear, "for I care not whether I live or die."

"Go to, boaster!" cried another. "Who among us cares whether he lives or dies when the king commands?"

"That we shall know tomorrow," said Hokosa quietly, and the soldiers laughed at the retort.

"So be it," said the king, and while silently and swiftly he led off the regiments, keeping in the shadow of the huts, Hokosa and his hundred men posted themselves behind the weakened fence and wall. Now, for the fourth time the attacking regiment came forward grimly, on this occasion led by the prince himself. As they drew near, Hokosa leapt upon the wall, and standing there in the bright moonlight where all could see him, he called to them to halt. Instinctively they obeyed him.

"Is it Hafela whom I see yonder?" he asked.

"Ah! it is I," answered the prince. "What would you with me, wizard and traitor?"

"This only, Hafela: I would ask you what you seek here?"

"That which you promised me, Hokosa, the crown of my father and certain other things."

"Then get you back, Hafela, for you shall never win them.. Have I prophesied falsely to you at any time? Not so—neither do I prophesy falsely now. Get you back whence you came, and your wolves with you, else shall you bide here for ever."

"Do you dare to call down evil on me, Wizard?" shouted the prince furiously. "Your wife is mine, and now I take your life also," and with all his strength he hurled at him the great spear he held.

It hissed past Hokosa's head, touching his ear, but he never flinched from the steel.

"A poor cast, Prince," he said laughing; "but so it must have been, for I am guarded by that which you cannot see. My wife you have, and she shall be your ruin; my life you may take, but ere it leaves me, Hafela, I shall see you dead and your army scattered. The Messenger is passed away, but his power has fallen upon me and I speak the truth to you, O Prince and warriors, who are—already dead."

Now a shriek of dismay and fury rose from the hundreds who heard this prophesy of ill, for of Hokosa and his magic they were terribly afraid.

"Kill him! Kill the wizard!" they shouted, and a rain of spears rushed towards him on the wall.

They rushed towards him, they passed above, below, around; but, of them all, not one touched him.

"Did I not tell you that I was guarded by That which you cannot see?" Hokosa asked contemptuously. Then slowly he descended from the wall amidst a great silence.

"When men are scarce the tongue must play a part," he explained to his companions, who stared at him wondering. "By now the king and those with him should have reached the eastern gate; whereas, had we fought at once, Hafela would be hard upon his heels, for we are few, and who can hold a buffalo with a rope of grass? Yet I think that I spoke truth when I told him that the garment of the Messenger has fallen upon my shoulders, and that death awaits him and his companions, as it awaits me also and many of us. Now, friends, be ready, for the bull charges and soon we must feel his horns. This at least is left to you, to die gloriously."

While he was still speaking the first files of the regiment rushed upon the fence, tearing aside the thorns with their hands till a passage was made through them. Then they sprang upon the wall, there to be met by the spears of Hokosa and his men thrusting upward from beneath its shelter. Time after time they sprang, and time after time they fell back dead or wounded, till at last, dashing forward in one dense column, they poured over the stones as the rising tide pours over the rocks on the sea-shore, driving the defenders before them by the sheer weight of numbers.

"This game is played!" cried Hokosa. "Fly now to the eastern gate, for here we can do nothing more." So they fled, those who survived of them, and after them came the thousands of the foe, sacking and firing the deserted town as they advanced.

Hokosa and his men, or rather the half of them, reached the gate and passed it in safety, barring it after them, and thereby delaying the attackers till they could burst their way through. Now hundreds of huts were afire, and the flames spread swiftly, lighting up the country far and wide. In the glare of them, Hokosa could see that already a full two-thirds of the crowd of fugitives had passed the narrow arch; while Nodwengo and the soldiers were drawn up in companies upon the steep and rocky slope that led to it, protecting their retreat.

He advanced to the king and reported himself.

"So you have lived through it," said Nodwengo.

"I shall die when my hour comes, and not before," Hokosa answered. "We did well yonder, and yet the most of us are alive to tell the tale, for I knew when and how to go. Be ready, king, for the foe press us close, and that mob behind us crawls onward like a snail."

As he spoke the pursuers broke through the fence and gate of the burning town, and once more the fight began. They had the advantage of numbers; but Nodwengo and his troops stood in a wide road upon higher ground protected on either side by walls, and were, moreover, rested, not breathless and weary with travel like the men of Hafela. Slowly, fighting, every inch of the way, Nodwengo was pushed back, and slowly the long ant-like line of women and sick and cattle crept through the opening in the rock, till at length all of them were gone.

"It is time," said Nodwengo, glancing behind him, "for our arms grow weary."

Then he gave orders, and company by company the defending force followed on the path of the fugitives, till at length amidst a roar of rage and disappointment, the last of them vanished through the arch, Hokosa among them, and the place was blocked with stones, above which shone a hedge of spears.

CHAPTER 20

Noma Sets a Snare

Thus ended the first night's battle, since for this time the enemy had fought enough. Nodwengo and his men had also had enough, for out of the five thousand of them some eleven hundred were killed or wounded. Yet they might not rest, for all that night, assisted by the women, they laboured, building stone walls across the narrowest parts of the valley. Also the cattle, women and children were moved along the gorge, which in shape may be compared to a bottle with two necks, one at either end, and encamped in the opening of the second neck, where was the spring of water. This spot was chosen both because here alone water could be obtained, without which they could not hold out more than a single day, and because the *koppie* whereon grew the strange-looking euphorbia known as the Tree of Doom afforded a natural rampart against attack.

Shortly after dawn, while the soldiers were resting and eating of such food as could be procured—for the most part strips of raw or half-cooked meat cut from hastily killed cattle—the onslaught was renewed with vigour, Hafela directing his efforts to the forcing of the natural archway. But, strive as he would, this he could not do, for it was choked with stones and thorns and guarded by brave men.

"You do but waste your labour, Hafela," said Noma, who stood by him watching the assault.

"What then is to be done?" he asked, "for unless we come at them we cannot kill them. It was clever of them to take refuge in this hole. I thought surely that they would fight it out yonder, beneath the fences of the Great Place."

"Ah!" she answered, "you forgot that they had Hokosa on their side. Did you then think to catch him sleeping? This retreat was Hokosa's counsel. I learned it from the lips of that wounded captain before they killed him. Now, it seems that there are but two paths to follow, and you can choose between them. The one is to send a regiment a day and a half's journey across the cliff top to guard the further mouth of the valley and to wait till these jackals starve in their hole, for certainly they can never come out."

"It has started six hours since," said Hafela, "and though the precipices are steep, having the moon to travel by, it should reach the river mouth of the valley before dawn tomorrow, cutting Nodwengo off from the plains, if indeed he should dare to venture out upon them, which, with so small a force, he will not do. Yet this first plan of yours must fail, Noma, seeing that before they starve within, the generals of Nodwengo will be back upon us from the mountains, catching us between the hammer and the anvil, and I know not how that fight would go."

"Yet, soon or late, it must be fought."

"Nay," he answered, "for my hope is that should the *impi* return to find Nodwengo dead, they will surrender and acknowledge me as king, who am the first of the blood royal. But what is your second plan?"

By way of answer, she pointed to the cliff above them. On the right-hand side, facing the archway, was a flat ledge overhanging the valley, at a height of about a hundred feet.

"If you can come yonder," she said, "it will be easy to storm this gate, for there lie rocks in plenty, and men cannot fight when stones are dropping on their heads."

"But how can we come to that home of vultures, where never man has set a foot? Look, the cliff above is sheer; no rock-rabbit could stand upon it."

With her eye Noma measured the distance from the brink of the precipice to the broad ledge commanding the valley.

"Sixty paces, not more," she said. "Well, yonder are oxen in plenty, and out of their hides ropes can be made, and out of ropes a ladder, down which men may pass; ten, or even five, would be enough."

"Well thought of Noma," said Hafela. "Hokosa told us last night that to him had passed the wisdom of the Messenger; but if this be so, I think that to you has passed the guile of Hokosa."

"It seems to me that some of it abides with him," answered Noma laughing.

Then the prince gave orders, and, with many workers of hides toiling at it, within two hours the ladder was ready, its staves, set twenty inches apart, being formed of knob-*kerries*, or the broken shafts of stabbing spears. Now they lowered it from the top of the precipice so that its end rested upon the ledge, and down it came several men, who swung upon its giddy length like spiders on a web. Reaching this great shelf in safety and advancing to the edge of it, these men started a boulder, which, although as it chanced it hurt no one, fell in the midst of a group of the defenders and bounded away through them.

"Now we must be going," said Hokosa, looking up, "for no man can fight against rocks, and our spears cannot reach those birds. Had the army been taught the use of the bow, as I counselled in the past days, we might still have held the archway; but they called it a woman's weapon, and would have none of it."

As he spoke another stone fell, crushing the life out of a man who stood next to him. Then they retreated to the first wall, which had been piled up during the night, where it was not possible to roll rocks upon them from the cliffs above. This wall, and others reared at intervals behind it, they set to work to strengthen as much as they could, making the most of the time that was left to them before the enemy could clear the way and march on to attack.

Presently Hafela's men were through and sweeping down upon them with a roar, thinking to carry the wall at a single rush. But in this they failed; indeed, it as only after an hour's hard fighting and by the expedient of continually attacking the work with fresh companies that at length they stormed the wall.

When Hokosa saw that he could no longer hold the place, but before the foe was upon him, he drew off his soldiers to the second wall, a quarter of a mile or more away, and here the fight began again. And so it went on for hour after hour, as one by one the fortifications were carried by the weight of numbers, for the attackers fought desperately under the eye of their prince, caring nothing for the terrible loss they suffered in men. Twice the force of the defenders was changed by order of Nodwengo, fresh men being sent from the companies held in reserve to take the places of those who had borne the brunt of the battle. This indeed it was necessary to do, seeing that it was impossible to carry water to so many, and in that burning valley men could not fight for long athirst. Only Hokosa stayed on, for they brought him drink in a gourd, and wherever the fray was fiercest there he was always; nor although spears were rained upon him by hundreds, was he touched by one of them.

At length as the night fell the king's men were driven back from their last *scherm* in the western half of the valley, across the open space back upon the *koppie* where stood the Tree of Doom. Here they stayed a while till, overmatched and outworn, they were pushed from its rocks across the narrow stretch of broken ground into the shelter of the great stone *scherm* or wall that ran from side to side of the further neck of the valley, whereon thousands of women and such men as could be spared had been working incessantly during the past night and day.

It was as he retreated among the last upon this wall that Hokosa caught sight of Noma for the first time since they parted in the house of the Messenger. In the forefront of his troops, directing the attack, was Hafela the prince, and at his side stood Noma, carrying in her hand a little shield and a spear. At this moment also she saw him and called aloud to him:—

"You have fought well, Wizard, but tomorrow all your magic shall avail you nothing, for it will be your last day upon this earth."

"Ay, Noma," he answered, "and yours also."

Then of a sudden a company of the king's men rushed from the shelter of the wall upon the attackers driving them back to the *koppie* and killing several, so that in the confusion and gathering darkness Hokosa lost sight of her, though a man at his side declared that he saw her fall beneath the thrust of an assegai. Thus ended the second day.

Now when the watch had been set the king and his captains took counsel together, for their hearts were heavy.

"Listen," said Nodwengo: "out of five thousand soldiers a thousand have been killed and a thousand lie among us wounded. Hark to the groaning of them! Also we have with us women and children and sick to the number of twelve thousand, and between us and those who would butcher them every one there stands but a single wall. Nor is this the worst of it: the spring cannot supply the wants of so great a multitude in this hot place, and it is feared that presently the water will be done. What way shall we turn? If we surrender to Hafela, perhaps he will spare the lives of the women and children; but whatever he may promise, the most of us he will surely slay. If we fight and are defeated, then once his regiments are among us, all will be slain according to the ancient custom of our people. I have bethought me that we might retreat through the valley, but the river beyond is in flood; also it is certain that before this multitude could reach it, the prince will have sent a force to cut us off while he himself harasses our rear. Now let him who has counsel speak."

"King, I have counsel," said Hokosa. "What were the words that the Messenger spoke to us before he died? Did he not say: 'Even now the heathen is at your gates, and many of you shall perish on his spears; but I tell you that he shall not conquer'? Did he not say: 'Be faithful, cling to the Cross, and do not dare to doubt your Lord, for He will protect you, and your children after you, and He will be your Captain and you shall be His people'? Did he not bid you also to listen to my counsel? Then listen to it, for it is his: Your case seems desperate, but have no fear, and take no thought for the morrow, for all shall yet be well. Let us now pray to Him that the Messenger has revealed to us, and Whom now he implores on our behalf in that place where he is to guide us and to save us, for then surely He will hearken to our prayer."

"So be it," said Nodwengo, and going out he stood upon a pillar of stone in the moonlight and offered up his supplication in the hearing of the multitude.

Meanwhile, those of the camp of Hafela were also taking counsel. They had fought bravely indeed, and carried the *schanses*; but at great cost, since for every man that Nodwengo had lost, three of theirs had fallen. Moreover, they were in evil case with weariness and the want of water, as each drop they drank must be carried to them from the Great Place in bags made of raw hide, which caused it to stink, for they had but few gourds with them.

"Now it is strange," said Hafela, "that these men should fight so bravely, seeing that they are but a handful. There can be scarce three thousand of them left, and yet I doubt not that before we carry those last walls of theirs as many of us or more will be done. Ay! and after they are done with, we must meet their great *impi* when it returns, and of what will befall us then I scarcely like to think."

"Ill-fortune will befall you while Hokosa lives," broke in Noma. "Had it not been for him, this trouble would have been done with by now; but he is a wizard, and by his wizardries he defeats us and puts heart into Nodwengo and the warriors. You, yourself, have seen him this day defying us, not once but many times, for upon his flesh steel has no power. Ay! and this is but the beginning of evil, for I am sure that he leads you into some deep trap where you shall perish everlastingly. Did he not himself declare that the power of that dead white worker of miracles has fallen upon him, and who can fight against magic?"

"Who, indeed?" said Hafela humbly; for like all savages he was very superstitious, and, moreover, a sincere believer in Hokosa's supernatural capacities. "This wizard is too strong for us; he is invulnerable, and as I know well he can read the secret thoughts of men and can suck wisdom from the dead, while to his eyes the darkness is no blind."

"Nay, Hafela," answered Noma, "there is one crack in his shield. Hear me: if we can but catch him and hold him fast we shall have no need to fear him more, and I think that I know how to bait the trap."

"How will you bait it?" asked Hafela.

"Thus. Midway between the *koppie* and the wall behind which lie the men of the king stands a flat rock, and all about that rock are stretched the bodies of dead soldiers. Now, this is my plan: that when next one of those dark storm-clouds passes over the face of the moon six of the strongest of our warriors should creep upon their bellies down this way and that, as though they were also numbered with the slain. This done, you shall despatch a herald to call in the ears of the king that you desire to treat with him of peace. Then he will answer that if this be so you can come beneath the walls of his camp, and your herald shall refuse, saying that you fear treachery. But he must add that if Nodwengo will bid Hokosa to advance alone to the flat rock, you will bid me, Noma, whom none can fear, to do likewise, and that there we can talk in sight of both armies, and returning thence, make report to you and to Nodwengo. Afterwards, so soon as Hokosa has set his foot upon the rock, those men who seem to be dead shall spring upon him and drag him to our camp, where we can deal with him; for once the wizard is taken, the cause of Nodwengo is lost."

"A good pitfall," said the prince; "but will Hokosa walk into the trap?"

"I think so, Hafela, for three reasons. He is altogether without fear; he will desire, if may be, to make peace on behalf of the king; and he has this strange weakness, that he still loves me, and will scarcely suffer an occasion of speaking with me to go past, although he has divorced me."

"So be it," said the prince; "the game can be tried, and if it fails, why we lose nothing, whereas if it succeeds we gain Hokosa, which is much; for with you I think that our arms will never prosper while that accursed wizard sits yonder weaving his spells against us, and bringing our men to death by hundreds and by thousands."

Then he gave his orders, and presently, when a cloud passed over the face of the moon, six chosen men crept forward under the lee of the flat rock and threw themselves down here and there amongst the dead.

Soon the cloud passed, and the herald advanced across the open space blowing a horn, and waving a branch in his hand to show that he came upon a mission of peace.

CHAPTER 21

Hokosa is Lifted Up

"What would you?" asked Hokosa of the herald as he halted a short spear-cast from the wall.

"My master, the Prince Hafela, desires to treat with your master, Nodwengo. Many men have fallen on either side, and if this war goes on, though victory must be his at last, many more will fall. Therefore, if any plan can be found, he desires to spare their lives."

Now Hokosa spoke with the king, and answered:—

"Then let Hafela come beneath the wall and we will talk with him."

"Not so," answered the herald. "Does a buck walk into an open pit? Were the prince to come here it might chance that your spears would talk with him. Let Nodwengo follow me to the camp yonder, where we promise him safe conduct."

"Not so," answered Hokosa. "'Does a buck walk into an open pit?' Set out your message, and we will consider it."

"Nay, I am but a common man without authority; but I am charged to make you another offer, and if you will not hear it then there is an end. Let Hokosa advance alone to that flat rock you see yonder, and there he shall be met, also alone, by one having power to talk with him, namely, by the Lady Noma, who was once his wife. Thus they can confer together midway between the camps and in full sight of both of them, nor, no man being near, can he find cause to be afraid of an unarmed girl. What say you?"

Hokosa turned and talked with the king.

"I think it well that you should not go," said Nodwengo. "The offer seems fair, and the stone is out of reach of their spears; still, behind it may lurk a scheme to kill or capture you, for Hafela is very cunning."

"It may be so, King," answered Hokosa; "still, my heart tells me it is wisest that I should do this thing, for our case is desperate, and if I do it not, that may be the cause of the death of all of us tomorrow. At

533

the worst, I am but one man, and it matters little what may chance to me; nor shall I come to any harm unless it is the will of Heaven that it should be so; and be sure of this, that out of the harm will arise good, for where I go there the spirit of the Messenger goes with me. Remember that he bade you listen to my counsel while I remain with you, seeing that I do not speak of my own wisdom. Therefore let me go, and if it should chance that I am taken, trouble not about the matter, for thus it will be fated to some great end. Above all, though often enough I have been a traitor in the past, do not dream that I betray you, keeping in mind that so to do would be to betray my own soul, which very soon must render its account on high."

"As you will, Hokosa," answered the king. "And now tell those rebel dogs that on these terms only will I make peace with them— that they withdraw across the mountains by the path which their women and children have taken, leaving this land for ever without lifting another spear against us. If they will do this, notwithstanding all the wickedness and slaughter that they have worked, I will send command to my *impi* to let them go unharmed. If they will not do this, I put my trust in the God I worship and will fight this fray out to the end, knowing that if I and my people perish, they shall perish also."

Now Nodwengo himself spoke to the herald who was waiting beyond the wall.

"Go back to him you serve," he said, "and say that Hokosa will meet her who was his wife upon the flat stone and talk with her in the sight of both armies, bearing my word with him. At the sound of the blowing of a horn shall each of them advance unarmed and alone from either camp. Say to my brother also that it will indeed be ill for him if he attempts treachery upon Hokosa, for the man who causes his blood to flow will surely die, and after death shall be accursed for ever."

The herald went, and presently a horn was blown.

"Now it comes into my mind that we part for the last time," said Nodwengo in a troubled voice as he took the hand of Hokosa.

"It may be so, King; in my heart I think that it is so; yet I do not altogether grieve thereat, for the burden of my past sins crushes me, and I am weary and seek for rest. Yet we do not part for the last time, because whatever chances, in the end I shall make my report to you yonder"—and he pointed upwards. "Reign on for long years, King— reign well and wisely, clinging to the Faith, for thus at the last shall you reap your reward. Farewell!"

Now again the horn blew, and in the bright moonlight the slight figure of Noma could be seen advancing towards the stone.

534

Then Hokosa sprang from the wall and advanced also, till at the same moment they climbed upon the stone.

"Greeting, Hokosa," said Noma, and she stretched out her hand to him.

By way of answer he placed his own behind his back, saying: "To your business, woman." Yet his eyes searched her face—the face which in his folly he still loved; and thus it came about that he never saw sundry of the dead bodies, which lay in the shadow of the stone, begin to quicken into life, and inch by inch to arise, first to their knees and next to their feet. He never saw or heard them, yet, as the words left his lips, they sprang upon him from every side, holding him so that he could not move.

"Away with him!" cried Noma with a laugh of triumph; and at her command he was half-dragged and half-carried across the open space and thrust violently over a stone wall into the camp of Hafela.

Now Nodwengo and his soldiers saw what had happened, and with a shout of "Treachery!" some hundreds of them leapt into the plain and began to run towards the *koppie* to rescue their envoy.

Hokosa heard the shout, and wrenching himself round, beheld them.

"Back!" he cried in a clear, shrill voice. "Back! children of Nodwengo, and leave me to my fate, for the foe waits for you by thousands behind the wall!"

A soldier struck him across the mouth, bidding him be silent; but his warning had come to the ears of Nodwengo, causing him and his warriors to halt and begin a retreat. It was well that they did so, for seeing that they would not come on, from under the shelter of the wall and of every rock and stone soldiers jumped up by companies and charged, driving them back to their own *schanse*. But the king's men had the start of them, and had taken shelter behind it, whence they greeted them with a volley of spears, killing ten and wounding twice as many more.

Now it was Hokosa's turn to laugh, and laugh he did, saying:—

"My taking is well paid for already, Prince. A score of your best warriors is a heavy price to give for the carcase of one weary and aging man. But since I am here among you, captured with so much pain and loss, tell me of your courtesy why I have been brought."

Then the prince shook his spear at him and cursed him.

"Would you learn, wizard and traitor?" he cried. "We have caught you because we know well that while you stay yonder your magic counsel will prevail against our might; whereas, when once we hold

535

you fast, Nodwengo will wander to his ruin like a blind and moon-struck man, for you were to him both eyes and brain."

"I understand," said Hokosa calmly. "But, Prince, how if I left my wisdom behind me?"

"That may not be," answered Hafela, "since even a wizard cannot throw his thoughts into the heart of another from afar."

"Ah! you think so, Prince. Well, ask Noma yonder if I cannot throw my thoughts into her heart from afar: though of late I have not chosen to do so, having put aside such spells. But let it pass, and tell me, having taken me, what is it you propose to do with me? First, however, I will give you for nothing some of that wisdom which you grudge to Nodwengo the king. Be advised by me, Prince, and take the terms that he offers to you—namely, to turn this very night and begone from the land without harm or hindrance. Will you receive my gift, Hafela?"

"What will happen if I refuse it?" asked the prince slowly.

Now Hokosa looked at the dust at his feet, then he gazed upwards searching the heavens, and answered:—

"Did not I tell you yesterday? I think that this will happen. I think—but who can be quite sure of the future, Hafela?—that you and the most of your army by this hour tomorrow night will be lying fast asleep about this place, with jackals for your bedfellows."

The prince heard and trembled at his words, for he believed that if he willed it, Hokosa could prophesy the truth.

"Accursed dog!" he said. "I am minded to be guided by your saying; but be sure of this, that if I follow it, you shall stay here to sleep with jackals, yes, this very night."

Then Noma broke in.

"Be not mad, Hafela!" she said. "Will you listen to the lies that this renegade tells to work upon your fears? Will you abandon victory when it lies within your grasp, and in place of a great king become a fugitive whom all men mock at, an outcast to be hunted down at leisure by that brother against whom you dared to rebel, but on whom you did not dare to shut your hand when he lay in its hollow? Silence the tongue of this captive rogue for ever and become a man again, with the heart of a man."

"Now," said Hokosa gently; "many would find it hard to believe that I reared this woman from childhood, nursing her with my own hands when she was sick and giving her of the best I had; that afterwards, when you stole her from me, Prince, I sinned deeply to win her back. That I married her and sinned yet more deeply to give her the greatness she desired; and at last, of my own will, I loosed the bonds by which I held her, although I could not thrust her memory from my heart. Yet I have earned it all, for I made her the tool of my witchcraft, and therefore it is just that she should turn and rend me. Well, if you like it, take her counsel, Prince, and let mine go, for I care nothing which you take; only, forgive me if I prophesy once more and for the last time—I am sure that Nodwengo yonder spoke truth when he bade your herald tell me that he who causes my blood to flow shall surely die and for it be called to a strict account. Prince, I am a Christian now, and believe me, whatever you may do, I seek no revenge upon you; having been myself forgiven so much, in my turn I have learned to forgive. Yet it may be ill for that man who causes my blood to flow."

"Let him be strangled," said a captain who stood near by, "and then there will be no blood in the matter."

"Friend," answered Hokosa, "you should have been not a soldier but a pleader of causes. True it is then that the prince will only cause my life to fly, but whether that is a smaller sin I leave you to judge."

"Keep him prisoner," said another, "till we learn how these matters end."

"Nay," answered Hafela, "for then he will surely outwit us and escape. Noma, what shall we do with this man who was your husband? Tell us, for you should know best how to deal with him."

"Let me think," she answered, and she looked first at the ground beneath her, next around her, then upwards toward the skies.

Now they stood at the foot of the *koppie*, on the flat top of which grew the great Tree of Doom, that for generations had served the People of Fire as a place of execution of their criminals, or of those who fell under the ban of the king or of the witch-doctors. Among and above the finger-like fronds of this strange and dreadful-looking tree towered that white dead limb shaped like a cross, which Owen had pointed out to his disciple John, taking it to be a sign and a promise. This cross stood out clear against the sinking moon. It caught Noma's eye, and a devilish thought entered into her heart. "You would keep this fellow alive?" she said, "and yet you would not suffer him to escape. See, there above you is a cross such as he worships. Bind him to it as he says the Man whom he worships was bound, and let that dead Man help him if he may."

The prince and those about Noma shrank back a little in horror. They were cruel men rendered more cruel by their superstitious fear of one whom they believed to be uncanny; one to whom they attributed inhuman powers which he was exercising to their destruction, but still this doom seemed dreadful to them. Noma read their minds and went on passionately:

"You deem me unmerciful, but you do not know what I have suffered at this wizard's hands. For his sake and because of him I am haunted. For his own purposes he opened the gates of Distance, he sent me down among the dwellers in Death, causing me to interpret their words for him. I did so, but the dwellers came back out of Death with me, and from that hour they have not left me, nor will they ever leave me; for night by night they sojourn at my side, tormenting me with terrors. He has told me that through my mouth that spirit whom he drew into my body prophesied that he should be 'lifted up above the people.' Let the prophecy be fulfilled, let him be lifted up, for then perchance the ghosts will depart from me and I shall win peace and sleep. Also, thus alone can you hold him safe and yet shed no blood."

"Be it so," said the prince. "When we plotted together of the death of the king, and as your price, Hokosa, you bargained for the girl whom I had chosen to wife, did I not warn you that this witch of many spells, who holds both our hearts in her little hands, should yet hound you to death and mock you while you perished by an end of shame? What did I tell you, Hokosa?"

Now when he heard his fate, Hokosa bowed his head and trembled a little. Then he lifted it, and exclaimed in a clear voice:—

"It is true, Prince, but I will add to your words. She shall bring *both* of us to death. For me, I am honoured indeed in that there has been allotted to me that same end which my Master chose. To that cross let my sins be fastened and with them my body."

Now the moon sank, but in the darkness men were found who dared to climb the tree, taking with them strips of raw hide. They reached the top of it, four of them, and seating themselves upon the arms of the cross, they let down a rope, the noose of which was placed about the body of Hokosa. As it tightened upon him, he turned his calm and dreadful eyes on to the eyes of Noma and said to her:—

"Woman, I do not reproach you; but I lay this fate upon you, that you shall watch me die. Thereafter, let God deal with you as He may choose."

Now, when she heard these words Noma shrieked aloud, for of a sudden she felt that the power of the will of Hokosa, from which she had been freed by him, had once more fallen upon her, and that come what might she was doomed to obey his last commands.

Little by little the soldiers drew him up and in the darkness they bound him fast there upon the lofty cross. Then they descended and left him, and would have led Noma with them from the tree. But this they could not do, for always she broke from them screaming, and fled back to its shadow.

Then, seeing that she was bewitched, Hafela commanded that they should bind a cloth about her mouth and leave her there till her senses returned to her in the sunlight—for none of them dared to stop with her in the shadow of that tree, since the odours of it were poisonous to man. Also they believed the place to be haunted by evil spirits.

CHAPTER 22

The Victory of the Cross

The sun rose suddenly over the edge of the cliffs, and while it was yet deep shadow in the valley, its red light struck upon the white cross of perished wood that towered above the Tree of Doom and on the black shape of Hokosa crucified to it living. The camp of the king saw and understood, and from every throat of the thousands of men, women and children gathered there, went up a roar of rage and horror. The king lifted his hand, and silence fell upon the place; then he mounted on the wall and cried aloud:—

"Do you yet live, Hokosa, or is it your body only that those traitors have fastened to the tree?"

Back came the answer through the clear still air:—

"I live, O King!"

"Endure then a little while," called Nodwengo, "and we will storm the tree and save you."

"Nay," answered Hokosa, "you cannot save me; yet before I die I shall see you saved."

Then his words were lost in tumult, for the third day's fighting began. Desperately the regiments of Hafela rushing across the open space, hurled themselves upon the fortifications, which, during the night, had been strengthened by the building of two inner walls. Nor was this all, for suddenly a cry told those in front that the regiment which Hafela had despatched across the mountains had travelled up the eastern neck of the valley, and were attacking the position in their rear. Well was it for Nodwengo now that he had listened to the counsel of Hokosa, and, wearied as his soldiers were, had commanded that here also a great wall should be built.

For two hours the fight raged, and then on either side the foe fell back, not beaten indeed, though their dead were many, but to rest and take counsel. But now a new trouble arose: from all the camp of Nod-

540

wengo there went up a moan of pain to Heaven, for since the evening of yesterday the spring had given out, and they had found no water wherewith to wet their lips. During the night they bore it; but now the sun beating down on the black rocks with fearful force scorched them to the marrow, till they began to wither like fallen leaves, and already wounded men and children died, while the warriors cut the throats of oxen and drank their blood.

Hokosa hanging on his cross heard this moaning and divined its cause. "Be of good comfort, children of Nodwengo," he cried; "for I will pray that rain be sent upon you." And he lifted his head and prayed.

Now, whether it was by chance or whether his prayer was heard, who can say? At least it happened that immediately thereafter clouds began to gather and to thicken in the blue of Heaven, and within two hours rain fell in torrents, so that every one could drink his fill, and the spring being replenished at its sources, flowed again strongly.

After the rain came cold and moaning winds, and after the wind a great gloom and thunder.

Now, taking advantage of the shadow, the regiments of Hafela renewed their attack, and this time they carried the first of the three walls, for its defenders grew feeble and few in number. There they paused a while, and save for the cries of the wounded and of frightened women, the silence was great.

"Let your hearts be filled up!" cried the voice of Hokosa through the silence; "for the sunlight shines upon the plain of the Great Place yonder, and in it I see the sheen of spears. The *impi* travels to your aid, O children of Nodwengo."

Now, at this tidings the people of the king shouted for joy; but Hafela called to his regiments to make an end of them, and they hurled themselves upon the second wall, fighting desperately. Again and again they were beaten back, and again and again they came on, till at length they carried this wall also, driving its defenders, or those who remained alive of them, into the third entrenchment, and paused to rest awhile.

"Pray for us, O Prophet who are set on high!" cried a voice from the camp, "for if succour do not reach us speedily, we are sped."

Before the echoes of the voice had died away, a flash of lightning flared through the gloom, and in the light of it Hokosa saw that the king's *impi* was rushing up the gorge.

"Fight on! Fight on!" he called in answer. "I have prayed to Heaven, and your succour is at hand."

Then, with a howl of rage, Hafela's regiments hurled themselves upon the third and last entrenchment, attacking it at once in front and rear. Twice they nearly carried it, but each time the wild scream of Hokosa on high was heard above the din, conjuring its defenders to fight on and fear not, for Heaven had sent them help. They fought as men have seldom fought before, and with them fought the women and even the children. They were few and the foe was still many, but they listened to the urging of him whom they believed to be inspired in his death-agony upon the cross above them, and still they held their own. Twice portions of the wall were torn down, but they filled the breach with the corpses of the dead, ay! and with the bodies of the living, for the wounded, the old men and the very women piled themselves there in the place of stones. No such fray was told of in the annals of the People of Fire as this, the last stand of Nodwengo against the thousands of Hafela. Now all the shouting had died away, for men had no breath left wherewith to shout, only from the gloomy place of battle came low groans and the deep sobbing sighs of warriors gripped in the death-hug.

"*Fight on! Fight on!*" shrilled the voice of Hokosa on high. "Lo! the skies are open to my dying sight, and I see the *impis* of Heaven sweeping to succour you. *Behold!*"

They dashed the sweat from their eyes and looked forth, and as they looked, the pall of gloom was lifted, and in the golden glow of many-shafted light, they saw, not the legions of Heaven indeed, but the regiments of Nodwengo rushing round the bend of the valley, as dogs rush upon a scent, with heads held low and spears outstretched.

Hafela saw them also.

"Back to the *koppie*," he cried, "there to die like men, for the wizardries of Hokosa have been too strong for us, and lost is this my last battle and the crown I came to seek!"

They obeyed, and all that were left of them, some ten thousand men, they ran to the *koppie* and formed themselves upon it, ring above ring, and here the soldiers of Nodwengo closed in upon them.

Again and for the last time the voice of Hokosa rang out above the fray.

"Nodwengo," he cried, "with my passing breath I charge you have mercy and spare these men, so many of them as will surrender. The day of bloodshed has gone by, the fray is finished, the Cross has conquered. Let there be peace in the land."

All men heard him, for his piercing scream, echoed from the precipices, came to the ears of each. All men heard him, and, even in that fierce hour of vengeance, all obeyed. The spear that was poised was not thrown, and the *kerry* lifted over the fallen did not descend to dash away his life.

"Hearken, Hafela!" called the king, stepping forward from the ranks of the attackers. "He whom you have set on high to bring defeat upon you charges me to give you peace, and in the name of the conquering Cross I give peace. All who surrender shall dwell henceforth in my shadow, nor shall the head or the heel of one of them be harmed, although their sin is great. One life only will I take, the life of that witch who brought your armies down upon me to burn my town and slay my people by thousands, and who but last night betrayed Hokosa to his death of torment. All shall go free, I say, save the witch; and for you, you shall be given cattle and such servants as will cling to you to the number of a hundred, and driven from the land. Now, what say you? Will you yield or be slain? Swift with your answer; for the sun sinks, and ere it is set there must be an end in this way or in that."

The regiments of Hafela heard, and shouted in answer as with one voice:—

"We take your mercy, King! We fought bravely while we could, and now we take your mercy, King!"

"What say you, Hafela?" repeated Nodwengo, addressing the prince, who stood upon a point of rock above him in full sight of both armies.

Hafela turned and looked at Hokosa hanging high in mid-air.

"What say I?" he answered in a slow and quiet voice. "I say that the Cross and its Prophet have been too strong for me, and that I should have done well to follow the one and to listen to the counsel of the other. My brother, you tell me that I may go free, taking servants with me. I thank you and I will go—alone."

And setting the handle of his spear upon the rock, with a sudden movement he fell forward, transfixing his heart with its broad blade, and lay still.

"At least he died like one of the blood-royal of the Sons of Fire!" cried Nodwengo, while the armies stood silent and awestruck, "and with the blood-royal he shall be buried. Lay down your arms, you who followed him and fought for him, fearing nothing, and give over to me the witch that she may be slain."

"She hides under the tree yonder!" cried a voice.

"Go up and take her," said Nodwengo to some of his captains.

Now Noma, crouched on the ground beneath the tree, had seen and heard all that passed. Perceiving the captains making their way to-

543

wards her through the lines of the soldiers, who opened out a path for them, she rose and for a moment stood bewildered. Then, as though drawn by some strange attraction, she turned, and seizing hold of the creeper that clung about it, she began to climb the Tree of Doom swiftly. Up she went while all men watched, higher and higher yet, till passing out of the finger-like foliage she reached the cross of dead wood whereto Hokosa hung, and placing her feet upon one arm of it, stood there, supporting herself by the broken top of the upright.

Hokosa was not yet dead, though he was very near to death. Lifting his glazing eyes, he knew her and said, speaking thickly:—

"What do you here, Noma, and wherefore have you come?"

"I come because you draw me," she answered, "and because they seek my life below."

"Repent, repent!" he whispered, "there is yet time and Heaven is very merciful."

She heard, and a fury seized her.

"Be silent, dog!" she cried. "Having defied your God so long, shall I grovel to Him at the last? Having hated you so much, shall I seek your forgiveness now? At least of one thing I am glad—it was I who brought you here, and with me and through me you shall die."

Then, placing one foot upon his bent head as if in scorn, she leaned forward, her long hair flying to the wind, and cursed Nodwengo and his people, naming them renegades and apostates, and cursed the soldiers of Hafela, naming them cowards, calling down upon them the *malison* of their ancestors.

Hokosa heard and muttered:—

"For your soul's sake, woman, repent! repent, ere it be too late!"

"Repent!" she screamed, catching at his words. "Thus do I repent!" and drawing the knife from her girdle, she leant over him and drove it hilt-deep into his breast.

Then with a sudden movement she sprang upwards and outwards into the air, and rushing down through a hundred feet of space, was struck dead upon that very rock where the corpse of Hafela lay.

Now, beneath the agony of the life Hokosa lifted his head for the last time, crying in a great voice:—

"Messenger, I come, be you my guide," and with the words his soul passed.

"All is over and ended," said a voice. "Soldiers, salute the king with the royal salute."

"Nay," answered Nodwengo. "Salute me not, salute the Cross and him who hangs thereon."

So, while the rays of the setting sun shone about it, regiment by regiment that great army rushed past the *koppie*, and pausing opposite to the cross and its burden, they rendered to it the royal salute of kings.

****

Then the night fell, and thus through the power of Faith that now, as of old, is the only true and efficient magic, was accomplished the mission to the Sons of Fire of the Saint and Martyr, Thomas Owen, and of his murderer and disciple, the Wizard Hokosa.

Lightning Source UK Ltd.
Milton Keynes UK

177582UK00001B/93/P